A
SHATTERED
EMPIRE

ALSO BY MITCHELL HOGAN

A Crucible of Souls

Blood of Innocents

A
SHATTERED
EMPIRE

Sorcery Ascendant Sequence

Book Three

MITCHELL HOGAN

HARPER Voyager
An Imprint of HarperCollins*Publishers*

HarperCollins books may be purchased for educational, business, or sales promotional use. For information please e-mail the Special Markets Department at SPsales@harpercollins.com.

FIRST EDITION

Designed by Katy Riegel

Maps designed by Maxime Plasse

Library of Congress Cataloging-in-Publication Data has been applied for.

ISBN 978-0-06-240728-3

16 17 18 19 20   OV/RRD   10 9 8 7 6 5 4 3 2 1

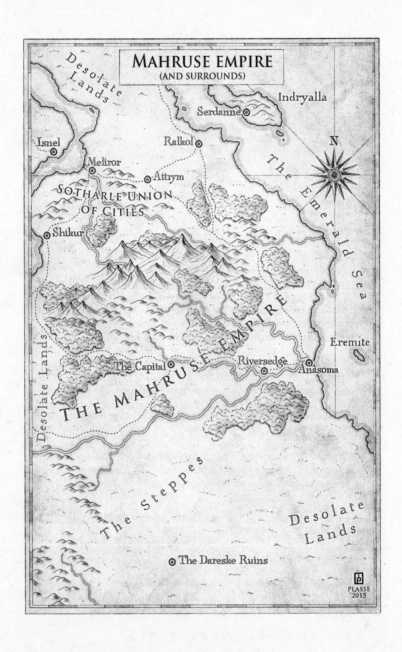

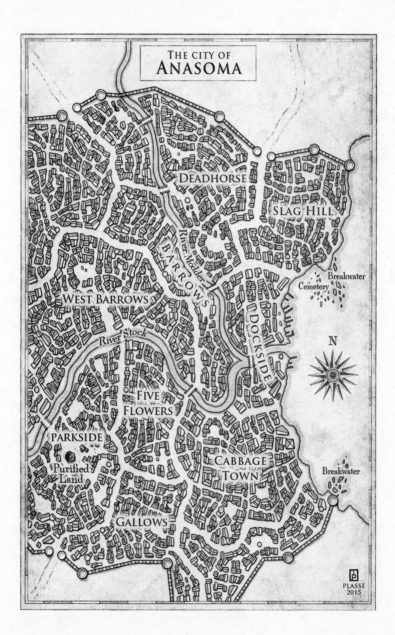

THE CITY OF
ANASOMA

DEADHORSE

SLAG HILL

River Mother

BARROWS

WEST BARROWS

Breakwater

Cemetery

DOCKSIDE

River Stock

N

FIVE
FLOWERS

PARKSIDE

*Purified
Land*

CABBAGE
TOWN

Breakwater

GALLOWS

PLASSE
2015

DRAMATIS PERSONAE

CALDAN, an orphan and an apprentice sorcerer in the Protectors
MIRANDA, an entrepreneur and ex-sailor
AMERDAN LEPHAR, a shopkeeper
VASILE LAURIS, a magistrate, once head investigator for the Chancellor's Guard
ELPIDIA, a physiker
IZAK FOURIE, a noble
LADY FELICIENNE SHYRISE (FELICE), Third Adjudicator to the emperor

THE PROTECTORS AND THE SORCERERS' GUILD
SIMMON, a master, Caldan's mentor
ANNELIE, a master
MOLD, a master

FIVE OCEANS MERCANTILE CONCERN
GAZIJA, the First Deliverer
SAVINE KHEDEVIS, a head trader
LUPHILDERN QUISS, a head trader
MAZOET MIANGLINE, a sorcerer
REBECCI WALRAFFEN, a sorcerer

LADY CAITLYN'S BAND
LADY CAITLYN, a noble crusader
AIDAN, Caitlyn's second-in-command
CHALAYAN, a tribal sorcerer
ANSHUL CEL RAU, a swordsman from the Steppes

INDRYALLANS
KELHAK, God-Emperor of Indryalla
BELLS, a sorcerer

A
SHATTERED
EMPIRE

PROLOGUE

Councillor Radgir winced as the Indryallan soldier behind him prodded his back with the tip of his spear. The point broke through his thin nightshirt and his skin, not deep enough to cause serious injury, but enough to send a warm trickle down his back.

He shifted his weight uncomfortably. He should have known to keep his mouth shut, foolish old man.

Radgir shuffled forward, away from the guards. Shackles around his ankles bit into skin rubbed raw, and he gritted his teeth.

He knew the mistake he'd made. The mistake of considering Indryalla first and mentioning his fears to Councillor Tadeas. He should have known the conniving old bastard would use any advantage over him to further his own position. His excuse, one he kept telling himself over and over, was that he was in the right. The God-Emperor wasn't Indryalla. Indryalla wasn't the God-Emperor.

Unfortunately, far too few of his countrymen separated the two.

This war with the Mahruse Empire was madness. Not only was it without purpose, it was futile. Indryalla was prosperous on its own, with trade burgeoning between it and many other countries, and Indryallans' crafting was the finest in the world. At least that was one thing Kelhak had done: developed their sorcerous knowledge far beyond what had been known, built schools to teach crafting, and made sure no one with the gift of a well went unnoticed.

Except it had all been for his own ends: to develop a fighting force beholden only to the God-Emperor. Most were his own blood, so many generations had Kelhak been among them, spreading his seed to anyone willing.

And plenty were.

Kelhak had changed—from a kindhearted ruler beloved of all his people to what he was now: a despotic tyrant. And Indryalla had been altered along with him. No longer was it the country Radgir had grown up in and loved.

And he didn't think that just because he was in chains now.

He raised his eyes and looked around, careful not to turn his head and give the guards behind him another excuse. A few dozen others were waiting nervously with him, all with shackled feet and shocked, fearful expressions. Nobles, councillors, and a couple of high-ranking Indryallan sorcerers. Crude bandages covered the sorcerers' hands, stained red with blood—their fingers had been cut off. One of them was leaking drops of crimson onto the floor, and both whimpered softly, unable to control their sobs.

A *purging. That's what this is.* Predawn arrests of supposed traitors and malcontents. This wasn't justice. This was butchery.

Radgir met the gaze of another councillor, Dorota, also in her nightclothes, although she'd managed to put a robe on before they took her. She was someone he trusted, and the first person he'd brought his misgivings to.

You've killed us, her eyes said as she stared at Radgir.

And he had.

He averted his gaze and rubbed his wrinkled, clammy hands together. When had he gotten so old?

To his left, a lock clicked, and double doors opened onto a courtyard. Torches flickered in their sconces as a breeze fluttered in, curling around his bare shins and feet. More soldiers approached from outside, stopping at the entrance and beckoning to the guards holding them prisoner.

"Listen up," shouted one of the guards from behind him, so close Radgir could smell the ale on his breath. "Form a line outside, single file. You'll be shown where to stand. Each of you will have a proper trial, overseen by the God-Emperor, may he live forever."

Radgir squeezed his lips tight but could hear some of the prisoners muttering the response: "May he live forever." He shook his head. Even now—dragged from their beds, the doors of their homes broken open—they couldn't shake a lifetime of conditioning.

Once outside, he shuffled across cobblestones to where he was directed and came to a halt. He realized he didn't care how the next part played out, because he knew he wouldn't survive it. Somehow, that thought calmed him.

Radgir breathed in the cool night air. Stars twinkled above him. A clear night. Still. As fine a night as any he'd experienced.

Soldiers carried a table and chair, placing them close to a wall. One of the God-Emperor's Silent Companions came and stood to the left of the table. A beast of a man, even taller than most of the others in his order. Both of his leather-gloved hands clasped the hilt of a massive greatsword, its point resting on the ground. An officious-looking man followed, clutching a thick leather-bound book, a sheaf of papers, and writing implements. He took a seat and began setting up. Radgir recognized him: Preben, a magistrate with a weakness for spirits and too-young women.

Radgir's stomach sank. Preben would do what was best for Preben, and he'd become one of Kelhak's most vocal supporters as the coins flowing into his pockets had increased over the years.

As Radgir had suspected, this whole thing was a sham.

A woman in chains stood next to Radgir, a noble. She hadn't been in bed like most others. Her fine dress was ripped and stained from her struggles, her curled red hair tangled. Her hands were trembling, and she was muttering. Radgir tilted his head to catch her words, but they remained indecipherable. He glanced around to see if there were any soldiers close by. There weren't. Good.

Radgir reached up and squeezed the woman's shoulder. She flinched at his touch, quivering violently.

"Shh," he whispered, and he gave another squeeze before dropping his hand to his side. "It'll all be over soon." It was the best he could manage under the circumstances. He sounded pathetic to his own ears.

"Do . . . do you think they'll let some of us go? I didn't do anything. Just talk, that's all."

Radgir swallowed the lump in his throat. "Perhaps." Again he cursed inwardly at his deplorable response. "I'm sure they will, my lady. The God-Emperor is known for his leniency."

At least he used to be.

The noblewoman sniffed, keeping her face downcast.

Radgir turned his attention to Preben, who said something to the soldier near him. They both laughed, then Preben dipped a pen in his ink bottle. The soldier and another of his fellows strode over to the first person in the line of prisoners, took the man by the arms, and half dragged, half hoisted him over to Preben's table.

"Name?" asked Preben, voice carrying over the sudden hush in the courtyard.

The man mumbled too low to be heard.

Preben frowned and leaned forward. "Speak up, man! We don't have all night."

The man cleared his throat and raised his head, looking straight at Preben. "Sir Krugert of House Fruin-Dolandrar," he said in a clear, loud voice.

"Ah yes, Krugert." Preben looked through his papers until he found the one he wanted. He read for a few moments, then spoke.

"Sir Krugert, you are charged with high treason, inciting others to violence against the God-Emperor, failing to report acts of treason, and intimate relations with a goat. How do you plead?"

At the last charge, a few of the soldiers jeered, while Preben's lips twisted with amusement.

"That's a lie! They all are! What's the meaning of this?" protested Krugert, red-faced. He struggled vainly against the soldiers holding his arms. "I demand to speak with the God-Emperor. He knows I'm loyal!"

Preben scowled and leaned forward. "If you were loyal, you wouldn't be here!" he shouted, spittle flying across the table. He wiped at his book and parchment with a sleeve. "You *demand* to speak with him? Such arrogance."

Krugert's shoulders slumped as whatever reserves of strength he'd gathered seemed to fail him. "Do your worst, then," he said. "Indryallans shouldn't live this way. We've lost sight of what we were."

"You deny it," Preben said, "yet treasonous thoughts spill from your own tongue. I have no choice but to find you guilty. May the ancestors have mercy on you." He gestured to the guards.

Krugert remained silent as he was hauled away. They manhandled him over to the Silent Companion and forced him to his knees. The guards twisted Krugert's arms behind his back until he cried out in pain, and they bent his torso over so he faced the ground.

The Silent Companion stirred. He looked down at the man forced to kneel in front of him.

Radgir wanted to avert his gaze but couldn't. He was transfixed by what he knew was about to happen.

Slowly, almost leisurely, the Silent Companion's greatsword rose, then blurred into motion, slicing down into Krugert's neck—and through. Gouts of blood spurted from the stump, leaving steaming strings across the stone.

Radgir heard someone whimper, only to realize he'd made the sound. Beside him, the noblewoman swooned and collapsed in a heap, while other prisoners cried out in shock and dismay.

The guards dragged Krugert's headless corpse into a corner and dropped it unceremoniously. One went back for the head, grasping it by the hair. He threw it toward Krugert's body, where it landed with a thump and rolled to a stop.

Radgir dragged his eyes from the grisly sight, his heart thudding in his chest. Brutality for brutality's sake. There was no one here to witness this, no object lesson for onlookers to learn. It was a show of cruelty toward them in their final moments. Inhumanity. That was it. Only someone inhuman would order this.

He looked around to find Preben staring at him. Radgir straightened up and drew his shoulders back.

"Leave the woman for now," Preben told the guards. "She'll be no fun unless she's conscious. Bring the old man."

Without waiting for the guards, Radgir walked over to the table. His legs wobbled, but he remained standing.

"Name?" asked Preben, following his little routine.

"Radgir of House Celespanna. Councillor of the First Circle. Beholden only to . . ." *The God-Emperor?* " . . . to someone I don't recognize anymore."

"Guilty, then," remarked Preben with a smile.

"You have no jurisdiction over me."

"You'd be surprised what I have jurisdiction over. Tonight's a special night. We're cutting away the deadwood."

Radgir sighed and tilted his head back in order to gaze one last time at the stars. As he did, he saw a figure at a third-floor window looking down at them. There was light behind the person, casting his face into shadow, but Radgir would know that silhouette anywhere: Kelhak. Watching how this played out.

Why?

Radgir shook his head. *Don't waste this moment*, he thought. It was an especially fine night. He breathed in the air. Sweet and cold.

He barely felt himself being pulled over to the Silent Companion. Pain erupted in his arms, and he sank to his knees. He bent over. On the stone in front of him were gouts of glistening scarlet. Two booted feet to his left shifted, and the tip of a sword that had been resting on the ground rose out of his sight.

He closed his eyes and breathed a prayer to the ances—

CHAPTER 1

Horns resounded through the air. Regiments of Quivers called to arms, woken from fitful sleep in hastily erected camps surrounded by their dead comrades. Caldan watched as hurried breakfasts of cornmeal bread and cheap red wine were consumed before armor was donned and weapons checked. He hadn't slept much himself, just a few brief spurts in between worrying over his encounter with the emperor and what would happen to him now that he was in the hands of the warlocks.

Long lines of soldiers snaked in from the front ranks, exhausted from battling the jukari in the darkness and holding them off until dawn broke. There had been dozens of isolated pitched battles, both sides hampered by the lack of light, which was mercifully clear of the lurid taint of destructive sorcery. The vormag, and it seemed the warlocks, were content to wait.

Or perhaps they were also exhausted.

The returning soldiers passed formations of fresh troops, dirt- and blood-splattered armor contrasting with gleaming hauberks, to collapse at the rear of the army in relative safety. Wounded Quivers were dragged or carried to the physikers, who were set up in lines—implements still dirty from being used throughout the night. There would be no rest for the physikers and their assistants for some time.

Now, hundreds of horsemen were saddled and waiting on the edges of the emperor's main forces. Commanders rode among the cavalry and foot-troops—bowmen and spear carriers—while the warlocks split into small groups and placed themselves in scattered locations among the forces.

From the river, hundreds of soldiers were swarming out of the recently docked ships. They formed up in ranks, bearing great round shields and broadswords, while those behind them wielded two-handed axes or long spears. Who they were still puzzled Caldan, but it seemed safe to assume they were reinforcements the emperor had arranged.

Except, of course, Devenish had been surprised at their arrival. But maybe the emperor hadn't felt the need to inform the warlocks of his plan.

One of the Quivers guarding the warlocks' tents came up to Caldan and handed him a wooden plate filled with cornbread and cheese, along with dried fruit and nuts. He also gave Caldan a steaming mug of honeyed and salted coffee. Caldan ate the food absentmindedly, keeping his eyes on what was happening.

To one side were the walls of Riversedge, and to the other they relied on a series of hills to offer some protection. And then there was the river itself, stretching mirror-bright to the east as they looked into the sun, and pale upstream to the west. A massive stretch of water, a barrier to the jukari—one they'd already shown kept them at bay.

Quivers formed up—as large a force as any the Mahruse Empire had gathered in centuries. The Noble Houses amassed their troops and assembled behind the Quivers. Having followed the emperor and his army—expecting to merely attend the fighting in name only, to be recognized in the honor rolls when the Indryallans were pushed back into the sea—the nobles now found themselves in the middle of a fight against a monstrous horde of creatures from the Shattering.

It wasn't clear to Caldan if they were more afraid of the jukari or of disobeying the emperor.

All around the army, warriors and nobles alike made familial gestures and mumbled prayers to their ancestors to keep them from harm. Some burned offerings, and along with the campfires, smoke hung thick above the host, obscuring the standards flapping in the breeze.

From Caldan's position close to Devenish's tent, the army seemed composed of chaos with only a few pockets of order.

There was movement in the front ranks, and shouts broke out. Caldan stood and looked past the human army. Farther away, he saw streams of jukari approaching, far less orderly than the Quivers. They stopped a few hundred yards away, the tips of their lines swelling like water pooling, until their numbers grew past his counting. They bellowed and snarled, a terrible, animal sound.

Commands roared throughout the emperor's army, along with curses and battle songs.

The Quivers marched out to answer the jukari, armor and weapons flashing in the sun. Drums pounded, horns pealed, booted feet stamped. Commanders dispersed among their troops, though Caldan noted that most led from the rear.

The jukari came on.

Heavy thumps sounded from Riversedge, and at first Caldan couldn't work out what was happening. Then he saw specks arcing into the sky: missiles thrown from counterweighted trebuchets. He squinted as they reached their zenith and began plummeting to the earth. A low rumbling sounded. Clouds of dust and clods of dirt erupted where the stones landed—but nowhere near the jukari. All the missiles fell short by hundreds of yards, with more following in the air.

Hoots and barking came from the jukari, who stood their ground, attention on the falling rocks.

Overeager? wondered Caldan. They had to know their shots would fall short.

Then he saw that while the jukari's attention was on the siege engine missiles, groups of Quivers had run to the front of their ranks, using the gaps between cohorts. They dropped baskets of arrows, raised their bows, and began firing. Missiles streaked into the sky, a dark rain ascending to the heavens, only to fall. Their shafts plunged into the jukari—failing, as far as Caldan could see, to do much damage. But some jukari did fall: tiny figures in their front lines stumbled. The holes opened up by wounded or dead jukari were quickly filled.

Thunder rumbled, and Caldan frowned. He glanced to the sky, fearing sorcery, of which there was no sign—but there was movement on the hills. He squinted . . .

And let out a gasp.

Hundreds of Quiver cavalry crested the hills and poured toward the jukari—steel-tipped lances gleaming, iron-rimmed shields hanging by their sides, hooves trampling the grass.

Both the trebuchet missiles and the flights of arrows had been a distraction.

The distance between the cavalry and the jukari closed with frightening swiftness. Then the horses were among the creatures. Caldan could hear lances snapping from where he was—although it could also have been bones—along with the squealing of horses and barks from the jukari. Splintered wood filled the air. Shouts and screams erupted. Lances now abandoned, swords were dragged from sheaths and flashed down. Injured horses toppled and flailed.

Riderless mounts bounded away in a lather.

The archers positioned themselves in the corridors between the armies, which were now advancing steadily on each other. Arrows still peppered the enemy, though now they were aimed farther behind and to the other side of the cavalry charge.

Foot soldiers broke into a trot, urged on by their commanders, and then they were in the melee. Shields rose to meet jukari weapons, and more often than not were broken by the force of the blows. Short spears and swords darted out in response. Yells and screams went up. Everywhere, Quivers hacked and slashed, weapons covered with black jukari blood.

More arrows rained down like angry insects. The cavalry withdrew and gathered themselves for another charge, while the jukari milled in confusion. They turned their attention to the foot soldiers, only to once again get hammered with a howling rush of horsemen. They crashed through scattered lines with barely a pause until they found themselves slowed as an organized mass of jukari came to the fore.

Blood pitched into the sky and to the ground, both red and black. It sprayed and spattered. Wooden shields cracked, arms broke. Quiver and jukari scalps split, skulls smashed. Those unfortunate enough to lose their footing or fall injured to the ground were finished off in short order, either by enemy weapons or the trampling feet of those around them.

The soldiers from the ships joined the fray, coming at a rush into the unprotected side of the jukari host, and for a few breathless minutes, all was chaos.

Across the battlefield, injured men dragged themselves back behind the front lines, allowing eager—and some not-so-eager—soldiers to replace them. They hauled shattered weapons and hacked armor, notched swords and shields sporting broken shafts of arrows and javelins.

Thousands sprawled dead and dying—men and jukari and horses, some so mangled they were indistinguishable from one another.

Then the jukari retreated, horns of their own sounding above the tumult.

Quivers dragged wounded comrades to safety, while the cavalry urged their mounts out of the throng and to the side. Men-at-arms surrounding nobles and their sons backed away as quickly as they could. Fallen standards were raised again, dirt-stained and bloody.

And the Quivers kept shooting flights of arrows, with a greater intensity than Caldan had seen before. Shafts made a thatch of the sky, chasing the jukari like an advancing storm cloud, peppering them with injury and death.

The retreat turned to outright flight as the creatures turned tail and fled.

The Quivers' drums ceased pounding. Horns blasted multiple notes, and the rain of arrows ceased.

There was a movement beside Caldan, and one of the warlocks assigned to watch over him came closer. Despite Caldan's insistence on staying with cel Rau, they had left the swordsman in the care of the army's physikers and told him in no uncertain terms that Caldan would be coming with them.

His keepers were middle-aged men with hard eyes, and he could sense both of them had accessed their wells and were linked to various craftings they wore. One sported a bushy beard streaked with gray. Gorton was his name. His companion, called Melker, was a thinner man with pale skin and freckles. Both were clothed in black, with silver flower-shaped buttons, as Joachim had been. A warlock's signature apparel, Caldan supposed.

Caldan's skin itched from the vibrations caused by so many craftings and trinkets in close proximity. So overwhelming was the feeling, his hair stood on end, and he found himself rubbing his arms. The air was filled with alternating scent-bursts of lemon and hot metal, as the warlocks had been using sorcery almost constantly. This close to Gorton and Melker, he could sense them drawing from their wells in spurts, but there was no visible sign of what they were doing. Outwardly, they looked like any normal persons.

Then again, I suppose I do, too.

"Devenish wants to see you," Melker said. "Now, if you please, while there's a lull in the fighting."

"What does he want?"

"Who cares?" Gorton said harshly. "Just hurry up."

"Gently, Gorton."

"Forget that," Gorton snapped. "We shouldn't be here babysitting, and you know it. We should be striking now with the others."

"All in good time," Melker replied smoothly. "You'll get your chance, don't you worry." He turned back to Caldan. "Coming?"

Caldan nodded.

In the distance, the jukari horde regrouped, bloodied but far from defeated. The superior tactics, armor, and weapons of the emperor's army had slaughtered many of them, but today was only one day, and there were many more to come. And the losses had been great on both sides.

Caldan turned from the torn-up field and followed the warlocks.

CHAPTER 2

aldan didn't expect Devenish and the warlocks to trust him, but his show of sorcery in breaking through Bells's shield—and his part in stopping the slaughter her crafting had wreaked among the emperor's forces—had gone some way to proving to them where his allegiance lay.

Or so he hoped.

He knew the warlocks weren't stupid. Like him, they would know fealty and obedience were sometimes only a surface detail. Underneath, though . . . that's where someone's true nature lay.

As Joachim and Amerdan had shown him.

Caldan and his escort approached Devenish's tent, but the warlock leader barely spared them a glance. The young man swept his mousy hair out of his eyes and shook his head at a question another warlock put to him. Then, with a few sharp commands, they all began walking toward the docks by the river.

Melker and Gorton pushed Caldan to the back of the group, and they trailed after Devenish and five other warlocks. One of them was

Thenna, an older, sun-touched woman whom Devenish had seemingly pulled rank on a couple of times when they'd first met. She'd had it out for Caldan from the get-go, and now kept glancing back at him with a frown on her face. He did his best to keep his expression neutral.

"Do you know what's going on in Anasoma?" Caldan asked Melker. "I left there a while ago and—"

"Shut it!" barked Gorton.

"What my colleague means," Melker said, "is that your questions will be answered in good time. There's much to do first before we'll be able to give you all the answers you want. Devenish wants to speak to you himself. And Thenna seems to have taken a disliking to you."

As had the emperor. *What have I gotten myself into?*

Gorton snorted. "She'll find something to dislike in most everything."

"Not Devenish, though."

"Oh no, not him."

Caldan kept silent.

So Thenna was infatuated with Devenish, and Gorton and Melker didn't much like her. He didn't know if this insight would be useful later, but when you're completely in the dark, any illumination might come in handy. Especially if there were factions he could exploit.

They trudged toward eastern Riversedge, where the dozens of mysterious ships were docked. Clouds of smoke filled the gray sky, twisting in the breeze. Surrounding Caldan, the ground looked as if a giant plow had furrowed the earth. Splashes of carmine stained the grass and dirt, and a multitude of corpses lay with limbs locked in rigor, clutching despairingly at themselves, their weapons, the grass. All had looks of horror frozen on their faces—mouths open, stretched and grimacing, as if they couldn't believe what was happening.

Caldan could barely believe it himself.

"Why don't they bury them?"

"I'll get you a shovel," Gorton said.

The stench of death and blood filled his nostrils, overlaid with the lingering scent of lemons. Weapons and armor forged by the empire's greatest smiths had been no match for the sorcery Bells had wrought. Black smoke from spot fires rose from the carnage, whether caused by the sorcery or something else, he couldn't tell.

Teams of Quivers were stripping the dead soldiers of their valuables, then dragging the despoiled bodies into carts to be taken care of later. Crows cawed and fought among themselves atop the piles, as if worried there would be a shortage of food for them soon.

So like most men. Squabbling over tidbits while there was more than enough for all. Shortsighted, and foolish in the extreme.

The birds at least had an excuse.

And he'd been the biggest fool of them all, the one who'd brought Bells to Riversedge. She'd played him, and he had let her, because there was a promise in there he'd wanted to believe.

It had been just another lie.

But that was what she did, lie, including to herself. He still wasn't sure she'd known what she was doing, but the results of her actions couldn't be denied. Caldan's stomach twisted at the thought, and he swallowed bile rising in his throat. The world spun, and he knelt to steady himself, fearing he might fall. He turned his burning eyes from the corpses and covered his face with his hands.

By the ancestors, he was glad Bells was dead.

"Unpleasant, isn't it?" remarked Melker.

Caldan realized the distaste on his face had been misinterpreted by the warlock. "It's more than unpleasant," he said. "It's repulsive. To use sorcery like this. To kill so many . . ." He shook his head in disgust.

"You had a hand in stopping it, which we're grateful for. As is the emperor."

"I didn't do it for any reward or recognition."

Gorton chuckled at his words. "Of course not."

"I didn't," repeated Caldan firmly.

Melker slapped Caldan on the back. "Whatever your reason, you've caused quite a stir. Just don't be too keen to draw attention to yourself. Some people don't take too well to that."

"That they don't," Gorton said.

"And it brings a person under scrutiny. If someone had things they'd rather keep to themselves, well, they'd have a way of becoming known." Melker gave Caldan a sidelong glance before looking away.

Caldan tensed. *What do they know?* He resolved to keep his eyes and ears open and remain vigilant.

A short time later, they left the fields of dead behind and passed ramshackle dwellings outside the walls of Riversedge. This area close to the wall was a shantytown, buildings shoddily made from whatever leftover pieces of lumber and discards their owners could lay their hands on. And despite the arrival of the Quivers, and the jukari horde close by, the residents were still here, going about their business.

There was nowhere for them to go.

Dirty faces with hollow eyes peered at them as they passed. Naked children ran between buildings, screeching and laughing. A grandmother bent over a large frayed basket, permanently hunched. She squinted at them and went back to her task of sorting rags into piles, knowing what was more important to her.

The Mahruse Empire isn't all it's cracked up to be, and I suspect most of its citizens know it. Only naive outsiders don't know better.

Like me, for far too long.

As they approached the river, two of the warlocks with Devenish split off and made their way east along the bank. Here, the ground sloped down sharply and disappeared into a swath of reeds growing along the water. Wooden wharves stretched out into the river, fifteen or so. Berths normally used for traders and fishermen were taken up with oceangoing ships. Sails were furled, and all of the ships had oar holes along the sides, out of which stuck the ends of paddles. A strange combination, for oceangoing vessels rarely required oars, or so he'd seen. Only some warships had them, so they could maneuver against the wind.

Clearly ideal for taking the ships upriver, though.

Even stranger was that none of them flew the same flags. Caldan squinted and shaded his eyes. Five different designs: a black circle on a white background, a white sword broken into three on a blue flag, a white diamond on yellow, a red shield, and an ominous silver skull on black.

"What do the flags mean?" Caldan asked the warlocks. "Do you know?"

Gorton grunted. "Mercenaries, I'd say. I wouldn't have thought the emperor needed them."

"He wouldn't," Melker said. "Though he does now. Devenish was as surprised as us to hear of the ships, and if anyone knew what the emperor had planned, it would be him. Looks like the mercenaries arrived just in time. Convenient, that."

Too convenient, thought Caldan, and he could see Melker had the same thought. The warlock's eyes narrowed as he surveyed the ships.

Contingents of mercenaries arriving soon after a large part of the emperor's forces were decimated? He knew something about percentages and possibilities from his study of Dominion, and the odds of this being an accident were low to nil. But with the jukari horde still at large, and supported by vormag sorcery, it seemed the emperor and his warlocks wouldn't have much choice but to pay whatever the mercenaries demanded. Unless they wanted Riversedge to be overrun and its inhabitants slaughtered.

He looked back at the destruction Bells and the warlocks had wrought, and he wondered if such concerns crossed the emperor's mind.

Melker pushed Caldan in the back. "Come on," the warlock said. "We're to stay close to Devenish until he decides what to do with you. And no sorcery, if you know what's good for you. I'll boil your brain in your skull before you can blink."

Caldan swallowed and nodded. He'd better tread carefully, or he'd find himself in deep water.

Melker and Gorton kept to either side of Caldan as they took up positions behind Devenish and the remaining three warlocks.

Thenna looked back and fixed Caldan with a cold stare. He held her gaze for a few moments before thinking better of it and lowering his eyes. He couldn't stop her thinking whatever she wanted, but it wouldn't do him any good to antagonize her further.

"There," Caldan heard Devenish say, and the warlock pointed to a group of people coming along the wharves toward the riverbank.

One of them was an elderly gentleman, tottering along. Withered, liver-spotted hands clutched two canes for balance. He was flanked by two men, one of considerable bulk and another who was stork thin . . .

Caldan squinted. It was the strange banker from Anasoma. What was his name? *Sir Quiss.*

What is he doing here?

A humming filled the air and penetrated deep into Caldan's bones. Shields sprang up around Devenish and the other warlocks close to him. Melker and Gorton followed suit an instant later. Interestingly, only Devenish, Thenna, Melker, and one other warlock's shields were multicolored and had an extra denseness to them. The remainder were the standard sorcerer blue. Which meant their wells couldn't handle the added strain. It followed that becoming a warlock wasn't all about strength.

Caldan filed that thought away.

"If you're expecting trouble, may I . . . ?" Caldan looked askance at Melker, who deliberated for a moment, then nodded.

Caldan accessed his well, touched his shield crafting, and linked to it. His skin tightened as multicolored energy covered him. Gorton whistled in surprise, while Melker merely gave Caldan an approving smile before turning his attention back to Devenish, who'd started toward the wharves.

With the warlocks' eyes away from him, Caldan slipped a hand into his pocket and drew out his beetle automaton. As gently as he could, he teased a few more strings from his well, drawing as little power from it as possible, and linked to his creation. He didn't know if it would be any use, but he wanted to be ready.

As they neared the group, Caldan's attention was drawn back to Quiss. As it had the first time he'd met him, in Anasoma, Quiss's form blurred, and Caldan couldn't help but think the banker looked denser than ordinary men, harder somehow. And so did the big man. *And* the old man with the canes. Caldan looked at Melker, then at Gorton. Did they see it? Should he tell them? Would they think he was crazy?

Caldan blinked rapidly, but they remained the same. And he remained quiet . . . for now.

The warlocks' boots scuffed across hard timber, and they came to a stop about ten paces from the three denser-men.

The old man faltered forward a pace. "I am Gazija," he said, voice wavering. "I'm the head of the Five Oceans Mercantile Concern, and some among my people call me the First Deliverer. I don't care for it much, but it's as good a title as any."

Devenish bowed. A touch too low, giving his deference a tinge of mockery. "I'm Devenish. They call me the First Warlock . . . and it's as good a title as any."

The warlocks around him chuckled, Thenna's false laugh the loudest of them all.

Sycophants. Caldan wondered if Devenish deserved their obsequiousness, or just received it because he was in the emperor's favor.

Either way, it soured his stomach.

"Your shields won't be as effective against the vormag as you think," Gazija said softly.

Devenish laughed, a surprisingly high-pitched sound. "You profess to know much, elder. How is it you came by such information?"

Gazija waved a hand, dismissing the question as unimportant. "We can swap stories later." He gestured across the terrain littered with bodies and smoke. "I can see we arrived just in time. What of the jukari forces? With my mercenaries helping, did you manage to hold against them? They must have taken significant losses for—"

"Enough, old man!" barked Devenish. "Many died here today, and not from the jukari."

The thin man, Quiss, leaned forward and whispered in Gazija's ear. Gazija listened and then nodded.

"Sorcery, then," said Gazija. "The stench of it reached us on the river. You fought against the vormag?"

"No. A rogue sorcerer, one of the Indryallans. Tell me what you want, *First Deliverer*." Devenish spat the title. "Then get out of our way before your ashes are scattered on the river." Devenish's face had gone a few shades redder in anger.

Probably won't take much to send him over the edge.

Gazija apparently thought the same thing and frowned. "That

is . . . unexpected. I'm here because I imagined my mercenaries would be of some use against the jukari. But I don't suppose you need to imagine, do you, seeing how they supported the emperor's forces during the last battle? Lucky for you, too—those monsters were an unexpected complication, I'd wager."

Devenish's mouth worked as he came to terms with what Gazija said. "Five companies of mercenaries, at the opportune time we'd need them . . . A suspicious mind would worry at such events transpiring so happily."

Gazija grinned, showing missing teeth. "Suspicious minds jump at shadows and eventually go insane. Our appearance is fortuitous, and you'd be a fool to refuse our help." Gazija fixed Devenish with a challenging stare. "And you don't strike me as a fool."

The old man was clearly up to something. He wasn't just here to help. But Caldan couldn't figure out what his game was . . . yet.

Devenish hesitated for a few moments. "On behalf of the emperor, I accept your offer. Bring their captains to me so I can brief them. And you'll need to hand over their signed contracts, of course."

"You mistake me, *First Warlock*. I didn't offer to hand them over to you. The contracts and command of the mercenaries will stay with me," Gazija said firmly. "And I'll be at every briefing to ensure they're used wisely."

"This isn't a negotiation, old man. We'll take your gift and do as we see fit. You'll not be able to stop us."

Gazija's eyes flashed with anger, and he drew himself up. "You have no idea what I'm capable of." An almost overpowering odor of lemons filled the air.

Caldan gasped and drew as much as he could from his well to bolster his shield. Melker glanced at him quizzically, as if he couldn't sense the sorcery.

Which, Caldan realized, the warlock couldn't.

"Beware!" he shouted. "Sorcery!"

Caldan's feet grew cold, and he looked down. Ice crystals were forming on his boots. Faint cracklings sounded as they grew before his eyes. He lifted his gaze to see shields surround the three denser-men.

Shields as dark as night, similar in nature to the impressive dome Bells had crafted, and the shield Amerdan used when he'd fled.

A sheet of ice solidified outward over the water. Rending snaps split the air as fractures crackled through rapidly freezing water. Growing swiftly, it froze the ships moored around them in place. Icicles formed on the masts and ropes. Steam billowed from the warlocks' and Caldan's shields as the temperature of the air around them plummeted.

Devenish and his warlocks struck back. Caldan sensed them somehow send the power of their wells toward Devenish, who gathered the force and fired a single glowing orange strand straight at Gazija.

Which the First Deliverer's shield absorbed without a trace.

Devenish's jaw dropped in surprise, and Thenna cried out in dismay.

The shield around Gazija winked out, as if the old man could handle whatever the warlocks threw at him without it. He took another step forward.

"Now that foolishness is out of the way," he said, breath steaming, "perhaps—"

Lemons again warned Caldan.

Devenish's face screwed up in concentration, but nothing was happening, so far as Caldan could see.

Gazija passed a hand over his face and shook his head, as if wearied by the foolishness of a child . . . and no more inconvenienced.

"Coercive sorcery isn't something to be trifled with," the old man said. "Especially as inept at it as you are."

Impressive, thought Caldan. *Shrugging off Devenish like he's nothing.* The denser-men were strange, but perhaps that was part of what they were, a stain of their particular brand of sorcery.

Devenish and Gazija locked gazes. For a moment, everything was quiet. Blood suffused Devenish's face, and beads of sweat broke out on his forehead. He snarled, hands clenching into fists until his knuckles turned white.

Then suddenly he relaxed, shaking his head. He uttered a low laugh.

"So be it," he said. "Bring the mercenary captains to my tent in one hour, where we can introduce them to the other commanders.

I'll leave someone here to show them the way. And you can . . . join them. I'll inform the emperor of our good fortune."

Gazija nodded. "You are most kind," he said, words tinged with sarcasm.

Caldan realized he was holding his breath and forced himself to breathe.

Devenish turned his back on the old man. He motioned to the others around him. "Come. We still have much to do." He strode back along the wharf, ice crunching underfoot.

Gorton and Melker watched him pass, then gestured for Caldan to follow behind his group.

With a last fleeting glance at Quiss, Caldan turned his thoughts to coercive sorcery and Miranda. Having hired five mercenary companies, and as head of the Five Oceans Mercantile Concern, Gazija was unlikely to want ducats in exchange for his help. Which meant Caldan had to come up with something else the man wanted if he approached him. But what?

CHAPTER 3

"ell, well. That was mighty interesting," remarked Melker. He licked his lips and looked back over his shoulder at the frost-rimed wharves.

To Caldan's right, Gorton bent down and picked a blade of grass. He put the end in his mouth and chewed thoughtfully. They were a few dozen paces from Devenish's tent, the warlock having told Caldan's escort to keep him with them.

From their position, Caldan could see the front line between the emperor's forces and the jukari horde. The occasional volley of arrows punctuated the sky, but this time they mostly broke up in midflight, their shafts falling aimlessly to the ground trailing smoke.

The vormag.

At this distance, Caldan couldn't sense anything, try as he might. But the lull in fighting, combined with Melker's and Gorton's comments about the warlocks joining the fight, led him to believe there was another battle being waged mostly unnoticed while the armies faced each other.

Sorcery.

And while the warlocks tested the vormag and kept them occupied, too busy to direct the jukari, the emperor's forces had time to recover. Heavy cavalry scattered across the field slowly formed once more into a cohesive force; Quivers, both foot soldiers and archers, took much-needed rest and nourishment. And all the while, more sprightly leather-armored cavalry harassed the jukari's flanks—peppering them with arrows and cutting down the creatures that broke from their lines with flashing sabers.

Melker sent some soldiers to fetch stools and firewood, and he set up their own campfire a dozen paces from the tent's entrance. Caldan almost jumped when the wood erupted into flame, as Melker and Gorton were testing the wind and positioning their stools away from the direction smoke would blow. It had been a tightly controlled burst, and too quick for Caldan to discern much, but an instant before it happened, a line in the air between Melker and the fire turned hazy.

It confirmed what he'd deduced from the warlocks' use of destructive sorcery when they had tried to kill Bells. And now that there had been such a display of devastation that no one could have missed for miles, what restraints the warlocks had on its use were fading. The long-held secret of destructive sorcery had been let out of the bag.

Caldan wasn't sure the world would be better off for it. He felt the Protectors went too far in restricting it, but the warlocks went too far in its use.

The two warlocks set themselves down, as if for a long wait. Gorton took his boots off and warmed his yellow-nailed feet by the fire. It seemed he'd resigned himself to missing the fighting with his fellow warlocks. Melker started picking up bits of stick and grass and threw them into the flames one by one.

"Cold down there on the docks," commented Gorton.

Melker nodded slowly, then groaned as he stretched. "Must be seasonal."

Gorton and Melker both chuckled, but Caldan could sense they were disturbed. He couldn't reason out how Gazija had sucked the heat from the very air, and it seemed the warlocks didn't know, either.

Caldan picked up a third stool and was about to move it out of the smoke when his knees wobbled. He breathed deeply and leaned on the stool to steady himself. There was a knifing pain in his legs, and a prickling beneath his skin. He swallowed and sucked in air, trying not to throw up.

"You all right there, Caldan?" asked Melker.

Caldan nodded as best he could, not sure what was wrong. He managed to stagger out of the smoke and slumped on his stool, head between his knees. Cold. He felt so cold; but his skin was slimy with sweat.

A hand grasped his shoulder.

"He doesn't look well . . ." said Gorton.

"Fetch some water, will you?" said Melker.

Caldan heard Gorton pulling on his boots and cursing under his breath. Melker's hand squeezed in reassurance.

"You'll be fine this time. It can take a day or more, from what I understand, for the full effects to manifest."

"What can? I think . . . maybe it's a reaction . . . to the stress of the last few days."

"Don't worry. Devenish told us what you were, and Kristof is probably on his way."

Melker could mean only one thing. They already knew he was a sorcerer, so he meant being Touched. "Who's Kristof?"

"He's one of you. Most others look to him. Most."

Caldan's mind was fuzzy, but hadn't Melker said something about full effects? "You know why I'm sick."

"Aye. Wait till you speak to Kristof. I don't have any answers."

"You do, you're just not telling me."

"That's right. It's not for me to say."

Caldan heard the finality in Melker's tone. He wouldn't say more on the subject. Gingerly, Caldan raised his head and breathed in lungfuls of air.

Gorton arrived with a jug of water, which Caldan took from his hands and sipped at. After a few swallows, he felt his nausea subside, and he drank deeply. He placed the jug next to his stool and sat up straight.

Gorton was eyeing him warily, but Melker offered him a smile.

"Feeling better?" Melker asked.

"Yes. A little."

"Maybe we can talk shop, take your mind off it."

"What do you mean?"

"You knew he was about to use sorcery, that Gazija. How?"

Caldan paused. *Why should I just dole out information to them for nothing in return?* "I'll answer any questions you have," he replied, "but in return, you have to answer some of mine. Fair?"

Gorton grunted and looked to Melker.

The pale, freckled warlock was regarding Caldan warily, plainly thinking his proposal through. "We won't be able to answer all your questions," Melker said eventually. "Some answers are not ours to divulge. Others . . . well, you're new here, and we have to determine where your loyalties lie."

"In other words, you don't trust me yet."

"I'm sure you feel the same way about us. But in time, you'll realize where your best interests lie."

"So I guess we'll just sit here quietly, if we can't trust each other."

Melker shrugged. "If you like. But we might find trust, you know. Not all of us are cut from the same cloth as Devenish and Thenna. Warlocks come from all walks of life, from the poor to the nobles. In time, we learn to trust each other about most things. It's just that some of us react to situations differently."

"But in the meantime," Caldan said, "we've determined neither of us will be totally forthcoming with the other. I'd rather not have a conversation where I can't trust anything the other person says."

"Then let's talk about something else. Your shield, for instance. Where did you get the crafting for it? And how did you learn to split your well into so many strings?"

A couple of fairly innocuous questions. Caldan couldn't see any harm in answering. "I smith-crafted the shield medallion." He noted Gorton's eyes widen. "Based on one an Indryallan sorcerer had. As for the strings, when I was in Anasoma, I worked out how to split my well. And since the city was invaded and we had to flee, I've been stretching myself as much as I can."

"How many strings can you manage?" Melker asked curiously.

Despite his casual question, Caldan sensed an intentness to him, as if the number of strings he could manage was important somehow. And it was, realized Caldan. For complex sorcery required controlling many strings, and this was an easy way to size up his strength. *No*, he thought, *nothing for free, Melker.*

"Four," lied Caldan, settling on that number because it was the minimum needed for the shield he'd shown them. "But it's a stretch. The fourth one is hard, and it's unstable."

Even as he said it, though, he thought back to his fight against the jukari with cel Rau. There, he'd pushed himself to control both his beetle and his shield . . . and his breath caught in his throat as a realization hit him: in the heat of battle, with no time to think, he'd forced himself to manage ten strings at once.

Ten.

The thought of doing that now, even in a quiet place with no distractions, made him feel ill. But he knew he *could* do it. He had done it before, which meant he could do it again . . . and maybe he could do even more.

Caldan's thoughts turned to Mahsonn's crafting, which he'd sensed required thirteen strings. He'd guessed that the medallion was what made Mahsonn invisible, but what if this was also the crafting that allowed him to control hundreds of destructive needles in mere instants? If Mahsonn's trickle of a well could use it to kill with such effectiveness, then what would Caldan be capable of if he could maintain thirteen strings? The idea was both terrifying and seductive. He wouldn't have anything to fear from most of the warlocks, that was certain.

"Four isn't bad, for a sorcerer. Warlocks have . . . more stringent criteria, shall we say. The strength of your well isn't that important, if you have other talents. Gorton here doesn't have the well to sustain a four-string shield, but he can do a few other things."

Caldan looked at Gorton. "Such as?"

Gorton chuckled, a sound with a slightly dangerous undertone. "I can burst a man's heart, if he stays still long enough to give me a fix on its location. Even through a shield, four strings or no."

Caldan shifted uncomfortably on his stool under Gorton's gaze. Despite the weakness he still felt, he stood up and began pacing along one side of the fire.

Both Melker and Gorton burst out laughing when he did so, and Caldan felt heat rise to his face. Were they joking with him? Or was their mirth to hide the truth just spoken?

"One of Gorton's talents," said Melker. "Many of which are very rare, the reason why he is valued highly." Gorton tilted his head in Melker's direction at this. "As for me, I don't have any rare talents. But I have a potent well and can handle quite a few strings. Is there anything you've noticed you can do better than other sorcerers?"

Caldan shook his head. "Not that I've noticed. I have a project I've been working on for a few years, but I wouldn't call it a talent. It's more a curiosity of mine." He would keep his abilities close to his chest. The warlocks might find out eventually, but under his terms.

"Don't be shy," Melker said. "What is it? Gorton's been trying to craft a rock that gives out heat so he's kept warm at night. I keep telling him there are better ways to stave off the night's chill." He winked at Caldan.

"I'll get it to work," said Gorton. "If we can then tie off the feedback loop like—" He cut off as Melker gave him a sharp look. "It'll benefit a lot of people someday."

"Indeed," replied Melker. "So, young Caldan, what's this 'project' of yours?"

Caldan swallowed. It really was just something he'd tinkered with, albeit with what he thought great success. But was this a talent like the ones the warlocks alluded to? He remembered that Mold and the other two masters hadn't been impressed with his automaton, though, and that made him think it was okay—in this instance—to be truthful. The fewer lies he told, the better—in order to keep track of them, if anything.

He reached into his pocket and drew out his rune-covered metal beetle, but hesitated. The construct required three strings for movement, hearing, and sight, and one more each for its shield and wings—and he had said he only had four strings. *Oh well—I'll just have to stick with four and choose which to use.*

He held the beetle between index finger and thumb and placed it on his stool. Accessing his well, he linked to the legs and wings, with another string for the eyes. Three should be enough. Runes flashed, then subsided to a muted glow.

"Lochner," said Gorton suddenly.

Melker grunted in agreement. He rubbed his chin. "Could be. That was a long time ago, though."

"Who's Lochner?" asked Caldan. "Did he also experiment with automatons?"

"He did. Years ago. A sorcerer who came to the warlocks hoping to be admitted. He stayed with us for a while, smith-crafting different items in hopes of proving his theories. In the end, it didn't amount to much." Melker went silent.

But Caldan could tell a lot was being left unsaid—the story just didn't feel right. He decided to push the issue. "Why do you both remember him, if he wasn't someone of note?"

The two warlocks exchanged glances.

Melker cleared his throat, then spoke. "Lochner grew increasingly frantic when his progress stalled. He felt he was close to making a breakthrough and refused to sleep until he did. One night, he was working alone on a crafting much like yours, except his was a rodent. In the morning, a servant found his door locked from within, and he didn't respond to knocking or requests to let anyone in. Eventually, the servant left to find a warlock, and when she arrived, she used sorcery to open the lock. Inside, Lochner was found sitting in his favorite chair in front of a cold fireplace. His automaton was clutched in both hands, but he was dead. Not a mark on him. And he was only twenty-seven years old. We were never able to find out how he died. He's one of the reasons experimenting with automatons is considered . . . perilous. They may not be related to what happened to him, but in the absence of anything else to go on, it's the most likely theory."

"But his crafting couldn't have killed him. I mean, it wasn't damaged, was it?"

Gorton shook his head. "No. I saw it. It was intact and showed no signs of having failed. I still remember the ruby eyes he used. Gave me the creeps. Like it was looking at me."

The warlocks had obviously turned Lochner's death into a cautionary tale of the dangers of sorcery, and tinkering with forces you weren't sure of. *Which I get . . . except that, without experimentation, how is progress to be made?*

Unless, of course, the warlocks weren't interested in progress.

Seeing how secretive they could be about the powers they were allowed to use and those that were forbidden to others, it wasn't the craziest theory he'd come up with.

At Caldan's urging, the beetle turned, skittering on its legs. Another thought from him, and its wings buzzed and it rose into the air. He sent it in a wide circle around them, enjoying the look of wonder on Gorton's face.

Just then, Gorton stood abruptly, gazing back down the trodden path away from Devenish's tent. When he did, Caldan sensed Melker open his well. A moment later, Gorton did the same. Not knowing what had been observed, Caldan made his automaton hover above them and reached for his shield crafting—then knew he'd made a mistake. He couldn't split his well into more strings, or the warlocks would know he'd lied to them. He cursed under his breath.

Coming toward them was a group of around twenty people. Most looked to be hard-bitten soldiers wearing motley gear and mismatched weapons. Among them were the denser-men, Gazija and his companions.

They trampled past Caldan and the warlocks with barely a glance in their direction, no doubt having gotten accustomed to being stared at as they made their way through the emperor's army from the wharves to the warlocks' location. Caldan watched their backs as they were ushered inside Devenish's tent by two blond women—warlocks, by their dress—who were positioned outside. He turned back to Melker and Gorton, intending to ask them if they knew much about the mercenaries. But they were glaring at Quiss, who stood not ten paces away. The banker must have been trailing the group, otherwise Caldan would have seen him break off.

"Forgive me," Quiss said in his curious melodic accent. "I don't mean to intrude—"

"And yet here you are," growled Melker.

Quiss ignored the warlock and looked at Caldan. "I believe we've met." Both warlocks turned suspicious eyes on Caldan. This was the last thing he needed. "Head Trader Quiss, isn't it? You did some business with my friend Miranda."

"Ah yes, so I did. How is she? Well, I hope. She has a fine business sense."

Caldan's reply stuck in his throat. "She's . . . not well," he finished lamely. "An accident." Was this a chance to find out more about these odd sorcerers? If they had far greater skill with coercive sorcery than Devenish and the warlocks, then why not?

"Oh dear," said Quiss. "She's not a sorcerer, though, so . . . was she hurt in the fighting?"

"No. It was before that, when we were escaping from Anasoma. She wasn't physically hurt; coercive sorcery damaged her mind. I came here looking for a way to heal her."

Quiss's eyes narrowed, and he gave Caldan a thoughtful look. He nodded slightly. "That's a shame. I'm sure the warlocks will try something." His tone left Caldan in no doubt he thought they wouldn't succeed.

"Shouldn't you be with your master?" interrupted Melker.

Quiss turned to the warlock, smiling. "He's the First Deliverer, not our master. And yes, I should accompany him. But I couldn't help but notice this fabulous creation." Quiss gestured to Caldan's beetle automaton. "I've never seen the like before. It's a hybrid, isn't it? Of sorcery and what?"

"And clockwork mechanisms." Caldan shrugged, unsure of what to say. He didn't want the warlocks to associate him with these newcomers, but he was also proud of his automaton. "It's something I've been tinkering with. Not much use, really."

"It flew. It can move on its own."

So Quiss hadn't been trailing the others. He couldn't have been, if he'd seen the beetle fly. He must have come from a different direction.

"It can, but you need to be able to control a few strings to make it function properly."

Quiss frowned. "What do you mean by strings?"

An odd question coming from him, thought Caldan. Then again, he'd only assumed Quiss was a sorcerer after Gazija's display.

Caldan quested his senses out and found that Quiss did indeed have a well, but where most others he'd felt were rough, torn, this one was perfectly smooth and gaping wide. It felt natural, right, somehow. His own well felt malformed in comparison. Then, in an instant, Quiss's well changed, folding in on itself until it disappeared. He'd allowed Caldan a glimpse of his true well before disguising it, as Simmon had his.

Caldan looked at Quiss in surprise, but the sorcerer merely bent over for a closer examination of his beetle.

"Strings?" Quiss prompted.

"If he doesn't know, don't say another word," warned Gorton.

"He has to know," said Melker. And then to Quiss, "Stop playing games."

The look Quiss gave the two warlocks was filled with pity. "Strings. Threads. Strands. Filaments. Whatever you call them, if you're still using them in your sorcery, then you've a long way to go."

"Pfft," scoffed Melker, glaring at Quiss. "There is no other way. You're just trying to get into our heads."

Quiss shrugged nonchalantly. "Think what you like." He turned to Caldan. "Come see me when you can. I'd like to hear more about what ails Miranda. I liked her, and I'll do what I can to help her. Which is far more than these warlocks can do."

"Bah!" exclaimed Melker. "A fool who doesn't know sorcery uses strings?" But underneath his words, Caldan sensed something. There was a quaver in the warlock's voice. Fear. The display of sorcery on the wharf had shaken him, seeing his leader's power so easily dealt with. Perhaps it had never happened before. After all, the warlocks were at the pinnacle of power, as far as Caldan knew. Certainly as far as *they* knew.

No wonder they were so disturbed. In a few moments, their entire dominance had been shaken, and reverberations from the meeting would likely be felt for years to come. As someone whose world had been turned upside down many times, Caldan could imagine what was going through all their minds meeting Gazija and these strange, dense men.

Quiss took a few steps back over the rough ground, inclining his head to each of them in turn. "I must be going, or I'll miss the meeting." He regarded Caldan evenly. "I'll see what I can do for Miranda."

Skirting their fire in an arc, Quiss walked up to Devenish's tent to be ushered inside.

"Don't listen to him, Caldan. Full of lies and misdirection, that one was."

Caldan agreed with Melker out loud, but he wasn't so sure. Master Annelie hadn't been able to heal Miranda, and she'd been hesitant to confirm that anyone else could. It wouldn't hurt to see what the denser-men were able to do, if they were willing.

Would it?

The only problem was, what would they ask in return?

And will I be able to pay their price?

CHAPTER 4

Aidan lounged in a faded red armchair with padding erupting from several holes in the middle of patches of frayed material. A warm fire crackled nearby, and he'd placed a jug of spiced wine next to it to heat. His arm was tightly bound in a sling against his chest. The physikers had taken their sweet time seeing to it. After they'd set the arm, they'd tried to give him more oil of the poppy, but he'd had enough of dulled senses for the time being.

Riversedge was almost in chaos. From what he'd heard, the jukari horde hadn't even reached the city when the emperor's forces had been butchered. With only a fraction of that army remaining, Aidan doubted the vormag would hesitate. They would set the jukari on the remnants and use their foul sorcery to destroy what they could.

He reached across and poured himself a mug of the wine, sipping at it without noticing the taste.

Across the room from him, Vasile was fast asleep in his own dilapidated armchair. The magistrate's arm was in worse shape than Aidan's, and they'd almost amputated the limb. *As bad a break as we've ever seen,* one of the physikers had said. Only Aidan interceding on Vasile's behalf had stopped them. Eventually, they'd agreed there was a slight chance the arm could be saved.

It hadn't been easy for Aidan to find Vasile, but his writ from the emperor opened doors and mouths that would normally have remained closed to him. He'd found the magistrate being tended to by the physikers seconded to Riversedge's Quivers. Aidan had followed the trail cel Rau had left and barged his way into the Quivers' main barracks, disappointed at finding only Vasile, but at the same time relieved the magistrate had made it to safety.

Word of his writ had spread throughout the Quivers, and soon he'd been summoned to a meeting with Riversedge's commander, a man by the name of Cilliers. From what Aidan could tell, Commander Cilliers hadn't left his "strategy room" to observe the jukari forces, let alone address the Quivers holding the walls.

He snorted in disgust at the thought of meeting the man, and Vasile stirred, disturbed by the noise.

Aidan sipped at his wine and realized the cup was empty. He began to refill it, paused, then continued to pour.

Vasile shifted and opened one eye. It was a few moments before he seemed able to focus his gaze on Aidan. He ran his tongue over parched lips and cleared his throat.

"I . . . don't suppose that's . . . water?"

"There's some next to you. The physikers said you'd wake soon. I don't think you'll want to move just yet. You need time to adjust." Aidan slurped a mouthful from his cup and set it down. With a groan, he levered himself to his feet and shuffled over to Vasile. He reached down and handed a jug filled with water to the magistrate. There was a hollow reed poking out the top, which Vasile looked askance at.

"Use it," said Aidan. "The physikers keep them for patients who have limited use of their arms and hands."

Vasile sucked water through the reed while Aidan restrained himself from asking the hundred questions he had tumbling around in his mind.

Vasile drained more than half the jug before pushing the reed out with his tongue and turning his head away. "Thank you," he said.

Aidan set the water down and returned to his chair. "Tell me what happened to you, cel Rau, and Chalayan at the bridge. And what happened after."

Vasile screwed his face up in a grimace. He looked sicker than before, if that were possible.

"You're not going to like what I have to say."

"There are many things I don't like in this world, bad news among them. But I've heard enough terrible things not to balk at hearing any now. I need to know what's going on."

Vasile nodded. "Cel Rau . . . killed Chalayan. Right after the sorcery on the bridge. He—we—thought you were dead. How is it you're alive?"

"All in good time, Vasile. Tell me of Chalayan's death, and what came after."

Swallowing, Vasile nodded again.

CHAPTER 5

Amerdan's father, now probably no more than a skeleton in a shallow grave behind their childhood home, had always said to him, "Look after your sisters, boy. You're the eldest, and stronger than them. It's up to you to make sure they come to no harm."

The fool of a farmer hadn't realized there were different types of strength. That which was visible, and that which was hidden. But his words stayed with Amerdan to this very day. He had been young when he realized the talents you were born with didn't really matter. It was what you *became* that determined your strength. Your power. And there were many ways to change what you were. His great misfortune—the imprisonment of him and his sisters for experiments—had eventually turned to fortune when he'd stumbled onto one of the more potent ways to alter what a person was, to change one's limits. Or perhaps it wasn't luck, but meant to be.

Was I chosen? Did the ancestors reach through the veil separating life from death to influence my fate?

He supposed it was possible. How else could you explain what had happened to him? And he was fine with that. What bothered him was the question of whether he had been selected before or after his sisters were abused and slaughtered.

Amerdan ground his teeth, shuddering at the thought. If their deaths had been essential to his . . . becoming, then someone would still have to pay. Whoever, or whatever, had chosen him would have to be punished.

And if I have to exact revenge on a capricious god, then I need to become powerful enough to do so.

Dotty knew this. He didn't know how his sisters had transferred their awareness into the rag doll, for she hardly ever spoke. He only knew he was glad of their comforting presence, and the knowledge that they hadn't left him alone in the dungeon with the sorcerer.

A shadow moved in the corridor ahead of him, flickering in the light cast by a lone oil lantern. An unwelcome visitor, and one who might come to regret his intrusion.

Amerdan ducked down a side passage and flattened himself against the stone wall. He knew he could kill or disable anyone who found him, but it was necessary to remain unnoticed, at least for the time being. Riversedge was a dangerous place for him now, but this building was close to the wall, and he could easily leave the city whenever he wanted. For now, he needed to wait and see if he could find Caldan again. Although he felt a certain kinship with the man, he would need his talent for sorcery, along with, eventually, his well.

And that meant avoiding anyone who came down to the third basement level. Hardly anyone found themselves here, but there was the occasional interloper into his new domain, for the most part easily avoided.

He hated waiting. But wait he had to, if he was to take possession of his prize. Caldan first, then he should look toward the Mahruse emperor and the other sorcerers who'd come against Bells—the warlocks. There was much he could absorb from them all.

But if they found him before he was skilled enough, then all his plans would unravel.

Footsteps in the distance became louder as the person approached, then stopped. Keys rattled, and a lock clicked. Hinges screeched in protest as a door opened. There wasn't much stored down here, and the rooms Amerdan had investigated contained mostly dust and long-dead spiders. Usually, the only things moving around were the rats. The moldy rugs and forgotten tapestries fallen from walls made for comfortable nests, and the rodents could forage above for food.

This place made his skin crawl, and he desperately wanted to wash.

Amerdan shifted his focus internally, using his senses to touch the spaces Bells had opened in his mind. Wells, she called them. One was smaller than the other and felt coarser somehow, as if a carpenter had bored two holes in a piece of wood and filed and sanded only one of them.

But it was to the new well his attention shifted. Bells had given him one last gift as she died. He couldn't usually tell what talents his trinket would transfer to him, and he was often surprised—and delighted—at what transpired. Randomness was to be avoided, but sometimes . . . it was sweeter when he discovered an ability he'd never had, rather than just had one enhanced.

The sorcerer's apprentice in Anasoma was an example. Reading was something Amerdan had never had the advantage of learning. Yet after he'd absorbed the apprentice, he just . . . *knew*. Knew without learning. With the experiments he'd conducted over the years, he thought he'd found out everything there was to know about his trinket, but it always seemed to surprise him. It certainly had when Bells told him he could be a sorcerer.

Extending his senses, he scratched at the blocked well. *Bells's* well. It hadn't been there before, and now it was.

Amerdan frowned with annoyance. His scratching had the same effect as someone using a fingernail to try to break through a wall. Try as he might, he couldn't find any purchase, any crack with which to force a breach.

Someone moved a few dozen paces away, and Amerdan's heart hammered. How . . . how had he sensed them move? He closed his eyes and concentrated. There was a mark of some kind he could feel, though there were walls between him and it, whatever it was. It seemed to call to him, as if it were a gash in the sorcerous senses he was only just learning how to use.

No, not a gash. A well.

A sorcerer.

Amerdan stumbled backward a step, then recovered, and understood something else in that moment.

Someone's hunting me.

He took a deep breath and crept to the door. There was only one way out of this room, and he wouldn't let himself be trapped like an animal. His abilities as a sorcerer were still mostly unknown to him, and if he came up against one of the warlocks or Protectors, he wasn't sure he'd be able to defeat them.

That fact galled and intrigued him at the same time. Amerdan shook his head. He could learn more about crafting later; now he needed to make sure he was safe. They were after him, and as weak as he was, he should flee.

Run, Dotty said, squirming against his chest. *Coward.*

Amerdan winced at her harsh tone. She was right, but she was also wrong. How could she be both? He carefully lifted the latch on the door, and seeing there was no light in the corridor, he slipped outside and felt his way through the pitch-blackness away from the sorcerer.

Illumination erupted behind him, throwing his shadow against a wall directly in front of him. He was almost at a corner. He quickly ducked around it and hid as voices drifted down the corridor.

"I thought I felt something," a woman said.

"Where?" said a man. "This is the fifth building we've searched, and there's been no sign. Whoever you're after, he's long gone."

"No," the woman said. "There was . . . bah! Perhaps you're right. But Gazija said we should check this area, and we will."

"It's your ducats, and this is better than fighting the jukari."

There were laughs following the man's statement. A sorcerer and at least four men, probably all warriors of some kind. Mercenaries, from what they'd said about ducats.

Dotty wouldn't like it, but he had to run. One day, though, they'd be the ones to flee from him.

Amerdan moved stealthily down the corridor until the light they carried faded. He felt his way along the wall. In this section, he knew where he was going—some narrow servants' stairs at the back of the building. Then he'd be out a side door and on the streets.

Dotty's words followed him all the way.

Coward.

That he might be, but he wasn't worried about himself at the moment. Who was Gazija, and why had he or she sent sorcerers and mercenaries after him? Whoever it was knew he was in this part of Riversedge, and that was not good at all. As much as he hated to, Amerdan had no option but to leave the city until he knew more.

CHAPTER 6

ootsteps approached Caldan from behind. He turned to see
Thenna striding toward him, gingerly lifting the hem of her
skirt above the blood and gore.

What does she want?

He brushed at his eyes and took a deep breath to calm himself.

She stopped a few steps away and looked down at him. After a
moment, her wrinkled, suntanned face screwed up in contempt.

"Where are Melker and Gorton?" she demanded.

Caldan pointed to a squad of Quivers some distance away. The
two warlocks were among their number, all of them taking swigs from
a bottle. "They're still keeping an eye on me. I needed some time to
myself. To think."

"Devenish wants to talk to you, though I don't know what he
expects to get out of you. Waste of time, if you ask me. He should be
dealing with the jukari."

This not being his first time around her, Caldan felt pretty confident in his assessment that Thenna often spoke without consider-

ing her thoughts. It made him wonder how high the warlocks placed wisdom on their list of priorities for membership. Not that he doubted her intelligence—only her shrewdness.

But that's her problem . . . and maybe my advantage.

So Caldan just nodded, then stood. His legs wobbled for a moment, and he feared he might lose his balance. When he felt a bit sturdier, he asked, "Where is he now?"

Thenna jerked her head back the way she'd come. "In the command tent, talking with that swordsman of yours."

"He's not mine," replied Caldan. "I just met him myself." Anshul cel Rau was his own man, as far as Caldan could tell. But the fact he was meeting with the leader of the warlocks surprised him.

"Bloody savage, too. From the Steppes," she added, not even hearing Caldan.

"I think he's much more than he seems." Cel Rau had risked his life to save people he didn't know from the jukari and vormag. Then he'd joined Caldan as he'd tried to defeat Bells. Not the actions of your average barbarian.

The warlock's eyes narrowed, and she sniffed. "Swords are no match for crafting."

The sight of Caldan's sword sliding through the sorcerer's shield and into his chest flooded his vision. It seemed so long ago, in Anasoma. He twisted his trinket ring on his finger but kept his disagreement to himself. "No match for your sorcery," he said. "It seems that you and the Indryallans have something in common."

"That's none of your business. I don't like you, Caldan. You look dishonest. And despite your *story*, I think you're hiding something. I'll find out what it is, and then we'll see how useful Devenish thinks you are."

Caldan shrugged, and without waiting for Thenna, he trudged across the devastated ground.

Thenna followed him all the way to Devenish's tent. Caldan could feel her eyes boring into his back, and it gave him an itch between his shoulder blades—one he resisted scratching while she watched him.

Let her think what she thinks. I'm sure she's dangerous, but she's not who I need to convince.

Now, if Devenish turns on me, then I'll need to worry . . .

Two young women were still on guard outside the tent, one on either side of the opening. Their long blond hair hung loose, and their dark eyes seemed to miss nothing. By their clothes—black, with silver flower buttons—Caldan was sure they were warlocks. Obviously, he could confirm that if he sensed their wells, but he didn't want to expose himself. Still, it was a reminder that he swam in unknown waters now. The appearance the warlocks put on was just that, a veneer hiding their true purpose. And until he could determine what that was, observation was his best weapon.

As he approached, the women looked him up and down before opening the tent flaps and gesturing him inside. They then looked over his shoulder at Thenna, and Caldan was surprised to see one of them sneer.

Professional or personal contempt? wondered Caldan. He pretended not to notice, but filed the exchange away. Small actions like this— little remarks, or the way people reacted around others—were helping him piece together a picture of this strange new world he found himself in. And the first image that was coming into focus was the fact that the warlocks were not some singular, unified entity. There were factions and schisms. And while he couldn't be sure *why* that was important right now, he was certainly going to keep his eyes out for who was aligned with whom.

As the monks had taught him all those years, *No knowledge is useless knowledge.*

"The Protector only," said one of the women. "You can wait outside, Thenna."

"Devenish sent me to collect him," spluttered Thenna. "And I'll deliver him myself."

"You have. We don't have orders to admit you as well."

Caldan glanced behind him to see a red-faced Thenna glaring at the other warlocks. He thought for a moment, then spoke.

"Devenish assigned Thenna to watch over me. If you send her away, you'll just have to chase after her when he realizes you didn't let her in."

Both of the young warlocks turned hard eyes on him. "Is that so?"

Caldan nodded. "Come on, Thenna, let's go inside. I'm sure Devenish doesn't want to be kept waiting." He stepped into the tent opening, one foot inside and one out, and beckoned to Thenna. She hesitated for a heartbeat, then strode through the opening. As she passed him, she gave him a frown, but she also narrowed her eyes and nodded minutely.

Now, it didn't matter to him whether Thenna was present when he talked to Devenish, but it mattered to *her*.

Small steps.

Inside, rugs lay on the ground, and the space was dominated by a map-covered table, the corners of paper held down with river stones. The uppermost map looked to be of Riversedge, with groupings of small black and white stones denoting what he assumed to be positions of the jukari forces and the emperor's own.

Devenish stood on the other side of the table, conversing with cel Rau in terse, hushed tones. When they saw Caldan enter, they broke their conversation off abruptly.

"We'll take this up again later," Devenish said.

Cel Rau nodded, hands resting on his sword pommels. He smiled at Caldan, tight-lipped, then looked at the maps, as if they were of interest to him.

"He came quietly," blurted Thenna, moving to stand beside Caldan. "Found him staring at the mess the Indryallan sorcery caused."

"Of course he did," replied Devenish, stepping toward them. "What else could he do? Thenna, would you be kind enough to find Kristof and bring him here? Oh, and that new physiker—what's her name?"

"Tamara."

"Yes, that's it. Bring her as well."

"But why?" protested Thenna. "Are you ill? I can—"

"It's not for me." Devenish placed a hand on her shoulder and kept his eyes on hers. "Please, Thenna."

She looked down and away. "Of course. I'll be back as soon as I can." She turned and left the tent.

Devenish went to a side table and poured wine into two bronze goblets. He handed one to Caldan before taking a sip. Caldan followed suit and forced himself to swallow. The wine was excellent, with a hint of black cherries and pepper.

"So, Caldan," Devenish said, "cel Rau here tells me you also had a hand in fighting some of the jukari away from people fleeing the horde. Your actions allowed a good many more to reach the safety of Riversedge."

Caldan inclined his head in affirmation, not trusting himself to speak. How much had cel Rau told Devenish? Caldan himself had revealed to the warlock that he was both Touched and a sorcerer. But the thought of Devenish knowing exactly what he was capable of filled him with unease.

Devenish studied Caldan's face. "I understand your reticence. It's a valuable gift you have, and rare. Very rare. The emperor likes to keep those we know are Touched close to him and in his service. You can understand why."

"Yes. They . . . we would be useful."

"Yes, useful. But not just for the emperor, Caldan—for you, too. What you don't know is that the more you use your unique abilities, the harder it will go for you. It's the strain, you see. On your muscles. Your bones. Your *mind*. If left uncontrolled, you'll use your abilities whenever they're triggered by stress or a threat. Who wouldn't? That's when they're most useful. But go down that path, and you'll be unable to hold off the side effects. Only a few trinkets can help you with this. And only the emperor's warlocks can provide them, if you want to survive more than a few years longer."

"So you say. How do I know you're telling the truth?"

Devenish shook his head. "You don't. But you'll soon come to realize I am. And the only way you can avoid, ah . . . unpleasantness . . . is to swear to serve your emperor. And what could be a finer, more important calling than that?"

"And what about crafting? That's all I really want to do."

"I've a few ideas about how your talents can greatly benefit the empire. But first, I have a task for you."

He evaded the question, Caldan thought. *And what is this about a task?* He glanced at the swordsman to find cel Rau staring at him, maps forgotten. "What do you want me to do?" he asked Devenish.

"Kill jukari and vormag, of course. What else is there to do at the moment?"

"Why me, though? I'm sure you have enough warlocks and Quivers. And now you also have the mercenary bands."

Devenish's mouth twisted with distaste. "Sellswords won't help us much."

That's not what you thought before, when the mercenaries rescued the Quivers.

And you want me to trust you? Well, I can play that game, too.

"If you say so, but I don't see what good I'd be: I'm a sorcerer, and the finer points of battle elude me."

Devenish's eyes narrowed, and he stared at Caldan for a moment. *You're more than just a sorcerer,* the look seemed to say, *and we both know that.*

"The mercenaries can't be trusted, though they'll be useful for softening up the jukari. The warlocks have their own tasks, and you can be sure they'll be fighting the vormag. But many are needed to defend Riversedge, and, of course, the emperor."

Caldan suppressed a sigh. He had no idea what Devenish's intentions toward him were, but if the warlock wanted him to kill jukari, then he'd have his wish. If anything, it would give him time to learn a bit more about the warlocks and come to a decision about serving the emperor . . . or not.

He nodded his agreement. "I'll do it."

"Of course you will," said Devenish. "Oh, and Thenna will go along with you. She'll be able to judge the strength of your sorcery and see your craftings at work. I assume you have some you've made?"

Caldan was about to reply when a wave of nausea flowed through him. His stomach churned, and he felt blood rush to his face. "Excuse me," he managed to mumble weakly. "Do you mind if I . . ." Without waiting for a response, he staggered over to the map table and rested his weight on it. His hands felt slick, as if he was sweating profusely, which he then realized he was. He breathed deeply, trying to banish his queasiness, which eased a little. "I'm sorry. I don't know what's . . ." What had Devenish asked him about? *Oh, yes, my craftings.*

Caldan turned to see Devenish regarding him calmly. "Yes," he replied belatedly. "I have three craftings I've made: a shield crafting and two automatons. I'm sure you'll see how advanced they are."

He could feel sweat snaking down his scalp, and he still felt weak. Taking a breath, he straightened and tried to pretend he'd recovered.

"Good," said Devenish. "But automatons are mostly useless. You'll need to craft more usable pieces soon, if you're to be any help. Then—"

Devenish paused as the tent flap opened and Thenna entered, followed by one of the biggest men Caldan had ever seen and a slender, dark-haired woman.

The man limped, and he looked like a grizzled veteran, but he wore a sword with a crafted hilt, along with many silver rings. Caldan could feel them vibrating at the edge of his awareness. *Trinkets.* The woman had none, but instead carried a leather kit similar to Elpidia's. At the thought of her, Caldan's throat tightened, and he swallowed with difficulty.

"Ah, Kristof!" exclaimed Devenish, as if greeting an old friend. "And Tamara."

"Oh, you remembered!" the physiker remarked with a simper. She glanced at Devenish, then looked down and away.

Beside her, Thenna crossed her arms, and her mouth drew into a thin line. "I brought them, as you wanted. Though fetching isn't my strongest skill."

"I know, Thenna. My thanks."

Thenna scowled at Devenish, then glanced at Tamara. Her scowl deepened.

Devenish approached Kristof, and they clasped hands.

"Wine?" asked the warlock.

"No," replied Kristof in a deep voice. "It interferes with the effectiveness of the herbs I'm taking. Or so they tell me."

"Ah. Well, later, perhaps. Tamara?"

"Oh, no. Thank you for asking. Not while I'm working. Is there someone I'm here to treat? I don't see anyone who looks injured."

"There will be." Devenish cleared his throat. "Caldan here is a . . . special one."

At his words, Kristof's eyes bored into Caldan's.

"He used his talents to help save some refugees from the jukari earlier. For an extended period. Or so I was told."

Devenish and Kristof exchanged a meaningful look, then Kristof grunted. Tamara nodded knowingly.

"Kristof, you'll need to assess him. I know there's plenty of work here with the jukari to keep you occupied, but obviously this is important—and he might be able to help. And Tamara, you know what to do. He'll need something to keep him going and get him through a few rough days."

Caldan didn't like the fact that they were talking about him as if he weren't there. And why would he need a physiker to get him through the next few days? "What do you mean?" he asked warily.

Devenish waved at Kristof. "He'll explain on the way. Kristof, be so good as to escort Caldan to your encampment. Find him any equipment he needs, and a bedroll or some such out of the way of the others. You'll both need your rest before tomorrow."

Tamara was nodding, while Kristof gave Caldan a penetrating look.

"Come with me," the big man said. "I'm sure you've a lot of questions."

"Wait," Caldan said. "Devenish, I need to talk to you about Joachim and what happened to me in Riversedge."

"Tomorrow," replied the warlock.

"Maybe," said Kristof, and Devenish nodded.

"Maybe, then," the warlock said. "We'll be busy with the jukari for a while, so whatever you need to speak about, it can wait. The vormag are proving troublesome. They've learned some things I wouldn't have expected, as if someone's been teaching them sorcery . . ." He shook his head. "No matter. Be off with you. Oh, and Kristof, Caldan is also a sorcerer." It sounded like a warning. "Thenna will question him when he's recovered. But for the moment, I need to talk to her."

He turned back to the map-covered table.

Caldan frowned at Devenish's back. He glanced at cel Rau, and the swordsman gave a minute shrug.

"Come on," growled Kristof once more, and he strode to the tent flap. He opened it and looked at Caldan expectantly.

Caldan hesitated. He had so many questions—about Joachim, the Touched, sorcery, his parents, even. The answers were at his fingertips, he could sense it. But he could also sense that those answers were going to remain just out of reach for the time being. It was frustrating, with so many unknowns whirling around him: Miranda, Amerdan, why he was feeling this way, the denser-men . . .

He was a patient man—the monks had trained him in that, if nothing else—but there was only so much longer he would play their game.

Caldan nodded to Thenna and left the tent, Tamara following at his heels.

Kristof set off, limping through the camp. Around them, soldiers were gathered into groups, talking and repairing equipment, sharpening weapons. There weren't as many as when Caldan and cel Rau first came here. Most of them must have been out patrolling or fighting the jukari, although he also knew many of them probably didn't return from the first encounter with the monsters . . . and Bells's havoc. A few of the soldiers noted Kristof passing and kept their eyes on him, whether out of curiosity, fear, or something else, Caldan was hard-pressed to decide.

Caldan's nausea subsided until it only niggled at him. A couple of times, he stumbled, and Tamara came to his aid, steadying him with a firm grip. He thanked her when she did, and she smiled in return.

They followed Kristof until they came to a bunch of tents separated from the others. They were larger than the regular soldiers' tents by a good margin, and beside each was a wagon. A wide clear space surrounded them, and the tents were all facing inward toward a smoldering fire. Situated around the fire were seven stools, and on two of them sat a man and woman conversing in hushed tones.

"Here we are," Kristof said. He limped over to the fire.

"Where is here, exactly?" asked Caldan. "I want to know what's going on."

By the fire, the man and woman stood. Both were nondescript, clothed in shirts and pants any commoner would wear. The man wore a short sword at his belt, while the woman sported numerous daggers. What marked them as different to Caldan were their adornments. Like Kristof, they carried a number of trinket rings and an amulet or two, if what he sensed was correct.

"What's this, Kristof?" said the woman. "You know strangers are to keep away from our area."

Kristof grimaced and rubbed his hip. "Tamara you know, and this is Caldan. He's one of us. Don't know where he's from yet."

"A feral one, eh?" she replied with a smirk. "That's rare. You'll have your work cut out for you."

Enough, thought Caldan. He was tired of being treated like a child. They were obviously Touched, as he was.

Maybe I am in the dark about a lot of things, he thought, *but do you all know you're going to be used up and drained of your blood? A final indignity; your reward for a lifetime of service.*

Surely they didn't, or they wouldn't be here still serving the emperor. But how do you tell someone that? How could he possibly make them believe him, let alone ensure his revelation didn't lead to his own death?

"All I know," Caldan said, interrupting their conversation, "is that one of my ancestors was someone called Karrin Wraythe." He felt that was enough for now—he kept the trinket ring to himself, keeping the hand wearing the ring firmly in his pocket. These people weren't sorcerers—he couldn't sense a well in any of them—so chances were they didn't know he had a trinket. He felt better among these strangers knowing they couldn't craft, while he had access to his shield crafting and beetle automaton. With these, he doubted they'd be able to do anything to harm him.

"Never heard of her," said Kristof in response to Caldan's declaration. "I need to rest. My leg is killing me." He sat on one of the stools. "Caldan, sit with us. We probably have a little time to fill you in on some details. Tamara, you can set your things in my wagon over there. You'll need to prepare a few mixtures."

The physiker nodded and bustled off to the wagon. She climbed inside and busied herself with her kit, taking out bottles and vials and a mortar and pestle, with which she began grinding herbs.

The man and woman resumed their seats. Both stared at Caldan, as if thinking he might make a break for it at any moment.

But where would I go?

Caldan kept his hand in his pocket, touching his shield crafting, and sat across from Kristof. He tried to appear at ease, stretching his legs out, but the truth was that he was anxious for . . . something. Anything. Action, information, a test.

Anything.

"Are you all Touched?" Caldan asked.

"In the head, maybe," the other man muttered, and the woman laughed. Kristof just shook his head at them before returning his attention to Caldan. He pointed at the man. "Edelgard here, and his sister, Lisanette"—the finger moved to indicate the woman—"are. As am I. We were raised in the capital, though, as are most of us. It is . . . unusual for someone to come into our ranks from outside."

Because the emperor keeps a tight control on the bloodlines, and any-one who tries to escape is killed—like my parents.

But it wasn't his place to say that, at least for now. "Why is that?" Caldan asked, affecting a puzzled frown.

"Whatever you think you know about your abilities is probably wrong," growled Kristof. "You don't know what you don't know. And that's dangerous. For you, for me, for everyone. If Devenish is right, and he almost always is, you'll learn something over the next few days. A lesson we've all had to learn. So . . . tell me what you *think* you know."

Obvious facts only, Caldan warned himself. "We're different some-how. What it is, I haven't the faintest idea. It's passed down from generation to generation. All I have to go on is what I've experienced. It's like my blood heats up . . . I can feel it pumping through me, beat-ing like a drum. I get hot. And I can move fast." Out of the corner of his eye, he could see Lisanette nodding. "And I must get stronger, too. When I've used a sword, it seems to weigh less. Others around me move so slow compared to me. It's an almost overwhelming advantage. But I can't control it. Can you?"

"Sometimes," said Kristof quickly, as if he wanted to answer before Edelgard or Lisanette did. "There are ways. Techniques you can use, and items."

He means trinkets, thought Caldan. Though Kristof obviously didn't want to reveal too much to him.

"But what you may not know," continued Kristof, "is that we walk a knife's edge. Tell me, Caldan, how many times has this happened to you? The heat, the speed? And what transpired the first time?"

An image of Caldan's wooden sword sticking out of Marlon's chest flashed in his mind. The first time was when he'd almost killed Jemma's brother. *Oh, Jemma.* She felt like so long ago now. Did he really care about her anymore? Honestly, did she ever really care about him? He was pretty sure it didn't matter, because what he had with Miranda felt more real to him.

Now, thinking about *her* and the condition she was in—being cared for by some nurse in Riversedge—definitely brought on deep feelings. For a moment, he forgot Kristof's question.

"I blacked out," he said finally. "For a long time. Almost two days. Since then it's only happened a few times. But with the jukari, it lasted much longer. It wasn't like the other times, when it left me as quickly as it came."

"What happened when it left you before? Did you feel sick?"

Caldan thought for a moment, then shook his head. "No, not really. Weak, a little dizzy, maybe. And . . . hungry."

Kristof grunted. "Lucky is what you've been. You didn't look well in Devenish's tent, and you stumbled on the way here."

"I'm fine—"

"No, you're not. You got away with it a few times before. I don't know how. But an extended use of your abilities, as Devenish described with the jukari, is going to affect you. This is one of the main reasons we are beholden to the emperor and the warlocks. They have trinkets that can help us. Only they can provide them. But they need to be earned."

So that's it—my trinket. And because Kristof doesn't know about it, he assumes it's all been luck. But, actually, it explained so much. Caldan had felt it bite into his finger when the heat of his abilities came over him, but afterward, when he'd taken the ring off, his skin remained unbroken. One of its uses, perhaps its only one, had to be mitigating the aftereffects of his Touched abilities. So far he'd recovered well, but the nausea and weakness he'd felt recently made him wonder if that meant it wasn't coping now. Which went a good way toward explaining why the three Touched around him had multiple trinkets. Rewards, yes. But rewards that also bound. Gifts to be used that remained the property of the emperor.

And Kristof said that only the warlocks could provide them. Why was that the case? Did the warlocks know the secret of creating trinkets? It was a possibility.

A cramp twisted in Caldan's stomach, and he bent over, grimacing in pain. If he hadn't been sitting, he would have fallen to the ground. "By the ancestors," he muttered. He pressed his hands into his stomach and tried to massage the pain away. After a few moments, it subsided, and he looked up to find Kristof, Edelgard, and Lisanette staring at him.

"Is this what I can expect? More of these cramps? And what do these trinkets do? How would I earn one?"

"You have many questions, I know," replied Kristof, "and we'll try to answer them as best we can. But for now, I'll need to be brief. Being Touched means your body has changed. You eat more, you put on muscle, and you're actually heavier than a normal person of the same size. Your body needs to do this to cope with the stresses your abilities put on it. And the heat, as we call it, accelerates certain functions of your body. It amplifies those changes, but there's a cost, as you're clearly feeling now. Wear and tear."

Like a crafting, realized Caldan. Touched abilities put a body under unusually high stresses. There would be corrosion, irreparable damage.

"That's why you limp," he said.

Kristof blinked in surprise. "Yes. The more you use your abilities, the worse it gets. Trinkets go some way to helping limit the damage, but they're not perfect."

Caldan nodded. "So, if I want to stay alive and in good health for as long as possible, then I really have no choice, do I? I have to join you." *And if I don't, then I'll likely be killed.*

Although, if I do, I'll likely be killed when I'm worn out and they take my blood.

Damned if I do . . .

Tamara approached bearing a wooden cup, which she held out to him. "Drink this," she said sternly. "All of it. I put some honey in, but it'll still taste bitter."

Caldan took the cup and swirled the contents. It contained murky water with a thick layer of ground herbs floating on the surface. He sniffed it suspiciously, recognizing the astringent scent of neem root, usually prescribed for swelling, along with the old-sock smell from tiny foxberry leaves, which helped to relieve anxiety. "What's in it? Apart from neem root and foxberry leaves?"

"I see you know something about physiking," remarked Tamara, impressed.

"A little. From where I was raised." Master Hagan had taught herbalism. He was a kindly old man who liked to take them into the countryside to collect specimens and replenish the monastery's stores. That seemed like a lifetime ago.

"There are eleven additives to this tonic, some of which are to relieve pain and swelling, while others help settle the blood. Some of them are extracts from rare plants and flowers. Very expensive, and paid for by the emperor. He looks after you, as he does us all."

Kristof cleared his throat. "Best to do as she says, Caldan. Without a few trinkets to mitigate them, you'll be feeling the side effects of your abilities soon. The nausea, cramps, and dizziness are the start."

If they meant to do me harm, they could have already, Caldan reasoned. And if they were all Touched and in control of their abilities, they could force the concoction down him anyway. The aftereffects Kristof hinted at wouldn't be pleasant, and if they thought he needed help to weather what was coming, it had to be bad. He smiled wryly and gulped the mixture down, coughing at the bitterness.

What honey?

A furry film of ground herbs was left in his mouth, and Caldan swallowed as much as he could.

"Edelgard," said Kristof, "can he lie down in your tent for the night? I'd prefer it if we had rooms in Riversedge for our use, but I'm working on that issue. You'll have to sleep in Lisanette's, but I'm sure that won't be a problem."

His tone indicated it better not be.

Edelgard inclined his head in acquiescence. "As you wish."

"Caldan," continued Kristof. "Edelgard will show you to his tent. It's just for tonight."

Caldan ran his tongue around his teeth to wipe away the last remaining bits of herb, swallowed, and stood. "I have many more questions . . ."

"Tomorrow," replied Kristof. "You'll see things clearer then."

Always tomorrow. Always later.

That's starting to get old.

But another cramp hit him, and he was pretty sure tomorrow sounded like a good idea. Although he did wish Edelgard hadn't started chuckling at Kristof's last remark.

Lisanette shot her brother an annoyed look.

"I'll show him," she said. "Tamara, will you want to stay for the night? I assume you'll need to look in on Caldan."

Tamara nodded.

"Good. You can stay with me, then. Edelgard can find somewhere else."

Edelgard shook his head ruefully. "Don't worry, sister. There's plenty of tents to share."

Lisanette took Caldan by the elbow. Up close, he smelled a whiff of lavender from her hair, but his breath caught in his throat when he noticed one of her rings. It was exactly the same as his: a knotwork pattern with stylized lions and onyx eyes. So his wasn't unique. That was interesting.

With a final farewell to Kristof and Edelgard, Caldan accompanied the two women to another tent. Inside, rugs covered the ground, and there was an actual bed with a straw mattress, as well as a chest of drawers, a writing desk, and a chair. Now he understood why each of the tents had a wagon. It was apparent the Touched held a privileged position and had luxuries denied most others, especially those in the army.

Tamara sat him down on the bed.

"Take your boots off and get under the blanket. You'll become quite cold soon, if I'm any judge."

Caldan followed her instructions as Lisanette poured a cup of water from a jug on top of the desk. She placed it on the rug next to the head of the bed, where he could easily reach it.

"That's for you," she said. "You'll need it. The men always hedge around the truth, as if somehow not knowing makes it easier. It doesn't. So I'll tell you: it'll be bad. You might want Tamara to mix you something a little stronger."

"I'll see," replied Caldan tentatively.

"Just don't try to brave it out. If you think you'll need something soon, tell Tamara, don't wait."

Caldan nodded. He'd been keeping the hand with his ring out of sight and had to resist the urge to twist it on his finger. He bit his lip and swallowed nervously. Surely she was exaggerating?

"All right," said Lisanette. "I'll leave you alone. Tamara will stay with you for a while, though." She was almost at the tent flap when she stopped and looked over her shoulder. "Word reached us of what you did. How you used your abilities, and sorcery, to protect people fleeing the jukari. Putting yourself in harm's way to clear a path for them."

"It wasn't just me," Caldan mumbled, heat flushing his face. "There were others."

"You're the talk of Riversedge. They say you're a Protector wielding trinkets and sorcery unknown since the Shattering."

Caldan shifted under the blanket. Neither the Protectors nor the warlocks would be happy with those rumors. Moreover, what did it mean that she'd heard such talk and hadn't asked about his trinket? Did it mean she didn't care?

For some reason he doubted that, and continued to keep his hand hidden.

Lisanette left the tent and closed the flaps behind her. Caldan heard her walk over to the fire, where Kristof and Edelgard were talking quietly.

"Try to relax," said Tamara. "It'll make it easier for you."

"It's hard to relax when everyone tells me I'm in for a rough time."

"I know. Just rest, then."

Caldan tried to follow her advice, lying back on Edelgard's soft pillow. He had a lot to think about already.

Another cramp ripped through his stomach, and he gasped. Then his legs and arms began to ache. A ripple of agony threaded its way from his calves to his head. He drew his knees up and pressed his palms to the side of his head.

"I think . . . it's started."

His muscles burned with a fire hotter than a crafting forge, and his joints ignited as if a thousand needles jabbed into them. He gave a wordless cry of agony.

And then the *real* pain hit.

CHAPTER 7

Felice covered her mouth with a hand and tried to suppress a cough. It was immune to her will, though, and she almost bent double as she hacked up phlegm. She looked around and, seeing no one was close, spat onto the cobbles. She was recovering slowly. Too slowly for her liking. But a physiker had told her the worst was over and given her a pouch of vile herbs to make tea from. Every morning and every night, she followed the woman's directions and drank a cup of the bitter brew. She was paying a heavy price for her brief splash into the Stock.

Still, it beat torture at the hands of the God-Emperor and his cronies.

It was just past midnight, and Felice was dressed in a motley assortment of clothes: stained and patched pants and shirt covered by a tattered cloak with a hood. She looked like a thousand other people wandering the streets—not well off, and not someone to bother, unless you knew them.

With all her coughing, maybe not even then.

From her vantage point, she could see a brightly lit window far above the street. Behind the glass was the room Kelhak had taken over as his bedchamber. The God-Emperor liked to burn far more lamps and candles than needed, even during daylight hours, and the window stood out like a beacon.

Felice scanned the street for anything untoward before returning her gaze to the window. She didn't want to find herself recaptured just because she'd become complacent. Indryallan soldiers scoured the streets for the remains of any resistance, and they knew what she looked like. Despite her disguise, she thought it unlikely she'd be able to evade detection if seriously scrutinized.

Shadows flickered across the window momentarily as someone passed in front of the light. It could have been anybody: Kelhak, a functionary, or some servant. Or it could even have been one of his Silent Companions.

That thought made her shudder. She'd found out little about them over the past few days, other than the fact that they were elite warriors, and that scared her. If she was to kill Kelhak, they'd need to be dealt with somehow, but she had even less information about them than she did about Kelhak himself.

There, at least, she had a bit more detail, especially concerning just how legitimate his title really was—considering she'd heard the "God-Emperor" had executed a significant number of his own nobles and counselors. She couldn't help but wonder if that was a move to keep his origins under wraps. Regardless, it was one more thing she was itching to find out.

A scuffling came from her right, and she reached for her dagger, ready to lash out—

Ah . . . it's only one of my informants.

Felice released her grip on the hilt. She was becoming twitchy. Too many sleepless nights and too much looking over her shoulder.

The street urchin Poppy sidled up to her. Tangled brown hair atop a gaunt face stained with dirt. The intelligence in her eyes was sharp and wary, like that of a wild animal. In one hand she clutched a wooden rod a few feet long and as thick as Felice's thumb. She was too young to be fending for herself. She should be playing with other children. Laughing and running around, with a mother who cared for her . . .

"Miss, are you all right?" asked Poppy. "Why are you crying?"

Felice wiped her eyes. *What is happening to me?* Not long ago, she wouldn't have paid the girl much mind if she'd passed her in the street. *Oh, how the mighty can fall,* she thought with a touch of bitterness. "No reason, little one. Did you spend the ducats I gave you on food, like I told you?"

Poppy's eyes flicked away. "Some. Had to pay most for my sleeping spot. The gang has rules. Didn't have much left over."

"Ah. Well, next time buy some food first. And I'll make sure you have something to eat after this." The homeless children on the street had proven themselves adept at extracting information from the Indryallan soldiers. Wide eyes, innocence, and childish curiosity often elicited candid responses that questions from an adult wouldn't. They risked much for her, and when this was over, she swore she'd do right by them. In the meantime, if she could keep them fed, she was—if not content—satisfied. "Did you find out anything about the Silent Companions?"

A scrawny arm extended as Poppy held out a hand, palm up.

Felice dug into a pocket and removed a copper ducat, which she handed over. The girl snatched her hand back, and the coin disappeared somewhere under her rags.

There was a faint squeaking as two rats scurried past them across the street. Poppy leaped at them, startling Felice with her quickness. The wooden rod flashed down, whacking one rat on the head, while the other fled for its life. Poppy picked up the dead rat by the tail, its tongue lolling out the side of its mouth, and secreted it beneath her stained clothes.

"They don't speak," she said seriously. "Ever."

"The rats?" replied Felice, puzzled.

"No, silly. The Silent Companions."

"Really? Never ever?"

Poppy shook her head. "Not to anyone."

"Thank you, my dear."

Poppy gave her a strange look, half-afraid and half-wary, and took a step back. "I ain't no one's dear."

Felice smiled and nodded, a lump forming in her throat. "As you wish, little one. Did you learn anything else?" She held up another copper ducat, which the girl eyed greedily.

"Maybe I did, and maybe it'll cost you two coins."

Without pause, Felice added a second ducat to the first. "Go on."

"He *does* something to them," Poppy whispered. "And they don't talk ever again."

"Kelhak?"

Poppy nodded.

"What does he do?" Felice asked.

"Something. He takes them, and when they come out, they don't talk anymore. Or laugh. Or get angry. Nothing. Maybe he takes their pain away. Can someone do that? That would be . . . nice."

Felice's chest tightened, and she drew in a breath. "Pain can be taken away, but not like that."

A look of disappointment came over Poppy's face.

"There's a pie vendor the next street over," added Felice. "Maybe you'd like a hot pie?" She had other lines out, trying to gather as much information as she could, but they knew the locations she frequented. If they had anything to report, they'd find her.

Poppy nodded eagerly, and Felice handed over the two ducats, which disappeared just as quickly as the others. Together, they walked away from the brightly lit window, looking to anyone passing just like a mother and her daughter.

FELICE SLIPPED TOWARD a side door and used a rusty key Rebecci, the wild-haired sorcerer, had given her to enter the offices of the Five Oceans Mercantile Concern. Once inside, she paused, listening. She couldn't be too careful these days.

The side entrance opened onto a narrow hallway in a storage area for records. A rickety flight of stairs led up to more of the same, and at their base an old man sat snoring in a chair—a sign that all was normal and the building hadn't been cleared out by the Indryallans.

She tiptoed past the sleeping record keeper and made her way to Rebecci's office, returning the nods of acknowledgment from a few employees on the way. She'd become a familiar sight to them recently, although Felice wasn't sure that was a good thing. She'd have to limit her visits or send someone else, like Izak. And that reminded her: yesterday, she'd sent him with a few men to sort out her quarters in the Cemetery, and she hadn't seen him since. She'd ordered another man to follow up, and apparently, in her absence, someone had moved in and appropriated her belongings, such as they were.

She tapped softly on Rebecci's door and waited a few moments. When there was no answer, she let herself in. As usual, the room was empty, save for the padded armchairs and desk, along with the sorcerer's glass figurines on the windowsill.

On the desk sat an envelope addressed to her.

Pignuts, cursed Felice to herself. So Rebecci was dodging her. It was incredibly frustrating. After all they'd been through to capture Savine in the diamond-caged crafting—or his essence, or whatever it was—Rebecci avoided her like she had the pox. And Rebecci was Felice's primary source of information.

Perhaps she thinks she'll eventually reveal too much.

One can hope.

Felice scoffed and picked up the envelope. It wasn't sealed, and she unfolded the letter inside, scanning the text. Hastily scrawled apologies, excuses, and urgent matters to attend to. Not a word about Kelhak or his Silent Companions, or whether she'd found out what they were up to.

Felice pushed those thoughts aside. Rebecci had promised to try to get word to the emperor about how Anasoma was a trap, through her leader Gazija. The exact nature of what Kelhak could do from here was uncertain, but Felice was sure it would be sorcerous. The Indryallans had proven themselves to be adept at crafting so far. Where were the Protectors when you needed them?

Felice ran her hands through her hair, feeling guilty almost immediately.

Dead, that's where they were.

Voices sounded outside the door, and Felice stepped quickly to stand with her back against the wall, beside the hinges. The door creaked open, and the thin figure of Rebecci walked in. The sorcerer strode to her desk, leaving the door ajar.

"Can you close the door, Felice? Thank you."

Another sorcerous trick, thought Felice. *Knowing I was behind the door. A handy one, at that.*

She closed and locked the door.

Rebecci's face was even more pale and drawn than usual, if that was possible. Her expression was grim as she looked at Felice. Her fingers clutched at a pendant around her neck so tightly her knuckles were white.

"Please, sit down, Felice. Here." Rebecci opened a drawer and removed a bottle filled with a greenish-blue liquid. Faint golden sparkles shone from it, even in the dim light. Sorcerous crafted wine. Expensive.

Rebecci took out a small glass, glanced at Felice, and then put it back. She placed the bottle on the edge of the desk closest to Felice. "You'll need this."

Felice bit her lip. "Bad news?"

Rebecci nodded. "Take the wine and sit down."

"We obviously haven't been found out, otherwise we'd be in chains or dead. Is Izak all right? Or have those two child sorcerers done something?"

Rebecci shook her head. "None of that. Please." She gestured to the wine, and Felice reluctantly grasped the bottle.

Heeding Rebecci's advice, she sat in one of the armchairs, removed the cork, and took a sip. A warm tingling swept through her, though she hadn't swallowed any of the fine liquor. Peaches and candied cherries, with a hint of something indefinable—a swirling energy from the sorcery. This was some of the best wine she'd ever tasted. Rebecci's news must be dire indeed.

Felice swallowed. "Out with it," she demanded.

Rebecci dropped her gaze to her desk and pretended to rearrange a pile of papers with one hand, while the other remained clutching her pendant, the metal-and-diamond crafting she'd used to contain Savine.

If Felice had had her way, she'd have taken a ship out to sea and dropped the pendant in the deepest water she could find, but Rebecci insisted on keeping it.

"You were correct when you said the Indryallan occupation of Anasoma was a trap," Rebecci said. "Your emperor's forces were gathered outside Riversedge."

Were, noted Felice, with a horrible sinking feeling. *Surely not?* "They're on their way here? Or . . ."

"There was an outpouring of destructive sorcery. An Indryallan sorcerer named Bells used a crafting that—well, it destroyed a major portion of the emperor's forces."

"The warlocks—"

"Were not much use. They couldn't do anything."

Bells. Where had she heard that name before? Wasn't that one of the Indryallan leaders here in Anasoma? Felice rubbed her stinging eyes, and for the second time in two days found she was crying. Thousands must be dead.

"The emperor? Was he—"

"No, he was untouched. Apparently the warlocks weren't the ones to stop the sorcery, either. Credit for that goes to a young man called Caldan. A Protector, by all accounts."

Felice reeled. Too many coincidences. She drank deeply from the bottle, this time not noticing the exquisite flavor, only wanting the blessed numbness sure to follow. Had the young man Caldan deceived her? What part had he played in all this? She took a deep breath.

"You've a way of communicating as far as Riversedge?"

Rebecci nodded reluctantly. "With my . . . people."

Felice had never heard that was possible, but not much surprised her these days. "Can I talk with the warlocks? Why didn't you tell me this before? I could have warned them!" Her voice had risen to a screech.

Rebecci let go of the pendant and held up both hands. "My people only just arrived at Riversedge. They couldn't have done anything to stop this or been able to alert the emperor or the warlocks to the danger."

Felice blinked and let the tears flow freely. She fumbled the bottle to her lips for another mouthful and swallowed. "I still need to talk to the warlocks. Can that be arranged?"

With a grimace, Rebecci shrugged. "I can ask—"

"Don't ask! You demand! I need to explain the situation here to them. They're blind to what's happening."

"They've their own problems as well."

Felice paused. "Of course, the dead. But I need to tell them—"

"Not just that. There's a horde of creatures assailing Riversedge and what's left of the emperor's army. Jukari and vormag. I assume you know what they are?"

That was impossible. A horde? "That can't be right. A few dozen, maybe."

"Hundreds, I was told. Perhaps many more."

Felice cursed under her breath. This situation was going from bad to worse. The Indryallans had to be behind this. Somehow. She didn't believe in coincidences. As in Dominion, everything had a pattern that could be teased into the light by someone with enough conceptual reasoning. The Indryallan invasion was years in the planning, perhaps decades. And this war wouldn't be won in a few weeks. A jukari horde had to have taken months to assemble; their numbers were scattered across the Desolate Lands.

She looked at the bottle of wine before standing and reluctantly placing it back on the desk.

Rebecci came around and enfolded her in a hug. At first Felice resisted, then found herself surrendering to the embrace. *Just a few moments,* she told herself. Then she sobbed, and the tears started anew.

CHAPTER 8

A high-pitched laugh woke Caldan. He groaned and tried to sit up, then stopped himself as his muscles cramped and his head felt about to explode. Every fiber of his being ached as if it had been trampled by a horse.

Clothes rustled, and he heard a squeak as someone unstoppered a bottle, then the clinking of a spoon stirring a cup.

"Here, drink this."

He knew that voice.

Tamara?

Caldan cracked open one eye and flinched as the bright light in the tent sent a spike of pain into his skull. The physiker held a cup to his lips, and he drank, hoping it was something, anything, that would take some of the pain away. He didn't even try to ascertain what herbs she was dosing him with.

Once he had finished the cup, she left the tent and returned a short time later carrying a bowl.

"It's not as warm as I'd like it, but I'm sure you won't mind."

Caldan caught the faint aroma of chicken. It was some sort of broth, and the moment he sipped, his stomach twisted with hunger. He slurped at the broth, and it quickly disappeared.

"I'll be back with another."

Caldan watched Tamara leave. It was bright outside, and judging by the shadows, the sun had been up a few hours.

He glanced around the tent. Everything looked the same as when he'd first arrived. A surreptitious check confirmed his ring and beetle hadn't been taken from him while he'd been unconscious, nor Bells's and Mahsonn's craftings. The parts of his other automaton were still in the room he'd rented after escaping from the Protectors. He'd better get back there soon, in case the landlord thought he wouldn't be returning and sold his valuables for a pittance.

Footsteps sounded outside the tent, then Tamara entered again, carrying another bowl of broth and a plate filled with chunks of roast meat and potatoes.

Caldan's stomach grumbled as he drank from the second bowl. Tamara handed him the plate when he was finished, along with a fork, and he attacked the dish with a ravenous hunger. It was a wonder he was so famished after last night's illness.

Before long, he shoveled in the last of the potatoes and meat—spiced goat. He looked up to see Tamara smiling at him, and he realized he'd ignored her the whole time he was eating.

"I'm sorry," he said. "I was . . . very hungry."

"No need to apologize. I know a lot about what you're going through, mostly from books, admittedly. You'll need more food soon, and plenty to drink."

"You've only read about it?" Caldan recalled that Devenish hadn't remembered the name of the "new" physiker.

Tamara lowered her gaze and stared at her hands. "I've trained for this. I was the best in my year at the university. They said the emperor himself selected me for this role, but . . ." She laughed, a gentle, self-deprecating sound. "Of course, he wouldn't know who I am. But the old physiker couldn't cope anymore. His eyesight was going, though he tried to hide it. Mixed the wrong extracts and gave one of the Touched a bad case of the runs."

An involuntary snort escaped Caldan, and Tamara giggled.

"It's not right to laugh at someone's misfortune," she said in an amused tone.

Touched. Caldan knew the term, of course, and a bit from what Joachim had told him, but Tamara had stressed the word oddly, almost reverently. "What do you mean by Touched, exactly?"

"Kristof will tell you more, but I don't think it can hurt to let you know. *You* are. Kristof, Edelgard, and Lisanette are. And the rest. You have the blood of the ancestors in you. You're all Touched. It's my honor to serve you."

It could explain much, or it could be misdirection. Except when Tamara used the word, she really believed what she said. But it did make sense—Joachim had told Caldan the abilities were hereditary. But weren't the ancestors just people they were all descended from?

Everyone revered their ancestors, those who'd passed from this world to the spirit world. The common curse he'd uttered a thousand times was part of his culture, and he'd never thought to question its roots: *By the ancestors.* Had it started out as something more than filial duty or veneration? If what Tamara said could be believed, then the ancestors were different from most people. What were they?

And perhaps more immediate a question: If he—and others like him—had some of their blood, a dilution, then what would the ancestors have been capable of?

He shook his head, dumbfounded and disturbed. There'd been so much lost during the Shattering. Invaluable knowledge that put civilization back hundreds of years, if not more. He'd thought the more unbelievable tales from before the Shattering were merely that: tales. But he had seen the jukari, fought them. And he had always been told they were nothing more than bogeymen, when in fact they were very, *very* real.

What if the others were true as well?

"Now that you're conscious," said Tamara, interrupting his thoughts,

"I need to tell Kristof you're awake, and not too much worse for wear. You're lucky you weren't affected badly. You put your body under a great deal of strain without trinkets to mitigate the effects. I saw someone once, early in my training: one of the Touched who pushed herself too far. She'd run a great distance, as fast as she could, reveling in her gifts. She . . ." Tamara paused, as if the words were difficult to get out. "She was bedridden for a few days, screaming with the pain in her legs. She was sure it would pass and she'd recover. As with all of you, she healed quickly." The physiker shook her head. "But she didn't—at least, not completely. The ancestors' blood is potent, you see. Her muscles and tendons were damaged beyond repair. She never walked again. Or I assume so. The warlocks took her away to care for her—because of her condition. I haven't seen her since."

Caldan was careful to keep his expression neutral. He could guess what had happened to the woman the warlocks took away. If she was useless, they would have drained her of her blood, likely keeping her alive as long as they could before disposing of her. *In the end, that will be my fate. And the fate of anyone who is Touched. We're just cows to be milked, then slaughtered.*

The canvas of the tent rippled as a gust of wind blew, causing the door flap to wave, and a waft of air brought with it a foul stench. Tamara's face went pale, and she rummaged in a pocket, drawing out a kerchief, which she held to her nose.

"It's the bodies," she said faintly. "There's not enough soldiers to bury them. The jukari are causing problems, and it looks like we'll have to deal with them first before worrying about Anasoma and the Indryallans."

Of course, thought Caldan. But shouldn't the newly arrived mercenary companies—not to mention the warlocks and what was left of the emperor's forces—be enough to cope? It seemed not. His body still ached as if he'd been trampled by a herd of bison, but he had to help, if he could.

He sat up, letting out a pained groan, and swung his legs over the side of the bed.

Tamara rushed to his side, placing her hands on his shoulders, and tried to push him back down. "What are you doing? Please, don't sit up. You must rest."

Caldan shook his head and brushed her away. He stood on trembling legs. "I can't. The destruction of the emperor's army . . . it was . . ." My *fault*, he wanted to say. He'd brought Bells with him to Riversedge. And though he knew it had to have been her destination anyway, part of him couldn't help but hold himself responsible. "A tragedy," was all he managed. "Everyone needs to do their part. Whatever needs doing to help. I can't just lie here and do nothing."

He exited and squinted in the bright sunlight as his eyes adjusted. The graveyard stink he had caught a whiff of hit him full-blast, and it was all he could do not to reel from the stench.

Rustling sounded from inside the tent behind him as Tamara hastily packed up her herbs and implements.

"Wait," she called, voice muffled behind the canvas.

Caldan checked the distance from where he stood to the walls of Riversedge. A few hundred yards, give or take. The clearing outside his tent was empty, save for the black coals and gray ash of the fire that Kristof, Edelgard, and Lisanette had been sitting around. The emperor must have been keeping them busy, which was no surprise. They wouldn't be idle while waiting for Caldan to recover.

He heard Tamara exiting the tent, and she came and stood beside him.

"You shouldn't be out of bed yet. Kristof will get mad at me if I let you exhaust yourself so soon."

Caldan felt his body tremble. He *was* weak, there was no doubting that. But not as feeble as Tamara thought he was. With none of the Touched around, and no idea when they'd be back, he could use the time to do a few things of his own.

Like check on Miranda.

"I'm not going to lie around," he said to Tamara. "There are things I need to do. People I need to see."

"I can't order you to do anything. But if Kristof were here, he'd—"

"He can't order me, either," interrupted Caldan, more harshly than he intended. He rubbed tired eyes and ran a hand over his hair. "I'm sorry, but I'm not part of the . . . Touched yet. Nor am I one of the warlocks. My talents don't automatically make me one of them. I'm not a possession to be owned. No human should own another. We'll work something out. But not today."

It wasn't clear who would even get to "keep" him. It wasn't immodest to think that with his talents, the warlocks and the Touched would most likely fight over who held his leash.

Caldan took a step in the direction of Riversedge, then turned to Tamara. She clutched her leather kit close to her chest, biting her lip and looking worried.

"I'm sure there are others who could use your skills more than me today, Tamara. When Kristof returns, tell him I'll be back. I have to tie up a few loose ends."

"You're not going anywhere," Kristof said from behind him.

Ancestors! cursed Caldan. He turned to regard the big man. There was no way he'd be able to escape from a Touched who had full use of his abilities.

Should he risk it?

No.

For the time being, he had to show both the Touched and the warlocks that he was pliable and willing to serve. Caldan inclined his head in Kristof's direction.

"As you wish."

For now.

A SHORT WHILE later, it began drizzling at the Touched camp, and Caldan kept blinking water from his eyes. He sheltered his face from the rain with a hand and examined the campfire. Nothing more than cold ashes surrounded by stones. A canvas tarpaulin had been stretched between two wagons, and the rain it collected poured off a crease at the back, creating a patch of sodden grass and mud.

Tamara and Kristof both sat on stools under the makeshift shelter. She looked miserable, while he calmly drew on a bone pipe, smoke curling around him.

When Caldan strode from his borrowed tent, Tamara stood and took a step toward him, before stopping and glancing at Kristof. Kristof said something to her Caldan couldn't catch, and she returned to her seat, wringing her hands. Then he beckoned Caldan to join them.

"Tamara said you wanted to leave to tie up some loose ends," Kristof growled. "Mind if I ask what they were?"

"I do mind," Caldan replied firmly. "My business is my own."

Kristof grunted. "Your business is now the warlocks' and the emperor's. Best you remember that." He took another puff on his pipe and let the smoke out slowly.

Caldan caught the faint scent of hawksclaw buds. Expensive and rare. Normally used to deaden pain, they were also extremely addictive. The monks grew some in their herbarium to sell to the people on the island. Kristof's limp and the hawksclaw pointed to only one conclusion: his body was failing him. Kristof looked to be in his fifties, but was he? Or was he just prematurely aged? A hard truth struck Caldan: *This is my future as well.* A slow, painful, debilitating slide into obsolescence. And then, in both their cases, they'd be drained and killed.

That is what he would choose to remember.

Caldan opened his mouth to ask if he could go into Riversedge to retrieve his belongings, then thought better of it. "How old are you?" he asked instead.

The look on Tamara's face told Caldan what he needed to know. Kristof's mouth curled into a sneer.

"Old? What does it matter? I've seen and done things ordinary people would be lucky to experience in a dozen lifetimes. I've . . . *we've* kept the empire together, along with the warlocks, for centuries. How old am I?" Kristof's voice rose in volume. "I've battled jukari and vormag in the Desolate Lands, along with other creatures that would have you shitting yourself. I've searched the Dareske Ruins for treasures and trinkets. I've killed too many to count, rulers among them. I've seen with my own eyes what the Shattering did to the world. Walked abandoned cities bigger than Riversedge." Kristof poked his chest with a finger. "Me. The son of a baker who tarried with someone above herself. I'm thirty-one. And I don't regret a single thing. What

I've done, I've done for the good of the empire, and for the emperor, may he live forever. I won't lock my gift away and die wondering what I could have been."

Tamara nodded all the way through Kristof's speech. Her eyes glistened with tears, and she gazed at Kristof with pride.

Is everyone mad? wondered Caldan with rising dread. How was he supposed to extricate himself from these fanatics? If he ran, they would come after him, and they wouldn't stop. No matter where he went, how he tried to cover his tracks, they'd find him. Not using himself up in the emperor's service would be a betrayal to them. All they saw was a tool, like a sword. One that, when it was old and its edges dull, could be melted down and reused.

He didn't understand how they could so blindly follow.

But he said, quietly, "I understand," and Tamara beamed at him with approval.

"That remains to be seen," said Kristof. "Tamara, you'll need to check Caldan for any lingering signs. But I trust you won't take long?"

"No, Kristof. A few minutes. Maybe a little longer, to mix some herbs in order to ease any lasting effects."

"I'm fine," Caldan said.

"You're fine when Tamara says you're fine, and not before."

Tamara stood and reached for her kit on the ground behind her. "This won't take long."

"See that it doesn't," growled Kristof. "Devenish has been asking after Caldan. I'm to take him to the warlocks as soon as I can. Which is now."

Kristof moved back and let Tamara poke and prod Caldan. She lifted his arms and ordered him to bend different ways. Caldan did as he was asked, telling her truthfully that he didn't feel any lingering pains when she questioned him. She looked into his eyes, and even his ears. Apparently he passed her inspection, as she pursed her lips and frowned once she'd finished.

"I don't think I'll give you anything at this stage. The less medicine you use, the better. If you develop any aches or pains, though, come and see me right away."

Her tone brooked no argument, and Caldan nodded his understanding. Tamara didn't have an agenda, other than helping the Touched.

"Come on," Kristof said. "Time to see Devenish. He'll decide what to do with you."

"I thought you were the leader of the Touched."

Kristof shook his head. "No leader. We're all equals. Though some are more talented than others. Grab your belongings. And don't annoy Devenish. He has a short temper, and more power than you or I will ever have. Both among the emperor and his armies, and as a sorcerer."

Caldan thought back to Gazija shrugging off what Devenish threw at him, and worried he wouldn't be able to defend himself against any coercive sorcery Devenish tried. For what other way did Devenish have of controlling him?

As they made their way to the warlock's tent, Caldan paused briefly to take stock. He had Bells's and Mahsonn's craftings—his, now—and trinkets, in addition to a few paper birds he'd folded last night from paper he'd found in Lisanette's tent. They always came in handy, but their simplicity was far removed from his smith-crafted automatons, and they certainly wouldn't be able to weather the coercive or destructive sorcery he'd seen over the last few days.

"Having second thoughts, are you?" Kristof asked, cutting through Caldan's mental inventory.

Caldan looked up to find himself being scrutinized intently. "Fine. I'm fine. It's such a lot to take in."

Kristof nodded. "You don't get something for free in this world. Our abilities come with a price. But the more useful you make yourself, the more trinkets you earn, and the longer you last."

Couldn't someone just not use their abilities? The idea wasn't without its problems, since Caldan himself didn't have full control over his abilities, so far.

But perhaps, with time . . . ?

"Come on," said Kristof. "Devenish has a job for us. I'm guessing he wants you brought into the fold quickly. This'll be an initiation of sorts. Don't muck it up."

Caldan did his best to look eager. "I'll try not to."

Not that he thought it would be all that difficult. If Devenish wanted him to go out and kill a few jukari, he could do that. All he really needed for that was a sword and his shield crafting. Once they considered him one of their own, their suspicions would wane, and he could figure a way out of this mess.

I wonder if this was how my parents thought about leaving, too.

Caldan sniffed and realized that either the stench of corpses had lessened or he was getting used to it. With the combination of the rain and the fact many of them had been carried away to be burned, he suspected the former. According to Kristof, Riversedge's poorest were helping dispose of the bodies for a coin or two a day, leaving the rest of the army to focus on the jukari. The horde had retreated even farther as the emperor's forces gained ground, but they were still very much a threat, and one the emperor could do without, with the Indryallans still to be dealt with. Warning horns and trumpets pealed occasionally, and soldiers rushed past on their way to the front lines. Far in the distance, Caldan could sense outpourings of sorcery—flashes flickered and faint rumbles of thunder reached his ears. This far away, he couldn't tell what was happening, but it looked like the warlocks and vormag were going hard at each other.

As usual, the same two blond women were on guard outside Devenish's tent. They eyed both Caldan and Kristof with suspicion, but Kristof paid them no mind. He pushed between them and held the tent flap open for Caldan.

Inside, it was dark and musty. Caldan's eyes adjusted quickly to the light, and he looked around. Maps still covered the center table, and Devenish was alone. The warlock stood next to a desk on one side of the tent, where he was fiddling with a glass vial.

"One moment, please," Devenish said. "I've caught a cold or some such. Just mixing something my physiker concocted."

Caldan shoved his hands in his pockets and watched as Devenish poured himself half a glass of water and unstoppered the vial. He added two drops of a reddish liquid to the glass, hesitated, and then added one more. As he moved, Caldan caught a glimpse of his face. He looked pale and haggard, and older than before.

"I swear you always think you're coming down with something, Devenish," Kristof said, half joking. "But you never get sick. You need to get out in the fresh air. You're always cooped up inside with hardly any light."

Devenish raised his glass and swirled the liquid. The water turned a pinkish hue. "Prevention is better than the cure, I find." He smirked at Kristof and downed the potion in one swallow. His eyes closed, and he shook himself all over for a few moments. "I'll never get used to the taste, but it keeps me healthy."

And indeed, Devenish's face had already regained some of its color. His cheeks turned pink, and he stood up straighter.

He couldn't have, could he . . . ? wondered Caldan.

Had Devenish just drunk some of the Touched blood in front of them?

Caldan glanced surreptitiously at Kristof, who had wandered over to the map table and was peering intently at tiny markings penned next to strategic points. He seemed to have no idea that anything was amiss.

Heat rose to Caldan's face, and he felt his blood boil at what Devenish had done. He fought back a snarl that threatened to give him away. The warlocks were rotten to the core. Whatever they'd started out as, they'd been warped into something . . . evil.

Caldan clenched his fists in his pockets. It was all he could do to resist calling Devenish out then and there. Only the fact that Kristof wouldn't believe him, and Devenish would likely kill him, stopped him saying something.

He turned away, afraid to speak, face burning with shame. *Calm down,* he admonished himself. *There will come a time when you can do something to stop this. But not now.* There was nothing to gain by acting at this moment, and everything to lose. It took Caldan a while to stop himself shaking, and when he did, he looked up to find both Devenish and Kristof staring at him.

"I'm sorry," Caldan said quickly. "I'm still recovering from using my abilities the other day. Tamara gave me something to help, but I suspect it'll take more than a day or two to recuperate."

Kristof nodded, but Devenish narrowed his eyes in suspicion.

"Do you have need of me?" asked Caldan, hoping to move on. "I'm eager to prove my worth."

That seemed to allay any worries Devenish had, as his face lit up, and he smiled. A feral grin.

"I'm sure Kristof has told you some of what he does, and why you are so essential to the Mahruse Empire's protection. Yes?"

"He has. And I understand."

"Such gifts as you have," Devenish continued, "are easily abused. And it's only by using them for the greater good that we can ensure they aren't used for nefarious purposes. If one of the Touched thought to go off on their own, not only would they be abusing a great gift, but they wouldn't last long. We have to take care of you. You've now seen the side effects of using your abilities for a prolonged period. There's no hiding the truth. And that's the reason the emperor, through the warlocks, must maintain strict control of certain trinkets. The more you show you will use yourself for the benefit of the empire, the greater trust we will have in you. And the more we trust, the easier we will feel about helping you mitigate the side effects of your abilities."

Yes—I get it. Toe the line, die, or be killed.

A wonderful life they offered him . . .

Caldan gave Devenish a brief smile. "I hope to prove myself worthy. I want to be in service to the empire, whether as one of the Touched, or using sorcery." A subtle reminder that he was also a sorcerer wouldn't harm him, and it might just sway Devenish from deciding he wasn't worth keeping around. Caldan guessed the warlock would realize his potential and want to take advantage of him in ways he couldn't with a normal Touched.

"Ah, yes. We'll talk about that once you return. But for now, we need your other talents. And yours, too, Kristof, my friend."

Kristof gave Caldan a measuring look. Something flitted across his face for an instant, then was gone. Fear, or hatred?

"A sorcerer as well as one of the Touched . . ." Devenish mused. "In time, Caldan will be a force to be reckoned with. But as he is, untrained, untested, he'll need guidance."

Kristof's face had gone dark, then he smiled with false brightness. "I hope you're not planning on Caldan replacing me anytime soon, Devenish. Though a Touched using sorcery would be capable of much more than the rest of us, it'll take years before Caldan is ready for some responsibility."

Devenish gave an indelicate snort. "Kristof, my good friend, you are beyond value to me, to the warlocks, to the emperor."

His blood is, thought Caldan. *But I'd wager Devenish thinks his abilities can be replaced by any other Touched.*

"Put any thoughts you have of retiring out of your mind," continued Devenish. "We are as one on this. Rest easy."

Kristof nodded. "Whatever you need. You know I'll do my best."

Devenish clapped Kristof on the shoulder. "Excellent. I can always count on you. But I'm remiss. How are you holding up? Are you keeping the pain at bay?"

"Barely. I'm still useful, though. I have to save myself for important missions."

"You'll be well looked after once it becomes too much for you. Don't fear on that count."

Lies and more lies, thought Caldan.

"Now, to business," continued Devenish. "Recent events have caused me to rethink our plans. The Indryallans have proven stronger and more resourceful than we anticipated. The jukari horde is something we didn't expect, and it is a massive issue. The Quiver commanders are stretched to their limits just dealing with the jukari. If the Indryallans come upon us now, we're finished."

Kristof frowned. "Where are they? Still holed up in Anasoma?"

"Apparently," Devenish said. "Maybe they've realized they bit off more than they could chew. The emperor certainly gave them something to think about."

"That he did. May he live forever."

Caldan couldn't believe what he was hearing. The emperor had been afraid and had used the warlocks to prevent himself from being targeted by the Indryallan sorcery. They were so worshipful of the emperor that they didn't realize he was a man out of his depth. But why would they? To them, he was almost a god.

And that's who they wanted him to serve?

"Take Caldan and strike at the jukari and vormag. A small group, only a few Touched. This can be Caldan's first test. I've another one for when . . . if he gets back."

So, it was a test they wanted. *As if I haven't proven enough, with just cel Rau at my side.*

Test me all you want. Knowing what impresses you only tells me more about what you all can't do.

And with that, I can break free.

CALDAN RAN BESIDE Kristof. For the third time in as many minutes, he opened his well and sent his senses out, searching for any sign they were in danger; and for the third time there was nothing. The sun edged down toward the horizon, bathing the trees with orange, but there was also a shadowy darkness. As if chasing the sun, dark clouds swept in from the east.

Kristof set the pace, though Caldan could see how he favored one leg. They ran onward: Caldan, Kristof, and Florian and Alasdair, both Touched. A sister and brother from Meliror in the Sotharle Union of Cities.

Florian wore her shoulder-length red hair in a multitude of braids, each tied at the end with a leather thong. Her body was well muscled, trim but solid—probably an effect of being Touched. She carried a short spear in one hand and a dagger tucked into her belt, as did Alasdair. His hair was more brown than red, and it was hacked short, close to his skull. They didn't say much, grunting and nodding curtly in response to orders from Kristof.

Caldan constantly scanned the area through the trees. He knew what they were about—hunting jukari—but at times he felt they were being watched.

Kristof carried an unusually long sword strapped to his back. A buckle on the harness would let him easily swing it to his hip—in order to draw it—at the first sign of danger. Two sturdy gloves were tucked into his belt, and Caldan noticed that the palms and inside fingers were padded with hard-boiled leather. A terrible design, if you relied on them for a firm grip. Caldan's curiosity got the better of him.

"What are your gloves for, Kristof?"

Behind him, he could hear that either Florian or Alasdair stumbled. Alasdair cursed, and Florian laughed.

Alasdair, then.

Kristof's brow furrowed. He lessened his pace until they came to a stop. They were almost atop a slight rise in the forest. "We'll take a break here," he said. "A few moments only."

Florian and Alasdair separated, making their way to opposite sides of the rise from Kristof and Caldan. They were sweating only slightly, while Caldan was dripping. He was also breathing heavily, while the others hardly seemed to be straining. Either they were in much better shape than him, or they had greater control over their abilities, using them to augment their stamina somehow. Part of Caldan was eager to learn more about what he could do, what he was capable of. But . . . looking at Kristof and his injured leg, another part of him knew every time he used his abilities, he was gradually wearing his body down. Prolonged use would see him assigned to an early grave, after years of pain and debilitation. He understood the danger and the attraction. The sacrifice and pain adding up to more trinkets . . . a vicious cycle. And yet . . .

If the deteriorating side effects could be lessened by certain trinkets, could they be halted altogether? Was this another secret kept from the Touched?

"Not everyone can master a long blade," Kristof murmured.

Caldan looked up. Kristof was leaning against the trunk of a moss-covered tree. He took one of the gloves from his belt and tossed it to Caldan. It was as he'd seen, thicker leather exactly where it was least useful.

Kristof continued. "The Touched come from all different backgrounds and have diverse talents. What are the chances every one of us is capable of becoming a blade master? Or master of other weapons?"

"Low," answered Caldan. "But . . . we don't need to be, if we have enough control."

"Exactly! Fancy blade-work is all well and good, if you train every day and have a talent for it. And if your opponent isn't armored. Or a sorcerer. Or a jukari or vormag. Against virtually any other man, you'll likely be the victor. In most situations we encounter, though, your blade-work won't be enough. Take me, for instance. I'm terrible with a sword."

"So am I," Caldan admitted. "I'm improving, but I'm only alive so far thanks to being Touched."

Kristof nodded. "Like most of us. We're all different, and only a handful of us are better than average with weapons. So I use an old technique." He tugged the other glove onto his left hand and unbuckled his sheath, then drew the blade.

Lifting his weapon, Kristof gripped the blade with his gloved right hand about a third of the way from the tip, holding it as you might a stave. He ran through a few moves, making as if to block a strike coming toward him, and using the pommel to bash and the tip to make short, sharp jabs. His movements were fluid, and Caldan could see straightaway the advantage such a technique gave.

"I don't think anyone's given it a fancy name yet, so we just call it 'shortened sword fighting,'" said Kristof. "It's easier to block, to get in close and render a swordsman's slashes ineffective. The glove protects your palm and fingers from the edge. It's . . . effective."

Caldan nodded eagerly. "You can change the direction of your blade much easier than usual. Your control is better."

"Yes. Take a glove and try it. You'll never go back to one-handed moves. Well . . . *never* might be too strong a word, but this technique will do the job. You'll see. Keep that glove, and give it a try. We'll practice more when we get back, but nothing is better than experience in the field, so they say."

Caldan tucked the glove into his belt. Florian and Alasdair moved in to rejoin them, and Kristof sheathed his sword and buckled it back over his shoulder.

"Time to keep moving," he said and broke into a jog once more.

Caldan followed, while the other two remained twenty paces behind. Trees flashed past, and the sun's glow faltered. Kristof didn't let the rapidly approaching darkness slow him and maintained his pace. As Caldan's vision quickly adjusted to the gloom, he realized the others had no problems with the lack of light, either. A common trait they shared, it seemed. Kristof kept glancing at a piece of paper in his hand.

After a while, the trees thinned and the undergrowth became thicker. They skirted around large boulders strewn across the ground as it transitioned from fairly flat to rocky and uneven. They slowed slightly, the uncertain footing lending itself to injury. A short time later, Kristof indicated another halt. Caldan sighed with relief and bent over to massage his thighs. His legs and lungs were burning. Kristof and the others might be able to keep this pace up, but he was struggling.

Without speaking, Kristof indicated for Florian and Alasdair to come closer. When they did, he brought his face near to theirs.

"In and out. No messing about. You know what to do."

The brother and sister nodded. Kristof turned to Caldan.

"There's a jukari force not far from here."

Caldan frowned. He hadn't seen any signs, and there were no campfires in the night. "How do you know?"

Kristof pointed to the paper he held. "The warlocks have been tracking them. Whoever is leading the jukari sent a portion of their forces in a wide arc in order to surprise us. What their purpose is, we don't know, but it's not a large group. Perhaps a specific target?" Kristof shook his head. "We can only guess, but right now it's unimportant. What we have been tasked with is stopping them."

"How many are there?"

"Thirty or forty. Around that number."

"You're serious? There are only four of us."

"Yes. We hit and move. Take some out and leave them in disarray.

Then hit them again. It's dark; jukari don't see well in the dark. We have the advantage."

Caldan rubbed damp palms on his pants. He wasn't as confident as Kristof appeared to be. Four of them against forty jukari? He'd killed a few before, but not many at a time. And even then, he'd somehow been able to push his sorcery to heights he'd never dreamed possible, maintaining threads without thinking.

"I . . . I'm not in control of my abilities like you and the others are. I don't have trinkets to help me, nor your experience." Caldan made sure the hand wearing his ring was out of Kristof's sight.

"That's fine. You'll do well. You'll eventually earn yourself trinkets. But that's not why you're here, right now."

"Then what am I—?" Caldan paused. "Vormag," he said, and Kristof nodded.

"Just in case. If we surprise them, they'll be dead before they can craft anything. If not, they'll have shields and destructive sorcery. That's where you come in."

So they trusted him enough to bring him along and see how he fared. But he'd be left out of the fighting and held in reserve to counteract any sorcery. If Caldan was honest with himself, he was a little relieved. He'd killed the jukari before out of necessity. Ambushing and slaughtering as many of them as he could didn't sit well with him. But this was what the Touched did, wasn't it? If he couldn't defeat the vormag and their sorcery, what would Kristof and the others do? Leave him there? No, Devenish wouldn't allow that. Restrain him and bring his body back, most likely. Then the warlocks could do what they wanted with his body. Once more, he was in a lose-lose situation.

All he did was nod his readiness to Kristof, who slapped him on the back.

"Let's go," Kristof said.

They moved through the darkness until they came across a narrow trail trodden into the short grass among the rocky ground. A snarl sounded ahead, and they paused. When no other sound reached them, they continued, this time with more stealth. They crouched low and slowed their pace.

With trepidation, Caldan opened his well. He followed Kristof's lead and took out his own sword, pulling the leather glove onto his left hand. There were three other wells out there, somewhere in the night. He had a sense of them, but not their exact location. Two were drawing power, while the third was quiet. But from what he could sense, it was larger and smoother than the other two. Possibly the leader, and as such, more dangerous.

He picked up his pace and tapped Kristof on the shoulder.

"There are three vormag out there."

"You're sure?"

Caldan nodded firmly. "Two of them don't have much power. Barely able to shield themselves, I'd say. But the third . . . could be troublesome. Depends on their training and experience, and their craftings."

"Assume they have craftings as good as our sorcerers can produce."

Caldan grimaced. "Three sorcerers might be beyond me."

"You'll have to manage."

Kristof turned his back to Caldan and continued ahead.

Caldan blinked and shook his head. He hoped they weren't trying to get him killed. And then, almost as one, three pinpricks of power pulsed from the Touched. *Trinkets*, realized Caldan. *They're readying themselves*. Two more trinkets pulsed, from Kristof and Alasdair.

A rock clattered to their left, tumbling down a slope. Kristof, Florian, and Alasdair stopped immediately. They scanned the darkness, turning their heads in a constant sweep. For long moments, no one moved.

A howl came from their left, where the rock had moved.

Jukari appeared out of the night, charging them.

Caldan had time to raise his sword and link to his shield crafting before the first of the beasts was upon them, slavering and snarling through its fanged mouth. Towering over the smaller form of Kristof, it hammered a rusty axe down toward him—only to miss completely, as Kristof stepped aside and battered the axe away with his sword. He jerked the blade forward, and before the jukari could recover its balance, it was bleeding from a thrust to the stomach. Kristof yanked his sword to the side and eviscerated the jukari. It fell to the ground, clutching at a coiled mass of intestines, and Kristof leaped over it toward another.

Caldan glanced frantically at Florian and Alasdair, both of whom were darting and weaving between a few of the beasts. Spears flashed faster than Caldan could follow. Black blood splashed across rocks and stained the grass.

A jukari loomed large in Caldan's vision. He dodged desperately as a wooden club the size of a log crashed toward him—too late. It thundered into Caldan with the force of a falling tree, throwing him backward. He landed hard on a rock, shoulder erupting in pain. His shield saved him from severe injury, but it didn't stop momentum.

Caldan caught sight of more jukari rushing toward them. The surprise Kristof had relied upon had been lost. Instead of facing a few at a time, they were outnumbered and fighting for their lives. He staggered upright and caught a flash of the assault. Kristof, a blur of steel, eliciting wet gurgles as he chopped and thrust. A shrieking Florian, stabbing like a maniac, leaping and cavorting among the jukari. Alasdair wheeling from a blow to his shoulder, teeth bared. Everywhere, jukari were injured and dying.

There was no time for thought, for suddenly they were in front of him. A wicked spiked club plummeted toward him. Caldan pivoted and parried just in time, holding his sword with both hands as Kristof had demonstrated. He moved forward and shoved two feet of blade into the side of his opponent. His leather-gloved hand stopped it from penetrating farther, and he quickly loosened his grip and shoved harder, the blade pushing deeper before he jerked it out.

"Legs!" Kristof shouted over the din.

And Caldan understood. The jukari were too tall. He stepped away from the creature he'd just killed and confronted another. It barked a gruff exclamation and slashed a sword down toward his head. He parried, again with both hands, then chopped into its thigh. With a howl, it sank to its knees. Caldan finished it with a thrust to its throat, and it fell down, gushing black, viscous fluid.

Where were his Touched abilities when he needed them?

He searched inside himself for the feeling, the heat of his blood, but found nothing other than his own gasps for breath and a drumming in his ears.

He ran for Florian, who was struggling against three jukari. Boots slipped on footing made treacherous by blood and bile, and he stumbled toward her. A wounded jukari lying close to Florian clawed at her ankle, and she cried out in pain. She hopped away awkwardly. Snarls erupted around her, and jukari closed in. Caldan yelled and stabbed one in the back. It slammed an elbow into his shield, and sparks flew. He staggered but stayed upright, leaping at it. Steel penetrated gray flesh, again and again.

Florian fell to her knees, spear gripped in one red-covered hand, while her other clutched at her ruined ankle. Three jukari loomed over her.

Caldan cursed, running again for Florian. Where were Kristof and Alasdair? Somewhere out there, he caught a fleeting glimpse of trinkets burning with power. He drew from his well and dived for Florian. He latched onto her arm. Clawed hands and weapons reaching for the woman met his impervious shield and skittered above her skin. Dismayed howls bayed from animal mouths. Florian looked at him, lips twisted into a grimace. Her teeth were covered in red blood. Her own, then, not jukari.

Bladed and blunt weapons hammered into them. Caldan's shield held, motes and sparkles erupting from the blows. He ground his teeth and *pushed*. As with his construct in the tunnels under Anasoma, his shield bulged outward. Only, this time, it went from a tight skin covering him and Florian to a dome in an instant. Jukari were thrown aside, like drops of water from a shaking dog. One slammed into a boulder, bones cracking. The other two tumbled across the ground, trailing clouds of dust.

"Caldan!" roared Kristof.

Caldan pulled Florian to her feet, and she leaned her weight on him. Kristof and Alasdair came barreling toward them, blood-covered apparitions, scarcely a patch of them unsullied by black gore and dirt. Even their hands and faces were spattered. Hot whiteness pulsed at their fingers and chests: their trinkets, perhaps the only things on them still clean. They skidded to a halt near him, and he cut the link to his shield. Alasdair grabbed Florian, and she smiled weakly. Deep gashes and bite marks covered her arms.

"You'll make it!" whispered Alasdair feverishly.

"I know," Florian said. "You won't leave me."

"Caldan," Kristof commanded, "if you're going to do something, do it now!"

Do something? I just saved Florian . . .

Caldan looked numbly around him. At least fifteen jukari lay dead and dying. Those remaining had backed away, hooting and snarling at them. They spread out in a circle surrounding them, jaws snapping and weapons waving. They were retreating, weren't they?

Then he sensed them: Sorcerers. Vormag.

The jukari were keeping Caldan and the others from fleeing. They were waiting for their masters.

He drew a breath, fighting back fear, and stepped toward the oncoming wells. Caldan reached inside himself, as deep as he could go. He wrapped his mind around his well, immersing himself in its leashed vitriol. Was he not a trained sorcerer? He'd created craftings that journeymen, even masters, would be proud of. He'd fought Bells twice and come out alive. Survived even Joachim's deception. But what tools did he have on him?

Bells's and Mahsonn's craftings—and he didn't know what many of them did.

A shield crafting.

His beetle.

Hardly anything he could use—and certainly nothing to combat three vormag. Controlled destructive sorcery was still beyond him. What he was capable of, raw destructive sorcery, would be no match for the vormags' shields.

Caldan realized they were hemmed in and trapped.

"We need to punch a hole through them!" Alasdair shouted to Kristof. "Now!"

Kristof glanced at Florian. "I . . ." He hesitated, eyes flicking left and right.

By the ancestors, he doesn't know what to do. "We can't run," Caldan said. "Vormag are coming. They'll cut us down."

"Can't you shield us?" Alasdair said.

Caldan shook his head. "Not if we're running away. I need to maintain contact with all of you. And if we stay here, we're done for. I'm no warlock. I can't do what they can."

The animal stench of the jukari was all around them, hanging heavily in the air. And the wells were coming closer. Soon they'd be right on top of them. Whatever vormag sorcery they'd use, Caldan was sure he didn't want to wait and find out.

"Run and die, or stay and die," muttered Kristof.

"We make a break for it and take our chances," Alasdair said.

Shaking his head, Kristof urged them to retreat to a boulder ten paces behind them. They put their backs to it and kept an eye on either side, should some jukari try their luck. Florian pulled strips of cloth from a belt pouch and set to busily bandaging her ankle. Alasdair looked at her, worry in his expression. She wouldn't be running anywhere for a while. Even with their regenerative powers.

"Give me your ring. You know which one."

Caldan's breath caught in his throat, and he looked at Kristof—only to find he'd spoken to Alasdair.

The brother glared at Kristof. "Why? It's mine. I earned it."

Kristof, never taking his eyes off Alasdair, held up his hand and removed one of his trinket rings. He offered it to Caldan. "For him," he told Alasdair. "He'll need them to get to the vormag. Otherwise, we're all dead."

Alasdair licked his lips. He glanced down at Florian, then to Caldan, then back again to Kristof. He cursed under his breath. "I . . ." He shook his head.

Florian tugged at Alasdair's shirt with bloody hands, leaving red smears over black. "Don't be a fool," she hissed. "He can take mine. It won't be much use to me now. But I'll want it back."

"Of course," Kristof said.

She pulled a ring from her hand and held it out to Caldan. Her blood-soaked fingers trembled.

There were now two trinket rings being offered to him. Caldan met both of the Touched's eyes. He knew what they were asking of him, but a small part of him was fearful of the result. What if he came to enjoy using his abilities? What if he decided to stay among the Touched, to earn more of these trinkets?

Stifling a curse, Kristof took Florian's ring and shoved it into Caldan's hand, along with his own. "Put them on," the big man commanded. "Might work, might not. But you need to get to the vormag. We'll hold off the jukari. Maybe try and clear you a path."

"I'm not leaving Florian," Alasdair said.

Kristof nodded grimly. "Stay with her, then."

Florian struggled to her feet. "I'm not bloody staying here. We don't split up."

"Good," Kristof said. He closed Caldan's fingers around the rings. "Put them on. You need to kill the vormag. That's your task."

Caldan swallowed and nodded. He slid the rings on as quickly as he could. He waited for something to occur, to feel their effect.

Nothing happened.

Alasdair shouted in alarm, leaping to their left at an incoming jukari. He dodged and weaved around its axe. Uttering foul curses, he yelled as his spear pierced the beast's hide. Gouts of black blood spurted from the wound. He backed away as a few jukari came at him, but they didn't attack. Instead, they dragged their wounded fellow away into the dark.

Alasdair turned his back to them and spat into the dirt. "Abominations. Should never have been created. It's a defilement, is what it is."

"Enough of that!" Kristof said. "Caldan, where are the vormag?"

Caldan pulled his gaze from the three trinkets on his fingers and shook his head. The vormag would be upon them soon. "Close," he said. "But the rings! They aren't doing anything."

Pain lanced his thigh. Florian jerked her spear back, tip red. Caldan pressed his palm to his leg, feeling warm blood leaking through his pants. Florian smirked at him. "A prick is sometimes all it takes."

In an instant, one of the rings clamped into his finger. The metal grew hot, so much so that Caldan feared his skin would burn. Warmth spread from his finger, trailing through his palm and up his arm. As the wave passed through muscles, they seemed to shiver beneath his flesh. An unpleasant feeling, like something alive crawled under his skin.

Florian placed her palms on the side of his head and drew his face close to hers. "Feel it," she whispered fiercely. "Breathe it. Follow it."

Caldan's blood drummed in his ears. It was as if molten metal pumped through his veins. He cried out, falling to his knees. Around him, the night grew lighter, as though dawn's glow broke over them. His senses sharpened; he could almost taste what Florian had eaten recently on her breath. She and Kristof and Alasdair seemed both closer and yet farther away. Kristof stepped toward them, slowly . . . so slowly. Caldan couldn't stand Florian's touch on his face. He twisted his head away from her and staggered to one side. He squinted at the stars of light twinkling on his fingers. The trinkets sang to him, coaxing his awareness toward them. Each one pulsed with its own heartbeat. He let himself be drawn toward them.

A slap rocked his head to the side. Florian.

Caldan snarled at her, surprising himself that he reacted so violently. She pushed him in the chest and backed away.

"The vormag," Kristof commanded.

"Yes," Florian whispered. "Go now. Kill them."

Yes. The vormag were coming. They had to be stopped. Sorcery was coming to kill Caldan and his companions, and he was the only one who could stop them. He bolted in the direction of the three wells coming toward them.

Behind him, Florian shouted at Kristof, "This had better work. I want my trinket back."

Booted feet thudded on the ground as they followed. Caldan barely felt his other two trinkets biting deep into his fingers. More pain blossomed. More heat suffused him, bringing a surge of excitement and strength. His sword felt as light as a twig. There were other sources of power out there, impinging less on his senses: candles held to the bonfires of the trinkets. Craftings created by the vormag.

A rock clattered to his left. A jukari, peering into the night. It couldn't see as well as him, realized Caldan. He sensed others close by, somehow. Three to his left, two more to his right. They moved toward him as if intending to cut him off. Ahead, between Caldan and the vormag, were two jukari lying in wait.

Teeth clenched, he rushed forward. The nearest jukari heard him coming and stood from a crouch.

Caldan sprang; his sword sliced clean through its neck. The decapitated head twisted in the air, falling with a thump and rolling to the side.

Caldan landed lightly on his feet and kept moving. Left now, another jukari. Boulders passed him in a blur. He caught the creature before it could raise its spiked club. A downward slash severed its leg halfway up its thigh, edge cutting and snapping the thighbone. Thick black blood sprayed across the ground. Orange eyes were wide with pain and fright. He heard a slavering snarl, then drove his sword into the beast's chest as its injured leg buckled. It twisted to the dirt, and Caldan tore his blade free.

Behind him, as if from a vast distance, Kristof, Florian, and Alasdair were shouting. Steel clanged on steel. Jukari bayed and howled—one beast's cries cut off abruptly. Caldan glanced over his shoulder. The other Touched had formed a knot, Kristof and Alasdair supporting Florian in her wounded state, as they followed his trail. A pack of seven jukari made sporadic attacks against them, falling short in most cases, as if they feared coming too close. Three came from the rear, with another two on both sides.

Caldan growled. The jukari were herding them. They'd lost many lives already and wanted the vormag to take care of these dangerous interlopers.

Well, let the vormag come, Caldan thought with excitement as the power coursed through him.

A brief thought flashed through his mind: *How bad will the after-effects be?* But he tossed it aside. There was no time to dwell on the future; the here and now was all that mattered. Survival. Kill the jukari and vormag.

Caldan urged himself forward, aiming himself at the wells he sensed ahead—and noticed another oddity: his sorcerous senses were magnified as well. Though they were still far away, the nature of the vormags' wells was in stark relief. Two of them small and rough, their edges felt jagged, almost as if they'd been hacked open with a blunt knife. Behind those two came the third, a smooth, wide borehole compared to its ragged companions. There was an ominous power to the third vormag's well. It surged and receded like waves on a beach, as if straining to be released. Swirling and caustic, it set his teeth on edge. All three tasted unnatural to him. *Wounds.* Not a natural pairing, as his was, these were holes gouged out of minds and sewn to power.

He almost stumbled at the realization. Of course, they had to be. These creatures were unnatural. *Created.* It made sense, then, that if there were sorcerers among them, they had to be *made* into sorcerers.

Caldan shook his head to clear his thoughts. He had to concentrate. Sweat flew. He could hear it hit the ground, like fat drops of rain at the start of a storm.

"Caldan!"

He ignored Kristof's shout. On his left, a jukari came for him, feet slapping, lips peeled back in a feral snarl. Almost without thinking, Caldan turned aside a chop from its massive sword. His own rang and quivered at the impact. He was no blade master, but he didn't need to be. The jukari stumbled, its momentum too great to stop. Its sword thudded deep into the earth, shuddering as it hit a buried stone.

Leaving its head down, neck and shoulders exposed.

Caldan drew back his arm and cleaved through its shoulder. His blade drove deep into the jukari's chest, slicing muscle and sinew and shearing bone.

He dragged his blade free, leaving the jukari twitching in the dirt. Black blood drained from the wound, pooling underneath the body.

Caldan looked around and saw that the jukari were pulling back. Not too far, but enough to give them space. In a moment, the other Touched caught up. A couple of jukari lunged toward them, only to quickly withdraw before coming too close. They growled and slavered, hooting and goading each other on. He looked back and estimated they'd traveled a hundred yards or so. It had felt like only twenty.

Florian was breathing heavily. She leaned on Alasdair and hopped a few steps. Not good. Whether it was her wound or the loss of her trinket, she was definitely weakened. If Caldan rushed ahead, she'd fall behind, and they'd be separated.

A shorter, stocky jukari began pelting them with rocks. Kristof and Alasdair swayed to avoid the improvised missiles, which clattered around them. A head-sized rock slammed into the ground next to Alasdair, and broken chips of stone sprayed him. One sliced a thin gash across his arm. Drawing his mouth into a tight line, Alasdair shrugged Florian's weight to Kristof. Once sure she was safe, he stepped to his right and calmly hefted his short spear, transferring his hand from close to the point to the middle of the shaft. With a blur of movement, he launched it. The stocky jukari's eyes widened. That was all the time it had before the spear buried deep into its chest. It fell backward, dead before it hit the ground.

Calmly, as if he did this every day, Alasdair walked over to the jukari and retrieved his weapon. The remaining jukari backed away, though they still stamped around and snarled with agitation. Alasdair turned his back on the creatures and rejoined Caldan and the others.

Caldan felt Alasdair's trinkets, like thin threads tugging at his skin. They were shining brightly to his vision and drawing power from . . . somewhere within. He smelled the jukari's putrid blood and sweat. He was light-headed but itching to do something.

Closer the vormag wells came. Caldan knew they would attack from a distance. He would be their target. A powerful surge of sorcery would descend on him, splashing and overflowing. The Touched would be on the edges, but they'd also be struck. It would be best if he weren't close to them.

"Stay here," he urged them. His words came out as a snarl. Whatever the trinkets were doing to him, they remained active. He spared them a glance and shielded his eyes from their terrible intensity— though most of their glare impacted only his sorcerous senses. Caldan caught an impression of a well to the north before it flitted away. He blinked, trying to catch it again but failing. Vormag, it had to be. He hesitated, torn between wanting to investigate further and needing to guard against the danger coming toward them.

No time. There's no time to waste.

Though his back was now to the Touched, he could feel their eyes on him as he strode off into the night, aiming directly at the vormag.

Two jukari broke from the others and shadowed him, one on either side. He ignored them, but was conscious of their hate-filled eyes. Their crude leather and cloth coverings gave off a fetid stench, and one made sure to clang the head of its axe on every passing stone.

Caldan shrugged, loosening his shoulders. His fingers ached where the trinkets bit into them.

The jukari he dismissed. In his current state, they were no match for him. He still had his well open, ready to draw on its power, but so far it wasn't needed. Vormag were the real threat to him. Or . . . perhaps they were secondary, too.

Because he couldn't shake the feeling that maybe this had all been contrived—that this really was a test, and one that had been planned from the outset. Even as he crept closer to the vormag, he wondered why else he would be out here. They wanted to see what he could do with the extra trinkets . . . and one way or another, they would have ended up on his hands tonight. Which is why it wasn't a leap to think that if he survived this night, the Touched and warlocks would pose a greater danger.

And if that was the case, then they needed to understand something about the danger Caldan posed.

He needed to send a message, one Kristof would deliver to Devenish without realizing its import: that Caldan wasn't to be trifled with. They thought him weak and inexperienced, easily swayed to join them with unspoken promises of power and glory. Dangling trinkets in front of him like carrots, with his own deteriorating body acting as the stick.

They'd overplayed their hand, though. Because none of these Touched had ever really experienced anything but their mundane lives before joining, and their lives as slaves after.

But I have. I have worked with sorcerers. I have fought sorcerers. I have seen the deceit of warlocks and the weakness of Protectors. And because I have lived, they will find it's not so easy to kill me.

And that's when another plan came to Caldan. One that showed his strength, throwing the unexpected at those who tried to control him: break the vormag, not just using the trinkets, but also with sorcery. He glanced around him, thinking furiously on what he had in his pockets to work with. Craftings he had no idea how to use, his beetle, two pieces of paper, hastily shoved in and crumpled. Nothing else.

Paper it had to be, then. Time was draining away, but he stopped stalking the vormag for a moment; he'd have to work fast. He took out both sheets of paper, then drew his left palm across his blade. Clenching his fist to hold his blood in, he dropped his sword. The two jukari made angry, questioning sounds but didn't edge closer.

Caldan loosened his fist slightly, letting his blood trickle down it like crimson ink. Using his right hand, he pressed the paper against his thigh and began scrawling with his index finger. Nothing fancy. Crude, misshapen runes, but drawn with the power of his trinket-infused, Touched blood.

Blood. It always comes down to blood.

His escape from the cell in Anasoma. His abilities. Joachim's depraved craving. Elpidia's cure. The trinkets biting into his flesh. And now sorcery.

As quickly as he could, he folded both pieces of paper into birds. His practiced hands made short work of the simple folds, even as he kept an eye on the jukari on either side and the vormag closing in.

There. It was done.

Caldan broke into a run, leaving his jukari watchers behind. He veered around a large boulder twice as tall as he was and sprang over another waist-high stone, all the while making a beeline for the vormag. They had to sense him coming; at least, he had to assume the most powerful one could. They would be shielded and ready.

Booted steps thudded behind him as Kristof and Alasdair came after him, though they were hampered as they struggled with Florian. Sprinting, he launched both birds into the air and linked to his shield crafting, enveloping himself in its protection. Two strings for the paper, and four for the shield. Maintaining so many at once was getting easier for him, and under the effect of his Touched abilities, the complexity of the task seemed to be reduced tenfold. Caldan felt he could split as many strings again as he already had, without much trouble.

No, he decided. *There's no time to experiment.*

There was a thunderous concussion, and Caldan was thrown off his feet. He tumbled and rolled, crashing into rocks and bouncing off, gasping with pain. His shield saved his skin from injury, but force still traveled through it. A second reverberation caught him on the hip as he scrabbled upright, spinning him in a circle. He fell again, squeezing his eyes shut at the agony spreading from the blow.

He couldn't see this sorcery. Whatever the vormag were doing, it was invisible to even his enhanced vision. Ignoring the ache, Caldan struggled to his feet. *There.* He staggered to a boulder and hid behind the bulk of it. He heard the harsh cries of jukari. They sensed what was happening, in some animal way, and thought he'd be defeated.

Not today, he vowed, spit thick in his mouth.

The vormag must have sensed his well as he sensed theirs, using it as a lodestone for their sorcery. He reached to both his paper birds, directing them toward the vormag. He couldn't see the creatures, couldn't determine whether they were shielded. But did it matter? If they could target him, he could target them.

There were no jukari close, and the Touched were nowhere to be seen. Good. They could look after themselves, and he wouldn't have to worry about defending them from sorcery. His chest heaving, he ran to another nearby boulder. *Keep moving*, he told himself. *Make it hard for them to send anything against you.* His birds were closing in on the vormag. They'd spread out, presumably to catch more in their net.

Caldan skirted around the boulder and sprinted in the direction his birds had taken. They'd be distractions, nothing more. If he were to kill the vormag, he'd have to do it himself.

Time to increase the odds in his favor.

Directing his birds toward the closest, weakest vormag, Caldan extended a string from one paper crafting to the other. He formed the thread like a modified shield crafting, stretched from bird to bird. It was a channel, transferring energy from his well between them and nothing else. It had no practical purpose, but like any string, he could push as much power through it as it could handle.

Which was exactly what he did.

A coruscant line split the night, a bedizened streak of dazzling violet. Caldan hissed a breath and sucked more power from his well, pushing it into the bridge between the birds, hoping the paper would weather the erosion.

His birds swooped down to the lone vormag, just as Caldan emerged from behind a boulder. Its back was to him. Its head tilted, gaze up, arms outstretched toward the paper birds as its well pulsed. The vormag screeched. Clawed hands clenched to fists as it prepared to unleash a sorcerous response against what it perceived to be the real threat.

Caldan leaped, uttering a savage cry. He hurtled into the astonished vormag and barreled it over. The vormag tumbled in a blur of shielded sparkles. It scrabbled to its feet, clutching at bruised and broken ribs. Its shield faltered as the pain diverted its attention. Caldan grinned in triumph. He jumped again and bore it to the ground, pounding his shielded fist into its face. In moments, the vormag went limp, and its shield winked out of existence. Caldan fumbled around for a rock, found nothing, then spotted a dagger hilt poking out the top of the creature's ragged leather belt. He pulled the blade clear and stabbed the vormag in the stomach. And again. Hot sticky wetness gushed over his hand.

He stood, panting, sweat dripping into his eyes.

One down.

Caldan whirled. He quickly sheltered near another boulder. A crack reverberated close by—a stone detonating. Jagged chips scattered across his shield. Sorcery meant for him had hammered down, missing its target and pulverizing the rock.

He bolted from his cover. The next-weakest vormag was farther away than the strong one. He'd have to skirt around in an arc. It would take longer, and give them time to launch more counters, but it couldn't be helped. He cut the thread between the two birds, and the power they drew diminished to a vanishingly small pulse. Let the vormag worry what had happened to the sorcery. They'd sense their companion had been killed, believe sorcery was the cause, and be focused on defending themselves from it.

Again, Caldan sprinted, still holding the dagger, legs moving in a blur. A jukari appeared in front of him. He dodged and sliced, and was past. It clutched at the gash in its throat, sinking with a gurgling moan.

There: the vormag was close.

Caldan split a string from his well, and for the second time, brilliant light erupted between his craftings. The vormag shrieked and looked up. Caldan barreled into it, battering the vormag with his shoulder, and sending it tumbling. With a horrible crunch, its head struck a stone in the grass. Its shield disappeared. *Lucky*, he thought, but didn't begrudge himself the opportunity. Caldan thrust, sending his blade into its chest, punching through tattered cloth and ribs. Cleaving its heart.

Dragging the steel free, he jumped to his feet. He glimpsed a shadow and sensed a well.

Two.

He ducked and rolled across rocky ground when he heard crackling air as filaments, glowing silver, flailed above him. The third vormag.

Without thinking, Caldan dropped his birds from the sky, the threads between them searing the night. He dived behind a rock. More vormag silver strands skittered around the space he'd just left. They brushed across grass and rocks, leaving a trail of scorched squiggles, stone charred and glowing orange from the heat.

By the ancestors!

Once again he was reminded that if he was going to survive long in this world, he was going to have to learn focused destructive sorcery—and how to counter it.

I just need to figure out how to get Devenish to teach it to me without becoming completely beholden to him.

Another blast of sorcery exploded above him, and it was all his shield could do to fend off the force.

Right—first things first.

Caldan crouched and darted around his cover, propelling his birds to where he sensed the vormag's well. Directing them to circle around the creature, hoping to distract it, he charged . . .

. . . into a massive, looming jukari.

Caldan managed to check his momentum at the last instant. Between the two of them, he would have come off second best. The creature was huge. Its sword swung for him, and Caldan dodged, the jukari's rancid stench wafting over him as he rushed past.

Vormag first.

Aiming for his bright line, Caldan searched the darkness. A smaller figure huddled by a stunted tree. The telltale shimmer of a shield surrounded it. Silver tendrils burst from its outstretched hands, wrapping around his birds.

Caldan could feel the paper begin to give way.

Ancestors!

It was too soon. But there was nothing he could do. They were lost. Drawing power from his well, he pushed it into the birds and ruptured their anchors. Corrosive forces instantly destroyed them. Two thunderous reverberations cracked, so close together they were almost one. Filaments of lightning burst from their remains, surging outward. Caldan sensed the vormag strengthen its shield. It sparkled a deep blue, then purple. Patches of red appeared, only to be washed away by purple, which then changed to the original blue.

Despite the immense blast of Caldan's destroyed craftings, the warded vormag shield was unscathed by his crude destructive sorcery.

So he rammed into it at full speed, wrapping his arms around the vormag's body.

Both of them crashed into the stunted trunk, sending splinters flying. Caldan's shoulder gave an agonizing twinge in protest, and his chest squeezed tight. The astonished vormag shrieked loudly, either in pain or sounding an alarm call for help.

Either way, it was right in Caldan's talent-enhanced ear.

Its bloody shield is too strong, thought Caldan. Still, his dagger flashed in furious shining arcs. His assault was enraged; all thought vanished. Warded bodies pressed together, throwing sparks where they touched. The vormag hammered him back, claws raking over his bare arms and clothes, unable to find purchase on his sleek shield.

A horse drove into Caldan's back, sending him flying. He rolled and staggered to his feet. Not a horse. The giant jukari. Caldan's side pained him as if a horse had kicked him, but it had been the enormous blade. Only his shield had saved him from being cleaved in two. He sucked a deep breath in, wincing at the sharp pain. The jukari came toward him. The vormag skittered to the side, and tendrils of silver slithered across Caldan's shield. He gasped. As he saw them coming, he strengthened his shield to repel an assault. But as the vormag sorcery contacted his, instead of retracting, the tendrils did the opposite: they pulled at his shield, draining it.

Like the arrows used on Joachim.

The creature was trying to exhaust his shield, while the jukari kept him busy. He could feel the tendrils latching on and leeching his power. Already he had to draw further from his well.

Caldan ducked, and the jukari's blade swooped over his head. He couldn't fight the two of them together. His rings pulsed on his fingers, still shining brightly. Blood coursed through his veins, scorching him inside.

Delay the vormag. Kill the jukari.

Cursing, he snarled and ran at the sword-wielding beast. At the same instant, Caldan immersed himself in his well, drawing as much power as he could. When he could hold no more, he flooded it down the tendrils draining his shield.

The vormag cried out, unprepared to cope with the surge. It fell to the ground, hands clutching at its head.

Caldan kicked the jukari in the knee, shattering the joint. His dagger, though tiny compared to the sword, slashed at the jukari with ferocity. On the first strike, it fractured against the hastily raised sword. The second strike, he shoved the jagged end into its belly. And again.

And again.

A yowl deafened Caldan, and a giant fist crashed into his shoulder. His weakened shield did little to soften the blow, and his left arm went numb. He thrust the dagger in again, as the jukari's good leg buckled. Hard yellow eyes stared into his. Putrid breath hissed through its mouth.

Stabbing the knife in one more time, Caldan left it there so that he could seize the jukari's matted hair. With sheer might, he wrenched its head to his left, slamming it into the ground. Its eyes rolled back, senseless.

He rubbed at his shoulder, trying to massage some feeling into his limb. A few moments was all he could spare. He glanced toward the vormag, which was slowly dragging itself to its feet.

Howls and snarls in the night indicated other jukari were coming. Caldan wrung more from his well, his mind beginning to dissolve with the power he was drawing. He bent over and grabbed the discarded jukari sword—a blade as tall as he was. Despite its apparent weight, he lifted it easily, holding the hilt and the blade a third of the way up with his shielded left hand. He almost laughed then. With sorcery, he wouldn't need a thick leather glove like Kristof did.

What the jukari did to Caldan, he could do to the vormag. So once more he rushed the creature, weaving between the silver filaments. It launched a fizzing sphere at him, which he easily avoided. Panic filled the vormag's features.

Caldan drew back his arm and launched the sword. It sailed in a perfect line, as if drawn by a string. Steel chopped into the vormag—halted by the shield with a ringing clang. But the bruising force cracked its ribs, doubling it over.

Then Caldan was upon it.

He screamed with agony as he sucked more power from his well—he was at the end, but somehow found just a bit more—shoving it down the vormag's conduits, overloading its craftings. Flesh sizzled and scorched as an amulet around its neck glowed orange. Flames burst through its tattered clothes.

It uttered a despairing cry, and its shield winked out. The drain on Caldan's shield eased, and he almost collapsed with relief.

Instead, he pummeled the vormag in the face.

Bones cracked, and blood oozed from splits opened up in the creature's gray skin. Sharp-nailed hands clawed weakly at Caldan. He pushed it away, searching for the sword and finding it to his right. He picked it up. The vormag gave him a hate-filled look. Caldan removed that look when he split its head in two.

His body dripping sweat, chest heaving, Caldan looked around. Jukari who'd come upon the scene too late to help were fleeing into the night.

Steel dropped from his fingers, clanging to the ground. Caldan grimaced as he tried to roll his shoulder. His arm tingled, a sign he was regaining feeling . . . and that feeling was pain.

The three Touched appeared.

Kristof took in the carnage. Three vormag and the jukari.

"Bloody work, Caldan, bloody work."

Caldan looked at the hacked corpses of the vormag and staggered away to a nearby bush, vomiting whatever was left in his stomach. He spat to clear his mouth and strode to Kristof.

Then his trinkets winked out.

His knees trembled, and his strength left him. He sank to the ground on all fours, chest heaving. This was what they wanted from him: Killing. Death. Using his sorcery. To turn him into a monster.

He tugged the two borrowed rings from his fingers. He held them out to Kristof and Florian, black blood-crusted circles of not-quite silver.

"Take them back," he croaked. "I killed them for you. That's what you wanted."

Kristof shook his head. "Not I, Caldan. The emperor. We all serve him."

Some more willingly than others.

CHAPTER 9

Leaving the vormag corpses behind, Caldan wandered among the boulders. He trailed after Kristof and Alasdair as they streaked through the receding darkness, finishing off the jukari too slow to flee. Florian hobbled beside him, and he offered her his arm, weak and pained though he was.

Together, they followed a wide spiral of jukari corpses littered across the ground. Most had died with their backs to their foes. One or two had been killed putting up a fight. Slashes and punctures oozed black blood on their torsos, arms, and thighs.

Gray light stained the horizon to the east. He'd lost track of time. A crow cawed. Larger birds began circling high above them—vultures and other scavengers. A pale-eyed crow alighted on a jukari corpse, skipping from leg to leg to stomach. It hopped to the jukari's head and pecked at its eyes.

"You did well," Florian said quietly.

She seemed a pale imitation of her previous savage self: calm and withdrawn.

"It is . . ." Florian began, but hesitated. She cleared her throat. "It is my hope you'll find a place among us, the Touched."

Scenes flashed through Caldan's mind, broken images: the sorcerer he'd killed in Anasoma, Keys's charred body, the soldiers he'd slaughtered at the abandoned mill, jukari and vormag hacked and slashed to death. His Touched abilities weren't a gift; they were a noose around his neck.

Caldan stiffened against Florian's firm softness leaning on him. Was this another of their lures, or merely Florian baring her thoughts? He almost shook his head. He couldn't know. And that, he realized, meant there was no trust between them. There could never be. He'd been pushed by Kristof into the jukari and vormag to show him, again, what he was capable of—and when he was vulnerable, comforted by a woman's welcoming words and touch. By design or by accident?

Did it matter?

His thoughts came with a clarity they hadn't in weeks. It felt like whatever had coursed through his veins this night had cleared away cobwebs he didn't know he'd had. Molten heat had scoured his body and mind clear.

"I am a sorcerer." There. He'd said it. *I will never be considered one of you.*

"There are many sorcerers."

"And not many Touched."

She nodded. "We are encouraged to have as many partners as we want. Our bloodlines are . . . valued. We are valued." She shrugged. "It's a good life. We don't want for anything, and we serve an important purpose."

Death. Killing. Slaughter. "Blood seeks blood," he whispered.

"We're a gift, handed down from ancient times. Remnants—"

"We're used by the empire. Told to kill until the damaging side effects of our own abilities render us useless to them."

Florian uttered no response to his baiting. She paused for a while, as if to give him time to consider his words. "Yes," she eventually said. "You're right."

He didn't betray his surprise at her admission. At least, he didn't think so.

She smiled slightly. "I know—there's nothing we've told you to make you believe anything I say now, even when I agree with you."

"Of course not. Trust is earned."

"Trust can be . . . hope."

"I hope for nothing."

"That's not true. All of us hope."

And this was why she was here with Kristof. A two-pronged attack. Words could accomplish what demonstration couldn't. She was to sway him. Her words were levers. But she didn't know the whole truth. She could admit that the Touched were used and discarded. But what she clearly didn't know was that before they were thrown away, they were bled dry, and that blood was used to fuel the power of the emperor and his warlocks.

That she would be used twice . . . just as they were all trying to use him in ways they wouldn't say aloud.

But I know.

They were unaware, ignorant. Immediately, Caldan lowered his head, ashamed of his thought. They lacked knowledge; that was all.

"The warlocks will want me to do their bidding." A small admission. Let her puzzle this one out.

"We all do their bidding."

Caldan studied Florian. Her lightly freckled face was pale against the dawn light, her red braided hair spattered with black, as were her supple leather clothes. She carried her short spear in one hand. It too was smeared with jukari blood.

Caldan smiled and shook his head. "But you are led by Kristof. I am a sorcerer, as well. With my Touched blood, what will I be capable of? They won't relinquish their leash."

Silence. Then, "You will have two masters."

"Never a good situation. Fraught with room for misunderstanding." Let her stew on his words. She needed to see that the warlocks' desires might not align with her own. But did she? What was he trying to accomplish here? What was the point of sowing dissent, if he wanted nothing to do with the warlocks *or* the Touched?

Because they should know the truth.

The thought hit him like a runaway horse. What use was the truth if it got you killed? If there was so much as a hint that he knew the truth, the warlocks would kill him, and anyone associated with him. Including Miranda. The potency of the Touched blood had been hidden from the world for centuries, and the emperor and his warlocks would ensure it remained hidden. At any cost.

He had no proof, and yet he was completely sure on that point.

What was a little more blood spilled to keep such a valuable truth hidden? How many others had died to keep the warlocks' secret?

Once again, it all came down to blood.

CHAPTER 10

Felice walked through the shadowy streets. She wasn't familiar with this section of Anasoma, but that wasn't surprising. The city was so large, not many could boast familiarity with all its streets and alleyways.

Perhaps that is especially true of those who supposedly ruled over it, she thought with a self-mocking twist.

Trailing a few steps behind her was one of Rebecci's hired hands, a short, squat man with shoulders as broad as an ox's. He carried no weapon that she could see, only hands the size of shovels that looked as if they could crush rock. His brown eyes, gleaming with intelligence he tried hard to hide, scanned their surroundings as they made their way to their destination—an address scrawled on a stained piece of paper handed to her by a fishwife down at the docks. It still had a fish scale stuck to it at the end of a sticky trail of . . . something from the insides of a fish.

She tried to engage the man in conversation again but wasn't holding her breath that he'd respond. He hadn't so far. There was something not quite right about him. Maybe she should try baiting him. She was about to ask him a question, one in a tone that implied he was slow of wit. Then Felice sighed, thinking better of it.

"I respect your wish not to speak to me," she said. "Whatever your reasons are. But I'd appreciate it if I knew your name. Otherwise, I might have to start calling you Big Ox."

The man glanced at her, then away.

"No?" she asked with amusement. "Fair enough."

She concentrated on putting one foot in front of the other. They'd begun to ascend a steep incline, and her lungs were burning. *Bloody fever*, she cursed inwardly. The sickness that had laid her out had gone, along with its lingering cough, but any exertion, and she gasped like a fish out of water. More fish! It was on her brain, no doubt because it was in her nostrils.

They passed a group of men and women congregating at a crossroads. All were hollow-eyed and hungry-looking, turning to stare at Felice and her companion as they walked past. She could sense their distrust of all people not native to Slag Hill, could almost smell their contempt . . . and jealousy.

Felice nodded to them, then kept her head down. Slag Hill had a bad reputation, even among the worst districts of Anasoma. And that was before the city had been besieged by the Indryallans' wall of fire. What the men and women were doing at this time of night, she didn't want to know. She wanted to avoid trouble—hence Big Ox.

Sweat poured from her brow and trickled down her face. She waited until they were a few dozen paces past the crossroads and stopped, opening the top of her shirt to let cool air in. They were almost to the crest of the slope, and to her right was a break in the buildings where an alley led down toward the sea cliffs. Through the gap, the sea was black and unfathomable. What lay beneath, she couldn't guess.

Just like with Kelhak.

"Pignuts," she whispered to herself. She was out of options. Which was why she was here in Slag Hill.

"Did you say something?" asked Big Ox. His voice sounded like she imagined a mountain's would, if one could talk.

Felice figured he was nervous, or he wouldn't have spoken.

Slag Hill had descended toward chaos once the Quivers patrolling the streets disappeared. The replacement Indryallan patrols hadn't done much to stabilize the neighborhood, sporadic as they were.

She shook her head. "It was nothing. Just talking to myself. It's the only way I can have an intelligent conversation."

Big Ox grunted, sounding amused and annoyed at the same time.

Felice looked up at the rest of the climb and winced. Not for the first time, she regretted embarking on this course of action, but she had no choice.

Keep telling yourself that.

She took a breath and continued up the steep incline.

"Gentle, they call me."

Felice almost stopped. Big Ox's words surprised her.

"Are 'they' being ironic?"

She walked another few steps before Gentle responded.

"No."

She waited for more but was left disappointed. So now she had a bodyguard who was known for being gentle? Or were they referring to the effect he had on those around him? She certainly wouldn't want to tangle with him. She flicked a quick glance back over her shoulder at the big man. Except in certain situations.

Felice snorted. *Keep your mind on the task,* she reminded herself.

When they finally reached the top of the hill, the buildings stopped abruptly at a run-down wall of crumbling stone breached by a twisted, rusting gate. Weeds sprouted atop the wall, which was also covered in bird droppings. The gate looked to have been unused for centuries. Luckily, it was open, as vines as thick as her wrist intertwined between the bars. Through the opening was the graveyard of Slag Hill. Their meeting place.

Around the graveyard, the buildings were squalid and falling apart. It didn't look like squatters had taken up residence, as if living this close to the graveyard was something even a fool wouldn't do. She was beginning to wonder what she was doing here as well.

Oh, right . . . I'm worse than a fool. I'm the fool who's following the orders of a fool.

Rebecci had arranged the meeting but had palmed it off to Felice, saying she had business to attend to.

A shiver ran down her spine as she passed through the opening in the wall. Spread out in front of her were tombs and gravestones, older than most of the districts in Anasoma. When the commoners spoke about local legends, those that were creepy or sinister often originated here. Even tales told to frighten children most often had Slag Hill in them, if only to set the scene.

Felice turned and addressed Gentle. "I have to check. Do you remember the terms of this meeting? You mustn't carry—"

"No pig iron, no crafted items, no trinkets, and nothing that illuminates."

Felice nodded. She was right that Gentle's huge exterior hid a sharp intelligence.

"The man I'm meeting was quite specific."

She expected Gentle to comment, but he didn't, and she sighed with relief. She was venturing into unknown territory and didn't want to explain herself. Not that she needed to, to this big ox, but . . . maybe she'd be able to come up with something to convince herself she was doing the right thing.

Ahead loomed a large tree. As they approached, she could see it was all but dead. A few leaves clung to branches, and the trunk leaned so far one way, she thought it would fall any day now. Someone had placed a few timber props underneath it in an effort to save the tree. One of them lay broken on the ground, snapped in two.

Felice skirted the tree and began counting her steps. At thirty, she turned to the east and counted fifty more. They were close to the edge of the cliffs, and the wind picked up, buffeting their clothes. She faced away from the gale and sidled closer to a marble tomb, atop which sat a weathered statue with both arms missing. Constant sea winds had worn the stone, so all that looked out was a sightless face with a nub of a nose and a gash for a mouth.

The faint sound of waves crashing reached her ears, brought all the way up the cliff by the wind. In the years to come, the cliff would also erode, taking the tomb with it.

Wait at the armless tomb, the message had said. It made sense now. At least one part of the instructions did.

Gentle made a circle around the tomb, then positioned himself behind her.

After the long walk, the cold wind cut Felice to the bone. Her warmth leached from her body, as if she'd traveled from the desert to the snow in a brief minute. She rubbed her arms and shivered. She had no idea how long they'd have to wait; perhaps she should—

Felice froze. The hair on the back of her neck stood up. She could hear Gentle shift his weight behind her. Something had . . . changed. In the blink of an eye, the atmosphere had somehow turned . . . bleak. It was as if the night became denser, darker, and sound was muffled.

She slowly turned her head and looked around.

There was nothing . . .

Beside the armless tomb, a shadow stirred. Something was there, where she would have sworn nothing had been moments ago. And Gentle had walked right past that spot.

It was too dark to make anything out, but the shadow grew until it towered over both her and Gentle. Felice swallowed, fear gripping her insides and twisting her stomach.

The shadow was tall and spindly. It looked like an oversize statue covered in strips of rag.

Gentle moved to her side and went to step in front of her, but she held out an arm and stopped him.

A soft hissing voice reached her ears, making Felice wish she was anywhere but here, and preferably snuggled up in a warm bed.

"Did you . . . abide by the terms?" the thing whispered. Words so soft they felt carried by the wind; if it had been calm, she wouldn't have heard them. Whatever it was, it felt ancient. And it was far removed from the assassin she thought she was meeting. Its words came out broken, as if it struggled to form them.

Felice shoved her shaking hands in her pants pockets. She squinted at the shape, but try as she might, she couldn't make any details out. At least she knew why whoever or whatever it was didn't want any light sources near, the better to maintain its disguise.

"Yes" was all she managed.

"No pig iron?"

Felice shook her head. "We have none."

"No craftings?"

"None."

"No trinkets?"

"No."

"No sources of light?"

"Again, no."

The mound moved back slightly, as if it had been leaning forward intently. "Say the name . . . and I'll name the price."

Felice steeled herself. It was too late to pull out of this now. "He's a sorcerer."

"Say the name."

"Kelhak. And there are two conditions. Myself and a . . . friend . . . need to be there when it's done. After he's dead, she needs to do something."

A sound like an exhalation escaped from the assassin. "Ah, ah, intriguing. Aligning maybe . . . death . . . maybe . . . must be done . . ."

Gentle's feet scuffed on dirt as he shifted his weight. He was nervous, and Felice didn't blame him. She waited until the assassin stopped talking to himself. She had to hand it to him: he'd worked hard on coming across as disturbing and sinister. But underneath the mummery, he was just a man with a knife. And that was all she needed. Albeit one who wasn't afraid of sorcerers.

"The price?" she reminded gently.

"Three trinkets. Three for what was . . . three for Kelhak."

Gentle gasped.

Felice cursed inwardly. Where was she going to get three trinkets? All the information she had was that he only ever asked for ducats.

"I thought you took payment in ducats? I hadn't heard you wanted trinkets."

"Not here. Not now. In payment . . . I do."

She tugged an earring and sighed. "I accept. I'll need a few days to gather the payment."

"A bargain sealed, then. Payment only when task is complete. You and your friend meet me here three nights hence."

"Agreed."

"Tell me, Felicienne . . . do you know why this place is called Slag Hill?"

She hadn't told anyone outside of Rebecci's circle her name. And all communication with the assassin's network had been anonymous so far. Felice's throat tightened. "This is where the old ironworks was located, before the sorcerers came up with a better way of smelting the metal. The old manufactories were shut down. I'd always thought it had something to do with that."

There was a pause. The only sound came from the wind gusting about them.

"No . . . before this city was another city. Ancient sorcerers created jukari here . . . among others."

Despite herself, Felice was intrigued. Knowledge was power, and she was never one to pass up learning something. "Vormag?"

"Among others."

Could she trust his information? And why was he telling her this?

"After the Shattering, the city was destroyed. Reduced to molten slag . . . killing almost everything here."

Almost? Some jukari escaped, then. They were confined to the Desolate Lands now. Still . . . she'd learned something, if it was true.

"Thank you," she said graciously. "I welcome all knowledge."

The assassin stirred, sounding like stones rattling down a hill.

"Knows . . . doesn't know . . . should she? . . . dangerous . . . yes, maybe . . ."

Felice drew herself up. Their business was done for now. And the sooner she left this place, the better. "If you've finished talking to yourself, we'll take our leave."

"Talking to myself is the only way I can have an intelligent conversation," the assassin said.

Was he mocking her? Had he heard what she'd said earlier? The realization he may have been following them all this time sent a chill along her spine.

With a creak, the assassin rose up until he was a few heads taller than Gentle. A whimper reached her ears, and Felice realized it came from her. A strong hand clasped her arm. Gentle.

"Be careful," the assassin whispered, "what you welcome, Felicienne."

"Enough of this mummery," growled Gentle. "Show yourself, assassin." He shoved Felice behind him, and light erupted, banishing shadows, as he drew out a sorcerous globe.

"Gentle, no!" Felice said.

There was a rustle of cloth as the assassin slammed into Gentle. Bones broke with an audible snap. The globe sailed over the cliffside like a falling star. Gentle sagged to his knees, one arm hanging limply by his side. The assassin withdrew into the darkness, back to his original position, then remained still.

Gentle keeled over, lifeless. Blood oozed from a wound in his chest, right where his heart would be.

Felice stumbled to her knees and pressed her hand against his chest to stop the bleeding. His eyes stared ahead, unfocused, unseeing. Felice felt hot tears trail down her cheeks.

"I warned you," the assassin said. "We have struck a deal. Honor it."

As the assassin finished speaking, there was a crack behind Felice, as if a frozen tree split in two. Her heart jumped at the sound. She twisted to look. Nothing.

Heart thumping in her chest, Felice jerked her head back to the assassin.

He was gone.

A shadow moved by the cliff edge.

"Pignuts," she said, looking down at Gentle. He was dead. There was nothing she could do.

Felice stood and wiped her bloody hands on her trousers. She wondered if she had the strength to go on.

Stumbling to the cliff, she used her boot to scuff at the edge. There was an overturned stone, some scrape marks.

He came—and left—over the edge.

Felice leaned as far out as she dared. A hundred yards below, the ocean crashed onto boulders. The wind rushed in her ears, blowing her hair straight up. It was so strong, it felt like a hand pushing her back.

She looked at Gentle, told him she was sorry.

What had Rebecci gotten her into?

"IT'S AN HERBAL mixture that will relieve the pain and swelling of the limb," Gerhard said, adding another spoonful of a dark green powder to a clear glass. The hot water inside turned a yellowy-green tinge as he stirred. "Only a few more ingredients, and we'll be ready."

Gerhard wore his pale hair swept back over his head and greased into place. He dressed like a sorcerer: dark robes, with craftings plainly visible, but the soles of his boots were worn almost through, and the elbows of his sleeves had been patched.

Here is a man who cares little for outward appearances, thought Aidan. He watched as Gerhard added a few drops of yellow liquid. Poppyseed oil, most likely, along with a dried leaf crushed between the palms of his hands and brushed into the cup.

Once Aidan's story had filtered up the hierarchy—helped along by the writ he carried—he had been questioned by a number of high-ranking Quivers and given privileges many couldn't afford. Gerhard was one: an expensive physiker.

Vasile was resting in the bed beside Aidan's. Both of them were to receive the expert ministrations of Gerhard, who by all accounts could speed the healing process, but whose main strength was setting broken and shattered bones in the right place. A badly set bone could restrict movement in an arm or leave a patient with a permanent limp. Through whatever arcane means he employed, Gerhard was supposed to be able to fix even the worst of splintered bones. A guard told Aidan he'd healed the daughter of one of the emperor's councillors, whose legs had been run over by a loaded wagon, and saved them from amputation.

As with most things, the wealthy and powerful were able to afford solutions those below them couldn't.

Gerhard thrust the cup into Aidan's hand. "Drink half; the rest is for your friend." The physiker then opened a flat leather folder and began removing small metal discs. He unwound the bandage on Aidan's arm to reveal the skin underneath, and Aidan had to clamp his jaw shut to prevent himself screaming with pain. Black and purple and swollen, the arm didn't look good to him.

And Vasile's was worse.

Aidan gulped down half the cup in one swallow. It was bitter and earthy, but not the worst he'd ever tasted.

Gerhard passed the cup to Vasile, who looked at the contents suspiciously before sipping at it like it was a fine wine. The magistrate sighed, then swallowed the rest as fast as he could with a grimace of distaste.

Gerhard nodded. He placed a dollop of a white paste on one side of a disc, then pressed it gently onto Aidan's arm, just below his elbow, where it stuck fast. As far as Aidan could tell, the disc was made from silver, with runes scribed into its surface. Three tiny rubies dotted it, seemingly at random.

The physiker repeated the process with four more discs, then did the same to Vasile. By the time he was finished, Aidan was feeling the effects of the medicine. The room was moving slightly, and his vision was blurry. Clinks and scrapings as Gerhard moved around became muted, as if the sound traveled through water.

"There," Gerhard said, seemingly from a long way away. "We'll wait a few moments, then begin."

Aidan tried to speak, but his lips and tongue were numb. He couldn't even move his fingers.

"The process is quite painful," continued Gerhard. "But thankfully, I've come up with a solution that dulls the senses enough that it shouldn't bother you. You might not even remember what happens. You'll be in much better shape to get around without as much pain after this. Perhaps you'll be able to resume limited duties."

Next to Aidan, Vasile sniggered. "Truths followed by a lie."

Aidan felt a twinge of alarm at Vasile's words.

Gerhard raised an eyebrow, floating across Aidan's field of view from left to right. The physiker lifted Aidan's uninjured arm a few inches, then let it go. It dropped back to the bed without resistance.

"Good. I'm sorry about this, but . . . I'm here to do my job. Whatever happens after is not my affair."

Gerhard went to the door and knocked. It opened, and in came four Quivers. Two stood next to Aidan, and the other pair beside Vasile.

"Once I'm finished, they'll take you to a secure cell. I'm afraid someone's brought some very serious charges against you. The Quivers thought you'd be easier to manage after I've finished my ministrations."

Aidan's thoughts were muddled, and he struggled to make sense of what was happening. *A cell? What charges?*

Gerhard sat next to him and began his sorcery.

Aidan lost track of time. Gerhard dissolved into a blur or colors and shapes, along with the Quivers. There was a faint memory of his arm being pulled, and agony. Some bumping and jostling.

Another bed, this one hard.

"Sleep," someone said.

And he did.

CHAPTER 11

Back at the army's encampment, Kristof jammed a key into the lock on the chest and twisted. It was a heavy iron box in the back of his wagon, and if Caldan had to guess, he'd say no two men could have lifted it. And that was probably the point. The lip opened slowly with a great shriek of grinding metal. Kristof rummaged around inside and came up with a sheathed dagger as long as his forearm. He ran a hand lovingly along the weapon before turning and presenting it to Caldan.

"Take this. It was given to me when I first joined. Now it's yours. Wear it with pride."

Kristof's voice was thick with suppressed emotion.

Caldan took the dagger and drew the blade. It was plain but well forged. It wasn't crafted, nor of any particularly valuable alloy he could determine. Both edges were razor sharp, though, and that's what mattered. It was what it was: a dagger for killing. Uneasily, he sheathed the weapon, feeling sick to his stomach.

"Now we have another mission," Kristof said.

Caldan looked to the Touched, whose face was grim, eyes hard.

"Devenish wants us to kill this Gazija," continued Kristof. "On orders from the emperor. Just you and me, and I'll judge how you perform."

Caldan swallowed. "I don't think—"

"You have no choice. We kill Gazija and anyone else who gets in our way. Quietly and discreetly. No one is to be able to trace it back to us, or the emperor. You'll prove you're truly part of our cause. He's a powerful sorcerer, though, so we'll have to be careful. Give him no chance to raise a shield."

Caldan had trouble forming words. A chill had traveled up his spine, as much at the man's blind acceptance of the order as at the order itself. It was all he could do to nod.

Kristof smiled, a baring of teeth. "An ensorcelled knife will be all we need for this mission. We've dealt with rogue sorcerers like Gazija before. I'll take whatever I need from the warlocks' stores."

Caldan wasn't going to stand back and let Kristof kill Gazija. Whatever the old man's motives, he'd shown he wanted to help defeat the jukari. And more than that, Caldan had witnessed the emperor's fear. If there was to be any chance of defeating Kelhak, he had a sense that Gazija would be vital . . .

But what were his options? Kristof wasn't going to be swayed by anything he said, and how could he possibly prove this order was a mistake? It would be one thing if he could convince Kristof of the emperor's duplicity when it came to the Touched—then the lie of this order would be apparent . . .

By the ancestors, think!

Kristof spoke again. "There's something else I need to tell you."

He drew a gold chain from around his neck and undid the clasp. From it he took a silver ring, which vibrated at the edge of Caldan's awareness. A trinket. Kristof held it out in his palm. The ring was startlingly similar to his own. It had a knotwork pattern, but instead of lions, there were ravens with tiny emerald eyes.

"I'm to give you this once tonight's mission is complete. A sign of how much we value you, and a show of trust. Over the next few days, I'll teach you about your abilities, and how to better control them, and how these trinkets affect you. For now, we have a job to do. Not a pleasant one, either, but one essential to the emperor's cause."

Killing an old man is essential? scoffed Caldan inwardly, but he couldn't contain himself. "Is it really for the good of the empire?"

"If Devenish says it is, then I believe him."

And that's part of the problem.

"Then let's get this over with" was all he said, though.

Kristof relocked the chest and shoved it back, covering it with canvas. He stood, jerked his head toward the docks outside Riversedge, then strode off.

Caldan was about to follow when he noticed four people, who could only be Touched, lined up in the camp. They must have congregated behind them, and Caldan had been too preoccupied to notice.

As Kristof passed each of them, they clasped his hand and spoke. Both of the women gave him a hug. It was a parting ritual of some kind.

Caldan took a step toward the first in line, a lean man with a hard face. They all had hard faces, with eyes that gave nothing away.

"I'm Rogget. Return to the Touched from whence you came. Keep the empire safe," said the man seriously, holding out a calloused hand.

Caldan clasped it in his. "What am I supposed to say in response?" he asked.

"Whatever you like. Most just keep their replies informal and friendly. Some don't like to speak. Especially on dangerous missions, from which they might not return."

Caldan smiled weakly. "Are there many of those?"

Rogget shook his head. "No. We're too valuable to waste. But sometimes . . . well, we can talk about that later. The others are waiting." He stepped back.

Caldan moved to the next Touched, a short-haired woman with an infectious smile. Caldan held out his hand, but she brushed it away and hugged him warmly.

"Welcome," she whispered kindly in his ear. "I'm Cherise, but most call me Cherry. Return to the Touched from whence you came. Keep the empire safe."

Caldan waited until she released her grip, then took half a step back. His eyes burned, and he blinked back tears. These were good people. They just didn't understand that their mission was terrible . . . and their fate even worse.

Clearing his throat, he took a few more steps back and turned to address the remaining Touched. Along with Rogget and Cherry, there was a tall, dark-skinned, muscular youth, sporting a light beard and a hawklike nose, and a middle-aged woman who would look more at home in a kitchen baking bread than here in the middle of an army.

"By the ancestors," he said firmly. "I promise to do what I can to protect the empire. From enemies without, and within."

Kristof frowned at his words, but only nodded.

Caldan made his way to the two remaining Touched and completed the ritual. They introduced themselves as Kra-bast from the western Desolate Lands, and Yiquin from Shikur in the Sotharle Union of Cities. The arm of the emperor and the Touched reached far indeed. If they were finding Touched outside of the empire and bringing them under their control, then their efforts reached much farther than he had suspected.

Caldan turned his back on Rogget, Cherry, Kra-bast, and Yiquin, and without waiting for Kristof, he strode off toward the docks. For a long time, he didn't speak, and after catching up, Kristof walked quietly beside him, sensing his need for silence.

After a while, Kristof touched him lightly on the shoulder. "This way," he said. "We can't go through the front door." He gave a short laugh. "A few of the old ones could, I have no doubt. But we need to be stealthier to get close."

"The old ones? Who are they?"

Caldan thought he saw a wistfulness come into Kristof's expression. It was gone in an instant, replaced by indifference.

"The Touched who were alive centuries ago, and those before them. That's how long we've been in service to the emperor. But from the records we keep, their skill far surpassed our own. Something's causing our talents to lessen with each generation, as if we're fading away. Nothing we have to worry about. That's a problem for the future. Can't waste time thinking about what we can't change."

It's the blood again, marveled Caldan. Something so simple, and yet Kristof and the others didn't see it. With each generation, the children of the Touched would inherit only part of their parents' abilities. Unless both were Touched.

Realization hit Caldan like a lightning bolt. "The warlocks encourage you to marry among yourselves, don't they?"

"Yes. That's a good guess. Our secrets must be maintained, and finding partners among ourselves entails less risk. Many don't, though. We lead a hard life, and most like to find solace outside our ranks."

It was interesting—it was the first time Caldan had heard Kristof even hint at the Touched remotely disagreeing with something the warlocks told them.

Although, in a few more generations, whether there were cracks in their alliance might become moot. The warlocks couldn't tell the Touched the truth of their blood's potency, because they would almost certainly figure out how precious it was. But that put the warlocks in a bind. The Touched were slowly but surely becoming less effective, both individually and as a force. It might take centuries, but they were doomed, as was the power the warlocks controlled through their blood. Unless the warlocks *forced* the Touched to inbreed . . .

Caldan sighed and rubbed his eyes. Wherever he turned, everything became more complicated.

They made their way parallel to the river and east of the docks. The vegetation became denser the farther away from Riversedge they went, but it never turned wild. They were too close to a major city for that. Houses and small towns dotted the countryside, though by now most were deserted because of the jukari.

Kristof led Caldan along a narrow, muddy path. Tall grasses on both sides soon had their pants soaked with dew. They followed the track a fair distance, with Kristof stopping occasionally to peer back at Riversedge, as if to gauge how far they'd come. When the river kicked back in the direction of the city, then sharply turned toward the coast in an S, he gestured for Caldan to follow him off the path.

They found a copse of willow trees growing close by the river. Tied to one was a rowboat with a pair of stowed oars. As they approached, a disreputable-looking man stepped from the shadow of one of the trees. He wore brown and greens—an obvious attempt to blend in with his surroundings—and a brimmed hat pulled low. As far as Caldan could tell, he wasn't a Touched, as he wore no trinkets.

"Wasn't expecting two of you," the man said, tone thick with distrust.

Kristof flicked a ducat toward him. Gold glinted in the fading light as the coin went tumbling.

The man snatched it from the air, and it disappeared into a pocket. "Nice night for a row," he said, and then backed away. Soon he was lost in the gloom under the willows.

"Get in," Kristof said. "I assume you can row?"

Caldan shook his head as he made for the boat. "No. But I've seen and read about it. I'm sure I'll get the hang of it."

The boat wobbled as he got in, but Caldan easily found his balance. He settled on a bench and unshipped the oars.

"You've read about it? This should be interesting."

"You're welcome to row."

Kristof shook his head and joined Caldan in the boat. It wobbled again, but like Caldan, Kristof settled himself easily.

We're not that different, Kristof and I, realized Caldan. It was hard not to feel some sort of kinship with the man, even though Caldan knew before the night was over he'd have to fight Kristof to protect Gazija—and there was a chance one of them would be dead.

"We're a fair way from the Riversedge docks," Kristof murmured. "By the time we get there, it'll be fully dark."

There was a sack at the bottom of the boat, its lower half wet from sitting in an inch of water. Kristof opened it and drew out a rope, along with a padded grappling hook.

"We make our way to the back of Gazija's ship, use the rope to climb up to his cabin, do the deed, and then we're out of there. Quick and easy."

Caldan bit his lip and twisted the ring on his finger. *Murder may be quick, but it's never easy.*

CHAPTER 12

Aidan threw his shoulder against the cell door. His jarred broken arm screamed in protest, and he groaned. The door rattled, but other than that, he had no effect.

"Leave it," Vasile said. "We're not getting out of here, and you might undo Gerhard's work."

"Traitor," spat Aidan. "Drugging us so they could take us prisoner. And for what?" He kicked the door. "Hey!" he shouted. "Why are we here? I have a writ from the emperor himself!"

Silence answered him.

Vasile was sitting on one of the two rickety cots in the cell, each with a ratty, stained blanket. The smell of mold and urine was strong enough to make breathing through their noses unpleasant. There were two buckets in a corner, one filled with stale water and the other empty. A tiny barred window let in some light, enough to see the cockroaches by.

"How long were we out?" Aidan asked.

Vasile shrugged. "How should I know? A few hours? A day?"

"How can you be so calm?"

"We haven't done anything wrong. This must be a mistake."

Aidan snorted. "No. Something's afoot. A power play . . . something. But what would anyone have to gain? It makes no sense."

The cell door shook as a boot slammed into it from the other side.

"Move to the back of the cell, or I'll be forced to make you comply." The guard's tone made it sound like their not complying was his preferred option.

Aidan shuffled backward, glancing around vainly for something to use as a weapon before thinking better of that idea. They wouldn't get out of this with violence.

A key turned in the lock. The door swung open, and a fat, bald guard came in. He wore a leather apron over filthy gray clothes and sported sweat-stained armpits. He smiled, revealing brown teeth.

"Back a bit farther, prisoners." He lifted an iron-shod wooden club and waved it at them. "Quickly like."

Vasile groaned as he lurched to his feet and backed against the far wall. Aidan joined him, clenching his fists as he seethed inside. After all he'd gone through, after all he'd endured for the Mahruse Empire, they had imprisoned him! There was no justice, but then again, he'd known this long ago.

Still keeping his eyes on them and the club pointed in their direction, the guard shuffled to the side, and a cloaked woman stepped gingerly through the doorway, face obscured by a hood. She carried a wooden staff, which she leaned on heavily, relying on it for support. She walked slowly, as if every move was excruciating. A soft wheezing sound came from her, along with a floral scent of perfume.

Aidan racked his brain to see if he could figure out who would want him imprisoned and came up empty. This was a new game, and one he didn't want to be embroiled in. Not with the emperor's forces in disarray and a jukari horde on their doorstep. His place, along with Vasile's and cel Rau's, was out doing what they could to help.

"What are the charges against me?" he demanded. "I've done nothing wrong. Reveal yourself, so I know who I'm dealing with. I've a writ from the emperor himself, exempting me from laws that would apply to others."

Behind the woman, Anshul cel Rau stepped into the cell. He regarded Aidan with disdain, mouth twisted, and leaned against the doorway, arms folded across his chest.

"Cel Rau!" said Aidan. "What's going on?"

The woman reached slender hands up. She grabbed her hood, fingers trembling, then pulled it back.

Caitlyn.

Aidan's eyes widened in shock, and his legs went weak. He fell to his knees as his strength left them. The cell closed in on him, pressing from all sides.

But she was dead. He'd seen her fall with a crossbow bolt through the chest. He'd been the one to do it. Her face was gaunt, almost emaciated, as if she'd fought off a nearly fatal illness and only just survived. Her eyes were bright with madness.

"That won't help you now, sweet Aidan," purred Caitlyn with ill-concealed malice. "The writ was presented to me. I don't have to tell you what happens to those who side with evil. You were corrupted, and I didn't see it. I don't know when it happened. But you'll be judged by your actions." She shook her head in sorrow. "Evil must be excised when it's found. You know that. No matter the cost."

Aidan sobbed and covered his face with his hands. "I had to," he croaked miserably. "I'm sorry."

Cel Rau had never forgiven him, and now that Caitlyn had returned, the swordsman sided with her.

"Sorry now, are you? Once you're caught and to be punished? Well, you'll have some time to think about repenting. Then, when you meet the ancestors, you can explain to them where you fell from the path, and why." Caitlyn tapped the end of her staff on the stone floor twice and cackled. "I won't listen to excuses. You're to be executed in a few days. Make peace with yourself."

"But Vasile here," Aidan protested, "he's innocent. He had nothing to do with—"

"With my attempted murder? He's guilty by association. And cel Rau's told me how he showed Chalayan the way down the dark path of destruction. No, Vasile isn't innocent."

Without another word, Caitlyn turned and limped away. Cel Rau backed out to let her pass. The guard followed, slamming the door shut. The lock snapped closed with a loud click, echoing around the cell with a chilling finality.

CHAPTER 13

Caldan shivered. It had nothing to do with the cold breeze blowing across the river and over his sweat-soaked body. Rowing was hard work, and he'd warmed up quickly; the chill he felt was not related to the air. He could die tonight. Either at Kristof's hands, or Gazija's, if the old man reacted as Caldan thought he was capable of.

And so he searched for an opening, a chance to make Kristof see the folly of what he was doing. The problem was, an unsteady rowboat was no place to confront him. Caldan cursed himself for not doing something sooner, on the bank of the river. But then he cursed himself again, because what could he have done?

For good measure, he cursed one more time.

After some fiddling about and practice, he'd worked out how to row with barely a splash on the water's surface. He maintained a slow but steady pace, telling Kristof he wanted to keep noise to a minimum, but the real reason was to give himself time to think and try to delay the inevitable.

Caldan sighed softly.

"It'll be all right," Kristof whispered. "You've been given a difficult first mission. That's why I'm with you."

And to kill me if I refuse. Let's not forget that part.

"But," Kristof continued, "once we're done, Devenish will trust you. And you'll truly be one of us."

"By murdering an old man?" Caldan blurted before he could stop himself.

"It needs doing. Best not to dwell on the details."

"Is that how you live with yourself? You just don't think about what you've become? Because I have to say: sticking a knife into someone is usually a last recourse."

Kristof was quiet for a time. The only noises were the oars dipping into the water and crickets from the nearby bank. Eventually he spoke. "Don't presume to judge me. Sometimes the emperor needs hard men for hard tasks." He leaned forward and poked a finger into Caldan's chest. "It remains to be seen whether you're fit for the Touched. But I'm hopeful. You've shown you're a fighter. And if you can use sorcery . . . well, then . . . you'll prove valuable in ways you can't imagine. I think Devenish is looking to replace me soon, and now he's found someone who's both Touched and a sorcerer."

"Right—I am those two things. But what if I don't want to be an assassin as well?"

Kristof shrugged. "You'll do whatever task the warlocks set you to. Either you can bitch and moan all the way, or you can accept your fate and come to terms with what you are. It's easier if you acknowledge the best use of your talents, and leave your conscience behind. But don't try to replace me, Caldan, I'm warning you."

Caldan could still feel where Kristof's finger had touched him. It ached more than it should have, as if reminding him of both their similarity and their differences.

"I'm not trying to replace you. I'm still not sure I want to *be* you."

Kristof said nothing, but by the expression on his face he seemed to accept Caldan's answer. The boat moved closer.

"Slow up a touch," Kristof said softly. "There are lights ahead.

Should be the ships moored at the docks." He half crouched and peered into the night. "Yes, that's them. Steer a bit to your right. We'll come at them from farther into the river."

Caldan did as he was told, hunching his shoulders in despair. So this was the start. Do this, do that, kill this person. He gripped the oars until his hands hurt.

Could he unship an oar and take Kristof unawares before they reached the ship? No—not with Kristof facing him. His options were becoming fewer and fewer, none of them good.

Kristof began coiling the rope attached to the padded grappling hook. "Slow down. We don't want to bump them and alert any guards."

Caldan glanced over his shoulder at Gazija's ship. They were closer than he'd thought. A few lights flickered on deck, but he couldn't see anyone on watch. Likely, there were guards at the gangplank but not patrolling the deck. No light came from the large window at the back—Gazija's cabin, Kristof had said earlier. Maybe he wasn't there, and they could give up for tonight . . .

Wishful thinking.

Without him rowing, they slowed considerably, until they were drifting. The current close to the wharves was slow but still noticeable. He'd have to move the boat nearer if they—

Kristof flung the grappling hook upward, and it arced over the gunwale, landing on the deck with a muffled thump. He quickly reeled slack rope in until the hook stuck fast on the side, then used the taut rope to steady them. With deft movements, he wound it around a cleat on the front of their rowboat and held them fast.

"You first," he said.

Caldan breathed deeply and nodded. His hands brushed his pockets to check that his craftings were still there, and he tugged his knife sheath, adjusting it so it wouldn't jab him in the leg when he climbed.

He gripped the rope and pulled himself up. In a few moments, he was outside Gazija's window. It was open a few inches. Caldan steadied himself, reached out, and pulled it open farther, just enough to create a gap he could squeeze through.

And then he was inside. The rope creaked, and a faint scuffing from outside told him Kristof was on his way.

He had to do something. But what? It would only be moments before Kristof made it inside.

Across the cabin, a shape in the bunk huddled under thick blankets. Caldan moved silently to the door and made sure it was latched. He rushed to the bunk and shook Gazija. "Wake up!" he whispered urgently. "You're in danger!"

The shape moaned and rolled over . . .

. . . and Miranda peered at him with sleepy half-lidded eyes under tousled hair.

"Mmmpf?" she murmured.

Caldan stepped back in horror. No. She shouldn't be here. Couldn't be here . . .

He turned to the window just as Kristof stepped down from it onto the floor.

Miranda sat up, clutching her blanket to her chest. She looked at him with wide eyes.

How did she get here? *By the ancestors!* Quiss had wanted to help her. Had he persuaded the physiker to release Miranda into his care? Or had he abducted her? Was there no limit to what the Five Oceans could do with their money?

If they had kidnapped her, then any reservations he had about killing Gazija would quickly disappear.

"Kristof," Caldan said. "We can't do this."

"What do you mean? We're here. Devenish gave us our orders. Whoever this girl is, she needs to be silenced. No one can know we were here. Do it now!"

"Oooh!" moaned Miranda. Clearly she hadn't been cured yet, was still unable to articulate, but even in her state, she recognized her life was in danger.

Caldan moved in between Miranda and Kristof. "I can't let you hurt her."

Kristof took a step toward him. "Out of my way, Caldan. When we see this through, I won't even tell Devenish you balked at the task."

"You think I care about Devenish? I care about killing an innocent girl!"

Blankets rustled behind him, but Caldan couldn't take his eyes off Kristof. He was hot, but not with the same heat that came to him when his Touched abilities awoke. He knew he couldn't rely on them. What worried him, though, was if Kristof was in full control of *his*. Caldan didn't know, and he wasn't waiting to find out. His fingers reached for his shield crafting.

Kristof's eyes followed the movement. And one moment he was by the window, the next slamming into Caldan.

Caldan's feet lifted off the ground, and all the air was driven from his lungs. He flew across the cabin and crashed into the wall. His stomach and chest burned with agony as he slumped to the floor.

"Stupid boy," Kristof hissed. "Did you think you would be a match for me?"

Caldan tried to groan but had no breath. He rolled onto his stomach and attempted to get up. Searing agony erupted in his side as Kristof's boot thudded into his chest. Multiple cracks echoed around the cabin as ribs fractured.

Through the pain, he heard Miranda draw breath to scream, only to be silenced as Kristof backhanded her across the face. She collapsed on the bunk, unmoving.

Miranda!

Kristof grabbed him by the scruff of the neck and pressed his face into the floor.

Caldan managed to draw a shallow breath, but his ribs hurt as if he'd been run over by a fully laden wagon. He gasped, and tears leaked from the corners of his eyes.

A weight descended on him: Kristof's knee in his back.

The Touched brought his face close to Caldan's. "You can't defeat me, boy. I've years of experience and training on you. Give up. You'll learn to follow the rules and do whatever I tell you. A little killing is part of protecting the empire."

Caldan tried to sneer at Kristof but only managed a wheeze. He sucked in a lungful of air. "You're doing this . . . because Devenish . . .

thinks he was slighted . . . in front of everyone . . . For no other reason . . . than that . . . he wants to kill Gazija . . . Even though . . . he brought mercenary companies . . . into the emperor's service . . . and . . . is helping save Riversedge . . . from the jukari."

"Not a man. Gazija and his ilk are an abomination. I can see they are, as I know you can. They're not natural."

"I'll judge a man . . . by his actions . . . not his words . . . or what others . . . think of him."

Kristof bore down on Caldan's throat, choking off his air. "Then you're a fool. Last chance, boy. Are you with us? Nod if you are. If you aren't . . . it's the knife for you."

My knife.

Caldan tried to reach it, but his arms were held tight by Kristof's legs. He couldn't activate his shield crafting without touching it, either. It was a flaw he hadn't considered when crafting it. If he poured his well into his beetle and ruptured the anchor, it would destroy the whole cabin, him and Miranda with it.

Caldan closed his eyes. There was nothing he could do.

He opened his well anyway, desperate to try something. Anything. But without a useful crafting, what could he do? He needed to create sorcery without one. His mind fled back to Anasoma, when he escaped from Bells the first time. His paper crafting had burned to nothing when he'd been desperate, but still melted the metal frame, sealing the door behind him.

Crafting when the paper was gone.

His vision blurred, darkness closing in from all sides.

There was a crash, and shards of pottery sprayed across the floor. Kristof bellowed, and the pressure on Caldan's throat eased. He gulped a breath and twisted onto his back, to see Miranda standing above Kristof, the handle of a broken jug in her hand.

Kristof leaped to his feet and punched Miranda in the jaw. She flew across the room, slamming into a wall above the bunk with a hard thump.

Caldan reached for his shield crafting—too late. Kristof's speed was incredible, and he was back astride Caldan in the blink of an eye.

Kristof's gleaming knife pressed against his neck, the blade cold and hard.

"Decide now, Caldan. What'll it be? Duty, or cowardice?"

Miranda screamed from behind Kristof. Metal gleamed as she raised her arm and plunged a small knife into Kristof's back. The Touched grimaced, and his grip slackened for an instant. Miranda staggered back and fell to the floor, eyes glazed.

But it should be enough.

She'd given Caldan time, a few more breaths, and he wasn't going to waste them. He calmed himself and thought about what craftings really were—materials that could hold the runes and withstand the corrosive force of his well. But they were, in the end, just a medium. So . . . couldn't his mind shape the runes? Act as the crafting itself?

Caldan frantically tried to focus his thoughts.

Acting intuitively, he began splitting strings and shaping them into runes around his well, linking, buffering, forming. A mishmash of coercive and destructive sorcery. A cobbled-together accident waiting to happen.

Either this would work . . . or his brain would boil inside his skull.

It was now or never. A trickle was all he needed.

He flooded his makeshift crafting with the corrosive power of his well and directed his crude, destructive sorcery. A tendril of energy snaked out.

Kristof grunted. Then coughed.

A warm wetness splashed Caldan's face and shirt.

Kristof's grip on Caldan's neck went slack, and the Touched keeled over, thumping onto the floor.

Caldan sucked in air, gasping. He wriggled and pushed Kristof's legs off him, ignoring the knifing pain from his ribs. A warm trickle flowed from his nose and into his mouth. He spat the blood out before pinching his nostrils. As he tilted his head forward, he winced. His brain ached inside his skull, as if it were bruised.

Kristof lay on the floor, eyes staring ahead, unseeing. A hole the size of a ducat in his throat bubbled with blood, and another through his chest smoked, charred around the edges.

Caldan dragged himself to Miranda, fighting off nausea and the soreness of his mind. She was sprawled across a rug, limp and unmoving.

"Miranda," he pleaded, touching her face. His fingers felt for a pulse.

He breathed a sigh of relief, which turned into a sob. She was alive.

Boots pounded along the corridor outside the door. Fists hammered on the wood.

"What's going on? Open up!"

"Out of the way. Let me through." He knew that voice.

Gazija.

Caldan staggered to the door and lifted the latch. The door flew open. He stumbled backward, resting against the wall, and slid down to the floor.

"She's all right," he said wearily. "She's not dead."

Quiss rushed into the room and headed straight for Miranda.

Gazija hobbled inside after him, eyes bright, concern on his face. "We felt the sorcery. You, I assume? Don't you know how foolish that was? You could have boiled your mind to porridge."

Caldan nodded, then winced again. He hugged his arms to his chest. His whole body trembled, and he couldn't stop it.

"I might have done just that," he said weakly. "I couldn't think of anything else. I thought it would probably kill me, but the alternative"—he glanced at Miranda—"was worse."

Gazija frowned with concern. "I can guess what happened here."

"Caldan's correct," Quiss said with relief. "Miranda is relatively unhurt. She'll wake with a sore head and bruised cheek. But she won't feel them much, not in her state." He turned to Caldan. "What's going on?"

"We all have questions for Caldan," Gazija said, giving Caldan a hostile glare.

Caldan held up a hand. "I didn't know what to do. I wasn't going to go along with him. But . . . why is Miranda here?" Quiss's words came to him, almost as if they were whispered into his ear: *I'll do what I can to help her, which is far more than these warlocks can do.*

But at what price? In Caldan's experience, everyone wanted something in return.

"Quiss came to me with your problem, and we decided to do what we could to help this poor lady. He thought she would be more comfortable in a bigger cabin, and I agreed. So who is this man?" Gazija tapped Kristof's body with one of his canes. "I assume Devenish sent him? What is he, one of their sorcerers?" Gazija spat the word with contempt.

"No," Caldan replied. "Something else."

Gazija grunted, even as Quiss moved to get Miranda back in the bed.

Clearly, Quiss had already decided to help Miranda. And for that, Caldan was more than grateful.

Of course, that might be all he would get to be. Because how could he explain this in a way that they'd believe? Kristof's body might help prove part of his innocence, but that could be explained away as protecting Miranda, not Gazija. No matter what, he had snuck into this cabin with a knife. He wouldn't blame them if they reached their own conclusions. Thinking back on the vormag from last night—and the dead man before him now—they might not be so far off.

I can only hope they don't take it out on her, he thought, looking at Miranda's lovely, sleeping form.

Ancestors knew it didn't look good for him.

CHAPTER 14

For some reason, they chose to believe him.

He had explained what he was doing there—and his role in trying to prevent it—and the two denser-men had taken him at his word.

It almost made him suspicious.

Quiss removed both his palms from Caldan's head. Caldan was still a bit unsure why that had gone so easily.

"You haven't sustained any permanent damage," the sorcerer pronounced. "You were lucky. Extremely lucky."

"You checked an hour ago—"

"And I'll check again in another hour. You could have fried your brain like an egg dropped into boiling oil. I've seen it happen—both the egg and the brain," Quiss said with a wry smile. "Seriously: it's not pleasant. The bones in the skull can't take the pressure buildup. Your head explodes."

Caldan swallowed and turned his ring on his finger nervously.

Yes—sounds distinctly unpleasant. He tried to push the thought from his mind, to no avail. "I was desperate." His voice sounded weak to him, small.

"So you've said. Do not do it again."

"I won't. I promise."

Quiss looked sidelong at him. "If you do, you'll most likely die."

"I promised not to—what more do you want from me?"

"Other than not leading assassins to the First Deliverer's cabin?" Another wry smile, but there was a bit more edge to it this time. "But maybe we can take some time to talk about what I saw in the camp the other day."

"What do you mean?"

"I mean, now that you're here, I have some questions about your automatons and how they work."

And there it was. The reason they'd decided to help Miranda. And possibly the reason they were so willing to accept his story about Kristof. They wanted something from him, and it had to do with his crafting. What bothered him, though, was what he could possibly know that these sorcerers didn't.

"Now, then," Quiss continued. "I'd like to go over what exactly you did to shape the destructive sorcery you used on Kristof, then discuss your automatons. We, ah, . . . can't seem to replicate what you've done." Quiss sounded embarrassed, almost annoyed.

"First, tell me about Miranda. Where is she? What are you doing to her?"

Quiss sighed.

"I'm serious—I'm not answering any of your questions until you answer mine. I played that game enough with the warlocks, and look where it got me."

"So little trust," said Quiss.

"Do you blame me?"

"I suppose not."

For some reason, Caldan felt he could at least trust that sentiment. So when Quiss continued, he tried to keep an open mind.

"We're trying to help her, as I said we would. She's had a nasty blow to the head as well. Our physikers are looking after her, the poor girl. How long has she been in such a state?"

"A few weeks," Caldan said. "There was . . . a fight."

"Coercive sorcery?"

Caldan nodded. "I didn't know what it was at the time. Just that it damaged Miranda's mind."

"That's what I feared."

"I want to be there when you try to heal her. I . . . I want to keep an eye on what goes on."

Quiss pursed his lips and frowned, looking like he was going to deny Caldan his request. Eventually, he nodded.

"All right," Quiss said. "But you won't understand much of what happens. Our sorcery is different from what you've learned your entire life."

Caldan almost snorted. He didn't believe they were so far removed. Quiss had shown him his well before, and if they had wells, then their sorcery still had to function in the same way his did. Perhaps through a different methodology, but the power of their wells had to be harnessed and shaped somehow.

He nodded, though, as if he agreed with Quiss. "When will you do it?"

"Try to heal her? Very soon. She's sleeping now, but I thought it best if I tended to you first."

"I don't need tending to. Please, can you just heal her?"

Quiss gave him a sympathetic look, then nodded. "Very well. Come with me."

"THE PATTERNS ARE the key. Each is ever changing. Some faster than others; some barely seem to move at all. They make shadows in the mind, dark and sharp. Each serves a function, the colored threads and the shadows they create. So when the threads shift, another pattern emerges: color and darkness. One the opposite of the other, yet two together, overlaid into a larger sequence."

Quiss's voice was soothing, almost hypnotic. An enclosed brazier designed for shipboard use gave off a welcome warmth, chasing the chill of the night away. The cramped cabin at the rear of the vessel had a window Quiss insisted on opening. Caldan felt suspended somehow between the comfort of the heat and the cold air's bite.

He sat cross-legged atop a blanket on a narrow bunk, his back resting against the hull. Another of Quiss's people had joined them after the sailors placed Miranda on the bunk opposite his. Unlike Quiss, the woman looked almost . . . normal. She did look denser to Caldan, but she was devoid of the half-starved look that seemed a characteristic of most of the sorcerers who followed Gazija.

The woman bent over Miranda. She was young, and her long red hair was tied in a braid. There were tiny embroidered purple flowers and blue birds scattered over her shirt and skirt. She placed a hand on Miranda's forehead, shook her head, and tsked in disapproval.

"Can you do it? Can you heal her?" asked Caldan. He didn't like the way his words came out, but he couldn't help his emotions. "I can offer ducats, but not much else."

The woman glanced at him, seemingly offended, then went back to examining Miranda.

Quiss took a blanket from the end of the bunk and covered Miranda's feet and the lower half of her body. "Oh, I think you'll find there's a lot you can offer. Quiet now. We have some serious sorcery to perform."

"Don't scare the man, Quiss," the woman said. Her voice was soft and husky. "I'm sure he's worried enough."

"My apologies, Adrienne. But he has to know this isn't without its risks. Damage caused by coercive sorcery is hard enough to fix when it was used by a skilled practitioner. When it's bungled like this, there are added complications. And it looks like someone's tried to heal her with . . . I don't know; what have they done? Made a mess of things."

Adrienne crinkled her nose. "Worse than a mess."

Caldan twisted the ring on his finger and bit his lip. "Joachim. I mean, one of the warlocks. He tried to heal her. I watched, but . . . all I saw was a jumbled mass of threads. There was no order I could see, and if I looked too long, it made me sick. He created a string of his own, a white one, and inserted it into the mess. He teased a few of the tangled threads away from others. To me, it looked like the threads became less chaotic."

"More rigid, you mean," said Adrienne. She shook her head. "Simpletons. Toying with what they don't understand."

Quiss snorted. "They're using what they've worked out so far. All sorcery starts that way. Experimentation and verification."

"A false path."

"One they don't know is false."

Adrienne gave a slight shrug of her shoulders. "They'll learn, eventually. But let's focus on this lovely young woman here. It distresses me to leave her like this. Come, Luphildern."

She knelt in front of Miranda and held a hand out to Quiss. He took it in his own and joined her, kneeling on the floor.

Caldan leaned to his right and saw they'd both closed their eyes. He fingered the crafted bell in his pocket and opened his well. A mere thought and he linked to the crafting's anchor. The colors of the cabin drained away, leaving a scene of washed-out grays. The only color came from Miranda's mind: a seething, tangled mess of roiling threads. Like it had the last time, Caldan's stomach rebelled, and he felt nauseated. The sense of wrongness was even greater than before.

Previously, he'd sensed that if he could bear to study the threads for long enough, a pattern would reveal itself. And Quiss's words confirmed his feeling. There *was* a complex arrangement in front of him; he just couldn't discern it yet. Caldan steeled himself and pushed away his queasiness. He hugged his knees to his chest, rocking back and forth. And waited.

As with Joachim's attempt, there was a movement at the edge of Miranda's mind. Two threads. Not white, but multicolored, like fish scales shining in the sun. Not altogether unlike the improved shield he was able to generate. Multicolored meant multiple threads from a well, at least three or four. He couldn't tell, and he didn't want to brush across Quiss's and Adrienne's wells to find out, for fear of disturbing their concentration.

Their threads were far thinner than Joachim's had been. They were delicate, and Caldan wondered how they'd be able to tease apart the tangled mess if they weren't strong enough. But Adrienne had said that wasn't the right way.

So what were these sorcerers going to do?

There was further movement, and two more multicolored threads joined the first. Then two more. Caldan pursed his lips and sucked in a breath as another two appeared for a total of eight. That had to be twelve strings at a minimum for each sorcerer, but could be much more—a feat they managed with what looked like relative ease. On that side of Miranda's mind, her colored threads twitched slightly, and the gap between them and the intruding threads grew minutely. It was as if they were repelled, like iron was from certain types of lodestones.

The multicolored threads moved together, weaving in and out and around each other. As Caldan watched, they formed patterns, almost like crafting runes, shapes he could nearly identify but not quite. Two threads formed an outline, until there were four configurations. Then the four came together, joining into a vastly more complex pattern, a weave of threads.

Caldan held his breath. For long moments, he sat there, waiting.

Then two more of the coercive sorcery threads appeared on the other side of Miranda's mind. Again, two became four. Then six. Then eight.

Caldan suppressed a groan. *Twenty-four strings*, he guessed. *At least. Each* of them.

The immense power and control shown by these sorcerers astounded him.

"Who are you people?" he muttered in wonderment, but Quiss and Adrienne remained silent and unmoving, engrossed in their work.

For the second time, the sorcerers guided their threads into an intricate pattern, identical to the first. And again, the coercive sorcery damaging Miranda's mind retreated. Now those threads took up half the space they had before. The roiling tangle in the center became even more chaotic and agitated.

As he watched, their two patterns stretched, elongating, until they formed hemispheres almost totally encasing Miranda's mind. Two of the edges touched, emitting a spark of energy, which quickly fizzled away to nothing. The joining grew, infinitesimally at first, then with increasing rapidity. Soon both patterns had merged into one multicolored sphere. Pulsing in the center was Bells's coercive sorcery, compressed even further into a tight ball as it pulled in on itself, away from the sphere.

Runes and patterns of pure energy. In one, Caldan thought he could discern an anchor; the shaping was foreign to him, but it would serve the same purpose. What interested him more than that, though, was that this was sorcery without a material crafting to weather the corrosive forces of the well. The similarities with what he'd divined of the warlocks' destructive sorcery didn't escape him.

The similarities to what he had done to Kristof startled him.

In this case, Quiss and Adrienne were creating a crafting *inside* Miranda's head, a place where they couldn't use a physical object. Yet, somehow, they seemed sure it would not destroy her mind, the way Quiss had warned Caldan his own attempts might.

He worried anyway.

The ball began to shrink, and as it did, the tangle of coercive sorcery compressed further.

Miranda moaned. Caldan drew his attention away from what the sorcerers were doing for a moment as Miranda's body twitched underneath the blanket. Her hands reached up to clutch at her head, twisting her hair.

"Don't move," Quiss whispered.

Caldan realized he'd leaned forward, and his hands were on the edge of the bunk. He'd been about to leap to Miranda's aid. He struggled with himself for what seemed like an eternity before heeding Quiss's command. He forced himself to lean back against the hull.

Miranda screeched. Her back arched, and the blanket was flung from her body.

"Don't!" barked Quiss.

"I . . ." Caldan swallowed as he once again moved to help her.

He clenched his fists, then slammed one into the wooden hull beside him. The pain didn't help, and besides, he had to remain still, lest he break the sorcerers' concentration. One misstep might shred her mind beyond repair.

Ancestors, give me strength . . .

Caldan forced his gaze away from Miranda, who was now lying still but emitting a faint keening sound from her slightly parted lips. He closed his eyes and compelled himself to concentrate his senses on the coercive sorcery being performed.

He regained his perspective and saw that the sphere had shrunk even further. But its effect on the coercive tangle had faded. It was as if the sorcery in Miranda's mind couldn't compress any more. The web of multicolored threads surrounding it drew closer . . .

There was a flash.

Caldan frowned. What had just happened?

Then another.

Something had moved from Bells's sorcery across to Quiss and Adrienne's.

Knowing what to look for now, he could see the next movement with more clarity. The arrangement of the sphere was changing. They were trying to match the pattern of the damaging sorcery. And when they managed to do so, one of the harmful threads was sucked out, as if drawn to the other pattern. When they matched, the sorceries didn't repel each other, they attracted.

One by one, Quiss and Adrienne were dismantling the tangled remnants of the coercive sorcery.

Caldan couldn't be sure how long it took. An hour? Longer? All he knew was that he couldn't look away. He could see Miranda's consciousness reorganizing itself as the knot in her mind was removed, little by little. There were breaks, pauses in what the sorcerers were doing. He couldn't work out why, but after each, Miranda's mind regained more of a sense of normalcy. Perhaps they were allowing it to reclaim itself, to restructure back to familiarity.

Caldan willed himself not to hope, but he knew it was wasted energy.

Finally, the last of the colored threads joined with a multicolored string and disappeared. The sphere expanded to its original size, then, before Caldan could blink, it dissolved. Threads vanished as Quiss and Adrienne closed their wells.

Miranda's mind was clear of any influence.

Adrienne groaned and levered herself to her feet. Quiss wiped his face, which was beaded with sweat, and rubbed the back of his neck. He rose, stumbling slightly, and met Caldan's eyes.

"She'll sleep for a time," Quiss said. "We did what we could. She should recover almost fully."

"Almost fully? What do you mean? I thought you cleared it all out."

"That we did. But it's not so simple," replied Adrienne. "Her mind will need time to sort itself out. It's spent a long time in a confused state. Some things, well, she may not remember. She will be unsteady on her feet for a while as well. You should stay here with her. If she wakes in the dark, not knowing where she is, she'll be frightened."

"Is that it, though? Just some confusion and disorientation."

"We can hope," she said.

"But—"

Quiss stepped to the door. "We'll send some food and water. Perhaps some wine as well? You look like you need it."

"Yes. Thank you. And thank you for healing Miranda. We're . . . in your debt." The words tumbled out of him, and he meant them. If Miranda was healed, there wasn't much he wouldn't do for these people.

Quiss smiled, not smugly, but with an expression tinged with sorrow. "We know."

Without another word, Quiss and Adrienne left the cabin, closing the door behind them.

Miranda's struggles had pushed the blanket lower, and it bunched around her knees. Caldan rearranged it to cover her up to her neck and closed the window. The air had turned even chillier, and the brazier was now struggling to hold the cold at bay.

He found himself kneeling beside Miranda. He brushed her hair over her ear and listened to her breathing. For the first time since Anasoma, she looked peaceful.

Caldan's eyes burned, and he wiped at them. The pressing weight he'd carried since Miranda was injured left him. It felt like he was released. A heaviness so great he'd become used to carrying it just vanished. His whole body shuddered at the sensation.

He shook his head despairingly. He hadn't realized how Miranda's condition had clouded his judgment. Looking back at the decisions he'd made since fleeing Anasoma, he knew there were some bad ones. Compromises and resolutions that now seemed flawed or downright stupid.

Things you would only do . . . for someone you loved.

He stood and tucked the blanket in. Miranda stirred, but she didn't wake.

Positioning himself back on his bunk, he contemplated his next move. Now that he could stop worrying about Miranda, it was time to look after himself. The problem was that he was in the middle of a war. Jukari and vormag on one side, the Indryallans on another, with the emperor's forces in the middle. And somewhere, seemingly lurking about the periphery, were Gazija and his people.

And, of course, there were the warlocks. Now that he'd killed Kristof, there would certainly be repercussions.

Because Devenish wouldn't let this slide . . .

CHAPTER 15

*P*link.

Another drop of water fell from the ceiling onto the floor.

Plink.

They were dripping from somewhere, and Vasile watched them fall. He'd lost count of how many somewhere after three hundred. His eyes hurt from following the droplets, and he massaged the back of his aching neck with one hand, grunting with pleasure.

By the ancestors, he needed a drink. And chicken poached in spiced cream, accompanied by an onion tart, finished with glazed strawberries and a piping-hot custard flavored with vanilla and toffee. Vasile's stomach rumbled at the thought.

There'd been no sign of anyone coming to release them. Their jailers had come and gone. And after a particularly spiteful visit yesterday, even Caitlyn had left them alone. Their cell had no window to the outside. Time was measured in sloppy meals, the jailers' shifts, and bowel movements.

Vasile stretched his back, grunting at the soreness that had crept in.

"Thank you for leaping to my defense with Caitlyn," Aidan said wryly.

"What did you want me to do? She's crazy. They both are."

"Yes. She's been driven mad, poor woman. But I put a crossbow bolt in her. The building was on fire. And they told me she was dead . . ."

He doesn't want to face Caitlyn. He's still haunted by what he did to her. "'Poor woman'?" said Vasile. "You've taken leave of your senses as well. What about us?"

"I knew her before all of this. When she was determined and idealistic."

Vasile's hands gripped Aidan's shoulders. Aidan's eyes were crinkled with concern, and his mouth was drawn into a tight line.

"What she was," Vasile said, "what caused her to begin her crusade against injustice and evil . . . that woman is long gone. I've seen it before, in my time as a magistrate. People start out with the best of intentions, and somehow, somewhere along the way, they make a choice that starts them down a different path. Then they make another bad choice, and so it goes. Soon they find they're stuck in a situation they can't see a way out of, wholly of their own making."

"It shouldn't have happened to her," said Aidan. "She was stronger than that."

"Maybe that's all she showed you. People can put on a decent front, but inside they can still be broken. You don't know her innermost thoughts. Everyone has demons."

"That's all too true. As I've seen. Some demons are worse than others. Maybe I was wrong to shoot her. What if I was the one who was deceived?"

"I don't believe that," Vasile said. "And all the wishing you do won't change a thing. You can't alter the past."

Aidan pushed Vasile's hands off him and stood. He brushed down his pants and shirt, failing to remove most of the grime that had accumulated over their stay in the cell so far, and not doing much to iron out the creases either.

"No," said Aidan. "But I can change the future. We need to get out of this cell and deal with Caitlyn."

"Be careful. You don't want to travel down the same dark path she did."

MADNESS SHONE FROM Caitlyn's eyes. Where, before Aidan shot her, it had been a mere spark, something fleeting, seen only briefly, it was now a bonfire. Droplets of spit flew from her mouth as she screamed, her expression twisted with hatred.

"Was it gold? What was it? Did they promise you power?"

Sitting on the floor with his back against the cold stone wall, Aidan shook his head. He rubbed his eyes. A tired ache was creeping into his mind from the constant battering of Caitlyn's words. This was the third time today she'd come to see him, each time trailed by cel Rau. And all she did was yell and accuse him of succumbing to evil, no matter how much he protested the opposite. Their jailer accepted a few ducats from her when she came and kept to himself, sitting on a low stool out of the way. So intent was Caitlyn, she failed to notice the man roll his eyes at some of her worse haranguing—but cel Rau did. His penetrating gaze missed nothing, and Vasile paled when the swordsman glared at him.

As usual when Caitlyn had appeared, Vasile edged to the back of their cell and tried becoming a statue.

"You were dead," said Aidan. "I killed you. I was told you were dead."

"They were simply following my orders. I told them to tell you I was dead. If you thought I was alive, you might have come back to finish the job. See, I still commanded their loyalty, whatever you may have thought. Not everyone's a turncoat. Not everyone succumbs to evil. And for your betrayal, I'll see you hang, you bastard."

Caitlyn's words struck home and stirred something inside Aidan. If he didn't do something, and soon, she could very well be right. He'd be swinging from a rope like a ham in a butcher's shop.

"It was you," he said.

"What was that? Confess, and I'll make sure they're lenient with you. A swift death."

"It was you," Aidan repeated, this time louder. Strength began to return to his limbs at the thought of doing something, anything, in response to Caitlyn's accusations and badgering. "Your actions turned me from the path you were following."

Caitlyn sneered at him. "Lies and more lies. Was anything you ever said to me the truth?"

"You lost your way," Aidan continued, voice rising. "The evil we confronted, that you saw so much more of . . . it twisted you. In the beginning, I noticed small things . . . roughing up a farmer to get information. It made me uneasy, but I thought no harm was done. No lasting harm. And we got what we wanted. A tiny discomfort weighed against the return. Easily justified, though with some misgivings and missed sleep. But as time went on, you became worse and worse. Torture, Caitlyn? Of people who were innocent?"

Caitlyn glanced at Vasile. "There are no innocents—"

"Yes, yes, there are. Your moral compass has failed you. It did a long time ago. I just couldn't see it. Our cause, and what we accomplished, blinded me too much."

"The sickness of evil can't be treated; it has to be cut out."

"Not along with those unwittingly caught up in it. Those with no choice in the matter."

"Wheat from the chaff, Aidan. You know that."

Aidan sighed wearily. "Not everyone is as strong as you. Or me. These are ordinary people who only wish to be left alone, to live as peacefully as they can."

"Left alone to help jukari or vormag?"

"For the safety of their families. Their wives. Their children. Sometimes you have to surrender in order to protect those most dear to you."

"I would never surrender to evil."

And Aidan realized she was right. She would never bend. Never compromise. Never consider that the ends sometimes didn't justify the means. Anything was on the table, no matter the wreckage left in her wake. It was why he'd had to kill her. Almost kill her . . .

It was why he had to finish the task.

"Leave me," Aidan demanded.

"I'll go when I'm—"

"Get out!" Aidan shouted. "I'll not going to listen to your demented raving any longer! Leave us be."

She backed away a step. "Tomorrow, it's all over for you, Aidan. Tomorrow." Caitlyn turned her back on him, slowly, a deliberate gesture, then left the cell.

Leaving them alone with cel Rau.

Far from relieved, the magistrate pressed his back against the wall and wrung his hands in front of him.

"Aidan," said cel Rau.

Aidan's heart thumped in his chest as he steeled himself for a fight. "I suppose you've thrown your lot in with Caitlyn," he said. "What do you want?"

"Cel Rau," Vasile said desperately. "Get us out of here! Caitlyn . . . whatever she once was to you . . . she isn't sane!"

Cel Rau glanced at Vasile, then away, as if dismissing him, then turned a cool look on Aidan. "Caitlyn hasn't been able to bring herself to say this, but the emperor needs her, and you."

Aidan could scarcely believe his ears. "Then it's all an act?"

"No act. She's a staunch opponent of evil. As am I. As should we all be."

"Ancestors," whispered Vasile.

"You've been thrown a lifeline. Join with Caitlyn and redeem yourself. We will hunt evil again. And we will be victorious. You weren't hard enough to survive the corruption she fought," said the swordsman with a slight shake of his head. "The weak fall by the wayside. Only the strong can bear witness to the frailties in men's hearts and endure."

Ancestors, thought Aidan, echoing Vasile. Were they *all* mad? No. Cel Rau was driven, perhaps more so than Caitlyn in some ways. "What are the terms?"

Cel Rau rolled his shoulders as if to loosen them. "Join with Caitlyn again. Return to what we were before. She has the emperor's favor, and he is our shining light against the darkness."

A *trifle melodramatic,* thought Aidan. But cel Rau was deadly serious. "And if I don't?"

Cel Rau shrugged. "Then you die tomorrow. And Vasile with you."

"He has nothing to do with this!"

"The emperor has decreed your fate. If you want to live, then you'll see the error of your ways." Cel Rau left them then, closing and locking the cell door behind him.

"He was lying," Vasile said. "Only, I'm not sure about what. Not without asking closed questions."

"I know, Vasile. I don't need you to tell me that."

"What should we do? I don't know anyone who could help us."

"The emperor is here," Aidan said. "That's why Gazija sent you with us. Weren't you supposed to obtain an audience with him and use your ability to convince him of the danger, and that Gazija could be trusted?"

"That plan fell apart the moment we started running from the jukari horde. We were too late to warn anyone. And cel Rau just said Caitlyn has the emperor's favor. No, that avenue is closed to us."

"And even if we manage to escape," said Aidan, "she won't give up. She'll keep coming after me. And you for aiding me. I'll have to figure out a way to deal with her once we're out of here. I need my neck intact to do it. So we lie. We lie, and live for another day."

He ignored Vasile's raised eyebrow at the irony.

WHEN CAITLYN VISITED again, Aidan bowed on bended knee to her. Words tumbled from his lips, hardly heard by Vasile over the roaring in his ears. As usual, cel Rau lurked behind Caitlyn like her shadow. This time, he carried Aidan's sword along with their other gear, as if there were no question Aidan would decide to join them.

This is not right, thought Vasile. But it needed to be done.

Caitlyn beamed at Aidan as lies flowed from his lips.

Vasile saw a good man bend before a monster, and a great man rise.

CHAPTER 16

Caldan roused himself from the bunk, where he'd tried in vain to find some semblance of sleep during the night. He checked on Miranda for what felt like the hundredth time and found her still sleeping peacefully, the corners of her lips turned up slightly, as if there were a smile on her face.

Ancestors, let her dreams be good ones.

Through the window, the river was shrouded in mist, a white cloud hovering above the water, barely lit by the dawn light. Smaller boats plowed through the fog, fishermen beginning their day, along with merchants and traders both coming and going from Riversedge. They moved slowly, careful to navigate the busy river in its hazardous state. The jukari rarely ventured near the water.

A knock sounded, startling Caldan. Miranda stirred but didn't wake. He opened the door to reveal Quiss, with a cloth-covered tray in one hand and a steaming jug in the other. Caldan caught scents of honey, fish, and eggs, along with coffee. The sorcerer lifted both up and looked at him expectantly.

"May I come in?"

"Oh. Yes, of course."

Caldan stepped away from the door, and Quiss deposited the tray on the end of the empty bunk, and the jug of coffee on a narrow shelf above it.

"How is she? I'm surprised she hasn't woken yet."

"Should she have?" asked Caldan with a tinge of worry. "Is something wrong?"

"She's fine. But we should try and have her eat and drink as soon as she can. She's lost a lot of weight and will need to regain her strength. There's—"

Miranda let out a yawn and opened her eyes. As Caldan moved to her side, she yawned again and rubbed her face.

"Caldan," she croaked. "Ow . . . my throat hurts. Where are we?" She smiled at Caldan, showing dimples in her cheeks.

A lump rose in Caldan's throat. After weeks spent with Miranda's slack-faced expressions, he'd forgotten how she looked.

Alive. She looks alive.

And beautiful.

She reached out a hand, and Caldan took it in his. "I feel like I haven't seen you in ages. But . . . Anasoma. We were running. It was only yesterday. What happened?"

Quiss cleared his throat. "Pardon me, Miranda, but your questions can wait for a few minutes. There's a bowl of porridge and stewed apples here for you. You should eat it while it's hot."

Miranda frowned, and Caldan almost sobbed out loud with relief. Just to see her conscious and talking again, to see her smile and frown . . . He backed away a few steps and sank onto the bunk where he'd spent the night, his legs weak.

"Sir Quiss? What are you doing here? And, Caldan, what's wrong? There's something you're not telling me."

Quiss turned to the tray on the bunk. "Caldan, why don't you help Miranda sit up? Then she can eat." He removed the cloth covering the tray and turned toward them, a green-glazed bowl in one hand.

Once Miranda was sitting up, Quiss made sure she ate half the contents of the bowl before he allowed either of them to speak, stifling any attempts at talk with stern looks.

"Enough," Miranda said, refusing the next spoon and holding up her hand. "I'm sorry. I feel so weak, I don't know what's come over me. And I can't finish the bowl!" Her expression grew troubled.

"That's fine," replied Quiss. He returned the glazed dish to the tray and brought Miranda a wooden mug. "No coffee for you, I'm afraid. You need to drink all of this. It'll help you recover."

Miranda eyed the drink suspiciously. "What's in it? And I think it's about time you told me what's going on."

Quiss nodded to Caldan. "I'll leave Caldan to explain. I'll come back soon with more food. In the meantime, please drink. I promise—it's something your body needs."

"Fine. But no more mush! I'll want something heartier. Meat and eggs, and some bread, if you have any."

"As you wish, young miss." Quiss quietly exited and closed the door behind him.

Miranda turned penetrating green eyes on Caldan. "What's going on? Your hair . . . it's grown. But that's impossible." She frowned, confused. "It's brown, by the way, in case you didn't know."

Caldan swallowed. He had no idea how to tell her about her condition and all that had happened since they'd fled Anasoma. But what he did know was that he wasn't going to keep the truth from her any longer. He didn't want to keep secrets between them. She deserved to know everything, not only because of what she'd suffered, but because . . . he realized she meant a great deal to him. He didn't want to be the cause of any hurt she felt.

He nudged her over to make room and sat on the bunk next to her. She placed an arm around his shoulders, and he could feel it trembling. Whether from weakness or emotion, he couldn't tell.

"This bunk's too small for both of us," Miranda said. "But don't leave me. I'm . . . scared." She tilted her head and rested it on his arm. Her long dark hair felt like silk on his skin.

"What's the last thing you remember?"

Miranda yawned again and wrinkled her nose. "I'm so tired," she murmured.

"I know. Here," he said, handing her the cup. "Drink."

She did, grimacing at the taste.

"Now . . . try to remember."

"Right. We were in the tunnels under Anasoma. There was a ladder and . . . after that it's all blank."

Caldan sighed, not sure how she'd react to what he was about to say. "All right. Here's what's happened since then . . ."

MIRANDA WAS ASLEEP again, hair spilling across the blanket and down the side of the bunk. Caldan pulled up the blanket to just under her chin to make sure she was warm. He then let her be and helped himself to what food was left on the tray. He wolfed down spiced eggs, mushrooms fried in butter and herbs, and three fish of some sort, the length of his hand, stuffed with greens and diced chicken, floured and fried to leave a crispy outside. After wiping greasy hands on the cloth, he drained the jug of the now-cold coffee, leaving only brown sediment at the bottom. Lack of sleep, combined with not having fully recovered from the use of destructive sorcery, was making him slightly dizzy.

A quick glance out the window told him the sun was high in the sky and the fog had burned off. Traffic on the river had lessened to a few lone boats paddling to their destinations.

There was still so much he had to do, but he was reluctant to leave Miranda on board alone. First, he had to talk with Quiss. Then Caldan had to scout the area around where he'd hidden the bone trinket. If it was clear of jukari, he had to take a chance and retrieve it. It had seemed like a good hiding place at the time, but now he wasn't so sure. The vormag were an unknown quantity, as were the warlocks. And now, with Quiss and his people in the mix, it was getting downright crowded around here. He worried, too, whether any of them could sense trinkets or craftings somehow. They could wander past, and he'd lose the bone ring forever, and with it, one of only two ties to his parents. And even though it was the only nonmetallic trinket he'd ever heard about, and was most likely worth a startlingly large sum, its value to him was far beyond its worth in ducats.

Finally, he still had to figure out what to do about Devenish, who would almost certainly come looking for him, seeing how Kristof had never returned and Gazija was very much alive.

Well—there was no putting things off. Better to face what was to come.

Quiss had sent someone to retrieve his belongings from his lodging in Riversedge yesterday, and Caldan grabbed the satchel. Nothing was missing, though the Bleeder Mahsonn's craftings were virtually useless to him, as was the trinket ring he'd found hidden in Joachim's residence. He made his way along narrow passageways, carefully retracing his steps from last night when Miranda had been carried to their cabin. Eventually he found his way onto the deck.

Apart from the sailors, there were a number of slender men and women about, dressed in a motley assortment of clothes. A short woman wore a mismatched yellow skirt and red shirt and examined what looked to be a dried lizard on a stick. Another man, dressed in brown woolen trousers and coat, stared at the sun, passing his hand back and forth across his eyes, shading them for a moment each time. Caldan decided against approaching the odd ones and headed for the gunwale. He stared into the murky river.

There was something about the woman and man . . . Caldan extended his senses and pulled back in shock. They were both sorcerers—he could feel their undisguised power—but . . . they had no wells. *Impossible* was Caldan's first thought, but he couldn't discount what he'd just felt. Quiss had a well; Caldan had sensed it before . . . or had he? Perhaps that was also a disguise. With the evidence right before him, though, how could he sense that they were sorcerers? And then something Kristof said came back to him:

Gazija and his ilk are an abomination. I can see they are, as I know you can. They're not natural.

Which meant Kristof had been able to see their denseness, too.

Caldan had always thought the way Quiss and the others appeared denser was somehow sorcerous in nature, but . . . there was another possibility that was starting to feel truer and truer: that the way he saw them was one of the abilities his Touched blood bequeathed to him.

"Caldan? Caldan, there you are."

Quiss hurried over to him. "I was trying to find out where you were." He took Caldan by the arm and led him away. "I went to see you and check on Miranda, and I discovered you'd gone. Come. Follow me belowdecks. There's someone I want you to meet. We've some questions for you. And a proposal."

Intrigued, though reluctant to leave the fresh air on deck, Caldan accompanied Quiss, and they once more entered the muggy gloom of the ship. Having been on only one other ship before, the *Loretta*, he could at least determine that they were heading for the captain's cabin situated at the rear. But somehow, Caldan suspected they wouldn't be meeting the captain.

They reached a varnished oak door, and Quiss stopped, knocking gently on the wood. Without waiting for a response, he entered, gesturing for Caldan to follow him inside.

The cabin was furnished much as Captain Charlotte's had been, with a desk full of maps held down with odds and ends, bound chests along one wall, and a luxurious bunk twice the width of the one he'd spent the night in. Wide windows let in copious amounts of light, and sitting in a chair in the sunlight was the sorcerer Gazija. The room had a sickly sweet scent, which Caldan traced to incense burning on a shelf.

This close, Gazija looked even more wizened than he had on the wharf the other day. Pale, liver-spotted hands held a piece of paper, and sunken eyes squinted at the writing. His skin was so thin it was translucent, and Caldan could make out the veins underneath.

Gazija turned to meet his gaze. Caldan found himself squirming and resisted the urge to leave, forcing himself to remain still. It was as if Gazija weighed every action he'd taken in his life with one look.

And found him wanting.

He tore his eyes away, and Gazija grunted.

"So this is the same man?" the old sorcerer asked Quiss, unimpressed.

"Yes. His crafting—"

Gazija cut Quiss off with a sharp gesture. "I'll ask the questions, and find out for myself." He folded the letter and placed it on the desk, then tapped his fingers on the paper, as if still considering its contents.

Caldan brought his eyes back up to old man's, not quite sure what to make of him. Gazija had used sorcery to drain the heat out of the very air, a display of power unheard of since the Shattering. Then he'd bested Devenish in some sort of coercive sorcery duel. More than bested; he'd made the warlock look like a child in comparison. No mean feat, and a deliberate one at that.

"What do you want?" Caldan asked hesitantly. "And why?"

Gazija barked a laugh. "No thanks for saving your fair maiden?"

Blood rushed to Caldan's face, and he looked down and away. "I meant no offense. I'm truly grateful. Without Quiss and Adrienne . . . I fear Miranda wouldn't have recovered."

"She wouldn't have, if you'd let the warlocks try to heal her," Gazija said. "They would have messed her up worse than they already did. But you did what was right for her. And that's my first question for you. Why?"

Caldan felt heat rise to his face and was suddenly self-conscious. "You mean, do I love her?"

"Ha! No. I've no interest in that. Why didn't you trust the warlocks to heal her?"

"I *did* ask them—or one of them. A warlock named Joachim. He was one of the most powerful sorcerers I'd ever met . . . and he clearly wasn't able to help her. I was still planning on asking other warlocks because I had no choice. But—"

"But what? Because you clearly lost faith in your own people?"

"What do you mean?"

"You're part of them, aren't you? Bound to them somehow?"

"No. I was an apprentice in the Protectors. Nothing more. For now."

"For now," echoed Gazija. "What are you to the warlocks, then?"

Caldan's thoughts returned to the bone ring. He had to keep his cards close to his chest. Although these people had healed Miranda, he wasn't about to trust them with all his secrets just yet. He had to be sure they wouldn't attempt to use him as well. "My parents, and possibly my grandparents, were linked to them. They left the emperor's service, though, and I was hoping to figure out why. As you can see, I have some sorcerous talent, and the warlocks want to keep me around, especially after I proved myself a few times against the jukari. I'm a tool to them, nothing more."

Nothing but a tool . . . and blood. While Caldan might be useful to Gazija, there was no telling how they would react to his being Touched.

"And so we begin to find the truth," Gazija said. "Quiss here tells me you have a bug you crafted. Do you have it here?"

"It's a beetle. And I do," said Caldan, reaching into his pocket.

He brought out his smith-crafted beetle and held it up between thumb and index finger. Gazija opened his hand, and Caldan passed him the crafting. If this was all they wanted in return for saving Miranda, then they could take it, with his blessing.

The old sorcerer ran his fingers over the rune-covered carapace and grunted. "A hard ink of some sort," he remarked. "Not the best method, wouldn't you agree?"

Caldan nodded. "It was all I had time for, and under the circumstances, I think I did quite well." For some reason, he felt the need to defend himself. Almost as if the old man were another master in the Sorcerers' Guild, and he was applying to become an apprentice. As the thought crossed his mind, Caldan realized that, while they weren't interviewing him for a position, they were very interested in his automaton, and he could also learn a great deal from them—if they were willing.

Gazija's expression turned to puzzlement. He poked at the beetle with a finger and lifted up one of the wings. "The metal parts—legs and wings—they can already move on their own, can't they? They just . . . don't have anything powering them yet."

"Until a sorcerer links with the beetle and operates the parts, no."

"So you've fused a mechanical creation with sorcery. In quite an ingenious way, I would add." Gazija glanced at Quiss. "And one we hadn't considered."

Caldan didn't sense anything, but the runes covering his beetle flashed, and it turned a quarter of a circle on Gazija's palm, gears and mechanisms whirring. Its wings flapped, once, twice, three times.

Gazija brought a hand to his lips and coughed until his frame shook with the effort. Quiss took a step toward the old man, then stopped, as if he thought whatever help he could offer would be rejected.

Once the coughing ceased, Gazija closed his eyes for a few moments before passing a trembling hand over his face.

"Gazija . . ." began Quiss.

"Not now!" barked Gazija.

His outburst brought on a fresh wave of coughing. Quiss moved to a side table and brought a mug to Gazija, who managed a few sips in between coughs until they calmed down. When they did, Gazija pushed Quiss away.

"Stop fussing over me. I'll be fine."

Veins throbbed in Quiss's neck, and his fists clenched. Eventually he nodded. "As you wish."

Gazija settled back in his chair. "So, Caldan, what does this bug of yours do?"

"Beetle," Caldan corrected again. "It's a simple design, so I guess the answer to your question is—not much. A sorcerer can see through its eyes, hear through the runes on the side."

"Yes, yes. Three of these . . . strings, as you call them, for the legs, sight, and hearing. And another two for the wings and a rather primitive shield. But what can you do with it?"

Caldan shrugged. "Scout an advance position? Watch your back? Spy, if the construct was small enough. I was going to test more options with others I craft in the future. I was able to use this one against the jukari and vormag, though. To drop sorcerous crafted globes near them and . . . overload the craftings."

Gazija grunted disapprovingly and shook his head. "Crude. But effective against those who aren't proficient in sorcery."

Caldan gave a slight smile. "Like I said, I have some ideas that I'll be exploring in the future."

Gazija gave him a strange look, then cackled. "I'd wager you do. You're a canny one. You saw the warlocks in action, then, against the Indryallan sorcerer? They must have been surprised."

There was an undercurrent of amusement in his tone that struck Caldan the wrong way. "You shouldn't sound pleased about it. Hundreds of people died."

"Oh, I know that, young man. But the warlocks were walking around with their eyes closed, as was your emperor. Now their eyes are wide open to the threat they face . . . and yet they aren't. They are still too sure of themselves. Secure in the power they've held for centuries."

Quiss's feet shuffled nervously beside him, and the hairs on the back of Caldan's neck stood on end. Gazija was too pleased with what had happened. And then he and the mercenary companies he controlled had arrived, just in time to turn the tide against the jukari and vormag.

Like Devenish had said, suspiciously good timing.

Careful, Caldan admonished himself. *Don't jump at shadows.* But they wouldn't be the first to use such a ruthless strategy. The book *Betrayers and Betrayals* by Caedmin Martorel was full of detailed instances of misleading and dishonesty across the ages. And many a Dominion game played with four or more players was won by the person with the greatest talent for deception.

He didn't think Gazija was such a pitiless man, someone who would sacrifice others to achieve his goals. But he couldn't ignore coincidences, either.

Caldan kept his face purposefully blank. If they wanted his beetle, they could have it. A few gold ducats' worth of materials was a small price to pay to see Miranda whole again.

And then maybe he could be done with these strange people forever.

"There are two more linking runes," Caldan said, breaking the silence that had formed. "I was going to add other functions, once I was able to hold that many strings."

Gazija gave him a penetrating stare. "Such as? Destructive or coercive sorcery, no doubt."

"No. Perhaps a mechanism of some sort, so it could move on its own without having to be constantly controlled. If I had time to experiment, I think I'd be able to craft one that could perform small tasks on its own."

"No doubt that's possible. But it's the potential for other things that interests us."

Other things? wondered Caldan. "Like what?"

Gazija waved away his question. "Nothing to concern you. But these runes, they're far too fragile. And so are the bug's wings and legs. And its body. It's hollow."

"The clockmaker I bought the parts from was used to making birds and other animals that moved on their own, using purely mechanical means, though. Most of the parts for the beetle were scavenged from other projects. They don't waste materials, if they can help it. And if I had time, I'd use a different method for the shaping runes. Etching or casting, probably. Filigree would be too fiddly."

"The runes are useless. One scratch or a chip, and the pattern would be broken."

Caldan bit back his frustration, seeing how he had just answered that. "Yes. But as I said, it was all I could do at the time. It's only an experiment."

Gazija nodded, almost as if he expected Caldan's response. "You have another in your satchel."

The flat confidence in Gazija's voice made it certain he knew. Maybe Quiss had searched his bag before turning it over. But for some reason, he felt like the old man had probably sensed the linking runes when he'd toyed with Caldan's beetle. Caldan knew, having seen Gazija's power on display, such a talent would be nothing to him.

Caldan placed his satchel on the floor. He reached into it and drew out his man-shaped metal doll. It was as tall as the length from his elbow to his wrist. Like the beetle, its brass surface was covered with hardened ink runes. Two tiny garnet eyes stood out from an otherwise featureless face.

"I didn't have much of a plan for this crafting," explained Caldan. "I kept adding linking runes. It just felt right. It can't fly like my beetle, obviously, but you can see and hear through it. It does have a better shield, too; one with multiple linking runes and anchors. The truth is . . . I'm not sure where I was going with all of these. They're more of a hobby than anything. I started out with paper folded into the shape I wanted, and then progressed to harder materials."

"Give it to me. Please."

Gazija held the beetle out, and Caldan swapped it for the small figure.

"Ten linking runes?" queried Gazija, raising an eyebrow. "How many can you handle now?"

Caldan kept his eyes on the beetle in his hand. "I'm not sure. When I'm relaxed and in control, maybe six. But . . ." he trailed off.

"But under pressure, a lot more," finished Gazija.

"When I don't think about them, it just happens. Outside Riversedge, with the jukari, I must have held on to ten at once. I didn't have time to think. I had to act, or I'd most likely be dead."

Gazija grunted.

"What do you think?" Quiss said, startling Caldan. He'd been so quiet, Caldan had almost forgotten he was there.

"It might work," replied Gazija. "But it would be a harsh existence."

Quiss wrung his hands together and shook his head. "We'll do what you want us to—"

"Some will," interrupted Gazija sadly. "Not all. As you well know."

Caldan looked from one man to the other, not understanding what they were discussing. There were tantalizing hints in what they'd said, but he couldn't quite see the pattern and reason out what was going on. He needed information. Without more clues, he was walking blind.

He had the sinking feeling that they wanted more from him than his crafting as payment for healing Miranda. He cleared his throat, and both sorcerers looked at him. Trying to look casual but feeling far from it, he wandered across the room and gazed out the window. His hands shook, and he clasped them together.

His eyes flicked to Gazija. Old and frail. Weakening with every day.

Were they only power-hungry sorcerers? The warlocks kept themselves hale and long-lived by drinking blood from the Touched; could these sorcerers be trying to make themselves immortal, too?

He'd stumbled into a mire, and one that might well suck him down to his death.

Don't be so morbid, he chastised himself. *You've found ways out of much more dire situations.*

Maybe not much more. But even if they want both craftings, what does it matter? They can do whatever they want with them after Miranda and I are gone.

"I'm grateful for what you've done for Miranda." He turned to face the two sorcerers. "I hope this crafting is enough thanks."

"It's a start," Gazija said. "But don't sell yourself—or the assets you possess—so short."

My trinkets? Does he know about the bone ring as well?

Does he know about my blood?

Gazija held up the figure, and the metallic legs and arms waved around. "This crafting is a beginning . . . I'll take this one, for now. But we also need your expertise. Show Quiss here how the crafting and the mechanical parts function together. He could figure it out on his own, but it will save time if you show him. And put him in touch with this clockmaker you mentioned."

"You're going to make more automatons? Why? For what purpose?"

"That's not for you to know. But remember, you owe us. You're bound to us now, and—"

So no—they do not trust me. Why, then, should I trust them?

"No," Caldan said firmly. "I'm tired of being pushed around, as if I were a piece on a Dominion board. I'm not bound. To you, or to anyone. I won't do anything I disagree with. Handing over my automaton repays the debt I owe you for healing Miranda, agreed?"

Gazija frowned, then glanced at Quiss. "Agreed," he said eventually. "But you're on the run from the warlocks now. You'll need our protection. You can't possibly go back, and even if you return to Riversedge, they'll likely hunt you down."

Of course he knew that, but it dawned on him that he'd never thought about the second half of the equation. The old sorcerer was right: he *was* bound to them now, any way you looked at it. "If you're offering it, I'll take it," Caldan said. "But I'll not enter servitude. If we are to do this, we must be open with each other."

"Fine—"

"And I'd like you to also teach me about destructive and coercive sorcery."

"Very well," agreed Gazija, too quickly for Caldan's liking. "But you'll find our sorcery almost incomprehensible compared with yours."

"All sorcery is the same. Anyone with the talent can do what another has done."

Gazija opened his mouth as if to speak, then paused. He smiled wryly at Caldan. "You're right." The old sorcerer reclined in his chair and closed his eyes. "Quiss, please take Caldan back to his cabin. I'm weary. I need to sleep."

Quiss motioned for Caldan to follow him, and they left Gazija alone, still clutching Caldan's smith-crafted automaton in one withered hand.

CHAPTER 17

Quiss directed Caldan to the cabin next door to Miranda's, and they positioned themselves comfortably on bunks, one on either side of the room.

"How did you shape the sorcery that killed Kristof?" asked Quiss.

"It was crude," Caldan said. "Coercive runes shaped the initial sorcery, twisting and guiding the power of my well."

"And I'm guessing it was instinctive; you did it in a desperate situation without really knowing how."

"Yes . . . and no. I'll start at the beginning." And he did . . . from the very beginning.

Caldan outlined his thoughts and experiences with destructive sorcery. First, his escape from the cell with Senira—before she'd died while under his protection. Then when he'd tried to lock the Sorcerers' Guild's door and his paper disintegrated, but the sorcery held anyway. But yes, that was while he was panicking and fearful. He'd seen Bells while she generated destructive sorcery, and the warlocks' retaliation. He'd discerned how they focused the raw, damaging force of their wells, and how they used the sorcery without a material craft-ing to take the strain. A crafting creating an invisible force immune to corrosion, which was then used to control destructive sorcery. It was . . . brilliant.

"And this time?" Quiss said. "You hadn't tried to replicate your sorcery since?"

"I didn't quite realize what I'd done at the time, back when I was escaping from Bells. I wasn't thinking clearly. I ran, and kept running. I was just trying to survive." Even now, it was hard to reconcile in his mind: coercive, shielding, and focused destructive sorcery, combined as one, with no physical crafting required.

Frowning, Quiss scratched his chin. "So would you say that you've only performed this type of sorcery under great duress? When the situation was overwhelming you? And you don't really know how you did it?"

Why was that point so important to Quiss? Caldan felt like he'd already answered the question, and yet Quiss kept pressing. Did Gazija and Quiss want him convinced this sorcery was dangerous because it really was, or because they thought it was their secret? Or were they unable to do this and wanted to find out how?

But Caldan meant what he had told Gazija: he wasn't going to operate in the dark anymore. If they wanted something from him, they could ask.

"Not really," lied Caldan. "Both times, it just happened. I couldn't think about anything but staying alive. My well was open. I had an idea of what needed doing. And . . . it was all so fast, without me knowing how I did it." But he did, and it was extremely difficult. It was all he could do to guide the forces before they burned his mind to cinders.

Quiss grunted and looked at Caldan with narrowed eyes.

Caldan uttered a nervous laugh he hoped sounded genuine. "If it happens again, it'll be because I'm about to die, so . . . it'll most likely kill me anyway, you said. I'll just have to make sure I'm never in such bad situations again, where I'm desperate enough to take that gamble."

"Easier said than done," Quiss said. "Still, don't try to replicate what you did. Not even for the purposes of experimentation. You wouldn't want Miranda to find you here, lying on the floor lifeless, would you? Your head splattered like a dropped watermelon."

"No," Caldan replied, and it took no effort to sound sincere. But it could be that, as with the number of strings sorcerers could split from their wells, a natural talent could enhance this knowledge. There could be sorcerers out there who performed this sorcery without straining themselves—everything was a possibility.

"Good. Now, about your automatons. We believe you may have a talent for this type of sorcery, one that neither Gazija nor I possess. We . . ." Quiss hesitated, seeming suddenly reticent. "We want you to augment the figure you gave Gazija."

That Gazija took as payment, you mean. "Of course."

"With coercive sorcery."

Caldan's mouth dropped open. "Coercive sorcery? What type? I mean, what do you need it to do?"

"Never you mind. We have put together some rune patterns, but they don't quite mesh. We know there's something we're missing, as we're not used to working with smith-craftings. Our sorcery sometimes fails to interact with the automaton. If you could please take a look."

Caldan's eyes narrowed. For them to have experimented already, they had to have seen his craftings. "You went through my belongings?" he said.

"Of course we did," said Quiss without a trace of guilt. He reached inside his shirt and removed a thick bundle of papers. He began laying them out on the bunk, separating them into different piles. Each page was covered with diagrams and notations in tiny script.

They must have worked nonstop on those for hours, realized Caldan. *And more than Gazija and Quiss; a few of them. This must be important to them.*

Caldan nodded as Quiss looked expectantly at him. "I'll take a look. It may be I can see what the problem is."

CHAPTER 18

Felice kept her eyes on Izak as he waved his drink in her direction. It sloshed up to the lip of the glass, and a trickle dribbled over the side.

"A shambling mound that disappears into thin air?" he said. "Or, rather, over the side of a sheer cliff? My dear Felice, what have you been drinking, and where can I get some?"

"First off, I think you've had more than enough. But I saw what I saw. It wasn't human. If I didn't know better, I would say it was a creature from the Shattering."

Izak shuddered. "At least they're confined to the Desolate Lands. But who knows what else is hidden there? Treasure hunters have come back with some wild tales. I could tell you about the time one of them—"

"Please don't. And stop drinking. This is serious business, and you need to play your part."

Izak gazed into his glass, apparently contemplating the golden liquid flecked with green particles. With a sigh, he set it down on a marble tabletop and settled back into his armchair.

Tonight, they were staying at an upmarket inn close to the center of Five Flowers. Just for the night, then they'd move. Since her capture by Savine, Felice hadn't spent more than two nights in the same place.

"You're right. I drink when I'm nervous. Or unhappy. Or happy."

"You'll need all your faculties over the next few days, so ease off. We have to see Rebecci. She has to know what this thing is; she put me onto it, after all. She's been withholding information, and I need to know everything, if I'm to get us through this."

"I still don't understand how they did that to Savine. Just sucked his mind out, like draining a bottle."

"We don't need to understand it. We just need it to work, which it has."

"I was curious." He sounded hurt.

"Then be curious about something that matters: Kelhak. He drove the Indryallans here, and they followed blindly. Most did, anyway. Those that didn't, well . . . they've been executed."

Izak looked grim. "I've heard the rumors as well. Apparently, it also took the Indryallans by surprise. Some of them are having second thoughts."

"And so they should. I don't know what's been happening outside of Anasoma, but capturing the city has to be a trap. If we can disrupt Kelhak's plans from this side, then we'll have done all we can."

"There are also rumors of Indryallan soldiers searching underneath the city. You know Anasoma was built over the ruins of a city from the Shattering?"

"I'd heard that," she said, remembering the strange assassin's words about Slag Hill. "But it's always been thought that city was long buried. And there are maps of disused tunnels, centuries old. Do you have any idea what they are looking for?"

"I don't. But maybe it's part of why they invaded Anasoma. You said yourself, it's a crazy plan to take over the city and just wait. Even as a trap."

Felice drew a sharp breath and stood from her chair. "That's . . . maybe." *Of course!* It had never made sense to her that this was solely a trap, because what about it was the trap? They had to be looking for something—searching through the old tunnels. What had the assassin said, exactly? *Before this city was another city. Ancient sorcerers created jukari here . . . among others.* "Izak, I could kiss you."

Izak grinned rakishly and stroked his goatee. "There's no need. But if you must, then—"

"They have to be looking for something specific," Felice declared. She began pacing back and forth across the thick carpet. "It's the only thing that makes sense." She snapped her fingers at Izak.

"What?"

"I want you to find out more about these rumors. Put your informants on it. I want to know how many Indryallans are searching, and where."

"I'll do my best."

"That's all I can ask." Felice nodded. "I sense we're close to something: a breakthrough. I can feel it in my gut. So are you ready?"

Izak looked longingly at the remains of his drink, then turned his gaze away and sighed. He stood and brushed down his coat. "Yes. Let's see what Rebecci has to say, now you've met with your . . . assassin."

CHAPTER 19

What about the body?"

Caldan shrugged, grimacing at the thought of Kristof's corpse. "I don't know," he said to Miranda. "But . . . I can't go back to the warlocks now. They'll kill me for what I've done, to say nothing of what the Touched would do to me."

"You can't run from both them and the warlocks for the rest of your life. They'll find you, sooner or later."

Caldan spread his hands helplessly. "I could take Kristof's body back to them—"

"And tell them Gazija killed him with destructive sorcery?"

"No. That sets them against Gazija more than they already are. I would have to tell them I did it. It was self-defense. He was trying to kill me."

Miranda grabbed his ear and tugged his head down.

"Ow!" Caldan said.

"You idiot!" she exclaimed. "You can't go back to the warlocks or the Touched. We've thrown our lot in with Gazija and his people, for better or for worse."

Caldan reached up and pried her fingers off. His ear throbbed, and he rubbed it gently. She was rapidly returning to her usual self. "Then what should we do?"

Miranda smiled briefly. "'We.' I like the sound of that. You thought the warlocks could help me, but that's no longer an issue. I'm fine now, thanks to Quiss. The Touched can be ignored. The warlocks have total control of them. You need to focus on the warlocks."

Caldan nodded. Miranda was right. The warlocks, and the emperor, were the real issues. Caldan moved to sit closer to her, and she rested her cheek against his chest. His arms wrapped around her, and he started to stroke her hair.

"It'll be all right," he said, scarcely believing the words himself. "I've come a long way since Anasoma. My sorcery is more powerful, and I'm more adept. I'm no longer that naive young man aboard your ship," he said, and looking down he could see a small smile on her face. "I can learn from Quiss and Gazija, if they're willing to teach me. It may be that the warlocks won't be able to touch me."

"You don't really believe that, do you?"

"I have to. I can't just give up. There's a way out of all this. We just have to find it." Caldan squeezed Miranda tighter in his embrace.

"Careful," she exclaimed. "You're squashing me."

"Sorry." He wasn't sorry at all. "Kristof and Devenish didn't part on the best of terms. There was tension in the air. I gather they'd had words about Kristof retiring for some time. I wonder if I could use that somehow . . ."

Miranda dug a knuckle into his ribs. "The warlocks, remember? They're who we need to focus on."

"Devenish . . . I have to assume all the warlocks . . . are immoral. What they are doing is a perversion. They have to be stopped."

Against his chest, Miranda stirred. She lifted a hand and then thumped him with it, *hard*.

"That's not what I mean. I'm not saying you need to go after the warlocks. Just figure out a way to keep them from coming after you. You can't take on every wrong you see."

"Someone has to do something."

"And the Indryallans?" Miranda said tightly. "Aren't you forgetting them? They're the greatest threat. What Kelhak is capable of . . . and what you told me about the emperor, leaves my blood cold." She shook her head. "Someone should do something . . . but not us. This is far bigger than what we can handle. Please, Caldan. There will be a time, but that time isn't now. Leave it. Concentrate on finding us a way out of this mess. We're in no position to do anything about it. The warlocks will come after you. Tell me you'll ask Quiss and Gazija for help. No, don't tell me. Promise me."

Caldan stared straight ahead. "We must make sure we survive. Of course I'll ask them for help. There's no other option open to me now."

"Another false step, and it will be all over. I . . . don't want to lose you. We can find our way out of this."

But he couldn't shake the thoughts from his head. *Why not us? If I stand back and do nothing, then what have I become? What would Simmon think of me, were he still alive?*

And yet . . . he knew she was right. It was too big for him to take on alone, and possibly at all. And it wasn't just him caught up in this; others were as well. Miranda was lucky to have survived.

But . . .

"I'm just glad you're all right," he said, throat thick. It sounded weak to him. His words didn't encompass what he felt for her. Perhaps no words could. Caldan gently cleared his throat. "I don't want to lose you, either."

He felt Miranda relax against him as she sighed. She tugged at a button of his shirt, picking at it with forefinger and thumb.

"Just . . . tell me we'll find a way out of this. And hold me closer."

Caldan reached up and stroked her hair. He meant it as a reassuring gesture, but the feel of her across his fingers and palm heightened his awareness. Now his blood hammered in his ears, drowning out almost every other sound. He could scarcely breathe. Gently, he brushed his thumb across her cheek and was surprised to find wetness. Tears. Whether of relief, fear, or something else, he couldn't say.

"We'll get through this," he reassured her. He had no right to be that confident. Warlocks, Indryallans, jukari and vormag, the Protectors—let alone Gazija and whatever he wanted . . . they would be lucky to escape unscathed.

And yet, holding her in his arms, he felt like he could take on the world.

"I know," Miranda replied, voice wavering. She wiped her face and looked up at him.

Her green eyes drew him in, and Caldan held his breath, not wanting this moment to end.

"Well, aren't you going to kiss me?" Miranda said slyly.

Caldan slid his fingers through her dark hair and cupped the back of her head. Then he drew her lips close to his.

CHAPTER 20

They entered the offices of the Five Oceans Mercantile Concern through an inconspicuous side door. Felice led the way, with Izak following. They passed storerooms and small out-of-the-way counting rooms, obvious by the wooden coin holders and beaded counters on desks. Felice ascended a staircase and passed through a door onto the first floor.

She paused.

Something isn't right.

The air felt dead. There were none of the familiar background sounds. No faint footfalls of people walking along corridors or rooms, conducting their usual business. Almost all the oil lamps burning in the hallway had gone out. Most of the illumination was provided by a sorcerous crafted globe suspended over the door to Rebecci's office.

From this angle, Felice could see the door was open a handspan. Unusual for Rebecci. And suspicious.

She turned to Izak and held a finger to her lips. He nodded his understanding, one hand going to the knife at his belt he always carried now. It didn't suit him, but then, they couldn't be too careful.

Holding her breath, she waited as patiently as she could, peering into the shadows and straining her ears for any sound someone was in the room. Finally, she was satisfied it was empty.

Felice bade Izak follow her, and she crept toward Rebecci's office, keeping to the side of the hallway to avoid their weight causing the floorboards to creak.

Heart pounding in her chest, she stepped gingerly to the door, pushed it open, and entered the room. She gagged as a putrefying stench assaulted her nostrils. She pinched her nose closed and covered her mouth with her palm.

Lying on the desk, arms and legs spread-eagled, was the source of the odor:

Rebecci.

A gash ran across her throat. Trails of scarlet splashed her neck, her dress, and the desk. Coarse ropes bound her wrists and ankles to the legs of the desk.

Felice swallowed. Behind her, Izak uttered a low moan.

Someone had breached her sorcerous defenses and killed her. But if she was like Savine, then . . . was she truly dead? Or had they captured her, like Rebecci had Savine?

Pignuts . . .

The diamond-caged crafting. Where was it?

Averting her eyes from the sight of the blood, Felice felt below the wound in Rebecci's neck for the chain and crafting.

Nothing. Whoever killed her had taken the gem with Savine in it. Which meant they almost certainly knew what had happened, and what to look for. Yes, they could have just robbed her for the diamond, but this . . . this was ritualistic. And with Rebecci's powers, Felice doubted a normal thief could have even gotten close to the sorcerer.

"Izak, search the desk. See if there's anything of interest."

"I . . . sure." Izak scurried around the desk and began opening drawers, shuffling through papers, and rummaging at the back.

It had to have been the two child sorcerers who'd confronted

Rebecci on the wharf, or Kelhak himself. There were no other sorcerers or Protectors left in Anasoma who could have done this.

Felice knew when she was out of her depth. They had to leave.

Quickly.

But . . . they should do something. It wouldn't be right to leave Rebecci here like this.

"Nothing," Izak said. "Just accounting records."

Felice nodded curtly. "Can you cut her bonds? We can't do much, but I can't bear to see her like this."

In the end, they placed her arms across her chest, and crossed her legs. Izak cut a piece of cloth from Rebecci's dress and used it to cover the jagged cut across her throat.

They left without a word.

CHAPTER 21

Caldan blinked against the sun, then peered over the gunwale toward the front lines, where the jukari horde was still skirmishing with the emperor's army. Columns of Quivers and trains of cavalry proceeded from the main encampment to relieve their comrades. He had been woken during the night by the sound of explosions and the humming of angry wasps, which quickly died away. It seemed the warlocks had been matched by the vormag. Whatever had happened, Caldan couldn't sense any sorcery now, and the two opposing forces eyed each other over a corridor strewn with dead bodies and discarded and broken weapons. Heavily armored men bearing shields made up the front line, with lighter armored spearmen behind them. A few buzzing arrows were still exchanged, but no more—perhaps the supply was running low. There was a constant drone in his ears, as the tumult of both sides merged into one discordant rumble.

This is a distraction, he thought once again. The real danger was Kelhak. The jukari and vormag were simply delaying the warlocks from confronting the Indryallans.

He turned to see Quiss approaching. The sorcerer's face was grim, but Caldan was pleased to see him. With all they'd done for Miranda, he'd be forever grateful, and yesterday, when Quiss had discussed sorcery with Caldan late into the night, it was one of the first times he actually felt like another sorcerer's, if not equal, at least colleague.

"There's a group of people approaching," said Quiss. "They are not sorcerers. But they have the same feel as you do. Why?"

Caldan ignored the question. "They're coming for Kristof," he said. "Me, they probably couldn't care less about. Either Kristof and I have been killed or captured, or I lacked the courage to go through with it. They know something went wrong, and they're coming to find out what happened."

Quiss placed a hand on Caldan's shoulder. "We're behind you, Caldan. We'll stand up for you from here."

I should take Kristof to them, as a gesture of respect. It's not much, and they'll likely scorn me, but I need to avoid more bloodshed.

"Can you organize a sled? I'll go below and retrieve Kristof's body."

"All right," Quiss said, but it was clear he didn't think that was the best idea in the world.

With a nod to Quiss, Caldan wiped damp hands on his pants and went below to retrieve the Touched. Kristof's skin was pale and clammy, but surprisingly wasn't as far gone as Caldan thought it would be. He asked a sailor for help, and together they wrestled Kristof through the ship and up on deck. By the time they did, Quiss had procured a sled and was standing near the gangplank. In the distance, a group of figures approached. A dozen men and women, all dressed in nondescript clothes but bristling with weapons and trinkets.

He was right: the Touched.

Caldan stifled a curse and set to transferring Kristof to the sled. He wrapped the body with a blanket, high enough to cover the charred hole in the chest. The second hole, in Kristof's neck, was still plainly visible. After a moment's thought, Caldan paused, then tugged the blanket up over the wound. He dragged the sled down the gangplank and onto the wharf, where he waited nervously for the Touched to arrive.

In the morning light, Kristof's features appeared peaceful, and the brightness and clear air seemed to make something of his return. Caldan felt it went some way to treating Kristof with respect. He couldn't do much more.

His thoughts touched on Miranda, and what had happened between them. He'd never experienced anything like it. Not just physically, but there was a strange feeling he'd never had before. Excitement and contentment combined, with a dash of longing. It was more than attraction and a deep affection. But not only did it make him question the danger he put Miranda in, it gave him a newfound determination to succeed. Only if he pushed himself and made hard decisions would they ever be free.

Which is why he'd wanted to go to the Touched first, to show them the body. To tell them his version of events. To make them see that the warlocks and what they did was evil. He knew that without evidence, many wouldn't believe him. And even with proof, some would deny what was before their eyes. But even if only one of them believed him, wouldn't it be worth it?

As they got closer, he realized with surprise that Devenish wasn't with them. Perhaps his presence would be an admission the warlocks were behind the assassination attempt? And the last thing Devenish needed was another confrontation at this stage. The warlock was no fool.

And yet, it also showed weakness. As if the chief warlock knew what had happened, but also knew he could do nothing about it.

The machinations were swirling, and enough to make his head hurt.

With a weary sigh, Caldan lowered his gaze from the approaching procession. He was under no illusions the path he and Miranda had chosen wasn't risky. The Touched approached, and Caldan could feel their eyes on him. With a grunt, he lifted the two arms of the sled and brought it before them.

Among the Touched were Lisanette and Edelgard, along with Tamara the physiker. All three stepped forward.

"And so we all come to this," Lisanette said sorrowfully.

To the side, Caldan saw Tamara's eyes widen as she recognized

Kristof. He turned his gaze away, not able to bear the sight as horror and grief flooded her face.

Lisanette fixed her now tear-streaked face on Kristof's body, her arms wrapped around her stomach.

Caldan began unstrapping Kristof, removing the blanket and dropping it on the ground.

"You'd better have a good explanation," Lisanette growled, voice breaking.

He spared her a quick glance and flinched at the animosity in her eyes. And he understood that all his thoughts about exposing the truth were simply wishes, now blowing away in the wind. There was no chance he would ever be able to overcome the doubt and distrust they now had for him.

And that made him angry. Caldan clenched his fists until his knuckles ached. *I could show them the light—show them everything, but they've already closed themselves off from me.* It was obvious in their expressions that none were in the mood for his explanations, let alone the information he could give them that would shatter their world.

No, the Touched would have to take care of themselves. Perhaps, so many years ago, his parents had had the exact same thought. Caldan felt he was right. Felt the certainty of his thoughts in his heart. Some things were too strong to fight against. The Touched could have their doomed life. With Miranda back, he now had a spark of hope.

So, knowing they could only trust in their hatred toward him, Caldan was more than a bit surprised when someone cleared his throat. He realized he'd stopped moving, crouched next to Kristof's corpse with his hands holding the straps. Dropping the leather, he stepped away from the sled, a silent offering of it to them, and turned to face the Touched and Tamara.

All three of them were facing him, expressions a mixture of anger and grief, hostility and disbelief.

Exactly as Devenish would want, ancestors curse him.

A dozen thoughts, excuses really, sprang to Caldan's mind. But none of them was worth speaking. He was walking a fine line already, and his best option was to try not to antagonize the Touched further.

But he felt that wasn't enough. He had to stop lying and make the hard decisions.

Caldan glanced behind him at Quiss and the other sorcerers lining the gunwale of the ship. If he slipped up, and the Touched attacked him, they'd all be slaughtered. And Caldan would be further bound to Gazija and Quiss.

Lisanette was the first to break their silence. "You keep away from him, Caldan. We'll take him from here. At least you didn't dump him in the river; he deserves better than that." Her voice was raw with emotion.

Caldan nodded and backed away another step.

Edelgard drew a cloth sheet and a scarf from a satchel. He covered Kristof up to his shoulders with the sheet and placed the scarf around his neck, covering the blackened wounds. When he finished, he came and stood in front of Caldan.

"How?" was all Edelgard said, as tonelessly as if asking a question about the weather.

Caldan steeled himself. "Devenish gave us a mission," he said softly. "But before we left, Kristof and Devenish had a disagreement. Kristof felt Devenish thought he was . . . past it and needed to be replaced. Kristof disagreed. Devenish reassured Kristof that everything was fine. They left it at that."

"That bastard Devenish," Lisanette cursed quietly, and Tamara looked at her in shock. "He never knows when to—"

"Enough, Lisanette!" Edelgard commanded. "Let Caldan speak."

"Why? So we can hear lies from his traitorous mouth?"

"So we can hear what he has to say, and then lay guilt where it belongs."

Lisanette subsided, but she was still seething.

"Thank you, Edelgard," Caldan said.

"Don't thank me," Edelgard snapped. "Just tell us what happened."

Caldan jerked his head in a nod, keeping his gaze averted. Maybe they'd see it as a sign of guilt, but he hoped they saw it for what it really was: contrition.

"We were in a rowboat that Kristof had arranged earlier. He was agitated. He accused me of wanting to replace him, or at least, he suspected that Devenish would want it, seeing as I'm Touched and a sorcerer."

Tamara cleared her throat. "Kristof didn't want any of you to know, but now . . . well, there's no harm. He needed strong painkillers just to get moving in the morning. I concocted an elixir for him, which he took a measure of in his tent before coming out. I . . . you should know the truth."

Thank you, Tamara. "When we entered the cabin, we found a woman I . . . love. Kristof wanted to kill her so there weren't any witnesses. I couldn't let him do that. So we fought."

Edelgard narrowed his eyes.

Lisanette flashed him a look of pure hatred. "You killed him!" she hissed with venom.

Caldan spread his hands slowly. "I had no choice. He was stronger than me. Faster. He was choking the life from me. I didn't want to die."

"Liar!"

"No. He had me on the ground. I was about to pass out. I had no choice."

"We all have choices," Edelgard said.

I used to believe that. It was an illusion. "I don't know what I was caught up in, but I chose not to be killed."

Lisanette looked at him like he was a spider she'd found in her bed. "You're a sorcerer. No wonder Devenish likes you."

"Far from it. He likes me about as much as you do." *And he likes me not because I'm a sorcerer, but for the same reason he likes you.*

My blood.

"You're in trouble then," Edelgard remarked.

It was all Caldan could do to nod his agreement.

"What was the mission?" Lisanette demanded.

"Ask Devenish, if you want to know."

"Oh, I will. You can be sure of that. Only, I can't be sure he'd tell the truth."

Tamara gasped again, and Edelgard came to stand next to Lisanette, placing one hand on her shoulder. She tried to shrug him off, but his grip remained firm.

"Now, now, Lisanette. That's no way to talk about Devenish."

She glared at Edelgard but held her tongue. Shoving his hand off, she stomped up to Caldan. "This isn't over," she snarled. "Devenish can join the ancestors, for all I care. I'll get to the bottom of what really happened."

"I told you the truth. It happened just like I said."

Lisanette scoffed and turned her back on Caldan. "Tamara," she said. "Go and notify as many of the other Touched as you can find. They'll want to pay their respects before the warlocks come to collect him. They always want to rush things."

And I know why. They'd want to take Kristof's body for their nefarious purposes.

Tamara rushed off, skirt flapping. Lisanette flashed Caldan another glare before moving to kneel beside Kristof's body. Edelgard watched her for a few moments.

He met Caldan's gaze and uttered a disgusted sigh. "How do you expect any of us to trust you after this?"

Caldan closed his eyes for a moment. "I don't. You can't. But maybe this will help: because I'm *not* one of you. I never wanted to be, and never will be. I could have killed Kristof to try to take his place, but I don't want it. So what other reason would I have, other than self-defense?"

"Who knows? Like you said, you're not one of us, so I wouldn't even try to delve into the mind of someone who could kill our friend. It doesn't matter what I think, anyway: Devenish will decide your fate. But right now we need to take care of Kristof. We'll leave now, before Lisanette does something stupid. And, Caldan, I agree with Lisanette on one thing: we never want to see you again. Is that understood?"

Caldan lowered his gaze and looked at the wooden planks between them. "Yes, I understand."

He watched as they knelt and paid their respects to Kristof before taking up the sled and dragging it away.

He had been convinced the Touched were disinclined to believe him, but perhaps a seed had been sown. Perhaps this was the first step to winning their trust and revealing to them what the warlocks were really up to.

Before Caldan could turn and head back to the ship, Devenish and Thenna stepped from the trees. Both of Devenish's blond-haired guards were flanking him as well.

"By the ancestors," cursed Caldan. They had obviously been waiting until the Touched left.

Or, he realized, killed him.

Caldan raised his eyes to meet theirs and straightened as they came toward him. Devenish glanced at the retreating Touched, as if to make sure they were out of earshot.

With a thought, Caldan opened his well and linked to his shield crafting. His skin tingled as the force slid over it. Devenish's guards stepped back, determined looks coming over their faces. In an instant, both of them were surrounded by similar multicolored shields.

"I don't want to fight you," Caldan grated. And he opened his well farther, as wide as he could. Power flowed from it into his shield. His teeth vibrated with the potential he drew forth, and he clenched his jaw against the sensation. An overpowering scent of lemons and hot metal filled the air.

"You can all see what I can do," he said firmly, and closed his well, shield winking out.

I am both Touched and a sorcerer. It's time I started acting the part.

Caldan held his well open, though he'd severed the link to his shield. In his mind, he went over the construction of a pattern Quiss had taught him, one of many. Like, and yet unlike, the same shield he'd just dropped. This one was pure coercive sorcery, a shield for his consciousness. It settled around his thoughts. He could feel it constricting them, pushing inside his head. A feeling he'd get used to in time, Quiss had told him.

"So," Devenish said. "Kristof is . . . dead."

The warlock's words hung in the air. To Caldan, they seemed to signify a step down an unalterable path. The warlock's expression remained blank. He stared at Caldan for long moments, then glanced up at Quiss and his people watching from the ship.

Eventually Thenna hissed, "I told you he was trouble. We should kill him—"

"Enough!" barked Devenish.

"But—"

"Another word, and you can leave. Be silent, and let your betters think."

Thenna subsided in a sullen sulk, shooting a murderous stare at Caldan.

Devenish moved to stand in front of him, and to Caldan's surprise he untucked his shirt and drew it over his head, so he stood there half-naked. His chest was crisscrossed with hair-thin scars, pale against his brown skin. He held Caldan's eye, then turned in a full circle on the spot. His back was worse. There were more scars than unblemished skin. Each looked not serious, barely enough to draw blood, but taken together, they were horrifying. What had happened to him?

"I was once like you," began the warlock. He smiled wryly, and one hand touched his trinket rings on the other. "Stubborn. Proud. A fool. I didn't know what was good for me. I had talent . . . considerable talent. But I was selfish. It took me a great deal of time, and punishment, to learn that what I wanted . . . well, that came a distant eighth or ninth on other people's lists. If they cared at all." Devenish paused. His eyes had taken on a faraway look. "For some people, learning their needs come after others' is a difficult lesson. But learn we all must. I don't want to put others though the ordeals I went through. So I'll ask you this only once. How did Kristof die?"

"I couldn't let him go through with it. I didn't know what to do, until we stumbled across an innocent woman. Kristof wanted to kill her. I disagreed."

"Huh," grunted Devenish.

"He's lying," spat Thenna.

Devenish grimaced, then glanced at Caldan, who remained silent.

Caldan sensed Thenna open her well, and he linked to both his shield and Bells's coercive sorcery craftings.

She glared at him. "Only someone guilty would shield themselves."

"A precaution," Caldan said calmly. "I'll defend myself, if I have to. He attacked me first."

Devenish met his eyes, giving him a considering look. The silence drew out. Neither of them broke it.

"Devenish," began Thenna. "Let me—"

Devenish struck.

Caldan felt the power building an instant before it hit him. He braced his shield and almost staggered off balance when it was completely ignored. A sorcerous net covered his mind, enclosing and trying to capture it. Blasts of coercive sorcery hammered against his hastily thrown-up defense, which buckled under the strain. Caldan groaned, bolstering his mental shield.

A look of surprise filled Devenish's face, quickly replaced by thoughtful determination. His onslaught strengthened, and another wave crashed into Caldan's barrier.

Drawing as much power from his well as he dared, Caldan tried to reinforce the screen Quiss had taught him. It was hard to concentrate; there were so many strings to hold. And Devenish's assault didn't let up; it kept coming, pounding like a hundred hammers on anvils.

But it was, Caldan realized, brute force. There was no subtlety to Devenish's attack. It was a far cry from the elegance he'd seen from Quiss and Adrienne when they dismantled the tangled remnants of the coercive sorcery inside Miranda's mind. Devenish's grasp of coercive sorcery was . . . crude. All Caldan had to do was withstand this attack, and they couldn't control him. And that simply meant strength, something he was realizing he had.

His *blood* had.

Abruptly, Devenish's assault ceased. This time, Caldan did stagger, so sudden was the withdrawal. Perspiration dripped from his face. His sorcery had held against Devenish. That had to worry the warlock, but also give him food for thought. He had to see that Caldan would be far more valuable alive than dead. One day, eventually, Devenish would see him suffer for this.

Or, at least, he would *try*.

Until then, let him sweat, thought Caldan. He could feel the presence of Quiss and his colleagues behind him on the ship. They'd gathered their power but had held back, waiting in case they needed to come to his aid.

He held on to his well and maintained his defenses in case another attack came. None did, though. Caldan looked up and saw Devenish frowning at him. Thenna was now standing by her leader's side, mouth twisted into a sneer.

"Together we could—"

"No, Thenna. Caldan has shown he's worthy enough to join our ranks."

"He's dangerous."

"Exactly. Enough now. Leave us."

"But—"

"I said leave us!"

Thenna fixed Caldan with a hate-filled look before leaving without a word. She stopped a few dozen paces from them, arms wrapped around herself, glaring.

"My mind is my own," Caldan said. "So what now? I told you the truth."

Devenish waved a hand. "It doesn't matter. You're strong enough to hide whatever happened. Whatever your version of events, *that's* now the truth."

"Is that how it works?"

"That's how it's always worked. For everyone, not just sorcerers. Warlocks, Quivers, Protectors, the emperor . . . The truth is what you can get away with."

"I don't believe that."

Devenish shrugged, then uttered a short laugh. "It doesn't matter what you believe. The world works the way it does without your belief. Get used to it." He pulled his shirt back over his head, tucking it into his pants. "The truth is, I had no idea what to do with you. Now my decision's made for me." Devenish gave Caldan a thin smile. "Join us. We'll train you. You'll control more power than you ever thought possible."

"No," Caldan said.

Devenish raised his eyebrows, then glanced at the ship behind Caldan, where Quiss was standing on deck.

"The emperor has need of your talents. By refusing me, you're refusing him. If you find me hard, he is steel to my butter. Do you understand?"

Caldan nodded he did.

"Good. Then there's nothing left to discuss—you'll come with us."

"No."

Devenish looked back at Caldan, almost as bewildered as he was angry. Then he looked to Quiss one last time, and his face was pure rage now. "You'll regret this," he said.

"Maybe," Caldan replied. "But I'm not so sure."

He turned and walked up the gangplank, leaving Devenish staring at his back.

CHAPTER 22

"Rebecci wanted to be there when the assassin makes his attempt on Kelhak's life," Izak said.

He couldn't sit still. One minute he was by the fireplace, and the next close to Felice, wringing his hands and looking at her like she had all the answers. The truth was, she had none. As soon as they reached their apartment, Izak had poured himself another glass, but he had taken only a few sips. He held on to it tightly, as if it were a talisman.

Felice paused, considering her response. "I assume she wanted to capture Kelhak like she did Savine. But that doesn't matter now. Savine's been taken, and Rebecci is dead."

"Would killing Kelhak actually just . . . kill him?"

"Or would he be able to find another body, you mean? I don't know. There's too much I don't know. And unfortunately, the one person who probably could answer is now dead."

"Some of her people may have escaped," suggested Izak.

"Yes, but finding them in this city, when they've gone to ground, will be close to impossible. It looks like we're on our own. Again."

Izak gave her a smile—a weak one that he meant to be reassuring, except it was anything but. "Is Rebecci truly dead, then? Could she also have survived?"

"I don't know," Felice admitted with a sigh. "I have no idea, and it's so frustrating. Can they even *be* killed? Sorcerers, that is. Or is capturing the best that can be done?"

"There's only one way to find out."

There was a hardness in Izak's voice that she'd never heard before. The invasion had rattled him. Now, though, Rebecci's murder had changed him.

"Let's get some sleep," she said. "We've a few hours until our next meeting with the assassin."

"Does he have a name, the assassin?"

Felice shook her head. "Not that I know of." But she'd certainly like to find out.

CHAPTER 23

Behind them, the guard slammed the door shut with a clang that echoed around the jail.

Vasile wondered why Caitlyn had returned Aidan's sword to him and could think of only two reasons. She was either sure Aidan had converted back to her cause and her leadership, or confident cel Rau could defeat Aidan. If he had to guess, he thought the second reason more likely.

Caitlyn and cel Rau escorted them along dank corridors that housed many more cells. Moans and whimpering came from some, and Vasile tried not to look inside. Cel Rau lent Caitlyn his arm and helped her ascend a flight of stairs, then they were outside.

Vasile blinked in the too-bright sunlight and sneezed. He wiped his nose and noticed his hand was both filthy and trembling.

They were free. Released from prison and spared death. But at what cost? For the both of them: enforced service to Caitlyn, or execution. At least they weren't still rotting in their cell.

A four-horse carriage made of polished rosewood waited in a court-yard outside, with a squad of mounted Quivers as an escort. The soldiers saluted Caitlyn as she exited the prison, and one of them hurried over to assist her. She brushed the offer away and turned to Aidan.

"We've a stop to make first." She looked at their soiled clothes and sniffed. "Well, I'm sure he's seen worse."

"Where are we going?" Aidan asked. "Vasile and I need a bath, a change of clothes, and a good meal or two."

"All in good time," Caitlyn replied. "For now, we have an appointment with the emperor."

Vasile half gasped before he could stop himself. *Let's hope he doesn't remember me.*

"May he live forever," muttered cel Rau.

Caitlyn turned an inquiring look on Vasile.

"That's right," she said. "A privilege not afforded to many. You'd do well to watch your tongue, and your manners. The emperor has heard all about your treachery, but apparently he was also told you'd done some good, fighting the jukari and vormag. It was he who convinced me to give you one last chance. And as always, the emperor's wisdom is unsurpassed."

Vasile nodded, not trusting himself to speak. Caitlyn wasn't being entirely truthful—but without asking specific questions, he couldn't be sure what was really going on. *Not now*, he decided. *There will be time to dig out the truth.*

Aidan cleared his throat. "And for that, we are thankful."

"Don't thank me," Caitlyn said. "Thank the emperor in person. And watch yourselves. He could crush you with a thought."

Despite her rejection of the offer of assistance, Caitlyn couldn't manage the steps into the carriage. Her injuries restricted her movement, and after a few false starts, she irritably gestured for cel Rau to help her. When Vasile entered behind her, Caitlyn's face was pale and drawn, as if such a small effort had drained her of energy.

The emperor's entourage was no longer with the Quivers camped outside the city walls, having moved to more luxurious and secure surroundings inside Riversedge.

They followed a road for some time before ending up at what looked like a noble's manor, commandeered for the emperor's stay. They entered through manicured gardens surrounding the triple-story whitewashed mansion with terra-cotta roof tiles. River pebble paths split the grounds into sections, and far to their left the trimmed grass and plants degraded into a wilder landscape. As they walked, Vasile heard the roar of a wild cat, followed by the cry of a peacock. For the owners to have their own menagerie spoke of great wealth.

And now it was all the emperor's.

Once inside, Caitlyn spoke to various functionaries, and her party was directed to the emperor's audience chamber. The passageways Vasile and the others walked were cluttered with servants, Quivers, functionaries, nobles, and hangers-on. The air smelled of stale sweat and sour wine, along with dust and dirt. Carpets underfoot were stained with mud and bits of grass, courtesy of the bustle, which left no time or space for cleaning. Frescoes covered the walls, their paint cracked and dark with age. Torch sconces held sorcerous globes, each casting a cold light.

Caitlyn was muttering to herself, eyes glued to the doors. Cel Rau stood close by her side, but his eyes were always on Aidan and Vasile. Aidan fidgeted nervously, probably having never met the emperor before, and that Vasile could understand. The emperor was the source of a thousand rumors and legends.

In his heart, Vasile knew the tales might not be true. He'd met the emperor before, disturbing experiences he'd hoped would never happen again. But what troubled him, the reason he'd fled the capital, was much more sinister. Something he'd never told anyone, for fear it would be traced back to him, and he'd be killed.

When Vasile had been dragooned into helping the councillors root out a plot to kill many of them, they'd presented him to the emperor, ostensibly as part of his reward. A brief encounter, a few moments only. But the next day, Vasile had joined the crowd of onlookers that always congregated around the emperor's audiences. And one of the warlocks had confronted the emperor, accusing him of kidnapping and killing a promising apprentice and somehow assimilating his well.

The emperor denied it, and disturbingly, the warlock had suffered a heart attack on the spot, dying moments later.

But the emperor had been lying.

Vasile had fled back to Anasoma, counting himself lucky to leave the capital alive. He'd thanked the ancestors when he'd arrived back home in one piece.

He just needed to have the same fortune again.

His thoughts turned to cel Rau. Suddenly, the man he'd fought alongside was a stranger. They'd survived against the jukari together, and Aidan had known him for years and trusted him without reservation.

Vasile wagered Aidan would have reservations now.

"Well, well," said someone from behind them.

Vasile turned and came face-to-face with Gazija. He struggled to keep his expression neutral. The old man was here? Now? This couldn't be a coincidence. Vasile glanced at Aidan, who was staring at Gazija, hand resting on his sword.

Gazija walked slowly, as if every movement was excruciating. He tapped his two canes on the floor, and the noise caught Caitlyn's attention.

"Sorcerer," cel Rau said. "What are you doing here?" He moved to block Gazija's view of Caitlyn and to give himself room to draw.

Vasile took a step backward.

"I'm here to see the emperor," Gazija said. He waved a piece of paper with an official-looking seal. "I have an *invitation*. I presume you're here to see him as well? Aidan? Vasile? You look the worse for wear."

Caitlyn pushed past cel Rau, who looked none too pleased. "I've heard of you," she said. "Don't think your mercenaries aiding the emperor absolves you of your evil sorcery."

Gazija frowned, though the corners of his mouth turned up in a half smile. "Yes. I'm sure cel Rau has told you what he knows. And I've heard of you, Lady Caitlyn. A fearless, tireless crusader against evil. As you call it."

"I know evil when I see it."

"I daresay you do," Gazija said dryly. He met Aidan's gaze, then flicked his eyes toward Caitlyn. "I'd like a few words with Vasile," he said softly, "in private."

Aidan frowned, then his eyes widened as comprehension dawned. He schooled his expression, nodded minutely, then turned to cel Rau. "I need to speak with you," he said. "And Caitlyn. I want to beg forgiveness."

"Not now, Aidan," said Caitlyn.

"Yes. Now." Aidan grabbed Caitlyn's elbow.

A hiss of breath escaped cel Rau's lips, and Vasile realized his sword was half out of its sheath.

Aidan let go of Caitlyn and raised his hands in a nonthreatening gesture. He sidled away, down the hallway. "I don't want them to hear my pleas. I'm . . . ashamed."

Caitlyn's eyes narrowed, but after a pause, she nodded. "All right. I don't know how long we'll be kept waiting, and I want to hear what you have to say."

"Thank you, my lady," Aidan said, gesturing for her to follow. Cel Rau kept close to them, as if expecting Aidan to wring her neck at any moment.

Taking advantage of the distraction, Gazija latched a bony hand onto Vasile's arm, pulling him closer.

"Do not be alarmed," Gazija said. "And please, we don't have much time."

"What's going on?" Vasile said. He looked into Gazija's rheumy eyes, all the while keeping an ear on the low murmurings coming from Aidan and Caitlyn.

"Ostensibly," Gazija said, "I'm here to receive the emperor's thanks for our mercenaries, which have proved useful in the battle against the jukari. But there's more going on. You, Vasile, are key."

Vasile shook his head. "Now's as good a time as ever to explain yourself, Gazija. You pointed me at the emperor from the beginning, and now I'll be put before him. Tell me what's going on."

"Very well," Gazija said. "It is almost time. I need to know if I can trust the emperor. He will do what's best for himself and the empire, this I believe. But what I have to know is, will he honor the agreement I strike with him here today? Vasile, you will know. There is more at stake than you realize. Not only is the world on a precipice, but my people have to survive this. I cannot ensure their safety if they are imprisoned, or worse, when this is over."

Or worse . . .

Vasile glanced at Aidan, Caitlyn, and cel Rau. Aidan was gesturing with his hands—*lying*—while Caitlyn nodded in agreement and said words Vasile couldn't hear—*also lying*.

"You must help me," Gazija implored Vasile. "You must help us."

"Why?" Vasile said. "You've lied to us from the beginning. Tell me the truth, and then I'll decide whether to help you."

"I have told you the truth."

Vasile glared at Gazija, hoping the depth of his displeasure came across. "The *whole* truth."

Gazija seemed to shrink, like a man too tired to continue. He nodded curtly. "We are sorcerers, this you know. And we are more skillful than the warlocks. They need us to combat the Indryallans, both with our sorcery and our mercenaries. This puts them in our debt. But we fear the emperor will not like the fact there are sorcerers more powerful than his warlocks. And if a person is dead, then you don't need to pay them back."

Truth. "You think the emperor will use you and your mercenaries, then dispose of you? That's crazy! Everyone would know."

"So?" hissed Gazija. "What would they care? They won't speak out against the emperor. Everyone lives in fear of him, but why? Because they think he's too powerful to take on. He has trod a dangerous path to obtain that power, but it isn't enough to defeat Kelhak. And if he takes any more, it could put him over the edge."

"Takes more what?" Vasile said, fearing he already knew the answer.

"More sorcerers."

So he knows the emperor's secret. Somehow he's seen what I heard the emperor lie about all those years ago. But . . . how?

"What do you know about that?" Vasile said.

Gazija sniffed. "Everything, and nothing."

"This is no time for games, old man."

"What I know," said Gazija, "is that we have a slight chance of defeating Kelhak, and then only if we're lucky. But like any leader, I'm also looking beyond this event to what comes after." His eyes bored into Vasile's. "Can I trust the emperor? Will he let us go, once Kelhak and the Indryallans are defeated? Will he honor our bargain? These are the questions I need answers to. This is why Quiss brought you to me in the first place."

"What are you two talking about?" Caitlyn said.

Vasile looked around as she limped over to them, with Aidan and cel Rau trailing behind her.

"We were just discussing evil," Gazija said. "And the forms it takes."

"Evil is obvious to those who look for the signs," Caitlyn said.

Gazija met Vasile's eye, then Aidan's. "You can see evil in many things, if you look hard enough. Perhaps, Lady Caitlyn, you should look for the good in people?"

Before Caitlyn could answer, the door to the emperor's audience chamber creaked open, and a harried-looking functionary came out.

The balding man looked around, annoyance on his face. "Head Trader Gazija of the Five Oceans Mercantile Concern," he said. "You're next."

"Here," Gazija said. "I'm here. I'll go in together with the Lady Caitlyn and her entourage. She's been waiting longer than I have."

Caitlyn shot Gazija a suspicious look, glanced at cel Rau, who said nothing, then shrugged. "Fine," she said. "The sooner we're done here, the sooner we can get to work."

"And what work would that be?" Gazija asked.

"Never you mind, sorcerer."

The functionary came over and looked them up and down. Vasile became more aware of their rumpled and stained clothes.

"Do you think this is appropriate?" the man snapped. "I've a mind to—"

A multicolored shield sprang into life around Gazija, and the sorcerous globes brightened, each glowing like the sun. Gasps echoed around the hallway.

"Take us inside," said Gazija imperiously. His shield disappeared. "And keep quiet, unless I ask a question."

"Cel Rau!" Caitlyn said.

The swordsman shifted his weight but didn't make a move. "It's a show," he said flatly.

The functionary's mouth closed with an audible clack. "The emperor has warlocks defending him. You'd better not—"

"I won't do anything," Gazija said testily. "Take us inside, now."

They followed the flustered man through the doorway and into a large ballroom. The entire space was lit by sorcerous globes attached to three chandeliers, illuminating paintings adorning the walls and sculptures in alcoves.

Quivers lined the passage that led from the entrance door to a dais, behind which was a crowd of nobles and spectators, along with their servants and men-at-arms. Atop the dais was the emperor, sitting on a padded chair. And still, despite his longevity, no gray touched his platinum hair.

As they entered, a dozen black-clad warlocks came toward them, forming a barrier.

"We sensed you," said one, a middle-aged man with a short-cropped black beard. "There is to be no unsanctioned sorcery in here, or you will be destroyed. Am I clear?"

"It was a display only," replied Gazija. "I find those can help with hardheaded individuals. Like your man Devenish."

The warlock grunted, then rubbed his chin, as if trying to decide if Gazija was a danger to the emperor.

A voice came from the far end of the chamber. "Let them pass," a man said, and once again—as he had been all those years ago—Vasile was struck by how the emperor sounded: resonant and profound.

"He is no threat to me," continued the emperor. "Though he might be to you."

Chuckles and titters came from the massed onlookers, and the warlocks parted to let them through.

They followed the functionary and approached. The conversational hum, which had been loud when they'd entered, dropped the closer they came to the emperor. Then a hush fell over the room, deep enough that Vasile could have been there alone.

Zerach-Sangur—the Mahruse Emperor—waved a hand, and the functionary who'd escorted them bowed his head low and backed away.

Gazija took a step forward and bowed as well. Caitlyn, with a stern look at Gazija, followed suit.

He obviously doesn't want to annoy the emperor, thought Vasile. He took that for a good sign.

Cel Rau dropped to one knee, and after a moment, Vasile and Aidan did the same.

"Lady Caitlyn," the emperor said, "you will have to wait until I've . . . dealt with Gazija here. I'm sure you won't mind."

Caitlyn kept her head bowed. "Yes, Your Imperial Majesty."

"Come closer, Head Trader Gazija," the emperor said.

Gazija hesitated, and the emperor sat up straighter, fixing violet eyes on him in displeasure.

"I like to move these old bones as little as possible, Your . . . Imperial Majesty," Gazija said, tapping his canes on the floor. "I'm sure you'll also forgive me if I don't kneel."

The emperor smiled. "Of course. I'm told you are the one to thank for the mercenaries who appeared on the river, and who have been instrumental in our fight with the jukari. So . . . you have our gratitude."

"You are most welcome, Your Majesty. My mercenaries—"

"Will be handed over to my commanders by tomorrow."

There was a long pause. "As you request," Gazija said eventually. "The jukari are a nuisance, but I have every confidence they'll be dealt with in short order. It's the Indryallans that worry me, and their leader, Kelhak. There are a *multitude* of reasons why he should be our focus."

The emperor laughed. A brief, fleeting sound. There was answering laughter from the assembled crowd. But Vasile could sense an edge to their response, as if they had no idea how the emperor would react.

"Perhaps," the emperor said, "you should give some thought to your own business affairs and leave the Indryallans to us. The warlocks have Kelhak well in hand, and I bloodied his nose the other day. He'll be no trouble to be rid of."

Vasile held his breath. *Lies*. The emperor was lying. He didn't believe the warlocks were able to do anything, *and* he hadn't defeated or damaged Kelhak. Vasile's heart pounded in his chest.

Gazija inclined his head. "As you say, Your Majesty."

Zerach-Sangur paused, a slight frown creasing his brow. "As I say," he repeated. "Now, tell me, First Deliverer—"

Gazija jerked at the title, as if stung.

"—will you and your fellow sorcerers do your utmost to assist the warlocks with defeating Kelhak?"

Another pause from Gazija, who looked to be choosing his words carefully. "Yes, Your Majesty."

The emperor smiled, teeth white and even. "Good."

"And after?" Gazija said.

"After is for after," came the emperor's reply.

"That's not good enough," Gazija said.

Horrified gasps came from around them. A thump sounded behind Vasile, and he turned to see that a noblewoman had fainted.

"I want assurances," Gazija continued, "that after we assist you— the warlocks, I mean—against the *multitude* of threats that Kelhak represents, you will allow us to go in peace. We will not be beholden to anyone, not the warlocks . . . or even you."

"First Deliverer Gazija," the emperor said, his voice at once cold and hard, and grating with violence. "You do not make demands. Not here. Not with me. All bow to my will, as it has been since I came to power."

"May you live forever . . ." muttered multiple people around Vasile.

"If you do not obey, then I shall bring such devastating sorcery upon you and your people that the flesh shall be scorched from your bones. Your buildings will burn. Their stones will crack and shatter. The gold you've taken pains to amass will run like water through the streets. And anyone who escapes, I shall hunt to the horizons! You will be wiped from existence, your memory a shadow dissolved by the sun. Men will tremble when considering your fate."

Vasile shuddered, rattled by the emperor's vehemence. He'd told the truth, and Vasile's soul shrank from the rage and the power behind the man, and from his very certainty that he'd be able to do as he said.

But Gazija withstood the verbal onslaught. He weathered the violence of the emperor's words without wilting, without bending.

"As you wish, Your Majesty," Gazija said. "We are here to help and offer our assistance without reservation. Kelhak must be defeated. I believe we both know this."

"What you shall do, Gazija, is go to the warlocks. You shall answer any questions they have. You shall hand your people over to them, and they shall obey the warlocks' commands. And you shall make sure they understand they need to give full cooperation to the warlocks, or else they shall be cleansed from the earth. And after, then we shall talk. I would welcome one such as you into our fold, along with your people. Together, we can ensure that the might of the Mahruse Empire endures."

Lies, the emperor's words fairly hissed to Vasile. Gazija was as good as dead.

"Now," the emperor said, "Lady Caitlyn. You've been gracious enough to wait."

Caitlyn rose to her feet slowly, grimacing in pain. "Thank you, Your Majesty. I've brought with me Aidan and Vasile, the men I told you about."

"They don't concern me." A *lie*, knew Vasile. "They're under your authority now. If they step out of line, you'll deal with them. In the coming times, we'll need everyone to do their part."

The menace in his tone was unmistakable. Vasile's hands trembled, and he clasped them together.

"I'll make sure Aidan doesn't stray again," Caitlyn said. "And I could use a man with Vasile's talents. They'll do what's right or suffer the consequences. We must fight evil—"

"Yes, of course. And Kelhak must be our focus now. We'll summon you for further duties, but there's another reason I called you here." The emperor snapped his fingers, and a warlock with long dark hair moved to his side. She held out a vial the size of a thumb, filled with a dark red liquid. Surprised murmurs filled the room. They trailed into silence as the emperor looked up.

"This is my reward to you," he said. "Drink it. Here. Now. In front of me."

The warlock approached Caitlyn and held out the vial. Vasile noted many of the nobles' eyes were fixed on the vessel, and not the emperor. A few expressions were openly desirous, while others were irritated.

They want it, thought Vasile. *And some wonder why the emperor is giving it to Caitlyn. What is it?*

Caitlyn frowned with puzzlement. "A potion?"

"Does my gift not please you?" the emperor said.

Caitlyn inclined her head, a pleased smile on her face. "Of course, Your Majesty. But there's no need to reward me. Fighting evil is its own reward."

Vasile could have sworn the emperor suppressed a smirk. Caitlyn was . . . unsure. She didn't know what its effect would be—but the nobles did, and they were jealous.

"You'll want this gift," the emperor said. "Do I need to repeat myself?"

"No," Caitlyn replied. "Of course not." She took the vial and unscrewed its silver stopper. With a glance at cel Rau, she brought it to her lips. Her hand trembled as she drained the contents. Caitlyn's mouth twisted at the taste, then she forced her expression neutral.

The warlock took the empty vial back and retreated.

The emperor smiled. "You get used to the taste. And you'll enjoy the benefits. For you to have suffered in your lifelong pursuit was tragic. I hope my reward shows how much I value you. Your writ will be returned to you. Be careful not to lose it again."

Half-truths, thought Vasile.

"Thank you, Your Majesty," Caitlyn said. "And if I may ask, what does the potion do?"

"You'll see. Go," the emperor said with finality. "We are done here."

Gazija coughed, then bowed low. Tapping his canes against the floor, he turned and gestured for Vasile and Aidan to follow, as if he, and not Caitlyn, were in charge of them. "Come," he said softly. "The emperor is right.

"We are done here."

CHAPTER 24

Amerdan woke and found himself shirtless, his chest covered in scratches as if he'd run through a patch of brambles. He clasped his hands over his head and rocked back and forth. *Not again. Not now.* Dirt crusted his fingers and was jammed under his nails, as though he'd been digging barehanded. He'd need to give them a hard scrubbing to get rid of the filth. At least he still had his pants and boots.

He reached for his trinket, his heart in his throat. Without it, how would he become what he was meant to be? Without it, he would be lost. Undeserving vessels would be everywhere, and he'd have no way of absorbing them. His fingers touched the chain and followed the links around until he had the trinket in his hand, closing his eyes with relief. Then he checked for Dotty. She was where he'd left her before falling asleep, tucked between the folds of his blanket. One of his greatest fears was that he'd lose the rag doll during these episodes. It had been years since he'd had one this bad.

Why now?

What he did during his blackouts, he'd never been able to find out. Except that one time in Meliror, in the Sotharle Union of Cities, but only because it was all anyone could talk about. They'd never found who'd gone on the killing spree. He chuckled at the thought, though the memory was many years old.

His eyes flicked open as a grunt sounded outside his shelter—probably a wild pig or some such. He was in a shallow cave in a small section of cliff carved from the side of a hill. It stank of animal, though whatever had used it was long gone, leaving dry, old shit and scratch marks in the dirt. Half a loaf of bread and some preserved sausage lay on a cloth, along with two bottles of water. He'd taken the food and drink from a farmhouse a few days ago. The bottles had contained raw spirits, and he'd emptied out the disgusting drink and replaced it with water from a stream. His only other comfort was the blanket.

He'd stumbled onto the cave on his second day outside of Riversedge. The city was too dangerous for him now. Amerdan didn't know what the emperor's warlocks were capable of, and he wasn't foolish enough to stick around and find out. His best option was to lie low for a time, then sneak back in and find Caldan. And then the emperor. He'd thought Bells would be his key to gaining access to the emperor, but she'd lied to him.

It was good he'd killed her.

What Amerdan knew for certain was that there was much talent on offer. His for the taking. His for the absorbing. And now, with his wells and newfound knowledge of sorcery, he was nigh unstoppable.

Amerdan stood and adjusted his plums. They ached, for no reason he could determine. Ah, there was his shirt, crumpled and discarded to the side. He picked it up and shook dirt from it, then slipped it over his head. With careful strokes, he brushed it down and removed a few burrs and tiny twigs stuck to the material. Uttering a satisfied sigh, he tucked Dotty inside, close to his heart.

Another grunt from outside, and a rustle of bushes and dry leaves as something moved around.

He reached for his knives and drew them both. He tilted his head and listened. The shuffling and grunting continued. A thick branch snapped with a crack, and a growl reached his ears—a deep guttural sound.

That's no pig.

Amerdan stood and stepped toward the narrow entrance. He blinked, waiting for his eyes to adjust to the bright light outside. After a few moments, he left the cave.

Its back was to him. It was a great hulking gray-skinned thing with black bristles on its head. The creature held a sword in one hand, but the thing's huge size made the weapon look like a dagger.

Without waiting, Amerdan leaped at the jukari and planted a knife in its back. As it howled, his other blade drove deep into its side. He clamped his arm around the jukari's torso, plunging his blade into its neck, again and again.

Eventually it stopped thrashing and collapsed to the ground, dropping its sword. A thick black liquid poured from its wounds. Its clawed hands scratched in the dirt, gradually slowing until it was still. Amerdan stepped away from it, frowning at his dirt- and black-blood-covered hands.

Filthy beast. He made his way to the stream at the bottom of the hill, where he could wash his hands. Dry leaves and twigs blanketed the ground on the way down. Amerdan took care to avoid making loud noises, but some sound was inevitable. At the stream, he took his time, scrubbing his hands and arms to the elbow with sand and repeatedly rinsing them. He washed his face and neck as well before drinking his fill.

Hoots and a low moaning call echoed from the cliffs. Someone, or something, had found the dead jukari. Likely another of its kind. Well, he was sick of staying in that cave, anyway, and had decided to move on.

Amerdan stood and turned . . . and came face-to-face with another creature. He frowned, opening his well and clutching his newfound power. He was confident his shield crafting would protect him, if he needed it, but he was concerned he hadn't heard the creature approach. It was shorter than the jukari, darker and somehow more sinister. Gray dreadlocked hair matted with muck fell past its shoulders. Its skin was wrinkled and spotted, signs of age. It wore rings and medallions, all covered with sorcerous runes. Amerdan found he could almost decipher some of them, but they were strange, unlike the shape and form of what Bells had taught him.

Then he discerned its well. Sharp edged, like a rent inside its mind to another place. It felt . . . artificial.

"I . . . sensed you," hissed the thing, surprising Amerdan. Its speech was hard to understand. Disjointed sounds, like the beast was gargling water. But he could comprehend it, and that left him an interesting dilemma.

This must be a vormag. Should I kill it now, or should I wait to see if it has something interesting to say?

For the time being, Amerdan stayed his hand. He tilted his head and took a closer look at the beast. Its eyes were set close together, but there was an intelligence in them. Its hide clothes were well made, double stitched and functional, though stained and dirt-encrusted. Metal buckles showed that it had access to metalworkers or stole what it needed.

It took half a step backward, eyeing him warily.

Amerdan took a full step forward. "What do you mean you sensed me?"

The vormag snuffled. A dark purple tongue licked its fangs. "Sorcery. Like . . . the Old Ones. Are you one of the Old Ones?"

Amerdan hadn't accessed his wells since he'd decided to hide from the warlocks and leave Riversedge. Which meant the vormag had sensed the power of his trinket. And in turn, that meant it had to die. But the Old Ones . . . Who were they?

"Yes," he lied. "I am."

With an unnatural reverence, the vormag knelt and bowed its head, baring the back of its neck. It was whispering quietly to itself, and Amerdan realized it was chanting a ritual.

Its words stopped abruptly, and it stood. Tears streaked its face, leaving trails in its filth. "We have waited for this day," it growled. "Come." The vormag shuffled backward and turned to face south. "Come. You will be honored."

By *filth such as you?* Amerdan sneered. He could kill it here and hope he subsumed its well. Or it could lead him to more of its kind, and he could possibly use them to get at Caldan and the emperor. It took him only an instant to decide.

"Do you have a name?"

The creature grinned, showing its yellow fangs and teeth. "Gamzegul. Gamzegul the Believer. They think to insult me by calling me that. But they'll see the truth."

Amerdan held out a hand, palm up. "Lead the way."

Gamzegul took him partway back up the hill before heading along a barely discernible animal run. Amerdan noted with interest the vormag frequently touched the leaves of plants and trunks of trees, and occasionally stooped to touch the earth, all the while muttering to itself.

"You were sent alone," Amerdan stated. The first words either of them had spoken for an hour.

Gamzegul stopped and regarded him with its slanted, pale orange eyes. "Alone, yes."

"Why?"

"Others not believe."

Amerdan grunted. He felt like he was starting to put it together. "The others don't believe any of the Old Ones survive from the Shattering."

"I believe."

"And it's good you do. Tell me, who do you serve?"

"Serve?"

"Yes. Who is in charge? Who gives you orders?"

"Talon Xarlas. It is . . . of the Old Ones . . . but not one of the Old Ones."

The vormag placed an emphasis on the word *talon*, as if it was an honorific. "Talon? Is that a name or a title, like lord?"

"It is . . . what they are. They are Talons."

"They? So, not one of you, or a jukari?"

The vormag shook its head. "Jukari are warriors, and servants, and slaves."

"Different castes, then," Amerdan mused. "So what is Xarlas?"

"Talon Xarlas—"

"Not Talon to me."

The vormag bowed his head jerkily, multiple times. "Yes. Talon Xarlas is . . . Talon Xarlas. After the Great Upheaval, the talons saved us all. Jukari and vormag."

Alive since the Shattering, what this creature called the Great Upheaval? Impossible. Except, as Amerdan had found out, many things that were thought impossible were actually quite the opposite.

Someone without a well becoming a sorcerer, for one.

"Xarlas and its kind have ruled you for thousands of years, then?"

Gamzegul blinked. "Yes. When the raging fires of the Great Upheaval were stamped out, there were many embers. But they will welcome you. I am sure."

It didn't sound sure. Embers from the Shattering . . . the jukari and vormag, and talons. Who knew what else survived from those times? "Power and influence are difficult to give up after so long. You understand this?"

Gamzegul nodded thoughtfully. "Yes."

"They will claim I am not an Old One. Do you understand?"

"Yes. They will see reason. You are proof."

"If they make me disappear, there is no proof. And they'll kill you as well."

"No . . ."

"Yes. Before they know of me, you must find as many of you who believe as possible. We must be sure our strength cannot be challenged. *Then* Xarlas and its kind can know of me. You must see this is the only way."

With a look Amerdan could interpret only as a mix between caution and fervor, Gamzegul slowly jerked its head forward in a nod.

"There are others that think as I do. They will decide."

Other ignorant vormag that clung to ancient myths and superstitions about the Old Ones, no doubt. But how best to take advantage of this? Amerdan needed more information. Yet the delay . . . Could he afford it? Anasoma beckoned him still. His sister's treatment . . .

the physiker Zakarius would need more ducats soon to continue her therapy, and to take care of the two other little ones he'd rescued— Annie and Pieter. They wouldn't be left alone and scared like he and his sisters had been.

"Old One? We must keep moving."

Amerdan shook the memory of the sorcerer's cages from his head and waved at the creature to lead the way.

They passed through the sparse forest. Most of the undergrowth consisted of wildflowers and grasses, and bushy plants he didn't recognize. Gamzegul paused occasionally, eyeing the sun and sniffing the breeze. The creature didn't try to keep quiet, clawed feet crunching on dried leaves and twigs, and Amerdan realized the vormag didn't need to keep their progress stealthy. The area around them must have been under total control of the jukari horde. Or rather, the talon horde.

Abruptly, the vormag stopped, holding up a hand. It snuffled, testing the air, and strode away from the dry streambed they'd been following for a good while. They pushed through a dense patch of shrubs and stopped at an abandoned campfire. Dry lumps that looked like the leavings of rats littered the ground, though they were far too large to be from any rodent. A rotting stench filled the air, and Amerdan's nostrils flared. Blackened bones stuck out from the cold ashes, and rags with dark patches were scattered across the area. Flies buzzed around them, and the rags swarmed with movement. *Maggots*, realized Amerdan. Feasting on rotting flesh.

Gamzegul snarled as he skirted around the fire. With a kick, he sent a pile of rags flying, scattering tiny white maggots across the dirt.

"Should have waited," it growled.

A straw figure caught Amerdan's eye: a doll made from bunches of dry grass, tightly wound with strips of cloth. Two buttons had been sewn onto its face in place of eyes. He examined the scorched bones carefully. Some were too small to be from an adult.

He reached for his knives. Under his shirt, Dotty shifted, the edges of her patches scratching his skin.

Not yet, she said, in the voice only he could hear. *Soon. It is needed, for now.*

Amerdan ground his teeth together. His hands gripped the hilts of his blades, while the vormag continued to pace the campsite, cursing in a guttural tongue.

Closing his eyes for a moment, Amerdan fought to clear the red haze that had overcome him. He released his hands from his weapons, one finger at a time.

"We should keep going," he said softly. "Is it far now?"

"No, not far. Close. These stupid jukari. I will punish them. They should have waited."

Amerdan stared at the soon-to-be-dead vormag, which was still walking and talking, for now.

"It's nothing for you to worry about." *Soon there'll be plenty of death for all of you.*

CHAPTER 25

A chilling sense of foreboding fell down onto Felice along with the rain. It had started as drizzle, strengthening to a downpour that threatened to flood the streets. The ominous feeling had stayed constant, a niggle at the back of her mind she couldn't shake, no matter how hard she tried.

Perhaps it was Rebecci's death, or maybe Felice's lingering feelings over Avigdor's mutilation and murder. The callousness of both acts still haunted her. Whatever the reason, she knew she couldn't let it get to her. She crushed her feelings into a tight ball and squeezed them to the back of her mind, where they would remain.

Or so she hoped.

A sheet of lightning flashed across the sky, illuminating the graveyard for a blink. Streams of water flowed between and over graves, following the path of least resistance. Most of them ran toward and off the cliff, where the wind whipped the muddy discharge into spray.

Felice tugged the hood of her cloak closer to her face to keep the downpour out. A crack of thunder made her jump. Ancestors, she was nervous tonight. After the lightning, she should have expected it. There was something in the air they all felt.

Izak, normally nervous, was standing as still as a corpse behind her. An apt metaphor, considering their surroundings. He hadn't said a word since they'd arrived at the graveyard. The place probably had him spooked. It was eerie enough at night, and now the drenching rain gave everything a washed-out, insubstantial look, as if they'd crossed over into a nightmare. The air reeked of decay and worse.

Enough of that. Where was the assassin? Were they early? Was he late? She couldn't gauge the time with the moon and stars obscured by the clouds. She should buy herself another pocket watch, having lost hers when hiding during the Indryallan invasion. The bloody mechanical things were expensive, though.

"Felice," Izak hissed.

"Now you decide to talk? What is it?"

"Turn around. Please."

There was an edge to Izak's voice. A terrified edge.

Felice turned slowly. Not three paces from her was the assassin. She had to crane her neck to look up into his face, which was obscured by a voluminous hood. Again, lightning flashed across the sky, illuminating the graveyard for an instant.

Felice swallowed, mouth suddenly dry.

As before, the assassin was clad in little more than rags—shredded, washed-out cloth trailing fringes and threads. Didn't they get in the way? Trip him up? But he'd been so quiet, they hadn't known he was here until he'd chosen to reveal himself. He was a few steps from her, and her back had been exposed to him. Felice shivered, and not from the freezing rain.

"You're late."

"Are we? It's the rain, probably. And my pocket watch. I lost it somewhere . . ." Felice trailed off. This man wouldn't care for explanations, and she honestly didn't feel like giving any.

"Next time, you won't be late."

Felice sniffed and brushed water from her nose. "There won't be a next time."

The mountain of rags swayed back and forth. It took her a few moments, but Felice realized he was laughing quietly.

"There's always a next time. Always."

Izak skirted a grave with a cracked stone lid that had fallen into the tomb. He stood next to her, knife in hand. The assassin didn't move. She couldn't even be sure he'd noticed Izak. But of course he had. And dismissed him as no threat.

"Izak," she said gently. "Put it away. We're among . . . friends." She almost choked on the word.

Reluctantly, Izak sheathed his blade. He remained next to her, however, where a few weeks ago she figured he might have fled. The man was developing a backbone.

Rags at the assassin's side moved, and a cloth purse landed at Felice's feet with a wet plop.

"Payment, please."

Felice rummaged under her cloak and came up with three trinkets: an earring shaped like a mermaid, a brooch in the form of a twisting snake, and a flat plate the size of her palm, depicting a tree bearing fruit. Rare examples of their kind, they were worth a fortune; but these days, hardly anyone was buying. Markets had dried up in Anasoma because of the invasion, and everyone was keeping their heads down. As such, the trinkets had been both difficult *and* easy to obtain. Since it was her job to know secrets, she knew quite a number of nobles in Anasoma had stashes hidden away. It had only taken the time to find two different nobles who'd died recently, and then she'd simply raided their secret lockboxes.

She placed the trinkets in the purse and held it up.

Rags extended and enfolded her hand, brushing unsettlingly against her skin. She resisted the temptation to draw away. When she felt a tug on the purse, she let go, and the rags withdrew.

"Good. Come, follow."

Felice faltered. "What's your name?" she asked.

The assassin turned to her, visage still lost in the folds of his loose hood. "I don't remember."

A nutcase, Felice decided. Albeit a highly effective one. He'd better be, for all the trouble she'd gone to. "What do I call you, then?"

For a long time, there was no movement, no sound, save the wind and rain.

"You've called me an assassin so far."

"Well, Assassin. What next?"

"Follow."

Felice turned to Izak. "You heard our man. Let's go."

"Are you sure this is wise?"

"No. But we have to do something, and soon. This is the only way. Rebecci thought so as well."

"And look where she is now," Izak muttered.

Felice's face went hard. "We'll end up like her if we don't do this. Dying like Rebecci is what we're trying to avoid. And when we kill Kelhak, the Indryallans will fall apart. We've been over this already. Now's not the time for second thoughts."

"What about third? Or fourth?"

Despite herself, Felice smiled. "Those either. We're in this till the end." She briefly squeezed Izak's arm and turned to face the assassin. "What do you do with the trinkets?"

"Do? I release them from their servitude."

Definitely a nutcase. As mad as an alchemist who'd drunk too much quicksilver. If Rebecci had placed all her hopes in him . . . perhaps she should have looked at other options.

Felice knew, though, there *weren't* other options.

She sighed, rubbing her eyes. "Lead the way."

CHAPTER 26

I t cannot be!"

"We must hide him! The Talon will be angry."

"So long. We had almost given up hope."

"The scrolls did not lie!"

The night air was thick with chatter. There were now four vormag. All gray haired and wrinkled. Old, like Gamzegul.

When his guide had told him they were almost there, Amerdan had insisted on waiting until dusk, when they'd be less noticeable. He didn't want Talon Xarlas finding out about him too soon. Not until he'd cemented his hold over these ignorant vormag. In the distance, he could hear the low roar of battle—jukari fighting Quivers. The sound ebbed and flowed as the feel of the night did when he was out hunting alone.

As the sun had gone down, Gamzegul had made Amerdan take his trinket and leave it hanging outside his shirt.

"A sign," it had said.

Amerdan wasn't comfortable with it out in the open. His secret.

But if it bent the minds of these savages, then he could tolerate it for a short time. After all, they'd be dead soon. Amerdan had no doubt the warlocks and the emperor's forces would triumph over the jukari. The question was, why didn't the jukari realize this? Did they have something they thought would sway any battle? Sorcery? Reinforcements?

Some of the jukari bore signs of fighting: hastily bandaged injuries, stained black with leaking blood. Broken pieces of armor and weapons lay scattered around, as if clung on to while the jukari fled and discarded in favor of new ones once they were safe. Amerdan saw a few of the beasts lick open wounds.

"We must take him to Talon Xarlas!" one of the creatures said now. "If it's found out we hid the Old One, the Talon will kill us all."

"I'll kill you now," Amerdan said with a snarl, "if you don't do as I say." He briefly opened his well and fed a pulse of power to Bells's crafting. Around him, the black shield flicked into, then out of, existence. He'd sensed flashes of sorcery close by—vormag—and it was a safe bet his would be lost among them.

At his display, the vormag hissed and snarled. Some stepped back in fear, while others fell to their knees.

"The darkness of the Old Ones! It is true," howled one.

"Quiet!" Gamzegul snapped at them, and the other creatures backed away.

Interesting, thought Amerdan. They recognized the dense shield as an ability of the Old Ones. He held back a laugh. As always, his luck was almost palpable. A trinket, a crafting, and a show of confidence and authority, and these beasts from before the Shattering were bent to his will. Pathetic creatures. But what could you expect from such unnatural things? Were they even alive, or just sewn-together pieces made to move and speak like puppets?

"Tell me of the talons," Amerdan said. "How do they differ from you? Are they sorcerers as well . . ." He trailed off as some of the vormag began to look strangely at him. Then he saw his mistake. As an Old One, he should already know. They were stupid, but not immune to some critical thinking.

"Time changes all things," he extemporized. "I need to know how they have been altered, to best deal with them."

"Of course," Gamzegul replied. "Some are sorcerers, some are not. They have other powers. Some of stealth, some of strength, of quickness. Only the Keepers are sorcerers."

Muttering arose from the other vormag at the words. Gamzegul silenced them with a glare.

Amerdan withheld a sigh. "The Keepers?"

Another vormag nodded; this creature had only one ear. "The Keepers hold the relics of the Old Ones, to await their triumphant return."

I doubt that's how the talons see it, mused Amerdan. "Why are only the Keepers sorcerers?"

"We . . . we do not know."

"Huh. Do the talons all have a trinket like this one?" Amerdan touched his silver cage.

Gamzegul shook his head. "Only—"

"Only the Keepers do. The sorcerer talons. Of course. And how many talons are there? And how many of them are Keepers?" The thought of foul creatures such as these possessing trinkets similar to his filled him with revulsion. They shouldn't be defiled that way. They were only for those who had been chosen.

For him.

"Not many . . . tens. Of them, only three are Keepers. There may be others in the wastes. There are many clans, spread over vast distances."

Gamzegul looked concerned. If the vormag knew what Amerdan had planned, it'd look a lot more worried.

"And Talon Xarlas is a Keeper, I take it?"

Gamzegul nodded.

Amerdan couldn't stand it anymore. Dotty squirmed against his skin, whether to warn him from taking this path or encouraging him, he couldn't tell. She was silent.

He tucked his trinket back inside his shirt. Patience was usually his strength, but after running from the battle, then all this hiding while he thought, he itched to do something. Sometimes patience could work against you. He'd already slipped up once. And if the vormag figured out he wasn't an Old One before he made his move, then it could get messy . . .

"Take me to Xarlas. Now."

CHAPTER 27

Halfway up the riverbank, Gazija disturbed something.

A strange-looking furry animal scampered up the trunk of a tree, sharp claws offering purchase on the rough bark. It stopped when it reached an overhanging branch, huddling down and regarding him with wide, fearful eyes. He studied it in the moonlight. It wasn't like any animal he'd seen before, but then again, so much here was different. The nocturnal creature, along with everything else, was a reminder they didn't belong.

So much strangeness. No wonder some of us go mad.

If the trauma of losing all you were wasn't enough, this world grinds you down. And the way we were forced to survive . . . Gazija almost retched at the thought. *Not me again,* he cursed determinedly. *Never again.*

Quiss had wanted to follow him on his walk, but Gazija had dissuaded him with excuses about needing time to think. What he really needed was certainty. To know he was following the correct path, had made the right choices. But as he knew all too well in his position, sometimes the only choice was between two bad options. Evil ones, some would argue.

His people saw him as a savior. But Gazija knew he was nothing. He'd brought a terrible fate upon them. One that gnawed at him every waking moment.

He began breathing hard. He was climbing a shallow rise to the crest of a hill. Hardly even a hill, but to him it was hard going. His canes didn't seem to be helping as much as they had when he'd first started using them. He was about to curse the wretched sticks but stopped. It was his body he should curse. Such a short-lived thing, it was, prone to all manner of repulsive ailments.

At the top of the hill, Gazija rested for a long while, letting the breeze cool him down and dry his sweat. At least some sensations were familiar, but they brought with them memories of what once was. What they'd all lost. Even pleasant recollections burned to ashes.

Turning to face the river, he fixed his gaze on the wharves and ships. Most of his people were down there. And he had a choice to make.

He reached into a pocket and pulled out the crafting he'd taken from the sorcerer Caldan. Garnet eyes stared out from the brass face of the figurine. An automaton, he'd called it. Both mechanical and sorcerous. A creation capable of moving on its own, and even of following rudimentary commands. The young man probably hadn't realized how close to coercive sorcery some of the workings were. One of Caldan's earlier masters might have, though few of them really had much of an inkling. They thought such sorcery was an abomination, while others used it only to subjugate. Ignorant, superstitious peasants.

Gazija had replaced the hardened ink Caldan had used. It was too easily chipped or scratched. Now, fine grooves were etched into the metal, using delicate destructive sorcery, following the patterns of the ink exactly. To the original runes, Gazija had added his own sorcery of such complexity and power, it was able to alter the original purpose and change the very nature of the object. Between the runes and shapes, far too small for a naked eye to detect, was Gazija's most subtle addition: coercive sorcery, but unlike any even he'd practiced before.

It might work. It might not.

He wouldn't know until it was tried. But the risk of failure was so very great . . . and the consequences could be devastating. They could scarcely afford to lose another.

Gazija sat on the grass, evening dew soaking into his pants. There he remained while the moon tracked across the night sky.

CHAPTER 28

Felice tripped over a skull and stumbled, pressing a hand on a wall to steady herself before jerking it back, covered in cobwebs. The skull rolled across the stone and shattered, scattering bone fragments brittle with age.

"Cursed ancestors!" Izak exclaimed at the noise.

"Keep your voice down!" Felice whispered.

Izak glared at her and brushed his hands against each other in an attempt to rid himself of his own strands of spiderweb. "If I'd known we were going to descend into the bowels of the earth through forgotten crypts, I'd have brought a lamp."

"We'll just have to make do. The assassin says he knows a way through the sewers and old tunnels, and we just have to trust him."

Izak muttered something too low for Felice to hear.

"What was that?"

"Nothing."

Ahead of them, the assassin paused, yet again waiting for them to catch up. Their only light was a sorcerous crafted globe he'd revealed. It was tied to a piece of leather cord, and he'd flung it over his shoulder so it rested in the middle of his back, just below Felice's eye level. It seemed either the assassin knew these tunnels intimately enough to travel through them blind, or he could see without the illumination, and it was for their convenience. As disturbing as the latter thought was, it showed he cared about them enough to provide the light for them.

Izak leaned in close and spoke in her ear. "I'll wager you ten gold ducats he's going to kill us."

"You don't have ten ducats. And besides, he's gone to an awful lot of trouble so far. If he was going to kill us, you'd think he'd have done it by now."

"True." Izak pulled at his goatee. "Perhaps we're in for a lot worse. Five ducats says he delivers us into Kelhak's hands."

Felice grinned. "I'll accept that wager. If you win, you can't collect."

"I'll just have to be content with knowing I beat you."

A low grumbling came from the mountain of rags, and they both stopped talking.

Felice looked across the tunnel to the wall on her left. Bones were stacked neatly in rows forming patterns, with skulls on top. Sightless sockets had watched them pass for the last hour. Far beneath Anasoma were many forgotten crypts, and the ones they traveled through now were ancient. When stone corridors ended, a rough-hewn tunnel through rock or earth led to the next. Someone had spent a great deal of time connecting them all. It must have taken decades; and by the look of the work, it had been completed a long time ago. A thick layer of dust had settled in the newer tunnels, giving rise to the idea that they hadn't been "new" for a long, long time.

"I've heard rumors about creatures inhabiting the oldest, deepest tunnels."

Felice snorted with amusement. "Izak, those rumors are used to scare young children into obedience, or for late nights at the inn, when you've had too many drinks."

"I knew a man who knew a woman who was down in the sewers. She was a young thief, exploring—"

"Hearsay," interrupted Felice. "Reason and evidence, please."

Izak made a show of patting himself down, then looked at her with mock surprise. "Oh, I must have left it in my summer house."

A faint sound impinged on Felice's awareness. Not unlike a snapping of cloth in the wind. A breath of air brushed her cheek. Ahead of them, the assassin had disappeared. On the stone floor ten paces ahead was the sorcerous globe.

"Felice," Izak breathed, voice laden with dread.

He'd drawn his knife again.

"Wait," she said.

There was a side tunnel up ahead—a section of the wall that swallowed their light. She heard another ripple. There was a faint shriek, like a scalded cat. It lingered for a few moments before it was silenced abruptly.

Izak's breath came in rapid gasps. "Not good. This is not good."

Felice held up a hand, trying to remain calm, despite her heart in her throat and a voice inside her head telling her to grab the light and run. "Stay calm. I said wait."

Another snap of cloth. A movement of air. A shadow stepped out of the side passage. The assassin.

She took a few steps back and looked up at him. His head almost brushed the ceiling. He was a tall man, with a remarkably silent step. A valuable trait in his line of work. He faced them, which left the sorcerous globe at his feet and his hood lost in darkness. It was only then that she noticed the blade in his hand, dripping something dark onto the stones. Droplets spattered next to the globe. It had to be blood, but . . . it wasn't red. It was black. Her eyes traveled back to the blade, and she noticed a pattern of runes etched into the metal close to where it disappeared into the rags. It was smith-crafted, or a trinket.

"Beware. There are . . . creatures here . . . in these oldest, deepest tunnels."

Felice locked eyes with Izak. He gave her a pleading look, all but shouting for them to go back. She shook her head.

"Assassin, what are these creatures you speak of?" Felice peered into the recesses of the man's hood, trying yet again to discern his features. To no avail. The blade was gone, and she hadn't seen him move.

"Forgotten ones. Scavengers."

"How do they survive down here? Do you know?"

There was a long pause.

"Others . . . dispose of corpses . . . down here."

Again, the man's eerie habit of repeating their words. It was both irritating and disturbing. He probably meant people who wanted to get rid of bodies left them in the tunnels. Thugs and criminals, thieves and murderers.

Abruptly, the assassin turned, rags swirling, and started off back down the tunnel. Hardly any dust stirred with his passage. Felice and Izak followed, and after what could have been one hour or three, he stopped them again. A waterskin dropped to the floor.

"Drink," he said.

Felice picked it up and unstoppered it. She was desperately thirsty, and they were woefully unprepared for a trip such as this. She didn't like feeling unprepared, or at another's mercy. She sniffed at the mouth of the skin, then took a tiny sip. Thankfully, it contained water, but she hadn't known what to expect. So far, this had been weird enough to make her question the simplest things. She drank greedily and handed the waterskin to Izak.

"We are . . . almost there."

Felice frowned. By her calculations, they had a long way to go, even if time had slipped away from them. Their route had been relatively straight, with no crowds to navigate, but they couldn't possibly be close.

"We can't be. How much farther is it?"

"Some hundreds . . . of paces."

"Some? Does that mean?"

"Three hundred."

No. Impossible. "That's—"

Metal chiming on stone interrupted her. Two daggers had dropped out of the man's rags onto the floor. Both were thin, with blades as long as her hand. But . . . they were covered in patterns. She peered closer, leaning forward. Vines, or possibly a tree, with the hilt as the trunk, each pommel a ball of twisted silver wire. Felice bit her bottom lip. Were they trinkets?

"Take . . . for Kelhak."

She bent over and picked up both daggers. There was no mistaking them now: trinkets, for certain. The silver alloy that wasn't quite silver. Both daggers would have collectors salivating and eager to empty their coffers of ducats to own them. She examined the pommels closely. There was something familiar about them. Through the strands of wire, she could see each enclosed a gem, clear, possibly a diamond.

Savine.

The realization hit her like a bolt of lightning. Rebecci had trapped Savine in a crafting like this.

A chill swept through Felice, much like when an opponent's Dominion strategy all of a sudden became discernible to her, and she realized her position was precarious. Somehow, they'd traveled a far greater distance than was possible. The assassin was tall. In fact, she'd never seen a man of his height before. Wielding a smith-crafted blade, possibly even a trinket. The man's need for trinkets as payment. His reputation. And two blades, which could only have one purpose, if her reasoning was correct.

This man, this . . . assassin was a sorcerer—but something more. And they needn't have paid him. He wanted them here. More than that, he would be doing this even if they hadn't asked him.

Pignuts.

"You have your own reasons to kill Kelhak, don't you?"

The rags stirred. "Rebecci and I. We agreed."

"What did you agree?"

The ragged hood above her leaned forward. "It is a lich. An inhibitor. It dominates."

It, not *he*. The assassin's choice of words increased her already disturbed state of mind. It was as if he thought Kelhak wasn't a man. Except she'd met Kelhak; they'd played Dominion, and she thought he was. The term *lich* meant nothing to her.

And now this . . . assassin—and, it seemed, Rebecci—thought Kelhak was similar to Savine.

"Kelhak," Felice said. "He's not what he seems, is he? He's not Kelhak. Something has taken possession of him."

"Already . . . said."

Behind her, Izak hissed with surprise. There were layers here she wasn't aware of. And as reticent as the assassin was, she had to tease information from him. "And we're not really killing Kelhak, are we? We're going to capture whatever possesses him."

If she was expecting a response from the assassin to show she was correct, she was disappointed. He didn't move, didn't make a sound.

"Why do you need us? I would think you could get to him unawares far easier than we could."

He said nothing, but it didn't matter—she hadn't become a spymaster without piecing together clues. *We're a distraction. No . . . anyone would do for that. He isn't certain he'll succeed. We're insurance. Which means we have currency. Rebecci planned this . . . She knew she might be killed.* "Answer this, then: What stake do you have in all this? Because if you don't answer, we're going to turn around and leave."

"About time," Izak muttered.

Felice waited. She snorted in disgust and made to leave, placing the daggers back on the ground. The assassin spoke, breaking the silence.

"My master commanded me."

"Who is your master? Where is he?"

"Gone. Dead."

"And you're still following his commands?" Felice asked.

Without a hint of movement, the rag-clothed man seemed to expand, almost filling the tunnel. A hum filled the air, not quite out of her hearing. Felice swallowed. She felt the menace the assassin exuded. It was a palpable force, with a weight, and she steeled herself as it washed over her.

"Do not presume. The master was wise beyond all others."

Felice studied the assassin. An idea seeded in her mind, sprouted, and grew. *No . . . Yes, it fits.* She staggered, steadying herself with a hand. The walls closed in on her. She struggled to draw breath.

Breathe, damn you, she castigated herself. Weakly, she began to laugh. Once she started, she couldn't stop.

Izak said something, his words unintelligible.

Don't let it crush you. Pull yourself together.

Eventually, her mirth bubbled away, leaving her half smiling, half grimacing. She knew what the truth was. Knew with the crystal clarity that only one gifted in Dominion could have. There was no doubt.

"You're a . . . a . . ." Felice waved her hand, uncertain of what term to use. "A construct from before the Shattering. But you're not jukari or vormag . . . What are you?" *By the bloody ancestors, the creature has to be thousands of years old! What does it know? What could it reveal to me?* It was all she could do to quash her hunger for knowledge.

"I am made, yes. But more than that. I'm alive. I am a talon."

Felice nodded, even though she had no idea what most of that meant. "You're following your master's dying wishes. He perished in the Shattering."

The creature stirred. Now Felice didn't want to see inside the hood.

"As did all sorcerers."

All? No, that couldn't be. "That's not true. There are sorcerers alive today, working their craft, and have been since the Shattering."

"Not like the Old Ones, the liches. The sorcerers you know were born afterward."

History was vague for hundreds of years after the cataclysmic event. No written works from the time survived. If it were true, what had caused every sorcerer in the world to die?

"How did they die?"

"My master killed them."

The answer hit her like a hammer blow. The enormity of it. Both the wickedness and scale of such a task. But was it evil, or had it been necessary?

"Why did he kill them?" Felice whispered.

"They were accumulating power. It was evil. All of them had become liches, and they had to be stopped. Exterminated."

There was that word again. The creature, talon, had used it to describe Kelhak. *Lich.*

"What is Kelhak? What is a lich?"

"They take. Collect. Accumulate to gain strength. They imprison others . . . Eventually, all they feel is hunger and a need to survive."

Bloody ancestors. Savine. Rebecci's crafting. People's souls, their essence, could be *extracted*.

And used.

Felice briefly covered her face with her hands, then rubbed her eyes. "Kelhak absorbs the life force of others, presumably to keep him alive. He's also a powerful sorcerer. How can we hope to defeat him?"

"Yes . . . and yes. Kelhak is many, and many are Kelhak."

A lich. Pignuts. Another realization hit her. "How many wells does he have?"

"Many."

Felice sighed. "I see. And what does he, it, inhibit?"

"Death."

"His own death?"

The hood moved from side to side—a shake of the head. "Others . . . those he subsumes."

CHAPTER 29

Caldan traveled the short distance into Riversedge, finally able to find the apartment he'd rented days ago and collect the rest of his belongings Quiss had left behind—basically some spare sets of clothes and some odds and ends. The fact was, he didn't really care about those things, but he needed an excuse to retrieve the bone trinket, and he couldn't be sure if Gazija would have him followed. To be fair, he also didn't know if Devenish would be after him, or if Lisanette would track him down and try to get her revenge, but he felt he could make a quick trip and get back without anyone the wiser. He made sure his shield and coercive sorcery craftings were in easy reach. On his way out, the innkeeper offered him a breakfast of honeyed porridge and charred lizards dipped in yogurt—apparently a local specialty. Caldan declined, not feeling particularly hungry, but accepted a cup of steaming tea. It was hot and sweet and good.

A short way down the street, the gate was already busy with wagons and people carrying baskets passing through both ways. The loud noise of the throng irritated him, and he realized he was in a bad mood. The truth was, he had no real plan at the moment. Making things up as he went along wasn't his strong suit, especially when the stakes were so high.

It took Caldan some time to make his way through the gate. The arrival of the emperor's forces had calmed the population somewhat, even though they still battled with the jukari close by; and now they were making hay while the sun shone, selling as much of their produce and goods as possible before this unexpected source of demand dried up. The press of horses and mules and oxen and wagons clogged the passageway. Many men and women argued with the Quivers guarding the gate and with one another; it made his head ache. He clenched his jaw and pushed through them as best he could.

Caldan breathed a sigh of relief as the Quivers waved him through, and he joined the exodus leaving Riversedge for the river wharves. He squinted into the bright sun and paused, catching his breath, but in reality he knew he was merely delaying the inevitable.

He was taking a chance, but the jukari horde had been pushed back enough for the roads to be clear on the way to where he'd hidden his bone ring.

He sent out a short prayer to the ancestors, not only that the jukari were held at bay, but that he didn't run into any Quivers or warlocks.

Luck must have been with Caldan, for he made his way to the abandoned village without incident. Dust rose into the sky nearby, signaling jukari and Quivers fighting, but far enough away that he could hear the battle only as a faint roar. As quickly as he could, he made it to the well, looking around one more time to make sure he was alone. He saw no one—and sensed no nearby sorcery—and felt reasonably confident he was by himself. He hastily climbed over the top and descended into the stone shaft, pressing against the sides, until he reached the bottom. Groping around in the muck, he let his fingers search for the package he'd dropped in.

There.

Snatching up the small bundle, Caldan scaled back out and ripped it open. Inside was the trinket, and he breathed a sigh of relief. He quickly hung the bone ring back around his neck, tucking it out of sight underneath his shirt. He looked around once more, waiting to see if anyone came out to challenge him, but he could hear only the muted battle in the distance. With purpose, he left the village, and before long he was back within sight of Riversedge and joining a line of people entering a gate.

A cloud passed across the sun, leaving him in shadow. At the same time, he could sense something . . . a gossamer thread of threat at the edge of his awareness. Strange. There hadn't been any clouds before. He looked up to see a dark haze on the horizon. As he stood there watching, the bright spot of the sun was blotted out. It was . . . unnatural. Even at this distance, bright flashes spread across the cloud; except they weren't silver, like lightning.

The eruptions were green, mixed with violet.

Sorcery again. And from the direction of Anasoma. The Indryallans, it had to be. And it was obvious they were no longer content to wait for the Mahruse Empire to come to them—they were lashing out.

Whatever was coming, it would be powerful and dangerous. Outside was no place for someone unshielded. *Ancestors, maybe even a shield wouldn't be enough.*

"Back!" he yelled to those around him and pointed toward the storm. "There's more sorcery coming. Get back inside the city and find shelter."

Cries of dismay erupted as people noticed the storm for the first time.

Miranda. His first priority was her safety. Besides, there was almost nothing he could do here. Gazija and Quiss would be better able to fend off whatever virulent sorcery was coming their way. Leaving the spreading panic, Caldan broke into a sprint and left the road, heading for the wharves.

By the time he reached Gazija's ship, the storm covered half the sky, and the wind had picked up enough to tear at his clothes. Dust and leaves struck his face, and he shielded his eyes with a forearm.

The deck was crawling with sailors, bracing themselves against the strengthening gale as they made the ship fast. Sorcerers were huddled in a group, taking orders from a shouting Quiss. Whatever Quiss was saying was lost in the wind. The other sorcerers could hear him, though, and a few nodded. Two broke away and barged past Caldan, back down the gangplank onto the wharf.

"Quiss!" Caldan shouted over the tumult as he approached. "Where's Miranda?"

"Belowdecks" came the reply. Quiss grabbed his arm. "Did you see Gazija?"

"What? No. Is he missing?"

Quiss lowered his head. "Yes. Gone somewhere on his own again. I shouldn't have let him."

"It's not your fault."

"I'm supposed to protect him."

"He can protect himself."

Quiss shook his head. "I don't think so. I've seen this before. It's . . . not good. Not good at all."

"Where have you seen this? What can we do?"

"There's no time to explain. We'll shield as best we can. We should be able to save the ships and protect the mercenaries."

It'll have to do, thought Caldan. To survive another day. That was all that mattered at the moment.

"I have to find Gazija," Quiss said. "I can sense there's more sorcery building somewhere to the north, and more to the west. One of the sources might be Gazija, but I don't know what he's doing there."

Caldan hesitated, glimpsed images of Miranda, but also of Gazija and Kelhak.

"Are you certain Miranda will be safe?" he said.

Quiss nodded, wind whipping his hair. "Yes."

"Then I'll come with you."

Maybe one day, I'll remember I can't fix everything, he thought ruefully.

CHAPTER 30

Felice was both scared and hesitant.

Her booted feet cracked old, brittle bones with each step.
Here, the order of the previous cryptlike tunnels was gone.
What were once organized and systematic stacks of human bones were
now strewn across the tunnel floor, as if someone—or something—
had torn them down in a rage. A thick oak door had been left open,
leading into a cavernous room. Light from the sorcerous globe faded
to darkness before revealing walls at the side. Tessellated tiles covered
the illuminated section of floor, obscured with a thin layer of dust but
still showing a primitive scene of men and women hunting fantastical
animals and clubbing them to death.

Rusted, broken hinges had decayed to almost nothing. The wood
of the door was ancient, cracks splitting through carved runes and
symbols. A few Felice recognized, not from any sorcery she'd been
exposed to, but—she was surprised to discover—from Dominion.
There, a twisted square surrounding a seven-pointed star, which in
turn enclosed a tiny face. And another, a symbol always carved into

the robes of the Cybele piece—a woman meant to embody life, which in certain situations could propagate an extra piece during the game. She stopped, pausing to ponder the significance of the carvings. It once had value far greater than a mere door. *Why else go to the trouble of decorating it with intricate designs?*

"They thought it would ward off the dead," she said, answering her own question.

Cloth rustled as the talon turned at her words. "You see clearly."

Felice swallowed. "Did the dead need to be warded against, back then?"

"Some . . . not here."

Superstition, then. But which dead did they feel they needed protection from? *Bloody ancestors, Rebecci, why aren't you here? I'm lost. This was important to you, but I'm walking in blind.*

Her fingers brushed across the carvings as she passed through. The stale air of the tunnels was replaced by a fresher scent. Felice greedily took a few more breaths. She hadn't realized, but she'd been breathing dead air, devoid of odor except for a whiff of dust. It made sense—it was the kind you'd find inside a coffin or tomb.

Their light moved to the left as the talon did. Izak sidled up beside her, bones crunching underfoot.

"Something," he said, "or someone, scattered those bones across the floor."

All she could do was nod. He was confirming her earlier thoughts.

With hinges rusted to uselessness, the door couldn't be secured. Something had known. And had used the old bones as a . . . warning? Or as an alarm. But the bones rested atop the dust covering the floor, and they themselves were covered in only a thin layer, as if they'd been moved very recently.

Felice bit her bottom lip. The creature the talon had killed . . . it was one of many, it had said. And, it appeared, they were *aware*. After so many years alone down here in the hidden depths of Anasoma, they felt frightened enough to set up a warning system—crude though it was. But frightened of what?

Part of her wanted to plant her feet and not budge until the talon revealed all it knew. Another part knew that would be folly. She hadn't known it before, but they were on a timetable. It was something she'd always been good at gauging, and at the moment, urgency tugged at her with insistence. "How long do we have?" she asked the talon.

"Not long. But we are close."

"Close? Close to what?"

"The end."

"You mean Kelhak?"

"Yes."

Once more, though, Felice felt something was off about the talon's statements. In this case, she doubted not the distance but how long it would take to get to the God-Emperor. They were ancestors knew how far underground, and by all reports, Kelhak would be heavily guarded. Unless the talon knew he wouldn't be . . .

"Tell me," she demanded. "What's the distraction?"

Izak frowned, looking puzzled. He hadn't caught up yet.

"The lich is performing sorcery."

Felice grunted. "A big one, I'll wager."

"Yes . . . he has decided to reveal himself. His followers will be sent away."

"How do you know this?"

"Rebecci arranged for it. Her leader will expose himself. The lich will not be able to resist. Kelhak will be drawn, and weakened."

So that's what Rebecci's plan was. Her leader was Gazija, of course. It was a dangerous path the sorcerers were on. She had to admire their courage.

And Kelhak would be alone, distracted by a complex and draining crafting. Perfect.

Except, of course, that no matter how good a plan is, a thousand things could go wrong.

Izak's hand rested on her shoulder. It was warm and welcoming. She covered it with her own.

"We'll get through this," he reassured her. "This is Rebecci's plan, and she wasn't a fool. She trusted this . . . talon, and whatever this distraction is."

Felice gave him a brief smile. He was a good man. But many good people had died so far who shouldn't have. Rebecci wasn't a fool.

Are we?

"HERE . . ."

Izak stepped ahead of Felice and poked his head outside the large window. She latched the door behind them.

The talon stood in corner near a barrel of salted beef marked with two horns and a triangle. The storeroom was small, its contents sparse. She shifted uncomfortably. This close to the talon, she caught a whiff of its rags. Old, rotting cloth. Dust. Age.

"There's nothing outside to lower ourselves onto. We're two stories up." Izak pulled his head inside. "We'd injure ourselves if we jumped. We have to find another way down."

Felice shook her head. "We're not going down. We need to go up." Kelhak's rooms were at the top of the building—having been there before, she knew that much.

"There'll be too many guards, though, if we use the corridors and stairs. Not to mention sorcerers."

She became aware of the talon standing behind her. Felice's heart skipped a beat. She hadn't heard it move. Slowly, she pivoted to face it. Tilting her head back, she looked into the dark, hooded face.

"Well? I assume this was also planned for?"

"Yes. We go up."

"How?"

Rough, musty rags enfolded her, and she yelped. Dimly, she was aware of Izak cursing. She hurtled toward the window, back first. Felice struggled to suppress a scream, knowing it could give them away. But the talon's arm held her tightly, almost squeezing the breath from her lungs. Her feet scraped against the sill as the talon pushed them both outside the window. Her feet dangled above the courtyard below. With a jerk, it fell beneath her. Wind rushed into her face with the swiftness of their passage, her hair whipping around her.

The talon ascended the wall with frightening speed, then stopped so suddenly Felice's stomach lurched upward, and she fought down nausea. They were in front of another window, this one glass. The room inside was dark. Rags pressed against the window frame, and with a crack, the latch broke. The window opened with a faint squeak from its hinges. She jerked forward as the talon entered the room, and she and Izak were unceremoniously deposited on the floor. Luckily, a luxurious rug padded their landing. Felice's fingers tangled in the long weave as she struggled to control herself.

Already, the talon was in the corner, as if it had touched them as long as it could bear.

Well, the feeling is mutual.

Izak staggered to his feet, muttering.

"How? Did it use sorcery to hold on to us?" He rubbed his arms, then straightened his shirt, all with sidelong glances at the talon. "It moved so fast . . ." He broke off, shaking his head.

Felice could still feel the sinewy muscle and bone of the arm that had clutched her tightly during the ascent. *By the bloody ancestors . . .* She took a breath. It had more than two arms. It couldn't have held on to them and scaled the wall otherwise. A chill ran through her. What else did the rags conceal?

Actually . . . I don't want to know.

"Yes," Felice said, mouth dry. "Sorcery."

Izak might fall to pieces if she told him the truth. They were both on edge as it was. He was putting on a brave face for what he thought was her sake, but cracks were starting to show. She didn't know if they needed him for when they confronted Kelhak, but she did know she needed *someone* besides the talon, lest she lose grip on her own mind. Because what they were doing was crazy. All she was going on was the fact that Rebecci trusted this creature. For there wasn't any doubt now. It wasn't just an act put on by someone trying to craft themselves a reputation. The rags, the halting speech, the oddness of the talon were real. It was what it was.

"Felice?"

Izak interrupted her thoughts.

"Yes? I'm sorry, I was thinking."

"Hopefully about what to do next?"

They both turned to the talon.

The sorcerous globe appeared again from somewhere underneath the talon's coverings. They were in a bedroom. A massive carved blackwood bed was against one wall, with dressers on either side. Expensive wall hangings surrounded them, and an exquisite Dominion board stood in a corner.

Felice couldn't help herself. She moved to the board and touched a few of the pieces, fingers coming away with a smear of dust. Whoever had furnished this room had a lot of ducats. And they hadn't been here for a while. Dead. Or imprisoned. Or they'd fled. It didn't matter.

"Is Kelhak on this floor?" she asked the assassin.

"No. The one below."

Ah, crafty. No one would expect an assault from above. Not here. Not once they'd cleared the levels and made certain they were empty.

"Lead the way, then. Izak, are you ready?"

He fidgeted and ran a hand through his hair. The other strayed to his knife. "Yes. For . . . whatever we're about to do. For Anasoma."

He surprised her. He had more heart than he let on. *Good.*

"Yes—for Anasoma." *And I suspect there's more than Anasoma at stake here.* There were wheels within wheels. Machinations within machinations.

Through the bedroom door was a carpeted corridor with wood-paneled walls. Their footfalls fell soundlessly as they followed the talon, stopping at a wide staircase down.

"Wait . . ." the talon said.

Izak brandished the trinket dagger. He looked ill at ease. Felice drew her own. She was certain she knew what it would do—capture Kelhak's essence. But what would they do with it once they had it confined? It had to be guarded, possibly hidden. Or sunk in the depths of the ocean.

And this all depended on them not only getting close enough for the daggers to work, but then getting far enough away to not be killed by anyone who was upset by the fact they'd just stolen their God-Emperor.

She joined Izak, and they sat on the carpet. If they had to wait, they might as well be comfortable.

"I hope we succeed," Felice whispered.

Izak smiled at her. The smile was weak, but he hadn't given up hope.

"We will. Then you can go back to spying on everyone, and I can get back to enjoying myself."

"I don't spy on everyone," she protested.

"But you would, if you could."

She had to chuckle. "Maybe. But that's not needed. Only a few people need watching closely."

"You see everyone as a piece on a Dominion board, don't you?"

Felice began to protest again, but something stopped her. *Do I? Are people game pieces to me?* She really thought about it for a moment, until she was finally able to answer herself truthfully.

No. But they acted as if they were. If this happened, that person would act a certain way. Another would react differently. So—no, they weren't all pieces. But they were all predictable.

"I see patterns, that's all."

She was glad Izak didn't reply, leaving her to examine her thoughts.

Felice didn't know how long they waited. After a while, she had to stand to return blood to her legs. A few moments after she stood, the talon stirred.

"Soon . . ." it rasped.

Now that it had spoken, Felice was aware of a change. A pressure had built, like the air before a storm, so gradually she hadn't noticed it. A faint, warm breeze wafted up the stairs, laden with the acrid smell of burning wood and scorched metal.

She clutched her dagger tightly, motioning for Izak to stand. He did, and they both watched the talon for a sign. Izak shifted his weight constantly from foot to foot. She could hear him breathing through his mouth, shallow and fast.

The rags stirred. "Come."

The creature descended the stairs without hurrying, tattered cloth sliding down the treads. At the bottom, it hesitated, hood moving from side to side, as if searching. Ahead was another carpeted corridor. A light-filled opening broke the darkness in the distance.

The talon moved away from the light, a few short steps to the wall on their right. There was a *snick* of metal, and a panel in the wall jutted open a finger's width. A concealed door.

They followed the talon inside, along a narrow passage. They turned left and continued farther. The corridor opened into an alcove, barely big enough for the three of them, especially considering the talon's size. Pinholes of light shone through the wall in front of them. It looked to be made from strips of wood with a thin layer of plaster covering them. On the other side, Felice could guess, was a fresco of some kind, all the better to hide the spy holes.

Felice pressed her eye to one of them and looked out at a strange tableau.

Kelhak knelt in the middle of the room, naked and glistening, like an ancient marble statue of a hero. Sweat dripped down his skin, joining a puddle underneath his legs. He was in the center of a circle delineated by a thumb-thick braided rope of . . . silver and gold? Gemstones the size of hen's eggs shone from bulges in the cord.

Despite the situation, Felice felt a catch in her throat. Even though it had been only a week or so at most since she'd seen him, she had forgotten that Kelhak was so . . . beautiful. *Except*, she reminded herself, *he isn't Kelhak anymore. Whoever Kelhak was, could have been, is gone.*

Surrounding him were crafted globes, enough to brighten the room as if it were bathed in broad daylight. True to Felice's guess, the walls were covered with paintings—scenes from the Shattering, mostly destructive and tragic, all loosely based on the famous illustrations in the *Paluruk Codex*, by an unknown author. Reclaimed in the Desolate Lands hundreds of years ago, the codex was cited as the oldest record known of the times during the Shattering.

One wall detailed a massive battle between sorcerers and their minions. Vormag and jukari beyond number fought ahead of tall, robed sorcerers, and behind them stood men and women with glowing hands and eyes.

Wait . . . Felice had seen similar paintings before, and books with colored illustrations. Histories pieced together from the Shattering. But this time, something stirred within her at the sight of the tall sorcerers directing the jukari. Scholars all agreed they were sorcerers, though they couldn't agree on why they towered over the jukari. Consensus was that it was stylistic, an embellishment on the artists' part to show the power of the sorcerers of the time.

But I know that's not true . . .

She flicked a glance at the talon beside her, taking her eyes off Kelhak for an instant. The talon was what was depicted in the paintings, not grandiose ideas of human sorcerers.

She looked back and saw how those tall, cloaked beings were clearly in charge.

So what was it doing living beneath Anasoma? And why is it here now? What does it have to gain from killing the lich?

Its power.

Rebecci had placed her trust in the talon, but what if she was wrong? Or what if she was right and had always meant for this talon to take the lich's power—and somehow that would benefit her? But she wasn't here anymore. Felice was, scant yards from Kelhak, and about to attempt to kill him.

She bit her lip in indecision, hard enough to draw blood.

"Look at that!" hissed Izak in barely a whisper.

The talon's hood jerked around at the sound, dark interior facing Izak, who swallowed and smiled weakly. Gradually, the talon returned to face the wall, presumably peering through its own spy hole.

Felice ignored their byplay. Kelhak hadn't moved from his position. What had caused Izak to exclaim was the air around Kelhak. It shimmered like the air above the ground baking in the desert, except light flashed from something it carried. Felice squinted, straining to make out what it was. Glimmering threads of different colors—green, blue, and violet. Once seen, they became more noticeable to her, snaking and twisting around Kelhak.

She could sense fate surrounding them. The stakes in this moment were high. She almost laughed at the understatement. Before, she had thought that more than just Anasoma was at risk. Now she *knew* it to her very core. It wasn't the thunderstorm feel of Kelhak's sorcery. Nor the presence of the talon, crouched as it was next to her, ready to pounce. Or even the cold metallic touch of the trinket dagger she found herself gripping tightly in her sweaty hand. There was a weight to this moment, a ponderous importance she could ascribe only to her inner mind teasing out a reasoning her conscious mind had yet to determine.

And that thought terrified her. To not know what hung in the balance . . . and to have to act and hope the consequences were an improvement over the original state of affairs.

She glanced at the talon, who remained glued to the peephole. Then at Izak, who had abandoned his. He sat on the floor, knees to his chest, breathing heavily, like a sick dog. He offered her a weak smile, which faltered. But he still clutched his dagger, a good sign.

This was one of those moments she dreaded. You swallowed whatever fears you had, hardened your face, and did what needed doing.

The tension swelled with every beat of her heart.

Reaching a hand to Izak, she grasped his. *You can do this*, she mouthed, and nodded firmly. Izak's nod in reply was short, but it was there.

She turned her head and fixed on Kelhak again. Nothing had changed. Perhaps the threads were more energetic, but it was hard to tell.

A rag-covered hand landed on her shoulder, and she flinched. Slowly she faced the talon. It bent down and leaned close to her, so its cowl was next to her ear. Cloth brushed her hair, cheek, and neck, and her skin cringed at the touch. Fetid mustiness filled her nostrils.

"Wait . . ." A breathless pause. "Soon . . ."

The rags withdrew, and Felice sucked in a breath.

A crack echoed in the chamber, as if a tree split in two. She jumped, startled.

The talon didn't move, and Kelhak remained still.

Felice gripped her dagger even tighter, skin slick. She licked her lips, tasting her salt.

Another crack. Around Kelhak, the air shimmered further, distorting his body. It rolled over him like waves. Soon his form lost all definition. Felice's teeth rattled along with a vibration, and a hum filled the air.

Light as bright as the sun erupted. Felice flinched and fell backward onto her ass, blinking tears from her eyes. It was too dark. She couldn't see. The flash had ruined her night vision.

She scrambled to her left, questing hand grabbing onto the talon's coarse rags.

The hum rose in volume, and the vibration was enough to make her bones ache.

"Soon . . ."

Soon what? We run in there blindly? But her eyes slowly adjusted. She could now see the spy holes and again pressed her eye to one. Kelhak was virtually invisible. Glimmering sorcery surrounded him, so intense it obscured everything within the circle.

Abruptly, the vibration, noise, and movement ceased.

Felice's mouth dropped open. Izak let loose a string of curses.

Kelhak had disappeared.

Pignuts. "Where is he?" she hissed at the talon.

"Gone . . ." the black pit of the talon's hood whispered at her.

"I can see that. Where?"

The rags rippled. Felice guessed it was a shrug.

Izak chuckled nervously. "Well, that was a letdown. I could use a cold drink and a warm barmaid."

"Wait," the talon said. "We strike when the lich returns. Rebecci was to disrupt the lich's sorcery and force him to return in a weakened state."

"But Rebecci is dead."

"We wait."

Felice wiped her forehead with the back of her arm, doing little, as both were soaked with sweat. She throttled her own mirth at the absurdity of it all, for fear that once she started laughing, she wouldn't stop. She sat in the dust, bewildered and stressed, waiting.

CHAPTER 31

Another boom of thunder washed over Caldan, and he shivered. The wind had whipped into a gale, and the dark clouds overhead roiled with animosity. Blue and violet streaks flashed among them, like glowing snakes racing amid smoke.

Caldan and Quiss stumbled across uneven ground, scuffed grass, and mud and stones.

Far in the distance, Quiver horns pierced the tumult, no doubt sounding a retreat for the forces warring with the jukari. Caldan doubted they could do much but huddle together and wait for the sorcery to dissipate. But there was something different about this storm that he couldn't quite name. It seemed less virulent and more focused, as if its purpose wasn't destruction.

Quiss looked at him with wild eyes.

"It has to be him," the sorcerer shouted. "Now that we're closer, I can feel his signature."

"How far?" Caldan said, having to raise his voice to be heard.

"A hundred yards perhaps."

Caldan squinted into the wind, which blew dirt and dust, obscuring their vision. There was a copse of trees in the direction Quiss pointed, by the bank of a stream.

Quiss quickened his pace, and Caldan hurried to catch up. Far above their heads, the clouds circled, and Caldan didn't like the look of them. They weren't centered over the emperor's forces, but improbably, they were directly atop where Quiss thought Gazija was.

By the ancestors, what was going on?

Caldan felt a surge of sorcery and heard Quiss gasp. A shield dome covered the trees, not pitch-black as Bells's had been, but barely a haze, like a ripple in the atmosphere. From a distance, they might have missed it—and perhaps that was the point.

Quiss and Caldan rushed toward it but stopped at its edge. Quiss placed both hands against it, as if trying to push his way inside.

"What are you—"

"Quiet!" Quiss said. "Yes, it's Gazija." The sorcerer glanced up at the clouds, then uttered a curse in an unknown tongue. "This way!"

He ran along the edge of the shield, and Caldan followed. Quiss kept peering through the barrier, then stopped abruptly.

"Here! Look!"

Caldan could see through the trees. A small figure sat on the trunk of a fallen tree, the stream flowing past in front of him.

Gazija.

From inside the shield, he turned to regard them with a look of chagrin, like a child caught stealing sweets. Then he turned his face from them.

He was only fifteen paces away, and they couldn't reach him.

"Fool! Fool!" Quiss said. "We're in this together!"

Caldan grabbed his arm. "What's happening?"

Quiss turned to face Caldan, looking like someone whose child had just died. Tears streaked his face, blown sideways by the wind.

"Gazija has somehow led Kelhak to him. He must have a plan he thinks will defeat him."

"Can we get through the shield? Can we help him?"

Quiss shook his head. "No. For the moment, all we can do is watch."

They turned to look through the shield, just as Gazija reached down and drew something out of a sack at his feet: Caldan's smith-crafted figure. But something about it was different. He could sense it from here. He knew his own work, and this one had been altered. Runes inscribed in lines finer than the thinnest hair, many symbols smaller than a grain of sand. They complemented what Caldan had started, altering and enhancing original elements. What resulted was a smith-crafting many times more complex. Gazija had taken the crafting to its logical conclusion.

Gusts of wind swirled, and Caldan shielded his eyes from the dust and leaves. Most blew around him, but some detritus hit his skin with a force that stung. A heavy, metallic scent filled the air. He tilted his head back and squinted at the roiling clouds. Glowing filaments of sorcery churned among them, green, blue, and violet. Caldan knew there was a pattern to them, but it was far beyond his ken.

In the center of the whirlwind, the clouds were now halfway to the ground. As he watched, they accelerated rapidly. Down the clouds came, twisting and spinning, to strike the other side of the stream.

Caldan's guts churned as reality folded in on itself. He doubled over, hands clawing at his stomach. He vomited bile onto the dirt. It didn't seem to help. Gagging and nauseated, he staggered a few steps before sinking to his knees.

And then, just as suddenly as it had hit him, the sensation was gone. Calm settled over him. Leaves and dirt no longer stung. The wind had died, as if a door to it closed.

Caldan knelt there, knees digging into the soil, trying to pull himself together. He wiped his mouth with the back of his hand and spat.

"Slave!" came a booming voice.

Caldan lurched to his feet, shaking his head to clear it.

"It's here," Quiss said with despair. "The lich is here."

Lich?

A man stood across the stream from Gazija.

"Kelhak," Quiss breathed.

The God-Emperor was tall and muscular, blue eyes glowing as if lit with an inner fire. Naked as a newborn babe. He wore not a single crafting or trinket.

"*Ik'zvime*," Gazija spat, standing.

"Just so." Kelhak's face was expressionless as he stared.

Caldan opened his well. To his crafting senses, the man was transformed: a sorcerous construct housed in flesh. Lines of power radiated throughout his body, never seeming to start or end. But they had to. And the wells . . . Caldan flinched, powerless to stop himself. Two dozen. Three dozen. More. He stopped counting, unable and unwilling to estimate how many there were.

What need did such a being have for trinkets or craftings? It breathed sorcery. Lived inside power untold.

"Why do you do this?" Gazija croaked.

"You would not understand, slave."

Gazija drew himself up straighter. "Slave no longer."

"One cannot escape one's nature."

"So you will get your revenge on me. For what reason? Why did you have to chase us such a long distance, and for centuries?"

The lich sneered. "No one escapes me."

"Then do it."

"I grow stronger than you can imagine. Where are the rest of your people? I will find them after this and consume them, as I did with Savine after he failed me and was imprisoned. Then this world will be mine."

"For what reason? You are nothing. You exist for no purpose, other than to exist."

Caldan didn't know what Gazija thought he could accomplish by arguing with the lich. Perhaps it was to delay his inevitable death. But no, there was design here—Gazija had a plan. Sorcery on such a scale had to have weakened Kelhak, and that had to be part of it. Gazija had forced him to come here, to face him and leave himself vulnerable.

Gazija's trembling hands clenched his canes. And there was a faint burst of sorcery from him, linked to a tiny crafting suspended around his neck.

"A message," Quiss murmured with puzzlement. "A signal. But to who?"

Gazija's shoulders slumped, and he shook his head. He turned to face Caldan and Quiss, fear contorting his face.

Whatever he'd planned wasn't working. He obviously expected something to have happened, and nothing had.

"Rebecci is dead," Kelhak said. "You should have guessed when I told you I consumed Savine. It was she who had possession of him. As always, you're two steps behind."

Kelhak didn't follow Gazija's glance, but all of a sudden, boiling clouds of darkness crashed down upon Caldan and Quiss. Caldan felt his shield waver under the onslaught, and his crafting keened from the strain. Streams of fire snaked through the obscuring sorcery, scorching trails across his shield. He groaned and drew more from his well, bolstering his wards lest they break. But it was no use. Lights flashed, and hammers pummeled his shield.

He couldn't take much more, and the metal of his shield crafting grew uncomfortably hot.

Several moments passed. Waves of heat pounded him. The air shivered. The tide of sorcery was too great. Too powerful.

Caldan waited for his shield to break.

But the screeching sorceries dampened, then disappeared. The pressure on Caldan's mind eased.

Quiss was still standing beside him, covered in his own shield. And a dome surrounded him and Caldan both. He traced the origin of the sorcery to Gazija.

The old sorcerer glared at Kelhak, mouth twisted in pained determination. Glittering lines skittered across the dome, and though Gazija bore the brunt of Kelhak's destructive sorcery, he managed to turn to face them.

"Save yourselves," Gazija cried. "You can do no more here."

Kelhak's sorcery trailed into nothingness. The dome covering Caldan and Quiss winked out of existence. Gazija had saved them from certain death, at the cost of depleting his own reserves.

Fumes of charred grass and earth floated around them like mist.

Caldan pressed his sleeve to his face. It came away damp with sweat and ash. He was alive only because of Gazija's intervention. And the old man had likely doomed himself.

Caldan felt Kelhak draw more power. It was a buildup that far exceeded anything Caldan could handle—more than a score of sorcerers would struggle to match Kelhak.

"The lich is going to absorb him," Quiss said. "There's nothing we can do. Oh, Gazija!"

Kelhak stepped toward Gazija. "Why do you not plead for your life, slave?"

Gazija shook his head and backed away. Another pulse of power came from him. Another signal. "What use is begging?"

Kelhak's laughter cut through Caldan like a blade. "All vessels beg at the end. Pitiful, mewling animals."

Gazija opened his mouth to reply, then closed it. Through the shield, Caldan saw the old man's face screw up in pain, and a hand dropped a cane to clutch at his chest. Gazija staggered and fell to one knee, still holding Caldan's altered smith-crafted figurine. Gasping, he drew a breath. Then another. Gazija opened his eyes.

Kelhak stepped nearer. "You feel it, then: the fear. I remember . . . eons ago, I was once something like you."

Gazija blinked rapidly, tears streaming down his face.

He knows he's failed, Caldan thought. *He knows he's a dead man.*

"Do it!" Gazija roared at Kelhak.

Silence greeted his outburst. Caldan's arm hairs stood on end as power built around him.

The lich began a slow walk toward Gazija, its eyes shining with an inner glow. As it approached, its mouth opened, lit by an incandescent light.

Gazija stumbled backward, hand clenched around the automaton, knuckles white. Power flooded through him.

"No," Quiss whispered.

A great rending threatened Caldan's eardrums. Behind Gazija, the air split in two. Through the crack poured a scalding heat laced with fumes of sulfur and putrefaction. Even at this distance, Caldan's skin could feel the baking temperature. And through his sorcerous senses, he realized that somehow Gazija had opened his well *outside of his mind.*

"Run, then!" shouted the lich. "There's nothing alive there. I know. I scorched the world, then came after you. Your essence will not survive, not without a life to cling to."

Gazija threw himself backward into the searing gash.

Quiss screamed with horror and rage.

The rent snapped shut with a screeching crack, closing Gazija's well from this world.

The shield dome winked out, and Quiss took a step forward, as if about to confront Kelhak, then faltered.

Kelhak howled with glee, a terrifying sound, as though it were uttered from a multitude of throats. Above him, his sorcerous design recoiled in on itself. Caldan sensed it pull back, like a drawn bowstring. It was about to disengage.

Kelhak raised his arms and sent his power upward to join with the storm. A funnel of clouds came down and snatched him up. For the third time that night, reality bent to a sorcerer's will.

CHAPTER 32

The vibration returned with a vengeance, threatening to shake Felice's teeth loose. She winced at the sensation. *Bloody sorcery.*

She placed her eye to a spy hole. The talon shifted as well. Roiling threads had returned. Heat shimmered from the gold-and-silver rope. A section jerked, buckling. Lightning arced along it, then traced a dome in the air.

Felice averted her eyes just before another bright flash.

Kelhak reappeared. One moment the chamber was empty, the next he was there, crouched and screaming with agony, limbs outstretched and mouth agape. He slumped to the floor, eyes squeezed closed, gasping like a fish.

"Now."

The talon burst through the wall. Plaster chips and white dust covered its rags and filled the air. Razor-sharp trinket daggers flashed toward the flaccid figure of Kelhak.

Felice whimpered and followed. Out of the corner of her eye, she saw Izak do the same.

The talon shouted in frenzied thunder. Felice found herself responding with a cry of her own, pent-up tension venting itself.

Silver blades aimed for vulnerable flesh. Kelhak's eyes opened. Two sorcerers shouted alien words. Kelhak and the talon. Glimmering chaotic lines coalesced into precise geometries. Sparks erupted as lines warred with others.

Felice pressed forward, all the while expecting Kelhak to shield himself, then end their lives. Izak screamed in terror.

Knives met flesh and sank deep. Two from the talon, hers, and Izak's.

Kelhak didn't flinch. A raised palm, and the mountain of rags was flung across the room. Bones cracked as the talon crashed into a stone wall. Frescoes shattered with the force, dust and fragments erupting into the air.

Felice tried to pull her dagger out for another thrust but couldn't. Kelhak smiled at her, blood dripping from his mouth.

Someone wailed like a baby. Her. The trinket blade slid free from Kelhak's flesh with a sucking sound.

Izak backed away, fear on his face, blood-smeared dagger in his hand. Booted steps thumped along the corridor outside.

They were done for. Rebecci's plan had failed. Four trinkets aimed at capturing Kelhak had no effect.

Felice retreated a step. *Flee!* she urged herself. *Where?* she answered back. Volcanic heat rose from the gem-studded rope behind her, scorching her back.

Out of nowhere, a mound of rags barreled into Kelhak, knocking him from his feet. They brushed Felice's shoulder, and she spun with the force.

Kelhak slammed into a wall and slid to the floor. Immediately, he regained his feet and let loose a growl. Felice noted with stunned shock his four puncture wounds no longer bled.

Scratchy mustiness enfolded Felice. Her head and stomach lurched.

She felt folded, somehow. Reality twisted. Thoughts spinning, she reeled. Embers filled her eyes, then faded.

FELICE LANDED FACE-FIRST. She couldn't breathe. Her eyes opened slowly. She was lying outside on the ground. On sparse grass and dry leaves. Beside her, Izak clawed at the dirt, sucking in lungfuls of air.

Felice wobbled to her feet. A black circle surrounded them, scorched into the earth, still smoking.

Where were they? What had happened to Kelhak?

A chattering behind her, followed by a rustle of rags. The talon.

It stood just inside the scorched circle. Their plan had failed. Kelhak had been about to kill them. The talon had done something, transported them here. It had saved them.

"You idiot!" Felice shouted, storming up to the talon. "You said you could kill it! What happened?"

The rags rippled. The talon's cowled head tilted to look up at the sky. Dark clouds stirred above them. "We weakened it."

"Enough to make a difference?"

A long pause. "Perhaps. We captured some of its power."

Izak levered himself to his feet. "Felice. Are you . . . are you hurt?"

She shook her head. "No. I'm fine." She realized she still clutched her trinket dagger, as did Izak. Of the talon's, there was no sign. She offered hers to the creature. "Yours, I believe."

The hood moved, left then right. "Keep it. You will need it."

"Gazija!" A shout echoed around them. A man yelling.

Cloth snapped, and before Felice could say anything, the talon shot away from them. In moments, it disappeared into the trees.

"Lady Felicienne!"

Felice turned to face who'd spoken her name.

Two men came toward her, on the other side of a stream. One was tall and spindly, and the other she recognized: Caldan.

Felice collapsed to the ground. She couldn't help herself. Tears flowed as she half sobbed, half laughed with relief.

CHAPTER 33

Smoke rose across a desolate landscape covered with rock fragments and pebbles—gray and black and dull. Cracks in the ground spewed gases, orange light, and heat. Lightning flashed from dark roiling clouds, but no rain fell. It wasn't sorcery, but neither was it natural. Craters spotted the ground as far as the eye could see, pooling with water no animal could drink. And irregularly spattered about the landscape were night-black circles as smooth as glass. It was . . . desolation. There was no movement, save for the wind and smoke. No animals moved. No ants, no insects. Not the faintest speck of green. No life of any kind.

One of the craters was recently formed. Raised edges of overturned ash hadn't yet been blown away by the wind or washed away by toxic rain.

In the center of the depression shone a glint of gold—something metal covered with a layer of fine dirt. A swirling current of air brushed the object, and more metal was revealed.

It moved, desiccated gray dirt falling from it. Shiny, rune-covered rods shook and twisted.

The smith-crafted figure sat up, gemstone eyes flashing with life.

GAZIJA GAZED ABOUT him. For a long time, he contemplated his surroundings: his world, shattered. Despair drove into him, hard and edged and furious. If he could have wept, he would have. If he'd had a voice, the hills would have echoed with howls of anguish. Anger began to build, overlaying the grief that threatened to swallow him. He pushed it aside. No longer did he have the strength to fight. It returned, and he shoved at it again.

Leave me. Let me be.

But it would not. It niggled at his misery. Poked and prodded him. His world was dead, consumed by its own private Shattering.

But he was still alive.

Eventually, his thoughts returned to his own body. Kelhak had been right: there had been no life here to sustain his essence. Only one option had been left to him. He hadn't known whether the sorcery would work. A way to contain a sorcerer's essence was known to him, but to allow the captured sorcerer control of its prison was fraught with danger.

His own improvements combined with Caldan's smith-crafting had worked to fashion a vessel of sorts for him, though his mind recoiled at the use of the word *vessel*. It was apt, but reminded him of the lich's existence.

Gazija lifted an arm and took in the pattern-covered brass limb. He lurched to his feet and wobbled upright, unsteady.

He was indeed now a vessel.

Which left the question: *Am I still Gazija?*

CHAPTER 34

Caldan stood at the end of a black circle scorched into the ground. Above him, the agitated clouds had dissipated somewhat. The concentrated scent of sorcery pervaded the air, so strong he felt it seeping into his clothes: hot metal and lemons, overlaid with something else . . . a putrid stench.

Quiss was overwrought, stumbling around the circle, tearing at his hair and garb. Words tumbled from his mouth in a tongue Caldan didn't recognize.

Felice looked like she'd taken a tumble off a cart and rolled in the dust. And considering that she'd seemed to appear out of nowhere, he could only imagine she had gone through something much worse. Her clothes were dirty, and every inch of exposed skin was covered with grime. And was that . . . yes, a splinter of aged bone stuck out from the cuff of her pants. Where had that come from? Clear trails ran down her cheeks from tears washing away the dirt. And Izak looked just as bad. Their eyes had a wild yet tired look to them, as if they'd stayed awake all night only to see the spirit of an ancestor pass in front of them.

Both carried silver trinket daggers with gemstone pommels, and both blades were streaked with blood.

"What happened?" he asked Felice.

She held up a hand, asking him to wait, while she drew deep breaths and wiped tears from her cheeks.

As a precautionary measure, Caldan expanded his sorcerous sense, searching around them, through the trees and bushes. Nothing. Apart from himself and Quiss, there wasn't a sorcerer close. The trinket blades, though . . . they virtually buzzed with suppressed energy, although, as with other trinkets, he couldn't find any familiar patterns or runes to latch onto. There was something . . . an odd power in them, unlike any he'd felt before. Questing, Caldan pushed himself deeper. It was supremely smith-crafted, a dense metal bound and held together.

Bound . . .

That's what was so different. The blade felt like a conduit . . . a drain. To where? He forced himself toward the opening. The closer he came, the harder it was. The crafting was corrosive, washing against his mind like burning acid. But he persisted, struggling to a point where all that existed was himself and the sorcery.

Filaments of power led from the blade down into the hilt, ending at the gemstone pommel. Caldan let his senses envelop the jewel. It was almost perfect, structurally. Only a few tiny flaws marked the crystal lattice. But there was something else . . . an ephemeral power throughout the stone. He had a sense of . . . confinement.

Caldan wanted to explore the gem more, but the caustic nature of the power was too much. He couldn't hold on anymore. With a gasp, he pulled himself clear and shook himself. He felt wrung out like a wet rag.

Those daggers were intriguing. Not only for the fact Felice and Izak carried them, but for their purpose. Something other than just killing. Something somehow even more sinister . . .

"Caldan!"

Caldan jerked his head up at the sound.

Felice.

He blinked distractedly. "Sorry. I was . . . never mind. Lady Felicienne. What . . . how did you get here?"

"I . . . I'm not entirely sure," Felice said. Her hair looked like she'd stood in a strong wind. Leaves and a fine white dust clung to it. She kept looking about her, as if she'd lost something, or expected someone to appear from behind a bush. "Where is 'here'?"

"Riversedge."

"Riversedge?" She looked at Izak. "Pignuts," she muttered. Izak gave a coughing chuckle.

"I didn't know sorcery could do such a thing," Izak said. "That's quite a trick."

Felice's eyes narrowed. "Yes. Yes, it is."

"What are you—" began Caldan.

"Later," Felice said. "Give us time to recover. We've been through quite a bit." She ran her hands through her hair, pulling out leaves and dust.

Caldan approached Izak. Though he grinned at Caldan, it was a sickly smile. Caldan clasped his shoulder. "It's good to see you, Izak."

"And you," offered Izak weakly. "I'm just glad I'm alive. Any chance of a drink around here?"

Caldan smiled, pleased to see Izak hadn't lost his cheer. "No, but once we get you two to safety, I'm sure we can arrange something. Sir Avigdor isn't with you?"

At his words, a bleak look came across Izak's face.

"Avigdor . . . well, he didn't make it."

"They killed him," Felice said. "Hacked his feet off and left him for dead."

Caldan felt the blood drain from his face. The brutality—and finality—of her account left him cold. Eventually, he said, "Who did?"

"A sorcerer calling himself Savine."

Quiss lurched over to Felice, face twisted with grief. "Savine, did you say? Where is he?" His words were urgent, intense.

"Another sorcerer named Rebecci did for him." Felice looked Quiss up and down. "You've the look she had. Half-starved. I take it your name is Luphildern Quiss?"

Quiss moved closer to Felice, wringing his hands. "Where is Savine?" he hissed, ignoring her question.

"Rebecci captured him, but someone killed her as well, and took the crafting that confined him."

Quiss dropped his arms to his sides, as if in defeat.

Another of Quiss's people dead, with another, Savine, captured . . . by a crafting?

Thoughts and impressions snapped into place in Caldan's mind, like the tumblers of a lock. The binding trinket daggers, capturing with craftings, the wrongness of Quiss when he'd first met him . . .

"How was Savine trapped?" Caldan said.

"The daggers," Quiss said, making the connection at the same time.

"No—it was a diamond," said Felicienne. "What—"

Quiss stepped up to Felicienne and held his hand out. She slowly handed her dagger over, as if reluctant to part with it.

"Here," Quiss continued, showing the trinket to Caldan. "This must have been part of Gazija and Rebecci's plan. There's a way to imprison someone's mind using coercive sorcery, and they tried to capture Kelhak. Though I don't know where these trinkets came from. Gazija thought one of us was a traitor, reporting to Savine, and he obviously kept his plan to himself." He gave a sad smile. "Except for Rebecci, of course. Gazija knew I'd join him if I knew. He . . . he excluded me to ensure one of us survived."

"I'm sorry," Felicienne said. "The daggers were given to us by a . . . friend."

Izak gave her a puzzled look. There was obviously a story there, and one Caldan would have to question Izak about later.

Izak took a step closer, glancing over his shoulder, back the way Caldan and Quiss had come. "Er, excuse me. Who are they?"

A group approached, hurrying toward them. Men and women all dressed in black.

Warlocks.

Hastily, Caldan extended his sorcerous sense. At least five wells. He didn't want to confront them just yet, but it seemed they had other ideas. One well was particularly wide and smooth: Devenish. And he'd warrant Thenna was by his side as well.

As the assembly of warlocks neared, they split into two separate groups: sorcerers and Quivers. For each warlock, there were two Quivers, armored and armed to the teeth. Five sorcerers and ten veteran soldiers. There seemed no alternative but to wait for them to approach. Running or fighting would get them nowhere, except possibly an early grave.

As Caldan guessed, Devenish led the pack, with Thenna a step behind. The Quivers spread out to surround them.

"Well, well," said the warlocks' leader. "When we felt the focus of the powerful sorcery end up here, I didn't expect to find you, Caldan." He pointed briefly at Quiss. "And I see your new owner is here. Perhaps you're following him around like a puppy?"

Thenna glared at Caldan, and it looked like it was all she could do to remain silent.

"Perhaps you should look toward your own puppy," he said, jutting his chin at Thenna. "It looks like she wants off her leash."

"How dare—"

"Be still!" Devenish snapped at Thenna. He turned back to Caldan. "So you've grown some teeth, it seems."

"I've always had teeth, Devenish. I guess I'm just not as eager to use them as you are."

At that, Devenish laughed.

"Oh, what I could have done with you," the warlock said, shaking his head. "So tell me, what are you doing—once again—in the middle of something that you should have no business with?"

"We sensed the sorcery as well and came as fast as we could. Not in time, though. I don't know what happened here, but I know these people. From Anasoma."

Devenish narrowed his eyes at Caldan. Maybe he bought the story, and maybe he didn't.

The warlock turned to Felicienne.

"You're familiar. Have we met?"

Felicienne gave Devenish a chilly smile. "We have, Devenish, in passing. I am Lady Felicienne Shyrise, Third Adjudicator to the emperor, and I demand to see him. I assume he came with his forces?"

A flash of fear crossed Devenish's face, gone in an instant. Devenish eyed her warily, then bowed his head in acknowledgment. "He did. And you may see him. We *all* will."

Caldan didn't like the sound of that. But with Felice as an ally, someone who clearly exerted some influence over Devenish, he felt like they weren't in immediate danger from the warlocks. Whatever their plans for him or for Quiss and his people, there was the greater Indryallan threat to deal with. They *had* to know this, even as arrogant as they were. Which meant that as much as it galled Caldan, they all needed to work together.

If we don't kill each other first.

"BY THE ANCESTORS!" exclaimed Izak. "The Quivers here are thicker than flies on . . . honey." He turned his head and coughed into a hand.

And so are the warlocks, thought Caldan. Aside from Devenish and Thenna, there were at least ten wells in close proximity. The other three warlocks who'd accompanied Devenish had left before they got back to Riversedge, after a whispered conversation with their fellows.

Scarce words had been exchanged between them all on the way here. Caldan surmised that no one knew who could be trusted. Even Izak was reluctant to talk, and after a few attempts to engage him in conversation, Caldan had given up.

A dozen Quivers guarded wrought-iron gates set in an imposing stone wall, with more stationed at intervals along a broad entry path. Six more stood outside the front doors of a massive mansion, which were open wide. Numerous functionaries and messengers made a continual procession, both into and out of the house. And a line of petitioners snaked from the interior, over the veranda, and onto the grounds.

Devenish led the way, seemingly at home, with Felice close behind him. Thenna had drifted to the rear of their group, and Caldan could sense her eyes burning into his back. For a noble himself, Izak looked distinctly uncomfortable, eyes shifting this way and that, face shiny with perspiration.

Following Devenish's lead, they were soon ushered into a side parlor and offered refreshments. Chilled cider and wines, along with fresh fruit and berries. There were also a few bowls and towels brought in for them to clean up, which the four of them from the hill used liberally.

Devenish surveyed them all. His Quivers arrayed themselves around the room. "Relax and have a drink. We might be waiting for some time. The emperor is very busy. Perhaps this might be a good opportunity for you to tell me what happened to you, Lady Shyrise."

Felice shook her head. She opened her mouth to reply but paused as a woman entered the room, flanked by armed guardsmen. The woman looked old, but there was a youthfulness to her step that made Caldan's heart ache. She was obviously important, and he knew why she felt so sprightly: it was at the cost of a Touched life, and their misery. She was impeccably clothed in a severe light-gray dress, and her skin was thin, almost translucent, but stretched tight. Exactly how old she was, Caldan couldn't tell, but over sixty, at least. Her guards were cold-eyed and devoid of expression. Each bore a long blade in a scabbard worn from use.

She stopped a few steps into the room, casting her eyes over them all imperiously. She dominated the space with an air of command. Turning her gaze to Devenish, she spoke. "It's good you're here, Devenish. We were going to send for you."

"Lady Porhilde," said Devenish. "I didn't realize you were here. What—"

"I'm sure there's a lot you don't realize, Devenish," Porhilde snapped. "For one, that the emperor requested your presence hours ago, but you weren't in your tent."

Devenish scowled. "There was the sorcery we had to investigate—"

"You have people for that," said Porhilde. "Did it cause any damage? Was anyone killed?"

"Not that I know of. But that's—"

"Then why did it warrant your personal attention? Bah. Spare me your explanations. He'll determine the truth of things."

Devenish bowed his head. "As you wish."

Lady Porhilde wasn't a sorcerer, but she must wield a much greater power if she could strong-arm Devenish.

"You'll come with me," she said firmly. "Now."

"Excellent." Devenish turned to Felice and Caldan. "Speak only if addressed directly—"

"Just you," interrupted Porhilde. "The emperor will see you one at a time. Separately. Individually."

A fleeting look of irritation passed across Devenish's face. "As you wish," he repeated.

"Not my wish, warlock," said Porhilde. "His. Defy him at your peril."

Devenish inclined his head and exited the parlor, followed closely by Porhilde and her guards.

Izak's sigh as the door closed behind them was audible.

"Who was that?" Quiss asked Felice.

"Lady Porhilde," she replied. "She's the emperor's First Concubine and Chief Advisor."

"Concubine?" Izak said. "Porhilde's a little . . . aged. And not like a fine wine, either."

The depravity of what the emperor and the warlocks were doing sickened Caldan, and he poured himself a cider to rinse his mouth and settle his stomach.

"He can't want to see me," Izak said with a frantic edge. "I don't know anything."

"Calm down, Izak," Felice said. "I'll vouch for you. No doubt I'll be questioned next. Just tell the truth, and you'll be fine."

"Should we tell them everything? What about the talon? And the lich?"

Caldan's ears pricked up at the unfamiliar words. The way Izak said them, they sounded like appellations. Quiss went pale and flinched, as if the names had a physical weight that struck him like blows.

"It's about time you told us more of Kelhak, and this lich," Caldan said, frightened by Quiss's reaction, and not a little concerned.

The sorcerer seemed to wilt. He sank onto a nearby chair, head in his hands. "Tell me what you know first," Quiss said weakly. "I don't know what a talon is, but the other . . . I know only too well."

Izak looked to Felice, as if for permission. She held a hand up to stop him saying anything, though, then began pacing back and forth.

"First," she said. "Izak, tell the emperor everything. He has to be told everything; and only tell him the truth. He'll know otherwise. Hold nothing back. If I'm correct, the very future of the Mahruse Empire is at stake."

But there was no time for "second," because the door opened and Porhilde entered, without Devenish. She pointed at Izak. "You next."

"No," Felice said, standing in front of Porhilde. "He needs to see me next. You know who I am, Lady Porhilde. I have information he needs to know. It may save time, and possibly thousands of lives."

For a long moment, Porhilde examined Felice. Then she nodded. "Very well, Lady Shyrise. I had better not regret this."

Again the door closed, leaving Izak, Quiss, and Caldan alone, aside from the Quivers positioned around the room. They'd heard what had been said, but Caldan supposed it didn't matter now.

Izak's turn came next, then Quiss's, leaving Caldan alone with the Quivers. He sipped cautiously at his cider and nibbled a few pieces of fruit and some nuts, but he was too nervous to eat more. He was about to have an audience with the emperor.

And that meant being face-to-face with a man Caldan knew was the living embodiment of a lie.

Caldan shook his head and snorted to himself. *So what? It's not like I can run away. All I can do is answer his questions honestly.* Devenish would have reported all he knew to the emperor and his advisors, so there was no room for Caldan to keep any knowledge to himself.

He looked up as the door opened and Porhilde entered. She eyed him sympathetically.

"Come with me."

Caldan stood and placed his cup of cider on a table. He smoothed his shirt and ran a hand through his hair.

"If you're ready?" Porhilde said with a hint of impatience.

"Yes," Caldan replied. He steeled himself, preparing to open his well at the slightest hint of danger. He was pretty sure he could hold Devenish off, as he had done so before, but the emperor was in a different class. Caldan's defenses would be no match, but he wouldn't go down without a fight if it came to that.

Outside, Caldan caught a glimpse of Quiss's back as he exited the building, before Porhilde led him along a carpeted corridor, passing squads of Quivers posted along the way, and stopped in front of wide double doors. She eyed him critically and clucked her tongue.

"I suppose you'll do," she said. "Some of the others looked worse off than you, especially Lady Shyrise and that Izak fellow. I don't know where they'd been, but they smelled like a graveyard."

Caldan only nodded, unable to focus much on what she was saying.

Porhilde raised her eyebrows at him, then opened the doors onto what looked like a ballroom commandeered for the emperor's use as an audience chamber. Three massive chandeliers lit the room by means of countless sorcerous globes of all sizes. To the right, behind a line of Quivers standing to attention, were curtain-covered windows, presumably leading out onto a veranda or gardens.

Inside, a long line of Quivers extended from the door on the left and right. A few had bows ready with arrows nocked. Behind them, Caldan could sense numerous sorcerers with wells of all types, enough to make his skin crawl and set his teeth on edge. For such rare items, there was a heavy concentration of trinkets in the room, too. Understandable, given that in here must be gathered some of the most powerful and wealthy people in the empire.

At the end of the line of Quivers was a raised semicircular dais, probably meant for musicians, but now holding a thronelike chair padded with red velvet. And sitting on the chair was a man clad in loose white cotton clothes. The emperor. His dark skin marked his ancestors as coming from the scorched, arid regions in the south, which Caldan found interesting—there wasn't much there except the Desolate Lands.

Surrounding the chair, a little behind and to both sides, were what Caldan assumed were the emperor's various advisors: men and women, old and young, some sorcerers, but most not. The emperor's multiple wells tingled at the edge of Caldan's awareness.

The emperor looked much younger than Caldan had first thought when he'd confronted the jukari. Lithe and well muscled. Smooth skinned and clean shaven, platinum hair not yet dulled by gray. Far too young to have Lady Porhilde as a concubine.

But he knew the reason for the emperor's appearance, and Caldan kept his face impassive at the disturbing thought.

Here was the source of the dreadful fate awaiting everyone who was Touched. The empire was built on the blood of innocents. But what empire wasn't built on death? Wars, assassinations, conflict . . . was this any different?

Yes. It had to be, Caldan was certain.

Porhilde cleared her throat loudly, and Caldan looked up, becoming aware he'd just stood there staring at the emperor. She gestured for him to walk between the lines of Quivers and approach the emperor.

"I'm sorry," he said. "I'm . . . in awe."

"As you should be."

"He's so . . . young. Younger than I thought he would be, I mean."

"The emperor and his family have been blessed with long, fruitful lives. It's because of this they've been able to guide the empire so successfully."

Porhilde smiled briefly, and Caldan detected a hint of sadness.

"Come on," she continued. "He isn't to be kept waiting. I shouldn't have to tell you this, but be careful. The emperor doesn't sit idle if action is needed. And suspicions can all too often lead to decisions that all parties regret later—if they're alive."

Caldan swallowed his fear and nodded. "Yes. Of course."

As they approached, the emperor shifted his weight in his chair and rested his chin on one hand.

"That's close enough," Porhilde said firmly as they reached a plush rug in front of the dais.

Caldan halted, acutely aware of the Quiver bodyguards, and sorcerers with open wells close by. He knew better than to open his own well, for such an action would be perceived as a threat. He wasn't sure why he'd only worried about confronting Devenish—of course the emperor would be surrounded by guards upon guards, sorcerers and warlocks. And as far as he'd come in developing his talent, as complex as his shield was, he'd likely be crushed like an ant under a booted foot by all the power surrounding him.

But leaving his well closed meant he was vulnerable to them. Coercive sorcery could take him with no resistance.

And that was probably the point.

Caldan licked his lips.

He kept his gaze on the floor and bent to one knee. What the protocol was, he wasn't sure, but this was better than standing there. Porhilde's hand touched his shoulder.

"Rise," she said.

Caldan did so, glancing at the emperor. He averted his gaze as he saw the man appraising him with penetrating, pale blue eyes. Caldan stood still, not daring to move or raise his head. Waiting. The silence lengthened, the only sounds in the room those of fidgeting courtiers and Quivers, the rustle of cloth and creak of armor. Someone coughed.

"Devenish told me about you," the emperor said. His words rolled off his tongue like honeyed thunder, deep and resonant. "I'd like to hear your story in your own words. As a newly raised warlock, you will work to my desires to help build a better empire."

So Devenish had told him lies.

Caldan didn't know how much—or even what—the emperor knew, but given Felice's warning, he decided to tell the emperor the truth about himself.

He met the emperor's gaze. "My parents were in the service of the empire. One or both was a sorcerer, possibly a warlock, but I don't know. One or both was Touched. They left the empire for some reason . . . and they were found and murdered."

Hisses and exclamations of surprise rose at his words. He felt Porhilde stiffen at his side. The murmurs increased in volume. A number of the Quivers looked to the emperor and his advisors, waiting for a sign to intervene. Caldan tensed, his mind on the edge of his well in case he needed it.

Nothing happened.

Caldan swallowed, throat dry, but pressed on. "I was raised as an orphan among the monks on Eremite. They . . . cast me out for injuring a noble's son, and I traveled to Anasoma. The Protectors took me in. Master Simmon, who . . ." Caldan's voice caught. "Who died during the Indryallan invasion, was my teacher. I fled to Riversedge, where I learned I was not only a sorcerer, but one of the Touched." He expected a reaction from the emperor or his advisors, but the room was still.

So Devenish had told them that much, at least.

"Devenish saw that my talents would be useful," Caldan continued. "So he tried to make me a warlock." He decided to finish there. If the emperor wanted more information, he'd have to ask for it.

Abruptly, the emperor stood. Any background rumblings faded quickly. He was tall, a good few inches taller than Caldan, and the pedestal only added to that height. He looked down on Caldan thoughtfully.

"Your honesty is . . . refreshing," remarked the emperor with a slight smile. "The bones of a story, without much meat, though. I often have to stop people embellishing their tales. Here, I find I'll have to do the opposite. Your parents, what were their names?"

Caldan's heart clenched in his chest, and he had to school his expression into neutrality. There was danger here, and he wasn't sure of his position. One false move, one perceived insult, and he might very well end up imprisoned, or worse.

"Our family name is Wraythe," he said carefully, a tinge of fear in his gut. "And from what I've been told, at least one of my ancestors, Karrin Wraythe, was in your service. She was presented with a trinket, which I now wear."

The emperor's eyes went wide, then narrowed. "And the ring on your finger is all you have of them? Nothing else?"

He was asking about the bone ring, just as Felice had in Anasoma. "Your Majesty, this is all I have left of my family. On the island of Eremite, my parents and my sister were killed when I was young."

The emperor blinked slowly. A slight smile curled the corners of his lips. He looked past Caldan to the mass of people in the chamber. "An end all traitors can look forward to," he said loudly. Then softer, "Though I regret your sister died. She would have been as you are. Useful."

For a long few moments, Caldan didn't trust himself to speak. Blood roared in his ears, and the room spun. Emotions warred within him: rage and hate and fear, and a need for vengeance. His hands clenched into fists, nails digging into his palms. When he mastered his emotions and spoke, it came out as a croak. "The good of the empire is paramount." He felt sick as he said the words, but nothing would be accomplished if he lashed out here.

"Indeed it is," the emperor said. "So, tell me, Caldan, young warlock, Touched—what do you desire?"

I desire my family back.

For a heartbeat, Caldan considered asking to be free of the warlocks and Touched. It seemed Devenish had presented him as still affiliated with those groups, glossing over the choice Caldan had made when he returned Kristof's body. The warlock had kept Caldan's "betrayal" to himself, and that meant Caldan would have to say it once more, only this time to the emperor himself.

A move he'd be sure to regret the moment the words were out of his mouth.

Because there was no way the emperor would let someone like him get away so easily, if at all. He'd had a hand in murdering Caldan's parents and didn't care who knew it. At the thought, once again Caldan had to suppress the rising anger that threatened to overwhelm him. He steadied himself, took a few deep breaths.

It was one thing to defy Devenish—*I can fight Devenish*—but the emperor? Caldan could feel the power coming off him, and no matter how afraid he might be of Kelhak, the emperor was certainly not afraid of a young man just learning to harness his talents.

Which meant he would certainly not brook any impertinence—let alone treason.

Caldan frowned, taking his time to answer. Because as all that passed through his mind, another thought kept coming to the forefront:

Why would he ask that? Couldn't he just command me, or dismiss me, or kill me? It's obviously a test, but of what? My loyalty? My cleverness? Ancestors . . .

His thoughts raced, off balance. Was the emperor offering him what he wanted most? It hardly seemed likely. And he certainly couldn't demand revenge for his parents and sister. So what, then?

Miranda.

What Caldan wanted was to live in peace. Whatever the outcome of the battle between the empire and the lich, the world would be forever changed. If the lich won, then, according to Quiss, there wouldn't be much of a world left. If it was defeated, Caldan would still be under the thumb of the warlocks, and the emperor. Which left only one answer.

"I want," he began hesitantly, "to go back to my studies. To develop my smith-crafting skills as best I can. To live a peaceful life. But . . . if that means I'm first needed to help defeat the Indryallans, then so be it."

"A peaceful warlock and Touched . . ." the emperor said dryly.

Chuckles rose at the emperor's comment, and Caldan felt heat rise to his face. He'd given an honest reply. Respect was too much to expect from those used to everyone else bowing down before them, but it still rankled to have their disrespect so casually thrown in his face.

"Tell me, young Caldan, did your parents have a bone ring in their possession?"

Caldan almost froze, and was about to keep his face expressionless, but at the last instant—fearing that would give him away—he affected a puzzled frown. Inside his shirt, the bone ring burned against his chest, as if it were on fire. "No," he managed. "I don't think so. They . . . died when I was young. I know very little about them."

"Except for what you've deduced from your trinket ring, of course . . ."

Caldan held up the hand with the ring. "This? Yes, it's the only thing of theirs I have. They'd given it to the monks for study, and the monks were kind enough to return it to me before I left."

The emperor held Caldan's gaze, and he struggled to keep his eyes level. Eventually the emperor nodded.

"What do you know of the lich?"

Again the question and sudden subject change threw Caldan off balance. But here, at least, he could be completely honest. "Nothing," he said, "other than what Felice—Lady Shyrise—and Sir Quiss told me. If it's true, then we need to do something."

"And what would you suggest we do?" the emperor asked, an amused look on his face.

Caldan's tongue stumbled. "I . . . I don't know. Kill him? Capture him?"

"That is the end result, not the process. But no matter—I hardly expect an untrained boy to save the empire." The room exploded into laughter—and Caldan couldn't help but feel it was more than a bit forced. "Anyway, we have known about the lich for some time. Devenish has a number of plans in motion. We expect to be victorious soon."

Victorious? You could barely take on Bells, *let alone Kelhak, whom you cowered away from like a frightened child. Appearances,* realized Caldan. The emperor was powerful—Caldan could feel that just standing here—but there was another type of power, such as that Lady Porhilde displayed. And unless he could use coercive sorcery over an entire empire, it was that kind of power that really held sway here. If the emperor showed any signs of weakness, there were those who would take advantage.

However, it didn't change the fact that the emperor held considerable control over Caldan's fate.

Caldan nodded slowly. "As you say."

"Good. Remember, Caldan, you are Touched, and as such, you will use your gifts for me, and for the empire. And as a sorcerer, you will have to work with the warlocks, however much you might dislike the idea." He looked at Caldan with a sad expression. "I'm afraid a peaceful life isn't your lot. In times such as these, when conflicts arise, your talents will be made use of. Lady Felicienne knows my thoughts, and she'll arrange things in my absence." The emperor waved a ringed hand. "Go now."

"But—"

"Be quiet," Porhilde snapped.

She grabbed him by the shoulder and directed him to turn. Caldan followed her directions, and they walked back to the entry door.

Caldan's thoughts tumbled inside his head. He was trapped. There was no way out. The emperor, the warlocks, the Touched, they'd all keep track of him, making sure he did what they wanted. No matter how much he rebelled against it, they'd find a way to force him to comply. He could run, but look where that had gotten his family. Dead. He needed a way to stop them from coming after him—if he could extricate himself from this mess and leave it behind.

This man had no way to destroy Kelhak, so he would destroy Caldan's life instead.

Porhilde escorted him out of the mansion. At the front entrance, she paused, giving Caldan a calculating look.

"Sometimes, what we want in life doesn't matter." Her eyes drifted to the side, and an expression of longing and pain crossed her face. "Do what the emperor wants, and you'll have a good life. Ducats, knowledge, respect. You'll be taught by gifted sorcerers. All will be yours. Many would be jealous to have your talents. Be content." Her eyes hardened. "After all, you don't want to end up like your parents, do you?"

Porhilde turned on her heel and left Caldan standing alone.

He felt exhausted and wrung out. Only now did he become aware that his skin was hot, and he was covered with a sheen of sweat. As quickly as he could, he strode along the path and exited the gates. He needed to find Felice and talk to her. And Quiss. And Izak.

And Miranda.

CHAPTER 35

Amerdan followed the vormag, Gamzegul, as they rounded a hillside, following a worn path, until he found himself among the jukari. Snarls and slavering mouths greeted him from mottled gray-skinned faces. Wiry black hair sprouted from the creatures' heads, thick and stiff. Gamzegul snapped at the jukari, speaking vile-sounding phrases in a base tongue. The creatures backed away, a few howling, some sniffing the air as if Amerdan were the one polluting it with a stench. They were beasts, even worse than the useless vessels Amerdan usually walked among.

As they passed, Amerdan was conscious of jukari falling into a group behind them. He glanced back, keeping his expression neutral so as not to alarm these animals. It seemed as if those jukari who saw him were all following in a pack. They were a motley bunch of monsters clad in mismatched pieces of armor, all sporting different weapons—spears, swords, daggers and cudgels, axes and staves—an assortment that spoke volumes about their organization, or lack thereof. And they weren't much for cleanliness, as their equipment was often rust stained and dusty. But their weapon edges were clean and sharp.

One jukari, bolder than the others, came close on his left side and walked beside him. A head taller than the rest, it towered over Amerdan. It carried a massive axe in one hand, the haft resting on its shoulder. Gamzegul barked at it, but it didn't back away.

Slanted yellow eyes bored into Amerdan's. He knew it was trying to intimidate him, in a simplistic, vulgar show of physical superiority. He considered a few options, but decided to leave it alone for now.

The jukari edged closer and nudged Amerdan with its elbow, hard enough to shove him a foot to the right. He didn't stumble, though, his nimble feet able to cope with the momentum change.

Gamzegul stopped and shouted at it. The jukari came to a halt, staring silently at the vormag. Hoots and snarls sounded around them.

Amerdan suppressed a sigh. These beasts understood only one thing: brute force. And Gamzegul was rapidly losing control of the situation. If something wasn't done soon, it would spiral out of control. The jukari were too stupid to realize there was a greater purpose to Amerdan coming among them. They had simple notions, basic thoughts. They'd treat him as they did all other prey.

Amerdan snorted, and the bullying jukari turned to face him. He smiled at it, revealing his teeth. More hoots broke out from the jukari—mirth, if Amerdan had to guess. He was unconcerned. And why not? The jukari was so huge, it would crush a normal man. Amerdan snorted again . . . then spat at it.

His wad of phlegm landed with a splat. Amerdan brushed his hands across the hilts of his knives. Sharpened to razor keenness, their cold hardness was ever comforting.

Gamzegul stared at him openmouthed. The immense jukari he'd defiled hesitated as the others quieted to a stunned silence. It blinked in surprise, and for the briefest moment, Amerdan thought that might be the end of it.

Wishful thinking.

Jerking into action, it roared, yellow fangs protruding between thin black lips, and attacked.

Amerdan darted to the right, ducking under a swing of the axe. It whistled over his head, barely missing. The jukari was faster than he'd thought. But it still didn't matter. His knives were free, but Amerdan held them back. As eager as he was to get this over with, as keen as his blades were to taste blood, the jukari—*all* the jukari—had to be shown he wasn't to be trifled with.

He twisted his body to avoid another hack of the axe. It thudded into the ground, and the jukari grunted. Amerdan backed away a few steps, and the jukari kept its eyes on him while it dragged the axe head free, clods of dirt clinging to the steel.

It came at him again, this time warily. A prod with the haft. A feint with the bladed head. Amerdan let his arms drop, feet planted firmly shoulder-width apart, as if inviting it to attack. A two-handed chop. Amerdan swayed aside and took a step forward—now inside the weapon's reach. And this time he didn't hold back. He leaped. Both knives ripped through gray flesh. Once, twice. Hardened steel grated across rib bones. Pointed tips searched for the beast's heart.

Amerdan landed lightly on his feet. The jukari uttered a bubbling howl, mouth frothing blackened foam. It staggered, falling to one knee, its face now level with Amerdan's. He drove a knife into its eye, rupturing the yellow orb. He yanked it free as the jukari toppled.

It lay there in the dirt, black rivulets of blood trickling from the puncture wounds he'd inflicted. Yelps and growls erupted. Jukari surged forward, then pulled back. Gamzegul shouted at them, pointing at Amerdan.

But they don't need the vormag's explanations, thought Amerdan. They'd seen what he could do. As simple as they were, they knew a greater force than any of them when they saw it. After all, it was in their nature.

He bent over and wiped his knives on the thing's ragged shirt, scowling at the result. He'd have to reclean them later. Amerdan sheathed his steel. He met the eyes of as many jukari as he could, unconcerned.

Gamzegul came up to him. "Unwise," the creature hissed.

"Necessary," Amerdan replied.

"The Talon will know."

Amerdan shrugged. It didn't matter. Couldn't this fool of a vormag see that?

Gamzegul must have taken his silence as some sort of answer. It bade Amerdan follow, then pushed its way through a wall of jukari. As Amerdan approached, the gap widened, enough to show him they were fearful. *Good.* They might be scared of the vormag's sorcery, but nothing frightened animals quite so much as bloodied steel and death. It spoke to them on a primal level.

They left the lifeless jukari behind, where its corpse was rapidly surrounded by others of its kind, bickering over its armor and weapons. Gamzegul quickened their pace until the crowd thinned.

As they continued, they wound their way around small campfires and sometimes sleeping jukari. Often, morsels of cooked meat were fought over, the largest of the jukari winning most of the food. Although they attempted to cook their meat, it looked charred black on the outside and raw within. Amerdan was surprised to see there were also dirt-covered tubers in piles, spilling from baskets, along with other vegetables, fruits, and nuts. *Perhaps not so savage,* he thought. Though the food had to have been pillaged from surrounding farms, the fact the jukari found it palatable and worth taking said much about them. It hinted that they might have their own farms somewhere, deep within the Desolate Lands . . .

Amerdan was still musing on this thought when Gamzegul stopped their progress. Ahead of them were two rows of jukari, all big and mean. Or, rather, bigger and seemingly meaner. All of them wore sets of armor that appeared less patched together than that of the other jukari he'd seen. And they all carried spears, along with long daggers hanging from belted hips.

"Talon Xarlas," Gamzegul said breathlessly, "is here. I will talk. The Talon . . . has to listen to me."

The vormag didn't sound certain.

"Come," the creature said. "Xarlas will test you. Are you ready?"

Amerdan nodded. The sooner this was over with, the better. Half-formed plans were all he had; he still wasn't sure what he should do in this situation—but one thing he was positive of was that he didn't have to hide who he was, his abilities, here. The jukari and vormag thought he was one of the "Old Ones," so let them. If it afforded him an edge with the animals, then all the better. If it gave him a way to control them . . . then what could he do? They were nothing, but the situation amused him.

It might be interesting to have an army of monsters at my beck and call.

A high-backed wooden chair dominated a cleared circle. A boundary of head-sized stones surrounded the chair, with jukari staying outside the insubstantial border. Inside were vormag, muttering and clutching crafted objects around their necks: medallions and amulets and the like.

Gamzegul strode forward confidently; all trace of the creature's uncertainty had vanished.

One of the vormag, a bald, skinny runt, barked a few harsh words at Gamzegul, who shook its head. The snarls and abrasive chatter of jukari filled the air, along with their rancid stench.

Gamzegul and the bald vormag exchanged heated words. Gamzegul stomped a foot. The opponent laughed shrilly. It seemed Gamzegul didn't have much standing with the other vormag. But the beast had practically said as much when they'd first met.

"Enough!"

The word boomed across the clearing. There was a powerful edge to it, an abrasiveness Amerdan found almost vicious. It had been voiced by a newcomer, who stood outside the stones. Xarlas, Amerdan presumed. A great hulking figure that somehow also looked like a scarecrow, patched clothes and tattered rags tied together. Its face was obscured by a hood, and yet somehow Amerdan had the feeling it watched his every movement. Hundreds of thin bones and metal objects were attached to the rags. As it moved to the high-backed chair, he could hear them tinkle and clatter.

Once seated, Xarlas brought up long, slender-fingered hands ending in clawlike nails. The hands reminded him of birds of prey, and

Amerdan could see why these creatures were called talons. It pushed its hood back, and cold, deep violet eyes peered out from under eye-browless sockets.

Amerdan blinked in astonishment. Xarlas's features had a distinctly feminine appearance to them. Slanted eyes like the jukari and vormag, but the talon's lips were fuller, cheekbones sharper. Casting his gaze about, Amerdan now saw there were other jukari and vormag with a softer appearance. Slightly longer hair, wider eyes.

They weren't remnants of creatures left over from the Shattering. The jukari, vormag, and talons were races in their own right. And with their newly minted craftings and the variety of food they ate . . . Amerdan realized they had to have a civilization deep inside the Desolate Lands, somewhere.

What is their purpose? What do they want?

Does it matter?

"Please," Xarlas said, waving to Amerdan, "be . . . at ease."

Her voice was rasping, like a file dragged across metal.

Amerdan looked around, unsure how he was supposed to make himself at ease. There were no other chairs or logs to sit on. Deciding to relax anyway, he sat cross-legged on the ground. *Let them see I don't think they're a threat. Let them see I'm unconcerned with being among creatures such as them.*

The jukari muttered and hooted and snarled, constantly in motion, occupied with doing one thing or another. Twitching, scratching, jostling for position. In stark contrast, the vormag were almost motionless. Their beastlike eyes regarded him with suspicion and awe. Xarlas gestured to the jukari and vormag, and they sat or squatted in the dirt.

Dotty moved inside his shirt, and Amerdan placed a hand on her to calm her. She was silent, though, which he hated. She was speaking to him less and less these days.

Amerdan ran his gaze over Xarlas, searching for strengths and weaknesses. He had no idea what she was, why she was so different from the other creatures. But he did sense she was a sorcerer . . . and that troubled him. She wore numerous craftings, whose purpose he couldn't discern. And there was something around her neck . . . an emptiness . . . no . . . a hot void.

Xarlas nodded to the vormag around her, who inclined their heads in return. They must have taken her gesture as permission, for they began murmuring among themselves. Gamzegul was the recipient of many a fleeting glance. The vormag stood there, though, unwavering.

That void . . . could it be a trinket? Amerdan could feel it pulsing, even at this distance from Xarlas. A bright burning so intense, he fancied he could feel it mirrored on his own chest.

A scuffle broke out between two vormag. Sorcerous sparks flew. The talon rose from her chair, tall and imperial, and swatted them both on the side of the head. The vormag subsided with sullen glances at each other.

Xarlas lifted a hand above her head. There was silence so deep, Amerdan could hear the flies buzzing.

Gamzegul stepped forward. "Talon Xarlas, I bring you one of the Old Ones. Returned to us—"

"Be quiet."

Gamzegul swallowed, casting a look back at Amerdan. Muttering resumed from the vormag, and some of the jukari hooted and howled, sensing the tension.

Amerdan couldn't take his mind off the pulsing heat the talon wore. It was a void, but also a livid scar. His chest hurt to be in such close proximity. He reached up to touch his own trinket through his shirt and jerked his hand back at the heat he felt. His trinket was burning, as if it had some sort of connection to the one Xarlas wore.

Amerdan hissed softly. He didn't like surprises unless he could benefit from them. It was hard to discern how he could turn this to his advantage.

Xarlas was staring at him. She pulled a ragged cloth away from her neck. Reaching in one clawed finger, she hooked it around a black metal chain and drew out the object that was burning Amerdan. A hush descended.

A trinket in the shape of a ball. Xarlas let it drop. It fell, hit the talon's chest, and rattled. Much like Amerdan's would.

Amerdan's chest hurt. It felt like he was clamped in a vise.

Impossible. But what was and wasn't possible was not for him to decide.

It looked smaller than his, but was that just in relation to Xarlas's greater mass? No, it was smaller. Whereas his was the size of a walnut, this one was only half as big.

Xarlas stepped toward him. "Gamzegul claims . . . you are . . . an Old One." She tapped her trinket ball with her nail. "This is proof I have walked among them. Proof they trusted me. I am a placeholder. We wait for their return."

Amerdan almost laughed. Her smaller trinket must be inferior to his. Why else the size difference? But the burning, the connection . . . it had to mean something. But what?

He stood slowly, brushing dust from his pants. Meeting the talon's eyes, he mimicked her movements. With one finger, he drew out his own secret, his trinket, and let it fall against his chest.

Exclamations of surprise came from the vormag, while the jukari twitched and moaned among themselves, agitated at the vormag's unease but clearly not knowing what was transpiring.

Less than animals, decided Amerdan. He could discount the jukari. The vormag and talon were a different matter. They were wary of him, and rightly so. But he could sense the desire in them. The longing for a return of the Old Ones.

For me to be what I claim.

Xarlas was hesitant, though. She ran her purple tongue over her lips. *What else is she waiting for? She is uncertain.* The Old Ones were sorcerers of great power. So . . .

A demonstration.

Amerdan opened his well and linked to the shield crafting he'd taken from Bells. Blackness surrounded him momentarily before turning transparent. He raised his arms in the air and turned a full circle. Jukari fell to their faces, prostrating themselves before him. Amerdan smiled at the feeling the sight gave him. He exulted.

Vormag bent their knees to him, lowering their heads until they stared at their own feet.

Only Xarlas remained standing. She stared at Amerdan for some time. He could almost hear her considering and discarding options. But eventually, even she bent to one knee. She bowed her head for a moment, placing a fist on the ground. Raising her head, she stood.

Her eyes were filled with hate.

Amerdan laughed. Xarlas's little world was in tatters. The talon had lost control and didn't like the feeling.

Too bad.

Xarlas tucked her trinket back under her rags. She came closer, and Amerdan could smell the stench of her. Stale sweat and mold. The mustiness of a long-closed room. She leaned in close.

"You are . . . false," she whispered threateningly. "There are no . . . Old Ones left." Then, though, louder: "An Old One . . . has returned! Let us . . . rejoice!"

Jukari howled and barked. Vormag pressed themselves even further into the dirt. Xarlas waited until the clamor subsided, then held a hand up for silence.

"But first . . . he must . . . be tested."

Ah . . . clever.

But Amerdan wasn't worried. And Gamzegul looked triumphant. The creature pointed a shaking hand at the bald vormag who'd challenged it earlier. "That one," he screeched. "Take that one!"

Settling old scores, thought Amerdan. *As always with these power struggles.*

The other vormag descended on the bald runt. It kicked and screamed, struggling in vain against their clutching hands.

"No!" Xarlas rasped, and the commotion ceased. The talon pointed a clawed finger at Gamzegul. "This one will be offered."

Gamzegul's face paled, eyes widening. The vormag shook his head. "No! I brought the Old One to you!"

"Take him," Xarlas said.

Feet scuffed across the dirt as the vormag came for Gamzegul. The creature resisted, futilely, as Amerdan watched.

They tore the vormag's clothes off and took all his craftings. They dragged Gamzegul, naked, gray skin trembling, in front of Xarlas and

Amerdan. The other creatures forced the quivering vormag to his knees, arms twisted painfully behind his back. He looked up at Amerdan, imploring.

"Please," Gamzegul whimpered to Amerdan. "I found you."

Xarlas smirked at Amerdan. "Show . . . us."

Gamzegul was not worth taking. The vormag were made creatures. And imperfect, at best. Amerdan swallowed. He didn't care about Gamzegul, but he was worried because he'd never absorbed a vessel like this before. What would it do to him? Would he sully himself? Would a small part of him become . . . infected?

Amerdan looked at the smirk on Xarlas's lips. The talon wanted Amerdan dead. If he failed this test, she would try to kill him. With the sorcerous might of the vormag to back her up, she might even succeed. He didn't know, and the not knowing made him more scared than he'd been in a long time. True, no one had bested him yet. But this situation was new.

It was also . . . delicious. Because, what if it worked? What would he be able to do, if he had such resources behind him? *In* him?

He looked down at Gamzegul. The vormag's mottled skin was dripping with sweat.

He knew what he had to do. There was only one way to show them.

Amerdan drew his knife.

Gamzegul threw himself against those restraining him and wailed with despair.

CHAPTER 36

Caitlyn brought them outside the city and into the emperor's army. It seemed her station afforded her the ability to requisition whatever she wanted from the Quivers, and she'd chosen a spot with a few vacant tents. Vasile gathered there had been quite a few Quivers killed now.

It was a smart move, actually. Vasile doubted he'd get far in the middle of the night before he was stopped by a sentry and questioned. He made a mental note: insane people were not necessarily stupid. Whatever happened from here on, whatever he decided to do, he'd better remember that.

Or he just might join Chalayan with the ancestors.

Around them were squads of Quivers settling in for the night. Most obtained their evening meal from the vast traveling kitchens that accompanied the army, though Vasile could smell roasted rabbit from somewhere close by. Quivers laughed at jokes, drank from flagons, polished weapons and armor, or collapsed exhausted into their bedrolls.

Vasile rubbed his arms, nerves on edge. *I don't belong here,* he thought. *Given to someone, traded like a cow.* He felt he'd been treated like an old nag, set to one last task before his usefulness was over—sure he was meant to die under Caitlyn's command. If not soon, then eventually.

"What are you thinking about?" Caitlyn said abruptly. "Don't be thinking you can get out of this. You're one of us now. Cel Rau's told me your secret, and you're going to help a great deal with our fight."

Vasile shook his head, then looked across the fire at her. Aidan sat on a stool, content to stare into the flames while contemplating his fate. Cel Rau kept himself busy around the camp: tightening tent ropes; removing leaves and twigs, which he threw onto the fire; casting a critical eye over his own and Caitlyn's gear. Right now, he was repairing a tear in one of her shirts, his fingers nimble with needle and thread.

"I was thinking," Vasile said, "that I could use a decent meal."

"Stew is what you'll get." Caitlyn nodded at the pot half in the coals. Steam poured from around its cast-iron lid. "You'll need to harden up, or you won't last long where we're going."

Vasile squared his shoulders. "I've done my fair share of fighting against the jukari and vormag. Cel Rau will tell you." But even to his own ears his words sounded weak. He'd been terrified. And Aidan and cel Rau would see through his bluster.

"'Fair share'?" spat Caitlyn. "Evil doesn't care about fair share. Would you put down your sword after killing one jukari?" She chuckled. "Or how about two? Or three? What's your fair share?"

"Forget I spoke," Vasile said. There was no reasoning with her.

"Aidan will be pleased you're joining us," Caitlyn said. "Our very own truth detector. We can cut to the heart of matters, root out evil, without spilling as much blood. He's always been soft, but now we'll be happy together. Won't we, Aidan?" She coughed into her hand and continued hacking for a while before she could again speak. "I said, won't we?"

"That's right," Aidan said, but he was lying. He met Vasile's gaze. "One big, happy family."

Cel Rau tied off a knot and bit through the thread with his front teeth. He slid the needle back into a small leather sewing kit. "Vasile was probably thinking about running. You're good at that, aren't you? Running away."

"You know, Anshul," Vasile said. "I often wanted you to speak more. But now, when you do, I wish you'd shut up." As the words tumbled out, Vasile clenched his fists, preparing for any backlash. He'd spoken rashly, unnerved by what was happening. And he knew how ruthless cel Rau was . . .

A laugh escaped Aidan.

And to Vasile's surprise, cel Rau began to chuckle. Caitlyn looked at them both with a tight smile on her face.

"I have my own truth-telling ability," cel Rau said, standing.

And the next moment, Vasile felt cold steel against his throat. The swordsman's blade had appeared as if from nowhere. He jerked back, but cel Rau gripped his hair with his other hand and held his head firm. Vasile felt a warm trickle run down his throat as his skin began to sting from the cut. He wanted to swallow, thought better of it.

"Sit down, Aidan," Caitlyn said firmly.

There was no sound for a few moments, apart from Vasile's own harsh breath. A creak of leather and wood indicated Aidan had sat back down. Vasile blinked sweat from his eyes.

"The magistrate will do what's right," cel Rau said. "Won't you, Vasile? You're too much of a coward to run. And now you have a chance to be part of something greater."

Vasile hissed with pain as his hair twisted in the swordsman's grip. "Yes," he said, panting. "I'll do what's right."

"You'll do what we tell you," Caitlyn said.

"I'll do what you tell me," Vasile repeated.

Cel Rau grunted. "Well, you haven't pissed yourself, so maybe you're telling the truth. But then, maybe my ability to discern isn't as good as yours."

Bastard.

"Stew's done," Caitlyn said brightly.

Vasile felt cel Rau release his grip, and the blade withdrew from his neck. The swordsman cleaned the edge on his pants and sheathed his steel. Vasile wiped blood from his neck.

"Dish up, would you, cel Rau? I'm not feeling my usual self. Haven't for a while, actually. Not since Aidan tried to kill me."

Cel Rau jumped to obey, like she'd issued a royal decree. He gathered four bowls and a wooden spoon, then dragged the pot off the coals with a stick.

"I think . . . none for me," Caitlyn said. "I don't feel well." Beads of perspiration dotted her brow, and she wiped them on her sleeve. "Not well at all."

"The emperor's 'reward,' is it?" Aidan said.

Caitlyn rose to her feet, staggering slightly. Her hands clutched at her chest. "I had to drink it."

"What was in the vial?" asked Vasile.

She looked at him, eyes wild. "I don't know."

"Neither do I," Aidan said.

"I know," said cel Rau quietly. "The emperor has a potion that only he knows the formula to. It is given to those who have earned a great reward. He has favored you, Caitlyn. You're to be rekindled."

Truth, realized Vasile.

Caitlyn stumbled over to cel Rau, grabbing his shirt and leaning her weight on him. "It burns!" she hissed. "I can feel my blood scalding through my body like acid. Cel Rau, what has he done to me?"

Wrapping his arms around Caitlyn, cel Rau lifted her off her feet and cradled her close to his chest. "You were broken. I asked the emperor to heal you. And in his wisdom, he granted my wish. With your wounds, you were unfit to lead again. It was either this, or you'd be discarded. I couldn't let that happen. You've been a shining light in the battle against evil."

A long speech for the swordsman, and a perplexing one. Had the emperor owed cel Rau a favor? For what? What was the connection between the two of them?

"Urgh," muttered Caitlyn. Her head lolled to the side. "Water. I need water."

Cel Rau stared at Vasile.

"All right," Vasile said. He grabbed a waterskin from their provisions and trickled some into Caitlyn's mouth. She gulped at it greedily, and it splashed from her mouth and down onto her shirt.

"Give it to me," cel Rau said.

Vasile looped its strap over the swordsman's head.

"If you run," cel Rau continued, "the Quivers will catch you. Then we'll have you executed." He didn't wait for a response, just strode off with Caitlyn to the tent she had designated as hers and disappeared inside.

Not long after, the screams began.

Soon after that, irate Quivers stormed into their camp demanding an explanation and some peace and quiet. Cel Rau marched out of the tent, and with stern looks from the swordsman, promises of violence, and displays of Caitlyn's writ, the Quivers retreated, grumbling under their breaths.

Caitlyn's screams continued, lasting well into the night.

VASILE STAGGERED OUT of his tent in the morning, bleary eyed from lack of sleep. To the east, the sky was beginning to lighten. He yawned. Around him, the Quivers' army began to stir. Smoke rose from cook fires, men and women coughed and spat, kettles boiled.

Cel Rau squatted by their fire, stirring the pot, which now contained bubbling porridge. He filled two bowls by the fire, then took the remainder with him into Caitlyn's tent.

It seemed cel Rau had stayed with Caitlyn the entire night. Maybe they were lovers. Or maybe he wanted only to ease her pain.

"There had to be enough left for ten men," Vasile muttered.

"What was that?" said Aidan as he emerged from his tent.

He looked better, to Vasile's eye. Less haggard and drawn. And he'd washed his face and hair. Vasile glanced down at his own dirty hands and felt ashamed. He hadn't thought to clean himself up. What would be the point?

He felt Aidan's strong hand lift his chin up. "Hold on to yourself," Aidan said. "It's all you have. All *we* have."

"All right," Vasile found himself saying. "All right."

"There's water and some rags in my tent. Clean up, then eat something."

A short while later, Vasile emerged feeling somewhat better. Aidan was right. As long as they were alive, there was hope. If he let himself slip into despair, then all was lost.

He moved to the fire and picked up both bowls, handing one to Aidan, who was again sitting on the camp stool and staring into the coals.

Aidan looked at the bowl in his hands with distaste. "Porridge," he said. "I don't think I'll ever eat it again." He scraped his portion into the fire and looked around. "Maybe someone else would be willing to share their breakfast."

"Maybe," Vasile said, spooning in a mouthful of porridge. It was better than anything they'd had in the previous few days, including the stew from last night. "What do we do now?"

"We wait," Aidan said, shrugging. "We're at Caitlyn's mercy, for the moment. All we can do is handle what she throws at us, while keeping our eye out for . . . something. Some way to get out of this mess."

"We should talk to Gazija. He's on our side, and he might be able to help."

Aidan pursed his lips. "I think the only side he's on is his own. But you're right: he might be our only hope."

Vasile was about to ask how they could contact Gazija when cel Rau emerged from Caitlyn's tent. The magistrate ate more porridge instead.

"She's asleep now, after eating," cel Rau said. "She suffered terribly last night, and she needs to gather her strength."

Both Vasile and Aidan remained quiet.

"The emperor has given her a great gift," cel Rau said. "One many are not so fortunate to receive. She has been favored and can now continue to fight in the emperor's name."

Whatever the swordsman was talking about, he believed it was true.

"What has happened to her?" Aidan said.

Cel Rau's mouth curled into the ghost of a smile. "She has been healed. The emperor has healed her. May he live forever."

CHAPTER 37

Several times Caldan glanced at Felice as they walked back toward Gazija's ships. The emperor had questioned them all, and let them go. Devenish was nowhere to be seen; presumably he'd scurried back to the warlocks as soon as he could. Same with Quiss. By Felice's side strode Izak, who seemed to stand straighter than he remembered. If Caldan had to guess, he'd been through harsh trials—worse than an encounter with the emperor—and come out the stronger for it.

"Come," Felice said, "I'll find us somewhere to stay. If you—"

"No," Caldan said. "I need to talk to Quiss. And so do you. There are things you need to know. We can't face this separately, or lacking information. It's for the best if I take you to see him."

Felice raised her eyebrows and gave him a calculating look. "Very well," she said after a pause. "I have questions for him anyway."

Caldan directed them down a busy street that led in the direction of the wharves. "And I'm sure he'll want to hear your story as well. How you came to appear right when Kelhak disappeared, for example."

"As long as there's something to drink," Izak said. "I've . . . *we've* been through a lot. I don't know about Felice, but I need something to settle my nerves. I never thought I'd get to meet the emperor."

Me neither.

And if Caldan never met the emperor again, he'd be happy. But he felt the chance of that was unlikely. There was too much at stake, and the emperor had to be central to any plan to defeat Kelhak.

Whether he's too afraid of the God-Emperor or not.

Felice remained silent as they wove their way through the crowded streets, and Caldan was content to think his own thoughts. It was only when they passed through a portcullised opening and onto the wharves outside the city that she spoke.

"The emperor has tasked me with gathering as much information as I can, so we can sift through it and assist with his plan to fight Kelhak."

Her words were slow and deliberate.

Caldan considered what she'd said for a moment. Despite her intelligence, Felice was just as blind to the emperor's true nature as others were. "From Quiss, and I assume the warlocks and Quivers. Along with the Touched. I don't envy you your task, Felice. There are too many secrets they'll never divulge."

"Well," Felice said, "it's my job to ferret out secrets and information. And I'm pretty good at it, if I do say so myself."

Ahead of them stood Quiss at the bottom of a gangplank. Felice stopped talking while Izak moved closer, as if he wanted to protect her.

"I felt you coming," said Quiss as they approached.

"You have some explaining to do," Felice said without preamble.

Quiss nodded. "As do you. We've lost our leader today, and I've also lost a friend. He kept his plans from me, for some reason. Perhaps he wasn't sure if I was a traitor or not. Whatever the reason, you know what happened in Anasoma."

"Yes."

"Well?" said Quiss. "What happened? You knew Rebecci, you said; did she tell you Gazija's plan?"

Felice shook her head. "I don't know the entirety of it, only that

Rebecci arranged for"—she glanced at Izak—"an assassin to make an attempt on Kelhak's life. I think Gazija's plan was to have Kelhak weaken himself by using sorcery to travel to Gazija in order to kill him, and then return to Anasoma. Once back, Rebecci and the assassin would try to kill Kelhak."

"So," Quiss said, "with Rebecci dead, you took it upon yourself to take over the plan."

"There was no one else," Felice said.

"We did what we could," said Izak. "The assassin gave us trinket daggers. But Kelhak was too strong."

"Yes," Felice said. "He wasn't as weak as Rebecci thought he would be."

Quiss's gaunt face grew grim. "He must be far more powerful than we suspected."

Caldan rubbed the back of his neck. He followed the conversation, but something else needled him. He sniffed the air, drawing a puzzled look from Felice. Underneath the usual smell of rank river water and fish was the scent of hot metal . . . but . . . this was also acrid.

Caldan opened his well, exposing himself to its power to link to his craftings, but not drawing from it. He pushed his heightened senses out, searching for what had caused his unease. He was dimly aware that Quiss also grasped his power in response. Caldan brushed over the sorcerer and stretched his awareness farther, past the ships and around the river. There was a tenseness to the air, a . . . darkness filled with an arcane mist. East. That was where . . .

Caldan's breath caught in his throat. He'd almost missed it.

"Something's coming," he whispered to himself, almost before he realized what he'd sensed.

A gust of wind ruffled the water's surface, then swirled around their legs.

Kelhak was striking again. *But so soon?* After an unleashing of such magnitude, he couldn't have recovered yet.

Caldan turned to Quiss, Felice, and Izak. "Another storm is coming." He reached for his well, keeping it open and ready to use.

Quiss faced east and squinted into the wind. Caldan could sense the sorcerer's awareness becoming distant as he searched.

"I think he's right," Quiss said.

A clap of thunder rolled across the city. Another gust of wind, this one stronger than the first, blew dirt with enough force, they shielded their eyes with hands and arms.

"What's going on?" Felice said. "What can you sense?"

"There aren't many clouds," Caldan said. "The thunder was caused by a sorcerous buildup."

Felice went very still, her face grim. "I need more information. What's going on?"

"It's coming this way," Quiss said. "But its focus is constantly shifting."

In the short time their exchange had taken, the wind had picked up substantially. There was still enough light in the sky that Caldan could see the beginnings of clouds forming to the east. And the sorcery was growing. Already, he could sense its immense power. The previous storm had been a trial, a test of their strength, what they could accomplish. Gathering on the horizon now was a mass of swirling sorcery like nothing he had ever witnessed. Was this how it had started thousands of years ago? Was this what it was like at the Shattering? Sorcerers vying for power, blind to the consequences of their actions. Sorcerers defending themselves against vicious attacks and lashing out in retaliation.

Across the horizon, as far as the eye could see, stretched a wall of black, silver-streaked clouds. It hung there with an immense weight of foreboding and . . . hunger. Caldan's skin tingled with a murmur of power. A surge washed over him, then retreated.

But something lingered: An emanation stuck to his skin like glue. A cold, tingling sensation covered him.

"What is this?" Caldan wondered aloud. "Quiss, can you feel this?"

Quiss shook his head. "There's nothing strange I can sense. What are—"

A sharp pain jabbed into Caldan's head as barbs latched onto his well. He clutched his head, reeling.

Hands steadied him from behind.

"Caldan!" said Izak.

"Something has his well," Quiss said. "I'll try to dislodge it."

The agony in Caldan's mind subsided somewhat, though it still felt like barbs were deep in his head. He closed his eyes and breathed deeply.

"I've lessened its effects," said Quiss. "But it's latched firmly onto Caldan. And I don't have a well, which is why I wasn't affected."

"Then that's it," Felice said. "Whatever it is, it's targeting wells."

"Of course," Quiss said. "Caldan, close it. Now!"

Caldan groaned with effort and closed his well. Immediately, the barbs slipped free, and the remaining pain vanished. Whatever had targeted him had gone.

"Then the focus isn't on the emperor's army," he said with difficulty. "It's on sorcerers. The warlocks are being targeted."

"That makes sense," Izak said. "The Quivers are already on the back foot. If the warlocks are taken out, the vormag will be hard to stop."

Felice grabbed Caldan by the arm. "We have to warn them."

She was right. They'd need all the sorcerers they could find in the coming days. But . . .

"Miranda will need my protection," Caldan said. "She could be hurt if anyone close to her is targeted."

"She won't be," Quiss said, shaking his head. "Whatever Kelhak's conjured, it won't find my people. She'll be safe with them."

Felice tugged on Caldan's arm, pulling him toward the warlocks' encampment. "Come on!" she said.

BY THE TIME the four of them reached the edges of the army, the sorcery had strengthened. They passed a few scattered campfires and tents, mostly empty of Quivers, since they were out battling the jukari. The warlocks' encampment was a fair distance away, but already the clouds loomed above them all like an overhanging cliff. Silver lines crackled and sparked across their surface, blooming from flashes of light, spreading a fine tracery of spiderweb.

"We need to move faster!" Caldan had to half shout to be heard over the wind and the thrum of sorcery.

Beside Felice, Izak flicked him a fear-filled glance. Caldan could sense Quiss was holding fast to his power, wherever it came from, and it looked like he was drawing as much as he could. His shield stuck to his skin and clothes, but his shoulders were hunched, mouth open and hands trembling.

Caldan was afraid he and Quiss wouldn't be able to withstand what was thrown against them. If he faced the might of Kelhak, if he was directly assaulted, his defenses would crumble like eggshell. As would the warlocks'. They'd all be killed.

Caldan broke into a sprint, urging the others on. He outpaced them all, glancing back to see if he was followed, then bent his head and surged to greater speed. He skirted around some tents, booted feet thudding across the heavily trafficked grass.

There was a shout behind him—Izak or Quiss, he couldn't be certain.

He slowed as he came across a particularly uneven stretch of ground churned by the constant coming and going of iron-shod hooves. Caldan paused for a few moments to catch his breath. The others were far behind him now, but he couldn't wait for them to catch up. He risked a quick look toward the warlock camp. He sensed the open well of a strong warlock, and the fainter well of another, a few hundred yards from his destination. Above his head, the sky swirled with a mass of clouds, and the wall had moved much closer. Its arrival was imminent.

Lightning crackled, and a second later, thunder ripped the sky apart. Sheets of rain pummeled him, lashing him with a force hard enough to sting. He blinked constantly to clear his eyes and sheltered them with his arm. Blue and violet filaments protruded from the roiling mass. They lengthened, stretching toward the warlocks, as if possessed of an intelligence driven by the desire to destroy.

Clouds churned, twisting to form a circle, a blemish amid the flat expanse. Caldan glanced away, stomach churning with nausea, feeling the earth spin around him. But his gaze was drawn to the cyclone again. Its rotation accelerated quickly, the mass growing in size as it gathered force. Abruptly, it protruded from the clouds, like a bone breaking through skin. It was a gaping maw, searching eagerly for blood. It curled lazily, slowly lengthening. Then it halted, like a wolf sensing prey. The funnel descended from the blanket of darkness. It corkscrewed as it fell, plunging straight for the two wells Caldan had sensed.

The funnel struck. Caldan lurched as the ground shifted under his feet, rippling. A wave of pressure broke over him, followed by the clap of a thousand lightning strikes. He flinched and almost fell to his knees as an immense weight pressed down on him. It grew greater, and he did buckle then. He whimpered in the hissing rain, hands clutching wet earth and grass. He smelled pungent lemons and scorched metal, so strong the scents seemed to assail him.

A detonation. For a moment, time stopped. All went silent. Then sound returned at full force. Sheeting rain pounded at Caldan, now so hot it scalded his skin. His chest ached and burned. The thrum of sorcery was so powerful, it rattled his bones. Screams reached his ears, even over the tumult. He added his to them.

Something horrible had just happened. A rending of the very fabric of reality.

The weight eased. He staggered to his feet and gaped at the sight of what the sorcery had wrought.

Where there had been grass and tents and wagons was now a black circle. Steam rose from the polished midnight surface, smooth enough it resembled a still lake. A hundred yards across, it sucked the light from the surrounding countryside. Caldan searched for signs of the two warlocks' wells but came up empty. They'd simply ceased to exist. Wiped from the face of the earth.

Purified land.

The ultimate sorcerous weapon, destructive sorcery, used during the final throes of the Shattering. Sorcerers with nothing to lose except their lives had imagined something undreamed of and unleashed it on their foes.

What had before been a fight between nations with sorcerers at their heads was now a fight for survival. Caldan's, the empire's, the sorcerers', the land's. Kelhak must be insane. A hand grasped Caldan's shoulder: Quiss.

"This is how a Shattering begins," the sorcerer shouted over the tumult. His face held a look of horror and awe. "I've seen it. Sorcery unleashed without thought of the consequences. This must be stopped!"

Caldan couldn't help it—the power discharged was phenomenal— he couldn't remain defenseless. He opened his well and shielded himself.

Felice and Izak reached them. Felice's hair was plastered to her face and they struggled with the wind, but both looked defiant.

Another funnel burst from the clouds. It hung there, moving back and forth like a snake. It rippled and turned, until Caldan was staring down the center hole into a violet churning mass of . . .

By the ancestors! Caldan snapped his well shut. His shield evaporated. He stood there, in the burning rain. He was scared to breathe. Had he closed his well in time before it fixed on him?

The maw seemed to look directly into his soul. He could feel the force of it—raging pain and glittering blades of hunger.

It swung away. Caldan sank to his haunches, relieved yet terrified. He watched as it moved away toward the warlock encampment. They had to be warned they were in danger if they fought back or used their shields. Anyone holding on to their well could be targeted. And if they were, then those within a hundred yards of them would also perish.

He took a few steps, then hesitated. Should he let the warlocks fend for themselves? They wouldn't think twice about tossing him into a fire, if it suited their purpose. If their numbers were reduced, it could be easier to break free from them. But that didn't mean he should do nothing to help them—they would be needed to defeat Kelhak, and at the end of the day, they were people, too. Caldan could see no way this task would be accomplished without the combined might of the warlocks, Quivers, Protectors, and Gazija's people. Kelhak's sorcery was too great for any one of those groups to face alone, unaided, unsupported.

Chaos ruled the emperor's encampment as Caldan and the others staggered among tents. Equipment lay abandoned; campfires extinguished by the downpour leaked black sludge from the coals. Rivers of rushing water flooded bedrolls and blankets. Everywhere, panicked faces were painted with garish violet-and-green-hued flashes of sorcery. Above them all, black clouds whipped and churned. And now there were three sinuous funnels descending from them. Quivers shouldered and jostled one another in terrified flight. Except, they ran aimlessly, not knowing what to do or where to go. Horns sounded from somewhere. Curses and shouts of alarm and warning filled the air, which vibrated, as if resounding with pounding drums.

A Quiver snagged Caldan's sleeve—a woman with bedraggled brown hair, eyes wide and fearful.

"You're a sorcerer!" she shouted over the tumult. "Do something!"

"I can't! They're targeting sorcerers. Run! Find shelter."

Caldan left her there, forlorn, staring at his back. He couldn't do anything against sorcery such as this. Could anyone? Was this beyond even Gazija's people?

Trailed by Felicienne, Izak, and Quiss, Caldan pushed his way through the hammering downpour, keeping his head lowered, else the rain made it almost impossible to see. Dismayed shouts brought his attention to his right. Wheeling clouds plummeted down—toward a lone figure dressed in black, shimmering with a multicolored shield, arms and face raised to the sky in defiance.

There was a flash and a thrum, and even though he wasn't in touch with his well, Caldan felt it ripple and twist. The ground lurched under him, and he staggered. A crushing weight pressed against him. There was a smack of detonation. Air cracked. Silence. Caldan hissed through clenched teeth. His well—he could feel his power sucked out of it, then it snapped back like a released bowstring. Coruscating fire burned within him. He shored up the barrier between his mind and his well, lest the surge break through and scour his brain with vitriol. Again, his chest burned, and he winced, as if his flesh sizzled.

It passed. Caldan groaned and rose to his feet, unaware that he'd fallen to the ground. He dragged himself up and helped Felicienne.

Izak and Quiss struggled against the force of the storm, getting to their feet, clothes muddied and wet.

Another circle of purified land lay where the defiant warlock had stood. A black stain on the landscape. Sorcery abused. The very life of the earth destroyed. There was a corruption to the black glass circle, a vileness that clawed at his sorcerous awareness.

Hoarse voices howled—Quivers writhing on the ground, clutching at their heads, tearing at their hair. Scarlet trails leaked from noses and ears.

Caldan's blood coursed through his body. A heat like molten metal surged in his veins. His trinket ring penetrated the flesh of his finger with white hot needles. He scarcely felt the pain. Everything around him and inside him clamored for him to flee. But he couldn't. Some things were greater than a single person, and though the warlocks' purpose wasn't his own, they would be needed.

And following his own advice to the Quiver, he ran, clutching the hilt of his sword so it didn't trip him up.

The newly forged purified land was between him and Devenish's tent. Caldan skirted the edge, feeling the *wrongness* to it, as if it had leached all that was life and sorcery from the world. And it pulled at him, as if wanting more sorcery, a giant drain dragging power toward it. Above him, clouds still wheeled, and the air crackled.

He dashed past bewildered Quivers, ignoring their cries and appeals, his booted feet stamping through puddles and streams. Despairing faces half glimpsed as he passed.

Devenish's tent was boiling with activity. Groups of warlocks rushed away from it in all directions. They must have gathered there when they sensed the coming storm and now dispersed to confuse their enemy and offer multiple targets. Devenish stood outside the tent, shouting instructions and reassurance to the departing warlocks.

As Caldan approached, he sensed shields spring up around warlocks. They hadn't succumbed to the utter confusion the Quivers had, but they still went to their inevitable deaths.

Devenish argued with Thenna. She tugged at his arm, and he shrugged her off. He yelled something lost in the wind and the downpour. She sank to her knees in front of him, hair plastered to her face and neck.

Caldan shot into their view and skidded to a halt.

"You have to stop the warlocks using sorcery!" Caldan pleaded. "They'll be killed!"

Devenish's mouth twisted into a grim smile. "They won't be. I'll see to it."

"No, Devenish," gasped Thenna. "You can't—"

"I will!" said Devenish. "Thenna, you must flee! Go with the others." Devenish looked at Caldan. "Take her, Caldan. Get her away from here!"

Thenna struggled to her feet. "I'm not leaving you."

"You must. I cannot protect you."

Thenna cursed viciously. She gave Devenish a despair-filled look and took a step back. Whatever defenses she had inside her crumbled, and she lowered her gaze.

Devenish turned to Caldan. "You must flee. Take Thenna. Carry her, else she won't make it in time. Go now!"

Caldan nodded. He understood Devenish had a plan, one that involved him taking on the might of the storm himself. But what could Devenish do on his own, unless he had something up his sleeve he hadn't revealed before?

The warlocks Caldan had seen were fleeing to safety, not to combat the sorcery. Devenish was sacrificing himself. But could he stand up to the reality—the lifeless voids that were the purified lands? The warlock leader thought he could, or at least that he had a chance.

Before Caldan could move or speak, power flooded out of Devenish. A tornado of fire and darkness. Caldan's well reverberated. A shield enveloped Devenish as the outpouring intensified. He was drawing the storm's fury upon himself.

Caldan didn't wait. He scooped Thenna up and sprinted away. He hardly felt her weight in his fired-up state. She pressed her face to his chest and sobbed.

He ran and didn't stop until he passed a few groups of warlocks. Only when Thenna struggled in his grasp and shouted at him to halt so she could watch what happened to Devenish did he stop. A hundred yards to their left, Caldan could see Quiss, Izak, and Felicienne struggling in their direction.

Thenna, soaked to the bone, the knees of her pants mud-stained, turned a tear-streaked face in the direction they'd come from. She hugged her arms to her chest and rocked back and forth.

Devenish stood still, a speck against the gray, washed-out landscape. But to Caldan's sorcerous senses, he pulsed with power.

An impossibly bright light flared from Devenish, immolating him. Caldan gasped and tensed, but Thenna didn't react. Caldan realized he could still feel Devenish's force. This, then, was the burst meant to attract the storm's fury.

Glowing spheres of light surrounded Devenish. Bubbles within bubbles. Caldan sensed the warlock's well intensify as each one came into existence.

Thenna uttered a despairing cry.

Spasms of power rolled out from Devenish. Clouds focused above him, circling as a shark might. All three funnels tracked toward him.

Lightning arced from Devenish as he loosed power with abandon. Brilliant golden tendrils of his own reached into the heart of the storm, only to be met with violet threads, twining around them and cutting them off. Again, Caldan sensed the underlying design. Crafted power used to create a barrier of force, which could contain the corrosion of destructive sorcery. The same power would disintegrate a well-made crafting in moments.

A funnel reached down to surround Devenish. Thenna screamed desolately, certain he would meet his doom.

Another rippling wave. A soundless flash, closely followed by a deafening clap of thunder. Pressure pushed Caldan down. The scent of lemons and molten metal flooded his nostrils. Thenna's wailing grew in intensity. He found himself face-first on the ground. Caldan clamped down on a primal need to scream.

The pressure relented, and Caldan and Thenna rose.

She let out a choking sob. Where Devenish had stood was another black glass circle.

Thenna sank back to the ground, head in her hands.

But the circle wasn't complete. In the center was a patch untouched by the purified land. Devenish.

"He's alive," Caldan gasped.

And the storm had shrunk, a fact Caldan hadn't noticed before. Whenever a patch of purified land was created, the storm lessened in fury, as if drained of power.

Thenna looked up, red-rimmed eyes searching for and finding the glowing sphere surrounding Devenish. Before she had time to react, another cloud funnel crashed down on the golden shield.

Brilliant agonizing light. Ground trembling with such a force it felt as if it should crack open. Purified land shattered, sending jagged splinters flying. Another black circle overlaid the first, fusing serrated spears of glass.

And still Devenish stood—though now he was surrounded by a spiked field of shattered purified land. The skin of Caldan's chest burned. He looked down to see a glow emanating from under his shirt.

His bone ring.

He tugged the chain around his neck, and the bone ring spilled out. It glowed a searing golden white, like Devenish's protections. Caldan lay in the mud, mouth open, as he worked through the implications.

A bone trinket he was all but certain was only a shield. It had previously reacted when Caldan's defenses had failed. But here it was answering the voice of the purified lands.

A golden glow, akin to that surrounding Devenish. Somehow, he could feel his trinket wanting to respond in kind. Caldan sensed the power flowing through it, searching, and an angry sensation—as if his bone ring sensed a rival.

The trinket was also a weapon, and that was why the warlocks and the emperor desired it.

Caldan knew by his ring's reaction that Devenish must also possess such a trinket.

Only one funnel remained, and Caldan allowed himself a glimmer of hope. Again the fury of the storm had abated. What had been driving rain was now a drizzling mist. Devenish had withstood two hammerings; hopefully he could weather a third. With the storm's ferocity diminished, he had to have most of the battle won. But there was something very wrong with what had happened.

With sickening dread, Caldan realized where this was leading. A slap for a slap. A strike for a strike. Devenish would focus on Kelhak and attempt to repay him for his affront. And if Kelhak survived, he would strike back. It would never end. Sorcery would run amok.

The Shattering all over again.

The last funnel boiled across the sky toward Devenish. It hung there, moving back and forth like a leech looking for a place to bite. Then it withdrew. Its maw retreated into the clouds and dissolved among them. Almost as if Kelhak recognized the futility of continuing.

The light from Caldan's bone ring winked out.

THENNA'S BACK REMAINED to Caldan. He shoved the bone ring under his shirt, heedless that it scorched his hair and flesh. He clenched his teeth against the pain. Bone it might be, but it somehow retained the heat of searing metal.

He regained his feet, and for heartbeats, all he could do was stare at the splintered mass of jagged glass surrounding a globe of brilliant light. Devenish amid destruction. Wielding a trinket no man or woman should have in their possession. This Caldan now understood.

They had to be destroyed, Devenish's and his. No one who'd felt the nonlife of purified land, the very corruption of creation, could deny this. And yet . . . Devenish clearly did.

Thenna shouted with joy and raced back toward the warlock. Around Caldan, groups of warlocks and Quivers were either lying on the ground, or on their knees, or standing on wobbly legs. All of them had eyes for Devenish's glowing sphere and the retreating storm.

Sunlight showered over them. Light gleamed off metal, rain-drenched Quivers and warlocks, and puddles of standing water.

Caldan blinked at the sudden painful glare. He rose to his feet, unsteady at first, then gaining strength.

"Caldan," Felice said as she approached. "What happened?"

Izak stared at the steaming circle of black glass, and Quiss's expression was one of pure horror.

Caldan blinked again, taking in the swath of smoking ground and the haze gathered above the newly created purified lands. He almost wept then, so great was his desire to flee and never look back, which warred with his sense of what was right, what he needed to do.

He turned and saw some of the Quivers hobbling away, reluctant to approach the areas where sorcery had erupted with such force. On the edges of the black circles, corpses lay burning.

He looked to the warlocks' encampment, now obliterated, where Devenish's shield had disappeared, leaving the warlock standing alone in the center of massive dark glasslike shards.

Caldan ignored Felicienne and jogged across the ground, past and through veils of smoke and scattered belongings. Around Quivers with harrowed eyes mirroring fear and confusion.

"I am alive!" Devenish shouted to the sky. "I defeated him!"

The warlock was cut and bleeding, his arms and legs slashed as he climbed through the shards surrounding him. But his expression was one of triumph and exultation. Thenna scrambled toward him, heedless of her own cuts.

Caldan halted on the edge of the purified land. One like no other. Shattered obsidian rose above his head. He could feel it, as close as he was: A void. Emptiness. Desecration.

The Quivers had been scattered but were slowly returning. Warlocks made their way toward Devenish.

Devenish was raving. "I am the only hope the emperor has! It is by my might alone that we all stand here, else you'd all be dead."

"Yes!" Thenna crowed. "My love. My savior!"

Madness. Devenish took advantage of Thenna's lack of knowledge, and no doubt would try the same trick with the other warlocks and the Quivers. His wasn't the power that saved him, it was his trinket. The emperor wouldn't fall for such deception.

More important, Devenish was setting himself as equal to the emperor. The problem was that, in a way, he was. Because just like the emperor, he wasn't actually strong enough to withstand Kelhak. He had a crutch—and who knew when it would break. The warlock had been swept up in the tide of power, and if he was left alone, there was a very real possibility of his doing much more harm than good.

Devenish thought he could stop the war. But instead, he would just escalate the devastation.

The wind continued to blow, chilling Caldan's clothes and skin. Insects buzzed and crows circled. Life continued unabated.

Thenna was with Devenish now, leading him out of the fragments of the purified land. The bare patch on which Devenish had made his stand was in the center of the circle—where he could still access his well. Here, where they stood upon the lifeless surface, sorcerers had no power. Crafting was impossible.

A shiver ran through Caldan. He reached for the buckle of his sword belt and released it. The blade swung to his hip. A furtive glance confirmed no warlocks were close as yet. There were a few Quivers, but they were no hurdle to him. Not now, not with everything he'd learned.

Caldan found himself gasping for breath.

Thenna and Devenish staggered toward him on bloodied feet, hands dripping crimson. Blood trails streaked their arms and legs.

Caldan's eyes moistened. Whether for the warlocks, or the loss of his innocence, or for the world in general, he knew not. Was he going mad? Had this crazed world unhinged him? Destroyed his moral compass?

Devenish and Thenna had stopped. They watched him, eyes laden with suspicion. Ten paces, and they would be clear of the purified land.

The warlock leader would wield a weapon that tore at the very fabric of life, and damn the consequences.

Devenish had already called out the emperor in front of hundreds of other sorcerers and warriors. He felt himself freed from whatever oaths he had taken to his liege, and free—and strong enough—to take on Kelhak. It was lunacy and hubris backed by sorcery.

A combination that could end only in disaster. The proof was standing before them . . . or, rather, they were standing on it. Devenish didn't understand what his arrogance meant, but Caldan did: a lifeless world, scorched and barren and ruined.

Caldan couldn't let that happen.

He glanced uneasily at his sword hilt, saw Devenish lick his lips, Thenna scowl.

"You can join us," Devenish was saying.

"Become one of us," Thenna echoed.

"Touched and a warlock," continued Devenish. "You'll be greater than you can imagine."

A tool, thought Caldan. *A potent implement to be used and discarded, like all the others.*

No—not like the others. A tool in the hands of someone almost purely evil now.

Devenish took a step toward him, hand outstretched, beseeching. "I will train you myself. Coercive and destructive sorcery will be yours to master. One day you'll be greater than me, and replace me as leader of the warlocks."

Thenna stared at Devenish in confusion. But Caldan wasn't buying into his lies. There was nothing he could offer. For one thing, Devenish wouldn't relinquish his position. Would never allow someone stronger than him, someone who could challenge him.

For another, there was no way Devenish would be in a position to offer any of this anyway, because by using purified land as a weapon he would destroy the world.

"No," said Caldan.

Devenish took another step. Thenna tried to push past him, but he shoved her behind him.

Caldan drew his sword, raised the freshly sharpened blade in the air before him. Sunlight covered the burnished metal.

"Caldan . . . lower your sword."

Another step.

"Stop," Caldan said, wincing at the weakness in his voice.

Behind him he heard Felicienne cry out in dismay. She would be here soon.

Devenish placed one foot in front of the other. "Together, we will discover new sorceries, the like of which the world has never seen! But you must join us, in spirit as well as body. There are no half measures. Become one of us. It is all you've ever dreamed of, is it not? Together, we will explore your treasured sorcery."

Devenish's soothing voice called to Caldan. He did want what Devenish offered. But only part of it. The other part was too repulsive to contemplate. He would forge his own path, away from the warlocks and the emperor, away from their machinations. Together with Miranda.

Yes, Kelhak still lay between him and his heart's desire. And yes, Devenish had been the one who had stopped Kelhak's assault. If Caldan allied himself with the warlock, Kelhak could be vanquished. But if Devenish was the rock that broke Kelhak's sorcery, then that rock was hollow, and already the cracks were showing. And that meant he wasn't a solid foundation on which to build a future—a future of peace. A future with Miranda.

Caldan had to take his place.

Devenish took another step. He held out his hand, palm up, pleading with Caldan to take it.

Caldan stepped onto the shattered surface, edges cutting deep into his boots.

"No," whispered Thenna.

Devenish shrank back, casting a panicked gaze around him. But there was no one to help. His well was blocked by the purified land. There was only the warlocks and Caldan.

And Caldan's sword.

Caldan's blade cleaved down. Thenna jerked back as Devenish tumbled, a surprised look on his face. The sword jutted from a gash in his shoulder; blood pumped from the wound. Caldan tugged his blade out and watched Devenish fall with a gurgling gasp, light leaving his eyes.

Thenna screamed, the sound returning to them a hundredfold off the hard glass splinters.

Caldan struck her across the temple with the flat of his blade, as he had done to Bells what seemed like so long ago in the cavern beneath

Anasoma. Thenna slumped in a heap, a red smear across her forehead. He was sure he would regret sparing her life later, but for now, in this moment, he just couldn't kill her.

Caldan wiped his sword on Devenish's shirt and sheathed it, refusing to think about what he'd done. He lifted Thenna's inert form and carried her off the jagged slivers. Placing her on the ground, he made sure none of her cuts were deep enough to be life threatening. Once satisfied, he returned to Devenish. He found the trinket on a silver chain around the warlock's neck, worn the same way as his own. A bone ring. Twin to the one he'd inherited. He tore the chain off and quickly fastened the ring next to his.

Then he left the purified land, opened his well, and poured power into his shield. He'd just killed Devenish, the leader of the warlocks and the man who they thought had saved them. Maybe some would realize why he'd struck Devenish down, but not enough.

Quivers nocked arrows; spears were leveled at him; cries went up from the soldiers. Warlocks gestured at Caldan—and focused sorcery came for him.

Sparks erupted from his shield as it buffered the attack. Glittering fire consumed the grass surrounding him—but he stood within the conflagration untouched. Arrows struck, most glancing away, iron points bending as they bounced off his wards. To Caldan, they were mere irritations. His skills had developed a great deal, and his complex, phased shield was equal to the task.

Ignoring the assault, Caldan began walking east, toward the river and Gazija's ships. If he stayed here, he might have to kill some of them before they backed off.

"Stop!" Caldan roared at the Quivers coming toward him.

Some of them faltered, and the rain of arrows lessened.

"Do not come against me!" he shouted. "Or you'll regret it."

As if they sensed the truth in his words, the warlocks' pummeling also tapered off.

Caldan resumed his march toward Quiss's ships, not caring whether Felice or Quiss followed.

After what he'd done, he hoped Miranda would forgive him.

CHAPTER 38

Amerdan sat cross-legged on patchy grass. Only the talon and the vormag had tents among these savages. Inside the talon's was a pile of rags that served as bedding and a wooden chest two feet wide and half as deep. It sported a heavy lock, though he hadn't tested it. He couldn't imagine what these beasts possessed that he'd want for his own. There was a musty scent in the air, overlaying a fetid stench of rotting meat.

Xarlas had bade him enter, then gone to talk with the jukari and vormag. Amerdan was grateful for the reprieve, as he was still light-headed from the gifts his trinket had delivered to him, whatever they were. He hoped for Gamzegul's well. The vessel wouldn't be needing it anymore, now that Amerdan had cut out its throat. He'd tried searching for the well, to no avail. Whatever his trinket had done to his mind left him unable to focus on sorcery.

But vast were the possibilities before him. Striking were the potential rewards.

First, though, the jukari and vormag must yield to him.

The tent flap rustled, and a draft washed over him, humid with the sharp scent of musk. It lay open a crack, a sheet of light cutting across the space, illuminating particles of dust. Leather-bound feet scuffed across dirt. Metal tinkled and bones clacked together. He opened himself to his wells, sensing the bruise of the talon's. He licked his lips, counting. Seventeen. She had seventeen! But they were blocked. A few were straining against the barrier separating the creature's mind from the source. There were thinner patches, as if the wall had been scraped at. Two of them had holes, but they were tiny. Only a trickle of power could seep through. Which meant she had taken wells much as he had, but hadn't been able to break the blockages. Whether it was because of the difference in their trinkets or a lack of sorcerous skill to help her break through was unsettled. Whatever the reason, the talon was stumbling along a similar path to Amerdan's. One that was for Amerdan alone. That couldn't be allowed.

How dare she?

He remained still, even when the talon came so close her rags brushed his back. Whatever her motives, his were above her.

"I would know," Xarlas said as she made her way to her nest of rags and sat down, "more of you." The talon rested her clawed hands on her knees and regarded him, violet eyes unblinking.

She was uncertain.

Amerdan marshaled his concentration. Here lay both opportunity and danger. Of all his encounters since childhood, no other had held more promise or more peril.

Dotty stirred against his chest, and he smiled.

"I am an Old One," he said.

Xarlas frowned, replacing the expression in an instant with blankness. "What city did you live in? Who was your master? What talons were yours?"

All questions Amerdan could not answer. But he didn't have to. How were these creatures used to being treated? Since the Shattering, they'd obviously assumed command, taken fragments of power unto themselves. But before . . . they were servants.

"Fool!" he hissed. "I had no master! I am beyond them!"

The talon stirred, clawed fingers clenching and unclenching. Amerdan deciphered her intent. Before, she had been a slave, but now she had tasted freedom for centuries. There would be no persuading her. Xarlas's actions were inevitable.

"You cannot kill me," he said anyway. "I have remained hidden for eons, gathering power to myself. Test me if you must. But know this: If you go against me, you will die. I will take you into myself, as I have done to others countless times."

"We have no wish to be servants again."

"But that is your place. You were created to serve. You know this. Denial ill suits you."

Xarlas shuddered, as if she could feel chains of cold steel sliding across her body, claiming it. "We will not—"

"You *will*."

She gazed at the ground between them, expression unreadable. Abruptly, she stood and moved to the chest. From around her neck, among the myriad metal and bone objects, she selected a key. Xarlas paused then, as if considering her actions, then unlocked the container.

I should kill it. Dotty brushed his skin, slid over his nipple. She had been quiet of late. *Speak to me!* he pleaded to his sisters.

Xarlas paused in the process of lifting the lid and turned. "Did you say something?"

"No. Open your box, talon. What is inside you're so eager to show me?"

A weapon? His death? No. If that were the goal, the talon would have taken it out before he was here.

I'll find out what's inside later.

Because with the talon dead, he could look at his leisure. And that's what he wanted: to kill it. His *trinket* wanted this. He could feel it. One hand reached into his shirt and drew it out. The spherical pendant rested in his clenched fist. His hand began to glow; light shone through the flesh of his fingers. The need filled him. He shivered with delight.

The talon had its back to him. It either didn't fear him or had defenses. Not sorcerous ones, judging from its blocked wells.

Amerdan's blade struck with barely a glimmer. The creature fell almost silently, choking on her own blood. He pushed it to the ground and sat astride it. It groaned faintly, lips bubbling scarlet. A radiance rose from its face, growing stronger as Amerdan sensed his trinket's power encompass the thing's essence. He raised his hand as a thread of sparkling light erupted from his trinket and snaked toward the vessel. The light thickened, swelling. Pulses traveled along the cord to him. Pain racked Amerdan's body, and he clenched his teeth together. Only a whimper escaped. Good. He was getting stronger.

As he watched, the skin covering the vessel's face leached of color, turning a corpse gray, its covering cracked, drained of vitality.

Which was now his.

The cord vanished, cutting Amerdan from the ecstasy, from the agony. The loss of any feeling was so sudden, the absence of pain became like pain itself. He gasped, and a shudder ran through him, tendons in his neck straining. With a croak, he collapsed onto the desiccated remains, panting.

A commotion outside reached his ears. Vormag arguing in hushed tones. Jukari howling and slavering.

Amerdan pushed himself to his feet.

He sawed at the vessel's neck until its head came free, defiling the corpse for following a path that was for him alone. The meat was like dried leather. He wiped his knife on the talon's rags, once more vowing to give the blade a proper cleaning later. The creature reeked of decay, of unopened tombs. The chain with the talon's trinket had slipped off the stump of its neck, and Amerdan picked it up to examine. He could sense it calling to him. Or was it the other way round? His called to this one?

Acting on impulse, he drew his spherical cage out and held it close to the talon's. A pulse of energy passed between them, a spark so faint he thought he'd imagined it.

Except now . . . he had a greater sense of the second trinket. He felt where it was, and, somehow, that it was now unbound to any creature. It was . . . enslaved to his.

Amerdan couldn't help himself. He laughed. Possibilities were opening up before him.

And another thing dawned on him: Where there was one, there were others. Like and unlike his own. He could pass one to his sister in the hospice. Would it be able to heal her? Could absorbing the contents of vessels lead to her cure? His salvation?

There were no certainties. But for the first time in many years, Amerdan felt he had a mission.

The contents of the chest lay in shadow, and he tilted it to the light beaming in from the tent flap. A few polished rocks. Scraps of metal with strange runes. Scraped leather covered in ancient writing. A dried flower? Personal items.

Junk.

Why did Xarlas move to open the chest, then? Was the rune-covered metal some sort of crafted weapon? Amerdan snorted, dismissing their importance. He was beyond such playthings.

He dropped the chest, and the contents scattered in the dirt. He tucked the talon's trinket into a belt pouch. The vormag must know where the other talons were. Killing Xarlas and assuming her place was only the start. The vormag would be uncertain. Hesitant. He had to take control of them.

They must fear him.

Amerdan opened his wells and strode from the tent.

CHAPTER 39

A cool breeze blew over Caldan from open windows. The captain's cabin. Luxurious, even though it was compact. He sat on a chair on which hung his sheathed sword. Drained, both emotionally and mentally, he held his face in his hands, resting his elbows on his knees.

Quiss stood by the windows. He was gaunt and pale, staring out into the night.

There was a knock at the door, and the latch turned.

"Come in," Quiss said in his strange accent.

When Quiss spoke, Caldan looked up. He wiped his tear-streaked cheeks. Seeing Felice, his eyes widened slightly.

Felice pursed her lips and entered. She examined Caldan, taking in the jagged cuts in his leather boots and the trinket ring on his finger. His hand reached up to touch the bone trinkets through his shirt, and her eyes followed his movement.

"I have to know why," Felice said plainly. "Devenish stood firm against the assault, and then you killed him when I was only a few dozen paces away. You walked calmly away while the warlocks and Quivers tried to kill you."

Caldan laughed softly. "You're wondering if I'm now a threat. Tell me, Felice, was the innocent man you played Dominion with a threat?"

"No. But people change. The warlocks think Devenish was killed by a rogue sorcerer. An infiltrator of Kelhak's, if the rumors are to be believed. A young man recently arrived in Riversedge. A false Protector from Anasoma. You. Except . . . I know you're not a spy. You're not a traitor. Which begs the question: Why did you behave like one?" She held up a hand to stop him answering. "You must have had a good reason. One you considered moral." She looked at Quiss meaningfully. "What does he know?"

"Everything," said Caldan.

Felice sighed. "I need to know—"

"No," growled Caldan. He stood, face twisted in barely constrained fury. "You'll tell *me* what you know about the bone trinkets. Now."

Felice took a half step back, swallowing. "During the Shattering," she said, "or before—no one really knows—the sorcerers created trinkets of immense power. A very few were . . . the antithesis of what many of them revered—sorcery. Instead, they expunged sorcerous power from an area. Destroyed all life. And the sorcerers didn't hesitate to use them."

"The Shattering," whispered Caldan.

Felice nodded. "Yes."

"Partly," broke in Quiss.

"What do you mean?" Felice asked.

"You're partly correct," Quiss said. "But do go on."

She looked at him in consternation, then turned back to Caldan. "Whatever happened thousands of years ago, the world was almost destroyed. A few brave men and women, heedless of losing their own lives, fought their way to and seized the trinkets. They saved all of us. Then one of their number betrayed them and took the artifacts for himself. He killed them all and reputedly destroyed the trinkets."

"Who was it?" Caldan said, then shook his head. "It doesn't matter who he was—"

"But it does. It was the emperor."

Caldan stared at her in disbelief. "The empire was created centuries after the Shattering. He couldn't have—"

"He already knew the secret of the Touched."

"You *knew* about their blood?" Caldan said.

"Yes."

"And did nothing?"

"And achieve what?" she snapped. "Commit suicide? You may think you know the truth, but you clearly haven't looked at it fully. Politics often trumps truth, young man."

"So the emperor took the bone trinkets," Quiss prompted.

"Yes. I thought," Felice said, "that there was only one such trinket left. I was mistaken."

Caldan nodded in agreement. He settled back into the chair, one hand close to his sword hilt. Quiss watched with emotionless eyes.

Felice continued. "My master called the trinket the Waster of Life. She told me everything she could about it before she died . . . except for the fact that there was more than one."

Caldan made the connection immediately. There was no mistaking the feel of the purified land, its deadness. A *Waster of Life*, he mused, *is a good description*. Then Felice had to have made the connection to his bone trinket. She knew he'd lied about not possessing it.

A silence hung in the air, broken only by the lap of water against the side of the ship.

Felice continued. "She said to me, 'If you ever get the chance, to possess or destroy one of these trinkets, take it. No matter what the cost.' You, Caldan, possess one: the bone ring. Stolen from the emperor decades ago by your family. Kept by them . . . They tried to keep it out of others' hands so it would never be used. And the warlocks have—*had*—one. Sorcery that didn't simply kill; it destroyed utterly. I didn't know what form the ancient relic took, only that it had to be in the warlocks' keeping. They hadn't used this knowledge for any ends, merely kept it in case it came in handy."

"Handy," snorted Caldan. "That's one word for it. So now you've worked it out, you understand why I had to kill Devenish."

Felice nodded and swallowed. "But it puts me in a difficult position."

"What are you going to do with me? Turn me in? Do you think I'll go quietly?"

"I don't expect so. Not after your display. I know a great deal about sorcery, both what is public knowledge and much that isn't. I know things I shouldn't." Felice wrung her hands. "Terrible things. But . . . what you did frightened me. And now I find you lied to me about the Waster of Life. You had it all along."

Caldan spread his hands. For some reason, he felt embarrassed. "I didn't know who to trust. I still don't."

"Do you trust this man?" She pointed at Quiss.

A fleeting smile passed across Caldan's face. "More than I trust you."

"I didn't know what it was, back then," she said. "I do now. And I believe you killed Devenish so that you could take his Waster of Life. Since you didn't immediately try to set yourself up as the new leader of the warlocks, I'm pretty sure it wasn't a power play. The man who defeated me at Dominion had been content to devote his life to studying crafting and had joined the Protectors. Except, he already possessed a Waster of Life, one kept hidden by his family for decades. Then you stumbled across another. And you had to follow your parents' path, their familial mission . . . to conceal a terrible artifact from those who would abuse its power. So you committed murder. Now, all you can do is run."

"I've had enough of running," Caldan said. He shifted in his chair.

"Yes," Felice said. "You'll be needed to fight Kelhak. We all will."

Caldan watched as her lips trembled and her legs wobbled. He felt ashamed. But he'd needed to know what she knew. She'd come alone against him, when she knew what he'd done to Devenish. And that implied she trusted him not to kill her. Perhaps she was on his side . . .

"You *do* have the Waster of Life Devenish used, am I correct?" Felice said.

Caldan nodded. "And mine."

"Beware calling it your own. And about Devenish: Why did you kill him?"

Guilt rose in Caldan, twisting his stomach and forming a lump in his throat. He swallowed. "Devenish wouldn't have stopped. He protected the warlocks and the Quivers from Kelhak's storm, and the purified lands. But he was . . . flawed. He only wanted power. He had to be stopped. It was the only choice."

"And who are you to make that judgment?"

"I'm no one. And I'd like to stay that way."

Felice studied him. He felt himself being evaluated, his actions weighed. Judged. It reminded him of the monks' gazes when they had found out he possessed a well. They'd looked at him as someone of consequence then. And now, he realized that's what he was. From the moment he'd been banished from the monastery, his path hadn't been his own. His blood, destructive and coercive sorcery—everything that had happened to him since would have happened no matter what path he'd taken. Of course it would; he was a fool to think otherwise. He'd stumbled along, blind to the future. He'd been content to live in the now, and look where it had taken him.

It seemed impossible that he hadn't realized this sooner. Killing Devenish had filled him with a clarity of thought he'd previously lacked. The clarity of someone with nothing, and everything, to lose.

"I—"

"You bring conflict with you," Felice said, before he could finish. "You are sorcerer and Touched both. Greater than the sum of the parts."

For several moments, he heard nothing but his own breath rasping through his throat, his own heart hammering in his chest.

"That's what Devenish said. He lusted after my abilities."

"And your blood."

"Yes. It came together for me with Elpidia. She didn't know about the Touched, but she knew the power I had flowing through me."

"Who is this Elpidia? And where is she?"

"Dead. Amerdan murdered her."

Felice frowned. "And who is he?"

"A shopkeeper. No—more than that. He's a danger."

"To who? You? Or to us?"

"Us? The Mahruse Empire and the emperor?"

"Of course."

"The empire is rotten to the core. There is no 'us' where they're concerned. And if you insist that you're still part of them, then we're done here." His words dripped with venom.

Grimacing, Felice shook her head. "We do good things, help many people. Without the empire, there would be disorder."

"The fact the empire does good things is testament to the fact that good people do good things. It has nothing to do with the emperor or those in his inner circle. The warlocks are corrupt. The Protectors are but a tool, whatever they once were. And they all hang on a secret—one they kill to keep, kill to maintain. Self-preservation and self-interest. Old and aging people clinging to power and to the only way they know of warding off sickness and frailty. Never mind that it comes at such a cost."

"Without the empire, the jukari and vormag would have overrun us. We'd have been slaughtered. We wouldn't exist today."

"I don't believe that. People would survive; they'd have found a way. Look at the Sotharle Union of Cities and the kingdoms to the south. Even Indryalla."

Felice looked at him with pity. "You think they don't know about Touched blood? You're fooling yourself. Of course they know! And a lot of them are less kind than the empire is."

"So I should be grateful for the chance to be used and worn out?" spat Caldan. "Then bled like a sacrificial animal?"

"That's not what I'm saying—"

"Stop. You may not realize it, but that's exactly what you're saying. The only way they expect me to serve is to kill and destroy for them, and then die in a place convenient for them to drink my blood."

Stepping between them, Quiss interrupted. "Now is not the time for this discussion. We have more important things to worry about. From what Caldan has explained, you now have no protection against the creation of these purified lands, as Caldan calls them. What he did was rash, but it's possible he's prevented much worse from happening. I'll admit, I don't know how they're created, but I've a better chance of working it out than either of you."

Felice's lips pressed together. "The warlocks will kill you all once they find out. I'm surprised they aren't here now. And there's no way I'm letting you take possession of one of the trinkets."

Quiss's laugh echoed around the cabin. "You have no choice. How would you stop me?"

"I've killed one of you before. One of your kind."

"Ah . . . Savine. I heard. You know you didn't kill him, not really. Besides, you were lucky."

"I make my own luck."

Quiss inclined his head. "As do I. In any case, Caldan has agreed to loan me a trinket to study. I'll admit, we haven't paid much attention to craftings or trinkets. We are beyond them. They're crutches."

"He's the only one who can help us," Caldan said. "What might take me months to figure out won't take Quiss nearly as long."

Felice nodded slowly. Her expression was blank, and Caldan couldn't decide what she was thinking. Likely, she knew she couldn't alter their path and would try something else in the future.

"It has started," she said, voice filled with fear.

Quiss nodded, but remained silent.

Caldan knew what Felice referred to. "A second Shattering," he said. "But this one we can prevent from happening, can't we, Quiss?"

The sorcerer shrugged, face bleak. "Perhaps. Perhaps not. We couldn't stop the lich, in our world. It's not a person. Or maybe it once was; no one really knows. It has taken over Kelhak's form. He is a vessel holding the entity, much as a cup holds water. It has learned how to absorb other people in some way. Their talents, their abilities. But what makes it dangerous, and powerful beyond anything you've ever encountered, is that it also absorbs wells. It makes them its own."

A gasp escaped Caldan. "It takes wells from sorcerers?" he repeated. "How many? Surely it couldn't use many at a time."

"Hundreds," said Quiss. "And you're right: its control isn't perfect. But it's enough."

"What does it want?" said Felice. "And how can we stop it? What has been tried before?"

"Before?" said Quiss incredulously. He shook his head. "It was all we could do to flee, else we would have perished. A few of us may have tried something, raw sorcery. But obviously nothing that worked."

"For someone who knows more than we do," Felice said, "you're surprisingly short of useful information."

"There has to be something!" Caldan exclaimed.

"If there is," Quiss said, "I don't know of it. If Gazija were here . . . but he isn't. We need the lich defeated, otherwise it'll come for us. For all of us. You have the trinkets now, which will stop the warlocks losing themselves in their power and causing another Shattering."

Caldan reached into his shirt and removed the chain from around his neck. He undid the clasp and removed Devenish's bone ring. It was identical to his own, but shinier, polished, as if caressed by many hands. He stood and held it out to Quiss. Felice's gaze followed the ring.

"Take it," he said. "We have to learn how to use it quickly. I've had mine for months, and its workings are an enigma to me. But I want it back in my possession when you're not examining it."

Quiss took the trinket but waved a hand dismissively. "Trinkets are just complex craftings. But I'll study this one soon, if you insist. Now, there's another urgent matter I must bring to your attention."

Felice smiled, as a mother might to a wayward child she knew was being evasive. "Then tell us," she said.

"We have another problem, one that we should sort out first. My people are far more sensitive than most sorcerers, and we've sensed some disturbing activity."

"Activity?" said Felice. "You mean sorcery."

"Yes," Quiss said. "I . . . I'll just come out and say it. There's another lich."

Another! Caldan felt weak. The air in the cabin pressed down on him, became too thick to breathe.

" . . . possibly more than one," Quiss was saying.

"Pignuts," gasped Felice.

"Where?" Caldan found himself saying. "Where are they? Are they as powerful as Kelhak?"

"All good questions," said Quiss. "Another one is: What is their intent?" He shook his head. "Without knowing who they are, we cannot say. But we know they are lesser than Kelhak."

Felice turned to Caldan. He looked into her eyes and saw not fear but determination. "We are alive so far, after all that's happened to us. We'll survive this."

"Quiss," Caldan said. "These others—you brought them to our attention because you fear what they might become."

"Yes."

As with any game of Dominion, you had to start somewhere. And a child had to play less complex games before he or she could comprehend the true scope of Dominion. What they had to do was clear to Caldan now. "We have to confront these liches first, while they're weak. They could provide insight into how we can defeat Kelhak."

Felice nodded. "I agree. Tell us more, Quiss. What do you know?"

"Much. And little."

Felice snorted a laugh. "We're not children, sorcerer. We don't need to be shielded."

Quiss paused, and then nodded himself. "Very well. The tearing of a well from one person is a painful experience. And one that requires great power, and art in sorcery. The reverberations echo through the air, as they do when the extracted well is . . . grafted to someone else. We felt such an occurrence a number of times. Some were weak, far away. We assumed these were Kelhak, or another."

The emperor, Caldan thought.

Quiss continued. "But a couple were closer, much closer. One we detected as we were approaching Riversedge. From among the emperor's army. I believe there was a sorcerous battle there."

Caldan clasped his hands to conceal their shaking. "There was bloodshed. The stench of sorcery."

"Anything else?" Quiss continued. "Something out of the ordinary?"

Pain. His broken sorcery. Hundreds of Quivers dying around him. A desiccated corpse with long black hair: Bells. Amerdan covered in a black shield. Amerdan. Amerdan, who when they'd first met had repulsed Caldan for an instant. Who'd revealed he was a sorcerer among the warlocks, among the destructive sorcery.

He looked up to find Quiss and Felice staring at him. They were waiting.

"Amerdan," he said. "A shopkeeper who fled Anasoma with us. He was . . . odd. I thought he was Touched. He had similar abilities to me. But he wasn't a sorcerer. Then he disappeared when we reached Riversedge, only to reappear with Bells. And he could shield himself. It has to be him."

"So . . . Touched and a sorcerer. Like you," said Felice.

Caldan met her gaze. "Yes. But . . . if he wasn't a sorcerer before, how could he claim another's well for his own? Bells, for all her tragic faults, I couldn't see doing something so horrible as tearing out another sorcerer's well and transferring it to Amerdan."

"Then he has to have a trinket that does it," Felice said.

A sensible thought, a highly probable path. But had it just occurred to Felice, or had she known all along?

"If a sorcerer can do it," Quiss said, "then a trinket can be made to do the same thing."

Caldan's thoughts churned. What was the truth of what Quiss and Felice knew? What were they holding back? Hiding? For everyone had secrets and kept them close.

"If Bells was the one to teach him, then she's dead. If it's a trinket, then he has it. Either way, our focus has to be finding Amerdan. If we can figure out how this process works, then we may have a hope of defeating Kelhak."

Felice was nodding, making Caldan wonder if she'd guided him to this path. But no, she couldn't have known about Amerdan—he'd just told her moments ago. It was one of her strengths, he realized. The projection of certainty, of purpose.

Quiss coughed. "Without Gazija, we are at a disadvantage. But my people and I may be able to find this man. We know what to look for: multiple wells. It will take time, but we can do it."

"How much time?" asked Felice.

"A day. Two."

"Then you'd better get started."

Caldan smiled, though he didn't feel like it. He was tired and wanted to sleep. Miranda was waiting for him, and he wanted to hold her. He needed some comfort. "This wasn't where I saw my life leading," he said wryly. "I'm not a hero. And hunting these liches sounds like a quick way to die. But it needs to be done."

Quiss nodded. "That it does."

Felice smiled, in the manner of someone who knew a truth you didn't. "There are many paths one can take, Caldan. It is the same as Dominion. Sorcery, war, life choices. You can see better than most which path will lead to where you want to end up. But some require sacrifice. A path that may seem easier also holds the risk of more going wrong, being open to disruption. You know this."

Before, when Caldan had been naive, he would have agreed. Before, he would have taken Felice at her word, taken her advice as a lesson he needed to learn. Now, everything had changed. Felice had come alone, unarmed, to a place she might have expected peril. A calculated move on her part. For Caldan realized everything she did was calculated. She'd put herself in danger's path, she spoke of helping them, of saving the empire, and she'd revealed knowledge they lacked. But could he take her at her word? The old Caldan would have.

Now he simply nodded, as he would have previously. But he reserved judgment.

"As for you, Quiss," Felice continued. "You know an awful lot about these liches. Is there something you should be telling us?"

Quiss averted his eyes. "The liches, and those trinket daggers you have, Felice—it's similar to what's happened to us. What we willingly did to ourselves."

Felice stared at Quiss, expression blank. Caldan frowned. He'd known these sorcerers were odd, but . . . Quiss had just implied they'd had their consciousnesses trapped.

"What do you mean?" Caldan said. "What's going on?"

Quiss sighed, his shoulders slumped. "You would have found out eventually. But we are not from here. There was a lich where we came from, the one inside Kelhak. It destroyed our world."

Caldan's mind reeled. *They are from another world! And Kelhak followed them here.* Felicienne was nodding, like she already knew.

"Is that why . . ." Caldan said. "I mean, your people: They have always looked different to me. Denser."

"Partly," admitted Quiss. "But mostly it's to do with our essence inhabiting people from your world. You're not quite strong enough to hold our essence, and there is . . . leakage."

He turned an imploring gaze on Caldan, as if he feared what his reaction would be.

"We found a way to escape," the sorcerer said. "We fled through our wells, but in the process, the flesh was scoured from our bones. We found a way for our . . . essence . . . to survive, though. We had to take over someone else. To use their bodies to house us."

"That's . . ." Words couldn't describe the disgust Caldan felt. And these were the sorcerers he'd thrown his lot in with? They were worse than the warlocks.

Felice cleared her throat. "Just so. Interesting, isn't it?"

Interesting? "What they're doing is an atrocity." Caldan's voice cracked on the last word. By the ancestors, was nothing what it seemed? He looked at Quiss, whose eyes were downcast, his expression pure contrition. It seemed he'd shrunk into himself further.

"We did what we had to do to survive," Quiss said, defiant and pleading all at once. "We're working on a solution."

"And your 'solution' was murder?"

"No! I mean . . ." He sighed. "I wish Gazija were here to explain. He thought he knew how, but . . ."

Caldan warred between his newfound revulsion and his desire to know more. "What happened to him? Did Kelhak really kill him?"

"Gone." Quiss's voice was flat, tinged with grief. "He killed himself, rather than let Kelhak take him. There's nothing on the other side to transfer his consciousness to. He's gone." Quiss breathed out heavily. "This is a night of revelations. We have all revealed much to each other, in order to show we are trustworthy. But in the end, what bonds we forge here tonight will all be tested in the coming days."

Caldan stood. The low cabin ceiling brushed his head. "Anasoma has fallen. The warlocks are in disarray. The Quivers are busy fighting jukari, when their attention should be turned to Kelhak. We are diminished, while Kelhak's plans come to fruition."

"This is true," Quiss said. "But what are his plans? You assume he must have a purpose, but your assumptions are based on false ideas. Whatever the lich once was, he . . . it . . . is no more human than a jukari. Less so. Whatever character he seems to possess is stolen. The body of Kelhak is a shell, a vessel."

"Then what do you suggest?" Felice asked.

Caldan wasn't sure she didn't know already. She was trying to subtly guide them. An impassioned speech here, a prod there. And he knew why.

She thought the end was coming. Another Shattering. And she would die to prevent it.

Which was one thing he knew he could trust.

Because he would do the same thing.

CHAPTER 40

"A ssume they know exactly what's going on," Miranda said with anger. "Then you won't be surprised."

He'd revealed everything to her during the last hour. She'd listened closely, interrupting only when she had a relevant question. When he was finished, Caldan felt wrung out but strangely relieved.

Caldan held her tighter. He sat on the narrow cabin bunk with his back to the wall. Miranda sat practically in his lap, his arms surrounding her warmth. Her hair tickled his nose, and he breathed in her scent. She fidgeted with the cloth of her shirt, her buttons. She sniffed, stiffened for an instant, then softened.

She thinks I reek. He was learning her ways. It felt strange being so close to her. He was embarrassed by his reactions, and yet . . . he didn't want anything else. The closer they became, the greater his desire to leave all of this—the warlocks and the Touched—behind him.

Miranda pinched his arm. "I worry for you, you know."

For some reason, the thought that she was concerned about him filled Caldan with uncertainty. They could run, leave this place. But he knew Felice was right. His path was set, and sometimes sacrifice was required to end the game. If he was giving up only a little time in order to help Quiss and Felice defeat Kelhak before extricating himself from the warlocks, then everything would be fine.

"We'll be all right" was all he said. It sounded lame to his ears.

Miranda shivered, as if cold, though the room and Caldan were warm. "You know sorcery far better than I do. Do you think they can catch Amerdan? And that this will lead to a way to defeat Kelhak?"

"I don't know. But I know we have to try."

"That's what I thought you'd say."

"You disagree?"

Miranda shrugged, then sighed. "If Quiss and his people combine with the warlocks, then what good will one more sorcerer do?"

"A sorcerer *and* Touched. Yes, I'm only beginning to understand my abilities, what I'm capable of, but it may be that I will be the tipping point." As much as the knowledge filled him with terror, it also filled him with elation. Terror, because using his abilities would hasten his death; because the fate of the world might rest in their hands. But the elation . . . the joy . . . That was what he felt when he practiced sorcery. Smith-crafting an item, filling himself with his well's power and controlling it to do whatever he wanted. His gifts were blooming like flowers in spring, and he wanted—needed—to explore them.

"You can't know that."

"I can't not know it, either."

Miranda punched his thigh. "Then we have to make sure we're prepared. What can we do? What do you need? What can I do?"

Caldan sensed her frustration. She felt useless. Her talent for merchanting and trading wouldn't be much use. But she could still help. "I don't know how long Quiss will take to find Amerdan. But there's a project I've started I want to finish. Another automaton. And I also have something I want to test. There's a blacksmith's near the closest gate, and I think it has all that I need. I'm only short a few raw materials."

"Tonight," Miranda said. "You want to get started tonight."

She was always quick to understand. "Yes."

"Tell me what you want me to do."

"There's a clockmaker; I'll tell you where she is. She has materials and parts she made for me. Would you be able to fetch them while I organize the forge? You'll have to wake her up."

"That I can do."

"The blacksmith's will be closed for the night, but there'll be someone there. Apprentices and workers. I'll persuade someone to let me in. You can meet me there."

"Do we . . . have to go right now?"

Caldan stirred. She was *so* warm . . . He stroked her hair. "In a little while."

Letting out a deep breath, Miranda sank farther into his embrace. She cleared her throat and turned so she could look at him. Her eyes were so dark, they were like black pools, staring at him seriously, yet one corner of her mouth tugged upward impiously. "Caldan," she whispered.

He tried to speak; words caught in his throat. He was still stroking her hair, didn't want to stop.

Miranda reached out and clasped the back of his head. She pulled his lips to hers.

CALDAN HAMMERED ON the blacksmith's door. He stepped back, glancing up and down the deserted street. It was after midnight, but the main thoroughfare close by was still bustling. An image of Miranda flooded his vision, her naked body glistening with sweat . . . He shook his head and hammered on the door again.

Metal scraped on metal as the door opened to reveal a young boy, eyes half-closed and blinking. Caldan shoved a silver ducat in front of him and they widened.

"I need some time at the forge. I was supposed to come during the day, but I was delayed. I want to do my work now."

The boy swallowed and glanced behind him. He turned back to Caldan and nodded, taking the coin. "All right. It's another two silvers for the space."

"Done. I'll pay when I'm finished."

The door opened wider, and the boy nodded. Caldan walked past him and into a packed-earth courtyard. Around the outside, what was probably originally a warehouse had been repurposed to house a dozen enclosures, each with its own anvil and forge equipment. The centermost room contained a long bank of glowing coals. Behind one stone wall, he could see the top of a waterwheel revolving. In front of the wall was a massive hammer, powered by the wheel. It was used for forging large pieces and cutting long ingots into smaller, workable sections.

He brought out a sorcerous crafted globe and placed it high up, where it would illuminate one of the enclosures. He turned to find the boy behind him, staring.

"I take it the forges are banked. Could you heat one up, hot enough for smelting?"

"Yes, sir." The boy stumbled off, half-asleep still but slowly waking up.

First, Caldan had to smith-craft an item to aid with his sorcery. Scribing runes and patterns into metal was hard work, and time consuming, and ink was temporary, so it was his least-favored option. He had an idea, though. He could use it to speed up the engraving process, if he had a crafting that could help. It would have to be subtle and under fine control, but he should be able to do it. The important parts of the construct still needed to be smith-crafted, cast using sorcery to maintain the links and his well's power flowing through them while they solidified. But the less important parts could be merely engraved, and for a construct of this size, if he didn't shorten the process, it could take weeks.

By the time he'd organized the workspace how he liked and the boy confirmed one of the forges was fired up, there was another pounding on the blacksmith's door. Caldan rushed over and let Miranda inside.

She dumped two sacks onto the packed earth with a clank and rubbed her wrists.

"You didn't tell me they'd be so heavy!"

"Ah, sorry." For some reason, Caldan couldn't meet her eye. Even fully dressed as she was, she distracted him. He was glad for the heat of the place—it might help him explain his flushed appearance.

"What is all this for?" asked Miranda. "I've seen your beetle; it's wonderful! But these plates of metal, I can't think what you'd do with them."

Caldan opened the sacks and began pulling out metal parts. Carefully, he ordered them across a workbench. Smaller, easier ones first, ending with the larger sections.

"My beetle is adequate," he explained. "It does what I want. But it doesn't have . . . menace. It's more of a curiosity. I want to create something that'll give people pause. And hopefully, a lot of confrontations can be avoided that way."

"But the warlocks will know what it is and how it works. So it'll be useless in case . . ."

Caldan knew why she trailed off. The warlocks were out for Caldan's blood. And there was no way he could avoid them forever, even with Felice and Quiss on his side. Miranda feared they'd attack him, and rightly so. But if he could make them pause . . .

"It's hard to judge other sorcerers' strength, or what they can do. Some sorcerers can sense another's well, but that still doesn't tell the whole story. It also depends on natural talents and the craftings they have, but . . . Like I said, if this works, it'll give even the warlocks pause. They'll see me, able to generate a powerful shield and control this construct. They'll know I'm not to be trifled with."

"I still don't understand. Couldn't they do the same thing? Won't you be revealing too much to them?"

"Strings," said Caldan. "Or threads."

"What about them . . . ?"

"Right—sorry. It's all about numbers. One of the tests to become a journeyman sorcerer is to be able to split your well into two strings. It means you can activate more powerful craftings. Masters can split their wells further, into three or more. The more strings you can control, the more powerful craftings you can use. But for each string you hold on to, maintaining control is harder. It's like splitting your mind into separate sections and having to focus on each one at the same time."

"So . . . you're telling me that if you're shielded, and controlling this new construct, a sorcerer will know you're the equivalent of a master?"

Caldan grinned. "Better. I can already do what few sorcerers can: maintain a powerful shield. The one I first used, when we fled Anasoma, that was a toy compared to what I can generate now. But on top of that, I can split my well further. The beetle takes another three to five strings. This construct will take . . ." He shook his head. "I don't know yet. A few more at least."

"Four strings, eight strings. There's not much of a difference."

"Ah, but there is! The more you hold, the slipperier each one becomes." Caldan took out a flat square of brass.

"So how many can you hold?"

"It . . . depends. I've managed more than eight, but I was under stress, not thinking about what I was doing. Just . . . doing it." Caldan spread his hands, unsure how to explain.

Miranda levered herself up onto a nearby table, her eyes glittering in Caldan's sorcerous light. "When you practice something," she said, "eventually, it becomes second nature. Like sword fighting. Blade masters are often unaware of reacting to threats. They just . . . move. It must be similar."

"Yes. That makes sense. But innate skill comes into it. Each section must work together to create something greater than the parts."

"As with sword fighting, so too with sorcery and your Touched gifts. If you can combine them, you'll be . . . the greatest sorcerer since the Shattering."

Caldan froze. What was it Devenish had said? *You'll be greater than you can imagine.* When all he meant was that Caldan would be a powerful tool for the warlock to use. Miranda's words echoed Devenish's, and they sent a chill deep inside his bones, even though he knew she couldn't possibly mean the same thing. For an instant, it seemed he was alone in a freezing wasteland, with no shelter, nowhere to run.

"And that means they'll never stop coming after me."

Miranda fixed him with a pity-filled gaze. She bit her bottom lip and turned her head away. Her hair slid across her face as she looked at the ground between them.

"There's a story I know," she said. "About a merchant who made some bad decisions. Very bad. He owed a lot of people a great many ducats. Some banks, some quite nasty moneylenders. One day, his house burned down, and they found his charred body inside. Luckily, his wife and daughter were staying at a friend's that night."

Caldan nodded, half listening. He laid out crafting sketches he'd penned earlier: runes and patterns to enable him to create a destructive sorcerous crafting. Not to kill, but to engrave metal.

"They knew it was him," continued Miranda, "because of the corpse. He'd taken to wearing a particular set of jewelry the last few months before the fire. Quite unique."

Caldan grunted. "Sounds like he should have sold it to pay some of his debts." He began inking his design on the brass plate.

"You'd think so, wouldn't you? I can't remember what it was—a medallion and something else. Anyway, they found a body burned beyond recognition, which they identified as the merchant's from the jewelry he was wearing. So the people he owed ducats to were disappointed. Perhaps they'd been the ones to kill him. But that would make for bad business. If you're dead, you can't pay back what you owe. Better to leave the debtor alive. The man's wife and daughter had nothing. The wife was forced to work . . . to do things she never thought she'd lower herself to do. All in order to feed her daughter. But that's slightly off story."

Caldan paused in his work. "I think I know how this ends. They found the man alive and well? Living somewhere else under another name?"

Miranda shook her head, leaning forward on her perch. "The moneylenders didn't. Once the daughter was older, she linked a few pieces of information together: stories from her mother, details of what businesses the father had interests in, who his friends and acquaintances were, where he would be . . . most comfortable, if he had to flee. You see, she was angry. A bitter, angry girl."

"So you're saying I should do something similar? Flee, but fake my own death." It made a good deal of sense. The only flaw in the idea was that he had nothing he could leave behind. His trinket ring was too valuable . . . Caldan glanced up at Miranda. She regarded him with hooded eyes.

He found his fingers had moved to turn the ring, and he stopped them. She shouldn't be asking this of him. It was one of only two links to his parents. To Caldan's past. But what had knowing more about his past delivered to him? The more he knew about himself, the less he wanted to. Then again, the metal ring was of far more value to him than just as a trinket. For Caldan, as a Touched, it functioned to enhance his abilities and mitigate their consequences. Without it, his body would degrade much more swiftly. Caldan returned to his scribing. "It's . . . I'll consider it" was all he said. Out of the corner of his eye, he saw Miranda nod.

"That's all I ask."

The trouble was, it was an excellent idea. And the sacrifice of his ring would make his death all the more believable. If they could escape unseen. They'd have to travel somewhere far away. There were many details that would need to be worked out.

There was also the fact that he didn't *want* to run. It was selfish, he knew—running might keep Miranda safer—but something told him he was *needed* in this. That he couldn't take the coward's way out.

"So what happened to the man and his daughter?" asked Caldan.

Miranda laughed feebly, causing Caldan to look up at her.

"She found him in another city. Living in a nice house, with another wife. Not a care in the world." She lowered her head. Her hair fell to cover her face. "She killed him. Took what she could easily sell. And went back to her mother."

Caldan heard the pain in her voice, felt her distress from where he sat. He lowered his pen and moved to comfort her. She trembled against him, letting out the occasional sob. Eventually she pushed him away and wiped her tears with the back of a hand. She smiled weakly, trying hard to show she was strong.

"Ancestors . . ." breathed Caldan.

"I'm sorry. It wasn't the best time to tell that story." Miranda sighed. "I've never told anyone before, even my mother. All she knew was that I made some ducats somehow and we had a better life. She no longer had to debase herself. She didn't ask me how. She was almost beyond caring then. Now you know my darkest secret. What must you think of me?"

Caldan wrapped his arms around her, ignoring her protests. When she realized he wouldn't be deterred, she relaxed. "We all have to make hard decisions sometimes. I'm just glad you came through unscathed."

Miranda kept her head buried in his chest. "I wouldn't say that. But I'm learning to forget."

"And your mother?"

"She . . . died, later. I think she wanted to for a long time, but couldn't because of me. Once she knew we had enough ducats to survive . . . she just sort of, let go. She wasn't well."

They held each other in silence for a while, until Miranda moved away. "Enough," she said firmly. "You've work to do."

Reluctantly, Caldan left her and returned to his crafting. When he looked at her, he saw anguish and guilt. A child, alone and mistreated. A mother and daughter squashed between starvation and an abusive world.

"We'll talk about this later," Caldan said. There were things in his past he needed to explain to her as well. They hadn't had enough time together. Maybe they never would.

"Perhaps," Miranda said with a sad smile.

And all Caldan could do was nod. He wouldn't push her to reopen old wounds. "As you wish."

They needed to be done with all this. To leave it all behind.

Amerdan, Kelhak, warlocks, Caldan recited. The path he had to take to finally be free. To rid himself of what he was becoming. All he had to do was defeat a being Gazija had failed to. One that had the warlocks and the emperor quailing in their boots.

No problem.

He returned to his work, and in a few minutes was finished. A crude crafting, he'd admit. But its only purpose was to assist him in crafting another construct. Caldan began assembling the parts, clicking rods into slots, fastening sections together with joints and screws. It was like a jigsaw. A rough one, but the clockmaker's craft had done wonders with the idea and refinements. Once it was assembled, Caldan sat back and surveyed the creature. He would have liked to give it wings as he had his beetle, but it weighed far too much. Before him was another doglike automaton, similar to the one he'd destroyed beneath Anasoma. But this one was far more complex. Not thin and spindly, the internal skeleton was covered with a protective shell. Lying in a jumble, unable to move, it still rose two feet above the workbench. It was beautiful, except for one thing:

Its surface was unblemished. Unmarked by the runes and patterns that would bring it to life.

Caldan stopped and checked on Miranda, who hadn't made a sound so far. She smiled and waved at him to continue.

"I'm enjoying watching you," she said with a smirk. "Forget I'm here and do your crafting."

He smiled back, his joy at both her words and his work genuine.

He turned to the brass plate and took it in his hands, opening his well and linking to the object. Hesitantly at first, then with more confidence, he poured his power through its pathways and patterns. He started with a basic design: a linking rune.

Sparks flew and metal shrieked, similar to the grinding wheel when it was scouring a blade. The scent of lemons filled the air. He stopped, checking the results both physically and with his sorcerous sense. The pattern was perfect. A fingernail-deep engraving embedded in the metal. The link felt strong, though it led nowhere.

For now.

Buoyed by his success, Caldan continued as quickly as he dared. The night was waning, and he'd lost a lot of time with everything that had happened. He needed to be finished and gone before the sun rose. This was draining, and he didn't want to be caught away from the safety of Quiss's ship, possibly unable to defend himself.

It took an hour, but at the end, even Caldan had to stare in wonder. The metal was not bright, but of a dull gray sheen. Fine dark lines flowed over the surface, occasionally sprouting into complex runic patterns, like flowers blooming from a vine. He ran a hand over it. It was hot to the touch, but cooling rapidly in the night air. The seams were still there, but as he'd been crafting the metal, he'd shaped them, so the articulations were less obvious. What resulted were almost unnoticeable joints. The wolf—for that was how Caldan thought of it—had two star sapphires implanted in its head for eyes—keys to its design, but also for the sorcerer who controlled it to see through. Quiss had given them to Caldan without blinking when he'd inquired if the sorcerer had any gems he could use.

"It looks like a suit of armor for a wolf," said Miranda. "It's a remarkable creation."

He could hear awe in her voice, and he flushed at her praise.

"Is it like your paper birds?" she continued. "And your beetle? It can move on its own like the others, can't it?"

"It is . . . more," whispered Caldan. "What I've learned from Quiss, seen him do . . . it has virtues I never dreamed of when I was at the monastery. And with the number of linking runes I've used, hardly anyone will be able to take control of it."

"The strings again?"

"Yes," replied Caldan with a smile. "There's a book in the monastery's library, *Devices and Mechanisms*, filled with schematics and illustrations supposedly from before the Shattering. I thought it was mostly fanciful invention. But I loved reading it, looking at the diagrams. I now think it wasn't too far off the mark. The author must know more than he revealed. I should find him."

"One day."

"Yes, one day."

"So you're finished? I'd like to see your wolf in action. I think it would scare most people, though."

Caldan nodded. "That's the idea. But before I show you, there is one thing we have left to do. It has been a day of secrets revealed. Let us see if we can unearth another."

"What do you mean?"

"The trinkets. Come, walk with me."

"But your construct?"

"Leave it there."

As Miranda slid off the bench he took her hand. Together they walked across the packed earth to the giant hammer powered by the waterwheel. Caldan pulled a few levers, and wood creaked and ropes groaned as water began turning the device.

"Caldan, you can't!" gasped Miranda, divining his intent.

From his pocket, he drew out the trinket ring he'd found secreted in Joachim's residence. He had no idea of its function, or its worth. Ghosts of ideas had come to Caldan of how trinkets could function, but none of the trinkets he'd ever seen had showed signs of crafting patterns. On the outside. Many had symbols whose meaning had been lost in antiquity, but they were a far cry from the complex designs required for sorcery.

"The alloy that trinkets are made from is incredibly strong, and I think I know why. It's to hide what's underneath."

He took the ring and placed it on the anvil, slightly to the side of the cutting edge of the hammer.

Miranda took half a step forward. "Caldan . . ."

He looked at her and smiled. "Sacrifices have to be made, if we're to survive and disentangle ourselves from the warlocks. This will be the first."

"People have killed for trinkets, and you're just going to . . ." She made a chopping motion with one hand.

He nodded. "I have to know if I'm right."

"Why? Isn't guessing their design enough?"

"No." Caldan paused, though, struck with a sudden sense of guilt. He was about to destroy an invaluable relic from before the Shattering.

You do what needs to be done, he told himself.

He struck another lever with the palm of his hand, and a rhythmic thumping filled the air. The immense hammer climbed slowly, tick by tick as gears turned. It rose above both of them, then halted, poised over the giant anvil underneath. One side sported a cutting edge of smith-crafted hardened steel. He could feel the warmth of the earth beneath his feet and a gentle breeze on his face, smell the scent of

Miranda close to him. An orange light was cast by the massive forge to his left, and the heat was oppressive, even though it was banked for the night.

With one finger, Caldan pushed the trinket ring until it was balanced over the opposite cutting edge on the anvil. He hesitated again, struck by a sense of loss and mortification. He shrugged, held his breath . . .

And released the hammer.

Down it came. Fashioned to flatten the heaviest ingots. Bladed to cut through hot steel. Heavy and immutable, as if it could crack the world. And with a flat metallic fracture, it split the ring in half.

The two pieces bounced off the anvil. He'd been expecting something more . . . a burst of power.

He didn't have to wait long.

He took a step toward the one half of the ring on the ground and gagged on an overpowering stench of lemons. He reached for his well and shielded himself, throwing himself in front of Miranda as he scrambled to expand it to protect her. He didn't have time to sigh with relief as his shield extended over her.

Thunder echoed in his bones. There was a geyser of coruscating fire. Caldan shut his eyes tight against the brilliance. Sorcery battered at his shield, working to crumble his wards. Heat cracked the stone of the floor as the air swam in waves. Caldan groaned and drew more from his well, strengthening his shield.

Miranda clutched him hard. He thought he heard her scream over the tumult.

Eventually, the lights and disturbance subsided, leaving them surrounded by scorched stone and blackened, smoking wood.

Caldan searched the ground for the sundered ring pieces. They were steaming, but dull and lifeless, as if whatever forces they'd contained had left completely.

At a safe distance, bleary-eyed apprentices stared with shock and horror at the destruction wrought on their masters' premises. Caldan grabbed a pair of tongs and picked up the halves of the ring, depositing them in a crucible he found nearby.

He dragged Miranda away from the hammer and anvil, as his shield was still being assailed by something, presumably the residual heat. They staggered farther away, and only when his shield didn't have to draw extra from his well did Caldan cut his link.

Cool air wafted over them, and they both gasped for breath. Apprentices ran up, babbling questions and exclamations.

"What happened?"

"Are you both all right?"

" . . . the masters are going to be right pissed off . . ."

Caldan didn't answer them. Turning to Miranda, he jerked his head toward the door they'd entered from.

"We should go. The warlocks would have sensed what happened. They'll send someone."

"Did it . . . did something come out?"

"I don't know. Maybe. Let's go." But it made no sense that trinkets had stored power. It would be a finite resource, and he'd never heard of trinkets failing to function and turning lifeless. Quiss might have an idea of what happened. He'd have to ask.

They pushed past the hands and bodies of protesting apprentices. Caldan grabbed his engraving crafting and sorcerous globe and shoved them in his pocket. He sent his sorcerous sense out and linked to the metal wolf. Six strings were enough to make it rise and leap off the workbench. He sent it barreling past wide-eyed boys and girls and out the side door.

"Run!" Caldan said to Miranda. And they did.

AS THEY LEFT the walls of Riversedge behind, Caldan held the two halves of the trinket ring in the palm of his hand. He discarded the crucible to the side of the road. The metal alloy that the ring was composed of had begun its life in a similar crucible, when it had been melted to be cast.

Caldan glanced around and, seeing they were alone on the road, brought out the sorcerous globe. Soon it lay glowing in his other palm. He peered at the broken halves of the ring. All four cut sections were the same. An outer layer of silver alloy, the rigid metal no current sorcerer could replicate, but inside was another, darker metal. A ring within a ring. A crafting within a crafting. He'd been right. Trinkets were merely complex craftings that were concealed inside objects.

Caldan snorted softly. *Merely.*

But the outpouring of energy when the ring had been cut meant there was more to this puzzle than he'd first thought. Somehow they also contained a source of power. It was the only thing that made sense.

The warlocks would surely come to investigate the damage wrought at the blacksmith's and evaluate the lingering sorcery.

And the apprentices will be able to give a description of me and Miranda.

Caldan laughed bitterly to himself.

"What's wrong?" asked Miranda.

Caldan shook his head. "Nothing." The warlocks had another reason to kill him now. As if they needed more than one.

CHAPTER 41

A young woman with gaunt cheeks and thin limbs came to his cabin and bade Caldan to follow, saying the new leader of the Five Oceans Mercantile Concern needed to talk with him. He left Miranda to sleep and followed the woman, but when Caldan arrived, Quiss was nowhere to be seen.

"Wait inside," the messenger said. Her hollow eyes were almost as dark as Miranda's.

The door closed behind him. A tiny window let in a faint light, enough to break the blackness up into shadowy shapes. After a few moments, he found his eyes adjusting, his Touched abilities kicking in, and he took the opportunity to examine his surroundings. *Bare.* It was the only word he could come up with. Some clothes were neatly folded and stacked on a stool. The bunk hadn't been slept in, and as dawn was about to break, that meant the sorcerer had been up all night.

Caldan turned his back to the window and sat on the bunk. It creaked under his weight, and he shifted until he was comfortable. As

Miranda was still asleep, and he had no idea how long Quiss would be, he might as well make use of his time.

One by one, he tested the craftings he had in his possession, checking them for any weaknesses that might have appeared. The last thing he needed was for one of them to have developed a flaw and to fail when he needed it. His power coursed through his shield medallion as he checked the links, buffers, anchors, and focuses. All seemed fine. His alloy was strong and resistant, and his smith-crafting was up to the task. More than adequate. His beetle was showing signs of wear, though: metal discoloration and a slight warping of the thinnest sheets. Caldan wasn't surprised, but he was disappointed. The metal he'd had to use was too soft, and he'd known it wouldn't last long. But still, it had served him well so far; saved him and cel Rau and that Vasile fellow from the jukari. The Bleeder Mahsonn's craftings he still had, but only one would be of use when he could control more strings.

As Caldan worked, his thoughts turned to the Touched. They were greater heroes than they themselves realized. Ostensibly an elite fighting force to the rest of the emperor's army, they quietly went about their missions, content to use their abilities to defend the empire. And the story the warlocks sold them was a tough one to refuse the call of.

You are unique.

Gifted.

You must use your talents for good.

We'll tell you how to use them, for the empire brings order and peace, and isn't that good?

Look—these trinkets will help you. Just do what we ask.

Miranda was right. There was only one way to free themselves, and that was to go far away from the empire. And she'd shown him the path . . . But could he do it? Was it possible to fool the warlocks? He could think of only one thing that would convince them he'd died, and that was his trinket ring. His fingers ran along its surface, feeling the patterns in the metal.

Amerdan, Kelhak, warlocks, hide, Caldan said to himself. He snorted. *Hide.* What a path he'd set himself on. The monks had taught him better than this. *Change what you can. Help who you can. Then, if you're still alive, think of yourself. And Miranda.*

The door opened without any precautionary knock, and Quiss entered, looking harried and weary. His hair was tousled, and his eyes were red-rimmed. His clothes were wrinkled, as if he'd slept in them, but Caldan doubted he'd snatched any time to relax. He fairly reeked of sorcery. And as he entered the cabin, Caldan's skin prickled. There was a lingering miasma surrounding Quiss, much like the heavy, charged air of a thunderstorm.

Quiss nodded to Caldan. He removed the clothes from the stool and placed them on the floor. In one hand he held slices of bread around a thick wedge of cheese. He took a bite and chewed slowly, thoughtfully.

"You've found Amerdan," stated Caldan.

Quiss squinted at him in the dim light, then nodded. "I've detected bursts of sorcery far from here. Nothing unusual in these turbulent times. There are vormag all around us with their primitive, twisted workings. But these were . . . different. Focused. Complex."

"Could it be another of Kelhak's sorcerers?"

"No. They are not so reckless. This close to the emperor and the warlocks, they wouldn't risk it."

"You sound certain."

"I am. The crafting was too complex, even for them. It had to be a trinket. We followed the scent"—Caldan's ears pricked up at the word *scent*; could Quiss and his companions smell sorcery like he was able to?—"and divined enough of the working to know it could be Amerdan. The stench of someone's well being ripped from them is quite unique. And overlaid on that were multiple wells being opened at once. Another lich."

"Bells had only one well," said Caldan. "Her own. This I know for a fact. If she knew how to steal wells from other sorcerers, then she would have had many more. I fear you're right. He has to be using a trinket, as we surmised. Nothing else makes sense."

Again, Quiss nodded slowly. He rubbed his chin, looking troubled.

"If this trinket has been fashioned to use coercive sorcery . . . then it's an abomination."

Caldan gave Quiss a sharp look. Did the kind of sorcery a crafting or trinket used make a difference? In his eyes, it didn't, but in Quiss's it obviously did.

"We know where he is," said Caldan. "There's no point delaying. We should confront him." He made to stand.

"He is within the forces of the jukari and vormag."

Caldan stopped. "Then he is attempting to control them, somehow."

Quiss nodded. "We think so. The emperor's Quivers and warlocks have pushed them back. The jukari are retreating now, and soon they'll be scattered. I've given orders to assemble a team. Some of the mercenaries will accompany us. We'll strike as soon as possible."

"How? They have to be miles away. It'll take time to find him again, even knowing where he is now."

"There is a way," Quiss said, "to travel there quickly. It's not without cost, but in these times, such trifles matter less and less."

He was talking about a special kind of sorcery. Kelhak had used it, as had the emperor, and Caldan had surmised it was an ability confined to those with multiple wells, but it seemed that wasn't the case. Which meant raw power was needed. "What do you need me to do?"

Quiss fixed Caldan with a stare. "Come with us. Use sorcery. Fight. I don't know what will happen, but your abilities could prove invaluable. You are growing, Caldan. Becoming dangerous. There are always choices. But some are less palatable than others."

Here, among Quiss and his people, Caldan was safe from the warlocks. But he couldn't hide forever.

He needed to see Miranda, to tell her what he was doing and say good-bye. But . . .

"When do we leave?"

GATHERED ON THE grassy slope of the riverbank in the dawning light, the host Quiss had gathered waited for others to join them. A small enough group, though, one that hopefully wouldn't draw the notice of the emperor's forces. Caldan stood to one side, one hand always near his craftings, the other resting on the buckle that dropped his sword from his back to his hip. Five mercenaries stood in a knot to one side, huge, hardened men wearing mismatched armor dented and scored from many a fight. And carrying too many weapons to count: swords, daggers, axes, and javelins. Each one also had a rectangular shield, tall enough for them to lean on when they rested. The mercenaries kept to themselves, speaking in hushed tones occasionally. A little away from them waited two emaciated sorcerers, obviously Quiss's colleagues. The brown-haired woman looked wan and sickly, her face pale and gaunt. The man was scarcely better, though he at least wasn't as thin. The woman looked like a strong breeze would blow her over.

Caldan had brought his wolf simulacrum along in case he would need it, guessing the chances he would were good. Not wanting to startle anyone, he directed it to stay a short distance away, hidden behind a tangle of blackberry bushes. It could follow them at a discreet distance and help him when he needed it.

Approaching from the ships, a large, middle-aged man walked toward Caldan. He was covered in a voluminous robe tied about his huge paunch with a sash. He smiled at Caldan and ran a hand through graying hair.

"I'm Mazoet Miangline," he said, bowing politely from the waist.

Caldan couldn't sense the man's well, but there was something else: a sorcerous *blurring* around his mind. His well hadn't just been disguised, as he'd sensed Simmon's had. It was totally obscured in some fashion.

"You're with Quiss," Caldan stated. He looked the man up and down. "But you're—"

"Fat?" Mazoet said with a wry smile. "Some of us cope with change better than others."

Caldan wasn't sure he understood Mazoet's meaning. "Is Quiss coming?"

Mazoet leaned forward. "Soon. He's finishing off a . . . crafting."

"How," Caldan ventured, "do you conceal your well?"

"You are a curious one, aren't you? Quiss told me as much. Very well, it's a simple thing. Coercive sorcery, of course. Does that bother you?"

It didn't—not really. But he thought back to the first time he'd encountered a hidden well: Simmon. Had the master known coercive sorcery? Or perhaps he didn't realize it was related? He wished Simmon were still here. He might have been blind to what the empire used him for, but he had been someone Caldan felt he could have counted on now. Not like the men he was surrounded by. Still, he didn't want to antagonize Mazoet, so he just said, "Not as much as it used to. Now I know more about it, is what I mean."

"Good. Then let's begin."

"Begin what?"

"Learning how to block your well."

"Really?" Caldan blinked.

"You want to learn, right?"

"Of course! But . . . out here?"

"No one will see. The mercenaries won't know." Mazoet gestured to the two thin sorcerers. "My friends won't care. We have time, so let's get started."

Caldan opened his well and sensed Mazoet's was already open. It had to be, for the man was suffused with power. He cast his senses over the other two sorcerers and found they were the same. There was no reason for them to be holding on to their power, and yet they were. What was he missing?

"It's quite simple, really," began Mazoet.

Caldan linked to his coercive sorcery crafting and prepared to follow Mazoet's instructions. And in the end, it really was simple. A basic pattern, a web of threads arranged a certain way, anchored around your well, covering it. Three strings were required, which meant it was beyond most journeymen sorcerers and even masters. But not warlocks and Quiss's people. Bells had told him coercive sorcery required a lot more strings than three. And if she was wrong about this, then she could have been wrong about many other things.

"I was told coercive sorcery required many more strings," Caldan said. "But this doesn't."

"Ah . . . that's true to an extent. Performing coercive sorcery on yourself is far easier than on others and requires less effort to maintain."

That made sense. His well needed to remain open but required only a trickle to keep his coercive crafting active.

It was a fortuitous encounter, meeting this Mazoet. This was an incredibly useful piece of sorcery that the man had simply given him for nothing. And yet it meant a great deal, seeing how invaluable it would be if he was going to escape from the warlocks.

"Caldan."

He looked up into the eyes of a man he'd just noticed standing to the side. Quiss. The sorcerer had come up to them without him realizing it. Caldan dropped his gaze to his feet. He was scared, he admitted to himself. His boots were damp, covered in dew from the walk through the grass, as were Mazoet's and Quiss's. A similar cold wetness had crept inside him since he'd woken. He was taking a step there could be no returning from until Kelhak was dead.

Or Caldan was.

"Is it time?" he said.

Quiss smiled pleasantly. In one hand he carried a cloth bag. "I see Mazoet has taught you how to obscure your power. There is much we can show you when we have the chance. But for now, yes, it's time to go."

A morsel of knowledge. Either shown out of friendship, or they were trying to manipulate him. Caldan regretted doubting them, but such was his existence now. Doubt everything. Trust no one.

"But," continued Quiss, "I must warn you—it is dangerous, and though you'll see what we do, you shouldn't try to replicate it yourself. Mazoet has a talent for this, so he'll be taking us through."

"Do you want me to promise?"

Quiss shook his head and smiled thinly. "No. I won't extract any more promises from you. You do what you think is best." He handed the cloth bag to Mazoet, and the sorcerer opened it and drew out a long, thin chain of gold links. At hand-length intervals along it were set faceted stones the size of his thumbnail—rubies, emeralds, sapphires, diamonds. Caldan had never seen so much wealth before. Beside each gem was a small flat disc of beaten silver covered with runes.

Caldan swallowed at the sight. The gold and gems that went into the crafting shocked him, the sheer expense of it. He watched as Mazoet unraveled the chain, making sure it wasn't tangled. It had to be thirty feet long.

"The crafting will be destroyed after we're through," Mazoet said. "We can't risk it falling into someone else's hands."

Caldan blinked. "That's . . . a waste." With such a chain, he and Miranda wouldn't have to worry about ducats for the rest of their lives. And their children's lives. He paused. Where had that thought come from?

Mazoet shrugged. "We don't place much value on wealth." Carefully he began laying the chain in a circle on the ground. When he was done, he was standing inside the crafting. The circle was about ten feet across.

"I thought you didn't know much about craftings?" Caldan asked. The golden rope said different.

"Mazoet is the expert here," replied Quiss. "And he finds it easier to delegate some of the task to the crafting." He shrugged. "It's crude, but it works."

Quiss turned his attention to the mercenaries and the two sorcerers. He waved a hand, beckoning them over. "Come. Everyone step inside."

Caldan expected questions from the mercenaries, but they obeyed Quiss's order without hesitation. *They've done this before,* he realized. *Interesting.*

A ten-foot-wide circle wasn't a lot of room, and Caldan, Quiss, Mazoet, the other two sorcerers, and the five mercenaries jostled one another until they were all inside. Caldan could smell the mercenaries' sweat, and the scent of steel and oil. They were big men, but he couldn't help noticing they flicked the occasional glance his way. No doubt wondering what Caldan's purpose was in all this.

As he was.

Caldan took up a position on the edge.

"Be prepared for anything," Quiss said seriously. "Keep inside the circle until it's over."

One of the mercenaries looked at Caldan. He wore a metal-scaled breastplate, and there was a huge sword strapped to his back. He sported a braided beard and a scowl. "When you throw up, boy, turn away from us!"

His companions laughed, and Caldan was surprised he didn't blush at the gibe.

"My name's Caldan." He held out a hand.

The mercenary looked at it for a moment, then shrugged and clasped it in his. "Selbourne. Captain of the Forgotten Company." He leaned closer to Caldan and whispered in his ear. "You hurt Miranda, and I'll find you and kill you."

Caldan's blood pounded in his ears. He stared into the mercenary's eyes. Hard eyes, used to violence and getting what they wanted. *How does he know her?* Maybe a better question was: Who was Miranda, really? He knew so little about her past. Not just a sailor, that's for certain.

"I wouldn't hurt her," he said. "I'd lay down my life for her." As he said it, the certainty of his statement rocked Caldan to the core. It was the truth. But this man, this mercenary, couldn't be left thinking he'd cowed him. He'd had enough of being pushed around. He kept his face as stony as he could.

"But if you come after me, it'll be your death."

Selbourne scowled at him and then guffawed with laughter. After a moment, the other mercenaries joined in. Selbourne's mirth settled down and he stopped.

"I've dealt with sorcerers before. I've a few tricks of my own." He paused, narrowed eyes drawn to Caldan's sword. "Not many carried a blade, though. None, actually. Can you use it?"

"I've been trained, but I'm not a blade master."

"Then you're outmatched."

Caldan merely shrugged, letting his gaze wander to the trees around them.

Mazoet moved his bulk closer to them both. "A gold ducat on Caldan!" he exclaimed.

Quiss snorted. "Enough, Mazoet. Don't encourage them."

Mazoet ignored him and looked to the other mercenaries. "No takers? Oh, well."

"So sure of him, are you?" asked Selbourne, voice filled with amusement.

"Not only is he a sorcerer, and an adept one, he's Touched."

At his words, the mercenaries let out wordless exclamations. Almost as one, they turned to stare at Caldan. A few of them made hand gestures he hadn't seen before. Superstitious, probably. A warding or a blessing, he couldn't be sure.

Selbourne took half a step back before catching himself and grinning wryly. He met Caldan's eyes and nodded formally. "You're welcome among us."

Another mercenary barked a laugh. "Leave some jukari for the rest of us!"

Caldan offered them a sardonic smile. "I have a feeling there'll be plenty to go around."

"Aye," Selbourne said. "That there will be. Ready weapons, men. Quiss here's waiting."

"Thank you, Selbourne," Quiss said wryly. "Everyone inside? Good. Mazoet, if you please."

Caldan opened his well and linked to his wolf simulacrum. It came toward them, sleek and fast, bounding across the uneven ground. There were gasps of surprise as it slowed to a stop and sat beside Caldan, just inside the circle.

"Don't worry," Caldan said. "It won't bite."

Quiss snorted, while Mazoet raised an eyebrow at him.

There was no warning. Caldan's head felt about to split in two. He spun, feet leaving the ground. Reality bent. There was a sharp cracking sound and a scent of lemons and hot metal so strong he retched. Everything went gray. His vision blurred. He reeled and stumbled, fearful he'd step outside the crafted circle. Except he couldn't feel the ground. There was nothing there. There was another crack. And another. Sparks blossomed before his eyes, sprinkling the gray with color, then faded.

He landed on something soft with a thump. He opened his mouth to breathe but couldn't draw any air in. His hands clawed at the ground. He managed a short breath. Then another deeper one. He gasped. Somewhere close by, someone was vomiting. Caldan levered himself to a sitting position. He was lying on a carpet of sodden dead leaves. There was no sign of the river, or the ships, or Riversedge. They were in a dense forest, the trees abundant enough to block out the light.

Mazoet stood beside him, regarding him with a calm, nonchalant expression. Selbourne was on his knees, doubled over, clutching his stomach. The retching came from one of the other mercenaries.

Thin streams of smoke rose from a charred circle in the ground. Caldan snorted air though his nose in an effort to remove the stench of sorcery. His eyes caught on tiny fragments of color around the circle. *The gems*, he realized. That's what the cracking sounds were: the jewels fracturing from the heat, the sorcerous forces destroying them.

Caldan checked that his automaton had come through unscathed, which it had.

In the distance, an animal-like howl sounded.

"Jukari," Selbourne said. He wiped spittle from his mouth and stood. "To arms, men! No time for sightseeing!"

Weapons were unsheathed, some more quickly than others, and the mercenaries fanned out in a line facing the direction the howl had come from. Shields were presented, while Selbourne stood to one side, presumably to give him room to swing his massive sword. The men's expressions were grim, but they didn't look nervous at all.

Quiss spoke to Selbourne in apologetic tones, voice raised slightly so everyone could hear. "We need to avoid using sorcery, if we can."

"So we're on our own then?" Selbourne didn't look impressed.

"No. If things get tough, we'll help. But we need to keep the element of surprise. There will be vormag about as well. We can take them out, and hopefully anyone who notices will think it's just another Quiver raiding party with a warlock or two."

"Right." Selbourne raised his voice. "You heard the man. If you have a shot at a vormag, take it. Otherwise, leave them for the sorcerers. You know the plan. We punch through and keep going. No looking back."

Caldan undid a buckle and swung his weapon to his hip. He took a breath, unsheathed the sword, and opened his well.

Mazoet placed a hand on his shoulder. "No shield. The vormag and the lich will sense it."

Reluctantly, Caldan used the technique Mazoet had taught him to disguise his well. He kept part of his awareness close to it, however, in case their situation deteriorated.

"Which direction?" asked Selbourne of Quiss.

The sorcerer pointed to the south, the direction the howl had come from.

"It figures," muttered Selbourne, then to his men, "Look lively now. I left a woman in my bed, and I mean to get back before she wakes."

One of the mercenaries chuckled. "Nothing you could do would wake her up."

Selbourne affected a look of hurt. "I'm only a man, and she is a demon."

"If Charlotte catches you talking about her like that, she'll have your plums."

"She already has them!"

More laughter, albeit slightly strained. Caldan knew they were attempting to make light of their situation to relieve the tension. They didn't know where they were and were about to go up against an unknown number of jukari and vormag and, from what they knew, a powerful sorcerer. He had to admire their gruff confidence and bravado.

But Charlotte . . . does he mean the captain of the Loretta? *Is that why he warned me about Miranda? And does Miranda know the captain is here?*

The mercenaries began moving through the trees, always keeping close, hardly leaving a gap between their shields except to pass around trees. Selbourne walked alongside them, the blade of his sword resting on his shoulder. Caldan trailed behind them, followed by Quiss and Mazoet and the other two sorcerers. Their feet brushed across the spongy leaves, scarcely leaving a trace of their passing.

The first jukari had its back to them. They'd been climbing a slight rise for a while, and it stood at the top, looking down the other side. Luckily, they were downwind of it.

Selbourne motioned for them to halt, while he crept toward its exposed back. Even as he stood behind it and raised his sword high above his head, it didn't stir.

Something had its attention. What?

Steel rent flesh, cracking bone and spilling black blood. The jukari toppled without a sound, skull split in two. Selbourne crouched beside the corpse, looking down at what had caught the creature's attention. He swiveled and crept back to them, surprisingly quiet and nimble for such a big man.

"There's a camp of them down there. There's some sort of commotion, but I couldn't see what. I saw a few vormag, as well."

"Anyone else? A man?" Quiss's voice was strained.

Selbourne shook his head. "No. But there's a tent, which is strange."

"In what way?" asked Caldan.

"Jukari and vormag don't use tents. They travel light. Whatever's using it, it probably isn't one of them."

Caldan looked to Quiss. "That's him, then."

Quiss frowned. "Maybe. We need to be sure."

"There were at least a few dozen jukari. We can't handle that many without sorcery. If you mean to keep hidden, then we can't do much."

Caldan fingered his ring and shield crafting. He also had his wolf, and his beetle . . . the trickle of power the beetle used shouldn't alert any vormag.

"I can scout the tent," he said. "To see what's inside."

HEAPS OF RAGS gathered into a pile. Patchy grass. A wooden chest with a heavy lock. And . . . Caldan squinted in the dim light. An automatic response, which didn't help this time. He could see only what his beetle saw.

There, over by one wall of the tent: another larger pile of rags, from which hung dried bones and metal objects. But this pile clothed someone . . . *something.* It was too tall to be a man. Leather-bound feet, and clawlike hands clenched into fists, nails digging into palms. Its decapitated head rested a few feet from its body. Its face . . . Far away, just past the crest of the hill, Caldan shivered. He urged his beetle closer to the figure. It scuttled along the side wall of the tent, sharp claws digging into the canvas. Sightless violet eyes stared from a bestial face. It looked like a jukari or vormag, only bigger, more *formed* somehow.

Caldan had to wonder: If jukari were soldiers, and vormag sorcerers, what then was this creature's purpose?

A shadow in the corner moved. Out of the darkness, Amerdan appeared. Caldan halted his beetle where it was and held his breath.

Amerdan stopped and frowned. He tilted his head to the side, and his gaze roved around the tent, as if searching for something.

He was different, to Caldan's eyes. The odd shopkeeper was completely absent, and in his place was something far more assured, far more . . . dangerous. But then, the shopkeeper guise had disappeared long ago, almost immediately after they'd left Anasoma. Amerdan's face was blank, but his bearing was straighter, and there was a sardonic twist to his mouth.

Abruptly, Amerdan shrugged one shoulder and removed something from under his shirt: a rag doll—the same one Caldan had seen on a shelf in his shop. He placed it atop the wooden chest, arranging its legs and body so it appeared to be sitting there, watching the inside of the tent. Amerdan knelt in front of it and placed a kiss on its cheek. He sat back on his heels and for a time didn't move. He shook his head, then waved a hand.

He's speaking to it, realized Caldan. Too softly for him to hear through his crafting. He sent a pulse to his simulacrum and made it move slowly across the canvas to a position where he could better see what was happening, but before it got there, Amerdan stood. The shopkeeper turned, and again his gaze roamed around the dimness of the tent. He looked directly at Caldan with empty eyes.

Ancestors! Caldan knew that he'd been found out. He directed his power through another sorcerous pattern on the beetle and blinked as a multitude of flashes in Amerdan's mind shone brightly in Caldan's sorcerous awareness. Wells. And a lot of them.

Caldan felt a clawing at his linkage to the beetle. He cursed and drew as deeply as he could in an attempt to cement his anchor. A sorcerous thread curled about his link and tried to force him away. Caldan's control slipped. It was as if he held a ball in his hand and someone was prying his fingers off one by one. He resisted with all his might, groaning with effort. Sweat dripped from his face, and he tried to fly his beetle out of there.

To no avail. Amerdan had wrested command of its movement from him. It would take moments for him to complete his control—and perhaps follow Caldan's strings back to him.

Caldan severed his links, and the forces assaulting his beetle faded. His threads whiplashed back and struck his mind like stinging slaps. He clutched his head, wincing at the pain.

Standing next to him, Quiss placed a stork-thin hand on Caldan's shoulder. Caldan realized he was on his knees.

"What did you see?" Quiss asked.

Caldan shook his head. "I lost control—"

"I know, I felt it. What did you see?"

"He was alone . . ." Quickly, Caldan recounted the details inside the tent, along with Amerdan's strange discussion with his rag doll.

"It was like . . . he was mad," continued Caldan.

"Are you sure?" Quiss asked. "What if the doll was a construct of some kind? What if it was ensouled?"

"No," Caldan said. "If it was, I'd have sensed it. It was just a doll. Then, at the end, when I knew he'd found me out, I tried to measure his well, so we'd have some insight into what we faced, but . . ." He looked up at Quiss. "There were so many."

Quiss's eyes narrowed. "How many? How strong were they?"

Caldan recalled the image in his mind and counted as best he could. It was a jumble, and he had trouble separating out the various wells. And there was something *wrong* with most of them. "At least fifteen," he said eventually.

Beside him, Quiss hissed with frustration. Farther back, his two companions began to argue, and the woman knelt and began drawing in the dirt with a stick.

"But they weren't all functional," Caldan hastily added. "Most were blocked somehow. I don't know why. There were only a few open wells, and these were jagged. The others . . ." He recalled the image again. "Someone had tried to open them, to remove the blockages."

Quiss nodded thoughtfully. "This process is unknown to us," he admitted. "The how of it. But if wells transferred by this process are blocked, then they need to be reopened. It doesn't make sense, though . . . How did this Amerdan stumble onto the process? You said he wasn't a sorcerer. Did Bells do something to him?"

Standing, Caldan brushed dirt from his knees. "She must have. But she's dead now, so she won't be providing any answers."

The sounds of the night hadn't changed, which meant for some reason, Amerdan hadn't alerted the jukari to their presence. But he might know it was Caldan, or perhaps suspect a vormag was spying on him. He'd seen Caldan's dog construct when they'd fled Anasoma, but he hadn't ever seen the beetle. Though now he had control of it.

Caldan said as much to Quiss.

The sorcerer stared at his hands. "If there's no ruckus, then we're safe. For now."

Safe? From Amerdan? That's not how Caldan would phrase it.

Selbourne came over to them, a penetrating look on his face. He obviously wanted to know what the situation was. He stood slightly to the side, face turned so he kept one eye on the rise and one on Caldan and Quiss.

"Well," continued Quiss. "Amerdan thinks he is safe. In the middle of this many jukari and vormag, only someone with no conscience would rest easy."

"He's not like anyone I've ever known," Caldan admitted. "I think he's Touched as well—"

"So you've said. But perhaps he isn't."

"What do you mean?" Caldan said. "He has to be."

Quiss raised a hand. "Hear me out. This trinket of his . . . it transfers wells, does it not?"

"Probably," Caldan said. He knew what Quiss was getting at, but this was all pure speculation. "You're about to suggest it does more."

"It makes sense. Perhaps he'd never used it on a sorcerer until recently. Then, all his other abilities were from ordinary people. It still transferred something from them. A piece of them."

Caldan glanced at Selbourne. "It doesn't matter. The result is the same. He can move as fast as a Touched. Is as strong as a Touched. And he also has at least fifteen wells. If he manages to unblock them, we're in trouble."

As Caldan spoke, Selbourne was nodding. "I agree. We strike now. As fast and as hard as we can. A smash and grab."

Then Caldan heard something. It intruded faintly against the sounds of the night, but intrude it did. He'd heard it before . . . tiny metallic wings, buzzing with the industry of a bee . . .

He squinted into the darkness, then extended his sorcerous senses. "My beetle," he said. "It's here, searching."

"We go now!" Selbourne said. He turned to Quiss. "Can you hold the vormag off for a time?"

Quiss nodded. "Yes. Of course we can. You take the lead. We'll deal with the vormag, you the jukari. We'll hit this tent with everything we have."

Sour spit filled Caldan's mouth. *Fear,* he realized, hands trembling. But they had to do this.

Selbourne and his men moved ahead, crouching low as they scuttled over the rise. Caldan followed, Quiss to his left, and the other two sorcerers close behind. He drew his sword, checked his craftings, and clenched his hands to still the tremors. His heart beat in his chest like a drum. He tasted his own sweat on his lips, breathed in the cool night air.

And needles pierced his finger. His trinket.

Caldan welcomed the pain. Needed to feel it.

On this mad expedition, he wanted all the help he could get. But a thought whispered to him . . . *It will damage me.* How much, he didn't know. A small amount, added to the total. But it needed doing.

"Are you all right?" whispered Quiss.

Caldan nodded, sweat dripping from his face.

Ahead of them, there was a gurgling sigh. One of Selbourne's men stepped from behind a tree as the body of a jukari slumped to the ground. At the bottom of the slope, Caldan could just make out the shape of Amerdan's tent.

Boots trampled grass, and leather and armor creaked as they rushed forward.

A howl sounded to their right as a jukari loomed out of the darkness. It was short and wielded a crude club, no more than a tree branch stripped of bark. Responding howls echoed from all directions. The jukari were alert to their presence.

Selbourne peeled off to confront it. "To me, men!" he shouted, dodging to the side as the club hammered down. Steel flashed, and Selbourne's blade thudded into the creature's neck. Dark blood spurted, and it stumbled, coughing. Selbourne's companion drove his sword into its chest.

Caldan's blood coursed through his veins, searing inside him.

When Selbourne ran toward the tent, he followed.

Around him, the mercenaries fended off more jukari. These were hardened men. Tall and physically powerful. But the jukari loomed over them, slavering creatures of nightmare. Caldan sensed Quiss open his well, and light erupted around one of the mercenaries. A jukari axe smashed into him. His shield lay to one side, split in two. Sparks erupted as the edge turned. But ribs cracked, and the man flew backward.

The jukari moved forward and lifted its axe. Caldan stepped into the breach, one foot on either side of the mercenary as he scrambled on the ground.

The axe hacked at him. He stepped calmly to one side and batted it away with a ringing clang. It thudded into the dirt. The jukari stumbled, pulled off balance. Caldan's sword flashed as he cut it down. It gurgled and then went limp.

He whirled, looking for Selbourne and Quiss. The sorcerer was facing him, but backing toward Selbourne. Mercenaries brushed past Caldan as they looked to their fallen comrade. Caldan ran to Quiss.

"Vormag are coming," Quiss said.

Caldan turned, opened his well, and sensed a number of wells racing toward them, irregular and unnatural, as if gashed into being. Quiss could handle these.

Beyond them, jukari grouped into threes and fours, reluctant to come at them alone. Some rushed around their flank and made darting feints. Animal grunts and yowls filled the air, until there was nothing except their clamor.

"Quiss!" Selbourne yelled.

Caldan felt power gathering.

Glittering lights pierced the blackness. The air hummed. Dazzling threads curved like sabers, danced across the ether.

Jukari and vormag alike raised their arms in defense, howls ringing. Flashes of incandescence. Screams abruptly cut off. Flesh sizzled. Dust blew and ground smoldered. Fire erupted from sorcerous-made flesh.

Vormag shields, wards raised against steel and fire and sorcery, parted like cotton under a knife. They thrashed and shrieked as death came for them.

And Caldan *saw*. He knew how Quiss was doing this. Shieldlike conduits contained the well's fury. Constrained it. Cajoled it. Shaped it.

Frantic sorcery from the vormag responded in turn. All to no avail.

Shields disappeared under hammering lights, as the vormag's furious bolts were devoured by Quiss's sorcery.

Vormag were left dead or screaming. Jukari lay shredded and burning like coals.

Caldan turned to Quiss with wonder and stopped. The man was weeping. Tears rolled down his cheeks, carving lines in ash.

And again, Caldan *saw*. Such power was horrifying to behold—and terrible to wield. It stained a sorcerer's soul. To take life so easily, no matter if it was jukari and vormag, was an atrocity. Such a use of power was grotesque, monstrous.

But there was something else . . . Around the charred remains of jukari and vormag, the ground steamed and cracked. The air seemed to *split*, and a fine layer of dust swirled on the breeze. The destructive sorcery wasn't just destroying their foes, it was destroying everything in its path. Reducing flesh and bone, grass and soil, the very air itself to ash and soot.

As had the Shattering been—sorcery gone mad, unleashed without restraint.

Whole cities reduced to dust. Populations slaughtered. Once fertile lands destroyed. The Desolate Lands: Had they once been lush and green?

This was what Gazija, and now Quiss, said they were trying to prevent, but the power they were unleashing was causing just the opposite.

"Stop!" Caldan shouted at Quiss. The vormag and jukari around them were dead; there was no need to continue.

Abruptly, the lights disappeared. Quiss wiped his cheeks. The mercenaries stared at Quiss, expressions fearful. Selbourne's face was grim.

A movement to their left—Amerdan stepping out of the tent.

The shopkeeper looked around him at the destruction and smiled. He smiled.

Caldan stepped toward him.

And Amerdan ran. A streak through the darkness.

At first toward them. Blood sprayed, and one of the mercenaries crumpled. And then Amerdan sped away.

Caldan surged after him, blood pounding in his ears.

Selbourne bellowed something Caldan couldn't decipher. Booted feet thudded after him. But they were all too slow to keep up with him.

Caldan ran past smoking bodies, charred ruins of mutilated vormag and jukari. Crunched through blackened debris and barely knew what his feet were touching.

Cool air caressed his skin as he raced after Amerdan. He left blackened grass behind. Caldan opened his well, casting his senses about . . . *There*. Amerdan was weaving among the trees, which made tracking him hard, and using any sorcery against him even harder.

Caldan stumbled into a dry riverbed and slowed. Amerdan was still ahead, but the round stones made for uncertain footing. They clattered and clacked together as he sprinted over them. The riverbed wound like a snake, and he caught momentary glimpses of Amerdan before he was lost to sight around a bend. As it turned again, Caldan raced up the bank, hoping he'd judged it right and he'd carve away some of the distance between them.

As he leaped down the bank and back onto the stony bed, he saw he'd been correct—Amerdan wasn't far ahead now.

A glittering light split the night. Caldan ducked, and it passed over his head. Heat assaulted him, then it winked out. But it hadn't been as stable as Quiss's sorcery. It had felt chaotic.

Which made sense, because other than from Bells, Amerdan wouldn't have had time to learn much sorcery.

He goes by instinct. The thought was a scary one, because it was rather similar to how Caldan was coming into his own powers.

Caldan scrambled across stones.

Amerdan glanced back at him. A whine sounded in Caldan's ears. He threw himself down, shield covering his vulnerable flesh.

Another line flashed above him, then another. The scent of lemons and hot metal. Caldan rolled to the side; his hand grabbed a stone. His heart hammered as he scrambled to his feet—and launched the stone at Amerdan with all his might.

It shattered against Amerdan's shield. One as black as midnight, covering him like a second skin.

The manlike dark void that was Amerdan stopped. For a moment, it didn't move.

Then it came back toward him.

Fear gripped Caldan, but he in turn gripped his sword hilt hard and drew as much power from his well as he could. His own shield roiled and churned as his sorcery flooded it.

Amerdan stopped ten paces from him. The darkness moved, much as Caldan's shield did, though lazily. Razor-sharp knives appeared at the ends of Amerdan's black arms.

Caldan's skin burned. His head ached.

The tips of Amerdan's knives came up, pointed at Caldan's eyes.

Without thinking, he raised his sword and linked to Bells's coercive crafting. *Alive*, he thought. *I need to take him alive, if I can. We need to know how he does it, to prepare for fighting Kelhak.*

"Your friends are far from here," Amerdan said flatly. "They're no help to you now."

Caldan lunged at him, blade thrusting. Amerdan swayed aside, batting the sword away. Caldan's left hand hammered into Amerdan's face, rocking his head back. It was like striking an anvil, though, hard and unyielding. There was a twinge in Caldan's wrist as something gave way. He cursed.

Amerdan's knives flashed at Caldan. He avoided them easily, then less so as they moved faster. One glanced off his shield, sending motes sparkling.

Amerdan was strong—very strong. He had unnatural reflexes, just as Caldan did now. But how strong and fast was he? How did he compare to Caldan?

Caldan revised his approach. Pitting raw strength against each other would put the conflict in fate's hands. He had no desire to do that. He needed a plan, one that didn't rely on strength alone.

He danced backward, out of reach. Amerdan didn't follow, but his knives continued to weave in a pattern in front of him.

This won't be won physically. At least, not by me alone . . .

Caldan commanded his wolf simulacrum, and it careened out of the darkness. Jaws closed on Amerdan's arm. Black limbs flailed, and sharp steel scraped against smith-crafted alloy. Amerdan stumbled, then one hand found purchase on the construct. He wrenched it, twisted—but its design was too rigid; it withstood his assault.

And Caldan split three more strings from his well and linked to his simulacrum—to the runes he'd copied from the arrows Joachim's men had used.

Amerdan's shield wavered. Caldan was almost through. He

clenched his teeth and drew more from his well. Power flowed from him, pulsed along his strings and into his construct. He felt Amerdan draw deeply, but although he had more wells, his were jagged and narrow.

Amerdan's shield dissolved.

Hard, pointed, metal teeth penetrated flesh, grinding against bone.

Amerdan's fist battered against alloy plates, breath hissing between teeth.

Caldan dove at him, chest heaving, blade slicing. Amerdan swerved, then pivoted. He swung Caldan's construct. It came crashing around and hammered into Caldan. He flew backward, landing on unyielding river stones, back slamming into them. Sparks flashed in Caldan's vision. He lost his link to his shield.

And Amerdan was upon him, one arm dragging the wolf. His weight settled on Caldan, knees squeezing his sides. Steel flashed.

Caldan threw his arms up in desperate defense. A burning sensation sliced along his forearm as flesh parted beneath the blade.

He thrust both palms upward with all his might. Amerdan grunted as he jerked back. Caldan clawed at Amerdan's shirt, desperate for purchase. Buttons popped. He held on with his left hand, punched out with his right.

Somehow, Amerdan was unmoved. Inhuman strength held Caldan tight. Amerdan grinned, teeth stained red with his own blood.

Caldan saw the knife descend just in time. He hooked his right arm in front of him, blocking Amerdan's. The point of the blade stopped an inch from his eye. Caldan tried to force the weapon away, pushing for all he was worth. It moved a fraction, then slid from side to side as they strained against each other, muscle against muscle, sweat mingling with sweat.

His metal wolf loomed large above him, blocking out the stars. It was still attached to Amerdan's arm and swung up, about to crash down on Caldan's skull. He made its jaws open and it dropped free. Suddenly relieved of weight, Amerdan's fist hammered into Caldan's face.

And again.

Caldan felt a crack. Hot wetness poured from his throbbing nose. He twisted and writhed, desperate for any advantage. From his position, though, his struggles barely had any force behind them.

Amerdan's fist struck again.

Caldan's vision blurred, edges closing in, darkness banishing light.

He spread his legs wide, bracing himself. He wriggled his free hand and grabbed Amerdan's shirt. His fingers closed about a hard ball. His sorcerous senses tingled, coming alive with a familiar vibration.

A trinket.

The trinket.

Amerdan's hand closed around his, squeezing. "It is *mine!*" he growled.

It was the leverage Caldan needed.

He wrenched Amerdan to the side, and they wheeled across the stones. He managed to grip the hand holding the knife in his and force Amerdan's arm straight out. They came to rest as before, with Amerdan on top of Caldan. And for a moment, they lay there, breath coming in gasps, sweat dripping, eyes locked, teeth bared, faces distorted with snarling desperation.

Amerdan grunted, hands shaking with strain. And with every heartbeat, Caldan was able to force him away, ever so minutely. He was stronger, or . . . Amerdan was tiring.

The shopkeeper seemed to sense this at the same time. He jerked and pushed, flailing mightily.

And Caldan held on. He tightened his grip, feeling his trinket ring barbs dig deeper into his flesh. Whatever was happening, Amerdan's Touched-like abilities clearly had a limit. Amerdan was slowing, becoming weaker.

Caldan yanked, heaved Amerdan over. Now he was the one on top. Legs entwined in deadlock.

Blood dripped from his lip onto Amerdan's face, the knife poised above him.

Amerdan laughed, but his eyes kept glancing to his trinket.

That is the key, realized Caldan. *He doesn't just want to kill me. He wants to take my well, and whatever else the trinket does.*

"Don't do this," grated Amerdan. "We're the same. Together, we can be more. Much more."

"You'll kill me."

"No! We'll be joined. Greater than what we were."

Amerdan continued to struggle, but his movements were weaker.

A deception. Don't trust anything he does.

With a groan of effort, Caldan pushed his bloodied hand closer to Amerdan, forcing Amerdan's knife toward his own face. Amerdan trembled underneath Caldan, then pushed, stopping the blade. But it was a momentary respite. Caldan leaned his weight forward, so his chest touched the handle of the knife.

The needle-sharp point pressed into Amerdan's collarbone and bit his skin. A bead of blood swelled around the tip.

"No . . ." Amerdan whispered. "Dotty."

Caldan frowned, but he couldn't decipher his meaning.

"They're afraid!" screamed Amerdan. A strange smile spread across his face, then he sobbed. "Please, don't."

What was happening? Amerdan had changed in a heartbeat. Why the sudden reversal? Caldan's limbs trembled, but his strength didn't wane.

Shouts echoed around the riverbed. Selbourne and his men. Amerdan's struggles began anew. Twisting, grunting, pushing, and pulling, searching for an opening. He was heedless of the knife, and it scored tracks across his skin.

Caldan met all of Amerdan's moves with counters. Often only his raw strength prevented Amerdan from breaking free.

More shouts. Closer this time.

Amerdan glanced frantically into the darkness. Then, all of a sudden, he stopped struggling. He looked at Caldan with intensity.

"There's a physiker in Anasoma," he said, as if the words were being dragged out of him. "Zakarius. A bald man. Find him. He's caring for my sister, and two others. Promise me you'll look after them."

Had his voice wavered? Why was Amerdan asking this of him? Why was he . . . *desperate*? "You can look after them yourself. We only want to . . . study what you are."

Amerdan laughed, as if Caldan had uttered a feeble joke. "Promise me?"

Puzzled, Caldan nodded. "I promise."

Amerdan relaxed slightly. "The sorcerers," he hissed. And Caldan had never before heard the word uttered with such hatred. "They are evil. Remember that."

"It's all right," Caldan said, attempting to reassure Amerdan. "We won't harm you."

"I am no slave," Amerdan said flatly.

"We don't—"

"I won't be imprisoned again. Tortured."

"Amerdan—"

"If I can't have your talents, then I'll become part of you."

What? And Caldan became acutely aware of their position: him on top of Amerdan, the knife turned to point downward, tracks of blood across Amerdan's collarbone and chest. And the only thing stopping the blade from sinking to the hilt was Amerdan's resistance.

"Don't," Caldan pleaded.

"You'll become greater than you can imagine. Something not . . . human. This flesh is but a vessel, and I am far more than you can imagine."

And though Amerdan's body was in its prime, his eyes possessed the wisdom of ages.

Wisdom or madness?

Or both?

In a sudden movement, Amerdan pulled Caldan's hands toward him. The blade disappeared, slipping between ribs. Amerdan's mouth opened, and he gasped.

Light and heat emanated from Caldan's hand—the trinket. He tried to pull the knife out, but Amerdan clutched him tight.

"Together," the shopkeeper whispered, "we will become even greater."

"What? What does that mean?"

"You'll see."

Glittering white light wormed its way between Caldan's clenched fist. A single thread. It wavered in the air. Caldan recoiled in horror. In moments, it thickened and extended, sliding behind Amerdan's neck. It latched onto Amerdan. He could feel it, sense its sorcery. Then a pulse traveled along it. Caldan tried to open his hand and drop the trinket, only to find one of Amerdan's hands tightly clasped around his. A smile came across Amerdan's face. Nothing evil. Nothing sinister.

No, it was . . . relief?

When the bulging pulse reached his hand, a blinding pain erupted in Caldan's mind. He screamed, unable to control himself. A massive pressure formed inside his head. His brain felt squeezed to the size of pea. Caldan roared again as another pulse entered him. And another. Agony lanced from all directions. Tears poured from his eyes. The pain . . . how long it went on for, he couldn't tell. But eventually, it lessened. Then disappeared completely.

Caldan came to lying prostrate on Amerdan. Shouts sounded from close by, one bellowing orders. Booted feet clattered over river stones. He opened his eyes and found himself atop a grotesque hundred-year-old corpse, gray skinned and desiccated, like it had been entombed and left to mummify. A husk, drained of all vitality.

He scrambled free, panting, exhausted to the point his limbs shook and his hands could barely hold on to the stones underneath them. The stench of the body flattened him, forced him to retch.

Selbourne ran into view, face dripping sweat. His greatsword held in both hands, he slowed and approached cautiously. "Here!" he bellowed. Answering shouts come from the darkness. "Are you all right?"

Caldan nodded. Tried to speak. Couldn't. He swallowed. Eventually he was able to get out, "I think so. He . . . killed himself." A few paces away, his wolf simulacrum stood motionless. Its surface was scratched and dented in places.

Selbourne grunted, looking pointedly at the hilt sticking out of Amerdan's chest. "Looks like you did for him. And not just the knife. You did something else."

"I didn't. He pulled the blade down."

"If you say so."

Caldan kept silent. He was in no mood to argue or explain. The implications of what Amerdan had done to him skittered about in his thoughts. He'd been violated, infected with corrupt sorcery.

He realized he still held the trinket in his hand. He opened it to reveal a spherical metal cage of tightly woven strands. A faint rattle came from it when it moved. He squinted but couldn't see inside.

He stood on wobbly legs and took a few shambling steps away from Amerdan's corpse. He was at once drained and energized. A peculiar feeling. He shuddered as a wave of heat ran through him. It was like, and yet unlike, the heat of his Touched abilities. Those were physical, he realized, while this was . . . something different.

The clatter of stones echoed; dead sticks snapped. Caldan waited for Quiss to join them.

Selbourne seemed to sense his mood and remained quiet. The mercenary knelt next to Amerdan's corpse and poked at a bulge beneath his shirt. He reached in and drew out the gray rag doll.

Caldan looked at the stained and patched thing. A toy for little girls. Whatever Amerdan's story, his mind hadn't survived the onslaught. His soul had been degraded. He'd killed for pleasure and to take possession of someone else. In the end, he'd been unhinged.

Would that be Caldan's fate? He knew not *how* the trinket had changed him, but he knew it *had*.

Quiss stumbled out of the night. Caldan tentatively reached into his own mind and searched, not for his well, but for others. And with numb certainty he found them and counted.

Eleven.

Somehow, his soul had been bound to others. Churning inside him, mixing and changing him . . . As molten metal and ores mixed within a crucible, so did a multitude of souls roil within the constraints of his body. They used to be a part of other sorcerers. Ones like him, with hopes and dreams. All ripped from them in death, along with the source of their power.

Caldan had been defiled.

I've become the thing I swore I'd fight against.

For some reason, not all of Amerdan's wells had transferred to him.

But most had. They were blocked, as expected, a hard, slippery barrier covering them—all except one, split by a hairline crack, through which flowed a trickle of power.

He realized Bells must have opened at least one for Amerdan. She'd shown him the way. After that, she'd probably been useless to him, and so she'd been killed.

"Caldan!"

Quiss. He was close. Caldan knew what he had to do. He opened his well and disguised it in the way he'd been taught, using its power to conceal and obscure, leaving only a faint shadow of it visible to sorcerers. Then, he sealed off the cracked well and completely covered all his new ones. Quiss mustn't find out. No one could. He feared he'd become a lich, or they'd brand him one, as they had the emperor and Kelhak.

Quiss came rushing up, stumbling over the uneven footing. "I sensed a burst of complex sorcery again. Then the lich's wells vanished. What happened?"

"It must have been his shield," Caldan replied, thinking quickly. "It was black, like the dome Bells used when she tore through the emperor's Quivers. And the wells must have dispersed when I killed him."

"Good work," Quiss said. He sounded relieved. "Where is the trinket?"

Ancestors . . . "I . . . I have it."

"Give it to me." Quiss held out his hand.

"We should get out of here first. The vormag and the warlocks had to have sensed what happened."

"We need to leave soon," Selbourne said. "But the main threat has been neutralized, and Quiss is more than a match for any vormag that stumble onto us."

Quiss's eyes narrowed, and he stared at Caldan intently. "Give it to me," he repeated.

Examining the trinket might be Caldan's only way of reversing what Amerdan had done to him. But it could also be the key to defeating Kelhak. Reluctantly, Caldan handed it over.

A wind blew along the riverbed, cooling Caldan's sweat and chilling him to the bone. He tasted dust on the air. Amerdan had found horrors and had reveled in them. He'd found a cup of malevolence and drunk deeply.

Then he'd forced Caldan to do the same.

Caldan stood, ignoring Quiss and Selbourne. The others came running toward them as they finally caught up.

Caldan looked out across the riverbed and spotted a pool of water. With faltering steps, he made his way to it. Along the way, he shrugged out of his shirt, then removed his boots and pants. Caldan stood there naked, as if newborn.

He entered the water and walked in up to his waist. He ducked his head and splashed water across his torso and arms. He washed his face clean of his own blood and rinsed his mouth.

The problem was that no amount of scrubbing would remove the stain Amerdan had forced upon him.

CHAPTER 42

Vasile walked reluctantly back from the Quivers' kitchens, through the encampment. He followed a path winding between jumbles of tents and wagons, carrying a tray of meat and vegetables and bread. Caitlyn had ordered him, and he had obeyed. Scents surrounded him: smoke, horses, human sweat. He stumbled over a tent rope and almost dropped his load. Rough laughter sounded from his left, but he didn't look.

Caitlyn was . . . changed. Remarkably so. Vasile reflected on the fact with curiosity and not a little wonder. What power did the emperor possess that he could heal someone so effectively? At least it explained the looks of greed and desire he'd seen on the faces of the emperor's hangers-on when Caitlyn had been given the vial.

He made it back to their tents and placed the tray by the fire. Aidan nodded his thanks, but he didn't move from his seat. He'd sat there for more than a full day, since the rejuvenated Caitlyn emerged from her tent. The only time he moved was to piss and eat.

Vasile squatted by the fire and dropped more peat on the coals. He could use some hot tea. Though the day was mild, he felt cold.

"A blind child could have made the trip quicker than you," Caitlyn said from behind him.

Vasile pulled himself to his feet. He dusted off his hands, then moved the kettle onto the heat. "Did you find out what that storm was all about yesterday? It wasn't natural."

Twisting clouds and tornadoes had appeared swiftly, blotting out the sun and creating detonations and chaos and confusion before disappearing. From overheard soldiers' conversations, they'd gathered the warlocks had been assaulted and lost someone important.

"Don't you worry about it, Vasile," Caitlyn replied curtly. "We've more important work to do."

"It wasn't the only unnatural thing to happen," Aidan growled.

Vasile looked at Caitlyn for the first time since he'd returned. Again, her transformation startled him. Gone were her limp and stoop, and her voice was strong, skin taut.

Not only did she look hale, but she looked younger.

And she bore herself with authority and grace. Her words dripped with conviction. Vasile could see how Aidan and others had followed her.

"What important work is that?" Vasile asked. "Where is cel Rau?"

Caitlyn ignored him, taking a couple of plates from the tray before sitting on a stool. She began wolfing down food like she was starving. Since her night of screams she'd eaten enough for all of them.

Her body is still healing, surmised Vasile. Aidan was right. This was unnatural.

Fork poised close to her mouth, Caitlyn chewed thoughtfully. In her other hand she clutched a greasy knife. "The emperor's work. Can anything be more important? We wait for his word. Then we move. Not before." As she spoke, she waved the knife.

Vasile edged away. Ever since cel Rau's blade had nicked his throat, he felt a strange anxiety around sharp instruments.

When his water boiled, he steeped some tea and waited.

A short time later, cel Rau strode into their camp. He was grinning like a wolf.

"Lady Caitlyn," the swordsman said. "We have a mission."

Caitlyn answered him with a grin of her own. "And?"

"Lady Porhilde has requested we meet with a Lady Felicienne Shyrise, over at the eastern docks."

Vasile sighed, rubbing his eyes. He swallowed some tea, then flicked the dregs onto the fire, where they hissed and steamed. He looked around to find Aidan staring at him. Aidan nodded slightly. Good. Caitlyn's transformation had been a shock to them both, but Aidan had taken it hard. A healthy Caitlyn was going to be far more difficult to get away from. Let alone dealing with cel Rau. Vasile gestured to the fire and plates.

"We'll clean up, then go."

Caitlyn shook her head. "No. As I said, we have more important work to do. Leave those."

Vasile shrugged. "As you say."

CHAPTER 43

As Caldan stepped from the water and stood dripping on rounded stones, Selbourne handed him his clothes. He took them with a brief nod of thanks and dressed slowly. They were soiled with dirt and sweat, and not a little blood, but they were all he had until they returned.

And it was chilly.

Quiss crouched some way away from their group. The mercenaries were all splashed with crimson. Surprisingly, only one was missing. The man who'd been killed by Amerdan as the shopkeeper fled, Caldan assumed.

Quiss held Amerdan's trinket, examining it with his sorcerous senses. The other two sorcerers stood a short distance away, staring at him.

"You've changed," Selbourne said gruffly. "What happened?"

Caldan looked up, then shrugged. "We fought. He almost killed me."

"It's more than that."

Caldan ignored the implied question. "What happened back

there, after Amerdan ran? I didn't expect to see you for some time, if at all."

"Huh. Something else occurred. When you chased after the lich, we regrouped and found there wasn't much opposition. There were already dead jukari and vormag everywhere. As if they'd met an over-whelming force. It was a pretty sight, and not only because it meant we'd have an easier time."

Amerdan had killed them. Because he was insane, or because he wanted to take them using his trinket? Either way, it didn't matter in the end. Amerdan hadn't known they were coming, and his actions had made it easier for them.

All Caldan did was shrug. That was in the past. Now he had to concentrate on the future. To work with Quiss to find a way to defeat Kelhak, all the while hiding his newfound, currently useless, wells. Which was an issue unto itself: *Should I even try to unblock them?* The very thought filled him with dread and loathing, yet that added power could be useful in taking down the God-Emperor.

At the monastery, he'd just had to do his duties, take his classes, and go about his life. Answers, there, were simple. The monks had trained him for so many tasks, but they forgot to mention one thing:

Outside those walls, no answers were easy.

Because even if he wanted to unblock each well, that would mean more strings to control—in *addition* to the ones he already used. He wasn't a "Bleeder," as Bells had called them; he didn't have a natural talent to split his well into dozens of strings. It had been hard work getting to where he was now.

"You look worried," Selbourne said.

Caldan affected a thin smile. "The sooner we're away from here, the better. I'll give Quiss a reminder. We need to get back. We're too exposed."

Selbourne grunted his agreement.

With a quick check on his wells to make sure they were concealed, Caldan approached Quiss and Mazoet. If the sorcerers heard him coming, they gave no sign, remaining still and intent on the trinket.

"I take it you haven't worked out how it functions?" Caldan said.

Quiss frowned and wrinkled his nose. "It will take a good deal of study to determine how it works, what it does exactly. And then we need to come up with a way of turning that knowledge against Kelhak."

Mazoet glanced at Caldan for an instant before returning his gaze to the trinket, then paused and turned back to Caldan. "You look different."

Caldan snorted. "That's what Selbourne said. I've never had someone force me to kill them before."

"I suppose not," said Mazoet.

I need to put Quiss and Mazoet on the right track and deflect attention from myself. Caldan nodded his head toward the trinket. "You've said you don't use them, right?"

"No," Quiss said. "I'll admit we are decidedly ignorant when it comes to trinkets and craftings, apart from using them for applications that require a great deal of raw power. It's one of the reasons I think Gazija was so intrigued by your automatons."

"That's actually perfect," Caldan muttered.

"What is?" Mazoet asked.

"Sorry—just thinking aloud. But the more I consider it, I'm realizing trinkets and my automatons are much more similar than I originally thought."

"How so?"

"Because, like the automatons, trinkets are really just complex craftings. They're made from an extremely hard alloy, but it's still just sorcery, at the end of the day."

"Go on."

"I think what kept everyone from truly studying them is the fact that they're so valuable. People have killed for them. Which is why the thought of deliberately damaging one is unheard of."

"But you have?"

"Yes. I . . . found a ring. And after I made my latest simulacrum, I used the blacksmith's waterwheel-powered hammer to cut the trinket in half. Inside was a hidden crafting. Here." Caldan rummaged in his pocket and brought out one section of the trinket ring. He handed it to Quiss.

Quiss took the segment and turned it over in his palm. His eyes became unfocused as he studied the trinket. For long moments, he remained still. Caldan was about to ask a question when all of a sudden Quiss hissed with disgust.

"Abomination," Quiss whispered.

"What is it?" Caldan asked.

Without warning, Quiss lunged for him and seized his arms, jerking Caldan toward him.

"Do you have more?" Quiss asked wildly. "Trinkets? Are there more here?"

"Quiss, what's wrong?" said Selbourne.

Caldan thrust Quiss away. "One. It's not what we need to study, though."

"Show me!" Quiss said, ignoring Selbourne's question.

Reluctantly, Caldan held up his hand.

Quiss's gaze fixed on his silver ring. "We didn't know. We dismissed these as advanced craftings, not worth our time to study."

"What is it?" repeated Caldan.

Quiss staggered back. He held on to Selbourne to support his weight and passed a hand over his eyes, as if suddenly weary. "I'm too weak for this," he muttered.

"Quiss," implored Caldan. "Tell us what you see."

"I see a well. Veiled. Hidden. Of course, these objects have to draw power from somewhere. We were mistaken when we thought them but craftings."

"They have a well inside them?" Caldan said.

Quiss nodded weakly.

"Inanimate objects can't have wells," said Selbourne. "Even I know this."

And Quiss nodded again.

Caldan caught his breath. "Then . . . each one had to take a well from a person? A sorcerer?"

"Take?" Quiss laughed, the brittle laugh of someone in disbelief. "Your well is part of you, your essence. You know this. To take it would be to kill you. No, they are not *taken*. The being is the well, and the well is the object. There is no separating them. Unlike Savine, when Rebecci captured him. In this case, the being is imprisoned. Forever. There is no release."

And Caldan understood. Each trinket housed a sorcerer's essence, stripped from them. Their physical bodies discarded in order to create the item. No sorcerer would do this willingly. To sacrifice themselves in this way, and for what? To create a trinket? No . . . they were unwilling participants, their powers and lives torn from them to construct artifacts.

Like stealing a Touched's blood.

And I've been wearing one the entire time . . .

Abomination, as Quiss had said.

Caldan held his clenched fist up to his gaze. On his finger shone his trinket ring, passed down to him by his parents. Whatever its powers, whatever benefits he would gain from it, the cost was too high. Too . . . immoral. Evil. There was no other word.

"Abomination," Caldan repeated numbly. He understood. But a part of him failed to grasp the enormity. "Show me," he asked of Quiss.

And Quiss did. He constructed a coercive sorcerous crafting, much as he had when Miranda was healed. Caldan, well open, followed what Quiss did. He sent his senses along the path Quiss took, down into the trinket.

Of course, coercive sorcery. A prison would be needed to hold the sorcerer and his or her well. What else would suffice? The patterns were complex and ever shifting. Caldan couldn't follow most of what Quiss did. But he could see the crafting inside revealed, when layers of camouflage were stripped away and the inner workings laid bare. Inside the trinket was a pulsing heart. A repository of power. But it was still a crafting.

Caldan hesitated, then sent his awareness to examine the inner workings of his bone trinket. Inside the bone ring, visible to him only now that Quiss had led the way, were familiar, yet distorted patterns. Carved inside the ring by a sorcerer with an extremely fine control of destructive sorcery. As Quiss had confirmed: Trinkets were advanced craftings. Extremely complex versions, their inner workings disguised and hidden, with a well taken from a hapless sorcerer.

It stood to reason that the function of the bone rings, the creation and control of the purified lands, wasn't the only reason their existence was kept hidden. They functioned as trinkets, yet they weren't made of the same hard alloy every other trinket was made of. Sorcerers and scholars believed the metal was designed that way both to weather the corrosive sorcerous forces, and so they couldn't be damaged from everyday use. But that was false, as Caldan had proven; the robust metal was to *conceal* a crafting.

Caldan drew his senses away from the bone ring. He rubbed the back of his neck, aware he was shaking. "What Quiss said is true," he found himself saying. "Trinkets are . . . enslaved sorcerers, housed in a shell."

Somewhere, probably during the casting, when someone had been embedding the coercive crafting through the patterns of the ring, a sorcerer's soul had been imprisoned within the object. Had they somehow added the soul into the crucible to mingle with the metal?

Sorcerers' souls ripped from them, compelled to serve a function.

And what's more, the warlocks must know. Kristof had said only the warlocks could provide the trinkets to mitigate the damaging effects of his Touched abilities. That was why the bone ring was so important to them and the emperor—it was the secret of trinkets revealed for everyone to see. Caldan suspected they knew how to create trinkets, which meant they continued the atrocity. Another black mark against them. As if he needed more to see how truly vile they were.

He'd been right to kill Devenish. The thought rocked Caldan to his core. Right to kill someone when he was defenseless? What was he becoming?

What I need to be . . . if I want to survive.

Another thought came to him. "Are they aware?" Caldan asked Quiss.

"No," Quiss said. "They couldn't be."

Caldan wasn't so sure. They knew so little. Miranda had thoughts and dreams while she was suffering from the backlash of Bells's sorcery—though she'd said they were scattered and ephemeral.

They are as I am, Caldan thought. *My brothers, and sisters. We weren't asked if we wanted to be sorcerers. And in their case, they were also given no choice about their fate.*

"But you don't know," Caldan said. "They could be. We should seek trinkets out and destroy them. Set them free."

"That would take centuries," Quiss said. He peered at the ring half on his palm. "And that is not a task I would relish taking on, and one that would have to wait anyway. Amerdan's trinket is more important. It holds the key to defeating Kelhak."

"Maybe," Caldan said quietly. "We're guessing it does."

"It is our best hope. If Gazija were here, then . . . but he's gone."

There was weariness in Quiss's voice. He'd obviously not only venerated Gazija, but relied on the old man's intelligence and wisdom.

Quiss met his eyes. "If we fail, there won't be anyone after us."

"Then we'd best get back. There are still jukari and vormag out there. We should leave while we can; there's no point fighting more of them."

Quiss looked away, then nodded. "You're right. Gather the others. We've got what we came for."

"We were lucky. It could have gone much worse."

"It will, Caldan. The worst is yet to come."

SINCE HE'D FIGURED out what the warlocks did with the Touched, a rage had burned within Caldan. Now, realizing another of their secrets, one they'd possibly killed his family to keep hidden, he possessed a strange vigor. He . . . seethed. An emotion so intense he hadn't recognized it for what it was. Hate.

It was like alcohol scorching through his veins. Similar to the heat of his Touched abilities. It was a heady feeling. A promise of violence to come.

The fact that the warlocks committed their obscene deeds for power was . . . grotesque. And it wasn't even as if they wanted to do anything with that power; they were simply scared of losing what they already had.

But their strength might be needed, if the lich was to be defeated. Because even with Quiss and his people, they were almost certainly overmatched. And the warlocks could be the force that turned the tide.

The question, then, was if they should be seen as allies or as sacrifices. Should they be warned, and strategies formed with their full knowledge? Or should they do the grunt work, possibly weakening Kelhak, but ultimately be wiped out by him and the Indryallan sorcerers that opposed them?

The problem was, Caldan didn't know the answer.

If Quiss was correct and they determined a way to combat the lich, should they save the warlocks, or let them be devastated, along with the empire?

REALITY TWISTED AGAIN. Caldan's stomach churned, and his head spun.

The ground fell out from under him, then thumped into the soles of his boots, as if he'd fallen from a height. Crackles and fizzles sounded close by. Again, the overpowering scent of scorched metal and lemons. The world turned dark gray.

He realized he was on his back, head pressing into damp grass. He took a painful breath.

Almost, Caldan thought. He'd opened his well and tried to discern what Quiss and the other sorcerers did to create the transition. They'd used at least ten strings, and the power it had required . . . There was no chance he'd be able to draw that much from his well.

He squeezed his eyes and rubbed them, then sat up. Groans came from the mercenaries as cloth rustled and leather creaked. Selbourne started barking orders.

Caldan stood and brushed pieces of dry grass and twigs from his clothes. It didn't help, as they remained filthy with dirt and dried blood. The dawning sun cast everything around them in pale light. He turned his face away from it.

Quiss was still examining the trinket and looked to be unaware of the goings-on around him.

"Let's get back to the ships," Mazoet said. "You can clean up a bit more there, and we can get started on figuring out this trinket."

A *few hours*, Caldan told himself. *That's what I'll give them, and then I can make a decision about what to do next.* He could wash, change his clothes, and, most important, make sure he had mastery of the concealment of his wells. *His wells.* Even the thought made him sick. They weren't his, they were someone else's. People who'd died as their powers were ripped from them. Whenever he opened his well, he could feel them. Even when his well was closed, he could still sense them, a similar feeling to when someone stood behind you: you couldn't *see* them, but you knew they were there.

He shuddered, glancing at his wolf, which sat on the ground beside him.

"I don't want Miranda to see me like this," Caldan said, though to his ears it sounded a weak excuse.

Quiss shook his head, tearing his gaze away from the trinket, and looked at him with sympathy. "She's stronger than you think. That you had to kill someone was . . . unavoidable. But it was a lich. He was tainted. Console yourself with the fact that, if left unchecked, he would likely have become another Kelhak. Though it's more likely he would have come to Kelhak's attention and been subsumed himself, his own wells adding to Kelhak's already considerable powers. We not only stopped that, but now we have a chance. A slim one, but it's there." Quiss smiled thinly. "What more can we ask, except for a chance? You're safe. For the time being."

Caldan drew a deep breath and walked a few paces, trying to settle his unease. But he couldn't forget Quiss's words.

Amerdan was tainted.

So that means I'm tainted, too? That I might become another Kelhak. That I'm a monster that may need to be killed as well . . .

He pushed those dark thoughts to the back of his mind, fearful of where they might lead him. He hadn't chosen to do this, and maybe that counted for something, but he would decide what to do about it on his own terms. The way Quiss spoke, there was no equivocation when it came to liches, and he was one . . .

"Caldan?"

"Sorry. It's a lot to take in. But of course you're right. Still, I can't let her see me in this state. I'll wash up first before I see her. But right now I need some time to collect myself."

"Very well," Quiss said. "Do not tarry, though. We've work to do."

Caldan left Quiss and Mazoet and made his way to Selbourne and his men, who were now waiting a short distance away. They'd left a trail in the dew-laden grass, and Caldan followed it. None of the mercenaries showed any signs of tiredness after the night's fighting and travel. A little dusty, some black blood spatters showing, but other than that, they looked ready to fight.

His fingers strayed to touch his trinket ring. Now that he knew how they were made, could he remain in possession of it? It weighed heavily on his hand, as if since he knew it contained another sorcerer's soul, just by wearing it he had a hand in the vile process. He could almost feel the corruption working its way into his finger, along his arm and up his veins into his heart.

But was it his problem to solve? There was much in the world he had no power over. And this was one thing he had no solution to.

"You did well," Selbourne said. He tugged on his beard and gave Caldan a shrewd look. "You're welcome to join us for a drink. A celebration that we're still alive, and a toast to the fallen."

"I . . . thank you. Perhaps another time." Caldan glanced back at Quiss and Mazoet, who were slowly trudging away, the other sorcerers behind them. They were all immersed in what Quiss held in his hand. The mercenaries followed, leaving Caldan alone with Selbourne.

The big man watched his men for a few moments, seemingly content not to say anything. Soon, the sorcerers and mercenaries were all aboard the ship and going below.

Caldan cleared his throat. "From what you said before, you must know Miranda. How? Where did—"

"I don't usually explain myself. She can tell you herself."

"I like to know who I'm dealing with."

Selbourne grunted in amusement. "That's wise. If she trusts you, she'll tell you. As for me, I don't trust you."

Caldan opened his mouth to protest.

"Not yet," continued Selbourne sharply. "Something happened to you out there. Quiss doesn't see it, but he's got a lot on his mind. I see it, though. You need to think long and hard about concealing something from him."

"The only thing that happened was I killed someone. I killed him for a trinket. What does that make me?"

"A realist. It had to be done." Selbourne turned away, as if to leave, then looked back. "Whatever happened, tell Quiss."

I can't.

But Caldan only nodded. If Selbourne told Quiss he was hiding something, then he'd have to come up with a plausible story. That was something he would have to deal with *if* it happened, though.

A featherlight touch brushed against his awareness.

He frowned, pausing.

What is that?

He waited for a few moments. It didn't return.

"Selbourne," Caldan warned, causing the mercenary to stop his progress toward the ships and come back.

"What is it?" said Selbourne.

Something wasn't quite right. Caldan's hand crept toward his sword, and when he clasped the hilt, his nerves steadied. Then, his threads leading to his wolf simulacrum were severed. It fell into a heap a dozen paces away.

Caldan clawed at his well.

Which was blocked.

By the ancestors . . . Mold must be here with the Protectors' trinket sword, probably with Thenna.

Figures appeared from the shadows.

There was no time to get back to the ship and under Quiss's protection. Selbourne should save himself. "Run," he told the mercenary. "The warlocks are here. They've come for me."

The mercenary glanced around them, squinting in the darkness. "I have your back—"

"Run!" Caldan said. "You've no chance against them without Quiss. Find him!"

Selbourne ran, cursing, while Caldan backed away from the ships, breath quickening. He drew his sword and peered around him.

They were out there, likely warlocks and their guards, blades bared, wells open and linked, waiting for him. Sorcery was his only option for escape, and yet it was barred to him.

His hand clenched into a fist. His trinket ring dug into his flesh. Caldan tried to trigger his Touched abilities. He thought dark, violent thoughts.

Nothing happened.

He bent and slammed his fist into the ground, pain exploding across his knuckles. And again.

Still nothing.

Blood trickled down his fingers and dripped onto the earth. Grasses parted to the clomp of booted footsteps. A faint scent of lemons and hot metal. As if that was needed, if he was blocked.

Caldan frowned. The blockage of his own well was startlingly similar to that of the others he'd acquired. Less solid somehow, but it had the same feel.

The smell of lemons became stronger.

"Don't do this," he shouted. "You know what I can do."

An amused laugh answered, coming from the trees. A woman's.

But the person who spoke next was a man Caldan recognized, as he'd suspected: Master Mold of the Protectors. He had to be the one using the trinket sword. The same one Caldan had carried all the way from Anasoma and delivered to them.

"You're unable to craft, and your strength and speed will be matched. You'll be overpowered." There was a pause. "Caldan, turn yourself in without any trouble. It will go easier for you. Thenna told us what you did."

For a moment, he almost abandoned all hope.

But he was tired, and hurt, and angry. And if he was to die here, he'd die with the truth known.

"And what did she say?" he yelled. "Did she tell you the warlocks kill Touched once they've outlived their usefulness?"

"Lies," hissed Thenna.

"Did she tell you about Devenish, how he could create purified land? That he wanted to pitch himself against Kelhak and didn't care what was destroyed along the way? Did she tell you the warlocks use destructive sorcery? But you already knew that, didn't you? And what about coercive sorcery—"

"Take him!" Thenna screamed.

Shadows broke from the trees. Warlocks and Protectors. Dozens of them. Armor and weapons gleamed in the moonlight.

Caldan let his sword slip from his fingers. He wouldn't give them any excuse to injure or kill him this day. Protectors rushed in, followed by the Touched Lisanette and Edelgard—both carrying weighted clubs.

His arms were pinned to his sides, then twisted behind his back as he was pushed to the ground, face grinding into the dirt. Rope encircled his wrists. A hand yanked his head roughly back.

"Gag him," Thenna said.

She stood in front of him, hatred on her face.

A cloth strip was forced between his teeth and tied behind his head.

Thenna took a step forward and spat in his face. Caldan closed his eyes. Warm saliva ran down his cheek.

"Not so tough now, are you?" Thenna said.

Surrounded and outnumbered? Of course he wasn't.

"That's enough, Thenna," Mold said. "He'll be tried and judged. We have a cell waiting—"

"No," Thenna snarled. "I'm taking him from here. You've done your job. He killed Devenish, and he's ours to do with as we will."

"Now, Thenna—"

"He'll greet the accursed ancestors in the hells. Lisanette . . ."

A booted heel smashed into Caldan's head.

CHAPTER 44

Felice waited on the deck of Quiss's ship, Izak by her side. The nobles of Riversedge had offered to supply lodgings, as was her right to demand, and their privilege, due to her rank as Third Adjudicator to the emperor, but she'd declined their offer. There was too much to do. Too much at stake. And inside Riversedge, she'd be too far from the action, removed from the pulse of the emperor's forces and the battle with the jukari. At least she'd been able to change her clothes and fill her pockets with purses of ducats before finding Izak—fleeing before an audience with Lady Porhilde wouldn't do her standing any good. She'd have some explaining to do.

She stretched her back and gave Izak a sidelong glance. He could be off drinking and whoring, and yet he hung around. Perhaps he realized the enormity of what they were doing. Or perhaps he sought to curry favor with her.

Or perhaps he's just overwhelmed by everything that's happened, and I'm a familiar face.

For some reason, she hoped it was the last one . . . probably because she was close to feeling the same.

She looked away from Izak, closing her eyes. Questions needed answering. The Indryallans had to be stopped. And the talon . . . She hadn't stopped thinking about it since it had disappeared. What was it? Where had it come from? What was its purpose? How did Quiss and his people fit into all this? And what of Caldan?

So many questions. Too many questions.

"There was a flash of light out there," Izak said.

Felice peered into the darkness but couldn't see anything.

"I saw it," Izak said.

"I don't doubt you."

After a few moments, Izak turned back to examining the men and women on watch, and she followed his gaze. From their look, they were mercenaries, and experienced ones at that. They all betrayed a nervousness, as if they were waiting for something to happen. Fidgeting hands. Biting lips. Furtive glances. All told a tale.

"Lady Felicienne," Izak said. "Perhaps, instead of waiting out here in the cold for Quiss, we could adjourn to a spare cabin? Partake of some spirits and keep the chill at bay." He smiled at her and raised an eyebrow.

Felice couldn't help but laugh. "Izak, are you propositioning me?" They'd been through a lot together, and the thought was tempting. She'd been alone for so long.

"I . . . well, yes."

She shook her head. "We'll talk when this is over."

Izak inclined his head. "I'll hold you to that. If we—"

Shadows moving caught Felice's eye. "Shh," she hissed.

Armored men appeared out of the blackness, illuminated by the sorcerous globes adorning the ship. Some limped, others winced at injuries. All looked battered and bloodied. Behind them walked Quiss and two of his colleagues.

The soldiers—mercenaries, surmised Felice—ascended the gangplank. Once on board, a few collapsed, and those on watch hurried over to administer aid.

Quiss strode onto the deck and eyed Felice and Izak.

"What are you doing back here?" he said.

The sorcerer looked tired. His face was pale, and he seemed skinnier than usual, if that were possible.

"How did it go? Did you catch the lich? Where's Caldan?" She might be acting above her station, but the ends justified the means, didn't they? The empire must survive, even if protecting it meant playing her own game of Dominion behind the emperor's back to ensure Kelhak was defeated.

And she still wasn't sure what to do about Caldan. She'd already gone out on a limb for him in Anasoma, and again when she'd decided not to turn him in for killing Devenish.

Quiss glanced into the darkness, as if expecting someone to appear. "I don't trust you."

Well, at least he's blunt. "There are those who would see what I'm doing in a treasonous light. I'm putting my faith in you, and require discretion. So where is Caldan? The warlocks are out for his blood."

"Would you hand him over to them?" Quiss said.

Felice shook her head. "No. Everyone will be needed in the coming days. There can be no separate strikes against Kelhak. We must work as one, or we'll perish." That was what the emperor would want, and it would save some time. He would be pleased. And if she could get closer to Quiss's people and learn more about them, then so much the better. Perhaps if she confided in them . . . "Listen," she said. "The emperor won't admit to needing alliances, but it's clear the empire and your people need to work together. That's why I'm here."

Quiss sniffed, then told the other two sorcerers to go below. He handed one a small item, which Felice couldn't see. They walked off, casting backward glances at him.

"Sir Quiss," Izak said. "Lady Felicienne speaks the truth. I've . . . *we've* seen things. We need to gather our forces, and our information. We worked with Rebecci in Anasoma before she . . ." He paused and cleared his throat. "You can trust us."

"Wait," Quiss said, his eyes narrowing. He held up a hand. "There are sorcerers out there."

"Not yours, I take it?" Felice said.

"No. The warlocks know they're no match for us. They wouldn't risk coming this close, unless—"

Suddenly, a large man rushed out of the darkness. He wore a greatsword strapped to his back and puffed mightily as he sped toward the ship.

"Quiss!" the man yelled. "They've taken Caldan!"

A YOUNG, DARK-HAIRED woman gasped for breath as she harangued Quiss. The mercenary's shouts had woken most of the ship, and she'd rushed onto the deck and headed straight for Quiss.

"You bloody find him!" the woman screamed at the sorcerer. "You took him with you. You put him in danger, after all he's been through. This is on you, Quiss."

The large mercenary—Selbourne, Felice had heard the woman call him—tried to placate her.

"Caldan went of his own accord, Miranda." He placed a meaty hand on her shoulder, which she shoved off.

So this is Miranda. I can see why Caldan is so entranced by her.

Although I'm guessing she doesn't normally yell this much . . .

"I don't care! I'm not leaving him to the warlocks. They'll kill him for certain. I'll find him on my own, if I have to." Miranda clutched at her hair, face twisted in distress. "They wouldn't take him back to their camp; it's too obvious and not secure enough. He has to be in the city somewhere."

Quiss stood rigid, hardly moving. His jaw worked for a few moments, then he spoke. "I don't know this city, and without knowing where Caldan is, there isn't much we can do. I tried searching for his well, but there was nothing. Either he's disguised it, or he could be dead."

Miranda kicked the deck and screamed an obscenity that would make a sailor blush. "He's not dead! I have my own resources. I'll find Caldan. Selbourne, come with me to see Charlotte. I know she's here on one of the ships."

"You didn't leave her on the best of terms, Miranda," Selbourne said.

Miranda grimaced. "I know. But there's nothing like a crisis to bring family together. And I think this qualifies."

Felice felt this was a good moment to interject.

"Perhaps I can help?" Felice said. Miranda reminded her of herself when she was younger: headstrong and unafraid to do what she thought was right. But in this case, if she confronted the warlocks, they might decide to make an example of her.

Miranda looked her up and down, as if examining a horse she was about to buy. "You must be Lady Felicienne," she said. "Caldan's told me about you. You wanted him to accompany you home after your game of Dominion."

Felice felt heat flush her face. "Ah . . ."

Miranda strode up to her and looked her in the eye. "Keep your hands off Caldan. I'll accept your help, but stay away from him."

Felice laughed out loud.

"What's so funny?"

"If you know I propositioned him, then you'll also know he rejected my advances soundly." She chuckled again. *She has courage, that's certain.*

"I'm serious," Miranda said.

"And so am I. I have no interest in Caldan other than trying to help him. I take it," Felice said, "that this Charlotte has sources here in the city we could use?"

"Yes," Miranda said. "Who do you know that could help?"

The chuckle became a full-throated laugh once more. "Me? I know the emperor."

Miranda didn't blink. "Good," she said. "Then you can help us find out where Caldan is." She turned to Selbourne. "Gather some men, quickly. We'll go with Lady Felicienne into the city."

Selbourne stood there, looking at the two of them, as if deciding whether to agree.

Miranda clapped her hands. "Go!"

With a nod, Selbourne left them.

"Now," Miranda said, turning back to Felice, "tell me how you'll help."

CHAPTER 45

Caldan's hand hurt. His head throbbed, and his tongue felt like it had swollen until it filled his mouth. His shoulders burned like they were on fire.

He remembered feverish dreams . . . Dreams both sharp and bludgeoning: Fog floating atop a river's surface, swirling and gliding around the hulls of ships. The pale mist's tentacles stretching up and over the sides of ships, igniting in furious incandescence. Hordes of jukari, goaded on by vormag, bristling with weapons newly forged, flooding the landscape like frenzied ants. Behind their gray, slavering ranks, huge misshapen creatures roared with bestial delight. Enormous metal maces thumped the earth. A city by the sea; a harbor, buildings cluttering every available space, flowing up the valley like a giant wave.

Water splashed his face. He blinked at sun-bright torchlight. Shadowed figures moved around him. Cold chains bit into his skin, grinding deep against the bone.

"He's awake," a man said.

"I can see that myself."

Thenna.

"He's still weak. You shouldn't—"

"He's one of the Touched. He'll survive until he's executed."

Silence greeted Thenna's words. The flickering too-bright torches shifted.

Caldan reached for his well—couldn't take hold of it.

The sword. It must be near.

He twisted in an effort to keep one of the figures in his vision. Agony flared.

"Caldan . . ." Thenna said, "try to keep movement to a minimum. You've received a rather nasty blow to the head. And your joints must be protesting their harsh treatment. But . . . I'm sure you'll do what you will." The glee in her voice was edged with malice.

Caldan was naked, chained. His arms were outstretched and pulled in different directions. His bare feet scraped against a stone floor, but only just. He lifted his heels and put his weight on the balls of his feet. The agony in his shoulders gradually subsided. He licked his lips, tasting his own sweat.

He was somewhere damp, neglected. White fungus grew on the wall in front of him, and the walls to either side were lost in gloom. A few torches dotted the stonework, and there must have been at least one behind him, as light shone on Thenna's sweaty face.

They'd blocked Caldan's well, but they didn't know he had more than one. Once they thought his contained, they had no reason to look further. He reached into his mind and brushed his senses over Amerdan's—his—wells. The trickle of power was still there. *Yes. I'm not defenseless.* Working through his pain, Caldan constructed a defense to protect his mind as best he could, then disguised the fractured well.

Thenna smiled thinly, watching his eyes dart around. "I've left you ungagged, to let you speak. No doubt you've already realized you can't access your well. The Protectors have their devices, some of which are useful. Annoyingly, they're reluctant to part with them, but it was only a small matter to remind them who is their master in Mahruse and persuade them to help us with your capture. Your actions have shown you're a rogue sorcerer, and not to be trusted. Not that it matters, since you've no craftings to use. We have them all now, and an interesting collection it is, too. You'll have to explain what they all do. We also have Devenish's trinket back." She stumbled over the warlock's name, the word catching in her throat. Her eyes flashed fire, filled with hate. A nervous muttering came from the warlocks around Caldan. "And also . . . a similar ring to his. You can imagine my surprise! The emperor will reward me handsomely for this."

They had everything of his, then—he had nothing left. *I'm going to die here,* Caldan realized. *As slowly and painfully as Thenna can manage.*

He twisted against his manacles and chains, metal biting into his skin, then sliding as his blood flowed. He bared his teeth in a soundless snarl. Searing agony traveled from his wrists down through his body as he writhed against his bonds.

He stopped, breathing heavily, and let his weight rest on the balls of his feet again.

Miranda . . .

Thenna laughed, a cruel sound with an edge of madness. "You may wonder why you're not dead already. No? I think you've been holding back. I never trusted you, and you proved me right. Maybe you're one of the Indryallans, or perhaps they bought you with promises of power and trinkets? No matter. We'll find out the truth."

"Truth!" spat Caldan, a dry thing that caused him to cough. Once he got control again, he said, "You already know the truth. What you want is an excuse to torture me! To make me feel pain. Revenge for Devenish's death." He cast his eyes around him to the other warlocks. "Can't you see what she's doing? She only wants to make me suffer."

Thenna stepped closer, her face inches from his. "Oh, they know already, Caldan. And they're of a similar mind. I can do what I want, and no one will ever know what happened to you. Your corpse will end up in the mud somewhere, food for animals.

"Except for your blood, of course," she added with a smile.

Caldan shook his head, causing beads of sweat to spatter the stone floor. He glared at Thenna.

I will see you dead!

Reining in his fury, he softened his gaze.

"You're making a mistake," Caldan said.

"How so?"

"I have secrets—"

"And we'll pry them out of you. By the time we're done, your mind will be scraped clean. There will be nothing left. If you can still form thoughts, you will beg for mercy, plead with us to be put out of your misery."

"Not these secrets. Send the others away. I can show you what I mean. A taste . . ."

With a puzzled frown, Thenna stared deep into Caldan's eyes. Eventually, she grunted. "You're harmless. And I already planned some time with you, alone." She turned and waved a hand at the other warlocks. "Leave us."

"But, Thenna—"

"Leave us," Thenna hissed. "He's mine to do with as I will."

One by one, the warlocks exited through the gloom to Caldan's left. A door closed with a clang.

"I know you're playing for time," Thenna said. "But no one will find you here. There is no rescue. This is the last place you'll ever know."

"You're not making me want to tell you anything."

Thenna laughed wildly. "I don't care! Don't you understand? Tell me or don't, it makes no difference. But you can't help thinking it might, so you can't take that chance. Once you tell me everything, I'll strip your mind bare and determine the truth."

She wouldn't let him leave here alive. But Caldan had to delay her in case she was wrong. Surely Quiss could find him. The question was: *Would* he find him? Because he already had what he wanted: Amerdan's trinket.

A weight descended on Caldan. Cold and heavy, pressing against his body and his mind. He quelled his rising panic.

"Have you examined my well?" Caldan asked.

"I imagine it's the same as it was before. Wells never change, though they can be concealed."

With a weak laugh of his own, Caldan drew himself up. He met Thenna's stare. "Look again, but not at my well. Around it."

"Why? There's nothing—" Thenna cut off with a sharp hiss of indrawn breath. Her eyes narrowed in puzzlement, then amazement. "How did you—?"

"They're blocked. I can't use them. But I know how the process to transfer them works." A lie, but he was relying on Thenna's lust for power to give him some breathing space.

"I would have seen them eventually," she said. "But it makes no difference. I'll drag their secret out of you while you scream."

"No, you won't. The knowledge can't be extracted through torture, given up unwillingly. Coercive sorcery makes sure of that."

"You're lying."

Caldan shrugged. *Of course I am.* "No, I'm not. If I'm pushed too far, coercive sorcery will snuff my mind out, like blowing out a candle. The secret of all this power will be lost to you, along with your revenge."

"They're not usable. So I'll take that chance."

"Will you? I think not. I can't open the wells now, but I was making progress. Imagine if you could do it yourself. Imagine the power you'd have. Think of how the other warlocks would see you . . . Thenna, you'd be like one of the sorcerers from before the Shattering. Far more powerful than anyone can imagine. Second only to the emperor."

Thenna retreated a few steps. "I'll make you howl with agony."

"You can't risk it."

"I'll ply you with coercive sorcery, along with the old methods: pincers and hot irons, sharp knives and serrated-edged saws. You'll beg to be put down, like a dog run over by a wagon."

"You won't."

No reply. Wetness trickled down his arms from the cuts in his wrists. Warm at the source, then cold as it descended. Ill-maintained hinges creaked. The door slammed.

Thenna was gone.

CALDAN SHRIEKED AND screamed his throat raw.

He'd lost track of time as Thenna made good on her promise. Misery piled atop misery. Glowing red irons seen through bleary eyes. The stench of his own burning flesh. Agony on agony. Subtle sorcerous webs scuttled about in his mind, tearing and rending, with no thought to the damage they caused—or the suffering.

The familiar feeling of his blood boiling in his veins returned as soon as they started to work on him—but chained as he was, he couldn't break free. They knew what he was, and they'd made sure even his enhanced strength was useless.

So far, Caldan's defenses had protected his mind, fending off their clumsy attempts. Quiss's lessons stood him in good stead, though with only a trickle of power from Amerdan's partially open well to work with, he was reduced to subtle tricks to unravel their coercive threads.

And frustrated, they applied themselves with vigor to the weakness of his flesh. He writhed and howled, swinging by his chains, until his throat was torn and bloody.

Time passed. But he didn't break. He didn't succumb.

He barricaded himself into a tiny kernel of thought. He was Touched. His body would heal, unless he was dead or sustained permanent injury. And as long as he could hold out, his mind was safe. And the longer he resisted, the greater their doubts would grow.

Searing agony flared again.

As long as I can hold out . . .

It took Caldan a few moments to realize the new agony was a result of his circulation being restored. He'd been lowered to the floor. Chains clinking, he curled himself into a fetal position, sliding in his own sweat and blood and filth.

Shadows moved around him. It was too much of an effort to try to make them out. He closed his eyes.

"Caldan . . ." a voice whispered.

A hateful voice, one he'd come to loathe. Thenna.

"I know you can hear me. You've proven yourself stubborn. But we both know where this will end. All you have to decide is how broken you'll be when death comes for you."

A strangled cough escaped Caldan's lips, tearing his throat, as if his own breath were composed of broken glass.

"Cl . . . close," he croaked.

"Hmmm . . . to what, though? To your secrets? Do you give up? Surrender your knowledge, Caldan. Maybe you can have some respite before the end."

Caldan uttered a weak laugh. "Close to . . . triggering . . . coercive . . ." It was all he could manage. They had to be doubting themselves now, didn't they?

"I think you're lying."

"He's weak." Another voice. A man's.

"He'll last a while yet," Thenna said.

"Maybe not."

"Don't question me."

"He's no good to us if you kill him before he spills his secrets."

Thenna snarled with disgust and frustration. "How long?"

"A few hours. Come back then."

Wiry fingers gripped his chin. "I'll see you soon, Caldan," Thenna said. "The time has come to use unconventional methods. I don't like this course, but you leave me no choice. When you see me again, you'll tell me everything. Or . . . I'll pay Miranda a visit. Yes, I know about her. And when she's here with you, you'll regret not being forth-coming with me."

Booted footsteps faded.

Miranda . . . no.

A hand cupped his head. Cool water trickled into his mouth, burn-ing his torn throat like acid. Caldan coughed most of it up.

"More," the man said. "Try to have more."

Eventually, he could swallow small amounts. Someone poured water over his face, and he spluttered. It pooled on the stone floor under his head. More footsteps faded. Hinges squealed.

Caldan groaned and tried to sit up. Failed. Tried again and managed to lever himself up on one arm until he half sat, half reclined.

He opened his eyes and blinked against the brightness and the water dripping into them. He squinted around him. Alone. They'd left him alone.

A brazier was against the wall in front of him, handles of metal implements poking out. Caldan looked at his chains. The brazier was too far away for him to reach.

Blood dried black crusted his manacles, and Caldan winced every time he moved his hands. But it couldn't be helped. He pushed himself into a sitting position, metal rattling against stone. The chains ran up to rings bolted to the ceiling, then trailed down to cleats in the walls on either side.

Clenching his jaw, Caldan twisted his forearms and wrapped the chains around them. Agony flared from his shredded wrists. He fought his way through it, pulling until the chains between him and the cleats were taut. He pulled, slowly at first, then with all his strength.

Nothing.

Again he heaved against the taut metal imprisoning him. He yanked and tugged until his vision went gray. Caldan ceased his struggle. It wouldn't do if he blacked out.

He closed his eyes. It was no use.

With a strangled cry of despair, he collapsed to the hard floor, face in his hands, weeping.

He didn't know how long he sat there before he pulled himself together. Numb, trembling hands wiped aching eyes.

The Touched had their trinkets, which offered more control over their abilities. Naked as he was, without craftings or trinkets, without being able to trigger his abilities himself, he was helpless.

Caldan cursed his manacles, his chains, Thenna, the warlocks, Joachim, Bells, everyone and everything that had led him to this. Gathering himself, he prepared for another struggle with the chains;

then his shoulders slumped, and his head lowered to his chest. There was no point. He was finished. Done. It would end here.

A band of steel around his wrist. All that was between him and freedom, perhaps some small measure of vengeance before he was recaptured. A ring of metal too small for his hand to fit through.

Caldan almost laughed then as a thought came to him. Would it be that simple? And that horrifying?

But the torturers' implements in the brazier were too far away. There was nothing else to use.

Quelling a rising dread, Caldan swallowed and licked salty lips. There was no point agonizing over this.

He placed his left manacle on the stone floor and raised his right hand high.

It didn't feel like it took bravery. All emotion and feeling had been wrung from him. He just didn't think about it, disconnected his thoughts from his actions.

The metal manacle slammed down on his left hand with a crack, shattering bones.

Caldan screamed once, then raised his arm again. As numb and damaged as his hands already were, it hadn't even hurt as much as he thought.

His hand came down again. And again.

His right hand curled around the manacle. His left hand looked strange to him, as limp as a sausage. Breath hissing between his teeth, Caldan pulled it through the manacle.

"Argh!" Waves of pain shot up his arm.

But it came free.

Caldan let out a throaty laugh. One tether no longer restrained him, and he could now reach the brazier. He staggered over to it, and taking a long metal rod he eyed the chain close to his remaining manacle. The rod made an effective lever, though it was a struggle to position it without using his mangled hand. But with the bar in the crook of his elbow, he yanked it down and one of the links broke. Loose chain clattered to the floor.

Caldan grasped the rod in his good hand and made for the door.

He banished all thought, wiping his mind clean. What remained was a semblance of his old self, but one with no emotion, no remorse, no feeling. To do what he needed to do, he could hold no mercy in his heart.

The warlocks were corrupt. The Protectors who worked with them were as well. As were the Touched. There were no innocents in this.

Caldan came to an iron-framed door. On the other side, somewhere, were his craftings and trinket, the sword barring him from his well, and Thenna.

He yanked the door open and looked into the eyes of a surprised guard. The man's mouth dropped open as he fumbled for his sheathed sword.

No innocents.

CALDAN ROAMED THE corridors and rooms of the building like an unforgiving spirit—hate and vengeance fueling his merciless rage.

A blind fury filled him, and he spilled blood and broke bone as a panicked beast would, with no thought to what was right or wrong, only of survival. Hurt or be hurt. Kill or be killed.

Trained guards fell before him. Too slow, barely moving when he came upon them. His boiling blood coursed through his veins, pushing him to extremes. A small part of his mind knew he was doing his body irreparable damage, but he cast it aside. For what use would he be dead?

He blew past the guards' feeble defenses. His metal rod slammed into skulls and necks, bludgeoning, hammering, leaving them limp or shrieking. Five were down now. And by the sounds of pain echoing throughout the building, the others would know he was loose and was coming for them.

Though Caldan's thoughts were reduced to the single imperative of survival, he still recognized goals he needed to fulfill to reach his end. Kill, find his craftings and trinkets, and find the sword.

He came across a group of guards cowering inside a carpeted room. The first one died with Caldan's rod buried in his brain. The second when Caldan broke the man's wrist and impaled him on his own sword. The third as Caldan yanked the blade out and hewed him from shoulder to hip. The fourth groveled, howling for mercy through tears streaming down his face.

But he died, too.

Caldan felt a warp in reality. The trickle of power he had was enough to indicate that open wells approached.

Let them come.

Caldan dropped his metal rod and took up a dripping short sword. He left a trail of sticky scarlet footprints behind him.

By their wells, he sensed sorcerers congregating in a group, no doubt shielded. Protectors or warlocks, it didn't matter. Shields would stop sorcery, or the blows of an axe, or the strike of an arrow, but unless these sorcerers were far more skilled than the masters Caldan had known, their defenses wouldn't arrest momentum. He would show them their protections were flawed. Sorcery was their crutch, and he would kick their support away and leave them reeling.

For an instant, Caldan paused. One sorcerer trailed the others, keeping always behind them. He laughed then and dashed toward the leftmost well. Once he got through or around that one, the sorcerer hiding behind the others would be his, and the trinket sword he no doubt carried.

There.

He blasted through a door. Splinters flew. Boards crashed against walls. A woman stood before him, covered in a blue haze. She snarled and opened her mouth to shout.

Caldan slammed into her, shoulder crashing into her chest. She flew across the room like she was drawn on a string, smashing into a stone wall. Her shield winked out as she slid to the floor, eyes rolling into her head. She slumped like a rag doll. Shouts came from somewhere to Caldan's right.

He ran.

Ahead was the lone sorcerer, moving quickly.

But nowhere near fast enough.

The blood of the ancestors churned through him, hot and turbulent and powerful. He laughed, shouting words he knew he'd never be able to recall.

A Protector stood in front of him, defiance on his face. He clutched a sword, the blade a ribbon of silver in moonlight. A multicolored fish-scale haze surrounded him, along with rune-covered crafted armor.

Caldan's elbow smashed into his head before he could move an inch. It snapped back, motes sparkling across his shield, and he fell unconscious onto the ground. Immediately, Caldan felt the barrier keeping him from his well dissolve, and he opened it and drank deeply of his power.

He dropped his short sword and grasped the hilt of the trinket. There was no time to learn how it worked, but that didn't matter. He now had access to his well, and his blood still burned like lava.

He ran a finger along the edge of the blade, slicing into his own flesh. His finger came away sticky and crimson. He drew symbols and runes on the trinket sword's blade, powerful permutations bound by a variation of the shield crafting.

He grasped the sword again.

Wells tracked toward him, gathering and combining.

With barely a thought, Caldan split his well into multiple strings. He gathered his power, sending it through the runes of blood on the sword.

And blew through stonework like it was paper.

The building rocked to its foundation. Shards of stone timber and dust blew in shredding gales. Those who rallied against him were as nothing. Shields, wards perfected over centuries, craftings and trinkets of incomparable power—they all failed as the sorcerers who possessed them parted before him like mist. Scintillating tendrils sheared through shrieking bodies.

Flesh split. Crimson flowed. Bones cracked.

Souls were sent screaming to the ancestors.

And through the destruction, Caldan strode.

There were no innocents. He destroyed them all.

When he could sense no more wells, Caldan turned to what trinkets and craftings he could feel. He left the ones on the bodies and parts of bodies; they were crude and unwieldy, proven worse than useless. But he backtracked to where he'd been held, and in a locked chest easily opened by his sorcery were his craftings and trinket ring. Everything but his bone trinket, and the one he'd taken from Devenish.

Thenna must have them.

Caldan was still naked, his body marked by the torments he'd endured—although the oldest of those wounds were already healing. He prowled the crumbling ruin of the building, searching, *wanting* to find more sorcerers to bring his vengeance upon. But there were none.

He passed broken walls and mutilated bodies. Rubble and dust, blood and flesh. Caused by his actions. Though this knowledge horrified him, that horror was so far removed from where he was right now that it seemed to be an echo of the person he used to be. At this moment Caldan was filled with righteous indignation, and a sense of wonder and elation. When he'd brought destruction, he hadn't thought—he'd been numb to what he was doing. And the elation was unforeseen. He reveled in his power's release, the complex application of destructive sorcery, wondering if there was anything that could stop him.

His uncanny strength left him in a rush. Weariness descended upon him, both physical and mental. He found a broken roof beam and sat down to rest. *A moment only.* He couldn't afford more. *They will be coming.* Warlocks and Protectors.

Ancestors—everyone would be coming, now.

Eventually he left the devastation.

Incredulous onlookers huddled in alleys and avenues outside—residents, traders, and merchants. They stared with shock at the destruction, and at Caldan as he trudged listlessly out of the smoking ruin, useless left hand hugged to his side. It ached abominably, and inside, he felt its loss keenly, as if part of him had been cut away. And it might as well have been.

Caldan ignored the people, looking up at the cloudy sky.

There was the dead body of a guard close by, a plump man with unseeing eyes. Caldan awkwardly stripped off the man's pants and shirt as best he could with only one working hand, and tugged them on. They were too big, but better than nothing.

Ancient stone walls surrounded him, and from the position of the sun, he was in the south of the city. That meant Miranda was east.

Caldan lifted the trinket sword and rested the flat of the blade against his shoulder, edge close to his neck. The guards at the gate would let him through; they wouldn't be able to stop him. Then he would go to Quiss's ships, clean himself and rest. A physiker would need to see to his hand. He'd healed flesh wounds quickly, but crushed bones were another matter. Perhaps they'd be able to set it so there was a chance he'd be able to use the hand again one day.

Perhaps.

He bowed his head and rubbed his eyes. He was weary, so weary.

Without warning, Caldan felt a surge of power and a whiff of lemons. He reacted instantly, his shield surrounding him the moment before gouts of light pummeled him. Dust stirred in great whirlwinds, and shadows thrashed among the wreckage he'd wrought.

He lashed out to where he sensed wells. Four, no, five of them.

Black-clad warlocks scrambled among the rubble, dodging behind cover. Thenna was with them.

Caldan whirled, searching for threats, promising violence to all who opposed him. Wood charred and stone cracked under his renewed fury.

"Stop!" someone shouted.

Caldan ignored them.

Thenna had tormented him past reasoning. Now she would reap her reward.

A shadow moved. He pitched sorcerous ruin at it. One of the warlocks floundered. Her shield dissolved under his onslaught, and as it fell, *she* fell flaming to the dust, screeching in agony.

Caldan opened bloodied arms and welcomed the warlocks. "Come against me!" he shouted, "and I'll destroy you all!"

"Caldan, stop!"

He sensed another well to his right. The warlock's wards crumbled beneath his hammering. Death came for that sorcerer, too, pulping his head to bloody ruin.

Hiding behind ruined walls, the remaining wells backed away. Slowly at first, then swifter. The warlocks were fleeing. Thenna knew they were no match for him. He would go after them and deliver their punishment.

"You look worse for wear."

Caldan turned sharply, eyes wide.

Lady Felicienne stood on a block of stone, thirty paces away. Her penetrating gaze roamed the ruins he'd created.

"This doesn't concern you, Lady Felicienne." Caldan's voice came out hoarse, raw.

"Destroying a city doesn't concern me? Watching someone I thought to be a good person kill warlocks doesn't concern me?"

"You have no idea what they did to me. They deserve this." And yet, even as he said it, emotional pain warred with physical pain, each as excruciating as the other. It was almost too much to bear, and he wanted to collapse into himself.

Rock clattered behind Caldan, and arms encircled him. He thrust them off, raised his sword to strike—

Miranda.

Tears streaked her face, leaving trails in the dust.

"Please stop," she begged him. She reached a hand toward Caldan.

He looked at it. Saw beyond it to the devastation he'd caused. It was Miranda's voice that had implored him to stop before, and he'd been too far gone in his fury to recognize it. "The warlocks took me prisoner. Tortured me."

Miranda nodded solemnly. "That wasn't right. But you have to stop."

"I . . . why?"

Miranda sobbed, drew a shuddering breath. "This is what you've warned against. Sorcery gone mad." She took a step toward him, hand still outstretched. "Please, Caldan. If you don't stop, you're no better than they are. And I know you. I've seen you help people when you could have just helped yourself. I know how much you did to help *me*.

You don't have to be them. You don't have to turn into them. Just . . . come back to the man you *are*. Not what they tried to make you."

Behind Felicienne, Quiss and Selbourne appeared. The mercenary was scowling fiercely, hands gripping his greatsword, while the sorcerer was fairly glowing with power to Caldan's senses. And behind them stood . . . Captain Charlotte?

Caldan's hand holding the sword twitched, and he realized it was still raised to strike Miranda. He lowered the blade.

"That's better," Miranda said. She took a step toward him.

"They deserved it," he said numbly.

"I'm sure they did. But it's over now. You're safe. We'll get you back to the ship."

"And Thenna?" He turned to Felice. "What about Thenna? She did this to me."

"She will be dealt with, I promise."

Could he believe Felice? Maybe. He looked at Miranda before turning his gaze from her. She was at once distressed and worried for him, and he couldn't face her disappointment at what he'd done.

"Let's leave here," he said, looking at the ground in front of him.

Miranda's arms were around him again, her head resting against his chest. "It'll be all right," she kept saying.

Caldan winced as she unwittingly rubbed tortured flesh. Fresh blood leaked through his clothes. He gently disentangled himself from Miranda, who gasped when she saw the red patches all over his shirt and pants.

Felice, Quiss, and Selbourne approached as he staggered out of the rubble with Miranda.

"Selbourne saw you'd been captured," Felice said. "Miranda and I found out you'd been spirited to this place, through the emperor's sources and a liberal use of ducats. Though it looks like we were too late to free you."

Her narrowed eyes regarded him like he was a rabid dog that needed putting down. And perhaps he was.

"I'm walking away from here," said Caldan. "It would be best if you didn't try to stop me."

Quiss gave him a disappointed look, and Selbourne shook his head. He ignored both of them.

"You've changed," Felice said.

Caldan nodded. *More than you know.* "When we first met, I was a different man. I'm stronger now."

Uttering a snort, Felice clasped her hands. "Or perhaps you're brittle and easily broken?"

"Time will tell," Caldan said. "I'm leaving now."

"I'll accompany you, then," Felice said. "I also need to speak with Quiss."

Caldan sighed, then regarded Felice thoughtfully, troubled for a reason he couldn't determine.

"It's all right, Caldan," Miranda said. "She helped me find you."

"Follow me or not," he said to Felice. "I don't care. But try anything, and you'll regret doing so."

"Tsk, tsk, young man. I've been nothing but forthright with you."

"So you say."

"You *have* changed."

"As I'm guessing you have." Suddenly restless, Caldan took a few steps east down the street. "I fear our chance of survival may already be lost." By the widening of her eyes, he knew she understood. But then again, how could she not? She could see the pieces on the board as well as he could.

The Indryallans. Kelhak. A second Shattering.

"Come with me, then," Caldan said. "We're going to try to save the world, with or without the warlocks and the Quivers."

Felice closed the gap between them, nodding with approval. "Then you'll need my help. I have some ideas. After all, this sort of thing is my specialty."

Caldan snorted and continued walking, leaning on Miranda.

Thenna and the warlocks had sharpened his soul with their torments until he hardly knew himself. But he would be among the first of many to be forged anew by events unfolding. For Kelhak the lich heralded a second Shattering . . .

CHAPTER 46

Caldan took the cup Felice offered him without a word. He clamped his good hand around it to stop it shaking. Fumes rose from the liquid inside: raw spirits, pungent and biting. He drained the contents and drew in a sharp breath. Miranda sat quietly on the bunk next to him, one hand on his thigh.

"Another?" Felice asked.

He nodded numbly and held out the empty cup, perversely enjoying the burning sensation in his throat and stomach.

Felice poured more of the pale green spirit from the bottle, evidently an expensive concoction, though he wouldn't know the difference between this and the cheapest rotgut.

This time, Caldan merely sipped at it, savoring the fiery taste in his mouth. Whenever he moved, his wounds pained him, still raw and fresh, though they were probably healing rapidly. Felice's nose had flared when she'd stepped close to fill his cup. No doubt he smelled of festering sweat and blood, along with smoke and the acrid stench of the destruction his sorcery had caused.

The one thing she didn't smell was effort—it had been so easy. In the end, destructive sorcery was simple. It was far easier to destroy than it was to create.

The trinket sword rested against his leg; he glanced down at the leather grip above the scratched and rust-spotted hilt. The plain exterior concealed a potency that was revealed only when the sword was unsheathed.

Felice thought she understood when she told Caldan he'd changed, but she didn't know what he'd become. As powerful as a warlock. More so. Yes, she could see that . . . but Felice would know there was more. There always was.

"What do you want, Felice?" Caldan asked. He wished she would leave. A physiker was supposedly on the way, to look at his hand and his other wounds. Then perhaps he could rest, alone with Miranda.

Felice leaned nonchalantly against the cabin wall, the bottle dangling from one hand. "I know you've been through a harrowing experience, but this is important. I want to marshal our forces. Strategize. Someone needs to take control and organize our defense."

"Our offense, you mean. If we fall back to defend, we're doomed to fail."

"I think so as well. The emperor—"

"Is scared to death of Kelhak. I saw it during the first sorcerous assault."

Felice paused. "Nevertheless, everyone will be needed." She indicated a pile of clothes on the bunk, along with a half-filled bucket, a rag, and a jar of ointment. "Quiss left these so you could clean up. But he didn't ask any questions. So, I thought to myself, why? What does he know?"

Caldan snorted. He removed his tattered and stained shirt, aware of Felice's gaze taking in the wounds across his chest and arms. Thenna's ministrations. Miranda moved to the bucket, wet the rag, and began wiping dirt from his skin as best she could.

"If it hurts," Miranda said, "I'm sorry." She shot a glare at Felice. "You should go. We won't be part of your plan. The warlocks have shown they can't be trusted."

Felice looked at her long and hard, then took a swig from the bottle. "Working together is the only way we'll make it through this alive. We found Caldan, didn't we, by working together?"

"Almost too late," muttered Miranda.

A cold knot began to form in Caldan's stomach. "I learned the truth from Quiss. He's desperate. If I had to guess, I'd say he doesn't think Kelhak can be stopped."

"We have to try—"

"I didn't say we wouldn't," Caldan growled at Felice. "But we don't even know how yet. We're working on something, but it's as if we only have a few pieces left, and Kelhak controls the whole Dominion board. One wrong move could mean disaster."

Miranda rinsed the rag again. Murky water joined the rest in the bucket. She was biting her bottom lip, and Caldan could tell the sight of his wounds was distressing her.

"We want assurances," Miranda said to Felice. "If Caldan is to be a part of this, then we need certainty that once it's over, he'll be left alone. Free to live his own life. Our own life."

Caldan smiled at her and gripped her hand.

"I promise," Felice said.

"Except you're lying," said Miranda bitterly. "The warlocks want Caldan's blood, literally. And the emperor sees another tool he can use to bolster his power. We're not stupid."

"I know you're not," Felice said, sighing. "All I can do is promise to do my best."

"Not good enough," Miranda replied.

"We won't win if we're divided," Felice said. "The warlocks, the Protectors, the Touched, the Quivers, even the mercenaries: all will have a part to play. Once it's over, then I can help you. The empire must survive. It *will* survive."

No mention of the emperor . . . perhaps we can use that. Caldan shifted his weight, then grimaced. "The warlocks are corrupt; the Protectors are blind; the Touched are puppets; the Quivers have already been decimated. They have the jukari and vormag to worry about, but they're a distraction."

"I know all this. And the trinkets? The Wasters of Life, does Thenna have them?"

"She has them both, that's my guess."

Felice cursed.

Caldan ran a hand across his face, feeling rough stubble, and exhaled, suddenly exhausted. He picked up the clean shirt Quiss had provided, pinched the fabric between his fingers. If this indeed were a game of Dominion, he had the sense he'd already used all his extra moves. "Miranda, do you know where my wolf is?"

She nodded. "Quiss has it. The warlocks either didn't see it or weren't bothered about it. They must have focused on capturing you and getting away as quickly as they could. Quiss said he wanted to study it."

"I'll get it back from him then," Caldan said. At least that was something.

Miranda wrung out the rag and stood. She hugged her arms across her chest. "Felicienne, it's clear you value the empire. It has your loyalty. But we can't be a part of saving it if you're likely to betray us. What are you going to do if Caldan refuses? Lock him up again? You saw how that worked out for Thenna. We want guarantees. Promise to aid us, to do whatever you can."

Caldan nodded. "We want out of this mess. And we need your help. Will you help us, Felice?"

"If I say yes, you'll think I'm lying. But . . . I think there's a way to reassure you. A certain magistrate I know."

Caldan thought she'd forgotten the bottle of spirits in her hand until she lifted it for another sip.

"There's another thing," he said. "Someone else needs to know, and I guess I can trust you with this. I made a promise to Amerdan before he died. He had a sister in Anasoma he wanted me to take care of, and two others. There should be someone else who can help them, if I don't make it. There's a physiker in Anasoma named Zakarius. I was told he's bald. When this is over, can you find him? And take care of them?"

Felice nodded. "Let's hope that doesn't happen and you can be the one to honor your promise."

The door opened, and a balding middle-aged man was ushered in by a mercenary. He carried a leather kit similar to the one Elpidia had.

"Who is . . ." The physiker saw Caldan standing there shirtless, torso dripping blood from wounds that had reopened when Miranda had cleaned his skin. "Ah, you, then."

Miranda took the bottle from Felice and drank a swig herself, eyes never leaving Caldan's damaged chest.

Caldan stood and held out his left hand. In the light of the lone sorcerous globe, it had a blue cast to it, and his fingers were swollen like sausages. Miranda pushed him toward the bunk and urged him to sit down. She joined him when he did.

"I'll leave you now," Felice said. "We can talk again once you've rested." She left the cabin.

The physiker gently took Caldan's ruined hand in both of his, muttering to himself under his breath. "A crush wound?" he said.

Caldan nodded. "Yes. I think most of the bones are broken."

The physiker scratched his chin. "I'd say you're right. This is going to hurt."

Caldan's jaw clenched against fresh agony as the physiker probed his hand, feeling for the bones. After a few moments, he shook his head.

"I'm afraid it's bad news."

"What is it?" Miranda said.

"I won't have to amputate, but he'll never regain use of the hand. Too many bones are broken. I'm sorry. I can bind it up so there's some cushioning until the pain goes away."

Miranda looked up at Caldan, who kept his face blank. He'd expected something like this. His Touched healing abilities wouldn't likely help here. If it couldn't be healed normally, then speeding up the process was useless. His chest grew tight, and for a few moments he couldn't breathe. His hand! It was as useless as a chunk of meat. Better if it had been cut off. Tears blurred his vision, and he blinked, wiping them away with his sleeve.

"Thank you," Caldan said, voice quivering. "Now, about my other wounds. Cuts and burns mostly. Nothing too deep."

FELICE WAS ABOUT to pour herself another drink when there was a pounding on her cabin door. It opened immediately, and a sailor poked her head inside.

"Quiss says to come on deck now. You're needed."

She emerged up top to see Caldan ahead of her, leaning on Miranda's shoulder. His fresh shirt now bore a bloodstain from where Miranda had touched him.

Felice felt sick to her stomach, but there was nothing she could do for him. What the warlocks had done to Caldan disgusted her. And they hadn't subjected him to torture for any reason other than revenge. Thenna, he'd said it was. She filed the name away on one of her special lists. She knew a little about that particular warlock, about her past, and none of it was good.

The humor had been wrenched from Caldan's face. All that was left was wariness and distrust. And hatred. He had been through a fire few escaped from with their sanity intact. And she wasn't even sure he had done that. Was he merely hiding a subtle madness? Had Thenna unleashed something dreadful?

The thing was, Felice didn't think the world was in a position to care about Caldan's pain. If he was mad and violent, then so be it—she would steer him to suit her needs. The man was no longer young after what he'd experienced, but he could still be guided.

Her eyes dropped to the sword he clutched in one hand, naked blade shimmering like water. Runes covered part of it, some filled with a reddish metal.

She quickened her pace and sidled up to Caldan. "Remember what I told you," she muttered to him. "Keep our secrets to yourself. We need to devise a plan and get everyone on board. You with Quiss. Me with the warlocks, Protectors, and the Quivers. Be careful, and speak as little as possible."

They followed the sailor up a short ladder to where the ship's wheel was located on a raised portion of the deck. Quiss was there, along with an immensely fat man with graying hair and a lined appearance. Facing them were three men, and a woman, who stared at Felice and Caldan like she was examining a suspicious-looking bug.

Felice almost stumbled. She recognized three of them. She'd seen all three together before. But where? She racked her memory. Some time ago in the capital. A fleeting glimpse only . . .

The woman had such cold eyes. She should remember seeing them before.

Ah! Now she recalled: Lady Caitlyn . . . the zealot who'd received her writ from the emperor himself. A foolish idea Felice had argued against. Sending out bands who were above the law. Two of the men had been with Caitlyn at the time. One of them was in his twenties, but with the hard-eyed look only veterans had. Aidan. And the swordsman, Anshul cel Rau, who looked to have originated from the Steppes.

The last man, however, was an enigma, but of all of them, it was he who arrested her breath. The eyes, her master had drummed into her: *You can tell much about a man from his eyes.* And this man's eyes were extraordinary. When he glanced at her as she approached, she felt penetrated to her soul. They were knowing.

Quiss spoke in hushed tones, mainly to Caitlyn. As Felice and Caldan approached, Quiss turned to give her a wan smile.

"You say Lady Porhilde told you to come here? Why? And why ask after Gazija as well? Did you have anything to do with his death?" the fat sorcerer was saying.

"Enough, Mazoet," Quiss said wearily. "Of course they didn't. I was there, remember?" His shoulders slumped, as if he was exhausted. "Felice, Caldan, I want you to meet some . . . friends of ours. Lady Caitlyn, Aidan, Anshul, and Vasile." Quiss indicated each in turn. "They joined our cause soon after Anasoma fell to the Indryallans. And it seems they've met up with their long-lost leader."

Felice inclined her head, but their focus was on Caldan, which didn't surprise or worry her. Let them think she wasn't a threat. She had to admit that the imposing form of Caldan, with his set jaw and wild eyes, made a good distraction. As did the sword still clutched in his grip.

She had her goal—to force the different organizations to work together to defeat Kelhak—but it would be akin to herding cats. Situations like this, the chance meeting with these people, she rarely entered with a definite plan. Usually, she examined people, asked a few questions, determined what their aims were and how she could push them in the direction she wanted.

She stepped forward and offered her hand to Caitlyn. "A pleasure," Felice said with just a hint of warmth.

The woman ignored her gesture. "Lady Porhilde requested we seek you out," she said. "You must have information we could use."

"Porhilde?" Felice said. "Ah, yes." The old manipulator must have found out where Felice was and deduced why. Nothing got past the wily fox.

Vasile, the man with knowing eyes, was the first to move. He lightly took her hand and held it for a moment before bowing his head.

"My lady," he said curtly. He stepped back, touching his other arm, as if it were injured, but she could see no sign of damage.

But what was odd was the position of Aidan's feet, his torso, shoulder turned, as if he were guarding Vasile. *This man has his loyalty, and not one bought with gold or power. An allegiance that goes far deeper than that.*

"I'm Vasile Lauris. In Anasoma I was—"

"A magistrate," finished Felice, as memories surfaced. If she recalled correctly, he was uncannily gifted at telling truth from falsehoods. He'd gathered quite a reputation, and not all of it good. "I have heard of you. Before that you were head investigator for the Chancellor's Guard, and his advisor. A man of prodigious talents." *Izak would find this Vasile useful in a gambling den.* Felice laughed to herself. She hoped Izak took her advice and kept his head down until this was all over. She'd buy him a drink, if she made it out alive.

She held her hand out to his companion. "I am Lady Felicienne Shyrise, Third Adjudicator to the emperor."

"We're all that's left of a special group commissioned by the emperor," Aidan said. "We hunt down and exterminate evildoers."

"Another important job" was all she said. Could they be used? Perhaps. Vasile was an interesting addition to the game. "I've seen you before, a long time ago." Felice met Anshul cel Rau's gaze and had to stop herself from flinching. There was violence and death promised in his eyes.

"Yes," Caitlyn said, annoyed, as if she felt left out. "Anshul is a peerless swordsman and staunch opponent of evil."

Felice risked a quick glance at Caldan, who stood removed, a few strides away. He was still obviously distraught and hurting from his experience at the warlocks' hands. This was no place for him.

When she looked back, Vasile had caught Caldan's eye and was nodding in recognition. The young man returned the gesture, barely.

Felice made her way to Caldan and clasped both his arms, forcing him to look at her. He trembled under her touch.

"Go below," Felice said. "You need rest."

"It's too late for that," Caldan said matter-of-factly, pointedly raising his eyes to stare over her shoulder.

She followed his gaze. A number of people approached in the distance. Two groups. One from Riversedge and another from the direction of the warlocks' encampment. Both groups were dressed in black.

"They all have wells," Caldan said. "The warlocks know I'm here. They've come for me."

His words were almost melancholic, as if he'd known this moment was coming but hadn't expected it so soon.

"Go!" she said. "Hide yourself below. I'll deal with them."

"No." Caldan's reply was quick, and firm. "I'm not running anymore."

"Caldan," Miranda said. "She makes sense."

Quiss frowned, taking a step closer to her. "We'll help see them off, Caldan. We can't let them take you. We need to speak again about your constructs. Until we know all you do, you're valuable to us."

"Very well," Caldan said, startling Felice with his control. "I owe you, Quiss. But once you have all I know, we're done. Am I clear?"

Quiss nodded, while behind him Mazoet looked upset.

The distant formations of somberly clad sorcerers approached faster than Felice would have liked. Caitlyn and her men moved away from them to the opposite gunwale, as if they had no stake in this encounter. But Felice knew almost everyone had something to gain or lose from this, even if they weren't aware of it. On encounters such as this hinged the fate of the empire.

She breathed deeply, trying to maintain her outward calm, while inside she seethed with conflicting emotions: anger at what the warlocks had subjected Caldan to, sympathy for him, but also irritation that he'd killed Devenish. They'd need every sorcerer they could lay their hands on in the coming times, and he'd brought the warlocks' focus on himself when it should be on the Indryallans. Quiss was also playing a game she hadn't had time to unravel yet; and Vasile and his companions . . . Were they working toward a goal, or merely being dragged along by circumstance?

The warlocks were nearly upon them. They came closer, heads rising and falling along with the land, bobbing up and down as they staggered over rough patches with unsure footing. Behind them came others, armored men and women. Protectors, most likely.

Quiss and Mazoet moved to where the gangplank met their ship, one on either side of the opening, but positioned ten paces back. Felice followed them. She trusted Quiss's and Mazoet's sorcery to be a match for the warlocks', if what she'd seen from Rebecci was anything to go by.

So she walked over and stopped in between the sorcerers, a pace in front of them. Ignoring their inquiring glances, she drew herself up and affected an irritated expression. Whoever represented the warlocks, probably Thenna, would see Felice first. And Felice would speak first, flanked by sorcerers more powerful than any of the warlocks were.

And they'd assume she was in charge.

The closer the warlocks came, the louder their passage. Night sounds were drowned out by their noise. Sorcerous globes lit their steps, so many it seemed they brought daylight with them. But a mob was just a mob, and that's what this was. A stupid distraction that never would have happened had Devenish still been in charge.

It seemed a few of the warlocks knew what Caldan looked like, for when they came close to the ship, some pointed at him, voices raised in anger. A palpable emotional wave passed through their ranks, one Felice understood. They'd had friends die by Caldan's sorcery. Probably all Thenna had told them. That she'd imprisoned Caldan and tortured him might not be known.

Felice shook her head. Thenna wasn't fit to lead the warlocks.

Thenna stamped up the gangplank, timbers quivering under her angry strides. Her skirt and shirt were ostentatiously embroidered with silver and gold threads, and her silver flower buttons each had a gemstone in the center. Whatever drove her, whatever tasks the warlocks had been set, she'd taken the time to commission new clothes—ones that marked her as separate from the other warlocks. Above them.

And that said as much about her character as anything else.

Thenna raked her searing gaze across Felice and Quiss and Mazoet before turning it to Caldan. She took half a step forward.

"Stop," Felice said calmly.

And to her surprise, Thenna did, then turned to confront her.

"I'm not going to be ordered around by you!" spat Thenna.

But despite her outrage, Felice saw her eyes flick to Quiss and Mazoet. A tiny lick of her lips. Thenna was unsure of herself, and hoping bluff and bluster would see her through. The warlock knew these people had more powerful sorcery, and she would likely back away from a fight.

Good. It was time she was put in her place. Distractions like this would do them no good. In the end, they all had to work together against Kelhak.

"I am Third Adjudicator to the emperor."

Thenna's lips tightened into a bitter line. "Stand aside, then. You have no authority over me."

Felice shook her head slowly, as a mother would at a wayward child. The other warlocks would see and take note. "I know why you're here, Thenna. You overreach yourself. This man, Caldan, is under my protection, and the protection of these two sorcerers as well. Do you dare risk the emperor's displeasure?"

"I'm on warlock business. Stand aside, or suffer our wrath."

"I will not," Felice said firmly, moving a pace closer to Thenna.

She was taking a risk, but she did have both Quiss and Mazoet at her back. Caldan wouldn't go quietly, and after what she'd seen of what remained of the building they'd imprisoned him in, she hoped Thenna didn't spark a fight. "What do you want, Thenna?" *Make her say it.*

Thenna pointed a trembling finger at Caldan. "Him. He murdered Devenish. He will be made to pay."

Caitlyn turned hard eyes on Caldan, and Anshul's hands dropped to his swords. Felice decided she'd best act quickly to forestall any violence from them.

"It seems to me," Felice said, "that he's already paid a heavy price. And one far more painful than mere death would bring."

"He has to suffer."

"He's suffered enough!" Miranda said. "Look at what you've done to Caldan. You tortured and almost killed him!"

"I agree," Felice said. "You did this to him out of anger, Thenna. It was not fitting behavior for a warlock."

"I'm the new leader of the warlocks. I'll decide what's fitting."

"That's for the emperor to determine."

"He'll appoint me."

"Will he? Not if I tell him not to."

"You're only a Third Adjudicator—"

"And as such I can bring any information or concern directly to the emperor that I see fit. Anything. You need to be anointed, and you're in a precarious position. Best you recognize it, warlock."

"What are you waiting for?" a warlock on the wharves shouted, and an angry muttering arose.

Thenna sneered at Felice. "They all know the truth. He'll be judged and executed." Unconsciously, her hands moved to touch a ring on her finger, then to an amulet at her throat. Craftings or trinkets. Either way, her movements betrayed her uncertainty.

Of course. Felice's path was clear now. "No, you're not taking Caldan. You've overstepped the mark. Your kidnap and torture of a suspect is criminal, and you're going to stand trial for it."

As for Caldan . . . he might be key to taking down Kelhak. The emperor needed to know of what had transpired, and perhaps pardon Caldan. At least until this was over.

"I saw him." Thenna shot a glare of pure hatred in Caldan's direction. "Devenish was helpless. Caldan cut him down without mercy, like he was an animal."

The troubling thing was, Thenna was right. Out of the corner of her eye, Felice caught a glimpse of Vasile nodding to Aidan.

Anshul glanced at Caitlyn, who nodded. The swordsman took a step forward.

"He was little more than that," Caldan said from right behind Felice, startling her. She'd missed his approach.

Thenna hissed between clenched teeth, lips peeled back. "You're dead. If I have to—"

"Enough, Thenna!" Felice said. If she didn't stop this, then Caitlyn and her killers might do something rash.

Thenna scoffed loudly. "This is a farce. Stand aside, or risk the wrath of the warlocks. I'll burn you all to cinders and take Caldan. You won't be able to stop me."

"She's opened her well," Quiss said. "But she's no danger."

Miranda sidled around and positioned herself behind Quiss.

"I'll see you all burn," hissed Thenna.

"Now, now," Felice said. Boots thudded on the deck as Caldan strode past Felice and stopped in front of Thenna. He stood straight, with his broad shoulders pulled back. The trinket sword dangled from his right hand, and Thenna's eyes kept darting toward it.

She fears the sword.

"Caldan," Felice said firmly. "Stay out of this."

"I will not," Caldan growled.

Bloody ancestors. "You are all witnesses," she said loudly for everyone to hear. "As Third Adjudicator, I order you, Thenna, to stand down. Your desire for revenge has left you without reason."

"You have no authority over me!" screamed Thenna.

Felice inclined her head. "That's true," she said calmly. "But I do have the authority to settle disputes, as long as it's done according to the law, and to bring urgent matters directly before the emperor. And I'm invoking my right to do both. After this, Thenna, we'll have an audience with the emperor. And I'll see to it he appoints someone more suited to leading the warlocks."

Grumbles from the other warlocks arose at Felice's pronouncement. Thenna looked about her anxiously before smoothing her face into an expression of contempt. Before she could respond, the grumbles faded to silence. They were waiting to hear what Thenna had to say. Anshul hadn't moved, though his hands remained on his sword hilts.

"We're taking Caldan now," Thenna said. "We'll leave with him, and there will be no more trouble."

Felice shook her head. "No, you won't. These are dangerous times, Thenna. The empire is in peril from the Indryallans and the sorcery they bring." There were mutterings of agreement from the warlocks behind Thenna. "Your focus on this one man has clouded your judgment. I don't excuse what he's done, or what you claim he's done. But you have gone too far. Leave here, and we'll settle this later."

Thenna licked her lips again, eyes darting.

Felice knew Thenna had no options—she wasn't going to start a sorcerous fight she knew she couldn't win, so she had to back down.

Instead, the warlock pointed an accusing finger at Caldan. "You murdered Devenish!"

Deny, thought Felice. *I need time*. She turned a pleading look on Caldan, hoping he saw.

"And I'd do it again," Caldan said, voice pitched low.

Felice closed her eyes for an instant. *Pignuts*.

Thenna shrieked in anger. The air around Felice seemed to solidify and bear down on her. There was an indrawn hiss of breath from Quiss. A vibration rattled her bones. Thenna and Caldan became surrounded by shimmering multicolored shields. Sunlight flashed from Thenna, striking Caldan. Motes sparkled across his shield.

Caldan chortled. The laugh of a man with nothing to lose, tinged with madness.

It was all Felice could do to turn and throw herself to the deck. Heat splashed across her back. The air cracked.

She pressed herself into the deck, arms covering her head, and waited for the backlash of sorcery. There were two wooden thumps. Miranda uttered a wordless cry.

When nothing else happened, she raised her head and turned.

Both Caldan and Thenna lay slumped lifeless on the deck. Quiss and Mazoet stood over them. Shielded warlocks backed away fearfully, hands raised in a gesture of submission. They exchanged wide-eyed, frantic looks from sweat-sheened faces and muttered nervously.

The warlocks were *terrified* of Quiss and Mazoet.

But the two sorcerers were not looking at the warlocks, as if they didn't care what they did. They both looked down at Caldan, faces twisted in a mixture of grief and disgust. Miranda pushed between them and sank to her knees beside Caldan.

Felice scrambled to her feet, brushing dust from her clothes as she carefully approached Quiss and Mazoet.

"What is it?" she asked Quiss.

He turned a sorrowful face toward her. He blinked, mouth drooping in sadness, then turned back to regard Caldan. "Not here," he said, voice cracking with pain.

Felice clutched her trembling hands together in an attempt to appear calm. Inside, she was anything but. Her guts quivered and roiled. She'd been certain she would die because she'd miscalculated. She bit down on a relieved laugh that bubbled from her chest.

"Are they . . . ?" Felice trailed off.

"No," Quiss said. "They're alive. We just had to . . . disable them. They were about to let loose with destructive sorcery, and I couldn't let that happen. As much as it pains me to say it, we need the warlocks. And now I think we need Caldan even more. This feud between him and Thenna has to be stopped."

Felice nodded agreement, edging closer. She bent over and rifled through Thenna's clothes, trying not to look at Miranda's tear-streaked face.

Ah.

In a belt pouch were two bone rings. Felice slipped them into her pocket. She noticed one warlock hadn't backed away like the others.

A middle-aged man with a short, sandy beard speckled with gray. He was off to the side, but he'd held his ground.

"You," Felice said. "Thenna is fine. Organize to have her carried away and taken care of."

The warlock regarded her steadily, and she could almost hear his thoughts turning. Eventually, he nodded. "All right," he said. "But Devenish's death—"

"Is my issue to resolve," Felice said. "In my authority as Third Adjudicator, I'm taking the decision of redress on myself." *Delay.* If she was right about what was coming, no decision might have to be made. They might all be dead. Everyone was needed, even Thenna. "Your name?" she asked the bearded warlock.

"Bernhard."

"You seem like a sensible man, Bernhard. So you'll lead the warlocks for the time being. Take Thenna to the emperor, speak to Lady Porhilde. Tell her everything that happened here, and everything I said. I'll follow shortly."

"But . . . Thenna—"

"Needs to be appointed by the emperor. As Devenish was. As were all the leaders of the warlocks before him."

There were nods from some of the warlocks. They knew she was right, and some of them obviously hadn't agreed with the way Thenna had taken power unto herself. Those nodding, and many others, looked to Bernhard and waited for his response. A sign they respected him.

Good.

Bernhard turned and beckoned a few of the burlier warlocks to join him. Together they picked Thenna up, taking care not to manhandle her too much. Bernhard directed them to leave, and the warlocks descended the gangplank to the wharf with Thenna.

"Lady Porhilde," Felice reminded Bernhard as he turned to go. "You know her, I assume?" Everyone did, or knew of her.

"Yes," Bernhard said, then hesitated. "Seven warlocks died when Caldan escaped, along with four Protectors. I don't care what the situation was. There will be a reckoning for those deaths."

Felice swallowed, then nodded curtly. "Of course. Tell Lady Porhilde everything. Then, when I join you, we can talk. The empire is in peril, and everyone must do their part. Until then, all else can wait."

Bernhard's gaze was drawn to the spots of blackness in the distance, the newly created purified lands, one of them erupting from the earth like sea urchin spikes. Felice met his eyes, and in them she read fear, and a desire to do his duty. *This man,* she realized, *isn't so unlike me.*

"I understand" was all he said.

He knows what must be done. All personal quarrels must be put aside. "Then go. I'll join you soon."

Bernhard left the ship, and the warlocks began tracking back to their encampment. Some split off and headed to Riversedge, their sorcerous globes lighting the way.

Felice drew a breath and turned to Quiss. "Now, Quiss, what is it? Why do you look like you've seen something terrible?"

"I . . . just hate to see Caldan in such distress. What Thenna did to him, the torture, the torment, must have unhinged him. He'll need plenty of time to recover. Which we'll provide, of course."

"Of course," Felice replied. But what caught her attention was Vasile's frown at Quiss's words. He thought the sorcerer was lying. Aidan had also caught the frown and looked at Vasile meaningfully for a moment before resuming a blank expression.

From Quiss's comment, Vasile's frown, and his companions' looks, there had to be something wrong with Caldan, but it wasn't what Quiss had said. *Bloody hells.* She needed to stay with him to get to the bottom of this, but she also needed to go after Bernhard and sort out this mess with Thenna, then bring the warlocks on her side.

Felice hesitated, unsure which option to pursue. Time; she needed time to do both.

She had to put Quiss on the spot. If he left with Caldan, for all she knew, they'd be gone when she returned.

"One moment, Quiss," Felice said in as commanding a voice as she could, considering she was facing two sorcerers who put the warlocks to shame. "I grant you Caldan has suffered tremendously, but that's not what has you concerned, is it?"

Quiss's eyes narrowed.

Felice decided to push the sorcerer before he could speak. "Out with it, Quiss. There can be no more secrets. The very fabric of the world is at stake."

As Felice said the words, she trembled, realizing she meant them. How would she tell what was demanded of her in such a time? The burden was great, and who was she? Who was she to decide who would be sacrificed in the upcoming fight for survival? For deaths would be inevitable.

The weight was too great, and her knees almost buckled, driving her to the deck.

Felice clenched her hands into fists, nails biting into the skin of her palms.

Someone must.

Quiss and his people mustn't be at odds with the warlocks. The Protectors must join them as well, along with the Quivers. And Caldan, somehow he was pivotal. She trembled anew. And the talon. All were linked. All had to move as one in order to defeat Kelhak.

The world was laid out before her like a Dominion board, the pieces transubstantiated into life. Her opponent was Kelhak, and who knew how many extra moves he had?

There was peril surrounding them all, and her steps needed to be measured and precise.

And Felice knew what she had to do. As in Dominion, she needed more extra moves. The talon. She must find it.

CHAPTER 47

Caldan groaned and squeezed his eyes tight against the pain it caused him. He took a few deep breaths to calm himself. The last thing he remembered was facing down Thenna on the deck of Quiss's ship. Then . . . nothing.

Fool. He'd been a fool again. His treatment at Thenna's hands had caused him to make unreasoned decisions. With everything he'd learned—both coercive and destructive sorcery—he'd been sure he was more than a match for the warlock. He hadn't even considered that Quiss might intervene.

Quiss.

Caldan's lips parted in a soft gasp. He opened his well and clumsily groped around in his mind. *By the ancestors.* The wards he'd constructed to mask his extra wells had been stripped away.

Though it caused a great deal of agony, he hastily reerected them, testing their efficacy until he was sure any sorcerer sensing him would find only his own well. But even as he did, he knew it was too late.

Quiss, and probably Mazoet, would have sensed what he'd tried to keep hidden.

His secret was unmasked.

And when they'd needed to, Quiss had sliced through his defenses as easily as a master would through an apprentice's. Their knowledge of sorcery was so far above his, the warlocks', and the Protectors' that there was nothing he could do to resist them.

And if they knew he was a lich, they'd not suffer him to live.

So why wasn't he dead? Then he remembered.

They'd needed him. Something about his simulacra was important enough it trumped even his corruption.

With trembling limbs, Caldan sat up, squinting in the dim light. Another cabin, this one tiny. A narrow bunk, cupboards on the other wall, the aisle between barely room enough to turn around in. He was still dressed, and the trinket sword was propped in a corner.

He breathed a sigh of relief when he saw it there. Then he confirmed he had all his other craftings on him. It looked like they'd left him here to recover, knowing he was no threat to them.

Miranda wasn't here, which was probably for the best. Though he wondered where she was. He didn't expect her to wait by his side every hour of the day, but it was nice having her close by, and he realized he didn't like when they were apart.

Caldan rose, intending to find Quiss, but stopped at the door. It was locked.

He opened his well and licked his index finger, tracing runes on the lock, using more saliva when he needed to. He connected a string to his rapidly drying linking rune, let his power flow through the crude crafting, and the lock clicked open. Steam clouded from his vaporized saliva.

Caldan took a moment to appreciate just how far he'd come since arriving in Anasoma. He'd known crude craftings like this were possible from Bells's escape attempt on the way to Riversedge, but they required control, an ability to precisely calculate how much energy was needed, and an efficient enough crafting to get the job done before it eroded. But there was something else, it occurred to him, about the corrosiveness of wells. This crafting had taken his expertise to control, that was true, but he'd poured his well into it, and it had flowed like a trickle of water—deliberate and calm, not turbulent. Perhaps this was why his paper craftings bore the strain so capably. He recalled Bells's words when he'd first met her: *Your well is remarkable, so smooth and stable.*

It made sense that the less turbulent the power of a sorcerer's well, the longer the sorcerer's craftings would last.

Caldan shook his head. A small piece of the puzzle that was sorcery, and not one that would help him in his situation.

He grabbed the sword and made his way on deck. Two of Quiss's colleagues were leaning on the gunwale on either side of the gangplank down to the wharf. Obviously there to make sure he didn't leave, or on the lookout in case the warlocks returned. Caldan ignored them and scanned the deck, noticing Quiss was standing by the wheel, talking to Mazoet, who pointed toward Riversedge, then back east toward Anasoma. When he did so, he noticed Caldan and smiled. Quiss turned and smiled as well, but there was sorrow in his eyes.

They know they can't let me live, thought Caldan. *It's up to me to make sure they think I don't know.*

"Where's Miranda?" Caldan said as he neared them.

"We persuaded her it would be best if you rested undisturbed," Quiss said. "She's on the ship, so you can see her if you like."

Caldan breathed a sigh of relief. She was still safe. "And Felice?"

Quiss shrugged. "In Riversedge. We don't know precisely where. She wants us to trust her with bringing the warlocks, Protectors, and Quivers to our side."

Before he could stop himself, Caldan snorted. "They'll do what they think is best for themselves, not for the world as a whole."

"Be that as it may," Quiss said, "we *will* need them. If only for a diversion. If we didn't, then we wouldn't be here, and we wouldn't have shown ourselves."

"Caldan," Mazoet said. "When did you regain consciousness? Did you feel anything?"

With a frown, Caldan shook his head. "Only just now. I came straight here. What's happened?"

Mazoet gaze Quiss a long look before replying. "There was a surge of sorcery. Close by, but it was over so quickly we couldn't tell where it came from. I'm not sure any of the warlocks could have created such a pulse. It was incredibly focused. It had the taste of when we travel, but it couldn't have been. It was too small."

"And you think if it was Kelhak, he wouldn't have bothered with this. He'd come at you with all he has."

"Yes. Exactly."

"Then," Caldan said, "could it have been someone else? The Indryallans?"

Mazoet growled under his breath. "I don't think so. It doesn't make sense, and that worries me."

"It's a distraction," Quiss said. "We need to focus on what we need to do to defeat Kelhak."

Caldan looked toward the walls of Riversedge, then to the dark marks spotting the countryside, his gaze coming to rest on the spiky, shattered purified land, where Devenish had made his stand, and Caldan had killed him for it.

The similarity to his own situation wasn't lost on him.

Mazoet cleared his throat. "We are . . . less . . . without Gazija, but we are still strong. And now, thanks to you, we have the trinket this Amerdan had in his possession. We're still hoping to unravel the secret of its workings and apply it to the, er, Kelhak problem."

Caldan looked down at the deck. Scratches and dents marred the hardwood surface. He knew they knew; there wasn't any reason to pussyfoot around the situation.

"I don't know how it happened," he confessed quietly. "We were struggling, and he just . . . he killed himself. He *knew* what would happen to me. It was as if he realized he would lose and decided to transfer what he had to me. Perhaps he thought he was making sure a part of himself survived."

Quiss and Mazoet were quiet for a long time. Water sloshed against the side of the ship, and crickets chirped.

Eventually, Quiss spoke. "It wasn't a gift, what he did to you. You wouldn't have chosen such a thing, under normal circumstances."

"Or even extraordinary circumstances," added Mazoet with a wry grin.

Caldan found himself smiling in return, though inside he knew they considered him a tool to be used and then discarded. Just like the warlocks had.

"I won't try to unblock them," Caldan said, lying through his teeth. For the truth was, he might have to, if he wanted to live. If he could learn to control such power, it would be an advantage when confronting Kelhak, and after, if he survived, would help him escape from those arrayed against him. Quiss included.

"I counted eleven," Quiss said. "Plus your own well. That makes twelve. Many different shapes and sizes, of course, which is to be expected. But twelve wells . . . Do you think you'll be able to resist the temptation?"

"My own well has sufficed so far. And what would I do with another eleven wells? I'd have to be able to manage many more strings than I can now. Plus, what situation would come up in which this much power would be useful? My own well—and talent—is sufficient to match the warlocks already."

Quiss gave him a level look. "I can think of one situation already: the one facing us."

Would they push him to truly become a lich, rather than let him leave the wells unblocked, then kill him because of what they forced upon him?

Of course they would. What was one life pitched against the world?

Caldan realized his hand was gripping the hilt of the sword so tightly it ached. With an effort, he relaxed his grip and carefully pried the hand away. Affecting a relaxed expression, he shaded his eyes against the sun and gazed out over the river. Birds with long beaks swam past, one diving underwater to return a short time later with a silver fish it swallowed whole.

"We'll get through this," Quiss said, the tremor in his voice giving lie to his words. "Miranda has been asking after you. You should see her. If you're open to advice, I'd tell her everything."

"No! Miranda can't know what I've done."

"Secrets between lovers always lead to trouble."

"We're not . . . It's none of your business."

"Caldan, don't be foolish. She deserves to know."

So you can justify removing me later? Caldan began to shake his head, then stopped. Maybe they were right . . . "Where is she?" he asked.

"Belowdecks somewhere, as far as I know."

Caldan nodded his thanks and left the two sorcerers there. He could feel their eyes on his back as he walked away, and he struggled to keep his steps slow and unhurried.

CALDAN HESITATED AT the cabin door, which was now locked from the inside. For a moment, his mask slipped, and he felt his face twist into an expression of guilt and self-pity. It took an effort to pull himself together, and a dozen heartbeats before he felt calm enough to knock.

Miranda opened the door and ushered him inside, then relocked it. She hugged him tight before suddenly letting him go and looking chagrined.

"I'm sorry," she said. "Your wounds."

"It's all right," Caldan said. "I'm healing quickly, and I'd prefer some hugs these days."

The room looked tidy; the bunk was made. Miranda's old habits, he assumed. There was a brush and comb on a shelf, along with a few sets of clothes. On a stool was a tray heaped with bread and dried fruit and chunks of meat on skewers.

Caldan sat on the bunk and almost immediately stood again. His mind wouldn't settle, and he was too nervous to sit. Then he realized there was something else making him jumpy. A sensation at the edge of his awareness, not unlike what he'd felt when he'd sensed Kelhak's storm approaching.

Sorcery. Coming from somewhere in the cabin. A trickle, but it was there.

He swallowed and reached for his shield crafting, preparing to open his well.

"Miranda, I want you to stay by the door."

"Why? What's wrong?"

Where was it? He stretched his senses, questing around him. "There's something here."

There. Under the blanket on the bunk. There was a slight lump. Could it be a trinket? But he didn't think Miranda possessed any of the artifacts, at least not the type he could sense.

The lump under the blanket moved.

Caldan blinked, unsure he'd seen it. Was it a rat? There were plenty about every ship . . . but that didn't make sense. There was an air of sorcery around it, and what's more, it had a familiar tang.

He gripped the sword firmly and stepped forward, prepared for anything.

He darted the blade forward, slipping it under the edge of the blanket, and yanked the material back. His eyes widened, and he staggered, clutching at the wall to support his legs.

Lying on the bunk was his smith-crafted automaton: the manlike figure. The one Gazija had taken from him.

Except it was different. Altered.

Its surface was scorched and marred, as if it had passed through a great heat. As he'd noted when he'd last seen it, intricate runes and patterns covered its surface, hair-thin lines etched into the metal. Shapes and designs far more complex than any he'd come up with.

"What is that?" said Miranda.

The automaton sat up.

Caldan's heart leaped into his throat, and Miranda yelped. He backed away, shield covering himself and her as he squeezed every ounce of power from his well.

There's nothing to be afraid of, said a voice in his mind.

Gazija. It sounded exactly like the old sorcerer. But he was dead.

I saw you die . . .

"Who . . ." Caldan croaked, voice quivering, then steeled himself. "*What* are you?"

I am who I always was. A long pause, as if the automaton sighed or was searching for the right words. *I am Gazija, First Deliverer to my people. After I saved you, when Kelhak attacked me, I was forced to flee back inside my own well. Transferring my consciousness to your crafting was the only way to survive.*

Caldan mulled this over, still alert for any sign of treachery.

"Caldan, what's happening?"

He clasped Miranda's hand to calm her. "It's talking to me."

"Sorcery?"

He nodded. "Yes. Wait while I find out what's going on." Caldan turned to the construct. "This was your plan all along, wasn't it?"

Yes.

"But . . . is it worth it? You stay alive, but is it really living?" Caldan knew that how Gazija's people currently survived was immoral and horrific. But was this the answer? Condemned to a bodiless existence forever? A harsh solution.

It is better than what we were before.

If Caldan were in Gazija's boots, what would he have done? Wasn't this a far more palatable existence than using and abusing other people's bodies?

The mere thought of what Gazija and his people did brought bile to Caldan's throat. He'd avoided thinking about it, because they were needed in the fight against Kelhak. But they were allowing a lesser evil to exist because of a greater one.

"I'll take you to Quiss," Caldan said. "No doubt you'll want to let him know you survived."

What, no more questions? I'd have thought you would have many.

Caldan shrugged. The warlocks and Protectors could deal with Gazija and his people. Once Kelhak was gone, he'd have to look after himself. Now, his survival and Miranda's was his only concern.

"Perhaps later," Caldan said. "I have more than enough on my plate as it is."

Then I'm afraid I'll have to add to your burden. You see, Quiss can't know that I'm still alive. And if the plan I have is successful, then you'll need to go far from here. Tell no one. Leave no trace.

"I NEED TO get off this ship," Caldan said irritably. "I've smith-crafting to do if I'm going to be any use."

"We have more important matters to attend to," Quiss said. "Your help is needed with Amerdan's trinket. If we're to have any chance against Kelhak, we're going to have to unravel its secrets, and soon."

Caldan placed his satchel gently on the deck. It contained some of his crafting materials, and Gazija, wrapped in a cloth. His mind was still reeling from the old man's story. It seemed incredible. Too fanciful to be believed, but the proof had been right in front of him.

Gazija's awareness housed inside a crafting, for all intents and purposes making him a self-aware trinket. One that had autonomy. Caldan was scarcely able to comprehend the possibilities. His own research and experimentation with craftings had been moving in a similar direction, but the idea of voluntarily giving up your own body for a fleshless existence sent shivers through him.

But it was better than the alternative, remaining the monsters they'd become in order to survive. In the end, he hadn't needed much persuasion to agree to help.

Caldan's eyes were drawn to the east, where he kept expecting the horizon to be blotted out by the dark clouds of another approaching storm. But luckily, there was no sign of sorcery.

Yet.

"Doesn't the trinket use coercive sorcery?" Caldan asked. "You're far more adept at it than I am. I won't be able to offer any insights."

Good, came Gazija's voice in his mind. *You need to get off the ship, otherwise I can't help you.*

"A new perspective is always welcome, Caldan. There may be angles we haven't considered, different lines of thought."

Quiss smiled encouragingly, but Caldan saw through his act. They wanted to make sure they had control over him. As everyone else did.

He means well, Gazija said. *And he's trying to cope as best he can.*

But Quiss never was one to make hard decisions. They don't sit well with him.

Caldan knew what Gazija really meant. Quiss had a conscience that some leaders lacked. And it seemed Gazija would do almost anything to achieve his goals. If that meant defeating Kelhak, then Caldan was happy to oblige him. But he knew Gazija wasn't concerned with Caldan's welfare, only with his own. If Gazija wanted off the ship, it was for his own reasons.

About to respond to Quiss, Caldan hesitated when a slender young girl came bounding up the gangplank. She wore a brown uniform of sorts, with a brimmed cap jammed over her short black hair. She was breathing heavily and covered with perspiration. The girl took a few moments to catch her breath, then her gaze traveled over both Quiss and Caldan. Reaching behind her shoulder, she pulled a flat satchel from her back to her stomach, and from it drew out a stack of envelopes. From the stack, she removed two.

"Are either of you Quiss or Caldan?" she said.

"I'm Caldan, and that's Quiss."

"Hmph," the girl snorted, then examined the backs of her two envelopes. She grunted and strode up to Caldan. "The description fits, so that's good enough for me. If you're lying, you'll likely be dead before tomorrow. So don't say no one warned you. Meeting's in two hours. Be there."

She handed Caldan that envelope and Quiss the other before turning and jogging back down the gangplank.

"What's this?" Quiss said, frowning with puzzlement.

Caldan examined his envelope. The front bore just his name, while the back had a bare-boned but accurate description of himself. He broke the wax seal, withdrew a single page from inside, and scanned the contents.

"It's from Felice," he said. "She's holding a meeting with representatives of everyone involved, from the warlocks to the Quivers, the Protectors, and Lady Porhilde. I've been asked to come alone. I'd guess yours says the same. It's . . . with the emperor."

Quiss stared at his letter as if it were a snake about to bite him.

"It must be a trap," he said quietly. "They're hoping to catch us off guard."

"What would they gain by trying something? I trust Felice, at least as much as I trust anyone." *Which isn't much.* "Her main concern is Kelhak, and she wouldn't do anything to jeopardize her goal."

"But how much control does she have over everyone else? Ask yourself that. Would you trust the Protectors not to try something? We use destructive and coercive sorcery, and they know it. And what about Thenna? I'm sure she'll be there."

"I can defend myself against Thenna," Caldan said.

"Not if she has the support of the warlocks and they strike all at once."

"Even then," he said, remembering his escape from their prison.

Enough of this, snapped Gazija. *Tell him Gazija would go. He'll know it for truth. Tell him, Gazija would want to evaluate the others and examine their plans, to see if they would help or hinder his mission.*

"Gazija would have gone," Caldan said carefully, keeping an eye on Quiss. Who knew what the sorcerer's reaction would be?

Quiss looked at Caldan sharply, mouth pressed into a tight line. "You have no idea what—"

"I know he was your leader. The First Deliverer, you called him. He would go. He would want to know firsthand what everyone else had planned. To see if he could help, or to find out if they would be thorns in his side. Kelhak is the only thing that matters now. Everything else is secondary."

"Gazija is gone. There's only me and Mazoet left to look after our people. I wish . . ." Quiss let out a lengthy sigh. "I just wish Gazija had told us more of what he planned. The best option I can see is for us to strike at Kelhak now. If we delay by trying to appease everyone else, then we're doomed to fail."

Not so. He needs to look beyond Kelhak, to what would happen if we are successful.

Caldan nodded minutely. He understood what Gazija was saying. Quiss and his people's secret was out now, and they had to show they could be trusted and weren't some type of monster. The warlocks,

Protectors, and Quivers needed to know they weren't trading Kelhak for another evil. Quiss was lost. He had been since Gazija had disappeared. The sorcerers were like a ship without a rudder. But what they should do, what they must do, was clear to Caldan.

"Quiss, you aren't Gazija," Caldan said, more harshly than he intended. "But you know what he'd do. You need to look further than Kelhak, to what your people will do once all this is over."

"He's gone," Quiss whispered.

His words were barely audible, voice quivering. He raised his gaze, and Caldan was surprised to see tears in his eyes.

"I can't . . ." Quiss continued. "Kelhak found him. The lich came for him and killed him or absorbed him. There's no appreciable difference. I can't follow in Gazija's footsteps."

"Quiss, you must . . ."

"No! You don't understand."

Tears were flowing freely now. Caldan turned his gaze away to give Quiss space. "Then tell me. What is it I'm missing?" Caldan was sure there was more to their story than had been revealed. There was always more, from small things people were ashamed to admit to larger, more unwholesome truths.

"Gazija . . . he did things others would have balked at. Things I argued against. But . . . he is . . . was . . . the First Deliverer. We owe our lives to him."

"He would have done what he felt was right. What he felt he had to do, to ensure your survival." Caldan stopped. What exactly had Gazija done that had Quiss so distressed?

Gazija's voice intruded on his thoughts. *Quiss has too big a heart. You have to realize, Caldan, our very survival is at stake, along with the world's.*

Caldan ignored Gazija's justifications. "Quiss, tell me."

Quiss gave him a look of such distraught guilt, Caldan almost staggered. Whatever it was, it wasn't good.

"The jukari and vormag," Quiss whispered.

What about them?

It was necessary, Gazija said.

"Gazija did what he felt he had to do," said Quiss. "The creatures from the Shattering, the mercenaries . . . it was all a setup."

Necessary, Gazija repeated. *To save the world.*

Caldan clenched his hands into fists. Surely Quiss wasn't suggesting . . .

"Kelhak didn't gather the jukari horde and direct them against the emperor's forces. It was us. We did it."

The emperor and warlocks were blind to what was going on. I had to show them the danger.

Caldan looked to Quiss, found the sorcerer's eyes squeezed shut, shame visible on his face.

"We hadn't counted on Kelhak's sorcery, through that woman, Bells. It struck while the Quivers and warlocks were preoccupied with the jukari. The horde we'd set in motion."

How many have the jukari and vormag killed? wondered Caldan. They'd left a trail of devastation all the way from the Desolate Lands—innocent people dead in their wake, buildings destroyed, fields ruined. Lives shattered. And part of the reason Bells's sorcery had been so devastating was because of the distraction of the jukari and vormag, but . . . she wouldn't have been in the position she'd been if it hadn't been for Caldan. He had his own guilt to bear. Many were dead because he'd captured Bells instead of killing her. Miranda had needed healing, and Bells had seemed his only option.

But the price . . .

"The mercenaries," Caldan said, throat thick. "They were supposed to join with the Quivers and save the day, weren't they?"

Quiss nodded grimly.

Instead of arriving to find the Quivers holding their own against the jukari, and joining to turn the tide, they'd found the emperor's forces already devastated. Caldan's fault.

"Quiss. We can't worry about the dead." Caldan could feel a coldness coming into his face, into his eyes. He could hear it in his own words. Thenna had scoured all emotion from him. He'd been thrust into a forge fire and hammered on an anvil. What shape he was now he didn't know, but he resembled a sword more than a horseshoe.

"What's done is done. The deaths are on Gazija's conscience, not yours." *As they are on mine.*

"Leave me," Quiss said flatly.

Caldan moved toward the sorcerer, but Quiss took a step back and held up both his hands.

"I said go," Quiss said hoarsely, voice tight with emotion. He glanced down at the deck, a gesture Caldan took to be an unconscious apology.

"All right. I'll leave you alone to think. But you need the Quivers, and the warlocks, and the Touched. You can't face Kelhak alone. That's what Gazija planned: you all have to face the lich together. If you're separated, you lose, and there's another Shattering. This world will be destroyed."

Quiss's expression was unreadable, and Caldan had no inkling whether his words had swayed him.

"We have to be at this meeting Felice has arranged," Caldan said. "I'm going to use the time before it starts to think about everything that has happened, and I suggest you do the same. Quiss . . . you need to be there. Nothing good will happen if you try to tackle Kelhak alone. I'll return and we can go together."

Caldan turned and strode down the gangplank and along the wharf, his booted feet thudding hard on the wood. Angry steps.

Good, Gazija said tonelessly. *Now, we have work to do.*

"By the ancestors," muttered Caldan harshly, "you'd best keep quiet or I'll—"

What? You'll do what?

Caldan clenched his jaw.

Kelhak can't know I'm still alive. I'll be your card in the hole, your extra move.

Caldan's steps faltered, and he almost stopped before resuming. "You're not alive."

I beg to differ. But never mind. Keep me a secret, and we have a chance. Now, tell me again what happened with Amerdan. Don't leave anything out.

Caldan didn't speak. Quiss had revealed the depths of Gazija's perfidy. The sorcerer had a conscience that didn't allow him to blithely condone the actions of his leaders, and the truth had spilled from his lips with hardly any prompting on Caldan's part. And Caldan found himself wondering whether Quiss was fit to lead in Gazija's absence. Should he be glad he was in charge? Or horrified at the thought that Quiss wouldn't do what was necessary when it came down to it?

When they were at the point of the sword. When life-or-death decisions had to be made. And when the fate of the world hung in the balance.

Perhaps Gazija sensed something of what Caldan was thinking, for he spoke again.

Quiss is a good person.

The implication was clear, both in Gazija's words and the fact he wanted to hide himself from Quiss, and the rest of his followers.

"But good people aren't going to win this battle," Caldan said numbly. "There will be hard decisions, and many will die."

Exactly. I remember . . . the slaughter on my world. We fought as best we could, but . . . everything died. Plants . . . animals . . . children . . . everything.

CHAPTER 48

Caldan sat alone on the bank of the river, a fair distance from the docks outside Riversedge. He was under no illusion he'd have any privacy on board the ship with Quiss and the other sorcerers around.

Slowly, carefully, Caldan scratched against the barrier between his mind and one of his new wells. *Scritch, scritch.* The sound was all in his head, for his scraping wasn't audible. But there was something else . . . a discharge so faint he almost missed it. A whiff of sorcerous energy. As if his workings had peeled off a layer of an onion. Except this layer was so thin, it would take a thousand more peels before he made any progress. *That's it*, Gazija said in his head. *Keep going. If you're going to survive this, you'll need all the help you can get.*

He wished he knew how to block Gazija out.

Gazija had been urging him to unblock his new wells since he'd appeared. He obviously had his own reasons, but whatever they were, Caldan didn't know. All he knew was that Gazija was right: he'd need more than the power of his own well if he was to have any hope of getting out of this alive.

Quiss and the others worried Caldan. More than worried him. His only avenue of escape from the warlocks and Touched had been Quiss and his colleagues, and now they were gone to him, too.

You can't let this setback get to you. You can't give in. There's always a way out of any situation; you just have to find it.

It was simply that the only solution he'd been able to come up with meant embracing the powers he'd been forced to take possession of.

A path he'd already vowed not to pursue.

There was also Miranda to think of. His chest tightened with grief and longing at the mere thought of her. She'd endured so much already. His plan would force her to give up even more: the life she'd made for herself; her friends like Charlotte; her possessions. And he'd feel guilty for asking her to do so, for the rest of his life.

Though the air was warm, he shivered. *I want her to give everything up for me. Ancestors take my guilt.* What was one more burden for him atop the rest?

He clasped his hands, weaving his fingers together. Out here, far from the moored ship, there was no one to detect his scraping and prying. He sent his will back into his mind, along sorcerous currents only those gifted would understand. The psyche was too nebulous, too indefinable for anything else. A well was somewhat more complex and tangible—but still a product of the mind.

And all he had to do was devise a coercive sorcerous crafting to breach the barriers separating him from the wells. For if he had to escape from here, from the emperor, and from Quiss, then he needed to fool them into thinking he was dead and travel far, far away.

His plan was dangerous. But it made sense. He required a body, his trinket ring, a crafting like Quiss had used to bring them to Amerdan, and a destructive sorcerous attack from the warlocks—with so much power thrown at him, it would hide his own sorcery in the tumult. Two parts of his plan required far more sorcerous power than he could currently produce on his own: warding off the warlocks' attack, and the traveling crafting. There was only one solution: he had to unblock and use the wells Amerdan had transferred to him. Doing so would confirm Quiss's worst suspicions about liches and mark him for death. But there was no other way.

If they failed in their attempt to defeat Kelhak, then it wouldn't matter. But on the slim chance they succeeded, he needed all the elements ready. There would be no second chances.

Steeling his resolve, Caldan once again sent his senses inward to the blocked well he'd been worrying at. The barrier felt hard, but at the same time there was a faint shifting current to it, as if it responded to an unseen pattern within itself. He drew back, considering his options. What was the barrier made of? There were no coercive sorcery components that he could discern. But then again, he was still learning, and far from being adept. His scrapings would eventually breach the obstruction, but something about the method didn't sit well with him.

It was crude, he realized. *And when I break through, what then?*

He'd be left with a tiny opening, from which power would trickle. A jagged, turbulent gash. Hardly conducive to crafting, and not what he needed at all. Such a small opening wouldn't serve his purpose. He'd need far more power than even ten such wells could provide, if he were to survive and free himself.

Forget the barrier, Gazija said. *Look to the edge.*

Caldan pulled back again and closed his well. It was easy to determine which of the marks in his mind were the foreign wells and which was his own. He just *knew,* in a way he couldn't explain. If he wanted to open his well and access his power, then it just happened. It was as natural to him as breathing. He'd never given thought to what he did, what the process was.

Thought became action, which in turn led to him accessing his well. It just *unfolded* and was done.

Caldan breathed deeply and sank himself deeper into concentration, pushing himself to summon all the sorcerous sense that he had. He opened his well, then closed it. Did so again. And again. And again. Each time, he focused on what happened, the process of unveiling his well that he'd never before thought about.

Again he went through the process, this time straining to slow it down, to give himself time to actually *see* what was happening. Normally, it happened so fast there was no in-between stage. One moment his well was closed, and the next it was open. But something had to happen; his own barrier had to disappear and reappear somehow.

He moved his awareness close, until all he could see was the mark of his well.

Open. Closed. Open. Closed. Just like the exercises the monks had made him do when they'd found he had a well.

Open. Closed.

They hadn't explained why he'd had to perform the exercise for hours on end, and being young and naive, he hadn't asked.

Open. Closed.

Where did the barrier go?

Open. Closed.

The barrier . . . he'd been thinking of it as one, but what if it wasn't? When his own well was closed, the covering wasn't something foreign like a trapdoor. It was just there. And then it wasn't.

He remembered something one of the monks had told him, a long time ago, when he'd just learned he was a sorcerer. It had been couched as a warning. *No sorcery is perfect, and the power flowing through a well is scalding and caustic, like boiling acid. There have been instances where unwary sorcerers were roasted by their own wells, much like with a failing crafting.*

The exercises he'd performed were training him. Training him to hold on to his power without thinking. Much like teaching a child to hold their pee so they wouldn't wet the bed. Or in this case, fry their mind.

Caldan narrowed his senses to a pinprick, zooming in close to the edge of one of the new wells. This near, there was a sense of *wrongness* to it he hadn't felt before. Darkness made up the edge of the barrier. Blackness so absolute it burned with intensity. It shrieked with abhorrence, seemed to seethe with insult. He shivered, but didn't look away.

Gathering a thread of his power, he created a crafting without thinking, coercive in nature, splitting the thread into four, then eight. It was coming more and more easily to him.

He shaped a probe and plunged it into the darkness, meeting resistance, tightly woven, that pushed him back. The sense of wrongness returned, this time magnified tenfold. It shivered from his mind to his heart, seeming to mortify his soul.

Why did it feel wrong?

He couldn't scratch or pierce it. And when he probed further, it seemed to respond in kind, gaining hardness, almost as if his prying lent it strength. He was missing something. Scraping or boring a hole, as Bells had done with Amerdan, wouldn't be sufficient for him. He needed to find another way.

Caldan grimaced, frustrated.

His own well accepted him; it was his, and his alone.

And then it hit him.

His own well couldn't be accessed by another sorcerer. He was trying to open another sorcerer's well, one that was someone else's. Theirs alone. The barrier was attuned to someone else. It prevented the well's forces from scouring their mind, as his did for him.

He drew back, turning his attention to his own well, his own barrier. It was sorcery of a sort, instinctive and natural, totally unlike crafting. It came from within.

Open. Close.

Caldan let his mind drift, allowing his subconscious to control what happened.

Open. Close. Open. Close.

He moved to one of the other wells, and, as subtly as he could, directed his thoughts around it—as he had so many years ago with the monks' tutelage.

Open. Close.

Barriers, resistance, had to remain. A sorcerer's mind couldn't allow unfettered power to escape.

Open. Close.

His own barrier covered the well.

Open. Close.

The wrongness he felt had to be another sorcerer's barrier. A binding that remained, even after the well had been torn from the sorcerer.

Open. Close.

Caldan molded his edges over the intense darkness. If he'd had to guess, he'd say it was the thoughts of the sorcerer. Or at least part of their consciousness. Holding on to their power, restraining it; because to let go would be to sear their mind to nothing.

Even lacking consciousness, their final essence clung to a primal desire. The well needed to be contained. But if he created his own barrier, would the previous one dissolve? How could he make it relinquish its grasp?

Open. Close.

Stretching himself further, Caldan split more strings from his well: two, then four. He deftly created hooks of shimmering sorcery, runes and patterns coalescing with light. He hardened his own covering, stretching it to match with the edge of the well.

Open. Close. Open. Close.

The old barrier *pushed* against his, and Caldan sucked in a sharp breath and held it. It was almost as if the barrier had tested his own.

Open. Close.

Another push, this one harder, sharper.

Warmth came from the well, slowly at first, then hotter.

Caldan drew more power and strengthened his barrier, then laughed out loud. He was still going about this the wrong way. Coercive sorcery would be a crutch. He couldn't hold on to this many strings for long, and he would certainly never be able to control more than one of these wells if he went about it this way.

He backed off, settling his mind, again letting himself drift. He mirrored his own well's barrier and placed it over the strange well.

Open. Close.

A hot tearing. Caldan ignored it, but a tear trickled down his face. The last thoughts of a sorcerer. That's what the barriers were. And he was dismantling them, showing the fragment of essence that there was another barrier now. One that could also contain the well.

And that the splinter of consciousness, the *wrongness* Caldan felt, could let go.

And, all of a sudden, it did.

Caldan's barrier fused with the edge of the well. The darkness dissolved, burning away, flinching from his mind's touch. His barrier settled into place.

Tendrils of blackness flittered this way and that, breaking into smaller pieces, dissolving, fading into oblivion. He was watching the final thoughts of a sorcerer disappear forever. Anguish racked him, deep inside his heart and mind.

More tears fell down his face.

"I'm sorry," Caldan said, knowing it was futile, that the sorcerer couldn't hear him.

He wiped his burning eyes with his fingers, then his wet fingers on his pants. It took him a few minutes before he could send his sight back inside. Caldan's thoughts immediately went to his well, and with an effort, he wrenched them aside. He directed them to the other well.

It sat there, looking and feeling similar to his own. The *wrongness* had vanished, though a barrier still remained.

His barrier. His to control.

Tentatively, Caldan reached out and opened the well.

Power flooded him. Pure and scorching. Corrosive and chaotic. A burning that would char worldly materials to ashes. Energy, power, radiant and magnificent. He held it, marveling in its feel.

Excellent, Gazija said, his voice tinged with pleasure.

It was Caldan's to control. And the well itself . . . smooth edged and wide. A gaping chasm compared to Amerdan's jagged boreholes.

It was done. He'd figured out a way to make the wells his own, as if they were born to him.

Hastily, he erected a concealment, disguising his second well until it vanished from his sorcerous sight.

Caldan opened his eyes and looked out across the river.

Boats sailed and rowed. Sailors called across the water to one another. The sun shone. Birds flew on the breeze. The day was no different from any other. Caldan smothered the urge to laugh hysterically.

He'd damned himself further in Quiss's eyes. First, when Amerdan had forced him to take on the wells, and now because he'd found a way to unlock their power. Was he so different from Kelhak, or whatever it was that inhabited his body? Had it made similar choices? Ones that seemed right at the time, the only way out of certain situations, to eventually have its humanity stripped from it, perhaps scourged clean by the vitriol of using so many wells?

A fish jumped from the water and splashed back down, startling him.

Just standing from his spot took all the will he had, strength, courage.

Miranda.

She was his anchor. He clung to her name like a shipwrecked sailor to a broken spar, murmured it like a benediction.

Something had changed inside Caldan, something greater than adding another well. And he didn't know what.

CHAPTER 49

With Quiss at his side, Caldan trudged back into Riversedge. Gazija had told Caldan that Vasile would pose a risk of finding out about him, just through noticing inconsistencies in what Caldan said and did. And from then it would take just one closed question for Vasile to know if Caldan was lying.

The prospect of another meeting with the man who'd all but said he'd ordered Caldan's parents to be killed filled him with dread and fury, but he kept a tight rein on his emotions. He had to focus on the present. Revenge, if that's what he wanted, could wait until Kelhak was dealt with.

Quiss was silent, refusing to speak when Caldan spoke or raised a question. Eventually, Caldan kept quiet himself. Often the sorcerer lagged behind, as if hesitant to arrive at the meeting with Felice and the emperor, and Caldan had to frequently stop and wait for him to catch up.

On one such stop, a cold wind whipped at Caldan's clothes, and he shivered, only partially from the chill air. In the east, clear sky gave way to dull gray. He scanned the horizon with careful eyes, searching for any sign the clouds were unnatural, but there was nothing.

It had been quiet, far too quiet recently.

Kelhak is up to something, Gazija said.

The ensouled construct was in a satchel Caldan had slung over his shoulder. Gazija had insisted on accompanying him.

Caldan grunted. "We're all up to something." This close to the emperor's mansion the streets were strangely deserted, and Caldan had no fear he'd be overheard. He reached across to adjust the sling that cradled his maimed hand. It still throbbed, but not as much as before, and the swelling had mostly subsided.

He should be striking again, continued Gazija.

"I, for one, am glad he isn't. You should be, too. It gives us time." Caldan glanced back at Quiss, who was slowly approaching.

It gives him more time, too.

"You have no idea what he wants, do you?"

His goal here doesn't seem to match what he did on my world. It's strange . . . He's changed . . . somehow.

That didn't sound good at all. "Kelhak's—the lich's—goals are different? So it might not want to destroy everything?"

Whatever it wants, you can count on it not being a good thing for you, or anyone else. Which is where Amerdan's trinket comes in. Quiss needs to find a weakness to exploit.

And the same weakness would apply to Caldan, with his numerous wells.

You are fearful of this, correct? You needn't be.

Caldan forced himself to scoff. "I'm not. Why would I be? It's just something that has occurred to me. The trinket is the key. What I don't understand is why *you're* not involved with dissecting it to reveal its workings."

I told you, no one can know I'm still alive. We can't risk anyone else knowing, not even Quiss. The more people know, the more likely it is Kelhak will be able to counter any plans we make. The element of surprise may be all we have left. Quiss and Mazoet can handle this task. They're actually better at it than I am. Surprise you, does it? Leaders don't have to be the best at everything. I'm confident they'll find something we can use.

"I hope so. No, that's not right. They *have* to."

Indeed.

"Shouldn't I be helping them? Why did you choose me? You could have revealed yourself to one of your people. They would have been glad to help you."

Because, Caldan, Quiss will not be able to do what's required to get us through this. It's not a weakness. Perhaps in another time it would be a strength. But not now.

Caldan wished he could see Gazija, to judge his expression. But even if the sorcerer were standing before him, his face would be a blank mask of crafted metal. Gazija knew about his multiple wells. He sought to use Caldan, where Quiss would seek to limit him and then kill him after Kelhak had been dealt with. Perhaps Gazija would kill him after, also.

Caldan realized he would be a second card up their sleeve. A second extra move.

He almost laughed aloud at the thought. It was insane. Gazija pitched himself and Caldan against Kelhak and hoped they would suffice.

Many would kill to gain access to the power you have, Caldan. You should rejoice in it.

"I know. But I'm not one of them. I'd prefer to be normal again." But that wasn't going to happen. And what really surprised him was that he wasn't even sure if he believed what he'd just said. His life would be simpler, but he was pretty sure he didn't *want* a simple life. He had the potential to do great things, to be someone remarkable . . . It was tempting, but . . .

Maybe a life not so dangerous, he thought ruefully, *but one where I can learn and grow. Where I can build my automatons and help people. Where I can be with Miranda.*

Except Gazija and Quiss wouldn't allow Caldan to live. It was too dangerous. *He* was too dangerous. This was his fate, and however much he wriggled and squirmed, like a worm on a hook, he couldn't escape it. Or so they thought.

But he could try. And try he would.

Massive iron gates appeared ahead—the emperor's compound. Caldan strode up and walked right through with barely a nod to the Quivers guarding the opening. A servant directed them along the path and into the mansion. At the doors leading to the audience chamber, Felice was waiting. Her hair was tied in an intricate braid, and her pants and shirt were dark red. She was staring at Caldan, and he gave her a short nod, which she returned before reaching up to straighten his collar.

"The others are inside. I was beginning to think you weren't coming. The warlocks and Protectors don't know what to make of you now," she said, brushing imaginary dust from his shirt. "But the emperor will know. He always knows."

Quiss watched them both. He glanced around at the guards along the hallway. "I'll wait and see what the emperor has to say."

"I'm at your disposal," Caldan said to Felice. "I'll do what's right."

Felice shook her head and let out a soft sigh. "No. We don't need you to do what's right. We need to get the job done. Whatever that entails." There was a calculated pause. "Do you understand?"

Quiss snorted and shook his head. "That's what Gazija would say," he muttered.

"It's as Rujandis wrote," Caldan said, "in *The Pillars of Society*: 'The meek must fall before the strong, for the needs of empire are greater than the needs of the individual.'" *Although the emperor obviously doesn't think so. He uses the empire to serve his own needs.*

But Felice agreed, or at least that's what she said. "Just so. We are falling toward an abyss, Caldan. One that would swallow us all. Everyone must play their part, but some can achieve more than others. Some people will be key. I believe you are one of them." She smiled thinly. "But I have been wrong before."

For a moment, Caldan thought about protesting. Who was he to be involved in such a high-stakes game as this? Except it wasn't a game.

Whether he liked it or not, Amerdan had thrust upon him the ability to do more than he ever thought possible, and he was now dealt in. Caldan drew himself up, squaring his shoulders. "I'll do my best. The Indryallans must be stopped, and Kelhak has to be defeated."

"Good," Felice said. "Then I think we're ready. And I think you should know: Thenna was incapacitated when you were, and I took the opportunity to take the trinkets from her. The bone rings."

Caldan scowled at her. "One was mine. You shouldn't—"

"It was the *emperor's*. And now I have them both, I'll decide what to do with them. You lied to him. I had to intervene on your behalf. You're lucky you're still alive."

He kept quiet, anger building inside. The ring had been one of his few links to his family, and presented an immense danger if used indiscriminately. And now it was gone.

Felice gestured for the Quivers to open the doors.

Metal hinges creaked, a sound Caldan decided was much like the winding of a massive iron trap.

They strode into the audience chamber, and this time the sides were empty. There was no crowd, no functionaries or hangers-on. No nobles come to bask in the emperor's presence.

Only the emperor, sitting on a throne-like chair atop the semicircular dais.

Gone was his exquisite smith-crafted armor. He was clothed in close-fitting pants and a red coat with gold embroidery at the collar and sleeves. His straight platinum hair hung over his shoulders, and his violet eyes stared intensely at them as they approached.

A group of people congregated off to the side, next to a large brazier. It was knee-high and a few yards across, and heavy enough it must have taken a few burly men to move it here. Heaped glowing coals gave everything an orange cast as the air above it rippled with heat.

It was Master Mold who Caldan recognized first. He looked older somehow, as if his face had gained more creases. A middle-aged warlock with a short, gray-speckled beard stood off to the side. Caldan assumed he was here representing the warlocks. But if so, where was

Thenna? Lady Porhilde sat demurely on a stool, skirts arranged around her so they didn't touch the floor. Vasile also stood there, looking strangely nervous, shifting his weight tentatively from foot to foot. Selbourne was also present, his eyes darting around. There was also a stranger: a tall man with brown hair cropped close to his skull. He wore a ceremonial uniform adorned with badges and marks of honor, though it was wrinkled and stained. Someone high ranking in the Quivers, then. His pale blue eyes took in everyone, devoid of emotion. A veteran, perhaps the commander of the Quivers that had arrived at Riversedge.

This is going to be interesting, Gazija said.

Caldan ignored him, deciding instead to just observe as much as possible.

As Caldan approached the warmth of the brazier, their reactions were as he'd expected: Porhilde, who was facing him, scarcely gave him heed; Selbourne gave him a brief smile, in the manner of men who'd fought together, knowing and brittle at the same time; but it was Mold who drew Caldan's attention. The Protector's mouth drew into a thin line, and his jaw worked, as if he chewed nails. He looked not so much at Caldan as at the trinket sword hanging by his side. Mold wanted it back, but Caldan wasn't of a mind to give it to him. The trinket would only be used against Caldan in the end, of this he was certain. He briefly wondered if the trinket could stop him using all his wells, before looking back at the master. Mold's glowering made him slightly uncomfortable, but that was all, and Caldan knew he'd come a long way from the person he was when he'd first met Mold. Joachim, Devenish, Kristof, and Thenna had seen to that. He put his hand on the hilt and smiled at Mold.

When the master scowled, Caldan smiled a bit broader—of all the people here, Mold was the one he had the least concern about.

What did concern him was that his skin was beginning to crawl. The emperor might not have been covered in craftings, but he had to be wearing a great number of trinkets—no doubt concealed under his clothes. Caldan sensed the potency of the emperor's wells and swallowed nervously, checking his own concealment yet again.

They stopped ten paces from the emperor, and Felice dropped to one knee. Caldan and Quiss copied her, and they waited.

And waited.

Felice fidgeted, touching an earring, then jerking her hand back down when she realized what she'd done. But she wasn't the one under scrutiny. Caldan was. A featherlight touch passed over his well, disappearing, then returning moments later. He stiffened when it brushed across his hidden wells.

The emperor, Zerach-Sangur, sighed deeply, then cloth rustled as he rose to his feet.

"You may stand," he said, voice smooth and fluid.

Caldan did as he was bidden, as did Felice.

"Excuse me, Your Majesty," Felice said. "But where is Thenna?"

"The warlock Thenna," said the emperor, "is dead. A terrible accident."

Caldan saw Felice swallow, and he looked up to meet the emperor's violet eyes. He had killed her, perhaps even absorbed her well. *Kelhak has him worried, and he's walking a knife's edge. Too many, and he'll slowly go mad like Kelhak. Still—I do not mourn for Thenna.*

The emperor gestured to the bearded warlock. "This is Bernhard, the new leader of the warlocks."

Bernhard inclined his head in Caldan's direction. "I've heard much about you, young man. And seen what you are capable of. Be warned, though. I'm not Thenna."

Caldan ignored Bernhard and met the emperor's gaze. Inside, he seethed just from being near the man.

"Master Mold here has something to say to you, young Caldan," Zerach-Sangur said. "I'll let him have his moment. Then we can all talk."

The emperor was playing with him, Caldan realized. He was probably playing with them all. It seemed . . . childish, somehow. *Don't we have better things to do than play these little games for your amusement?*

The scary answer was simply: *No.*

He turned to regard Mold, whose well tugged at the edge of his awareness. It was open, and he was drawing from it. Something inside Caldan rose: the animal side that sensed a threat.

"Mold," Caldan said. "Don't do something stupid."

The Protector shot Caldan a venom-filled look.

Caldan had betrayed the Protectors and then killed some of them when escaping from Thenna.

But that was *Mold's* impression of events. They were complicit in abetting the warlocks in keeping the people subject to their whims. And Mold himself had allowed Thenna to torture him.

So think what you think. I don't care.

"This man should be imprisoned," Mold said. "He's killed Protectors and warlocks, using forbidden sorcery. He must be questioned and punished."

"Executed, you mean," Caldan said.

Mold glared at him. "If that's what it takes."

"There is a great danger to us all," Felice said. "And we must put aside our differences to combat it. If we don't, we could all perish."

Mold snorted. "The warlocks will be enough to deal with the Indryallans. Devenish showed we were a match for their sorcery, as did His Majesty." He gestured at Quiss. "And these others as well. We don't need them."

This man is blind, Gazija remarked.

Caldan couldn't respond out loud, but that didn't stop him from thinking: *They all are.*

"I disagree, as does the emperor," Felice said to Mold. "May he live forever," she added, loud enough for everyone to hear.

Mold's mouth opened in surprise. "What is this? Have you all gone mad? This is what I've been fighting against my whole life! What the Protectors have been doing for centuries!"

Porhilde cleared her throat. "You forget yourself, Mold. Be careful who you call mad," she said, with a glance at the emperor, who looked amused.

Mold blanched.

"What Lady Felicienne says is true," continued Porhilde. "The warlocks will be . . . insufficient. The sorcery of these others, led by Luphildern Quiss, must be harnessed if we are to have a chance against the Indryallans."

Mold recovered quickly from his gaffe and now raked both Porhilde and Felice with an icy stare. He seemed to have trouble speaking for a few moments. "I'll work with them, then," he spluttered. "But not with Caldan. He's also stolen a trinket from us." Mold's hands clenched into fists. An instant later, his shield surrounded him.

This isn't going to end well, Caldan thought. He took a step toward Mold. Caldan knew he could defend himself against whatever sorcery the Protector threw at him, but the people around him wouldn't be able to, apart from Quiss and the emperor.

Caldan took another step toward Mold and drew the trinket sword.

The emperor held up a hand, stopping any reaction to Caldan's daring. "Do not intervene," he said to the others. He was smiling now, amused by the confrontation. He gestured at Mold to continue.

"Caldan," the master said, "that trinket belongs to the Protectors."

"It was used to subdue me so I could be tortured. By Thenna."

"Be that as it may . . . it belongs to us."

They think it can stop Kelhak. Can it? Caldan didn't know. But if they tried and were wrong, it would be disastrous. Mold had to know what Thenna had done to him—and he'd left the sword for another Protector in order to keep Caldan powerless. Mold was no ally; he'd decided Caldan knew too much, and that he had to be stopped. Caldan's transgressions of breaking into the library and using destructive sorcery had shown he was a rogue. Mold wanted to kill him, like an injured dog to be put down.

It was funny; Caldan didn't feel like he was doing the wrong thing. To him, the warlocks and Protectors were on the wrong side. *Perspective*, he realized, *is everything.*

This sword contained the well and essence of a sorcerer. It wouldn't be powerful enough to stop Kelhak. If it was an essential part of their plan to stop the God-Emperor, that would lead to their deaths.

"I want Kelhak dead," Caldan said. "As do you all. But I also want to do more than just survive. You're mistaken if you think this sword will help you. Kelhak is more powerful than you know."

"Then give it to me," Mold said. "It's no use to you; you can't even activate it."

Mold was right. There was a trick to activating the trinket Caldan hadn't been able to work out. Yet. But if he was correct, and it would be useless against Kelhak, then it would also be useless against him now.

Caldan stepped toward Mold. "Very well," he said. He reversed the blade so it rested against his forearm, the hilt toward Mold.

As I said, Gazija remarked, *this is interesting.*

Mold frowned, no doubt suspecting a trick. He looked to the emperor for permission.

Zerach-Sangur observed them both with a smile on his face, looking to be greatly enjoying himself. He gave both Mold and Caldan a calculating look, then nodded.

Mold's hand reached for the sword. It closed around the hilt, and Caldan let him take it.

Caldan opened his well and linked to his shield crafting. A multicolored haze surrounded him, and Mold took a few steps backward, still looking askance at Caldan.

Caldan drew as much power as he could to reinforce the shield, and to make the flow from his well a raging torrent. His arm hair stood on end. The very air seemed to hum, and the familiar stench of sorcery filled his nostrils: hot metal and lemons.

We'll see what the sword can do.

And his well slammed shut—the torrent ceasing in an instant— his shield winking out of existence. Caldan's mind recoiled, and he staggered, shivering violently. This time, he'd known what was happening, so he didn't fall, but nausea rose as his stomach roiled.

He looked up and saw sadness on Mold's face. Out of the corner of his eye, he could see the emperor's violet eyes taking in what was happening.

Sucking in air, Caldan forced himself to straighten.

"Stop, all of you!" said Felice.

"This is none of your concern," hissed Mold.

Caldan uttered a weak laugh. Mold *was* blind. He must be shown the truth: both that the plan to use the sword on Kelhak would fail, and that Caldan wouldn't . . . *couldn't* be chained anymore.

He broke his gaze from Mold's, and at the same time, he opened another of his wells. His shield surrounded him once again.

Mold gasped and staggered back a step; then a look of determination came across his face. And Caldan's second well closed. Not slammed: closed slowly, as if the ability of the sword were stretched.

Caldan opened a third well, and a fourth. Splitting out strings, he linked to his shield. The power flowing through him was immense.

"I . . . I can't," Mold groaned.

Abruptly, the blockages preventing Caldan from accessing his wells disappeared.

Mold shook his head, his jaw set. "It's . . . it isn't possible."

"It is," Caldan said. "How did I resist the trinket? No—don't answer that. Answer this instead: If I can do it, won't Kelhak be able to?" Caldan shook his head. "Your plan is flawed, if it's to use the sword on Kelhak. It won't work.

"Also," he said, coming closer to Mold, whispering so only the Protector could hear, "if you try to harm me again, I will *destroy* you."

Mold frowned, and Caldan could feel the Protector's sorcerous senses brush across his mind. He dropped his concealment of his wells.

With a gasp, blood drained from Mold's face. "You have more than one well. A lot more."

"Yes," Caldan said. "As does Kelhak."

"How did we not sense this before?" asked Mold.

Careful, warned Gazija. *Don't give too much away. They'll be looking for any weakness.*

"I concealed them," Caldan said simply. "If you knew I had multiple wells, who knows what you might have done?" He looked Mold in the eye. "Probably tried to kill me, as Kristof and Thenna tried to, and failed."

Felice clapped her hands, drawing their attention to her. "So, Mold, the plan you came up with isn't going to work. That's not good.

We need to know we have a chance at succeeding before attempting anything with Kelhak."

The emperor cleared his throat, and all eyes turned toward him.

"I'll ask again," the emperor said, words resonating around the room. "Tell me, Caldan, young warlock, Touched: What do you desire?"

Those were the exact same words he'd used before, Caldan recalled. *Either he didn't believe me then, or he thinks something has changed.*

"I . . ." He glanced at Felice. "We know what Kelhak really is: a lich. He left his humanity behind long ago. Now he exists only to absorb other sorcerers to increase his power and to keep him alive. What I want is to stop him. Kill, capture, whatever is necessary."

Beside Caldan, Felice was nodding.

The emperor's face was expressionless. He cleared his throat. "Anyone with multiple wells is a lich, then? And has to be . . . killed or captured?"

Caldan shook his head. *Careful.* "No, Your Majesty. Kelhak is out of control. Perhaps his power drove him to madness. But having more than one well doesn't mean you're a monster." He hesitated before adding, "You're living proof of that."

Mold gasped, while Porhilde glared at Caldan as if he'd turned into a snake.

The emperor nodded. His eyes went strangely unfocused for a moment before fixing Caldan with a piercing intensity. "As are you."

Caldan froze for an instant. "I don't know how it happened," he admitted. "The process, I mean. There was a trinket, and—"

"Where is it now?" the emperor said.

Felice spoke for the first time. "With Luphildern Quiss here. They're attempting to fathom how it works in order to combat Kelhak."

Behind her words was a truth Caldan knew the emperor wouldn't want to hear: If someone could destroy Kelhak, or neutralize his power, then they could do the same to him. And not only that, but there was another trinket that could transfer multiple wells to a sorcerer— which was the key to much of the emperor's power and influence.

Suddenly, Caldan bent his knee and knelt on the floor again. *Truth,* he thought. *Do not speak a lie.*

"I pledge myself to defeating Kelhak. I don't know why I was gifted these wells, but I will use them as best as I'm able to defeat the Indryallans and their leader."

He held his breath, waiting for a response.

The emperor remained quiet for a few moments, then spoke. "You have killed and injured a number of warlocks and Protectors."

Caldan could feel the ache of the wounds inflicted by Thenna. Though they were healing rapidly, the ghost of their pain still lingered. "I did. But it was no more than they tried to do to me. They tortured me," he said through clenched teeth. "Thenna especially. She took delight in it. She wanted revenge because I killed Devenish, whom she loved. But more than that, she wanted multiple wells for herself. For the mere power's sake."

"And you don't?"

Caldan met the emperor's eye. "No. I don't."

The emperor paused, then smiled. "Good. We need more sorcerers like you, Caldan." He turned to Felice. "Lady Felicienne, you must take Caldan under your wing. He is to be given access to all the warlocks' knowledge, and whatever training he requires. This trinket Quiss has must be brought to me, tonight. I will be able to divine its working better than any other."

"No," said Quiss. He drew himself up straight, squaring his shoulders.

Silence followed his denial. The emperor sneered at Quiss, and Caldan sensed him open a dozen wells. Raw power infused the emperor; so much coursed through him that Caldan had to withdraw his senses for fear of becoming engulfed himself.

"Say that again," the emperor said, voice dripping with menace.

Though he wasn't the object of the emperor's displeasure, Caldan nevertheless felt insignificant in the face of such a display.

Quiss remained still, one hand rubbing his chin. Bernhard stepped forward, only to stop at a sharp gesture from the emperor.

"As you wish," Quiss said eventually.

The emperor returned his gaze to Caldan, though he kept his wells open. "I need to know you'll obey me, as your emperor. After all, you lied to me about the bone trinket . . . We cannot afford to be faint-hearted in these times."

"I will," Caldan said. "You can rely on me."

"That remains to be seen. Tell me, then. Where is your bone ring now? And Devenish's?"

Caldan tensed, avoiding looking at Felice. "Thenna took them from me."

Irritation flashed across the emperor's face, gone in an instant. "They were not with her."

"Perhaps another warlock has them?" Caldan said.

"Perhaps. It is of no matter."

A lie, as Caldan knew.

The emperor raised his voice, his regal face surveying them all. "All of you, the time has come to reveal what I know of Kelhak's plan."

Felice frowned, and Caldan realized this was new to her.

"For too long," the emperor said, "we have allowed ourselves to be distracted. The Indryallans, the jukari, the sorcerous strikes against us, which I defeated—"

Caldan lowered his gaze.

"—allowing Kelhak time to reach his true goal, which lies beneath Anasoma. Ages ago, there were rumors, hints, but . . . I paid them no heed. Now my spies have revealed what I dared not dream was true. Ancient places still survive, mostly in ruins, crumbling with age. But a few endure, protected from the elements. Hidden. Sealed. And Kelhak has found one. His aim all along, it seems. I thought such a place lost forever, but now I know there is a laboratory underneath Anasoma. A workshop, of sorts. Where creatures were made. Evil things full of malice and spite."

Jukari and vormag, realized Caldan. *He's talking about their creation.*

"Kelhak doesn't want to destroy us," continued the emperor. "He wants to *enslave* us. With knowledge of these sorcerous workings, he'll be able to create not only more jukari and vormag, but other beasts. Foul and abominable. He must be stopped. And I fear if we wait here until we think we are ready, we'll be too late. Too late . . . Our survival swings in the balance."

The emperor's voice was hypnotic, and Caldan and those around him hung on every word.

"If we do not strike now, all will be lost."

Caldan calculated the import of the emperor's words. But he also saw the emperor himself: a desperate sorcerer, afraid for his life. He wouldn't put himself, and them, in danger unless he thought there was no other choice.

Which is why we've been sitting in Riversedge all this time. The emperor is strong when it comes to the rhetoric, but much weaker when it comes to the execution.

No one spoke, as if the emperor had woven sorcery over them all.

"Tomorrow, we set out," the emperor said abruptly. "We will use the mercenary ships to approach Anasoma. Lady Felicienne will arrange to breach the walls"—Caldan thought he heard Felice curse under her breath—"and we will fight off the Indryallans while searching for Kelhak. There can be no more delays. He must be stopped. There is a . . . the lich is making something. It has begun its task. We have to act now, before it's too late."

The emperor sat back in his thronelike chair, as if exhausted from speaking.

Felice stepped forward, her gaze moving from face to face, making sure she met all their eyes before moving on.

"Where is the leader of the Touched?" Caldan asked before she could speak.

"They'll do as they're told," the emperor said, confirming Caldan's fears.

The Touched were nothing more than expendable tools.

"They are under my direct control now," the emperor continued. "As are the warlocks. They have been apprised of the situation and stand ready to defend the empire, as all good citizens would."

Caldan grunted, not caring if his displeasure showed.

The emperor took no notice. "You are all here," he said, "so we can work together. We have lacked focus, and now I will remedy that error. Make no mistake: our lives, and the lives of those we love, are threatened. I will not lie to you. But at the same time, I will not tolerate dissent. If you pursue other agendas instead of focusing on the task at hand, you *will* be replaced. And most likely executed. We cannot afford any weakness. We must all work together under my command to defeat the lich. Are we in agreement? I must hear it from each of you." He looked to Vasile and beckoned him forward. "Magistrate Vasile, you will confirm who is speaking the truth, and who is lying."

Vasile took a few steps forward. He licked his lips, then nodded. "As you wish, Your Majesty."

The emperor turned his gaze to the veteran soldier. "Knight-Marshal Rakim?"

Rakim nodded to the emperor. "This has already taken too long," he said, words clipped and precise. "You have my word."

Everyone's eyes flicked to Vasile, who nodded. Caldan had no idea what was going on. Somehow, the emperor trusted Vasile to determine if someone was lying.

Porhilde spoke next. "I agree as well," she said with a hint of exasperation.

Another nod from Vasile.

"And you, mercenary?" the emperor said. "Selbourne."

The big man stroked a braid of his beard. "Our contract doesn't cover sorcery on such a scale," he said. "We cannot counter sorcerers, unless we have support. The jukari are still a menace, along with the vormag. I thought we'd be mopping them up, searching for any stragglers."

"And you will be," the emperor said. "But I need a group of you, around forty. Hard men. Men who won't fold when the situation becomes dire."

"A strike group?" Selbourne said, and the emperor nodded. "I think I know where this is going. What do you propose as payment?"

Ducats, Caldan guessed. Selbourne wanted to be paid more.

"Crafted armor and weapons for you and your men, and a trinket each, as well. Whoever survives gets to keep them."

Selbourne snorted, though he continued to stroke his beard. "I'll see who's interested," he said eventually.

"And you, sorcerer? Quiss," the emperor said.

Quiss looked at him with hollow eyes. To Caldan, he looked weary and almost broken. The sorcerer, Gazija's second-in-command, sat unmoving, hands clasped tightly in his lap.

Caldan remained silent, his gaze taking in the others in turn.

You must speak before he does, Gazija said suddenly. *He must join with the emperor. Tell him you don't want them all to just survive. There must be more beyond that.*

Without thinking, Caldan spoke. "A wise old man once said to me, 'When facing death, you must not focus on just surviving.'"

Quiss's head jerked up at that, and his eyes bored into Caldan's.

"You must do more than that," Caldan continued.

Quiss's face was drawn, and he stepped forward, almost stumbling. He gave Caldan a blank look. "We're with you. I want to do more than survive."

I knew he'd come through in the end, Gazija said.

But Caldan wasn't worried about Quiss or the others, only about the emperor.

CHAPTER 50

Felice stood on the veranda outside her lavish ground-floor room. Only those at the top knew her real role, and they made sure she was housed in luxury. The rooms chafed her like an ill-fitting dress, and she hadn't worn one of those for years. Squads of Quivers patrolled the manicured grounds around the mansion, which was owned by a wealthy noble. No doubt he thought to curry favor by housing her here. Beyond granite walls, the city spread out, and beyond the walls of the city were the jukari and vormag.

Then there were the Indryallans. She clasped her hands behind her back and walked to the edge of the tessellated veranda.

She glanced to the side, where a Quiver in full armor stood at attention. There were other nobles and officials of the empire here, and they valued their own skin. More than the empire's, Felice supposed. But she didn't. She felt distant; and the longer she stayed here, the worse she felt.

She stretched her back and made her way through curtained doors into her suite.

"You're making me nervous," Izak said from an armchair next to the fire.

"We all should be," Felice replied. "This plan of the emperor's . . . it's hasty. Not at all what I envisioned."

"You sound like you doubt him. I'm glad I'm not going along. Not that I couldn't handle myself."

Felice smirked at him. "But you are coming. I'll need you for protection."

"Eh?" exclaimed Izak. "What do . . . oh, very funny." He sank back down into his chair from which he'd half risen.

"You've done enough, Izak. This mission . . . it's far more dangerous—"

"I can come." Izak stared at her intently. "I can protect you . . . if you want me to."

Felice's chest grew tight. She shook her head and sighed. "You've done all you can. Now you're free to go. Perhaps when this is over . . . If the emperor believes this is our best hope, then I trust him."

But questions needed answering. Like the talon . . . She hadn't stopped thinking about it since it had disappeared. There was a bowl on a side table filled with fruit, along with a short knife. She slipped the knife up her sleeve—she couldn't be too careful these days—and resolved to find a blade easier to carry.

A soft breeze blew over her from the open window, bringing with it a scent of the flowers outside and a . . . mustiness.

It couldn't be . . .

Felice whirled.

The talon stood just inside the doorway. There was no outcry from the exterior guards.

"It's about time you showed up," Izak said. He stood and poured a yellow spirit into a glass. Sipping, he regarded the talon. "What's your poison?"

The creature moved to a position against a wall, deep in shadow. The black oval of its hood moved back and forth, as if examining the room.

"Heriotza-derrota," the talon said. "If you have any."

"Ah . . . no. Sorry." Izak shrugged and downed his drink, then returned to his armchair.

Felice's heart was racing, and she took a deep breath to calm herself. "I won't ask where you've been, or what you've been up to—"

"You've been looking for me. That's not a clever thing to do. I assume you want to pay for another attempt on Kelhak?"

"No," Felice said. "Well, maybe. But I also need to know about the old passages under Anasoma."

There was a long pause. "This is what I feared."

Izak leaped to his feet. "So you know! And you didn't tell us."

Felice was about to tell Izak to shush, but he had a point. "Well," she said to the talon, "do you want to tell us now?"

"I have . . . guarded the old ruins for centuries. I have failed."

Felice's thoughts swirled. "Can you get us there? Can you find Kelhak?"

The talon's hood dipped forward in a nod. "There is only one place for him to go, if he is to gain what he wants."

CALDAN WAITED FOR some time. The gloom pervading the workshop thickened, daylight fading to be replaced by the steady orange glow of the forge. By the door, two Protectors stood silently, as if waiting for him to steal something or do something they could take action against him for. He knew they hated him for the Protectors he'd killed, but the emperor's word was sacrosanct, and as little as they liked it, they obeyed. Mold had been livid when Caldan had appeared at the Protectors', refusing to speak or even listen to him. But he obeyed as well.

The emperor's word forced acquiescence.

The latch lifted and the door opened, admitting a master. She was short and stocky, with forge-scarred hands and arms. Caldan didn't remember seeing her before.

"Master Mold has asked me to deal with you," she said without emotion.

Caldan stirred from his spot by one of the walls. "Good," he said, ignoring that she said "deal with" instead of "help." "I know you have armor and weapons for your Protectors, and I need a piece."

The woman raised her eyebrows. "I can't hand over any crafted pieces. They're the property of the Protectors and owned by whoever made them or paid for them. And I think you'll find the Protectors' asking price far more than you can afford."

He knew they'd try to work around the emperor's command, but he wouldn't have expected less from them. That was fine, though, as he didn't want an actual crafting.

"I think you'd be surprised, but that's neither here nor there. I just need a gauntlet," Caldan said. "An uncrafted piece. No runes, no markings. Blank. I'm sure you have one of those."

The master sniffed. "Maybe. I'll check."

"I'll come with you. I'm looking for something particular." He didn't want her to sift through what they had and bring him only the poor-quality items.

Caldan followed the reluctant master to a storage room and was in turn followed by the two Protectors guarding the door. The space was small, so the guards remained in the corridor outside.

The master moved a few crates and began rummaging through sacks on the floor. She drew out a few items, all rusted and poorly made.

"These are all we have. I can—"

"I'll see what's in these boxes," Caldan said, ignoring her wilting stare. He knew the best items wouldn't be left to molder in sacks on the floor.

A short time later, he found what he wanted in a wooden box: an articulated left-hand gauntlet. He held it up, examining the metal used and the workmanship. He'd struggle to get his useless fingers into the glove, but it would suffice.

"You can't have that one," the master said. "It's a commission for a noble."

"A more important noble, the emperor, says I can have it. Tell Mold . . . tell him I'm sorry, for what it's worth."

Caldan strode out of the room and returned to the forge area. The two guards scurried after him. He didn't appreciate their looming presence, but it didn't really bother him either. Caldan simply focused on crafting the piece—there was no time to consider doing it elsewhere. And while he would have preferred to craft this in private, they wouldn't understand the complexity of it anyway, so he felt safe altering the gauntlet in front of them.

It was a nice piece of armor, Caldan admitted, and must have cost a fair few ducats. Jointed plates and fine mail mesh covered the hand and midway up the forearm. The dark alloy was one the Protectors used only rarely, despite its resistance to corrosion—it was also difficult to craft with. Still, it was light and flexible, and that made it perfect for Caldan's needs.

Caldan placed the armor piece on a bench top. He drew out the brass crafting he'd created to inscribe his wolf construct, which was back in his cabin with Miranda. With this, he should be able to craft the runes in no time. The tricky part would be to bind the gemstones to the metal, but he had an idea for how to do that as well.

Thoughts of Amerdan's trinket and how it worked swirled in his head, along with questions about Mold's trinket sword. Quiss and his sorcerers, and the warlocks, were churning out variations as fast as they could—craftings aimed at stripping wells and containing them, along with blocking them. But peeling layers from Kelhak like an onion would be a long process, and the lich would know what was happening. And if it decided to abandon the body of Kelhak and take another, it would live on. Quiss was confident they'd be able to follow it, but Caldan wasn't so sure.

And neither was Gazija.

Caldan drew out a few pages scrawled with patterns and runes: his schematics for a gauntlet. Ideally, he'd have smith-crafted the metal himself, but he had only a few hours until they'd leave Riversedge. The emperor wanted haste, and that meant cutting some corners.

But it didn't mean Caldan couldn't try a new theory . . . of buffers and cushions and shields. If he was ever completely blocked from his wells, then storing a surge of power might just save him one day.

Smoothing the paper on the bench top, Caldan took a breath and prepared himself. Once more, he opened his well and linked to the brass plate. He pulsed his power through its pathways and patterns. Metal screeched and sparks spattered across wood. The sour scent of lemons filled his nostrils. This time, he was more confident and worked faster, not stopping to check the results with his sorcerous sense.

Some time later, it was done. As with his construct, a fingernail-deep engraving was embedded in the metal of the gauntlet. Every finger, every metal plate, was covered with crafting runes and intricate patterns, swirling and flowing. Nodding with satisfaction, Caldan drew out a pouch and poured pea-sized gemstones—a "gift" from the emperor—across one of his sheets of paper. His brass engraving crafting could cut, but if he was careful, it could also bind. As with Felice's and Izak's daggers, something was required to house the wells. Caldan didn't know yet how trinkets managed it, but at the moment, gemstones would have to do.

Carefully, he held a sapphire against the back of the gauntlet, in the center of a circular rune. A flash of power, and it was done. He attached six more to the gauntlet, until it looked as if it were a costume piece, or something a too-wealthy noble would wear to a martial ceremony.

But it was far from a useless, gaudy thing.

Caldan linked to the gauntlet and coursed his power along the lines of his crafting, scouring the metal, testing, evaluating. Confining, catching, imprisoning—all virtues imbued in the metal and gemstones. On top of those, he'd included a catchment of power—a design based on the buffers of sorcerous shields that had to store sorcery for a limited time. If his wells were ever blocked again, he'd have a card up his sleeve. One more extra move.

It would do.

He sent a command to the gauntlet, and the fingers twitched. Frowning, he fine-tuned his control until one by one the fingers curled and uncurled. Then he sent it scuttling along the bench and back again.

Aware of the Protectors' eyes on him, Caldan donned the gauntlet. He grunted, fiddling with its fingers until his own were inside. Plate metal and silvery mesh encased his ruined hand.

Caldan held it up, gazing upon his latest, hastily crafted creation. Then he curled the fingers of the gauntlet into a fist.

He smiled then, with genuine pleasure, for the first time in days. If he controlled the gauntlet as he did his constructs, his left hand wasn't so useless now. It would take time to master, and would mean he'd constantly be using two strings, but it was worth it.

He was almost whole again.

Almost.

CHAPTER 51

The moon was obscured by clouds, but fire pits of glowing coals and a plethora of lanterns made navigating the tents and equipment easy. Many parts of the encampment were hives of activity, even this late at night. There had been a time, not long ago, when Caldan would have been uneasy walking through an army this large. Especially knowing that warlocks were close by, with their secrets and workings he wouldn't have been able to fathom. But no more.

To the south of Caldan and Miranda lay Riversedge. In front of them was the main military camp of the emperor's forces, spread out, with innumerable campsites missing Quivers, mostly because they were dead.

Miranda stumbled over a tent rope, and Caldan steadied her, his hand catching her elbow. Beside them padded Caldan's wolf construct, and Caldan tapped its side.

"Are you all right in there?" he whispered to Gazija, who was hiding inside the automaton.

I'm rattling around like a die in a cup, snapped Gazija. *The sooner I'm out of here the better. Felice better have made sure Aidan and Vasile will be here. We'll need their help, if you're to escape once this is all over.*

"I told her to bring them, like you asked," Caldan said. "Let's hope she listened."

Gazija snorted but said no more.

"Are you sure this meeting will be safe?" said Miranda.

Caldan shrugged, though she might not catch the movement in the shadowy light. "I trust Felice to do what she thinks is right. And the truth is, they want to use me now. If the warlocks or the emperor wanted me dead, then I would be. Thenna underestimated me before. She had no idea what I was capable of, though . . . neither did I. The warlocks won't make the same mistake a second time."

"Felice has to have a plan," Miranda said as they skirted another group of tents. "Or the beginnings of one. But it's obvious she needs more information, or she wants her own card up her sleeve."

"An extra move . . . just like any good Dominion player. She's right to do all she can. And perhaps we'll be able to take advantage of that. I have a few ideas."

"Then perhaps together we'll be able to think of something. I don't particularly like the emperor's plan of a full-on assault."

Caldan barely held back a snort. "Me either. But strength is what he's used to. It's what's enabled him to cling to power all these years. Ah, this looks like it."

An open tent had been erected close to the warlocks' encampment. Caldan had a fair idea why Felice had chosen this location. She was an astute woman, and careful. She wanted her audience to be cowed before they were gathered. She wanted them to be reminded of what was at stake, and how powerful a foe they faced. And what better way to do that than to hold a meeting in the shadow of the newly created purified land.

Felice had chosen the place where Devenish had made his stand against Kelhak. Where the warlock leader had mistakenly thought his sorcery was superior to the lich's, since he'd been able to weather two strikes—strikes sent all the way from Anasoma.

The place where Caldan had killed Devenish and taken his bone trinket.

Where the other warlocks had run, fleeing from what they faced.

And the location of so many Quivers' deaths.

Inside the shelter, there was a ring of camp stools set in a circle. In the center was a fire pit, in which a few logs burned merrily.

No guards stood around the tent. In fact, now that Caldan thought to look, the nearest Quiver was dozens of paces distant. Felice had made sure they wouldn't be overheard.

Two of the stools were occupied. There was Vasile, along with Aidan, whom Caldan had only recently met. Both looked haggard, faces drawn, as if they hadn't had much sleep. And there was Felice, standing silently at the edge of the covering.

I wonder if she'll be surprised, Gazija said.

Caldan ignored him. He couldn't let himself get distracted. He would need all his wits about him to come out of this meeting, for the reality was, Felice would sell him out if she thought it would save the Mahruse Empire, and the world.

Just as I would do to her, he thought, ashamed he would consider such a horrible thing. He wasn't liking the person he'd become . . . but he'd had no choice in the matter. Hard times made hard men. From now on, no decision would be an easy one, and likely the world hung in the balance.

Caldan took Miranda's hand in his. He gave Felice a final glance before they stepped into the warmth the fire radiated.

"You're late," Felice said.

Aidan and Vasile murmured a greeting.

"We had to discuss some things with a . . . friend, first," Miranda replied.

Felice raised her eyebrows. "I told you not to tell anyone about this meeting. If you can't—"

Miranda held up a hand, and Felice stopped. "We all have something in common, or so I'm told. We want to get through this alive, and escape those who currently have influence over us, who control us. For Caldan and me, that's the emperor." She smiled wryly at Felice. "No offense."

"None taken."

Aidan stood, one hand rubbing his chin. "We're in a similar predicament, Vasile and I. There are chains around us that won't be easily broken. We're here now, but we can't be gone for more than an hour or two, or things will become . . . difficult for us."

"We'll hear you out," Vasile said. "But make it short."

Felice toyed with an earring, pausing as if to choose her next words carefully. "You know the danger we face. Raw power might not carry the day. We need a backup plan with more . . . subtlety."

As I thought, Gazija said. *She'll listen.*

"I agree," Caldan said. "But first, there's something we need to show you, Felice. Or rather, we've been told to show you. We do need to come up with some extra moves, so to speak. We have a few ideas. And we know someone who can help. But you have to promise never to reveal who he is. Do you all agree?"

Vasile nodded, while Aidan gave a gruff affirmative. Felice pursed her lips, then she also nodded. *Which is what she would do no matter what she's decided,* Caldan thought.

Caldan and Miranda exchanged glances. Miranda shrugged. There was nothing left to decide. Indeed, their path had been set as soon as they'd decided to accept Felice's invitation.

He called his wolf and positioned it in front of Miranda. At his command, the side opened, and his—now Gazija's—manlike automaton tumbled out.

Puzzled frowns turned to confused wonder as the figure stood, then walked toward Felice. In the orange light of the fire, its rune-covered body glowed, arcane and otherworldly.

It stopped a few paces in front of Felice.

"This," Miranda said, "is Gazija, Quiss's leader. He's not dead."

Gasps came from Felice, Vasile, and Aidan. Vasile leaned so far forward on his stool, he almost fell off. Felice's expression turned thoughtful, and Caldan knew she was taking this new information on board and calculating possibilities.

"You'll be able to verify it really is Gazija," continued Miranda. "Or so he tells us."

Hello, everyone, Gazija said. And from the looks on Felice's, Aidan's, and Vasile's faces, Caldan knew they'd all heard him this time.

My trial has not broken me. Far from it—I no longer need canes to walk. I can be of great use against Kelhak. And all of you can be of great use to me. Kelhak will have a potent shield that's almost impossible to breach. It wards against not only sorcery, but physical intrusion as well. There might be a way to break through . . . if all else fails. Though it's a foolish plan and may get me killed. Still, if we're desperate . . .

Felice pursed her lips, then slowly nodded. "We're all ears."

CHAPTER 52

Dense mist swathed the river and its banks in a cold blanket of white, draining the morning of color. Dawn's first light didn't do much to alleviate the gloom, but the occasional gust of wind parted the haze enough for the captains to ensure they didn't run aground.

Caldan stood at the prow of the *Loretta*. He hadn't been able to sleep during the night; he'd slipped out of his cabin hours ago and wandered the deck, a cloak wrapped tightly around him to keep out the chill.

Ahead of them, the first vessel in their convoy slowed as it ceased rowing and shipped its oars. It was one of only a few to have oarsmen, which meant it wasn't totally useless on the river. He'd learned Gazija and his people had used sorcery to enable the ships to sail upriver, though on this journey they hadn't needed to, since traveling back down with the current was much easier. Caldan didn't know how they'd done it, but it was something he was interested in learning.

Trailing behind them was a cobbled-together armada of as many ships as they could scavenge from Riversedge. Each was filled to the brim with the emperor's Quivers, along with the warlocks. Decks bristled with spears and swords wielded by armored men and women. Some of the ships even held squads of light cavalry, who would be used to swiftly take control of sections of the city and set up safe areas for the strike force. The emperor was on the ship directly behind the *Loretta*, which was also crowded with warlocks and some of the Touched.

Far ahead, the mist swirled, and Caldan caught a brief glimpse of blue flames atop a wall before it was obscured again.

Anasoma.

That was why the ship ahead had slowed. Caldan peered at its deck, where vague shapes moved, and pulleys and ropes creaked as boats were lowered into the water. One sailor lashed the wheel into position before clambering over the side and down a rope ladder. She jumped sprightly into a boat and it pushed off, making for the *Loretta*.

It took only a few trips, since it was manned with a skeleton crew, before the ship ahead was deserted. *The Small Fist* was painted in red across the stern. And this would be her last voyage.

"Are you ready, Caldan?" Quiss said from behind him.

Caldan's shoulders tightened, and he loosened them while pretending to shrug. "No. But then, none of us are. We'll do what we can, and hope it's enough."

"Don't lose sight of our goal. Kelhak must be stopped. Everything else is chaff."

"What else is there? Quiss, if something happens . . . look after Miranda for me, please." More misdirection. But Caldan hoped little hints here and there would form a picture in Quiss's mind.

"She can look after herself," the sorcerer said. "So I wouldn't worry. But I'll do what I can."

Caldan turned to face him and nodded. "Thank you."

"I've got to organize my people. Make sure you join your group and stay with them." Quiss left Caldan at the gunwale.

Caldan unclenched his good fist beneath his cloak and stretched aching fingers. Selbourne had given him a sword to use, and it hung heavy from his hip. He wore his newly crafted gauntlet on his shattered hand. It still ached deep inside, but the skin was slightly numb to his touch. Standing by his side was his wolf automaton. He'd hammered out the dents and repaired its craftings, but it still looked battered. Earlier, belowdecks, he'd opened it up and Gazija had secreted himself inside once more. The wolf gave Gazija extra mobility and protection, and Caldan wouldn't have to carry him around like Amerdan had his doll. And if needed, Gazija could control the wolf himself.

A sailor came up to Caldan carrying a bowl of water. She placed it on the deck in front of the wolf. "There you go," she said. "Good dog."

"Ah, sorry," Caldan said. "It doesn't drink."

"It's alive, isn't it?"

"No, not really."

The sailor picked up the bowl, frowning. "What good is it, then?"

Caldan shrugged, and the woman turned and left, shaking her head.

He looked up to catch a glimpse of Miranda scurrying across some rigging. She and three other sailors shimmied along a crosspiece and began hauling up one of the sails. Once it was furled, they lashed the canvas into place. It seemed she hadn't lost her nautical skills, and her readoption into the crew had gone without a hitch.

Mercenaries started crowding onto the deck, boots thumping along narrow corridors and up stairs. They gathered in smaller clumps, checking and rechecking armor, shields, and weapons, keeping busy in an attempt not to think about what was coming.

Selbourne was among his band, his greatsword resting on one shoulder as he made his way among them, clapping backs and shoulders and speaking words of encouragement. The mercenary captain caught Caldan's eye and gave him a nod.

Felice stood to the side, taking in everything. Quiss and a few of his sorcerers concentrated on their sorcery. He'd abandoned his own ship to be on this one with the rest of them at the forefront. At the wheel, Captain Charlotte guided the *Loretta*. She'd spared the occasional glance for Caldan and waved once, but either she'd been too busy to see him or she was avoiding contact, because she had plenty of time for hushed conversations with Selbourne. Maybe she didn't approve of his relationship with Miranda. She'd seen them together, after all.

A tortured groan came from behind Caldan, from the lead ship, which now moved under a different means: sorcery. Quiss and his people were propelling the vessel at impossible speed toward the iron portcullis that blocked the river. Water churned in the ship's wake, and huge waves crashed into the riverbanks as it hurtled past.

By now, the fog had thinned, and it was almost possible to discern the walls of Anasoma. A blue glow emanated from ahead, casting the rapidly dissipating mist in a garish light—the Indryallan sorcery, which prevented people scaling the walls to get in or out, though the main defense was still the walls themselves.

Caldan turned from the sight and made his way to Selbourne, who was speaking with a stocky black-haired woman carrying two hatchets in belt loops. She wore light leather armor covered with crafted metal scales, and a crafted crossbow on her back. Two quivers bursting with quarrels hung from her belt.

" . . . and keep the others focused," Selbourne was saying to her. "They must not break from the path laid out."

"I hate to split us up like this—"

"I know. Hit hard, then get out. Stir the ants' nest, then run. We'll all meet at the designated points and regroup. We'll be constantly moving, so the Indryallans shouldn't have time to gather and catch us."

The woman nodded jerkily and then jutted her chin out at Caldan. "You have a visitor."

Selbourne and the woman clasped hands; then she left him, with a backward glance at Caldan.

The mercenary captain tugged at his beard and looked Caldan over. "Get rid of the cloak, it'll slow you down and probably tangle you up. Only an idiot wears a cloak when they're fighting."

Caldan undid the clasp and bundled the cloak up, placing it in an out-of-the-way spot. "Selbourne," he said, approaching, "I take it you have multiple strike groups heading to different parts of Anasoma. But where will you be?"

"With you and Quiss, of course. Sorcery can't solve every problem, and you'll need to conserve your power for . . . later on. We'll try to take care of normal resistance, and with any luck, there won't be much. At least until we find Kelhak."

Shouts echoed across the river as guards on the walls sighted the ship speeding toward them. Within moments, horns resonated through the air, sounding the alarm.

"And so it begins," Selbourne said without emotion. "Stay close. I hope whatever plan you and Quiss have works."

So do I, thought Caldan. But he wasn't so sure. The Protectors' sword hadn't been able to contain his wells—the wells he had now—and although Quiss and his people were smith-crafting similar items as fast as they could, how many wells did the lich have? A hundred? Two hundred? More? There was no way of knowing; and if they fell short, it was likely they wouldn't last long.

"She's about to hit!" exclaimed a sailor from behind them, and Caldan looked up toward the walls of Anasoma.

The Small Fist aimed directly at the massive portcullis. Its prow hit with a thunderous crash. Timber splintered and tortured metal groaned, but the barrier held.

Caldan extended his sorcerous senses as he felt a surge of power around him. An almost invisible cord coiled out and struck *The Small Fist*, sliding over its wooden hull.

A *conduit*, realized Caldan. What came next would be pure destructive sorcery.

Energy surged along the cord, sun-bright pulses that splashed over *The Small Fist*. Immediately, the deck erupted in orange flames, tongues of fire licking the sails and charring their edges. Soon they too were alight, burning furiously, waves of heat dispersing the faint mist that remained. Shouts of alarm came from atop the wall.

Behind Caldan, Felice hissed with displeasure.

"It's not quick enough," she said. "Get it done, Quiss. We need to be inside and scattering."

The sorcerer inclined his head toward her. Caldan felt another surge as more incandescent pulses raced along the conduit. These struck directly at the hull. A jagged hole opened in the seasoned timbers as power punctured it with a shattering of splintered wood. Sorcery streamed through the opening.

Quiss's sorcery broke the crates of alchemical ingredients Felice had sourced, and their contents mixed with fervor, the heat of sorcery hastening the reaction.

The Small Fist exploded in a ball of churning fire.

Chunks of timber flew in all directions. Both masts lifted, as if pulled up on a rope, then toppled. Flames rose into the sky, and black smoke plumed upward on a swell of incandescent heat. A wave of pressure rushed up the river toward them, whipping the surface into spray.

Caldan checked to see if Miranda was safe and found her sheltering with some sailors behind the gunwale.

"Down!" someone yelled.

Caldan crouched low just as the wave hit.

Thunder cracked, and scorching air whistled past. The deck lurched under Caldan as the ship jolted and shuddered. He waited a moment, then leaped to his feet and peered toward Anasoma.

The portcullis was a twisted ruin. Cracks had opened up in the surrounding wall, and chunks of stone fell, tumbling down into the river and onto its banks. Across the gap, from the top of the crumbling walls to either side, the blue flame stretched like a bridge of fire.

A cheer rose from the crew of the *Loretta*, quickly followed by answering calls from the ships following. Charlotte let loose a string of curses, exhorting her sailors to concentrate on their tasks.

Caldan gripped his sword hilt until his knuckles pained him. This was only the beginning, and he didn't think there would be much to celebrate with what came next.

Again the deck lurched, this time from the oarsmen propelling them forward. Caldan braced his legs against the periodic surges, then turned to find Selbourne gone. The mercenary captain was over with Felice. She was speaking heatedly with him and made a chopping motion with one hand into her other. Selbourne nodded and left her. She glanced at Caldan, then looked away as one of Quiss's colleagues came up to her.

Caldan wondered what that was all about.

Two mercenary groups gathered on the left side of the ship, each composed of around twenty men and women, all wearing crafted armor and armed to the teeth. They talked and joked among themselves, but there was a hard edge to them all. Violent people, used to using violence to get what they wanted.

Caldan made his way to Felice. She was berating a mercenary who was trying to hand her a sheathed sword.

"I don't know how to use one," she said.

"You need a weapon," the man said. "There's going to be fighting."

"I know that—I *planned* all this. I have a knife, and it'll do me. I'm sure there will be plenty of you around, plus the sorcerers. If they can't defend themselves, then I'm done for anyway."

The mercenary shrugged and returned to his group.

"Felice," Caldan said.

She turned her dark eyes on him. "Do you think he was propositioning me?" Felice gave a self-deprecating laugh. "I missed it. Must be the stress . . . all this organizing, and anticipation, it's enough to make your hair turn gray. Anyway, do you have the crafting Quiss's people gave you?"

Caldan patted his trouser pocket, where the metal disc was. He'd tested it the previous night, along with others. They worked to block a few wells, but no more than that. If the wells were narrow and jagged, the crafting was more effective, able to block more of them, but with wide, smooth wells, they were less effective. Caldan realized the smith-craftings he'd tested, along with others, could also be used against him, if Quiss wanted to. And perhaps that was Quiss's plan. Once Kelhak was defeated, Caldan himself, in their eyes a budding lich, would be a problem to take care of. He held the instrument of his own undoing in his pocket.

"Yes," he said. "Let's hope we have enough."

"There's not much we can do now. Where's Miranda?"

He nodded to the gunwale. "Helping the crew."

Miranda came over and clasped Caldan in a hug, and he had to bend to place a kiss on her cheek. He sighed into her hair, knowing nothing he could say would persuade her to stay out of harm's way.

Felice turned to Caldan. "Remember, regroup once Kelhak is dead, then head for the docks. It'll take a while for the Indryallan commanders to realize their God-Emperor has been defeated, so we need to survive until they do. We shouldn't have too much trouble with all these Quivers along with us."

"Find Kelhak," Caldan said, repeating the plan. "Kill him. Get to the docks. Commandeer ships and get them out into the harbor."

"Good," Felice said. "Then I'll leave you. Get to your group soon. Once we're inside, there's no time to waste." She turned and made her way to the band of mercenaries closest to where the gangplank would descend.

Miranda looked into Caldan's eyes. "Tell me it will all work out," she said.

"I hope it will. Get to the purified land; I'll meet you there."

"We'll succeed," she said. Then, stronger, "We will, I know it."

"I'll do all I can. I just hope it'll be enough."

"It's more than anyone else can," she said, and even though he didn't think that was true, it gave him heart all the same. He pulled her close and kissed her until he wasn't sure he'd be able to breathe anymore.

Enough of that! Gazija said.

Caldan reluctantly pulled away and cast a wry glance at his wolf.

A shadow covered the ship as Anasoma's walls loomed over them, and they passed the wreck of a portcullis. Above them blazed the blue flame. Jagged splinters of metal jutted from the stonework, which still radiated heat from the explosion. Citizens of Anasoma gawked at them from the surrounding streets. A few raised a ragged cheer, but no more than that.

"For the emperor!" yelled Felice.

"For the emperor!" returned some of the sailors.

The mercenaries and Quiss's people remained silent.

Along the river they went, Felice squinting behind them. "I can't see," she muttered.

Caldan leaned over the side and looked back at the ships in their wake. "Soon," he said. "The last ship will be through in moments."

"Get ready, men!" roared Selbourne. "You know the plan. Stick to it or die. It's that simple."

Ahead of them, a bridge grew larger the closer they came.

"Now!" said Felice as the ship drew near the river's stone embankment.

Sailors bounded over the side, and coils of thick rope followed. They scrambled as they landed, grabbing the ropes and tying them to metal rings bolted to the stone.

Fibers creaked as the ropes grew taut, taking the weight of the ship. The *Loretta* slowed and crashed into the embankment, timbers groaning in protest.

The gangplank slid over the side, and mercenaries rushed down it. Some of the lightly armored ones vaulted over the gunwale and started pushing amazed onlookers away, keeping a space clear for the mercenaries spewing from the ship.

They had established a firm foothold on solid land by the time the counterattack came.

Armored Indryallans began pouring from the mouths of alleys. Volleys of arrows descended, the missiles thudding into shields and the decks of the ships.

"Let's go," Caldan said. He grasped Miranda's hand, and they joined Felice's group.

CHAPTER 53

Only a hundred yards from the ships, and already their progress had halted. The Indryallans were all over them now, arrows falling thick and fast, streets and alleys blocked with wagons and carts, bristling with spears. Quivers spilled from the ships and clashed with Indryallans in a vicious melee of thrashing swords and splintering wood. Men and women died. Curses filled the air along with incoherent shouts. Shields and heads smashed. There was no break, no respite. Rivers of scarlet ran in the gutters. The wounded shrieked, and the dead lay silent.

To Caldan's left, Indryallan sorcery sliced through the shields of two warlocks, the stones underneath them scorched to black. They collapsed in a heap, charred and smoking. Ahead, firestorms raged where the warlocks tried to blast their way through the Indryallan line. The air vibrated to the hammering of sorcerous forces unleashed. Radiant threads whipped above the buildings as sorcery met sorcery.

Caldan sheltered with Miranda at the side of a warehouse, watching as more and more Quivers and warlocks disembarked from their ships and rushed to join the fray. He caught glimpses of Touched in the fighting, racing around with preternatural speed, showers of blood in their wake.

Knight-Marshal Rakim stood surrounded by a dozen other officers. Their eyes constantly scanned the streets and buildings, assessing and evaluating. Rakim shouted commands, and the others scurried to obey. More reinforcements rushed to the north when the Indryallans had weakened the Quivers and almost pushed through.

The knight-marshal strode over to the emperor, who was sitting on a low stone wall. Zerach-Sangur was clad in his plated smith-crafted armor once again. The workmanship put Caldan's gauntlet to shame. He was surrounded by Quivers and warlocks, and not a few Touched, Florian and Alasdair among them. The two siblings carried their usual short spears, with daggers tucked into their belts. Caldan caught sight of Felice watching the battle nervously. The swordsman, cel Rau, shadowed Lady Caitlyn; he'd not acknowledged Caldan or anyone else. Devenish's replacement, Bernhard, was issuing instructions to the warlocks. And then there was Master Mold with a dozen or so armed Protectors. Mold studiously avoided Caldan's eye. He couldn't blame the man—even though the master now had possession of the trinket sword, Caldan had proven it no long held sway over him.

Rakim and Bernhard spoke to the emperor, who nodded and waved a hand in dismissal. They each bowed and returned to directing their forces. They would stay here and command the beachhead in the emperor's absence.

"We'll never get through these Indryallans," Miranda said from beside Caldan.

"We're not meant to; this is a diversion. Kelhak is our goal. The Quivers' and warlocks' role is to keep the Indryallans busy while we go after him."

Abruptly, the emperor stood and gestured to Felice. They exchanged whispered words, and Felice nodded. She met Caldan's eye and beckoned him.

"I'll slip away as soon as it's safe," Miranda said. "Once I disappear into the city, no one will find me. Be careful."

"You too. We're in this together, don't forget."

By the time Caldan and Miranda made their way to Felice, she'd also been joined by Selbourne, a score of mercenaries, a dozen or so warlocks, Aidan and Vasile, and cel Rau. Lady Caitlyn stood next to cel Rau, but her attention was on the emperor.

Quiss, Mazoet, and the four sorcerers with them remained ten paces away, as if not wanting to be part of the group. Florian busily tied her braided red hair behind her head, pointedly ignoring Caldan, while Alasdair sneered openly at him.

Just like with Mold, he didn't blame them for their animosity. And just like with Mold, he didn't really care what they thought of him.

"Where are the rest of the Touched?" Caldan asked Felice.

"Fighting. This is our strike group."

"There are too many of us to be stealthy," Caldan said.

"We're not sneaking, we're striking."

The emperor approached and stood beside Felice.

"Be ready to move," he said, pitching his voice so all could hear. "Rakim and the warlocks will keep the Indryallans busy. As soon as they go on the offensive, we're to take advantage of it."

Felice nodded and began issuing orders.

Caldan swallowed and turned to look at Miranda, feeling the emperor's eyes on his back.

"Go," he told her. "When you think you're unobserved." He led Miranda away, and they stopped next to a building with an alley close by. Caldan looked around. The emperor was now directing warlocks, Felice beside to him.

Vasile was looking at them intently. Caldan gave him a nod, which the magistrate returned. Vasile said something to Aidan and began walking toward them. Cel Rau frowned at Vasile, but let him be.

Good, thought Caldan. Miranda and Vasile could slip away together. She would be safe waiting at the purified land while Vasile procured a getaway carriage.

Miranda wrapped her arms around Caldan, hugging with all her strength. She kissed him again, hot and passionate. After a few moments, she pushed him away, tears trailing down her cheeks. "Stay alive," she said. "I'll see you soon."

"Stay safe," Caldan said.

Glancing around her to make sure she wasn't observed, Miranda beckoned to Vasile, and they quickly ducked into the alley.

Caldan heard their footsteps fade as they raced away.

AIDAN STEPPED BETWEEN the mouth of the alley and cel Rau, who'd made to follow Vasile. "He's clear of this," Aidan said. "He can't fight, the same as the woman. They'd be a hindrance to us. Let them go."

Cel Rau's eyes narrowed, and his hand moved down to rest on his sword hilt. He sniffed. "Caitlyn will find him. We will find him. Once this is over."

"Who knows what will happen in the meantime."

"The emperor will survive. We will once again fight against evil under Caitlyn's command."

Not if I have any say in it, thought Aidan.

FELICE'S PLAN WAS to move to a location in West Barrows the talon had provided. It had told her there was an old distillery there that had been built over the ruins of a long-dead sorcerer's private mansion.

Felice kept her attention on the side roads they passed, aware of Aidan and Lady Caitlyn close behind her. Strangely, she felt she could trust Aidan, unlike many of the others. Cel Rau especially. She didn't know what his game was, but a tribal swordsman? His markings were incomprehensible at best, and no swordsman from the Steppes would wield two swords. His bearing and accoutrements screamed wrongness to her. But what did it matter, in the end? As long as he was as good with those blades as the others thought he was . . . and he stuck to the plan.

"We're being followed," the Touched man Alasdair said from his position flanking the emperor.

The talon.

Felice turned to face them. "Of course we are. Everyone we've passed wants to know what we're doing. Just keep moving."

She frowned at the men, daring them to keep talking, then returned to her path. *Kelhak. The lich.* Nothing else mattered.

Businesses and tenements passed in a blur. Old, new, decaying, brick, painted: Felice took no notice. Goad Street: left here. Coffer Road: turn right. Across a square and past the fountain—*Where was it . . . ?*

There.

Move, move!

Suddenly, pillars of white burst around them. Voices cried out as explosions struck the buildings. Felice threw herself to the ground. Shattered missiles of wood and stone whirled through the air. She glimpsed shielded sorcerers raising craftings and trinkets, while mercenaries scattered.

More explosions fanned into buildings and across the street. Cobblestones cracked, and unshielded bodies were flung like leaves. Blinding energies burned, and Felice threw up a hand against the glare. Ruler-straight lines burst from the emperor and his warlocks, knifing into the sky, then curling across the city and downward. Where they hit, discharges glittered and crashed. Howls and wails pierced air already clouded with smoke and ash.

"Keep moving!" the emperor commanded, heedless of the blood and flesh splashed across the ground.

It's easy to say that when your shields protect you, Felice thought, but even still, she scrambled to her feet, blinking through tears.

Caldan grabbed her arm, and she felt her skin tighten under his shield. A fish-scale film covered her.

Then the sorcery relented—the attack was over. The flashing assault petered out. Smoke and ruin surrounded them.

The emperor was standing, and that was the main thing.

"Selbourne, Mold—what's the damage?" Felice shouted.

The mercenary captain was moving among his men, making sure injuries were bound.

"Leave them," commanded the emperor. "We don't have time."

"They'll walk out of here," Selbourne growled. "A minute is all we need."

Mold came toward them, eyes on Caldan.

"The Protectors are fine. We did what we could to shield the mercenaries."

"They know where we are," the emperor said. "There will be more attacks. Move. *Now!*"

Felice wiped sweat from her forehead. She wanted badly to make sure the others were okay, but also knew the emperor was right. Looking at him, she almost needed to squint. His shield shone brighter than the others, bathing her in its brilliance. For the first time, she realized that its light gave off no warmth.

With the warlocks haranguing them, they continued. Felice marched onward in a kind of stupor, leading them all to the rendezvous. The rest of the group, their only hope for the world, trailed behind her.

A short time later, a gaggle of children interrupted her daze. They raced out of a side lane, girls and boys, squealing and shouting with fear, barely giving Felice and her retinue a passing look. She remembered who they were fighting for—not just the emperor, but for everyone.

For an instant, the lich and her mission were forgotten. The inexpressible weight pressing on her lifted; the abyssal precipice in front of her closed. A brief sense of wonder and responsibility transcended her fear.

Then she remembered herself. And her knees weakened under the heavy weight on her shoulders.

Bloody hells, she cursed herself. *Pull yourself together.*

Not long after, they arrived at the distillery. Its great wooden doors were locked and presumably barred on the inside. No matter. There was a smaller door twenty paces down.

Felice looked to Quiss. "Open it," she said.

There was a metallic click, and hinges moaned as the door came ajar.

Inside was cold air and silence, both disturbed as they entered. Felice stopped and stood a few dozen paces in. Huge copper boilers and vats stretched down both sides of a long room. A pungency in the air tickled her nostrils, slightly harsh and medicinal, yet flavored with many layers: blackberry and flowers, honeyed nuts and spice.

A draft ruffled her hair, caressed the back of her neck.

"Come," the talon said from beside her. It must have been waiting for them.

Weapons were brought to bear on the talon. Blades and spears pointed at the creature, but it made no move.

Felice became aware of the emperor as he took a step toward the talon, then stopped. The creature turned its hood in the direction of the emperor, and for long moments the two stared at each other— something unspoken passing between them. Whatever it was, the emperor gestured, and the weapons threatening the talon were pulled back.

"Come," the talon repeated, breaking away from the emperor. "We have no time to waste."

Which was true, but it wouldn't be a waste to set up a rear guard. There would be sorcerers coming after them, and soldiers. If they were attacked from behind while confronting Kelhak, they not only would be caught unaware but also would have any route of escape cut off.

"It's about time you showed up," Felice muttered. "How many can we leave behind?" she asked the others. "We can't have enemies at our backs."

"None!" snapped the emperor. "We'll create wards, enough to guard the rear."

Caldan shook his head. "We have to leave people here to guard the entrance. They sensed where we went, and they'll be chasing us." He placed a hand on the head of his wolf.

"He's right," Selbourne said.

The emperor hissed. "We need as many as we can to fight Kelhak, but . . . maybe a few warlocks can remain behind. Weaker ones." He issued orders, and some warlocks split from the others. Some pulled metal discs from pockets and pouches and began setting them up around the door and walls of the building.

In the end they left five warlocks and a dozen mercenaries. Too few and there would be no point, but too many and they'd compromise their chances with Kelhak.

Felice turned to face the people who'd come with her this far, aware of the emperor's eyes upon her. Those remaining were all they had against the lich. She hoped they would be enough.

"This is it!" she said, raising her voice slightly. "Keep your weapons ready and your wits about you. From now on, speak softly, and no rest breaks. Stay together, and you just might see the light of another day."

Nods and nervous mutterings answered her. She'd never been much for speeches, but it had seemed like the right time to say something. Aidan gave her a nod, while at his side cel Rau looked relaxed, as if this sort of thing was routine for him. Caitlyn paced around them, crafted armor glinting. She'd healed well, but Felice knew there would be scars left behind, and not all of them physical.

The talon led them to a trapdoor in the depths of the cellars. When they opened it, dank air escaped, and stone steps descended into absolute blackness.

THE REDUCED GROUP scuttled along damp and spiderweb-encrusted tunnels, barely pausing. Sorcerous globes lit their passage. The talon ranged ahead of them, urging them to maintain a fast pace. Dust stirred, and things crunched and squelched underfoot. They passed pitch-black openings emitting the same musty, decaying stink as a moldy tomb. Muffled sounds from the battle above reached them.

It went on like that for some time, until finally they emerged into a circular chamber, walls lined with fired brick, floor covered with a white lichenlike growth. Far above them, a faint light shone from an opening. Against the wall opposite, the talon swayed back and forth. He recognized the creature from what Felice had told him about her unplanned journey to Riversedge. A soft crooning came from it, sending shivers up Caldan's spine. He could sense sorcery building around the creature.

"What's it doing?" he asked.

"I—" Felice broke off as the emperor pushed past her and strode up to the talon.

It didn't indicate that it sensed his presence, merely kept swaying, humming.

The emperor reached up and placed a hand on the talon's back. Then Caldan sensed more wells opening—five. Quiss and his sorcerers stirred, some frowning.

In front of the emperor and the talon, the sun burst forth from the bricks. Shafts of brilliance sprayed outward, and underneath them the brick glowed orange. Black and gray smoke poured upward, and with a sharp crack, bricks crumbled into dust and rubble. The talon continued, aided by the emperor, until layers of bricks were stripped away to reveal gray stone—and still they kept going. Rock heated to glowing fractured and disintegrated, piling at their feet.

A tunnel—they were tunneling through the rock.

More sorcery and dust and smoke. Shattering and cracking and sorcerous lights. A dozen heartbeats passed—ten feet in and still going. The talon started singing, a high-pitched warbling song in a language Caldan realized probably hadn't been heard in thousands of years.

And the emperor joined it, his deeper voice underlying the talon's chant.

The floor beneath them hummed.

Caldan found himself struggling to breathe, so powerful and controlled were the sorceries in front of him.

Stone chips sprayed from the opening amid billowing dust and smoke.

An almighty crack rent the air. The ancient song ceased. Out of the heaving cloud came the talon.

"Come," it said.

They covered their mouths and noses with their sleeves and followed the creature, stumbling over debris. The end of the tunnel opened into another chamber. This one was lined with massive slabs of stone, and the air was tasteless, sterile.

To the left, great stone stairs descended into inky darkness. The emperor stood at their head, waiting.

"What is this place?" Aidan said.

Felice coughed and wiped gray dust from her face. "A buried city. Long forgotten."

And now, rediscovered.

"Hurry," the emperor said, gesturing for his warlocks to come to him. "Our sorcery might have been felt. Prepare yourselves."

Caldan's wolf loped down the stairs into the gloom.

"It can scout for us," Caldan said to Felice, and she nodded.

"As long as it doesn't give us away."

And the company descended into the ancient ruins beneath Anasoma.

"THIS HAS THE makings of a disaster," Aidan said to cel Rau. "You need to tell me what's going on."

Hammering drums sounded faintly above them, detonations so loud they could hear them even this far under the ground.

"You don't need to know more," Caitlyn said. "Other than what I tell you. We're here to help the emperor kill Kelhak."

Aidan ignored her. He glanced at cel Rau. "Are you a tool of the emperor?"

The tribesman's eyes flashed. "I'm no one's tool. I do what's right."

"And are paid handsomely for it, I'd wager," said Aidan.

Cel Rau remained motionless, both hands resting on the hilts of his swords.

"Defeating evil is its own reward." Caitlyn met Aidan's eye. "Though there are always casualties. Great causes require sacrifice. As I have suffered, and been born anew. The emperor has faith in me, as should you. Keep an eye on that Caldan, as well, both of you. The emperor has plans for him."

"What plans?" Aidan asked.

"That's not for you to worry about."

Nothing good, then, thought Aidan. But what did he expect? People like Caitlyn, cel Rau, and the emperor were blind to their own evil.

Aidan bent down and brushed at the dust covering the ends of his britches in an effort to hide his expression, though they were all cast of shadows down here in the darkness with only a few sorcerous globes for light. Ahead strode the emperor and Felice, while behind them, Caldan followed, along with Quiss, Mazoet, and their sorcerers. Aidan caught occasional glimpses of metal glinting in the darkness—Caldan's strange wolf as it roamed ahead of them.

"Vasile told me," he began, speaking to cel Rau, "that everyone wants one thing: to destroy Kelhak. So you needn't worry on that score. But you *should* worry about yourselves. Think of what we know now about forbidden sorcery. The best way to keep a secret is if only dead people know it."

With a cough, cel Rau frowned at Aidan. "The emperor wouldn't do that."

Even without Vasile, Aidan could tell cel Rau was lying. If they survived Kelhak, some people wouldn't leave here alive.

"You dare voice words against the emperor?" hissed Caitlyn with venom. "After he spared you? After he offered redemption?"

"Secrets must be kept," he said. "For the good of the empire. If a few people die for the greater good, then the cost is worth it. You taught me that."

Aidan kept his gaze on the people around them and the hoary surroundings. Some of the stones composing the walls revealed dust-covered carvings, as though the makers had taken it upon themselves to imbue decoration or life into this grim place. As they passed another carved block of stone, Aidan trailed his fingers over it, trying to hide his anxiety. An image of cel Rau's sword dripping blood appeared in his mind, with Chalayan's head neatly separated from his shoulders. A murder Aidan had condoned. Vasile had told him cel Rau carried out the act as soon as he was able. It had been done with eagerness . . . Cel Rau hadn't given the benefit of the doubt, given the sorcerer time to show whether he was truly corrupted by his newfound power. Instead, he'd killed Chalayan as soon as he'd seen they were relatively safe from the jukari and vormag. He'd been wanting to kill Chalayan . . . waiting to do the deed.

" . . . and the worst sorcerers are the ones who have let themselves be corrupted," Caitlyn was saying to cel Rau. "The Protectors do an adequate job of policing the cities and major towns, but there are innumerable out-of-the-way places that harbor evil."

"We will need to return to our role," cel Rau said, "and support the emperor outside the cities."

"Rogue behavior cannot be tolerated," Caitlyn said. "This Caldan, for instance." She lowered her voice. "He must be . . . contained. The emperor has decreed it."

"The emperor is wise and all-knowing, may he live forever," cel Rau said.

Aidan coughed as he realized cel Rau believed what he'd said. He turned. "Tell me, cel Rau, what do you make of our newfound friends here?" He waved a hand at Quiss's sorcerers.

The tribesman scowled and increased his pace for a few moments, until he walked ahead of him. Behind Aidan was Caitlyn, and an itch formed between his shoulder blades. *No, she won't kill me yet. But I suspect it's only a matter of time.*

"Well?" Aidan prompted.

"It's for the emperor to decide what to do with them."

"But will he kill them?"

"I don't know," cel Rau said. "The emperor's ways are beyond me, may he live forever." He glanced back at Aidan for an instant before returning to watch where he was going.

Cel Rau really did want the emperor to live forever. The thought was . . . disturbing. The swordsman knew more of the emperor than he let on.

Aidan watched cel Rau from behind, the sun-dark skin of his muscled arms, the rough leather and cloth of his hauberk. A mysterious and troubled man.

And Aidan realized he despised the tribesman. Though they'd traveled together for years. Though cel Rau had saved Vasile from the jukari as they'd approached Riversedge. Though they'd exchanged bread across an open fire. The merciless slaughter of Chalayan stood above all other acts. A defining moment. Cel Rau had always been an executioner, realized Aidan.

"You're here to kill them, aren't you?" Aidan said to cel Rau.

The swordsman kept walking, as if he hadn't heard.

"Answer me!" hissed Aidan. Behind him, Caitlyn laughed softly.

Cel Rau stopped, ancient dust swirling around his ankles. He turned to face Aidan and met his eye. "No," he said simply. "If you die, if *I* die, so be it."

"It's someone specific, isn't it?"

Cel Rau flashed him a sidelong glance.

"Quiss?"

No reaction from cel Rau.

"Lady Felicienne?"

Still nothing.

"Caldan?"

Cel Rau chuckled and shook his head.

IN HIS THIRST for knowledge, for all things related to crafting and sorcery, Caldan had read many tomes, from the brittle and dusty books and scrolls left to molder at the back of the monastery's libraries to newly penned theories detailing the time before the Shattering. What he hadn't realized, though, was that the old cities from that time might still exist. Not as cities in their own right, but as crumbling ruins. After all, it was thousands of years ago. Whatever was left had to have been destroyed by nature, after the bones were picked over by scavengers and treasure hunters. He was astounded to realize that it was possible semi-intact buildings, or even whole cities, might exist in places where nature and weather were less active: deserts, arid lands, the purified lands . . . or, as this one was, underground. Buried . . . forgotten.

Much like the talon that was leading them. At some point in the past, there must have been knowledge about this creature, but it had clearly been lost to time. It was here now, though, and with a turn of its head, the shadowed hood regarded him. Deep inside, Caldan thought he saw a faint reflection of light: eyes staring out at him.

"What is it?" he asked.

It loomed at his side. Frayed rags rustled. Caldan could smell something underneath its now-familiar stale scent: blood and urine. As if the creature exuded them or had encountered them recently. The stench of recent death.

"Walk with me," the talon said, drawing Caldan by the elbow away from the others.

The talon had birdlike fingers ending in . . . talons. Caldan had seen their like before, lying dead in Amerdan's tent. Amerdan had killed one of these creatures—had he absorbed something from it, which was now a part of Caldan?

Bony fingers dug into his arm, and Caldan glanced back at Felice, who watched as the talon drew him away. Her face was inscrutable. And the emperor . . . the emperor watched them like a hawk, but he didn't intervene.

The talon's well was jagged and fierce, a rupture that tugged at Caldan's awareness. It was uncomfortable to stand so close to this creature. A made thing, carrying the power of a long-dead sorcerer. His hands balled into fists, his nerves bristling in alarm, as if expecting violence.

"What is it?" Caldan said again. "We've no time for this."

The talon paused, brought the dark opening of its cowl to face him. "Why are you here?" it said.

Caldan held his breath, knowing he was on the precipice of something important but not yet understanding what it could be. From a few paces behind the talon, he could see Felice regarding them both, and behind her, the emperor and his warlocks.

"The lich must be stopped," Caldan said.

The hood bent toward the stone beneath their feet. "Ancient blood flows within you."

Ah, the ancestors' blood. "Weakly," admitted Caldan. How the talon knew about it wasn't clear.

"Your kind is lost. Your purpose . . . astray. But there is more. I sense a kinship in you, and that is impossible. I was created a long time ago."

Was the creature implying Caldan was now part talon? After all, he'd absorbed essences from Amerdan, who'd killed the other talon . . . "What do you mean?" Caldan wasn't sure he wanted to know the answer. He had enough weighing him down, and he feared another burden might break him.

Out of the corner of his eye, he saw Felice take a few steps closer.

The talon placed a large hand on Caldan's shoulder. Its weight pressed down, but Caldan remained unmoved. This close, he could see tiny details in the clawlike appendage: hard skin covered with lines and cracks. The creature looked particularly disturbing, limned in flickering torchlight overlaid with the sterile glow of sorcerous globes.

Be careful! an inner voice warned.

Rags rustled as the talon turned the void of his hood to regard Felice, then back to Caldan. "Everything . . . has reason."

"That's . . . true," Caldan said.

"They will try to kill you," the talon said.

Why was it telling him this? What did it want? Caldan twisted his elbow from its wiry grasp. "I know. How can I not?"

"I am of the Old Ones, but not one of them."

The sorcerers before the Shattering. Its masters. "They are all dead, except one," Caldan said. "They will not return."

"Perhaps you are wrong."

"You seek," Caldan said, "to bring them back? How?"

"To create anew."

Caldan trembled at the conviction in the talon's voice. Him. It was talking about him. The talon wanted a return to the time before the Shattering. First Gazija, and now this creature. Each had some plan for him, a design of their own making. None of them considered Caldan's own desires.

"We have other concerns at the moment. We don't even know if we'll survive this."

"The emperor must have a balance. A counterweight. He fears any of his kind. For thousands of years, he's suppressed sorcery. And when a test of his power came, his empire was shattered."

"I don't care," Caldan said, but he could feel the false note in his voice. Inwardly, he cursed himself. When Kelhak was gone, he wanted to be done with them all. There was no stable ground anymore. Not here. Not for Caldan. He'd been turned into a lich against his will. Wasn't that enough? Couldn't they leave him be?

"My name was . . . is . . . Inchariel. Seek me out."

Despite himself, Caldan's curiosity was piqued. He thought about it for a moment. What knowledge did the talon have? Perhaps far more than the warlocks, even as much as the emperor. Maybe he should find out what it wanted. But that was a decision for another time.

Caldan nodded, turned away from the unnerving creature.

The talon moved to the front of their group. Rag ends trailed in the dust. Mercenaries parted to let it through, fear and disgust writ large on their faces.

CHAPTER 54

Caldan's group stopped in a tight-knit bunch when an opening appeared. The emperor was in the lead, surrounded by warlocks, followed by cel Rau and Felice, then Mold and two Protectors. Selbourne and his mercenaries enclosed Caldan, along with Aidan, Caitlyn, Quiss, and the portly Mazoet, with the other stork-thin sorcerers bringing up the rear.

The entrance to the old city was open, a square of blackness bounded by blocks of stone. Patterned alloy edged the doorway, etched with indecipherable writing. Words as small as ants tracked across the ageless surface, and curled lines of metal spread across the stone walls, as if they had grown roots.

They stared into the impenetrable blackness, and while their reactions varied somewhat, it was apparent on most faces that they were all facing a horror none of them wanted to contemplate. And when they finally pulled their gazes away and turned back to the talon, it was gone. Vanished without a sound.

There were angry mutterings from the mercenaries, quickly hushed by Felice and Selbourne.

"Let it go," the emperor said. "It is far more useful than you know. And uneasy, around your kind."

Your kind, thought Caldan. *So the emperor doesn't consider himself one of us. But maybe I'm not either, now.*

Caldan lifted his sorcerous crafted globe and strode forward. Although he was surrounded by potent sorcerers and hard-bitten mercenaries, and he himself possessed multiple wells, he felt small and frail before the dark opening. And though his wolf was beside him, he hesitated to send it through, as if anything entering that maw would never return.

But there was no going back. He turned to regard the assembly behind him, his sorcerous globe banishing shadows. Felice regarded him with faint concern, her hand reaching up to toy with an earring. Quiss, his expression tinged with sorrow, looked all the more thin and frail in the meager yellow light. Selbourne, eyes squinted in scrutiny, remained hard-faced and unyielding. They'd stepped to the fore, their people behind them, as if they should be the first ones through the opening into the unknown. A show of leadership, of strength.

Skin prickling, Caldan met each of their eyes in turn as the silence grew. What lay beyond, they didn't know, but each of them was certain they wouldn't come out of this alive.

The emperor spoke softly. His voice seemed to reach all of them, even those at the rear, who looked up as he did so.

"We tread where no man has for hundreds of years," the emperor said. "Ruins from the Shattering, long sealed. *Ancient.*"

Caldan didn't need the emperor to tell him this. They could all feel it. Age was all around them. In the air they breathed. In the dust covering the floor.

"There may be treasures," the emperor continued. "Items far more valuable than gold or gems, trinkets and devices from before the Shattering. But we must leave them. We're not here for wealth."

Of course he'd want them all for himself, thought Caldan. Gazija had warned him of this.

The emperor turned his gaze to Felice, then to Caldan, and finally to Quiss. "We're here to fight our way to Kelhak, a lich, a sorcerer corrupted by the very power he thought to control. There can be no quarter. No hesitation. It is him or us. Everyone else around him is a distraction: his Silent Companions, his sorcerers. Our only goal is Kelhak." The emperor raised his voice further, as if heedless of who heard him. "For if we fail, the world tumbles into another Shattering. And this time, there will be no returning from oblivion for humanity. We kill Kelhak, or we fall. There are no other outcomes. Be vigilant. Be wary. Strike first, and strike hard. Hold nothing back. There are no innocents where we travel." He stepped into the pitch-black entrance, his sorcerous globe chasing away shadows that had been there so long it felt like they had substance.

ARMORED INDRYALLANS SWARMED them without warning. Caldan's wolf hadn't sensed them approach and had only caught a glimpse of steel in the darkness before it was too late.

Pouring from narrow side passages, their attack was swift and brutal. Huge men slammed into, and through, the mercenaries. Some mercenaries held their line, but others scattered while hacking at their opponents or crumpled under the onslaught. Mold and the other two Protectors managed to shield themselves in time but fell to the stone floor under crushing blows from massive axes and swords. Shrieks and howls and curses bellowed around them—all from the mercenaries, for the soldiers attacking them made no sound. *Kelhak's Silent Companions,* realized Caldan.

The stench of lemons and scorched metal filled the air. Caldan opened his well and covered himself with his shield. Nearby screams rang in his ears. He drew his sword just in time to parry a blow from a looming Indryallan. Its blade crashed into the ground as he sidestepped, sending sparks flying. He slashed desperately, opening a gash between armored plates. The man hopped back, dead eyes staring, and didn't utter a sound.

Out of the corner of his eye, he saw Selbourne wrestling with his opponent. Greatsword abandoned, the mercenary plunged a dagger deep into flesh. Around him, though, his soldiers dropped under the vicious assault. Blood spurted and bones broke. The ferocity of the Silent Companions was terrible to behold. Swords hacked and slashed as if raised by tireless arms. Some mercenaries managed to wound and even down Companions, but more of Kelhak's men crowded in to replace their dead or injured fellows.

A dark shape flitted among them like a giant swallow. Rags flapping, glittering blades protruding from somewhere among its clothes—the talon. Swords struck where it had been an instant ago, and its own blades carved through flesh and leather and armor as if it were gossamer.

Flashes of radiance came from the tunnel to Caldan's left, where the warlocks were. The emperor, along with Alasdair and Florian, had left to assist them when the fighting started. The sorcerers had insisted on staying separate from the rest of the group, and now he knew why: so they could use destructive sorcery without fear of injuring or killing their own comrades.

He swallowed and focused on the man in front of him, but part of him wished he had more control of his own abilities, like the other Touched did. To kill someone somehow felt fairer if you did it with a sword or other weapon.

Caldan charged, while sending his wolf to savage another Companion. He swung his sword low in a feint, then twisted it in an upward arc. Flesh parted as his blade hacked through mail and into the man's waist. He yanked it out, blood covering the metal, then his opponent's greatsword slammed into his shield, rocking his head to the side. Caldan stumbled, ears ringing, vision hazy. He fell to one knee, sucking in air and raising his sword weakly over his head for the expected follow-up blow.

But the blow never materialized.

Caldan lurched to his feet and shook his head. His opponent lay dead in front of him, sporting multiple wounds from Selbourne's blade—and to his surprise, Felice was withdrawing a dagger from the man's neck.

"I'm fine," she said. "Do what you need to."

Caldan shook his head. He'd been worried that she would be out of her depth here, amid the carnage, but she had proven him wrong.

He turned back to the battle and saw mercenaries clutching at terrible wounds, while others lay sprawled across the ground, eyes lifeless and staring. Silent Companion corpses were littered around them, but the men were big and strong and were hard to take down. Aidan, Caitlyn, and cel Rau were close together, and, as evidenced by the dead on the floor, were an effective team. Flashes and explosions of sorcery came from farther down the tunnel, which turned a corner— the emperor and his warlocks, who were focused on the Indryallan sorcerers supporting the Silent Companions. Mold and the Protectors had rallied and were fighting hard, but they couldn't take on many of the Companions at a time, and more were coming from the side passages, casting long and eerie shadows in the illumination of sorcerous globes.

There were too many. With the warlocks tied up countering sorcery, the Companions knew it was only a matter of time before they overwhelmed their opponents.

And Kelhak would have won.

No!

Caldan's trinket ring jabbed into his finger as the heat in his blood rose.

But sword work wouldn't suffice here and now; he needed to do more. Caldan focused on his multiple wells. It was about time he pushed himself. If he didn't, then it would all end here.

His control of his wolf was cut, and it took a few moments before he realized Gazija had taken it from him. The construct darted among the Companions, sparks of virulence leaping from its metal skin. When they struck, armor and flesh blistered and smoked, and men fell writhing to the ground.

A wild grin twisted Caldan's lips, and a growl sounded from deep in his throat.

He reached his senses out to Mahsonn's crafting in his pocket.

The Bleeder had been able to control bursts of extremely focused destructive sorcery because of his ability to manipulate many strings. Caldan knew he couldn't let loose his novice destructive sorcery. Though he could likely kill many Companions, it was too unfocused, and he'd probably kill many of the mercenaries as well, even warlocks, if they got in his way.

He needed pinpoint control. Powerful sorcery woven around allies.

Caldan linked to the crafting, split his well into two strings, then four, eight, then sixteen. His mind recoiled, and the strings became slick, threatening to slip from his grasp. He grappled with them; it was akin to trying to hold on to greased snakes. They squirmed and coiled, as if desperate to evade his grip, but he managed to settle them down. To his relief, once he corralled them, they quieted, even feeling less slippery. He was getting better at holding on to them, more practiced.

Sixteen strings. From what he sensed of Mahsonn's crafting, it would be enough.

Caldan connected all of them to the linking runes imbued in the crafting. His power and awareness flowed through its pattern as he tested it, figuring out its design through the shaping runes, buffers, and anchors. There were many loops forged separately, yet all working in harmony with each other. Complex transference runes merged with controlling loops.

And the pieces of the design clicked into place for Caldan.

He filled the crafting with the corrosive power of his well and focused his will.

The air vibrated, humming like a swarm of bees. Dozens of whiplike tendrils, visible only to his sorcerous senses, lashed from him. Caldan curved them around the mercenaries and into the Silent Companions assaulting them. These men would die as Breyton the Quiver had on their way to Riversedge: by hundreds of tiny cuts.

But something different happened.

Companions spun and twisted, as if scores of invisible sword blades slashed them. Dark blood sprayed. Limbs were severed. And for the first time, some made sounds. Anguished howls ripped from tortured mouths were silenced as throats were sliced. Hands clutched at leaking entrails before they themselves were severed.

Caldan almost let his strings slip from his grasp, so surprised was he at the carnage.

But in an instant, it was obvious to him what had happened. Mahsonn had only a constricted well. His sorcery was limited by it. Caldan's innate power was much greater. So were the results.

What would happen if he joined more of his wells to the crafting? Two or three or even more?

He walked forward, around the two fallen Companions. Selbourne was already rushing to fight more of the creatures, but he needn't have bothered. They would all be dead soon.

Somewhere to his right, Caldan sensed Quiss and his people add their sorcery to complement his. Incredibly complex waves crashed around allies and broke over enemies. Companions disappeared in puffs of swirling smoke, while dense shields protected the fallen.

Caldan opened another well and added its caustic fire to his own. In the gloom, Aidan, cel Rau, and Caitlyn traded blows with Companions, while Felice pressed her back against a wall. Caldan unleashed more destructive sorcery, spraying his whips across mail and plate and leather. Metal and flesh parted, and men fell, splattering crimson stains across the stones. The Companions were cut down and were replaced, only for the new soldiers to disintegrate under his onslaught. Some twitched and writhed before they ceased to breathe, while others blew apart in bloody chaos.

A Companion stood over a fallen mercenary whose broken shield lay at her feet. The mercenary raised a despairing arm as an immense sword was about to split her head open. Caldan lashed the Companion, who flew backward and crumpled into a heap.

Three Companions hacked at two Protectors, who stood over Mold's inert form. The Protectors warded off the blows, tiring rapidly under the assault. Caldan directed his sorcery past them and into their opponents. Blood spattered across the Protectors' shields, and

Caldan moved on, walking as calmly as he could through the dead and dying littering the flagstones.

He opened a third well, directing its surging energy through his strings and the Bleeder's crafting.

Companions jerked and shrieked and died in their dozens. They were no match for his focused sorcery. He released volley after volley, weaving it around mercenaries.

Silent Companions fell, their lives snatched from them by Caldan's carving tendrils.

As he killed, and the mercenaries found themselves saved, some yelled their thanks, while some backed away fearfully, knowing as Caldan did that what he was doing was a terrible thing.

But it needed to be done, if they were to survive.

Caldan walked among the dead, followed by the survivors. Glittering fire whipped and curled in his vision, slicing into flesh, through bone, spilling blood and viscera—and he knew that those watching without sorcerous ability saw nothing of what he did. Only men flayed and carved like meat in a butcher's shop.

And soon there were no more Companions standing.

Caldan ceased his relentless march and swallowed. The glittering lights in his sorcerous senses faded to motes, then to nothing.

At first, he was filled with euphoria.

Such power I possess! What can't I do, with more training and practice? With guidance from Quiss and Gazija, I could soon surpass the warlocks, if I haven't already. Except . . . Quiss and Gazija wouldn't allow it—and for good reason.

Or was it? Couldn't he achieve far more good with his power than others had? Or was that the path the emperor walked?

Was that the path Kelhak once walked?

A hand tugged at his sleeve. Felice.

She gazed at him in horror, and her bottom lip quivered. Shame, sympathy, or disgust? He couldn't tell.

"Enough," she said. "Please, Caldan."

He drew a deep breath, grounding himself in her eyes. "I'm sorry. I had to. I'm . . . done."

"I know," Felice said. "I know you had to do it. They're all . . . dead now."

Caldan turned to find Aidan and Caitlyn both staring at him, expressions blank. Behind them, mercenaries clutched weapons and shields tight, eyes wild and terrified, as if they expected the same fate that had befallen the Companions.

"It's all right," he said to them.

A few nodded, some muttering among themselves, looking around at the blood-splashed stones. As Caldan's wolf padded over to him, they made superstitious signs of warding.

Then the emperor laughed. And Caldan realized he'd left them so that he could see how Caldan and Quiss reacted. He'd wanted to gauge their power. The sound of his mirth sickened Caldan, and he turned his face away, but not before catching a glimpse of the emperor's expression.

Lust and greed.

Then Caldan noticed the Protectors were missing. Where were . . . There. They crouched over the fallen figure of Mold.

Caldan rushed over to them. He reached Mold's side just as they straightened, helping the master to his feet. A trail of scarlet leaked from Mold's mouth, and one eye had rolled up into his head, leaving only the white showing. One bloodied hand still held the trinket sword, red metal runes shining on the silvered blade.

"I'm fine. Leave me!" Mold cried. He blinked, as if the sight in his remaining eye was bleary. One of the Protectors offered him a vial, which he drank from. After a moment, Mold straightened. An alchemical stimulant and painkiller, Caldan surmised.

Mold peered around him at the destruction Caldan had wrought and shook his head despairingly. "What you did to the Indryallans . . . how? You're what we've spent our life fighting against."

"I am," Caldan said, unperturbed. "But then again, maybe not. Because in another time, I might have become a warlock. And then you'd be taking orders from me." He held up a hand as Mold began to protest. "You know it's the truth. They've held knowledge back from you, about what they know of sorcery. They don't respect the Protectors. But that argument's for another day. Right now, here, we work with what we have. If we don't, the lich will destroy us all.

"Just know that, for today, we *can't* be enemies."

Mold stared at him, revulsion warring with . . . sadness?

He might actually be starting to understand. Right now, though, all I care about is him not trying to stab me in the back.

Turning away from the Protectors, Caldan saw the mercenaries gathering behind him. While they'd waited, they'd been listening to every word he'd said. Many of them were injured, their fellows bandaging them up as best they could. And flasks were being handed around. Caldan guessed they contained oil of the poppy, as the mercenaries took only a small sip before passing them on.

To the side stood Felice, Aidan, and Caitlyn, along with the swordsman cel Rau. A few warlocks, along with Florian and Alasdair, had returned from the darkened passages where they'd battled their own Companions and sorcerers. Some were also injured; a number were supported by two of their brethren as they stumbled back to the main group. Drool trickled from slack mouths, and sightless eyes stared about them. Wounds of the mind, Caldan deduced. Fighting Indryallan sorcery was perilous for the weaker sorcerers among the warlocks.

Aidan caught Caldan's eye and nodded to him, expression bleak.

Caldan drew in a ragged breath. There would be worse to come.

THE TUNNEL THEY followed ended abruptly, opening onto a subterranean thoroughfare. Rubble was strewn in front of them; bricks lining the opening had fallen from crumbling mortar, one of the few signs they'd seen that the place was deteriorating. Before the Shattering, they'd certainly built things to last.

Geometrically perfect square pavers lined the road, the gaps between them thinner than a hair. What stone they were made from, Caldan couldn't tell. Perhaps it wasn't a natural substance at all, but a product of superior technology, or even sorcery.

Beyond the light their torches and sorcerous globes provided, the road stretched away in either direction, eventually fading into obsidian darkness. Their group congregated close to one another, as if their very nearness warded off the strangeness of the place.

Caldan understood what they were feeling, for he felt it himself. Their civilization, for all its advances and luxuries, for all its searching and knowledge, didn't compare to the time before the Shattering. They'd come here on a quest to prevent a second Shattering, but they had been confronted with the fact that, for all its supremacy, for all its accomplishments, a far greater civilization than theirs had succumbed to the very same forces they were to confront. They thought they had a chance to succeed. But this desolate, buried city told them otherwise.

The walls on either side of the road were blank, devoid of the images and symbols that decorated the side passages they'd traveled through so far. Their lights reflected against the polished rock walls, echoing from one to the other until they faded to nothing.

Word spread from the emperor up ahead: a short break, moments only.

A scrape reached Caldan's ears, and he turned. One of the mercenaries was attempting to scratch something into the paving stone at his feet with a dagger.

The man cursed, then looked up at everyone staring at him. "I can't mark it," he said, and shrugged. His words echoed around them, and several of the mercenaries flinched.

"There are tracks in the dust," Aidan said as Felice approached from the gloom in front of them.

Caldan looked over to where Aidan pointed. Many booted feet, coming from their right and disappearing down the road to their left. Was it Kelhak and his retinue? Or was it someone—or something—else?

"We follow them," Caldan said. "Whatever they're looking for, they can't know its exact location. Not after all this time. They'll have to search for it. Probably split into smaller groups. We can weaken them."

Felice looked askance at him, but he kept his expression neutral. They still had no idea if their plan would work.

Into the darkness they walked, and this time Aidan, cel Rau, Caitlyn, Caldan, and Quiss were at the fore, trailed by Felice and Selbourne, then Quiss's sorcerers surrounded by mercenaries. Mold and his Protectors came next, scarcely speaking as they took in the wonders of this ancient place. The emperor guarded their rear with his warlocks and the two Touched—strangely silent, though he should know more about this place than anyone. A few times, he had stopped, eyes unfocused, as though struggling to remember something . . .

Minutes passed as they followed the disturbed dust trail. Numerous openings appeared at either side, but they hurried past, as if exploring the passages would bring some unknown calamity down upon them. The darkness and the unknown was oppressive, an insubstantial presence that nevertheless weighed each of them down, almost like it had an otherworldly substance, which could only be sensed, never touched or seen.

Ahead of them, a set of burnished gates resolved out of the shadows, and they halted. At least three times their height and just as wide, the gates were polished to a mirror brightness, unblemished by age. Across their surface was an intricate mosaic of connecting symbols, etched into the metal with unerring accuracy. Tiny runes at the top of the gates merged to create other, larger patterns underneath, which themselves merged into even greater symbols below them. The complexity was bewildering, almost mesmerizing. Caldan blinked and had to look away to steady himself as the symbols began to swim before his eyes.

"It's not sorcerous," Quiss said, breaking the stunned silence.

Caldan opened his well and checked. Quiss was right, as far as he could tell. But so many of the runes and symbols were familiar to him, from what he knew of crafting. Like, and yet unlike—as if the shapes he'd been taught were crude approximations, a child's drawing compared to a master's painting. The gates themselves might not be sorcerous in nature, but they were an example of the complexity sorcery had ascended to thousands of years ago.

Quiss stretched out a hand and placed it on the metal. Several of the mercenaries gasped as he touched it, as if they feared some sort of reaction from the inanimate object.

Caldan narrowed his eyes. He brought his sorcerous globe close to the ground and examined the bottom of the gates. Illustrations of manlike figures lined the base. On both ends, they were hunched and crude. Closer in they changed into a second type, smaller, more detailed, each one with a sunlike symbol on its chest, a circle with radiating lines. Then, in the center, stood the tallest of the figures. Only some of these had the sun symbol, but—

They each had four arms.

The intricate geometries and runes on the gates dissolved into curves and spirals, all still descending until they coalesced around the figures.

Felice crouched at Caldan's side and placed a hand on his shoulder. She pointed to the figures on the farthest edges.

"Jukari," she said.

Her finger moved to the smaller shapes.

"Vormag."

Then she touched one of the four-armed figures, her finger leaving a shiny smear.

"Talon," she whispered.

And with that, he understood what the pictures meant.

The patterns etched into the alloy of the gates weren't just decoration. There were symbols and script, and pictograms. A few words Caldan could translate, and what he could, combined with the other details, filled him with dread. They were part memorial to the ancestors' triumph, imbuing the metal with their knowledge as a way of making their discovery immortal, and part instruction manual, information and details on how they'd achieved their goal. They'd conceived and spawned creatures through sorcery, servants to do their bidding.

They'd created life, of a sort, and then enslaved it.

And after they'd perished in a devastating war of their own creation, their monstrosities were free, left to roam, to do as they willed. The doors were part history, part schematic, and part warning.

Caldan shook himself, found his gaze continually drawn to the details of the gates.

He'd known, as they all had, that the jukari, vormag, and talons were constructed creatures. But now they were part of this world like any other. For thousands of years, they'd existed without the masters who'd created them. They could be pushed and prodded, but never again truly controlled.

For the first time, he believed he truly understood the entirety of Kelhak's horrific plan, his purpose in choosing Anasoma.

Beneath the city, in the ancient passages and rooms long unused, abandoned, forgotten, were the means to enslave the world. With its overpowering sorcery, its innumerable wells, its lack of morality, what monsters would the lich create?

"It's a schematic," Felice said, and the fact that she had figured it out didn't surprise him. "Can you decipher it? Would you be able to follow the instructions?"

Caldan shook his head, a heavy sense of doom settling over him, preventing him from speaking. The future was laid out before him, myriad possibilities narrowed down to hardly more than a few. If they failed, then months, perhaps years after they were killed, hordes of jukari and vormag would be unleashed on the empire. Not direction-less tribes like those that existed in the Desolate Lands, but well-equipped masses under the control of one leader: Kelhak.

This time, the Shattering wouldn't be one of sorcery destroying civilization, but one of murder and enslavement. The lich had burned Gazija and Quiss's world and learned from its mistakes. A dead world was useless.

It was far better to have one you controlled.

CHAPTER 55

After passing through the gates they walked along abandoned passageways, through the bowels of the earth, some winding, and some straight. Dust and chalky bones littered the ground, crumbling with age underfoot. Sometimes there were rust stains impregnating the stone, metal bruising the ground as it eroded to nothing.

A place where sorcerers worked and lived, so long ago. A place where sorcery was combined with lost arts of flesh crafting, gnawing at the boundary of what separated the inanimate from the animate, death from life.

They trudged through halls and corridors, a maze of passageways and galleries. Dust stirred with every step, swirling to their knees and caking their boots and legs. The air was lifeless, entombed here for so long it had taken on the stone taste of the walls and floor.

Selbourne constantly spoke with his mercenaries, words pitched low, barely heard over the slap of footfalls. From the look of some of them—wide eyed and jittery—Caldan thought he was reassuring them, calming their nerves. The weight of stone pressed down on them, along with the weight of ages. It wasn't an easy thing to dismiss.

But then again, he didn't have the time to think about it; his mind churned with other matters: Kelhak. Sorcery. What it meant to be a lich. The nature of wells, and trinkets.

Muffled words and curses filled the corridor. Caldan looked up, aware he'd not been concentrating on what was ahead.

He lifted his sorcerous globe in his gauntleted hand, but its light couldn't penetrate the darkness around them for very far.

"Bloody ancestors," cursed Felice.

"We must go this way," the talon said from right behind Caldan, making him flinch.

There was a long pause. The conversation of mercenaries and warlocks and Protectors murmured in the background.

Untarnished metallic doors had appeared in front of them, out of the darkness. Torches and sorcerous lights banished shadows, throwing the doors' surface into sharp relief. An intricate pattern was etched into their bronzelike metal, one seemingly without rhyme or reason.

The doors stood open on massive hinges, solid metal as thick as Caldan's extended hand.

"It's a maze," Aidan said, wonder on his face.

Caldan stepped back and peered at the etched pattern. He was right. At the center of each door was a blank circle, joined to the pattern by a single line. He followed the contour until he lost it among many others.

The emperor called them all, wanting to take the lead. Leather creaked and armor clanked as the mercenaries separated to make a path for him to the front.

Felice frowned, pulling again on her earring. "Can't Kelhak just . . . travel?" she asked Caldan, waving a hand. "And disappear? He's done that before. So have we."

The talon's hood moved from side to side slightly, as if the creature shook its head.

Before it said anything, the emperor's voice came from ahead of them. "Not without using a great deal of stored power. The lich won't want to do that. It cannot conceive of anything that will harm it, so it will not flee from us. When we fight it, by the time it realizes it's in trouble, it will be too late. Its sorcerous reserves will be depleted."

Caldan found himself nodding. It made sense. Quiss's craftings, based on the Protectors' trinket sword, would block as many of Kelhak's wells as they could, while others, based on both Felice's trinket dagger and Quiss's knowledge, would drain as many more from the lich as possible. With so many craftings aimed at blocking and absorbing its wells, the lich would die from a hundred tiny cuts.

But few things in life, as Caldan knew well, went according to design. As in Dominion, opponents usually had extra moves they could make.

AIDAN AND CAITLYN followed the emperor through the doors. The injured warlocks and mercenaries trailed behind the rest of the group as they marched down the tunnel and entered a vast chamber. There was a stillness to the room, more profound than anything else Aidan had felt since they left sunlight behind. Behind him, the company filed in through the open doorway. Holes in the stone revealed there had once been a door, but no more. Age had done to it what it did to everything: devoured and destroyed.

Sorcerous globes threw shadows, revealing ancient stones swirling with sections far darker than those they had been walking so far. Blackened, as if by great heat. But the patches were too inconsistent for that. Aidan scraped at the uneven rock with his boot. The very stones were stained with something.

"What do you think caused it?" Caitlyn said.

"Blood," the talon said from behind Aidan.

He turned. "What did you say?"

The towering, scruffy-looking thing turned this way and that, as if sniffing the air.

"The blood of generations," it said. "This is a womb. A slave pit. And a cemetery."

Aidan exchanged glances with Caitlyn, and they moved away, not wanting to be near the creature. *Once this is over,* he vowed, *I'll see it dead. Such evil cannot be allowed to exist.*

In the center of the immense chamber lay great slabs, dozens of them, rising from the floor as if carved from rock where they stood. He could not fathom their purpose. The walls to both sides and in front of him were tiered. Steps rose from one level to the next. Aidan left Caitlyn behind and ascended to the first tier.

Crumbling metal covered the ground, and he confirmed the next tier was the same. Iron would have corroded many years ago, but this brighter metal still endured, to a point. He bent and picked up a portion, squeezed until it disintegrated in his grasp. Flakes and splinters fell from his hand.

"It's an alloy of some kind," said Caldan.

The young man had followed him up, and now stood on the first tier.

"The ancients knew more of metallurgy than we do. They created marvels—"

"And horrors," Aidan said. "Don't forget that."

Caldan nodded. "What do you think this place was?"

Aidan's boot scuffed metal fragments. "The talon said it was . . . a womb. Among other things."

"A womb? What did it mean?" Suddenly, Caldan rushed back down the steps and hurtled toward one of the slabs.

Aidan followed, but at a slower pace. When he reached him, Caldan was kneeling, hands running over the side of the slab.

"There are patterns here," Caldan was saying to himself. His hands became gray as he brushed away dust. He grunted, then moved his attention to the top surface of the slab. More dust clouded the air as he wiped the stone. Taking a breath, he blew close to it, revealing intricate patterns and runic symbols.

More evil. "Sorcery," Aidan said.

"Yes," replied Caldan. "The gates we came across before—the ones with pictures of jukari, vormag, and talons—this is where the creatures were made."

"How long has Kelhak had access to this place? When did he find his way down here?"

Caldan sighed. "I don't know. It doesn't look like it's seen recent use, but if there are more, and the lich has started making more jukari—"

A cry from across the room interrupted them. Horrified murmurs broke the silence following it.

Aidan ran to a far corner, where a group of mercenaries and warlocks had gathered. He was aware of Caitlyn and cel Rau following his every move, but he didn't care. Lying on one of the slabs was a desiccated corpse. Though its gray, mottled skin was shrunken and wrinkled, its arms and legs were still bigger than a human's. A jukari.

More of the mummified corpses lay on slabs in the shadows. The same bright crumbling metal trailed from bands around their wrists and ankles.

"These things are almost worse like this than when they're alive," Aidan said. "It's good this place has remained buried for thousands of years."

"Well, it's been rediscovered now," said Felice. "What need does he have for people, if he controls his own army of monstrosities?"

"He learned his lesson before," Caldan said, "with Gazija's world. A completely shattered world is useless to the lich. It wants wells. It *needs* wells to make sure it's more powerful than everyone else, in order to survive."

"We already know this," Aidan said. "But only vormag have wells, not jukari."

Caldan met his eyes, a grim look on his face. "But their wells are inserted in them . . . having basically been ripped out of a sorcerer to create them. So he's not after more vormag, but jukari. Jukari who will obey him without question, who he can then, in turn, use to enslave us all. Or, at least, the sorcerers. That's what he cares about: a steady supply of sorcerers and their wells. The jukari will herd them like cattle. Then their wells will be stripped from them for whatever purpose the lich desires. Either to add to its own, or create vormag, or trinkets. Or even sustenance. An endless, compliant source."

"But they'll be sorcerers. Why wouldn't they rise up against the jukari?"

"Do you think the lich will let any sorcerer reach adulthood?"

"A well is there from birth," Felice breathed. "Possibly before. Bloody ancestors . . ."

Fear and revulsion flushed through Aidan. As the pregnant women he'd rescued had been used for their babies, so would humans be harvested for their wells.

And now that the idea had been planted, there was no reason that only Kelhak would be interested in such a plan . . .

He kept his head lowered but glanced toward the emperor, who was urging everyone to hurry and gather together before they resumed their march.

Such abhorrent knowledge couldn't be allowed to be used again.

CHAPTER 56

nother new chamber. Far in the distance shone a light. It flickered briefly, as if something had passed in front of it, then continued shining. Their sorcerous globes banished darkness, revealing tarnished vats in rows, not unlike the distillery where they entered this catacomb. Massive circular vessels made from copper-tinged metal stained with green patina. Except copper would have corroded long ago.

Another alloy, thought Caldan, calling his wolf to his side. Gazija had relinquished control as soon as the fight with the Silent Companions was over. He didn't want there to be any chance Kelhak could sense his sorcery.

Caldan turned to regard the warlocks and mercenaries as they entered behind him.

Felice held a hand to her nose. "It's rank in here."

The pinprick of light went out.

"Hush!" Felice hissed at them all, and after a few moments, shuffling feet, metal clanks, and creaking leather trailed into silence.

The emperor moved quietly to the side, Alasdair and Florian flanking him.

"Something's up ahead," Caldan whispered to Felice.

She nodded. "I saw it. And that's why I said 'hush' . . ."

Selbourne left his men and approached. He smelled of his metal cuirass and sweat. And slightly behind him, the talon also moved closer, its mustiness seeming to invade their space.

The talon stirred, and Caldan felt a flicker of sorcery, but whether from the made creature or a trinket, he couldn't tell. Rags moved as it raised its arms, two clawed hands emerging from the tatters. In each it held a dagger identical to the ones Caldan had seen Felice and Izak carrying when they'd appeared outside Riversedge.

Selbourne whispered orders to the mercenaries, as did the emperor to the warlocks and Touched. They fanned out, weapons drawn and ready, sorcerers clutching craftings and trinkets. Wells were opened and wards spread over as many as possible. To Caldan's sorcerous senses, trinkets shone like stars on fingers and from around necks. Felice stayed behind Caldan, where Aidan and Caitlyn and cel Rau and Felice gathered in nervous readiness.

From the darkness ahead, dozens of tiny sparkles glittered, floating and whirling like fireflies. Up and up they circled, until they reached the ceiling—where each erupted into a powerful sorcerous globe, casting harsh, cold light over the chamber.

Ages-old detritus and workings were revealed: smooth metal containers twice the height of a man and as shiny as if they were forged yesterday. Pipes protruded from them, some ending at guttering in the floor, while others snaked upward to smaller vessels. And bones were littered around them—knee-high piles of thicker, longer black bones mixed with human-sized chalky white. Metal glinted among them—weapons and armor and buckles—all made from the same corrosion-resistant alloy. Glass urns and jugs lay shattered and whole, whatever alchemical liquids they held drained and evaporated.

A battle had been fought here, thousands of years ago. And judging from the destruction and bones, the cost to both sides had been high.

The emperor strode forward just as more sorcerous globes illuminated the murk at the chamber's far end.

Where Kelhak stood.

As perfect as a marble statue. Tall and magnificent. And like Quiss
and his colleagues, he had an unnatural density to him. An otherworldly confluence of reality that seemed to push the weight of the
world away—or draw it into itself. To hoard intensity, as if to deny
that anything outside of its influence mattered.

All eyes were drawn to the sight, like iron to a lodestone.

"Kelhak!" the emperor shouted. "We're here to—"

The light surrounding Kelhak winked out. A shadow smothered
the emperor, then swept him up. There had been no sound, just a
darkness enfolding shining crafted armor. It rolled and let out a deep-
throated roar. A creature bigger than a draft horse, its gray mottled
hide studded with scales. Steam rose from it, and ichor dripped. It
was newly created, Caldan realized as a sulfurous, decaying scent
assailed him.

A lash of the abomination's tail knocked two mercenaries into
mewling piles. Twisting, glittering tendrils reached out to score its
hide—but somehow, impossibly, it resisted them. The beast raised
limbs as thick as tree trunks, ending in claws as sharp as blades. Mercenaries and warlocks scattered like rats in torchlight.

Blinding tendrils burst from the emperor as he writhed in its
clutches. Dozens of wells opened, and the walls and columns around
them were writ with sorcerous blooms and shaken with thunder. Warlocks shrieked and screamed, painting the creature with hissing lines.
Javelins poked into its skin, doing little more than annoy it.

A shape flashed past Caldan as the talon entered the fray, so close
the wind of its passing ruffled his hair. Its silver blades whirled, hacking chunks from the beast's armored hide.

Caldan added his sorcery to the warlocks', his boiling Touched
blood coursing through his veins.

A gaping maw dripping mucus closed about the emperor, who
was shouting, casting sorcery with abandon. Fangs grated against his
shield. Incandescent lines scissored, cutting and shearing and scorch-

ing. Alasdair, Florian, Caitlyn, and cel Rau bounded and danced among the thing's flailing limbs, blades and spears flashing.

"Everyone!" Alasdair cried. "The limbs. Hack its—" Swordlike talons slashed through him, and he fell in pieces, mouth working, making no sound.

Florian wailed in anguish, stabbing at the beast with renewed frenzy. Voracious tendrils roamed over the creature, slashing deep. Smoke and black blood spat from the wounds.

Caldan poured his sorcery into destruction. Hundreds of cuts scored the creation's scaled hide, but not deep enough. He abandoned Mahsonn's crafting and took another tack. Gathering his power, he pounded raw destruction upon the thing. Flame and anger, the raw energy of his wells.

But obviously this creature wasn't all Kelhak had in store, and Silent Companions began pouring out of the darkness. Mercenaries cursed and warlocks screamed. Blades clashed. Sorcery cut and burned. Men and women fell on both sides. Arms hacked and slashed with violence. Armored figures wrestled in the dust and bones. Sorcerers flailed under their shields while spewing dissecting lines. Mold and his Protectors were shining like beacons amid the carnage.

"Stand firm!" Selbourne shouted over the din.

How many of them were left to hear the mercenary captain?

Companions assaulted sorcerous wards and threw themselves at mercenaries, slashing and thrashing, blades shining and cutting, sparks flashing from armor. Caldan turned to them for a few moments, sorcery whirling and dismembering. Their armor glowed orange. Skin blistered and separated. Many fell, and not all of them were replaced.

Caldan's stomach clenched and twisted. A sickness rose in him, and his muscles weakened, scarcely holding him upright. His Touched abilities were damaging him, with only his one trinket ring to mitigate their aftereffects.

He sensed Quiss and Mazoet, and their sorcerers, shaping something, while warlock flames cascaded against the creature. Whatever they crafted was unleashed. The air shrieked and wailed. A stone column shattered, spraying debris over them all. Quiss and Mazoet shone with sorcery, limned in sickening light.

All of a sudden, the talon scaled the creature's back, nimble as a cat. Shining blades plunged deep into the creation's head.

And the back of its skull exploded. Viscous blood and brain misted the air. Fragments of skull splattered the ground, and the beast fell with a mammoth crash.

Caldan checked on Felice, who was safe with Aidan and Caitlyn, a shocked fright in her eyes.

Florian lurched from the beast. Cel Rau slipped in blood, falling to his knees. Caldan raced toward the emperor. A foul stench permeated the air, and the emperor's unsurpassed smith-crafted armor was dented and scratched.

But Zerach-Sangur rose to his feet, grinning like a madman.

He ignored the carnage around him and nodded to the talon, which backed away to the edge of their light.

The clamor quieted. All the Silent Companions were either dead or incapacitated. Mercenaries stumbled, blades notched and bloodied. So far, at least half were dead or injured, and the warlocks hadn't fared much better. Quiss and his people had lost one or two, and the survivors looked haggard and drawn.

"Anyone who can walk, gather around me," the emperor shouted. "Now! Everyone else, tend to your wounds."

Mercenaries began binding wounds, casting glances toward the back of the chamber, where Kelhak still stood, immobile and serene. The emperor strode toward Kelhak. Lights flickered in nearby tunnels—more Companions rushing to join the fight.

Selbourne yelled. "Form up on me and hold these bastards back!"

Armored figures spewed from the darkness, and the mercenaries met them with steel. Selbourne grabbed Felice's arm and dragged her back to his men, allowing Aidan, Caitlyn, and cel Rau room to move.

The emperor shrugged off concerned hands. His eyes flashed with anger and determination.

"To me, warlocks!" he roared.

The surviving sorcerers scrabbled to his side, weakened and weary, panicked and scared.

Quiss and his people joined them.

The emperor picked up his sword from where he'd dropped it. It was a smith-crafted blade covered with runic designs. He strode toward Kelhak, not waiting to see who followed.

Air wavered, as if heated around the lich, as a warded dome covered Kelhak.

The emperor pointed his sword at Kelhak, who stood rigid in the face of the threat. Runic armor glinted in sorcerous light, sparkling as the emperor's shield churned across its surface. Metal plates covered golden mail. Long platinum hair blew, as if in a subterranean wind, and the emperor's mouth worked as he silently cursed the lich before him.

Kelhak took a step forward, naked torso glistening. A score of sorcerous globes erupted in radiance from where they floated above him, bathing the lich in a cold blue light. Not a single crafting or trinket adorned Kelhak. Not one.

Caldan tried to swallow, though his mouth was dry. The lich was so far gone into his sorcery, he had no need of craftings. In essence, he was pure sorcery, a soul that had captured many others to do its bidding. The body of Kelhak had been used for a purpose. A puppet. A tool. A peerless mind squashed and subsumed without thought.

"Keep them from the sorcerers," shouted Selbourne over the din of clashing blades and screams as the mercenaries battled the Silent Companions.

"*Ik'zvime*," the emperor spat, half curse, half cry.

Kelhak raised his face to the ceiling far above, as if trying to see through the rock between him and open sky.

The emperor's face twisted in wrath. Flickered in fear. But this time, he wasn't going to take the coward's way out.

And he struck.

Caldan lunged for Selbourne in panic and shielded him, yanking him back from the impending eruption. Lemon and scorched metal scents filled his nostrils, so strong he almost gagged.

Streaks of black coursed from the emperor. Those that touched Kelhak's shield went no farther; they were absorbed and turned into sparkling motes. Others sprayed wide, cutting a swath through stone. Scorched lines appeared in their wake; molten stone poured from razor trenches, spitting orange and golden. A blistering wind blew, stinging with dust and heat and bone.

Caldan sensed the emperor's wells, power flowing through them thick and fast, barely under control. The emperor was pushing himself to his limits. And on the heels of his attack, arrows and javelins from the mercenaries struck the God-Emperor's shield, exploding and flashing to ashes.

And Kelhak remained untouched.

Behind Caldan, Quiss's sorcerers used craftings to drain and block Kelhak's wells. A dozen were consumed by them, and yet the obsidian lines of the emperor's sorcery still flailed in an attempt to penetrate the lich's shield. In the tumult, Caldan ceded control of his wolf to Gazija, and the construct slunk into the shadows.

Power spewed forth from Zerach-Sangur, and he yelled in defiance.

Lines of arcane energy whipped Caldan's shield, and he found himself dragged backward by Selbourne, who was shouting, spit spattering from his mouth. The noise of sorcery deafened Caldan, drowning out any other sound. Selbourne's words went unheard.

Caldan sent his own sorcery against Kelhak's shield, but it seemed feeble in comparison to the emperor's immense power.

Midnight tendrils bounced across walls, through columns, cutting swaths through stone. A mercenary cried out as one sliced through him. Another wailed as his arm was neatly severed and dropped to the ground. A warlock, confident her shield would protect her, darted forward, and her head was separated from her neck. The shield winked out. Crimson spurted, splashing warlocks nearby, who flinched as the hot liquid drenched their own shields.

Everywhere, men and women sobbed and mewled. Around them was sorcerous slaughter, while in front were foes who fought like madmen, soundless and vicious.

Kelhak's laughter boomed, a thousand-voiced sound. An ageless tormented clamor condensed into a single vocalization.

Caldan groped for courage as Selbourne continued to drag him across the floor.

"No!" he shouted to the mercenary, words whipped away like leaves in a storm.

"We need you at the rear!" Selbourne said. "We can't hold them off much longer."

"I can't," Caldan said. "Kelhak must be killed, or everyone has died for nothing."

Selbourne nodded grimly. "Go, then. We'll bloody hold." He gripped Caldan's shoulder briefly, then turned and raced to bolster his mercenaries.

Caldan felt a swell of pride at the man's courage, before he turned and rushed toward Kelhak.

A thunderous crack battered Caldan down, slapping him sideways. He scrambled to his feet, ribs aching. From nearby, he sensed Quiss, Mazoet, and their people hammering against the lich's shield.

Wave after wave after wave of sizzling brilliance. Blazing light that sparkled with violet incandescence so intense it hurt his eyes to look upon.

All washing like the sea against a rock. Withstood. Broken.

Smoke and cinders spat from Kelhak's spectral wards. Lights of all colors flashed and stamped the walls of the gallery. Surges of force made the air shimmer.

And the lich laughed all the while.

Until the talon darted forward—and straight through Kelhak's shield, as though it didn't exist. Caldan sensed its wells open, and a wave of cold poured forth. The lich screamed as the heat was sucked out of the air. Sharp cracks sounded as a mist swirled, and frost rimed stone as moisture froze. Silver blades slashed at Kelhak, sliced the skin of his upraised arms.

There was a thunderous clap. The talon wailed in agony, high and piercing, as a wave of force slammed it aside. It tumbled across the floor, rags flapping, leaving a trail of dark blood. Legs trailing limply behind it, the talon used its clawlike hands to crawl across the stone as it attempted to get away from Kelhak.

Caldan opened his wells and added his corrosive power to that assailing the lich. Everything he had learned. Every trick he had deduced. Every method of controlling destructive sorcery he had gathered, he melded into the Bleeder's crafting.

Sorcerous tendrils whipped through dust illuminated by flashing lights. The air shrieked. The glow of forbidden sorcery etched every surface.

Kelhak's shield whined as it was painted with motes. Purple and red sparkles swirled and churned. And the destructive sorcery dissipated to nothing.

Pinprick glitters were yanked from Kelhak—warlocks and Quiss's people draining wells from the lich. More were sucked from it, floating through the violence to their crafted prisons. And the vermillion glow of the lich's stolen wells dimmed minutely. But it wasn't enough. The lich was far stronger than they'd realized. The emperor's confidence had been a sham. He was only here because he had no choice—it was fight or die.

And when the lich rose from the tumult of their feeble sorcerous attacks, when they were depleted and it was still strong, they would be absorbed. And the wells they'd stripped and blocked would return to the creature.

The emperor shouted in defiance again.

Answering lines blacker than night glittered out to meet him. Dark yet blinding—precise and beautiful.

The emperor's shield broke under their onslaught. Metal and flesh and bone were severed. Zerach-Sangur, the emperor of the Mahruse Empire, toppled. Meat collapsed into slops and blood spurts. Intense heat blackened and charred what was left of him.

Caldan thought he heard the warlocks wailing over the tumult. A scream came from Caitlyn. She rushed Kelhak, sword raised over her head. And was tackled by cel Rau. They fell, tumbling in the dust. Caitlyn kicked and clawed the swordsman as he tried to stop her. Cel Rau wrestled himself on top of her. He pinned her arms, and she kneed him in the plums. He toppled to the side, and Caitlyn thrust him off. She lurched to her feet and grabbed her blade, rushing toward Kelhak again, screaming incoherently. Cel Rau stretched one hand toward her . . .

A bolt as bright as the sun came from Kelhak and struck Caitlyn—who evaporated in a scarlet mist. Her blade clanged to the stone. Her fight against evil was over.

And evil had won.

Coercive sorcery poured from the lich, assailing Quiss and his sorcerers. Quiss dropped, as if poleaxed, and Mazoet fell, howling, clutching at his head. He tore clumps of hair from his scalp. The sorcerous assault on the lich's wells ceased in an instant.

Caldan scrabbled across the cold stones, aiming for Quiss, who lay on the ground, writhing and moaning in agony. A short distance away, Mazoet's eyes and ears leaked blood. The sorcerer's mouth opened in a scream—but no sound emerged. A brilliant mote jerked from his head and shot toward Kelhak, and joined the other wells in his churning mass of power. Mazoet slumped to the cold stone. He twitched once, then his eyes remained open, staring lifelessly.

The many-throated voice of the lich roared in Caldan's ears.

"You know not what you do. But I forgive you. We forgive you. Come, join with me. With all of us."

By the ancestors. They were out of their depth. So far out, they were all likely dead.

Mold sat among his butchered Protectors. Scattered around him were chunks of flesh dripping red, white bones protruding from ragged meat. He blinked numbly at the sight, as if he didn't believe what he was seeing. Pressing one hand to the floor, he staggered to his feet and turned his gaze to the almost invisible barrier around Kelhak. Large though it was, it was small against the vaulted ceiling above them.

They hadn't even come close to the shield yet, and they were slaughtered, their numbers reduced to a fraction.

Mold shrieked—a sound drawn from the depths of his soul, rage filled and throat tearing.

Kelhak was slowly turning in a circle, as if searching for something, or someone. His manifold roar echoed between walls, compounding his alienness.

Mold stepped toward the shield, trinket sword in his hand. His shadow stretched out behind him, cast by the sorcery pouring from Kelhak.

Caldan knew it was no use. The shield would repel him. There was no way Mold could penetrate it and get to the lich.

The last remaining Protector stopped at the shield's edge, wild-eyed, maniacal face pale. Mold cried out—words lost in the uproar of sorcery crashing around them. He raised a fist to beat on the shield in frustration.

And his arm passed through.

Violet sorcery coated it like paint. Mold convulsed, tendons in his neck standing out like whipcord. His flesh dripped, splattering the stone, revealing the bones underneath. He wailed, feet scuffing the ground as he attempted to pull himself free, but couldn't. Corrosive fire burst from the shield and covered him. Bones cracked and twisted.

Felice cried out in horror.

Mold fell to the floor, lifeless, sword clanging on stone. And a bright spark was ripped from him, caged in patterns of coercive sorcery. It floated up, then toward Kelhak. The God-Emperor laughed again, a sound that wasn't loud but nevertheless reached Caldan where he crouched. So profound and diverse was it, the lich's voice penetrated his bones.

The spark contained a well, and whatever was left of Mold's awareness. It drifted in the air and found its way to Kelhak. Then it was gone, added to his host of wells. One more to the total. One more to replace those they'd already stripped from him.

Caldan trembled.

Even if his body survived this day, he knew a part of him wouldn't.

Kelhak, the lich, was horror. A carrion being that shouldn't exist.

Almost without thinking, he commanded his wolf to return to his side from the darkness. Sounds of fighting came from behind. Selbourne and his mercenaries still battling the Silent Companions and

Indryallans come upon them from the tunnels—their blood spilled and lives lost to give them this one chance.

Caldan had come into this wanting one only thing: to survive. But seeing the lich in the flesh, knowing it didn't require flesh itself, that it was the remnants of a decayed sentience, he knew his own life was a minuscule thing compared to stopping Kelhak.

He hoped . . . for who wouldn't? But he also despaired.

Urgency filled him, hot and pressing.

Mercenaries clashed around the chamber. Steel striking steel, flashing sparks, blades biting into leather and flesh. Snarls and words echoed between walls. He could sense them, their heartbeats, as booted feet stirred up clouds of dust that had remained untouched, unsullied, for thousands of years. More mercenaries fell, their ranks thinning. Selbourne was buying them scant extra minutes, at great cost.

Stone columns lay between Caldan and the lich. And that terrible shield.

Immune to destructive sorcery, Kelhak remained unharmed. The only sign of his weakness was the slightly diminished mass of his wells. But there were still *so* many . . . Lights flashed behind Caldan, uncertain at first, then steady, rolling back the blackness with globes of illumination. Quiss had recovered—enough to join with his remaining sorcerers.

Caldan felt more sorcery weaving out of the darkness. More tailored smith-craftings tore into the lich, stripping further wells from its voracious grasp.

Kelhak stood motionless. A smile played about his mouth. The God-Emperor's terrible voice rang out. "Come, all of you. There is peace within me."

He thinks we are defeated, Caldan thought. *And why shouldn't he?*

A putrid stench followed the wells pried from the lich, like the rot of human flesh.

Caldan stepped to the edge of the lich's shield and took the trinket sword in his right hand from where Mold had dropped it. His shield sprang up around him, but he stopped short of the line dividing safety from death. He couldn't risk testing his own wards against the lich's. Somewhere behind him, Selbourne shouted a warning.

Caldan clutched the Protectors' trinket sword, hand burning. His gauntleted hand clenched into a fist around Mahsonn's crafting, but he found he no longer needed contact with it, or the rest of his craftings. His power and finesse had grown, and he knew them now. His shield. His construct. The Bleeder's weapon.

He linked to the last.

Scores of tendrils whipped across the lich's shield. A hundred points of violet light sparked from the contact. The purple glare coalesced into one blinding flash, limning stone and corpses with its brilliance.

The barrier shrank as cascading motes scattered across its marble surface, then strengthened.

He'd barely scratched it.

Kelhak lashed out, a potent eruption that came for Caldan—only to splash harmlessly against a shield raised by Quiss and his people.

"We can't stand much more," Quiss yelled above the tumult.

Caldan felt a hand on his shoulder. Felice. She looked up at him, her face streaked with dirt and sweat. And pressed something into his hand.

The bone trinket rings.

"Use them," she said desperately. "If we don't try something, then we're all dead."

Caldan swallowed and closed his hand around them.

It was relatively easy now, to search for the hidden coercive link to them, to decipher their inner workings as his power flowed through them.

He took a breath and lashed at Kelhak—with the same sorcery he'd killed Devenish for using.

Blackness covered Kelhak's shield as burgeoning purified land tried to siphon life from everything it touched. The lich's wards exploded with light, the glow of sorcery coating everything with corrosive glitter. And once more the shield shrank, only to expand again as Kelhak resisted, somehow.

Caldan opened more wells. Four. Eight. He split strings and tapped their power. More clashes of sorcery. Caldan added a legion of slashes to buffet the lich's wards. Followed by more coalescing purified land. Again and again.

Blinding flashes painted every surface, dispelling shadows, and thunder cracked around him. Caldan's wells pummeled the lich's shield, trying to break it with frenzied onslaught. Coruscating lines scoured the air, hissing with violence. Flames erupted. Stone pavings closest to the shield crumbled and exploded, showering dust and shrapnel. Men and sorcerers cried out in terror, their wailing penetrating Caldan's awareness.

But he dared not pause.

Power smashed into power. Gouts of sorcery slopped across the floor.

Do not stop, Gazija said to him.

Caldan nodded, droplets of sweat falling from his brow, though he knew the old sorcerer couldn't see him.

He tried something different: a shaping of focused power, the kind he'd used when escaping from Thenna's torments. Modified through the bone rings, splitting its swath into segments.

Brilliant lines as sharp as razors sawed at the shield. Seething lightning crawled and pried, attempting to violate the sanctity of the lich's wards. Power bled over. Corpses smoked and charred. Selbourne cried out in pain. Caldan sensed the mercenaries retreat from the Silent Companions, then gather in a defiant cluster.

He drew even more power, feeling its corrosiveness wash over him.

And Kelhak's shield wavered. For an instant, it dimmed under the assault of the Wasters of Life. And the lich's attention drew away from everyone else. To focus on Caldan.

Kelhak frowned, head tilted to one side. He regarded Caldan as a curious child might a bug. A power grew within the lich, a swelling of sorcery so massive it dwarfed anything Caldan had ever sensed.

It hammered into Caldan, breaking over him. His mind recoiled from its intensity, and his body was crushed into the ground. He reeled, losing focus, but with an immense surge of will drew even more from his wells and reinforced his shield. He staggered to his feet—and sent surges of sorcery at Kelhak.

Caldan raged, pouring power into the bonfire.

And felt a break. Nothing physical, but something intrinsic to life. Perhaps it was the fabric of the world shredding.

A Shattering.

He was on the brink. His fight with the lich had begun to unravel reality.

Dismay crept up on Caldan. He withdrew some of his power. By attempting to kill Kelhak, he would destroy the world. He was no better than Devenish, whom he'd killed to prevent such a thing. He couldn't do it.

He faltered . . .

Caldan cried out, but he didn't know what he said. A prayer. A plea. A yell of defiance.

Kelhak took a step forward. Their eyes met, and like recognized like.

Liches.

One weaker than the other. Prey.

Caldan's wolf construct barreled out of the blackness, skittering across stone, metal claws scrabbling for purchase. There was a Silent Companion clinging to it, hands gripping around its runic neck. Inside, Gazija sent the construct toward the lich's shield. Through it. Human armor and flesh melted and sloughed, leaving a trail of bones, which scattered, clattering over stone. Kelhak's corrosive shield covered the wolf construct, scouring its metal skin. Sections glowed orange. Crafted metal liquefied and ran, leaving gaping holes.

It pushed farther inside before its legs collapsed beneath it. Then its corroded alloy split apart.

Gazija tumbled out, rune-covered limbs flailing. Along with him, smith-crafted discs attached to a golden chain spilled like a hoard of coins across the floor.

Caldan ceased his pummeling of the dome ward and gathered his strength. The shield sprang back, as strong as before. Kelhak's eyes turned from him, became aware of Gazija.

The manlike construct rose to stand, a smith-crafted figure two hands high. It ran, trailing the golden chain, not toward Kelhak, but in the beginnings of a circle.

"Do not break!" Selbourne bellowed in the gloom.

The captain and his remaining men formed an arc behind Caldan, along with Felice, Florian, Aidan, and cel Rau. Silent Companions came at them, weapons moving in a frenzy. Blood spilled like wine, splashing faces, arms, torsos, legs and feet. Boots slipped and skidded. Faces twisted in snarls. Metal clashed, striking sparks.

"Hold the line!" yelled Selbourne.

The mercenaries were giving Caldan a chance. Holding back the tide of slavering inhumanity.

Caldan sensed Gazija's power grow. He heard the sorcerer's design call to him.

Inside Kelhak's corrosive shield, Gazija's metal limbs extended, and he spread glistening sorcery at the lich. Luminous threads struck Kelhak, and he recoiled from their ferocity. But the sorcery encountered another shield covering the body it sought to destroy, an impenetrable barrier as invisible as air.

The hazy dome surrounding the lich, separating it from the outside world, dissolved as it marshaled its resources. It sucked its power back into itself, recoiling its strings and opening more wells.

Caldan stepped toward it, hesitated, glanced back at Selbourne and his men. They were falling fast.

There isn't time, he thought to himself. Then, *There has to be.*

He turned his sorcery to the Silent Companions. Sparkling destruction weaved among them. They screamed and flailed and were flayed. Bodies were wrenched and twisted, adding their charcoaled meat to the ground.

Reality wrenched around Kelhak as a hundred wells opened at once.

Hot air washed over Caldan, scalding him. He turned to the lich and saw Gazija's form smoldering under pummeling lights. But he still stood.

Caldan ran toward Kelhak, splitting strings from his wells, as many as he could handle. Bitter lemons and hot metal filled his mouth and nose. The sheer number of strings daunted him, and he swallowed, almost gagging at a pinching, sulfurous stench. The lich's sorcery rattled his bones.

Caldan staggered, head and body aching. But he was close now.

Waves of heat poured from Gazija. He lurched a few more steps, one hand gripping the end of the golden chain, a few feet from the beginning. The stone underneath his metal feet was a lake of fire, skittering with sparkling cinders. But Gazija's smith-crafted alloyed body withstood the sorcery.

For now.

Knowing time was short, Caldan linked to as many of the rune-covered discs as he could, questing his strings out, finding linkages and anchors, pulsing his power through runic patterns based on the trinket sword clutched in one hand.

Wells were stripped from the lich. Ten. Twenty. Fifty.

Not enough.

If they pulled a hundred more from the lich, then maybe they had a chance. Caldan clenched his teeth and opened more wells, splitting a dozen new strings and yanking power from the abomination.

Not enough.

Kelhak turned glowing eyes upon Caldan. For several heartbeats, they glared at each other.

Just as Gazija reached the other end of the chain, and fused the two together with a burst of sorcery, hairlike carvings appeared and connected the circular crafting.

Roaring, Caldan rushed forward as scorching hammers smashed into his shield. A weight descended on him, bending his back as his shield erupted in sparkling motes. The crafting whined under the strain—a fraction of Kelhak's power brought to bear. Caldan's blood rang in his ears. Heat penetrated the soles of his boots, and they began to smoke.

He stepped inside the circle the golden chain delineated and coursed his power through it. Foreign strings joined his—Gazija adding his own sorcery to the crafting.

Reality twisted, folded in on itself. A sudden gale dragged at Caldan.

The ground dropped from under his feet. Caldan's stomach recoiled, twisting and rebelling against the alien sensation.

He landed with a thump, raising a cloud of dust from his clothes. The wind ceased.

Caldan's clutching hands grabbed dry leaves and the dirt of centuries, the bone rings spilling to the dirt.

His wells disappeared.

A shrieking wail battered Caldan's eardrums.

The lich.

Caldan laughed weakly, tried to pull himself together. He struggled to his feet and stood in the center of the circle of the purified land in Parkside. It was a black stain on the landscape—sorcery abused, used to destroy the very life of the earth. Corruption and vileness clawed at his senses.

To his right, the construct housing Gazija lay, twisted and scorched.

Caldan dragged his gaze away toward Kelhak. The lich's eyes were fixed in front of him. His mouth was open, as if he couldn't quite believe what was happening. He raised trembling hands and stared at them.

"This cannot be," Kelhak said, words filled with fear and dread.

Caldan tried again to open his wells, but they were barred to him.

"Caldan!" he heard Miranda yell from somewhere far to his right. He risked a quick glance, and in the distance saw her race across the edge of the purified land toward him.

One of Kelhak's hands dropped to grab a dagger in his belt, while the other hand stopped it when it was half drawn. His face twisted into a grimace, then a scowl, then a half smile. He grunted, hands and arms working, as if he struggled with himself.

Then one foot stepped forward, toward the edge of the purified land. Growling with the effort, Kelhak dragged the other foot across the ground.

Kelhak. The *real* Kelhak.

He was still there, inside somewhere. The same Kelhak who'd been a student at the monastery. Who'd won the Dominion tournament at the Autumn Festival, then left Anasoma to make his way in the world. A course not unlike Caldan's own. And now Caldan was a lich as well.

The lich may have taken Kelhak's body, but here, with no sorcery to imprison him, he was trying to break free.

Caldan's own wells wriggled in his mind, suddenly becoming as slippery as eels as he grasped at them. He corralled his own well, then another. Sweat stinging his eyes, he managed to hold on to them with the force of his will alone. Except the more he gathered, the harder they were to control.

And the lich had hundreds.

Suddenly, tinted sparks broke away from Kelhak's head. They floated up, then spiraled down to the ground, where they vanished into the purified land. He trembled, panting hoarsely.

They must have been wells, and whatever remained of the sorcerers. The null of the purified land was unraveling the lich's absorbed power. But if Kelhak made it out of here, he would be free to resume as he had before.

And Caldan couldn't let that happen.

He stepped toward Kelhak.

The man, or the lich, looked at Caldan as he approached, but his dragging shuffle continued.

"No, no, no . . ." Kelhak panted under his laboring breath. Another mote rose away from his head, then drifted down to disappear into the ground—quickly followed by two more.

And then, Kelhak's eyes pierced Caldan's. "Kill me," he said. "No! Don't do that. I have power—*we* have power. A knowledge of sorcery that would make you a god." His face twisted. "Don't listen to it. Kill me, now." A feral snarl escaped his lips. "Noooo!" Another lurching step.

Palm sweat-slick, Caldan gripped the hilt of the Protectors' sword hard enough his hand ached. Simmon had asked Caldan to kill him, and he hadn't been able to. He'd been weak then, but now . . .

He swallowed and approached Kelhak, whose stagger had quickened. More glittering motes broke free and were absorbed by the sorcerous null.

A searing pain assailed Caldan's mind as one of his wells broke free. He staggered, screaming wordlessly. Through the agony he felt his remaining wells squirm, then settle as he reasserted his control. Caldan gripped the sword harder, forcing himself to go on.

Kelhak moaned. One hand slapped at his head. Another dragging step, then a second.

Perhaps Gazija was right. The lich couldn't be killed; it was too knowledgeable, too cunning, too innately sorcerous now. There was only one way to be sure. *I don't know* and *I think* weren't good enough.

He brought the trinket sword up, the blade a river of moonlight. Kelhak's eyes followed its arc, flickering between contempt and determination.

Caldan reached out with his smith-crafted gauntlet. A skein of symbols covered every surface. Each plate carpeted in one unbroken stroke formed into patterns. Sorcerous runes and gemstones sparkled with power, drawn from the reservoir he'd imbued in the crafting.

Kelhak hissed, spittle flying. He kept up his lurching march across the purified land.

Caldan opened the fingers of his gauntlet.

"No," Kelhak said, then his face twisted. "Do it."

Caldan stepped toward Kelhak, who lashed out, kicking and punching and screaming.

Caldan parried the blows, and the trinket sword slid easily into Kelhak's chest. Hands came up to clutch at the blade; blood dribbled from Kelhak's mouth like wine. Shimmering lights sprang from his head like disturbed butterflies, swirling and fluttering.

And with one quick thrust, Caldan placed his gauntleted hand against Kelhak's face.

Limbs twitched and jerked. Kelhak's knees buckled, and Caldan followed his descent to the ground, keeping the gauntlet in place. It grew cold to the touch and seemed to throb with power. Caldan almost sobbed with relief. It worked, and he'd stored enough sorcerous energy in its buffers to do its work, to function for a time inside the purified land.

Motes flew in glittering clouds around Kelhak's head. They swirled and roiled, forming into a spiral as they were sucked down into the gauntlet. Some motes—sorcerers—escaped the crafting's pull and fell toward the ground to vanish in a puff of sparkles, but most were caught in the winding suction of the gauntlet's sorcery.

Down into the crafting the colored motes went, and the gems flashed with inner light as they were trapped inside. Kelhak convulsed, almost dragging the hand away, but Caldan held on.

Fragments coursed from Kelhak's head, pulsing and writhing and coiling, before the crafting extracted them, snared them, imprisoned them forever.

And then the motes vanished, sucked into the crafted gauntlet like water down a drain.

Kelhak breathed once. Was still. Lifeless eyes stared.

Shouts came from somewhere, getting closer.

Miranda.

Caldan sat back, pulling the gauntlet and blade from Kelhak with palpable relief. They both glistened red, and the gemstones flickered with contained life: sorcerers, or what was left of them. Their wells. And the lich's awareness.

The gauntlet was no longer a silver alloy, but charred as black as midnight. Metal so cold the air steamed around it. Everything about the object screamed anathema to Caldan. It was all he feared—and mirrored what he was.

Caldan lay back, used his feet to push himself a few paces away from Kelhak's corpse. His head ached abominably from corrosive sorcery. His wells were blocked. He didn't know if forcing all that power through his mind before had damaged him permanently, but at least the lich had been contained.

Contained.

Not killed or destroyed. Its essence still existed. The power of many of its stolen wells also remained with it. As did its sorcerous knowledge.

People would kill to obtain such an artifact. Unscrupulous sorcerers who lusted after power. The warlocks.

Whoever succeeded the emperor.

That was why Gazija had pushed Caldan in this direction. To give him no option. No safe haven.

The crafting couldn't remain here; it wasn't safe. And Caldan couldn't stay, either, else he'd be killed. Two birds with one stone. That's what Gazija had planned for.

Caldan laughed weakly; all he could manage. Still he was being used.

He closed his eyes, body and mind aching. His muscles spasmed, sending waves of agony throughout him. Cramps ripped through his stomach, and it felt his bones would twist so much they'd break.

His Touched abilities had caught up with him. With prolonged use, and only one trinket to mitigate the effects, the damage to his body manifested quickly.

Just a minute, he thought. *Then I'll get up.*

Footsteps pounded close by.

Miranda.

CHAPTER 57

Caldan grimaced, wiped blood from his brow with a shaking hand. He tried to draw a deep breath, but a knifing pain in his chest stopped him. He swallowed, the inside of his mouth gritty with dust, and forced himself to take shallow breaths.

The purified land underneath him was hard, and he could feel its abyssal absence like a palpable force. Its very lifelessness leached strength from him, as if merely taking away his sorcery wasn't enough for it. As if it hungered for more.

Death came for all of them, he knew this with certainty. But he hadn't thought his would be so soon. Then again, he hadn't thought they'd be able to defeat Kelhak.

He tried to get up, but his legs refused to move. He coughed and spat, turning onto his back and looking up into the sky. A wave of agony threaded its way along his limbs and into his head.

The sky was still blue. A bright color that shouted life, after the dismal depths of the ancient ruins beneath Anasoma, and the darkness of the purified land pressing into his back.

Life.

Someone grabbed his outstretched arm and pulled, grunting with the effort. White-hot needles poked his joints and skin, and he gasped. He blinked, tried to focus on the indistinct figure. They tugged again, and he slid across the ground, slowly gaining momentum as they backpedaled. Then he ceased moving. There was a curse, then a sob.

"Bloody ancestors! Why are you so heavy?"

Miranda.

Now he recognized her scent, overlaid with sweat and fear and determination.

Gritting his teeth and groaning against the agony of his battered and bruised body, Caldan struggled to sit up. Pain pressed into his skull, hot spikes, the first of many.

"Caldan," she said. "Are you hurt? You were only out for a few minutes."

"Miranda," he managed to croak.

"Thank the ancestors! It worked! But we need to get out of here. You need to get up."

She was talking about their plan. For Caldan to transport Kelhak, so they'd be away from the others. And be able to save themselves and flee.

Caldan laughed weakly, then winced at the lancing pain in his skull. Nausea squeezed his stomach, and he turned his head to retch. Nothing came out.

"Wait," he said, then coughed. "A few . . . moments."

"They'll be coming," Miranda said. "You made such a ruckus, they couldn't have failed to notice. And I assume they'll have sensed the sorcery."

There was no need for her to state who "they" were. The Indryallans. Quiss and his people. The warlocks. All of them would be coming. And they all probably wanted Caldan's head.

"Kelhak's dead," Miranda said. "And I think Gazija is too. We have to run. Now. There are people watching us; they'll know which direction we go."

There was panic in her voice.

"Where's Vasile?" Caldan said.

"Gone to gather provisions, and a carriage to get us through the city quickly."

His left hand felt light. Caldan saw his own misshapen fingers, no longer enclosed in his gauntlet. "Where . . . is it?"

"Your gauntlet? Here. I put it my satchel while you were unconscious. That crafting . . . Caldan, I didn't like the feel of it. There's something wrong about it. It was icy cold, and I didn't want it touching you."

Gazija's words echoed in Caldan's head: *Go, far from here. Tell no one. Leave no trace.*

The old sorcerer had pulled Caldan's strings since the body of his altered construct had appeared in the cabin. Perhaps in case they were victorious and this very situation arose. But with the number of dead, Caldan thought this triumph tasted much the same as defeat. Ashes and blood and darkness.

It all made sense now. Gazija wanted Caldan to possess the gauntlet. To flee, and become its guardian. Or its destroyer. The warlocks, or the emperor had he survived—even his own people—couldn't be trusted with such a powerful artifact. Hundreds of wells, and possibly the essence of the lich, with all the knowledge it possessed.

He had to move, do something. But he had no strength left.

"The bone rings," Caldan said. "I dropped them, somewhere."

"I have them," Miranda said. "They're safe. Gazija . . . I'm sorry."

Again, her hands gripped his arms, and she began dragging him along the dirt-covered surface.

Get up! he implored himself.

"Miranda . . ."

She stopped pulling him. "What?" she said, breath coming in gasps.

Caldan rubbed his eyes, then opened and closed them a few times. His surroundings became clearer. Miranda stood above him, clothes torn and dirty, covered with dust and dried blood. There was a kind of shocked disbelief in her eyes. Perhaps she wondered how they were still alive. There was a crimson smear across one cheek, and sweat trickled down her grubby face. Her long, dark hair was plastered to her head.

She was beautiful.

He shook his head and managed to lever himself to his knees. He felt Miranda's hand on his shoulder.

"Easy," she said. "Take a breath. Then try to stand."

Off to the side was Kelhak's corpse. His body was bloody and raw, skin a bright red, as if scalded by boiling water. Once-bright blue eyes were now sightless white orbs.

The Protectors' sword was back in Caldan's scabbard. Miranda must have sheathed it.

"The emperor is dead," Caldan said.

Miranda gasped, then her mouth drew into a tight line. "Good riddance. But that brings its own troubles."

A few dozen paces away, Caldan glimpsed the blackened and furrowed metal form of the construct that housed Gazija. It lay facedown, unmoving. Many of the runes and patterns were disfigured or melted away.

"Gazija," Caldan called, coughing as his throat stuck together.

There was no answer.

"Gazija!" Caldan said again.

The figure twitched. *Leave me*, Gazija said, voice barely above a whisper.

Miranda ran to Gazija and picked him up. She cradled his damaged form in her hands.

Quiss . . . is coming. I'll hang on.

"No," Caldan said. "I'll not—"

Leave me. Flee.

"Caldan," Miranda said. "We should do as he says. He might be able to persuade Quiss not to come after you."

Reluctantly, Caldan had to agree with her. He thought the chance was slight, but if anyone could persuade Quiss, it was Gazija. And perhaps it was the sorcerer's way of trying to apologize for using Caldan.

They placed Gazija gently on the ground and made their way to the brink of the purified land. Ahead, Caldan could see startled and curious faces. Whoever had been close enough to observe or hear the final moments of his fight with the lich had come to see what the disturbance was about. The crowd they were heading toward was at least a few faces deep, but none of them seemed to want to step onto the null of the purified land.

Caldan did as Miranda had asked, but his legs were like jelly. He fell, and agony flared as he tumbled to the ground. The debilitating aftereffects of his Touched abilities had taken their toll. He'd damaged himself and needed time to recover. And right now, even the thought of opening his well made his mind flinch in expectation of the pain sure to follow. His senses were scraped raw, scalded and hurting from the power he'd drawn in the fight with Kelhak.

"It's no use," he said. "I'm too weak. Leave me."

Miranda stood above him, biting her lip. Tears trailed down her cheeks. "I'm not leaving you here. I'm not."

She grabbed his arm, and he winced as she started dragging him again. "You reek," she said.

Caldan managed a halfhearted chuckle. "I know. We'll clean up later. Once we're safe."

She paused and bent over, sucking in air. "Stop talking. I need to save my breath."

Even though moving hurt him, he forced himself to endure it. They had to run if they wanted to survive, but he also wanted to be off this accursed purified land. Its nothingness was soul destroying for a sorcerer, and without his wells, he was defenseless—if he hadn't damaged his mind permanently in the final battle with Kelhak.

"We'll get out of this," Caldan reassured her. "We've made it this far, haven't we?" His vision blurred and became gray. The pressure in his head increased, and he clenched his jaw. Miranda swayed in front of him.

No. It was him. He couldn't go on. It was all over.

Darkness came crashing down.

CHAPTER 58

When Kelhak and Caldan had disappeared, leaving behind only a smoking circle, Quiss and the other sorcerers were livid. And frightened. But that had lasted only a few minutes.

"Where did the talon go?" Aidan asked Lady Felicienne.

"It was injured," she said. "I saw it drag itself away, but it's disappeared."

She was shaking, and her eyes were wild. He couldn't blame her. Aidan never wanted to go through another fight like that.

"We have to get out of here," he said. "If Kelhak's not dead now, we've lost."

Felicienne shook her head. "We have to get to Caldan. He's the key now, if Kelhak survived."

They stumbled along behind Quiss and the others as they ran back the way they'd come, this time following the trail left in the dust by Kelhak's Silent Companions, hoping the route out of the ancient city would be shorter. Aidan checked on Felice often, making sure she kept up with the furious pace.

Then, as one, Quiss and his sorcerers stopped. They raised their faces upward, as if they could see through the rock above them. Quiss fell to his knees, head bowed, as if he were praying. And some of his people were weeping. Quiss took some aside and whispered urgently to them, before turning to the survivors.

"Kelhak is dead!" he crowed. "But there is another lich, somewhere near the purified land. A lesser one. We will deal with him."

"Don't you bloody dare touch Caldan!" Felice said.

Quiss ignored her. "We are too weak to travel there by sorcery," he said to those around him. "We must go quickly then. By the time we reach the lich, we'll have recovered enough of our strength to be able to defeat him."

Quiss and his sorcerers hurried their pace. Out of the corner of his eye, Aidan saw cel Rau dart off into the darkness of a tunnel.

Aidan grabbed Felice's sleeve, stopping her in her tracks. "They'll make it to the rendezvous quickly. Unless we get ahead of them."

With a nod of her head, Felice latched onto Aidan's arm and pulled him after Quiss. "You want to make sure Vasile is all right, don't you?"

"Yes. Though we have another problem. Cel Rau just disappeared down that side tunnel there. I don't know what he's up to, but . . ."

Felice pursed her lips. "You have to follow him. I'll stay with Quiss in case Caldan and Vasile are still at the purified land. But after that, they were meant to rendezvous at a warehouse in Dockside. I fear cel Rau has been tasked with killing Caldan. And that must not happen. I don't want to split up, but it can't be helped."

Aidan nodded reluctantly. Felice was right—they couldn't cover two places at once unless they separated. "If you find Vasile," he told Felice, "keep him safe. And if I find Caldan, I'll do my best to protect him. After what just happened, he doesn't deserve to die."

He left Felice to follow Quiss after taking a burning torch from one of the surviving mercenaries. The Silent Companions had come from these side passages, so it was a good bet cel Rau was following their trail in the dust. A flicker of light came from up ahead: cel Rau.

Aidan ran through ancient corridors, taking short walking breaks to catch his breath. Cel Rau remained a good distance ahead, and he caught glimpses of the swordsman's light only along particularly long passages. *He has to be running too,* thought Aidan.

After what seemed like an eternity, Aidan emerged into sewage tunnels, then finally into the streets of Anasoma.

Once outside, he stopped, blinking in the daylight. He panted like a dog, face dripping sweat.

A few passersby looked at him curiously but scurried about their business. Sounds of fighting came from all over the city: sorcerous detonations and keening, metal clanging. The Indryallans were retreating. Already, people were shouting that ships had left the harbor, and that the God-Emperor had been killed. But strangely, there wasn't much relief in their expressions.

He skirted the edge of a wide avenue, searching for cel Rau. In the distance, the docks of Anasoma glistened amid sparkling waves.

There. Cel Rau pushed his way through a crowd of people, then took off at a sprint once his passage was clear.

Aidan followed as fast as he could. Cel Rau never paused to glance behind him, so it was relatively easy to match his pace without worrying about being seen.

After a while, buildings grew sparser, then eventually petered out. Ahead of him, Aidan saw a vast, cleared area. The purified land.

Cel Rau stopped, and Aidan ducked against a wall, his face dripping sweat and his breath coming in gasps. There was no way Quiss and his people could have kept up such a punishing pace. They had to be far behind, which meant Aidan had time to deal with cel Rau.

Aidan loosened his sword in his sheath and glanced around. He began walking toward cel Rau, who was peering across the purified land, one hand shading his eyes.

Suddenly, cel Rau dashed away, sprinting toward a carriage. It was a hundred yards away, and rapidly gathering speed.

Was that . . . *Vasile!* The magistrate was driving the horses. Which meant Caldan and Miranda could be inside. And it seemed cel Rau had drawn the same conclusion.

CHAPTER 59

Caldan rocked like he was on a boat. Hooves clopping on paved streets drummed into his body through the floor of the carriage.

Fire lashed Caldan's mind from his wells, all of them open and leaking power. His sorcerous senses flinched from the corrosive onslaught. He suppressed a strangled groan and frantically closed them. He licked his lips when his original well closed, the last of them. Without the distraction, he could feel his skin tingling, his bones vibrating to the life all around him.

He was out of the null zone and was now able to defend himself. Except that his mind was still scraped raw from his fight with Kelhak and his sorcerers. And he was as weak as a newborn calf and walked just as well as one. Sure, he had access to his wells, but he wasn't even sure he'd be able to use them.

Caldan hesitated, then opened his well. Fire coursed across his nerves, and he flinched, both his body and his mind. But it was bearable, just. A tiny trickle was all he required, enough to disguise his wells, and in moments, he was done. There was nothing he could do about his trinkets, though. And there had to be sorcerers with the talent of sensing them, as he did. But at least he'd closed off one avenue of detection.

Sorcery flared all over the city, small eruptions, but intensely focused. Fights between opposing forces, neither of which probably knew Kelhak was vanquished. Horns pealed to the north. Answering calls came from the northeast and east. Indryallans or Quivers, it didn't matter. All that did was flight.

Their pursuers were invisible to Miranda and Vasile, but Caldan kept track of the wells he could, marking the most powerful. Those would be the ones to worry about, if it came down to a fight for survival.

Then, behind him, a few of the wells winked out, only to return a moment later.

The purified land. They'd reached it, and likely found Kelhak's body along with the ravaged smith-crafting that had housed Gazija. Caldan had no way to tell if they were Indryallans or someone else, but the reality was, it didn't matter. The crowd they'd left at the purified land would point them in this direction, and then the sorcerers would search for wells, and finding none, would turn to trinkets— then they would detect his ring and the Protectors' sword.

The buzz of a crowd. Unwashed people. Laughter. Cloth rustling.

He lay still for a while, but the swaying sensation was making him sick. He opened his eyes and sat up, wincing at the pain it caused.

Miranda was by his side. "Lie back down," she said. "Vasile's driving the horses, but I think he hasn't practiced for a while."

"Wh . . ." Caldan coughed, tried to swallow. "Where are we going?"

"My warehouse. We can hide out."

"Again," Caldan said.

Miranda smiled. "Yes. Just like before. Rest now. Only a little while longer, and we'll be safe."

Caldan loosed his senses, searching for signs of sorcerers close by. After a few moments, he nodded, relieved there were none near. But farther out, he could tell there were wells ranging from the north to the east—and some of them were powerful indeed, sparkling in his senses like glittering stars. And very faintly, the vibration of trinkets. He paused, concentrating on the sorcerers.

At this distance, it was hard to tell, but he was sure of it: they were coming closer.

"Miranda," he said. "They're coming for me." His hand came up to touch the bone rings through his shirt, where they nestled yet again.

As they descended toward the docks of Anasoma, Caldan lay back, too weak to do more.

An animal fear gripped him, a now-familiar feeling. Flight. Escape. Flee.

He knew they'd never be safe. Never again.

"We're here," Miranda said.

Caldan half woke from a daze. He'd lost track of time.

The carriage door opened. Vasile and Miranda dragged him out, and into her warehouse.

AIDAN CIRCLED THE building for the second time, nerves fraying. There were a few doors, but it looked like they were all locked. The carriage with heavily lathered horses was close by, but he'd lost sight of cel Rau in the narrow streets, and now the swordsman was nowhere to be seen.

He dropped his hand to his sword hilt and checked that it was still with him for the hundredth time. Moving into the alley behind the warehouse, he noticed a narrow door was ajar. When it hadn't been before.

Aidan cursed and drew his blade. He ran past piles of garbage and over the muddy trickle in the center of the alley. Through the gap in the doorway, he could see the inside was dark, and musty air wafted out.

A woman screamed.

Aidan shoved the door open and rushed in. He heard Vasile shout a curse. Aidan barreled around a corner, then skidded to a halt.

In front of him, Miranda was on her knees. Cel Rau had one hand twisted in her hair, while the other held a blade at her throat. Bleeding marks scored one of cel Rau's cheeks, where Miranda had managed to scratch him. To the side, Caldan lay in a tangled heap, unconscious. Vasile was between them, shielding Caldan, clutching a dagger and pointing the trembling blade at cel Rau.

Aidan held up a hand. Cel Rau was a better swordsman than he was. Could Aidan take him? Not without help . . . "Stop," he said calmly. He edged forward. "Why, Anshul?" Aidan said calmly. "This woman is innocent. We're all good people here."

Cel Rau shook his head. "We cannot suffer this man to live. The emperor has commanded it. Caitlyn cannot have died for nothing."

Vasile took a step toward cel Rau. "The emperor is dead. Whatever he wanted you to do—"

"Still holds," hissed cel Rau. "Caldan is worse than Chalayan."

Vasile's eyes widened, and Aidan knew cel Rau believed what he was saying. Bloody ancestors, how could he persuade him to stop?

"No. Please," begged Miranda, then yelped as cel Rau twisted her hair. Her hands clutched at his, but cel Rau's grip remained firm.

Something wild was in cel Rau's eyes, as if he were fighting inside himself. A pained smile spread across his face.

"We must destroy evil where we can," cel Rau said. "Caitlyn knew this. And I thought you did, too."

To Aidan's surprise, Vasile took another step toward cel Rau. The dagger in his hand shook even more. Vasile's mouth was drawn in a tight line, his face grim but determined.

"What are you going to do?" cel Rau said.

Vasile took another step. "What would you do, if faced with evil?"

Cel Rau's face twisted into a snarl, but then he hesitated. He nodded at Vasile with grudging respect.

Aidan took a step to his right, hand still outstretched, the other gripping his sword. "Caitlyn went too far. She was lost. As you are."

"No! The emperor—"

With a cry, Vasile darted at cel Rau. Cel Rau easily parried the blade aside. He pivoted, slicing a cut on the side of Vasile's head. The magistrate staggered away, one hand pressed to the wound.

Miranda plunged a knife into cel Rau's thigh. The swordsman hissed and wrenched her by the hair, swinging her in a half circle. She screamed. Aidan moved forward as Vasile writhed on the floor.

"Back!" cel Rau shouted. "Or I kill her, too." Blood seeped from around the blade embedded in his muscle.

A groan came from Caldan. Cel Rau's eyes flicked to him. Caldan groaned again and rolled onto his side.

"The threat is over," Vasile said quietly, one hand pressed to his head. Blood seeped from underneath it.

"Yes!" Miranda said. "Kelhak is dead. Caldan killed him! Leave him be. He's no threat to you."

"Lies!" cel Rau said.

"Truth," said Vasile.

Cel Rau's eyes narrowed in confusion.

Miranda jerked cel Rau's arm down, and the swordsman overbalanced. Aidan rushed forward.

"No!" shouted Vasile.

Sparks sprayed from clashing swords. Aidan slashed at cel Rau, was parried. Miranda clutched at cel Rau's leg, hampering him. Blades weaved and danced, opening gashes across Aidan's arm and cel Rau's side. Cel Rau jumped back, as best he could with Miranda clinging to him, opening a gap. He stomped on Miranda's ankle and shoved her away, raising his sword in time to deflect a thrust from Aidan, countering with a slash that cut deep into Aidan's thigh. It burned like fire.

Cel Rau came at him again. Aidan backed away, blade weaving in desperate defense. His blood splashed the floor.

Then Miranda lunged at cel Rau, shrieking and clawing. She hooked her legs around his, pulled him to his knees . . .

And Aidan thrust his sword through cel Rau's leather hauberk. He drove it down, with all his strength behind it. The blade penetrated deep, into the back of his shoulder and through to his chest. Cel Rau jerked. Aidan yanked his blade out. Cel Rau spasmed once, let out a gurgling moan, and collapsed on top of Miranda. She wriggled free, pushing and shoving.

Miranda stood, wild haired, and looked at them with fear.

"It's all right," Vasile said. "Aidan won't hurt you."

"They're coming for us. For him," she said. Her eyes strayed to cel Rau. "There will be more. They won't rest until Caldan's dead. He's saved us all. Saved everyone, and they'll kill him. It's not right."

Aidan glanced around him. The space was practically empty, with only a few barrels and crates against one wall.

"Aidan," Vasile said. "We have to help. We can't let them kill Caldan."

Aidan ran a hand through his hair. "I know. But there's nowhere to hide. Maybe . . . if we could get to the docks? Hide him on a ship?"

Miranda shook her head. "Quiss and his people can sense him. I have an idea." She looked at Aidan and Vasile. "But . . . you'll have to lie to Quiss and the warlocks. Can you do that?"

Vasile and Aidan exchanged glances. Aidan nodded.

"Yes," Vasile said. "We can do that."

"We need to see to your head," Aidan said.

"I'm fine," Vasile replied. "It's shallow. Probably looks worse than it is."

Miranda bent over Caldan. She took a ring from his finger, and a sword from his belt. "I can find somewhere to hide Caldan," she said. "But they'll keep looking for him. So we have to make them think he's dead."

They helped her drag cel Rau's body to a corner of the warehouse. Breaking open crates, they piled as much wood and straw around him as they could.

"The warehouse is old," Miranda said. "These places are a fire hazard. We'll burn it down. Then they'll find the body, and think it's Caldan."

She jammed the ring onto one of cel Rau's fingers and placed the sword by his side. "The ring is his last link to his family. It was the reason he ended up here. But . . ." Miranda hesitated. "It's the source of all his troubles. I hope he forgives me."

"I'm sure he will," Vasile said.

Miranda picked up cel Rau's swords and handed them to Aidan.

"Thank you," he said, accepting them solemnly. They were good blades, with much history. He would keep them as a reminder of cel Rau, the man he'd once considered his friend.

"This is the only way," Miranda said. "They won't suspect, if they find it here. Not only because it's his connection to his family, but because it helps with his Touched abilities, and with mitigating the damage they cause."

She straightened. "That barrel there, it's full of oil. Smash it open. There's a bucket in one of the rooms. Spread it around."

"And then leave us," said Caldan.

Miranda gasped and rushed to his side. "Can you stand?" she said. "We have to get out of here."

With an audible moan, Caldan levered himself to a sitting position. His face was pale, and he looked like he hadn't slept for days.

"I'll manage," Caldan said. "But Aidan and Vasile have to leave. Now. Please."

He obviously had a plan and didn't want them to know it. Aidan clasped his hand and gave him a nod of thanks. After Vasile did the same, they left.

A short time later, they were outside. Smoke billowed from the warehouse.

When the building was well ablaze, and a crowd had gathered around, Quiss and a few of his sorcerers arrived. Vasile and Aidan watched them pointing and gesturing to the warehouse. Trailing after them came Lady Felicienne, and the mercenary captain Selbourne with some of his men. All of them sported stained bandages, their clothes and skin and armor spattered with dirt and blood.

Felicienne grabbed Quiss's arm. "Don't do this," she shouted. "He saved us all. You know he did."

The sorcerer shook his head and pushed her away. "I can feel his power building! Wells have been opened. He's about to strike out at us. We have to stop him!"

Then Quiss and his people added their arcane power to the conflagration.

CALDAN REACHED FOR his ring, to find it missing. He sighed. He knew Miranda had been right to take it, but it still hurt. One of only two links to his heritage, to his family, gone.

His body and head ached, but he had no choice. Around them the heat from the fire was growing fast, and outside he sensed Quiss and his people approaching.

"Miranda, gather your belongings. It's time. We need to leave all of this behind."

Reaching into his pocket, Caldan took out a stick of chalk. It was broken, a small nub. The rest was powder. It would have to do.

His basic understanding of how the sorcery worked would be enough. But it was power he needed, and a lot of it.

"I'm going to draw a circle," he told Miranda. "Please don't scuff it. If there's any flaw, we'll likely not survive."

"Hurry," Miranda said. She coughed at the smoke and pulled her shirt up to cover her mouth.

Runic patterns took shape as Caldan marked the floor. Complex designs he'd only glimpsed when Mazoet had taken them to where Amerdan was and back again. Sorcery of a kind he'd never dreamed of.

Soon it was done.

Caldan had Miranda step gingerly over the chalk circle and sat her in the center. Flames crackled all around them. His skin was hot and smoke stung his eyes.

He squatted down next to her and opened his well. His mind recoiled from its stinging slap, and he hissed through clenched teeth. Caldan felt heat suffuse him: his Touched abilities again. Blood coursed like lava through his veins, filling him with unnatural vigor. It set hooks into his soul, drawing him away from despair. And the shadows of the world fell aside.

He was already exhausted and damaged from his abilities, and any more might do permanent damage.

Caldan clenched his jaw and sank deeper into his sorcery anyway.

Well after well he opened, splitting off strings and linking to his chalk crafting. His design was so frail, worse than paper. But it had to suffice; he had to make it last.

Ignoring his splitting headache, Caldan pulled Miranda close, hugging her to his chest. He gagged as the stench of hot metal and lemons assailed his nostrils.

A tremendous surge of sorcery grew around him, and he flooded his crafting with the corrosive power of all his wells.

Reality twisted.

A WAVE OF pressure drove Vasile into the ground, and Aidan alongside him. All around them, the streets were lit by a hellish glow. Thunder rumbled, a cacophony of fractures. Sorcerous fire lashed the building. Stone cracked, and the air rippled under the intense heat. Shimmering lights flickered against gray walls.

"He's dying!" Quiss crowed. "His wells are fading. Strike! Strike!"

Shadows were banished by boiling light. Violence shook the warehouse. Whips of sorcery pummeled from above. Virulent balls falling from the sky splashed waterlike across the roof, erupting in violet chaos.

Power of a kind never before seen in Anasoma scourged the warehouse clean.

"Enough!" commanded Quiss.

His sorcerers ceased their devastating conflagration. Tendrils of focused energy withered and died. Stone heated past melting ran in orange trickles, while black smoke billowed from blazing wood.

There was a groan, then a crack. Blocks of stone tumbled down the side, falling to the street below with shattering crashes, sending shards of splintered rock flying in all directions. Another moan came from the building, then a shriek of tortured wood. Sparks whooshed into the sky as the uppermost level collapsed, the burning timbers unable to support their own weight.

Whip cracks split the air.

"Back!" someone shouted.

Quiss and his sorcerers recognized the danger and retreated to a safe distance. Felicienne and Selbourne stood for a few moments longer, staring into the burning building, before they too ran.

After burning bright for a long time, the warehouse collapsed.

Vasile felt Aidan's hand on his shoulder.

"Let's get this over with."

Vasile nodded.

A SHORT TIME later, Vasile waited in the street with Aidan. Quiss paced back and forth in front of them. Wooden staves poked among the charcoal mess. Heat still radiated from stone, but Quiss had his people shield themselves and work in short shifts.

Curiously, one of his sorcerers clutched a blackened metal figurine. Selbourne crossed his arms over his chest and waited with Felicienne, a short distance from Quiss, as if they didn't want to stand near him. Tears streaked Felice's face, which was twisted with grief.

She's lost her emperor, Vasile thought, *and now the man who saved us all.*

"Here!" a woman said, and Quiss looked up. She strode from the cinders, carrying a sword covered with a film of gray ash.

Quiss took a staff from someone and jabbed it down on the sword. Metal clanged; the layer of ash dispersed. Reddish runes were revealed on the blade. Fragments of charred bone crumbled among the ash.

"He looks pleased," Aidan said.

Vasile grunted and scratched at the crude bandage wrapped around his head. "What they did . . . It is as Miranda said. It isn't right."

"Is there more?" Quiss said. "We need to be certain."

The ends of more staves rifled through black and gray detritus.

Metal clinked. Something rolled across the cracked ground. Stopped.

A ring. Quiss shielded himself and entered the ruin. He bent over and picked it up, then strode from the hazy air in the ruins. Taking a breath, he blew ash from it.

Vasile and Aidan leaned forward.

A silver ring; the outside surface was covered in a knotwork pattern into which two stylized lions with onyx eyes had been worked. Detailed enough that Vasile could see tiny claws and fangs. Inside the band, unfamiliar symbols were etched into the metal.

"It's his," Quiss said. "Good. I felt his wells disappear, but we need to be certain. Are you sure he was inside?"

"Yes," Aidan said.

Vasile nodded.

Quiss stared at him, but Vasile met his eyes and kept his gaze steady.

The sorcerer weighed the ring in his palm. He glanced toward the blackened bone in the ruins, and for a moment he seemed to wonder. Then his shoulders slumped. "So it's over, then," he murmured. "It's all over."

Felicienne spoke up from behind him. "No. It's not over, Quiss. You have much to answer for."

AFTERMATH

Quivers poured through the streets of Anasoma, clearing out the Indryallan soldiers and fighting running battles with their sorcerers. Thoroughfares were awash with clashes of steel, scourging detonations, and some cheering. Residents barricaded themselves inside their homes, leaving the streets to be violently contested.

Felice left Aidan and Vasile and strode over to a fountain in the center of the square. Around the edges of the space, squads of Quivers stood guard, while Knight-Marshal Rakim and the warlock leader Bernhard directed the cleanup operation.

A short distance away, Quiss rested with his people. Their heads were bowed as they held discussions in low tones. Quiss looked even more emaciated than normal, as if the final fight with Kelhak had drained him of vitality. Sunken cheeks and blood clotting his face and clothes made him look maniacal.

Felice washed her face and hands, then scrubbed her arms. The cool water felt good but did little to banish her bone weariness.

From behind her, someone cleared his throat. She turned.

"Knight-Marshall Rakim," Felice said. "I take it the operation is going well?"

Bernhard stood to the side, just behind Rakim. His beard was charred and patchy. It looked like he'd suffered a close call.

"First Adjudicator Shyrise . . ." Rakim began.

"It's Third, actually."

Rakim raised an eyebrow. "Then where are the Firsts? Or Seconds, for that matter? You were the only one to stay with . . . the emperor . . . and see this through." Pain etched his face. The only ruler he and generations of his family had known had died today.

"They stayed behind," Felice said plainly. "It was too dangerous for them." She shrugged. "The plan was partially mine, and I had to see it through."

Rakim grunted. He glanced at Bernhard, then back at her. Bowing low, he said, "Then we await your orders."

"Ah . . . excuse me?" Felice managed, thinking she'd misheard him.

"You are in charge," Bernhard said. "Not of Rakim's soldiers, or my warlocks, but overall. Someone has to assume command. At least until there's a new emperor selected from among his progeny."

Felice looked around her at the destruction. Dozens of plumes of smoke rose into the sky. Who would replace Zerach-Sangur, the emperor? Who *could*?

"I think," she said slowly, "the age of emperors is over."

Her thoughts turned to Caldan. Aidan and Vasile didn't fool her, however much Quiss believed he'd killed Caldan. She smiled, recalling their Dominion game: Caldan had made his extra move count.

But he must still possess the bone rings. Felice had to fulfill her vow to her mentor and destroy them. And such an uncontrollable person as Caldan couldn't be allowed to retain the trinkets.

First, though, she had to find him. And that could take months, if not years.

Perhaps she could ask Izak to send out feelers to his contacts . . . and curiously, she wanted to see the deceptively charming man again.

And the talon would be of use, wherever it had gone . . .

Also, perhaps she could do something to help Poppy and the other street urchins, now that she was in a position to.

Felice sighed.

There is so much for me to do.

CALDAN LAY THERE, simply too exhausted to do anything else. His back and limbs pressed into sun-warmed ground. His shirt and pants rasped against his skin at the slightest movement, as if they were coarse hessian rather than cloth. Other than that, he felt numb. There was a soothing sound to the wind as it gusted around him, warm and comforting. Faint murmurings and whistles reached his ears, almost creating a lyrical sound.

He barely moved, apart from his chest, which rose and fell with each agonizing breath. The insides of his eyelids glowed as a harsh sun beat down on him. Sweat trickled along his scalp.

There was a scrabbling sound beside him. He forced himself to half roll to one side and opened his eyes, trying to reach his well. And failing.

A spiny orange lizard sitting on top of a rock regarded him, unblinking.

Caldan licked parched lips.

Someone whimpered behind him. He moaned and rolled to the other side.

Miranda lay sprawled on dry, cracked earth. As Caldan watched, an ant crawled across her neck and over her face.

Alive. They were both alive.

In bad shape, but breathing.

Caldan looked up and squinted at the bright sun. He'd sent them south, that's all he could remember. How far, he had no idea.

He lurched to his feet, shaded his eyes, and peered about.

Arid earth extended as far as he could see in all directions.

Wait. No, there. He squinted through the haze at a mirror-bright square column rising into the sky. An artifact from before the Shattering, its purpose lost in the mists of time. A landmark in the wastes of the Desolate Lands.

Caldan laughed then. He'd done it, spirited them away to where no one would find them.

Miranda's satchel lay a few paces to his right, and he slung it over his shoulder. Then, as gently as he could, he lifted Miranda and cradled her in his arms.

His heart seemed to beat stronger.

And he began walking.

This ends the

Sorcery Ascendant Sequence.

To the Reader,

Having readers eager for the next installment of a series, or anticipating a new series, is the best motivation for a writer to create new stories.

New release sign-up. If you enjoy reading my novels as much as I enjoy writing them, then sign up to my mailing list at http://eepurl.com/BTefL. I promise to notify you only when a new novel is released, so no spam e-mails!

Share your opinion. If you would like to leave a review, it would be much appreciated! Reviews help new readers find my work and accurately decide if the book is for them as well as provide valuable feedback for my future writing.

You can return to where you purchased the novel or simply visit my website at http://www.mitchellhogan.com and follow the links.

There are also a number of websites like Goodreads where members discuss the books they've read, want to read, or want others to read.

Send me feedback. I love to hear from readers and try to answer every e-mail. If you would like to point out errors and typos or provide feedback on my novels, I urge you to send me an e-mail at: mitchhoganauthor@gmail.com.

Thank you for your support, and be sure to check out my other novels!

Kind regards,
Mitchell Hogan

ACKNOWLEDGMENTS

To my patient fans, who waited for this book even though it took a little longer.

To my editors, Derek Prior and David Pomerico, whose (sometimes harsh!) advice made this book far better than I could have on my own.

To my lovely wife, for her understanding and forbearance.

To my darlings Isabelle and Charlotte, who are too young to understand why Daddy has to stop playing with them and disappear all the time.

ABOUT THE AUTHOR

When he was eleven, Mitchell Hogan was given *The Hobbit* and the Lord of the Rings trilogy to read, and a love of fantasy novels was born. He spent the next ten years reading, rolling dice, and playing computer games, with some school and university thrown in. Along the way he accumulated numerous bookcases' worth of fantasy and sci-fi novels and doesn't look to stop anytime soon. For ten years he put off his dream of writing, then he quit his job and wrote *A Crucible of Souls*. He now writes full-time and is eternally grateful to the readers who took a chance on an unknown self-published author. He lives in Sydney, Australia, with his wife, Angela, and daughters, Isabelle and Charlotte.